STUDIES IN THE SHORT STORY

ALTERNATE EDITION

STUDIES IN THE SHORT STORY

EDITED BY
VIRGIL SCOTT
Michigan State University

HOLT, RINEHART AND WINSTON, INC.
New York Chicago San Francisco
Atlanta Dallas Montreal Toronto

Cover illustration: VICTOR VASARELY "Constructivism to Kinetic Art," Poster for the London Arts Group, Detroit and New York, Serigraph, 1968.

Library of Congress Catalog Card Number: 77-139000
SBN: 03-081159-7
Printed in the United States of America
1 2 3 4 40 9 8 7 6 5 4 3 2 1

For my mother

PREFACE

The first edition of *Studies in the Short Story* appeared in 1949, at a time when the analytical approach to the teaching of literature still had some claim on the adjective "new." Our intent in that edition and in the two editions to follow was to provide a text-anthology which, by adapting the "new critical" approach to the abilities of college freshmen and sophomores, would help instructors to broaden and deepen their students' understanding and appreciation of good fiction. With this in mind, we employed five basic methods. First, we organized the book so that it would move from the relatively simple to the relatively complex, from the comparatively obvious to the comparatively difficult. Second, we grouped our selections around a series of introductions designed to present to the student certain fundamental critical principles that would give him at once a vocabulary and a working basis for reading, understanding, and judging a variety of short stories. Third, we followed each story with a set of study questions designed to focus the student's attention on those aspects of a given story which at that point in the text we deemed most important. Fourth, in order to give the student some practice in criticism through comparison, we included some stories that were clearly inferior, either from the standpoint of method or from the standpoint of significance. Finally, we tried to include as wide a variety of *kind* of story as we could and still hold the book to a reasonable length.

This Alternate Edition, as its title implies, is intended to give the instructor a choice between two texts which employ fundamentally the same approach to fiction. However, even the most casual comparison will reveal a number of significant differences between the two texts. The most obvious, of course, is that this edition offers the instructor a different choice of stories—in this case forty-four as against the forty to be found in the Third Edition. But there are a number of other important changes. The Third Edition is divided into seven sections; the Alternate Edition is divided into nine. Where in the Third Edition the three basic elements of fiction—conflict, character, and theme—were telescoped into one section, the Alternate Edition devotes one section to each of these elements; this change has been prompted by my own experience in teaching fiction, where I have discovered that students in the beginning of a course in fiction are more comfortable if, for a short time, they are asked to concentrate on one fictional element at a time. Moreover, the sections on these basic elements are here preceded by a section whose intent is to suggest to the student the variety of reasons that can impel an author to write a story. Beyond this, three sections found in the Third Edition—the section on Honesty and Dishonesty in Fiction, the section on Humor, Satire, and Fantasy, and the section entitled Theme and Variation—have been omitted, and sections on Implication and Irony and on Contrast and Balance have been substituted. In the original text, two of these sections (the one on honesty and dishonesty and the one on thematic variation) were intended to introduce students to the critical process of comparison and contrast, and in the Alternate Edition, this basic principle of comparison has been adopted as the rationale of and the focus for the final section of the text.

Other changes and modifications are not so obvious but probably merit passing mention. First, where the Third Edition of *Studies in the Short Story* offered the instructor forty stories from forty different writers, the Alternate Edition gives him an opportunity to consider eight writers—Boyle, Conrad, Greene, Gordimer, Joyce, Lawrence, Malamud, and Flannery O'Conner—in some kind of "depth." Second, one type of "apparatus" found in the Third Edition is missing from the Alternate Edition. So many instructors have told me that the "study questions" found in the Third Edition tended to "get in the way" of what *they* wanted to do in the classroom with a given story that I have moved these from the text to the instructor's manual. Here they can be used by those instructors who find them useful and disregarded by those who do not. Third, the "unevenness" of the stories in this Alternate Edition is not so dramatic as it was in the Third Edition. My own experience in teaching fiction has convinced me that the freshman of 1971 is considerably more sophisticated than was the freshman of 1949. For this reason, I have incorporated, particularly in the final section, one or two stories which are probably inferior in technique or significance to most of the stories in the text, but no story in this edition is as obviously and as outrageously inferior as were two or three which I used in the Third Edition. And finally, I have very thoroughly revised all of the introductory discussions of fictional theory which appeared in the Third Edition.

In the preparation of this Alternate Edition, I have, of course, contracted far more debts than I can hope to acknowledge here. But I would like to express my gratitude to all those instructors at distant universities who have wrenched the time from out of their own busy schedules to write to me about their reactions to the Third Edition of *Studies in the Short Story,* reactions which have played a significant part in the preparation of this Alternate Edition. And I must also thank all of those in my own department who have experimented with this story or that one in their own classrooms, or who have made invaluable suggestions for this particular text.

V. S.

East Lansing, Michigan
October 1970

CONTENTS

STUDIES IN THE SHORT STORY

1

THE INTENT OF FICTION

The preface of a recent anthology of short fiction opens with the question, "If one doesn't get pleasure out of reading fiction, then what's the use of it?" The question is, of course, rhetorical; few would argue that anyone who sits down to a short story or a novel expects, and rightfully so, to derive pleasure from the experience. But the question poses others which are not rhetorical. What precisely do we mean by pleasure? How does one derive pleasure from reading fiction? Is it possible that one derives different kinds of pleasure from different kinds of stories, and if so, what kinds? And finally, there remains one further question, which, insofar as this text is concerned, is most pertinent of all. This anthology-text has been created for use in a classroom. Can a course in fiction in any way increase the pleasure we derive from reading fiction? Can it, further, show us how to enjoy fiction which we would not otherwise have enjoyed? *Studies in the Short Story* exists on the assumption that both of these questions can be answered affirmatively.

Most of you have been reading fiction for much of your life. And if you think about it, you will realize that you have gone through a number of changes in your reading tastes. At one stage, you found stories in a first-grade reader interesting. At another, you graduated to juvenile fiction. At a third, you found "adult" fiction more rewarding. You would probably describe these changes in reading tastes as "increased maturity." But if you further analyze your reading habits, you may discover that at some point in this maturation, your preferences stopped changing and became relatively fixed; that is, you stopped climbing and sat down on a plateau. This book and this course hope to show you that beyond this plateau are other mountains worth the ascent.

What is the nature of this plateau? Most of you are aware that at this moment you have certain preferences in fiction, that you like some kinds of stories but dislike others. If asked to define these preferences, you would very likely come up with a list of characteristics which are to be found in that large body of fiction which can be called "popular." To begin with, you probably prefer fiction with a strong story line to fiction in which "nothing much seems to happen." If, in addition, that story is "original" (that is, if the plot contains a surprise turn or an apparently new "gimmick") so much the better. You may prefer humorous stories to serious ones, and ones which end happily to ones which do not. Beyond this, you may have settled on what Robert Penn Warren has called "threshold interests" in fiction; you may read only stories which deal with sports or crime or love, or stories which project us into the future (science-fiction) or stories which purport to recreate the past (historical fiction). Finally, you probably prefer "easy" stories to "difficult" ones—not only those stories whose meaning and intent are easily grasped, but those stories that give easy solutions to the human problems with which they deal, and stories in which human existence is portrayed as neat, simple, and clean cut, in which villains are clearly villains, heroes are clearly heroes, evil is neatly and completely evil, and good is totally good.

Although fiction defies any attempt to break it down into neat subdivisions or to classify it the way a biologist classifies life forms, in the main we have described above what critics call escape fiction. In general, a story will either take us out of the life we know into a life we would prefer, or it will subject us more intensely than experience itself to that life; most readers prefer the first kind of story to the second. And what needs emphasis at the outset of a course in fiction is that one need not be apologetic about liking escape fiction. Most people in our culture lead routine and often monotonous lives; hence we can enjoy the vicarious escape which an exciting spy or adventure story can afford us. Most of us have discovered that sexual love lacks that perfection and total ecstasy which we could wish it to have, and so most of us can enjoy a story in which such love seems to be a possibility. We all live in a world whose faults are often more glaring than its virtues, and we can therefore appreciate an escape into a more perfect world. In short, even the most sophisticated reader reads, among other things, detective stories or spy stories or those ephemeral novels which are promoted by profit-oriented publishers and which are found on current best-seller lists.

But the sophisticated reader of fiction does not stop here; he has discovered that a different kind of fiction can also provide him with a very real pleasure. If one kind of fiction provides us with a vicarious escape from our world, our lives, our personal limitations, another kind increases our awareness of that same world, and of those same limitations. Most readers new to such fiction may find their introduction to it an unpleasant experience. Since the stories in this text are predominantly of this second type—partly because sophisticated readers have found them in the long run more rewarding, partly because I am assuming that such stories are new to you—some of the reasons for this initial reaction merit attention at the outset of a course in fiction.

To begin with, the writer of such stories is using fiction to interpret our lives or our world for us. Human nature and existence in its pure state tends to be, if not completely chaotic and senseless, at least so complex as to elude any comfortable and easy understanding of it. The writer of serious fiction is, among other things, concerned with making sense out of senselessness, with creating order out of chaos, with suggesting possible principles where there seem to be no perceptible principles. To put this in another way, he is concerned with trying to make us understand ourselves or our world better than we did before we read his story. But such self-knowledge can be unpleasant. We may, for example, sense unconsciously that man's condition is essentially tragic, but we may not want to believe it; and the story which makes a good case for this view of life is clearly not telling us what we would prefer to believe. To state this more broadly, serious writers usually are trying to tell us the "truth" about life insofar as they can perceive it, and the truth about life is never completely pleasant or reassuring. It is this aspect of serious fiction which prompts some readers to reject it on the grounds that life is depressing enough without adding to that depression through reading. What such a reader has not yet learned is that self-discovery and self-understanding can be more rewarding than self-delusion, that preparation for life can be more satisfying than escape from life.

Serious fiction, then, can add to your understanding of existence. But there is a more immediate reason for "studying" it in a formal course. The techniques and emphases of serious fiction are frequently not the same techniques and emphases as those which are employed by writers of escape fiction. If you have never learned to understand these differences in method, you may find serious fiction incomprehensible. Since various sections of this book are designed to introduce you to some of these differences, this is not the place to discuss them in any detail. We should, however, consider briefly one point. We said earlier that one element which you may look for in a story is a strong story line. Almost all escape stories offer such a line, and many serious stories follow suit. To cite one instance, an Isaac Asimov "space opera" will always tell an exciting story, though it will tell us little else about ourselves or our world; George Orwell's *1984,* which has behind it the deadly serious intention of telling us something about the nature of communism and totalitarianism, has an equally suspenseful narrative. But some fiction does not have this strong story line. Writers may find more significance in a very slight incident than they do in a more dramatic one, and that significance will often be brought out by a refocusing of emphasis away from plot and onto character or theme. The reader who looks for narrative above all else will find this type of story either dull or incomprehensible. He must, in short, learn to read stories which may not seem to him to be stories at all; he must learn how other devices in fiction—characterization, point of view, symbol, allusion, contrast, and the like—play their equally crucial part in helping a writer to achieve his purpose or effect.

In short, this course should help you to understand and appreciate stories which you may not, at the moment, understand or like. One final word needs to be said at this point about pedagogy in such a course. Fundamentally, the method employed in this course will be analytical, by which is meant that your approach will be to separate out of each story its separate elements and methods in order ultimately to better understand and appreciate the story. Such a method, you may discover, has its dangers as well as its advantages. For one thing, if the course is successful, it may change your reading tastes; you may discover that the course has "spoiled" some fiction for you which you now like. Beyond this, you may at the outset feel that "tearing a story apart" is not a superhighway to appreciation, that in fact it can (at least temporarily) "spoil" fiction in general for you. It may take some time to convince you that such is not the case, but meanwhile we can point out that probably the reader who derives most enjoyment from reading is the critic, and the critic's approach to literature is primarily analytical. True, the analytical approach involves hard work, but those who have learned to employ it have almost invariably found the results worth the effort.

W. SOMERSET MAUGHAM

The Facts of Life

It was Henry Garnet's habit on leaving the city of an afternoon to drop in at his club and play bridge before going home to dinner. He was a pleasant man to play with. He knew the game well, and you could be sure that he would make the best of his cards. He was a good loser; and when he won was more inclined to ascribe his success to his luck than to his skill. He was indulgent, and if his partner made a mistake, could be trusted to find an excuse for him. It was surprising then on this occasion to hear him telling his partner with unnecessary sharpness that he had never seen a hand worse played; and it was more surprising still to see him not only make a grave error himself, an error of which you would never have thought him capable, but when his partner, not unwilling to get a little of his own back, pointed it out, insist against all reason and with considerable heat that he was perfectly right. But they were all old friends, the men he was playing with, and none of them took his ill humour very seriously. Henry Garnet was a broker, a partner in a firm of repute, and it occurred to one of them that something had gone wrong with some stock he was interested in.

"How's the market today?" he asked.

"Booming. Even the suckers are making money."

It was evident that stocks and shares had nothing to do with Henry Garnet's vexation; but something was the matter; that was evident, too. He was a hearty fellow who enjoyed excellent health; he had plenty of money; he was fond of his wife and devoted to his children. As a rule he had high spirits, and he laughed easily at the nonsense they were apt to talk while they played; but today he sat glum and silent. His brows were crossly puckered, and there was a sulky look about his mouth. Presently, to ease the tension, one of the others mentioned a subject upon which they all knew Henry Garnet was glad to speak.

"How's your boy, Henry? I see he's done pretty well in the tournament."

Henry Garnet's frown grew darker.

"He's done no better than I expected him to."

"When does he come back from Monte?"

"He got back last night."

"Did he enjoy himself?"

"I suppose so; all I know is that he made a damned fool of himself."

"Oh. How?"

"I'd rather not talk about it if you don't mind."

The three men looked at him with curiosity. Henry Garnet scowled at the green baize.

"Sorry, old boy. Your call."

The game proceeded in a strained silence. Garnet got his bid, and when he played his cards so badly that he went three down not a word was said. Another rubber was begun, and in the second game Garnet denied a suit.

"Having none?" his partner asked him.

Garnet's irritability was such that he did not even reply, and when at the end of the hand it appeared that he had revoked, and that his revoke cost the rubber, it was not to be expected that his partner should let his carelessness go without remark.

"What the devil's the matter with you, Henry?" he said. "You're playing like a fool."

Garnet was disconcerted. He did not so much mind losing a big rubber himself, but he was sore that his inattention should have made his partner lose too. He pulled himself together.

"I'd better not play any more. I thought a few rubbers would calm me, but the fact is I can't give my mind to the game. To tell you the truth I'm in a hell of a temper."

They all burst out laughing.

"You don't have to tell us that, old boy. It's obvious."

Garnet gave them a rueful smile.

"Well, I bet you'd be in a temper if what's happened to me had happened to you. As a matter of fact I'm in a damned awkward situation, and if any of you fellows can give me any advice how to deal with it I'd be grateful."

"Let's have a drink and you tell us all about it. With a K.C., a Home Office official and an eminent surgeon—if we can't tell you how to deal with a situation, nobody can."

The K.C. got up and rang the bell for a waiter.

"It's about that damned boy of mine," said Henry Garnet.

Drinks were ordered and brought. And this is the story that Henry Garnet told them.

The boy of whom he spoke was his only son. His name was Nicholas, and of course he was called Nicky. He was eighteen. The Garnets had two daughters besides, one of sixteen and the other of twelve, but however unreasonable it seemed, for a father is generally supposed to like his daughters best, and though he did all he could not to show his preference, there was no doubt that the greater share of Henry Garnet's affection was given to his son. He was kind, in a chaffing, casual way, to his daughters, and gave them handsome presents on their birthdays and at Christmas; but he doted on Nicky. Nothing was too good for him. He thought the world of him. He could hardly take his eyes off him. You could not blame him, for Nicky was a son that any parent might have been proud of. He was six foot two, lithe but muscular, with broad shoulders and a slim waist, and he held himself gallantly erect; he had a charming head, well placed on the shoulders, with pale brown hair that waved slightly, blue eyes with long dark lashes under well-marked eyebrows, a full red mouth and a tanned, clean skin. When he smiled he showed very regular and very white teeth. He was not shy, but there was a modesty in his demeanour that was attractive. In social intercourse he was easy, polite and quietly gay. He was the offspring of nice, healthy, decent parents, he had been well brought up in a good home, he had been sent to a good school, and the general result was as engaging a specimen of young manhood as you were likely to find in a long time. You felt that he was as honest, open and virtuous as he looked. He had never given his parents a moment's uneasiness. As a child he was seldom ill and never naughty. As a boy he did everything that was expected of him. His school reports were excellent. He was wonderfully popular, and he ended his career, with a creditable number of prizes, as head of the school and captain of the football team. But this was not all. At the age of fourteen Nicky had developed an unexpected gift for lawn tennis. This was a game that his father not only was fond of, but played very well, and when he discerned in the boy the promise of a tennis player he fostered it. During the holidays he had him taught by the best professionals, and by the time he was sixteen he had won a number of tournaments for boys of his age. He could beat his father so badly that only parental affection reconciled the older player to the poor show he put up. At eighteen Nicky went to Cambridge and Henry Garnet conceived the ambition that before he was through with the university he should play for it. Nicky had all the qualifications for becoming a great tennis player. He was tall, he had a long reach, he was quick on his feet and his timing was perfect. He realized instinctively where the ball was coming and, seemingly without hurry, was there to take it. He had a powerful serve, with a nasty break that made it difficult to return, and his forehand drive, low, long and accurate, was deadly. He was not so good on the backhand and his volleying was wild, but all through the summer before he went to Cambridge Henry Garnet made him work on these points under the best teacher in England. At the back of his mind, though he did not even mention it to Nicky, he cherished a further ambition, to see his son play at Wimbledon, and who could tell, perhaps be chosen to represent his country in the Davis Cup. A great lump came into Henry Garnet's throat as he saw in fancy his son leap over the net to shake hands with the American champion whom he had just defeated, and walk off the court to the deafening plaudits of the multitude.

As an assiduous frequenter of Wimbledon, Henry Garnet had a good many friends in the tennis world, and one evening he found himself at a city dinner sitting next to one of them, a Colonel Brabazon, and in due course began talking to him of Nicky and what chance there might be of his being chosen to play for his university during the following season.

"Why don't you let him go down to Monte Carlo and play in the spring tournament there?" said the Colonel suddenly.

"Oh, I don't think he's good enough for that. He's not nineteen yet, he only went up to Cambridge last October; he wouldn't stand a chance against all those cracks."

"Of course, Austin and Von Cramm and so on would knock spots off him, but he might snatch a game or two; and if he got up against some of the smaller fry there's no reason why he shouldn't win two or three matches. He's never been up against any of the first-rate players, and it would be wonderful practice for him. He'd learn a lot more than he'll ever learn in the seaside tournaments you enter him for."

"I wouldn't dream of it. I'm not going to let him leave Cambridge in the middle of a term. I've always impressed upon him that tennis is only a game and it mustn't interfere with work."

Colonel Brabazon asked Garnet when the term ended.

"That's all right. He'd only have to cut about three days. Surely that could be arranged. You see, two of the men we were depending on have let us down, and we're in a hole. We want to send as good a team as we can. The Germans are sending their best players, and so are the Americans."

"Nothing doing, old boy. In the first place Nicky's not good enough, and secondly, I don't fancy the idea of sending a kid like that to Monte Carlo without anyone to look after him. If I could get away myself I might think of it, but that's out of the question."

"I shall be there. I'm going as the nonplaying captain of the English team. I'll keep an eye on him."

"You'll be busy, and besides, it's not a responsibility I'd like to ask you to take. He's never been abroad in his life, and to tell you the truth, I shouldn't have a moment's peace all the time he was there."

They left it at that, and presently Henry Garnet went home. He was so flattered by Colonel Brabazon's suggestion that he could not help telling his wife.

"Fancy his thinking Nicky's as good as that. He told me he'd seen him play and his style was fine. He only wants more practice to get into the first flight. We shall see the kid playing in the semi-finals at Wimbledon yet, old girl."

To his surprise Mrs. Garnet was not so much opposed to the notion as he would have expected.

"After all the boy's eighteen. Nicky's never got into mischief yet, and there's no reason to suppose he will now."

"There's his work to be considered; don't forget that. I think it would be a very bad precedent to let him cut the end of the term."

"But what can three days matter? It seems a shame to rob him of a chance like that. I'm sure he'd jump at it if you asked him."

"Well, I'm not going to. I haven't sent him to Cambridge just to play tennis. I know he's steady, but it's silly to put temptation in his way. He's much too young to go to Monte Carlo by himself."

"You say he won't have a chance against these crack players, but you can't tell."

Henry Garnet sighed a little. On the way home in the car it had struck him that Austin's health was uncertain and that Von Cramm had his off days. Supposing, just for the sake of argument, that Nicky had a bit of luck like that—then there would be no doubt that he would be chosen to play for Cambridge. But of course that was all nonsense.

"Nothing doing, my dear. I've made up my mind, and I'm not going to change it."

Mrs. Garnet held her peace. But next day she wrote to Nicky, telling him what had happened, and suggested to him what she would do in his place if, wanting to go, he wished to get his father's consent. A day or two later Henry Garnet received a letter from his son. He was bubbling over with excitement. He had seen his tutor, who was a tennis player himself, and the Provost of his college, who happened to know Colonel Brabazon, and no objection would be made to his leaving before the end of term; they both thought it an opportunity that shouldn't be missed. He didn't see what harm he could come to, and if only, just this once, his father would stretch a point, well, next term, he promised faithfully, he'd work like blazes. It was a very pretty letter. Mrs. Garnet watched her husband read it at the breakfast table; she was undisturbed by the frown on his face. He threw it over to her.

"I don't know why you thought it necessary to tell Nicky something I told you in confidence. It's too bad of you. Now you've thoroughly unsettled him."

"I'm so sorry. I thought it would please him to know that Colonel Brabazon had such a high opinion of him. I don't see why one should only tell people the disagreeable things that are said about them. Of course I made it quite clear that there could be no question of his going."

"You've put me in an odious position. If there's anything I hate it's for the boy to look upon me as a spoilsport and a tyrant."

"Oh, he'll never do that. He may think you rather silly and unreasonable, but I'm sure he'll understand that it's only for his own good that you're being so unkind."

"Christ," said Henry Garnet.

His wife had a great inclination to laugh. She knew the battle was won. Dear, oh dear, how easy it was to get men to do what you wanted. For appearance' sake Henry Garnet held out for forty-eight hours, but then he yielded, and a fortnight later Nicky came to London. He was to start for Monte Carlo next morning, and after dinner, when Mrs. Garnet and her elder daughter had left them, Henry took the opportunity to give his son some good advice.

"I don't feel quite comfortable about letting you go off to a place like Monte Carlo at your age practically by yourself," he finished, "but there it is, and I can only hope you'll be sensible. I don't want to play the heavy father, but there are three things especially that I want to warn you against: one is gambling, don't gamble; the second is money, don't lend anyone money; and the third is women, don't have anything to do with women. If you don't do any of those three things you can't come to much harm, so remember them well."

"All right, Father," Nicky smiled.

"That's my last word to you. I know the world pretty well, and believe me, my advice is sound."

"I won't forget it. I promise you."

"That's a good chap. Now let's go up and join the ladies."

Nicky beat neither Austin nor Von Cramm in the Monte Carlo tournament, but he did not disgrace himself. He snatched an unexpected victory over a Spanish player and gave one of the Austrians a closer match than anyone had thought possible. In the mixed doubles he got into the semifinals. His charm conquered everyone, and he vastly enjoyed himself. It was generally allowed that he showed promise, and Colonel Brabazon told him that when he was a little older and had had more practice with first-class players he would be a credit to his father. The tournament came to an end, and the day following he was to fly back to London. Anxious to play his best, he had lived very carefully, smoking little and drinking nothing, and going to bed early; but on his last evening he thought he would like to see something of the life in Monte Carlo of which he had heard so much. An official dinner was given to the tennis players, and after dinner with the rest of them he went into the Sporting Club. It was the first time he had been there. Monte Carlo was very full, and the rooms were crowded. Nicky had never before seen roulette played except in the pictures; in a maze he stopped at the first table he came to; chips of different sizes were scattered over the green cloth in what looked like a hopeless muddle; the croupier gave the wheel a sharp turn and with a flick threw in the little white ball. After what seemed an endless time the ball stopped and another croupier with a broad, indifferent gesture raked in the chips of those who had lost.

Presently Nicky wandered over to where they were playing *trente et quarante*, but he couldn't understand what it was all about, and he thought it dull. He saw a crowd in another room and sauntered in. A big game of baccara was in progress, and he was immediately conscious of the tension. The players were protected from the thronging bystanders by a brass rail; they sat round the table, nine on each side, with the dealer in the middle and the croupier facing him. Big money was changing hands. The dealer was a member of the Greek Syndicate. Nicky looked at his impassive face. His eyes were watchful, but his expression never changed whether he won or lost. It was a terrifying, strangely impressive sight. It gave Nicky, who had been thriftily brought up, a peculiar thrill to see someone risk a thousand pounds on the turn of a card and when he lost make a little joke and laugh. It was all terribly exciting. An acquaintance came up to him.

"Been doing any good?" he asked.

"I haven't been playing."

"Wise of you. Rotten game. Come and have a drink."

"All right."

While they were having it Nicky told his friend that this was the first time he had ever been in the rooms.

"Oh, but you must have one little flutter before you go. It's idiotic to leave Monte without having tried your luck. After all it won't hurt you to lose a hundred francs or so."

"I don't suppose it will, but my father wasn't any too keen on my coming at all, and one of the three things he particularly advised me not to do was to gamble."

But when Nicky left his companion he strolled back to one of the tables where they were playing roulette. He stood for a while looking at the losers' money being raked in by the croupier and the money that was won paid out to the winners. It was impossible to deny that it was thrilling. His friend was right, it did seem silly to leave Monte without putting something on the table just once. It would be an experience, and at his age you had to have all the experience you could get. He reflected that he hadn't promised his father not to gamble, he'd promised him not to forget his advice. It wasn't quite the same, was it? He took a hundred-franc note out of his pocket and rather shyly put it on number eighteen. He chose it because that was his age. With a wildly beating heart he watched the wheel turn; the little white ball whizzed about like a small demon of mischief; the wheel went round more slowly, the little white ball hesitated, it seemed about to stop, it went on again; Nicky could hardly believe his eyes when it fell into number eighteen. A lot of chips were passed over to him, and his hands trembled as he took them. It seemed to amount to a lot of money. He was so confused that he never thought of putting anything on the following round; in fact he had no intention of playing any more, once was enough; and he was surprised when eighteen again came up. There was only one chip on it.

"By George, you've won again," said a man who was standing near to him.

"Me? I hadn't got anything on."

"Yes, you had. Your original stake. They always leave it on unless you ask for it back. Didn't you know?"

Another packet of chips was handed over to him. Nicky's head reeled. He counted his gains: seven thousand francs. A queer sense of power seized him; he felt wonderfully clever. This was the easiest way of making money that he had ever heard of. His frank, charming face was wreathed in smiles. His bright eyes met those of a woman standing by his side. She smiled.

"You're in luck," she said.

She spoke English, but with a foreign accent.

"I can hardly believe it. It's the first time I've ever played."

"That explains it. Lend me a thousand francs, will you? I've lost everything I've got. I'll give it you back in half an hour."

"All right."

She took a large red chip from his pile and with a word of thanks disappeared. The man who had spoken to him before grunted.

"You'll never see that again."

Nicky was dashed. His father had particularly advised him not to lend anyone money. What a silly thing to do! And to somebody he'd never seen in his life. But the fact was, he felt at that moment such a love for the human race that it had never occurred to him to refuse. And that big red chip, it was almost impossible to realize that it had any value. Oh, well, it didn't matter, he still had six thousand francs, he'd just try his luck once or twice more, and if he didn't win he'd go home. He put a chip on sixteen, which was his elder sister's age, but it didn't come up; then on twelve, which was his younger sister's, and that didn't come up either; he tried various numbers at random, but without success. It was funny, he seemed to have lost his knack. He thought he would try just once more and then stop; he won. He had made up all his losses and had something over. At the end of an hour, after various ups and downs, having experienced such thrills as he had never known in his life, he found himself with so many chips that they would hardly go in his pockets. He decided to go. He went to the changers' office, and he gasped when twenty thousand-franc notes were spread out before him. He had never had so much money in his life. He put it in his pocket and was turning away when the woman to whom he had lent the thousand francs came up to him.

"I've been looking for you everywhere," she said. "I was afraid you'd gone. I was in a fever, I didn't know what you'd think of me. Here's your thousand francs and thank you so much for the loan."

Nicky, blushing scarlet, stared at her with amazement. How he had misjudged her! His father had said, don't gamble; well, he had, and he'd made twenty thousand francs; and his father had said, don't lend anyone money; well, he had, he'd lent quite a lot to a total stranger, and she'd returned it. The fact was that he wasn't nearly such a fool as his father thought: he'd had an instinct that he could lend her the money with safety, and you see, his instinct was right. But he was so obviously taken aback that the little lady was forced to laugh.

"What is the matter with you?" she asked.

"To tell you the truth I never expected to see the money back."

"What did you take me for? Did you think I was a—cocotte?"

Nicky reddened to the roots of his wavy hair.

"No, of course not."

"Do I look like one?"

"Not a bit."

She was dressed very quietly, in black, with a string of gold beads round her neck; her simple frock showed off a neat, slight figure; she had a pretty little face and a trim head. She was made up, but not excessively, and Nicky supposed that she was not more than three or four years older than himself. She gave him a friendly smile.

"My husband is in the administration in Morocco, and I've come to Monte Carlo for a few weeks because he thought I wanted a change."

"I was just going," said Nicky because he couldn't think of anything else to say.

"Already!"

"Well, I've got to get up early tomorrow. I'm going back to London by air."

"Of course. The tournament ended today, didn't it? I saw you play, you know, two or three times."

"Did you? I don't know why you should have noticed me."

"You've got a beautiful style. And you looked very sweet in your shorts."

Nicky was not an immodest youth, but it did cross his mind that perhaps she had borrowed that thousand francs in order to scrape acquaintance with him.

"Do you ever go to the Knickerbocker?" she asked.

"No. I never have."

"Oh, but you mustn't leave Monte without having been there. Why don't you come and dance a little? To tell you the truth, I'm starving with hunger, and I should adore some bacon and eggs."

Nicky remembered his father's advice not to have anything to do with women, but this was different; you had only to look at the pretty little thing to know at once that she was perfectly respectable. Her husband was in what corresponded, he supposed, to the civil service. His father and mother had friends who were civil servants, and they and their wives sometimes came to dinner. It was true that the wives were neither so young nor so pretty as this one, but she was just as ladylike as they were. And after winning twenty thousand francs he thought it wouldn't be a bad idea to have a little fun.

"I'd love to go with you," he said. "But you won't mind if I don't stay very long. I've left instructions at my hotel that I'm to be called at seven."

"We'll leave as soon as ever you like."

Nicky found it very pleasant at the Knickerbocker. He ate his bacon and eggs with appetite. They shared a bottle of champagne. They danced, and the little lady told him he danced beautifully. He knew he danced pretty well, and of course she was easy to dance with. As light as a feather. She laid her cheek against his and when their eyes met there was in hers a smile that made his heart go pit-a-pat. A coloured woman sang in a throaty, sensual voice. The floor was crowded.

"Have you ever been told that you're very good-looking?" she asked.

"I don't think so," he laughed. "Gosh" he thought, "I believe she's fallen for me."

Nicky was not such a fool as to be unaware that women often liked him, and when she made that remark he pressed her to him a little more closely. She closed her eyes, and a faint sigh escaped her lips.

"I suppose it wouldn't be quite nice if I kissed you before all these people," he said.

"What do you think they would take me for?"

It began to grow late, and Nicky said that really he thought he ought to be going.

"I shall go too," she said. "Will you drop me at my hotel on your way?"

Nicky paid the bill. He was rather surprised at its amount, but with all that money he had in his pocket he could afford not to care, and they got into a taxi. She snuggled up to him, and he kissed her. She seemed to like it.

"By Jove," he thought, "I wonder if there's anything doing."

It was true that she was a married woman, but her husband was in Morocco, and it certainly did look as if she'd fallen for him. Good and proper. It was true also that his father had warned him to have nothing to do with women, but, he reflected again, he hadn't actually promised he wouldn't, he'd only promised not to forget his advice. Well, he hadn't; he was bearing it in mind that very minute. But circumstances alter cases. She was a sweet little thing; it seemed silly to miss the chance of an adventure when it was handed to you like that on a tray. When they reached the hotel he paid off the taxi.

"I'll walk home," he said. "The air will do me good after the stuffy atmosphere of that place."

"Come up a moment," she said. "I'd like to show you the photo of my little boy."

"Oh, have you got a little boy?" he exclaimed, a trifle dashed.

"Yes, a sweet little boy."

He walked upstairs after her. He didn't in the least want to see the photograph of her little boy, but he thought it only civil to pretend he did. He was afraid he'd made a fool of himself; it occurred to him that she was taking him up to look at the photograph in order to show him in a nice way that he'd made a mistake. He'd told her he was eighteen.

"I suppose she thinks I'm just a kid."

He began to wish he hadn't spent all that money on champagne at the night club.

But she didn't show him the photograph of her little boy after all. They had no sooner got into her room than she turned to him, flung her arms round his neck, and kissed him full on the lips. He had never in all his life been kissed so passionately.

"Darling," she said.

For a brief moment his father's advice once more crossed Nicky's mind, and then he forgot it.

Nicky was a light sleeper, and the least sound was apt to wake him. Two or three hours later he awoke and for a moment could not imagine where he was. The room was not quite dark, for the door of the bathroom was ajar, and the light in it had been left on. Suddenly he was conscious that someone was moving about the room. Then he remembered. He saw that it was his little friend, and he was on the point of speaking when something in the way she was behaving stopped him.

She was walking very cautiously, as though she were afraid of waking him; she stopped once or twice and looked over at the bed. He wondered what she was after. He soon saw. She went over to the chair on which he had placed his clothes and once more looked in his direction. She waited for what seemed to him an interminable time. The silence was so intense that Nicky thought he could hear his own heart beating. Then, very slowly, very quietly, she took up his coat, slipped her hand into the inside pocket and drew out all those beautiful thousand-franc notes that Nicky had been so proud to win. She put the coat back and placed some other clothes on it so that it should look as though it had not been disturbed, then, with the bundle of notes in her hand, for an appreciable time stood once more stock-still. Nicky had repressed an instinctive impulse to jump up and grab her; it was partly surprise that had kept him quiet, partly the notion that he was in a strange hotel, in a foreign country, and if he made a row he didn't know what might happen. She looked at him. His eyes were partly closed, and he was sure that she thought he was asleep. In the silence she could hardly fail to hear his regular breathing. When she had reassured herself that her movements had not disturbed him, she stepped, with infinite caution, across the room. On a small table in the window a cineraria was growing in a pot. Nicky watched her now with his eyes wide open. The plant was evidently placed quite loosely in the pot, for, taking it by the stalks, she lifted it out; she put the bank notes in the bottom of the pot and replaced the plant. It was an excellent hiding place. No one could have guessed that anything was concealed under that richly flowering plant. She pressed the earth down with her fingers and then, very slowly, taking care not to make the smallest noise, crept across the room and slipped back into bed.

"Chéri," she said, in a caressing voice.

Nicky breathed steadily, like a man immersed in deep sleep. The little lady turned over on her side and disposed herself to slumber. But though Nicky lay so still, his thoughts worked busily. He was extremely indignant at the scene he had just witnessed, and to himself he spoke his thoughts with vigour.

"She's nothing but a damned tart. She and her dear little boy and her husband in Morocco. My eye! She's a rotten thief, that's what she is. Took me for a mug. If she thinks she's going to get away with anything like that, she's mistaken."

He had already made up his mind what he was going to do with the money he had so cleverly won. He had long wanted a car of his own and had thought it rather mean of his father not to have given him one. After all, a feller doesn't always want to drive about in the family bus. Well, he'd just teach the old man a lesson and buy one himself. For twenty thousand francs, two hundred pounds roughly, he could get a very decent second-hand car. He meant to get the money back, but just then he didn't quite know how. He didn't like the idea of kicking up a row, he was a stranger, in a hotel he knew nothing of; it might very well be that the beastly woman had friends there; he didn't mind facing anyone in a fair fight, but he'd look pretty foolish if someone pulled a gun on him. He reflected besides, very sensibly, that he had no proof the money was his. If it came to a showdown and she swore it was hers, he might very easily find himself hauled off to a police station. He really didn't know what to do. Presently by her regular breathing he knew that the little lady was asleep. She must have fallen asleep with an easy mind, for she had done her job without a hitch. It infuriated Nicky that she should rest so peacefully while he lay awake, worried to death. Suddenly an idea occurred to him. It was such a good one that it was only by the exercise of all his self-control that he prevented himself from jumping out of bed and carrying it out at once. Two could play at her game. She'd stolen his money; well, he'd steal it back again, and they'd be all square. He made up his mind to wait quite quietly until he was sure that deceitful woman was sound asleep. He waited for what seemed to him a very long time. She did not stir. Her breathing was as regular as a child's.

"Darling," he said at last.

No answer. No movement. She was dead to the world. Very slowly, pausing after every movement, very silently, he slipped out of bed. He stood still for a while, looking at her to see whether he had disturbed her. Her breathing was as regular as before. During the time he was waiting he had taken note carefully of the furniture in the room so that in crossing it he should not knock against a chair or a table and make a noise. He took a couple of steps and waited; he took a couple of steps more; he was very light on his feet and made no sound as he walked; he took fully five minutes to get to the window, and here he waited again. He started, for the bed slightly creaked, but it was only because the sleeper turned in her sleep. He forced himself to wait till he had counted one hundred. She was sleeping like a log. With infinite care he seized the cineraria by the stalks and gently pulled it out of the pot; he put his other hand in, his heart beat nineteen to the dozen as his fingers touched the notes, his hand closed on them and he slowly drew them out. He replaced the plant and in his turn carefully pressed down the earth. While he was doing all this he had kept one eye on the form lying in the bed. It remained still. After another pause he crept softly to the chair on which his clothes were lying. He first put the bundle of notes in his coat pocket and then proceeded to dress. It took him a good quarter of an hour, because he could afford to make no sound. He had been wearing a soft shirt with his dinner jacket, and he congratulated himself on this because it was easier to put on silently than a stiff one. He had some difficulty in tying his tie without a looking glass, but he very wisely reflected that it didn't really matter if it wasn't tied very well. His spirits were rising. The whole thing now began to seem rather a lark. At length he was completely dressed except for his shoes, which he took in his hand; he thought he would put them on when he got into the passage. Now he had to cross the room to get to the door. He reached it so quietly that he could not have disturbed the lightest sleeper. But the door had to be unlocked. He turned the key very slowly; it creaked.

"Who's that?"

The little woman suddenly sat up in bed. Nicky's heart jumped to his mouth. He made a great effort to keep his head.

"It's only me. It's six o'clock and I've got to go. I was trying not to wake you."

"Oh, I forgot."

She sank back onto the pillow.

"Now that you're awake I'll put on my shoes."

He sat down on the edge of the bed and did this.

"Don't make a noise when you go out. The hotel people don't like it. Oh, I'm so sleepy."

"You go right off to sleep again."

"Kiss me before you go." He bent down and kissed her. "You're a sweet boy and a wonderful lover. *Bon Voyage*."

Nicky did not feel quite safe till he got out of the hotel. The dawn had broken. The sky was unclouded, and in the harbour the yachts and the fishing boats lay motionless on the still water. On the quay fishermen were getting ready to start on their day's work. The streets were deserted. Nicky took a long breath of the sweet morning air. He felt alert and well. He also felt as pleased as Punch. With a swinging stride, his shoulders well thrown back, he walked up the hill and along the gardens in front of the Casino—the flowers in that clear light had a dewy brilliance that was delicious—till he came to his hotel. Here the day had already begun. In the hall porters with mufflers round their necks and berets on their heads were busy sweeping. Nicky went up to his room and had a hot bath. He lay in it and thought with satisfaction that he was not such a mug as some people might think. After his bath he did his exercises, dressed, packed and went down to breakfast. He had a grand appetite. No continental breakfast for him! He had grapefruit, porridge, bacon and eggs, rolls fresh from the oven, so crisp and delicious they melted in your mouth, marmalade and three cups of coffee. Though feeling perfectly well before, he felt better after that. He lit the pipe he had recently learnt to smoke, paid his bill and stepped into the car that was waiting to take him to the aerodrome on the other side of Cannes. The road as far as Nice ran over the hills, and below him was the blue sea and the coast line. He couldn't help thinking it damned pretty. They passed through Nice, so gay and friendly in the early morning, and presently they came to a long stretch of straight road that ran by the sea. Nicky had paid his bill, not with the money he had won the night before, but with the money his father had given him; he had changed a thousand francs to pay for supper at the Knickerbocker, but that deceitful little woman had returned him the thousand francs he had lent her, so that he still had twenty thousand-franc notes in his pocket. He thought he would like to have a look at them. He had so nearly lost them that they had a double value for him. He took them out of his hip pocket into which for safety's sake he had stuffed them when he put on the suit he was travelling in, and counted them one by one. Something very strange had happened to them. Instead of there being twenty notes, as there should have been, there were twenty-six. He couldn't understand it at all. He counted them twice more. There was no doubt about it; somehow or other he had twenty-six thousand francs instead of the twenty he should have had. He couldn't make it out. He asked himself if it was possible that he had won more at the Sporting Club than he had realized. But no, that was out of the question; he distinctly remembered the man at the desk laying the notes out in four rows of five, and he had counted them himself. Suddenly the explanation occurred to him; when he had put his hand into the flower pot, after taking out the cineraria, he had grabbed everything he felt there. The flower pot was the little hussy's money box, and he had taken out not only his own money, but her savings as well. Nicky leant back in the car and burst into a roar of laughter. It was the funniest thing he had ever heard in his life. And when he thought of her going to the flower pot sometime later in the morning when she awoke, expecting to find the money she had so cleverly got away with, and finding, not only that it wasn't there, but that her own had gone too, he laughed more than ever. And so far as he was concerned there was nothing to do about it, he knew neither her name nor the name of the hotel to which she had taken him. He couldn't return her money even if he wanted to.

"It serves her damned well right," he said.

This then was the story that Henry Garnet told his friends over the bridge table, for the night before, after dinner when his wife and daughter had left them to their port, Nicky had narrated it in full.

"And you know what infuriated me is that he's so damned pleased with himself. Talk of a cat swallowing a canary. And d'you know what he said to me when he'd finished? He looked at me with those innocent eyes of his and said: 'You know, Father, I can't help thinking there was something wrong about the advice you gave me. You said, don't gamble; well, I did, and I made a packet; you said, don't lend money; well, I did, and I got it back; and you said, don't have anything to do with women; well, I did, and I made six thousand francs on the deal.' "

It didn't make it any better for Henry Garnet that his three companions burst out laughing.

"It's all very well for you fellows to laugh, but you know, I'm in a damned awkward position. The boy looked up to me, he respected me, he took whatever I said as gospel truth, and now, I saw it in his eyes, he just looks upon me as a drivelling old fool. It's no good my saying one swallow doesn't make a summer; he doesn't see that it was just a fluke, he thinks the whole thing was due to his own cleverness. It may ruin him."

"You do look a bit of a damned fool, old man," said one of the others. "There's no denying that, is there?"

"I know I do, and I don't like it. It's so dashed unfair. Fate has no right to play one tricks like that. After all, you must admit that my advice was good."

"Very good."

"And the wretched boy ought to have burnt his fingers. Well, he hasn't. You're all men of the world, you tell me how I'm to deal with the situation now."

But they none of them could.

"Well, Henry, if I were you I wouldn't worry," said the lawyer. "My belief is that your boy's born lucky, and in the long run that's better than to be born clever or rich."

HUGH NISSENSON

The Well

Sunday. It's ten-year-old Micah, Aviva's kid, waiting in front of the dining-hall just before lunch, who brings us the news: One of the Bedouin camels from Ahmad's camp two kilometers south of the *kibbutz* has strayed into our date grove to give birth. "Come and thee! Come and thee!" Micah cried. Buck-toothed, and with ugly brick-red hair like his mother, he speaks with a lisp, spraying a fine mist of spit into the air that gives me the fantastic notion that he has somehow boiled over from the heat. "Juth for a minute," he insists.

Grossman the mechanic is with me, pale and drawn from his morning's work in the machine shop and his attack of *shil-shul,* the chronic dysentery from which he has suffered the last two days. "Pleath," the boy pleads, but bathed in sweat, and absent-mindedly chewing on the ragged end of his drooping mustache, Grossman refuses with a shake of his head, and goes inside, slamming the screen door behind him, and stirring up the flies. The boy takes hold of my hand.

"It'll only take a minute."

"Where's your mother?"

A hubbub around us, as more and more of the *chaverim*—the comrades, members of the collective settlement—arrive at the dining-hall from the work shops and the fields. They are in much the same state as Grossman and myself, and do not care who knows it; sullen, completely exhausted by the heat, and oppressed by the prospect of a meager meal and an afternoon's work still to be done.

"Oh pleath. Pleath," the boy begs, with the rising inflection, the sad whine of the ugly child who has already learned that he cannot command attention any other way. "You don't underthand."

"Maybe after lunch."

"But that'll be too late. He'th going to kill it."

"Kill what? Who?"

"Oh hurry!"

It's too much of an effort for me to argue or try to understand, and he knows it. Hand in mine, he leads me away, past the deserted machine shop and the cow shed where, attracted by the feed, literally hundreds of twittering sparrows are perched on the corrugated tin roof—the only life, it seems, besides ourselves, abroad on the desert at this hour of the day.

Just noon. At the date grove, row on row of the broad dusty leaves cast no shadow, offer no refuge from the terrific glare of the sun.

"Look!" says the boy.

"Where?"

I shield my eyes with my hand, and there, in the direction that he points, just beyond the line of trees to the south, is the camel with her colt that couldn't have been born more than an hour before. Beside them, on the ground and swarming with flies, is the bloody sac. A wonderful sight, I must admit. The colt, waist high, as yet with only a rudimentary hump, all knees and huge splayed toes, jerks its head convulsively as it sucks at the pendulous swollen udders of the mare.

"Promith me!"

"What?"

"You won't let him kill it, will you?"

This time, he only has to turn his head. To my left, not ten feet away, and apparently watching us all the while, is a young Bedouin with a rifle, squatting on his hams against one of the trees.

"Shalom."

"And peace; peace unto you," he replies, speaking Hebrew with a thick Arabic accent. Under the *kafiyah* that shadows his eyes, a rather handsome, intelligent face; high cheekbones, a hooked nose, and a thick black mustache that droops down to the corners of his mouth.

"Ask him yourself. He says he'th going to kill it. Why?" says the boy, and the Bedouin, for an answer, glances up to indicate—what? In the torpor engendered by the heat, it takes me a moment to understand fully. I too, as though compelled, look up at the cloudless sky from which the sun has bleached all the color, leaving a white, translucent haze that dazzles the eyes.

"Tell me why!"

It's the drought, of course. I try to explain to the boy. Now the middle of November, what little autumnal rains the Bedouins depend on to water their herds is more than six weeks overdue.

"But what about their well?"

"Ah, now that's just the trouble. Their well has all gone dry. The colt has to be killed so that their children will have the milk to drink. You wouldn't want the children to die of thirst, would you?"

"I don't care."

"Micah!"

"Is our well dry too?"

"Not yet; no."

"Why not?"

"It's deeper."

While we have been talking, the Bedouin has opened the bolt of his rifle—an old Lee Enfield .303, and inserted a cartridge with a click that rivets our attention to the oiled barrel gleaming in the sun. When he stands up in his soiled, billowing pantaloons, the boy cannot suppress a shout that makes the mare swivel her head in our direction. She apparently has just become aware of us, and with a kind of comical, bewildered ferocity, lets hang her protruding underlip, and bares her teeth. The startled colt has stopped sucking, and skitters backwards, with its shaky forelegs locked together, and the back spread awkwardly apart. For the first time, I catch a glimpse of its bitten cord, already withering from its belly like a dead vine.

"Chaver! . . . But comrade," the boy shouts.

"Micah, come here. Come away."

"Comrade, don't."

"Come away, I tell you. It's none of our business."

"You promithed."

"No. There's nothing I can do."

I catch him by the hand and drag him away. At the cowshed, the echoing crack of the shot rouses the sparrows who rise in a dark twittering mass, circle the silo twice, and begin once again to settle on the sloping tin roof.

Grossman is still in the dining-hall when I get back, sitting alone at a corner table.

"Where's the kid?" he asks.

"I left him at the nursery."

"Aviva was looking for him."

"I know. I saw her. How's the stomach?"

"Okay."

"Really better?"

Obviously forcing himself to keep up his strength, he is eating a plate of white goat's cheese and chopped cucumbers, washing down mouthfuls of the stuff with sips from a cup of cold water.

"The water'll give you cramps."

"No," he says, "I really feel better. . . . So the Bedouins are beginning to slaughter their herds."

"You heard the shot. . . . The kid was terribly upset."

"It's a shame."

"I read in yesterday's paper that the government says if the drought keeps up, they'll try and relocate the tribes to better grazing land up north."

"The government," he grimaces. A stomach spasm? It's hard to tell. With a sour expression on his face, wiping off his mustache, he pushes away the plate of food. "Who was doing the shooting?"

"One of the younger men. Good-looking. He speaks a little Hebrew, I think."

"Don't tell me. Not Ali?"

"Which one is Ali? . . . Oh." I remember, Ali, Sheik Ahmad's oldest son, with whom Grossman had struck up a friendship two years before, when for a season both of them were shepherds, pasturing their herds together some thirty kilometers or so north of here.

"Ah," he goes on. "It's a damn shame. By the time the government decides to do anything for them, it'll be too late."

"Not necessarily."

"You know it as well as I do. What's the use? By the time it goes through all the official channels to provide relief, they'll have slaughtered all their young animals. What'll they do come spring?"

"They'll manage."

"They'll starve. That's what."

Then absorbed in thought, he is silent. All around us, like insects in amber, each sound in the room seems embedded and preserved in the thick air, yellowed by the sunlight streaming through the windows; the clatter of tin forks, scrape of plates, murmur of the comrades' voices, and pervading all else the buzz of the flies that are so fat and lazy when they alight you can squash them with a finger.

"Ali, eh?" he asks. "I haven't seen him in over a year. What do you think? Maybe I ought to go over and have a talk with him."

"What you ought to do is go back to your room and lie down."

He gives me an ironic glance and is partly right. It's not his health alone that concerns me, but my reluctance, as elected secretary, more or less a kind of first among equals, general manager of the settlement, to allow the *kibbutz* to become officially involved in Bedouin affairs at all.

"No," I tell him.

"Why not? We were friends."

"You asked my advice and I'm telling you. If they really would like us to help them, let them take the initiative for once—just for once, and come to us."

"I can't see any harm in just talking to Ali."

But there is. That's the trouble, and Grossman knows it as well as I, in spite of any personal relationship he may have cultivated with the Sheik's son. For eleven years now, since the establishment of our settlement in the desert by force of arms, we have lived in a state of truce with Ahmad's tribe, no more and no less. Time and time again, experience has taught us that when we so much as offer them any material assistance, much less demonstrate a willingness for a real peace, it is refused, and taken for nothing but a display of weakness on our part, a loss of face as far as we are concerned.

"No," I continue, "I . . ." But Grossman interrupts by standing up. "No matter. It was just a thought."

He leaves, but all afternoon in the secretary's office—a desk, two rattan chairs, and a metal filing cabinet—I can think of nothing else while I should be at work checking a list of supplies to be bought tomorrow in Beersheba.

. . . One hundred kilos baking soda, one hundred salt . . .

Impossible to keep my mind on it. The office, adjacent to the radio shack, stands on a little rise behind the dining-hall, commanding a view of the desert to the south. Broken up by a network of wadis running east to west—dry water courses eroded by flash floods—the landscape always gives me the impression that it has been raked by the talons of some gigantic beast. Here and there, glaring in the sun, are white outcroppings of rock; ribs and spines and shoulder blades, only partly buried by the cracked earth. Yes. It is exactly as though some unimaginable animal has dug at the earth to bury the bones of its prey.

. . . Salt, one hundred kilos sugar, tea . . .

Again and again my gaze returns to the window, but at this distance, the black wool tents of the Bedouin encampment are indistinguishable in the chaotic pattern of the shadow cast by the afternoon sun on the broken ground. Once, and only for a moment, one of their camels is to be seen, silhouetted against the sky, and again—or is it my imagination?—I can hear the faint echo of a rifle shot borne on the rising wind.

Four-thirty. Finished by now with his work at the machine shop, Grossman is there, I am sure of it, but to speak with Ali means nothing. That's the whole point. It is Ahmad himself who has always been responsible for most of the difficulties that exist between us. The absolute ruler of the tribe for over twenty years, he is terrified—and with some justification—that even the minimal communication between the two communities will undermine his feudal authority. I have seen him only once or twice, at the Kassid or Morris, cafés in Beersheba; a great hulk of a man, not without dignity, who wears a pointed little beard, and whose dark, unhealthy-looking skin reminds me, for some reason, of the color of a slice of apple left exposed to the air. Purportedly still possessed of a harem of twenty women or more, his licentiousness is legendary. One story has it that one day, long ago, at the height of his powers, he came upon a beautiful fourteen-year-old Bedouin girl drawing water from a desert well, and unable to resist making overtures—pleading, threatening, promising her anything to get her to join his harem—he reduced the child to tears.

"Let me go," she begged. "If you don't let me go, I'll tell my father."

"And just who is that?" Ahmad wanted to know.

"A sheik. A very powerful sheik who'd have you gelded like a horse."

"Who?" he laughed.

"Ahmad. Do you realize that? Sheik Ahmad," was the reply.

Five-fifteen. Sure enough, Grossman shows up at the office, looking even worse than before; completely drained, with livid lips and feverish eyes.

"So you went."

"Yes . . ." We walk back to his room and he talks. "Things are terrible there, worse than I imagined. Their well has been dry since the day before yesterday. What water they have will only last them to the end of the week, if they're lucky . . . less . . . They've made up their minds to slaughter most of their herds by then, sell the meat for what they can get in Beersheba, and maybe buy enough water to last them until the rains come."

"Did you speak to Ali?"

"I was right. It was he that you saw. He agrees with me absolutely. If and when the government acts to help them, it'll be too late."

The evening breeze is blowing from the southwest, drying the sweat from our bodies with a chill, and whipping the sand across the ground with a rasping noise that sets the teeth on edge. We pause in front of the row of attached wooden shacks that serve as the bachelor quarters of the settlement.

"So Ali really was willing to speak with you."

"Of course. One must be willing simply to . . . make the effort."

"And Ahmad?"

Grossman laughs. "The old dog . . . would you believe it? Ali told me he's developed a taste for European women in his old age. He's actually gone so far as to place advertisements in three or four papers on the Continent for a new concubine . . . preferably young, fat, and blonde."

"But you didn't speak with him."

"It wasn't necessary."

"He refused to see you."

"Yes, but it doesn't make any difference. He'll soon be dead. Ali will be Sheik. He has most of the authority right now. . . . I tell you, this is something new. Times have changed."

"I see. And just what did Ali propose?"

"Nothing. He just told me what was happening. Of course, I could see it all with my own eyes. They're desperate. He . . . No. He didn't propose anything."

"But you did."

"No . . . That is, I suggested . . . Actually, I wanted to speak with you first."

We go inside his room that resembles nothing so much as a cell with its iron cot and tiled floor. Grossman insists on making coffee, squatting on his hams in front of the kerosene burner in the same posture as Ali against the date palm. Interesting, the similarities between them. It is never so apparent to me as now. Both of them, Arab and Jew, born in the country, reared here, feeling completely a part of it, even resemble each other physically, affecting the same drooping mustache that is probably Turkish in origin, signifying virility. The water begins to boil on the blue flame.

"Yes," repeats Grossman. "You'll see for yourself. Times have changed."

Does he really believe it? I don't know. Maybe it's so. In any case, what I as a European immigrant can never fully comprehend is the significance of that mustache or peculiar crouch; the sense of utterly belonging in this country of his birth. Whatever the truth concerning the Bedouins may be, it is that which is at the heart of Grossman's passionate desire to effect a rapprochement with the tribe. Knowing no other home, he appreciates and respects the Arab's sense of possession for a land that he loves as well. More, actually speaking fluent Arabic from his childhood, he can remember a time in the not too distant past, when the two populations lived side by side with no more than the usual conflicts that divide one man from another. The fact that he has fought them, has in fact, within my earliest memory of arriving here, fought bravely against Ahmad himself who attacked the settlement on the first night of its establishment, seems to him essentially beside the point. Being young, it is the present that counts for him—this moment alone, and the future, when the development of the land that he loves will depend first and foremost on peace.

"Sugar?"

"No thanks."

He hands me a cup, and sits on the cot which squeaks.

"You realize this is the chance we've been waiting for."

"Maybe."

"But I told you," he says. "Ali will soon be Sheik. If we can just establish good relations with him now . . ."

"But it isn't as if we haven't tried before. What about the drought four years ago? It was the same thing. They refused any help, and then—when was it? You remember. That little girl with appendicitis."

He remembers, nodding his head sadly in the diminishing light. Two summers ago, rather than trust us to take one of their children into Beersheba for an operation, they apparently preferred to see her die.

"Still, this is different," he insists. "Ali is different from the old man. He spent almost a year in Tel Aviv, did you know that? Working at the port. With Jews. That's where he learned to speak some Hebrew. For the first time, they're more than willing to accept our help."

"What exactly do you suggest?"

"What about our own well?"

"All right, so far as I understand."

"That's what I thought. We've probably more than enough water to see us all through."

"That I couldn't say."

"Well, enough for at least a week, surely, if we're careful. The rains will surely be here by then."

"Then what you want is to have us share our water."

"Exactly."

"That's, of course, a decision that neither of us can make alone."

"I realize that," he tells me. "The whole *kibbutz* will have to decide. That's why I wanted to speak with you. We'll hold a meeting."

"When?"

"You should have seen the camp. They're rationing what water they have, and the kids have sores on their lips . . . the corners of their mouths. . . . They surrounded me with tin cans, begging for water, as one would beg for alms."

He has neglected to light a lamp. In the gathering dark, his face is almost invisible, and his momentary anguish is communicated only by the timbre of his voice.

"When do you want me to call a meeting?"

"What? . . . Right away. The sooner the better. Tonight, if you can. Right after supper."

"I'll see what I can do."

"Wonderful. Oh. I almost forgot. Tell the night watch to let Ali through, will you?"

"You asked him to come here tonight?"

Under his mustache, his teeth gleam faintly as he grimaces with a stomach pang or smiles to himself in the dark.

"Yes," he tells me, "of course. About ten."

The meeting, held in the dining-hall, and attended by about sixty adult members of the settlement, is over by nine-forty-five. Grossman's motion is carried by almost two to one after Lev, the engineer who dug our artesian well four years ago, assures us that in all probability there will be enough water to supply the two communities for at least the next week if we are careful.

It's agreed that the Bedouins are to be permitted to take as much as they need every morning without charge—on one condition imposed by Zvika, who holds forth from his bench for more than five minutes, his round face shining with sweat, and his eyes bloodshot from the cigarette smoke that hangs in the air. He is a tractor driver, a man of about twenty-eight, completely bald, and intensely self-conscious about it, so that even indoors, his head is always covered by an army fatigue cap, with its peak turned up. A particularly doctrinaire and pedantic Socialist, and an author to boot, he has recently published a book comparing the life of the modern *kibbutz* to the ancient Hebrew Essenic and early Christian communes. His high-pitched voice drones on. Now, to illustrate some point he is making, he is actually quoting by heart from Philo—the Alexandrian writer of antiquity—describing the life of the Essenic communes near the Dead Sea that were so much like our own.

"For none of them wishes to have any property of his own, but rather by joining together everything without exception, they all have a common profit from it."

Grossman, glancing at his wrist watch, interrupts him impatiently:

"Philo! Who's Philo? What's this Philo got to do with it?"

"I'm discussing the principles upon which this *kibbutz* has been founded. Principles which . . ."

"But there's a motion on the floor. What's all this have to do with sharing the water with the Bedouins?"

"That's it. Aha! Exactly. Sharing . . . You are evidently proposing an equitable distribution of the water. All well and good, and in accordance with our principles. But we are dealing here with a feudal lord—a Sheik, don't forget that. What's there to guarantee that Ahmad will distribute our water fairly among his own people? How can we be absolutely sure, for example, that it's not his harem alone, or his relations—who knows—who are going to benefit. Do I have to tell you . . ."

"I've already explained," says Grossman. "Ali . . ."

"What do I care about Ali? Ahmad. Ahmad is still Sheik, and whether you remember it or not, it was Ahmad who . . ." His shrill voice breaks off, but the rest of the sentence hangs over us as tangibly as the blue smoke. It was Ahmad who ordered the surprise attack on the settlement eleven years ago, and who was responsible for the murder and mutilation of Zvika's first wife, a girl of seventeen. "As a matter of fact . . ." he resumes.

"I guarantee it," says Grossman.

"How?"

"You have my word. I guarantee a fair distribution of the water. I'll supervise myself."

Zvika shrugs. Aviva rises, yawning behind her hand, and suggests that such a guarantee be amended to the original motion. She is exhausted from working all day in the communal laundry, and wants only to be able to go to bed.

"Well?"

A show of hands, throwing a forest of shadows resembling pruned trees against the wall. The amended motion is carried unanimously, and we adjourn.

"Congratulations," I tell Grossman.

"Thanks. Yes. It's a beginning, at least. A step in the right direction."

Outside, the wind is blowing from a blue-black sky that is ablaze with the innumerable stars of the desert night. Grossman shivers as we walk back to his room. The cold is intense. It is as if the sun today had burned away the atmosphere of the earth, exposing us to a chill from outer space itself.

"Ali ought to be here by now. Would you like to come in for a cup of coffee?"

"No thanks. I'm tired. Bed for me."

A little later, while brushing my teeth at the pump outside the row of shacks, I catch a glimpse of them both through the window of Grossman's room. They are standing in the corner, by the orange crate that serves as a bookcase, talking together with cups of coffee in their hands. Once again, their physical resemblance is striking. They are even the same height and, but for the slightly darker cast of the Bedouin's skin, might be taken for blood relatives, cousins, or even brothers perhaps, with their high cheekbones, and long mustaches that emphasize their thin lips. Are they speaking Arabic or Hebrew? I am too far away to tell. The Bedouin suddenly laughs, touching Grossman on the upper arm. It is not hard to imagine that they are recalling the memories they have of shepherding together, near Halutza. Now Grossman is laughing too, holding his nose. I was right. They are talking about shepherding—the stench of the long-haired sheep, the lonely hours spent under the shade of the cypress tree, with the shared, stale loaf of bread on the grass between them and the goat skin water bag passed from hand to hand.

Monday, just after dawn, it begins. For almost four hours now, patiently queued in the blazing sun, a long line of Bedouin women—perhaps a hundred of them or more, dressed entirely in flowing robes of black wool, with only their eyes showing, and strings of Turkish coins sewed onto their veils—draw water from the spigot outside of the cow shed. There is no sound but the twittering of the sparrows and the tinkle of coins as one by one, they bend down and fill the tin cans they have brought with them. The silence is uncanny. Occasionally, on their arms, a naked infant, covered with flies, is to be seen, but it too, as though enjoined by some mysterious command, makes no noise, but only gazes about with solemn, feverish eyes.

Grossman and I are supervising. Just from the look of him, he feels no better, worse perhaps, than last night. The exhilaration of getting his motion passed and making arrangements with Ali has worn off. Periodically, he must excuse himself to go to the latrine, and when he returns with an embarrassed smile on his ravaged face, I plead with him to go back to his room and lie down.

"No, no, it's all right. I promised . . ."

He dozes a little, stretched out in the bar of shadow cast by the overhanging roof, while the black-robed women shuffle by. In the shed, a cow lows. I too began to fall asleep, only to be abruptly awakened by a confused babble of voices, and a piercing shriek.

"What is it? What's happened?" Grossman rubs his eyes.

At the spigot, two of the women have gotten into a row. For some reason, one of them, holding up the line, evidently cannot make up her mind whether to fill up her rusty can or not. With her hands at side, clenching and unclenching one fist, she stares at the stream of water that splashes over the hem of her robe and bare feet, while now four or five of the others flap their arms and rage about her. Then, with another shriek, she is shoved aside, stumbling against Grossman who has come up to them, shouting in Arabic at the top of his voice. Silence again, sudden and complete, broken only by the wail of an infant from somewhere in the crowd.

"What's the trouble?" I ask.

"Turn off the water. . . . Just a minute," he tells me, and then, in Arabic, speaks to the woman who has been thrown against him. In a huddle on the ground, apparently mortified by her physical contact with a strange man, she buries her veiled face in her hands and emits nothing but a high-pitched, quavering wail. It is more than a minute before he can get her to answer. Then, listening attentively, with a puzzled expression on his face, he turns to me.

"I don't understand."

"What does she say?"

"It just doesn't make sense. She says that she and her husband are very poor. They will starve because they own only two milch goats that will die of thirst unless they can get water."

"Then why doesn't she take it?"

"That's what's so confusing. She says she can't afford it."

"Are you sure?"

"Positive."

"But tell her it's free. She can take as much as she needs without charge. Didn't you explain that to Ali?"

"Of course."

"Well, didn't he tell them?"

Again, Grossman questions her, but this time she refuses to answer altogether. It is impossible to determine her age, or even the shape of her body underneath that robe. Only her eyes are visible, yellowed and contracted in the glare of sun.

"Useless . . ." Grossman straightens up. The other women have fallen back in a silent semicircle around us. "I just don't get it. There's obviously been a misunderstanding of some kind."

"What are you going to do?"

"I don't know. Ask Ali, I guess."

"Now?"

"I suppose so."

"Wait here, I'll bring the jeep and go with you."

"No, no, there's no need."

"Do as I say. You're in no condition to drive."

With one hand to his head, he closes his eyes and makes a gesture as if to shake off the weakness that has hold of him.

"I don't know," he says. "Maybe we ought to wait."

"For what?"

"They really can't afford it."

"Afford what? What are you talking about?"

"If we drive over to the camp now, we'll be considered guests. You know their laws of hospitality. They'll feel obliged to slaughter a sheep for a meal."

"You wait here."

The communal jeep is kept in the machine shop, but it takes me over twenty minutes to locate Chaim who has charge of the keys. He is working in the shack that houses our electric generator, repairing a worn fan belt. I could have spared myself the effort. By the time I drive back to the cow shed, Ali is there. He had apparently just ridden over from the encampment on a small white mare that one of the women holds by the bridle as he dismounts and shakes hands with Grossman who begins talking to him at once, in a low, anxious voice. They are speaking in Hebrew as I come up, each with his forehead almost touching that of the other, and their hands clasped behind them.

"Then you did tell them," Grossman is saying. The Bedouin nods.

"But I still don't understand. If they know we're not charging them anything, why does the woman say she can't afford it?"

"It's nothing."

"There must be a reason."

"She's talking about the tax."

"What tax?"

"A half a pound."

"For what? Whose?"

"My father's. For the use of the water."

Ali is smiling. He is having difficulty in speaking Hebrew so quickly. Now, very slowly, searching for each word, he says, "You mustn't bother yourself."

"Do you mean to tell me that your father is taxing them a half a pound per person for the use of water from our well?"

"But of course."

Grossman is silent. Behind us, an infant gives a stifled cry, and the mare tosses her head and chomps at her bit.

"Let me get this straight. . . ."

"But I have already explained," says Ali. "There's no need to concern yourself. This is—" He completes the sentence in Arabic.

" 'Our affair entirely.' "

"Yes, that's it. It's the law. The tribe must always pay the Sheik for the right to draw water from the well."

"But the water is ours."

The Bedouin gives a barely perceptible shrug.

"Don't you understand?" says Grossman. "It's impossible. It . . . what we want . . . what I promised . . . I gave my word. . . . The whole point is for us to share with all of your people fairly . . . an equal distribution."

Again, the Bedouin apparently cannot get the drift of the Hebrew. Grossman must translate.

"Equal?"

"Yes," says Grossman. "That woman, for example. What about those who can't afford it?"

"Equal?" the Bedouin repeats, and then, giving up, he lapses entirely into Arabic.

"What's he saying?" I ask Grossman.

"He says it's the law. It's always been the law. He says it's . . . the lord's . . . his father's right as Sheik to tax them, just as it was his father's before him, and before that, long before. . . ."

"Before what?"

"He didn't say."

I glance at the Bedouin who is looking beyond me, beyond the sloping tin roof of the cow shed and the date grove, toward the desert where the shadows are diminishing as the sun slowly ascends toward noon. . . . Before. Before us, is of course what he means; long before our possession of the land, our settlement and government, when free, or at least subject only to his own law, the Bedouin roamed the desert that belonged to him alone.

"No," says Grossman. "It's out of the question. At the meeting, I promised . . ." and then, in a final effort to make himself understood, he too continues in Arabic.

Before he has finished, the sun has reached its zenith. His eyes are glazed, his face streaked with sweat. The Bedouin says nothing until, with a hopeless gesture, one palm upraised, he abruptly turns on his naked heel and walks with dignity toward the waiting mare. The little horse takes a mincing step as he swings himself into the wooden saddle, and shouts a word of command to the waiting women, one of whom catches his reins as he leads them away. For almost a minute after they are out of sight, their dust hangs in the air. Grossman coughs, and with averted eyes and saying nothing, goes down on one knee to the spigot, where he catches a few drops of water that cling to the spout, and moistens his parched lips.

Tuesday and Wednesday. Not a cloud. No sign of rain. The colorless sky is empty but for the flocks of ravens that wheel in gigantic circles above the Bedouin camp. From morning to night they are to be seen like spots before the eyes, the symptom of some madness induced by the heat of the sun. Now there can be no doubt of it; without water, the Bedouins are slaughtering the remainder of their herds.

Although I am sure he is aware of what is happening, Grossman makes no mention of it. All day Tuesday he is too sick even to get out of bed. Some of the women take turns bringing him tea and toast, and emptying his bedpan, and for the rest of the time, he lies perfectly still, with his face to the wall. Then, as is sometimes the case, on Thursday morning, although greatly weakened, his stomach spasms have subsided sufficiently for him to get up. Restless and inordinately thirsty, he haunts my office where I am busy writing a letter to *Tnuva,* the co-operative marketing organization of the *kibbutzim* that is negotiating with us for the export of our dates overseas. For what seems to be an hour, he sits by the window facing south, sucking on an orange and brushing away the flies that settle on his face and arms.

"What do you think?" he asks at last. "I suppose it's really Ahmad's fault."

I put down my pen. "I guess so."

"Still, it's a shame. There must be something that can be done."

Then, for a while longer, he is silent again. A ray of sunlight, riddled with dust, illuminates his face. In the past few days he has lost weight and looks somehow five years younger and more vulnerable than he really is—twenty-six or twenty-seven at the most. The drooping mustache seems more of an affectation than ever, a pretense of manhood pasted on by a kid.

"I don't suppose Ali was here while I was sick."

"No."

"No, I didn't think so. He'll never come back now. Strange. How well it was going that night when he and I had coffee in my room. Ai, if you only knew how sick of it all I am!"

"Of what?"

"This . . . hatred. Did you know that eleven years ago, the night of the attack, I was the one who found Chava?"

"Chava?"

"You remember. Zvika's wife."

"Chava. Yes."

"She was sleeping in her tent when they came. They went at her with their knives when she was still alive. I've never told Zvika, of course, but she was still alive when I found her. Sometimes, you know, I still . . . have dreams."

"But you don't hate them."

"The Bedouins? I did. Oh, how I did. It's just—how can I possibly explain it? I told you. It makes me sick. All these years, one thing bringing another . . . endless."

More silence. He rises abruptly from his chair.

"Who can say? I wonder if it'll do any good now."

"What's that?" I ask.

"It couldn't do any harm."

"What?"

"It might still help. You never know."

"I see. You want to go to their camp and try to speak with Ali again."

"Yes."

Now it is my turn to say nothing. He shreds the pulp from the orange rind with his teeth.

"It'll be unofficial, of course. No one here will ever know, except you and me."

"Then why tell me?"

"Because I thought you understood. Don't you see? It's better than not doing anything . . . letting it go on and on. What is there to lose?"

"I don't know."

"Nothing, I tell you. Come with me," he says. "You'll see."

I screw on the top of the fountain pen. My sweating wrist has smudged the ink on the letter. It will have to be done over again. "If that's what you really want."

"Yes."

We take the jeep. South of the settlement, there is only a narrow dirt track that eventually leads to the Egyptian border, just north of Nitzana. Surrounded by the white rocks, we are in the valley of the bones, but even here, in the mouths of the wadis, there is still some scrub vegetation left alive, a gray-green stubble incrusted by the white shells of countless snails. Not a tree is to be seen.

"How far now?"

"A half a kilometer. Less," Grossman shouts. Ahead of us, and to the left, where the track intersects with still another narrower path that leads between the rocks, he slows down.

"Their well."

It takes me a moment to be able to distinguish the ruin as a ring of man-raised stones, about knee-high and plastered together with sun-baked mud. He shrugs and drives on, now off the track itself, and up the floor of a huge wadi that runs parallel to the path among the rocks. When he stops, only one black tent can be seen to our right. The rest are apparently hidden around the bend of the wadi walls that are over ten feet tall.

"Where is everybody?"

"Hiding," Grossman explains.

"Are they afraid?"

"It's just the way they are with strangers."

"Well, there's Ali, at any rate."

"Where?"

He is standing with another man in the shadow of a huge boulder about fifty yards away, near the half-skinned carcasses of four or five freshly-slaughtered sheep that lie on the ground covered by a cloud of flies. The blood and flies, the cry of the ravens whose shadows flit across the ground, even the untended fire of dried camel dung smoking in front of the tent give the impression that some kind of sudden catastrophe has overwhelmed the camp. The naked child completes the picture. A little boy, perhaps six years old, with a swollen belly and shaved skull, emerges from the tent at our approach with a tin can in his hands. "Brandied Apricots"—printed in English, coming from God knows where—part of the label is clearly visible as he thrusts it before us, begging for water without a sound.

"Give him your canteen," whispers Grossman, "and wait here." He starts forward. The child, for some reason, refuses to drink from the canteen itself. I must pour the water into the rusty can, but there is too much of it, and it spills to the ground.

"Wait!" I cry, but it is too late. He has already turned and disappeared once more into the tent. Now Grossman is talking, rapidly and in an undertone to Ali, in Arabic, standing with the bloody carcass of the sheep on the ground between them. The second Bedouin has taken a little step to the left, and for the first time, I can see him clearly. It's the old man himself, Ahmad, the Sheik, fatter and older than I remember him, with a fuller beard that has turned completely gray. Still, unmistakably, it is he; carrying himself erect, with his shoulders back, and one hand playing with the hilt of a silver dagger stuck in the yellow sash around his waist. Ali has begun to talk too, for the first time, in a loud, clear voice. The old man glances at him, and either because the sun is in his eyes, or because something his son has said amuses him, he screws up his face and shows his teeth in a grimace that could be taken for a smile.

Behind me, the child, or someone, stirs in the tent, and when again, I look around, what happens next, happens so quickly that it is only later, in retrospect, that I can visualize it all as a piece. Ali is talking, gesturing with his hands, and suddenly without warning, Grossman has lunged at him, slipping on the bloody ground, so that he is only able to give the Bedouin a glancing blow on the right cheek with his fist. They are down, the both of them, and for the moment, incredulous, neither I nor the old man can make a move. He is still grimacing, the smile frozen on his face, his fingers spread on the hilt of the knife. A moment more, and both of us still remain where we are. Grossman is the first to get to his feet, staring stupidly down at the Bedouin who holds his hand to his cheek and rocks his head slightly from side to side. When I come up, the old man retreats another step to the left.

"What's happened?" I ask.

No answer. "What is it?" Still no response. With his mouth open and the same stupefied expression on his face, Grossman reaches out his hand with the evident intention of helping Ali to his feet. "Tell me," I repeat. The hand smeared with sheep's blood, is still extended, but now the Bedouin drags himself back on his elbows and spits on the ground with disgust.

"He blames us for everything," says Grossman, getting behind the wheel of the jeep. "The fact that they've lost their herds . . . this morning, a child died . . . everything. There was nothing I could say. He says his father is right. We've taken their land, and now deny them water."

He tries to turn on the ignition but fumbles with the keys. His hand is trembling. I glance up. The two Bedouins are standing in front of the tent. Something apparently has struck them as funny. The old man, at least, is laughing deep in his throat, with his head thrown back and his hand still on the hilt of his dagger.

"Why did you hit him?" I ask.

The engine starts with a roar. I have to repeat the question.

"Ah, dog," Grossman replies, looking away. "What else could I do? He called me a dog of a Jew."

JEAN PAUL SARTRE

The Wall

They pushed us into a large white room and my eyes began to blink because the light hurt them. Then I saw a table and four fellows seated at the table, civilians, looking at some papers. The other prisoners were herded together at one end and we were obliged to cross the entire room to join them. There were several I knew, and others who must have been foreigners. The two in front of me were blond with round heads. They looked alike. I imagine they were French. The smaller one kept pulling at his trousers, out of nervousness.

This lasted about three hours. I was dog-tired and my head was empty. But the room was well-heated, which struck me as rather agreeable; we had not stopped shivering for twenty-four hours. The guards led the prisoners in one after another in front of the table. Then the four fellows asked them their names and what they did. Most of the time that was all—or perhaps from time to time they would ask such questions as: "Did you help sabotage the munitions?" or, "Where were you on the morning of the ninth and what were you doing?" They didn't even listen to the replies, or at least they didn't seem to. They just remained silent for a moment and looked straight ahead, then they began to write. They asked Tom if it was true he had served in the International Brigade. Tom couldn't say he hadn't because of the papers they had found in his jacket. They didn't ask Juan anything, but after he told them his name, they wrote for a long while.

"It's my brother José who's the anarchist," Juan said. "You know perfectly well he's not here now. I don't belong to any party. I never did take part in politics." They didn't answer.

Then Juan said, "I didn't do anything. And I'm not going to pay for what the others did."

His lips were trembling. A guard told him to stop talking and led him away. It was my turn.

"Your name is Pablo Ibbieta?"

I said yes.

The fellow looked at his papers and said, "Where is Ramon Gris?"

"I don't know."

"You hid him in your house from the sixth to the nineteenth."

"I did not."

They continued to write for a moment and the guards led me away. In the hall, Tom and Juan were waiting between two guards. We started walking. Tom asked one of the guards, "What's the idea?" "How do you mean?" the guard asked. "Was that just the preliminary questioning, or was that the trial?" "That was the trial," the guard said. "So now what? What are they going to do with us?" The guard answered drily, "The verdict will be told you in your cell."

In reality, our cell was one of the cellars of the hospital. It was terribly cold there because it was very drafty. We had been shivering all night long and it had hardly been any better during the day. I had spent the preceding five days in a cellar in the archbishop's palace, a sort of dungeon that must have dated back to the Middle Ages. There were lots of prisoners and not much room, so they housed them just anywhere. But I was not homesick for my dungeon. I hadn't been cold there, but I had been alone, and that gets to be irritating. In the cellar I had company. Juan didn't say a word; he was afraid, and besides, he was too young to have anything to say. But Tom was a good talker and knew Spanish well.

In the cellar there were a bench and four straw mattresses. When they led us back we sat down and waited in silence. After a while Tom said, "Our goose is cooked."

"I think so too," I said. "But I don't believe they'll do anything to the kid."

Tom said, "They haven't got anything on him. He's the brother of a fellow who's fighting, and that's all."

I looked at Juan. He didn't seem to have heard.

Tom continued, "You know what they do in Saragossa? They lay the guys across the road and then they drive over them with trucks. It was a Moroccan deserter who told us that. They say it's just to save ammunition."

I said, "Well, it doesn't save gasoline."

I was irritated with Tom; he shouldn't have said that.

He went on, "There are officers walking up and down the roads with their hands in their pockets, smoking, and they see that it's done right. Do you think they'd put 'em out of their misery? Like hell they do. They just let 'em holler. Sometimes as long as an hour. The Moroccan said the first time he almost puked."

"I don't believe they do that here," I said, "unless they really are short of ammunition."

The daylight came in through four air vents and a round opening that had been cut in the ceiling, to the left, and which opened directly onto the sky. It was through this hole, which was ordinarily closed by means of a trapdoor, that they unloaded coal into the cellar. Directly under the hole, there was a big pile of coal dust; it had been intended for heating the hospital, but at the beginning of the war they had evacuated the patients and the coal had stayed there unused; it even got rained on from time to time, when they forgot to close the trapdoor.

Tom started to shiver. "God damn it," he said, "I'm shivering. There, it is starting again."

He rose and began to do gymnastic exercises. At each movement, his shirt opened and showed his white, hairy chest. He lay down on his back, lifted his legs in the air and began to do the scissors movement. I watched his big buttocks tremble. Tom was tough, but he had too much fat on him. I kept thinking that soon bullets and bayonet points would sink into that mass of tender flesh as though it were a pat of butter.

I wasn't exactly cold, but I couldn't feel my shoulders or my arms. From time to time, I had the impression that something was missing and I began to look around for my jacket. Then I would suddenly remember they hadn't given me a jacket. It was rather awkward. They had taken our clothes to give them to their own soldiers and had left us only our shirts and these cotton trousers the hospital patients wore in mid-summer. After a moment, Tom got up and sat down beside me, breathless.

"Did you get warmed up?"

"Damn it, no. But I'm all out of breath."

Around eight o'clock in the evening, a Major came in with two falangists.

"What are the names of those three over there?" he asked the guard.

"Steinbock, Ibbieta and Mirbal," said the guard.

The major put on his glasses and examined his list.

"Steinbock—Steinbock . . . Here it is. You are condemned to death. You'll be shot tomorrow morning."

He looked at his list again.

"The other two, also," he said.

"That's not possible," said Juan. "Not me."

The Major looked at him with surprise. "What's your name?"

"Juan Mirbal."

"Well, your name is here," said the Major, "and you're condemned to death."

"I didn't do anything," said Juan.

The Major shrugged his shoulders and turned toward Tom and me.

"You are both Basque?

"No, nobody's Basque."

He appeared exasperated.

"I was told there were three Basques. I'm not going to waste my time running after them. I suppose you don't want a priest?"

We didn't even answer.

Then he said, "A Belgian doctor will be around in a little while. He has permission to stay with you all night."

He gave a military salute and left.

"What did I tell you?" Tom said. "We're in for something swell."

"Yes," I said. "It's a damned shame for the kid."

I said that to be fair, but I really didn't like the kid. His face was too refined and it was disfigured by fear and suffering, which had twisted all his features. Three days ago, he was just a kid with a kind of affected manner some people like. But now he looked like an aging fairy, and I thought to myself he would never be young again, even if they let him go. It wouldn't have been a bad thing to show him a little pity, but pity makes me sick, and besides, I couldn't stand him. He hadn't said anything more, but he turned gray. His face and hands were gray. He sat down again and stared, round-eyed, at the ground. Tom was good-hearted and tried to take him by the arm, but the kid drew himself away violently and made an ugly face. "Leave him alone," I said quietly. "Can't you see he's going to start to bawl?" Tom obeyed regretfully. He would have liked to console the kid; that would have kept him occupied and he wouldn't have been tempted to think about himself. But it got on my nerves. I had never thought about death, for the reason that the question had never come up. But now it had come up, and there was nothing else to do but think about it.

Tom started talking. "Say, did you ever bump anybody off?" he asked me. I didn't answer. He started to explain to me that he had bumped off six fellows since August. He hadn't yet realized what we were in for, and I saw clearly he didn't *want* to realize it. I myself hadn't quite taken it in. I wondered if it hurt very much. I thought about the bullets; I imagined their fiery hail going through my body. All that was beside the real question; but I was calm, we had all night in which to realize it. After a while Tom stopped talking and I looked at him out of the corner of my eye. I saw that he, too, had turned gray and that he looked pretty miserable. I said to myself, "It's starting." It was almost dark, a dull light filtered through the air vents across the coal pile and made a big spot under the sky. Through the hole in the ceiling I could already see a star. The night was going to be clear and cold.

The door opened and two guards entered. They were followed by a blond man in a tan uniform. He greeted us.

"I'm the doctor," he said. "I've been authorized to give you any assistance you may require in these painful circumstances."

He had an agreeable, cultivated voice.

I said to him, "What are you going to do here?"

"Whatever you want me to do. I shall do everything in my power to lighten these few hours."

"Why did you come to us? There are lots of others: the hospital's full of them."

"I was sent here," he answered vaguely. "You'd probably like to smoke, wouldn't you?" he added suddenly. "I've got some cigarettes and even some cigars."

He passed around some English cigarettes and some *puros,* but we refused them. I looked him straight in the eye and he appeared uncomfortable.

"You didn't come here out of compassion," I said to him. "In fact, I know who you are. I saw you with some fascists in the barracks yard the day I was arrested."

I was about to continue, when all at once something happened to me which surprised me: the presence of this doctor had suddenly ceased to interest me. Usually, when I've got hold of a man I don't let go. But somehow the desire to speak had left me. I shrugged my shoulders and turned away. A little later, I looked up and saw he was watching me with an air of curiosity. The guards had sat down on one of the mattresses. Pedro, the tall thin one, was twiddling his thumbs, while the other one shook his head occasionally to keep from falling asleep.

"Do you want some light?" Pedro suddenly asked the doctor. The other fellow nodded, "Yes." I think he was not over-intelligent, but doubtless he was not malicious. As I looked at his big, cold, blue eyes, it seemed to me the worst thing about him was his lack of imagination. Pedro went out and came back with an oil lamp which he set on the corner of the bench. It gave a poor light, but it was better than nothing; the night before we had been left in the dark. For a long while I stared at the circle of light the lamp threw on the ceiling. I was fascinated. Then, suddenly, I came to, the light circle paled, and I felt as if I were being crushed under an enormous weight. It wasn't the thought of death, and it wasn't fear; it was something anonymous. My cheeks were burning hot and my head ached.

I roused myself and looked at my two companions. Tom had his head in his hands and only the fat, white nape of his neck was visible. Juan was by far the worst off; his mouth was wide open and his nostrils were trembling. The doctor came over to him and touched him on the shoulder, as though to comfort him; but his eyes remained cold. Then I saw the Belgian slide his hand furtively down Juan's arm to his wrist. Indifferent, Juan let himself be handled. Then, as though absentmindedly, the Belgian laid three fingers over his wrist; at the same time, he drew away somewhat and managed to turn his back to me. But I leaned over backward and saw him take out his watch and look at it a moment before relinquishing the boy's wrist. After a moment, he let the inert hand fall and went and leaned against the wall. Then, as if he had suddenly remembered something very important that had to be noted down immediately, he took a notebook from his pocket and wrote a few lines in it. "The son-of-a-bitch," I thought angrily. "He better not come and feel my pulse; I'll give him a punch in his dirty jaw."

He didn't come near me, but I felt he was looking at me. I raised my head and looked back at him. In an impersonal voice, he said, "Don't you think it's frightfully cold here?"

He looked purple with cold.

"I'm not cold," I answered him.

He kept looking at me with a hard expression. Suddenly I understood, and I lifted my hands to my face. I was covered with sweat. Here, in this cellar, in mid-winter, right in a draft, I was sweating. I ran my fingers through my hair, which was stiff with sweat; at the same time, I realized my shirt was damp and sticking to my skin. I had been streaming with perspiration for an hour, at least, and had felt nothing. But this fact hadn't escaped that Belgian swine. He had seen the drops rolling down my face and had said to himself that it showed an almost pathological terror; and he himself had felt normal and proud of it because he was cold. I wanted to get up and go punch his face in, but I had hardly started to make a move before my shame and anger had disappeared. I dropped back onto the bench with indifference.

I was content to rub my neck with my handkerchief because now I felt the sweat dripping from my hair onto the nape of my neck and that was disagreeable. I soon gave up rubbing myself, however, for it didn't do any good; my handkerchief was already wringing wet and I was still sweating. My buttocks, too, were sweating, and my damp trousers stuck to the bench.

Suddenly, Juan said, "You're a doctor, aren't you?"

"Yes," said the Belgian.

"Do people suffer—very long?"

"Oh! When . . . ? No, no," said the Belgian, in a paternal voice, "it's quickly over."

His manner was as reassuring as if he had been answering a paying patient.

"But I . . . Somebody told me—they often have to fire two volleys."

"Sometimes," said the Belgian, raising his head, "it just happens that the first volley doesn't hit any of the vital organs."

"So then they have to reload their guns and aim all over again?" Juan thought for a moment, then added hoarsely, "But that takes time!"

He was terribly afraid of suffering. He couldn't think about anything else, but that went with his age. As for me, I hardly thought about it any more and it certainly was not fear of suffering that made me perspire.

I rose and walked toward the pile of coal dust. Tom gave a start and looked at me with a look of hate. I irritated him because my shoes squeaked. I wondered if my face was as putty-colored as his. Then I noticed that he, too, was sweating. The sky was magnificent; no light at all came into our dark corner and I had only to lift my head to see the Big Bear. But it didn't look the way it had looked before. Two days ago, from my cell in the archbishop's palaçe, I could see a big patch of sky and each time of day brought back a different memory. In the morning, when the sky was a deep blue, and light, I thought of beaches along the Atlantic; at noon, I could see the sun, and I remembered a bar in Seville where I used to drink manzanilla and eat anchovies and olives; in the afternoon, I was in the shade, and I thought of the deep shadow which covers half of the arena while the other half gleams in the sunlight: it really gave me a pang to see the whole earth reflected in the sky like that. Now, however, no matter how much I looked up in the air, the sky no longer recalled anything. I liked it better that way. I came back and sat down next to Tom. There was a long silence.

Then Tom began to talk in a low voice. He had to keep talking, otherwise he lost his way in his own thoughts. I believe he was talking to me, but he didn't look at me. No doubt he was afraid to look at me, because I was gray and sweating. We were both alike and worse than mirrors for each other. He looked at the Belgian, the only one who was alive.

"Say, do you understand? I don't."

Then I, too, began to talk in a low voice. I was watching the Belgian.

"Understand what? What's the matter?"

"Something's going to happen to us that I don't understand."

There was a strange odor about Tom. It seemed to me that I was more sensitive to odors than ordinarily. With a sneer, I said, "You'll understand, later."

"That's not so sure," he said stubbornly. "I'm willing to be courageous, but at least I ought to know . . . Listen, they're going to take us out into the courtyard. All right. The fellows will be standing in line in front of us. How many of them will there be?"

"Oh, I don't know. Five, or eight. Not more."

"That's enough. Let's say there'll be eight of them. Somebody will shout 'Shoulder arms!' and I'll see all eight rifles aimed at me. I'm sure I'm going to feel like going through the wall. I'll push against the wall as hard as I can with my back, and the wall won't give in. The way it is in a nightmare. . . . I can imagine all that. Ah, if you only knew how well I can imagine it!"

"Skip it!" I said. "I can imagine it too."

"It must hurt like the devil. You know they aim at your eyes and mouth so as to disfigure you," he added maliciously. "I can feel the wounds already. For the last hour I've been having pains in my head and neck. Not real pains—it's worse still. They're the pains I'll feel tomorrow morning. And after that, then what?"

I understood perfectly well what he meant, but I didn't want to seem to understand. As for the pains, I, too, felt them all through my body, like a lot of little gashes. I couldn't get used to them, but I was like him, I didn't think they were very important.

"After that," I said roughly, "you'll be eating daisies."

He started talking to himself, not taking his eyes off the Belgian, who didn't seem to be listening to him. I knew what he had come for, and that what we were thinking didn't interest him. He had come to look at our bodies, our bodies which were dying alive.

"It's like in a nightmare," said Tom. "You want to think of something, you keep having the impression you've got it, that you're going to understand, and then it slips away from you, it eludes you and it's gone again. I say to myself, afterwards, there won't be anything. But I don't really understand what that means. There are moments when I almost do—and then it's gone again. I start to think of the pains, the bullets, the noise of the shooting. I am a materialist, I swear it; and I'm not going crazy, either. But there's something wrong. I see my own corpse. That's not hard, but it's *I* who see it, with *my* eyes. I'll have to get to the point where I think—where I think I won't see anything more. I won't hear anything more, and the world will go on for the others. We're not made to think that way, Pablo. Believe me, I've already stayed awake all night waiting for something. But this is not the same thing. This will grab us from behind, Pablo, and we won't be ready for it."

"Shut up," I said. "Do you want me to call a father confessor?"

He didn't answer. I had already noticed that he had a tendency to prophesy and call me "Pablo" in a kind of pale voice. I didn't like that very much, but it seems all the Irish are like that. I had a vague impression that he smelled of urine. Actually, I didn't like Tom very much, and I didn't see why, just because we were going to die together, I should like him any better. There are certain fellows with whom it would be different—with Ramon Gris, for instance. But between Tom and Juan, I felt alone. In fact, I liked it better that way. With Ramon I might have grown soft. But I felt terribly hard at that moment, and I wanted to stay hard.

Tom kept on muttering, in a kind of absent-minded way. He was certainly talking to keep from thinking. Naturally, I agreed with him, and I could have said everything he was saying. It's not *natural* to die. And since I was going to die, nothing seemed natural any more: neither the coal pile, nor the bench, nor Pedro's dirty old face. Only it was disagreeable for me to think the same things Tom thought. And I knew perfectly well that all night long, within five minutes of each other, we would keep on thinking things at the same time, sweating or shivering at the same time. I looked at him sideways and, for the first time, he seemed strange to me. He had death written on his face. My pride was wounded. For twenty-four hours I had lived side by side with Tom, I had listened to him, I had talked to him, and I knew we had nothing in common. And now we were as alike as twin brothers, simply because we were going to die together. Tom took my hand without looking at me.

"Pablo, I wonder . . . I wonder if it's true that we just cease to exist."

I drew my hand away.

"Look between your feet, you dirty dog."

There was a puddle between his feet and water was dripping from his trousers.

"What's the matter?" he said, frightened.

"You're wetting your pants," I said to him.

"It's not true," he said furiously. "I can't be . . . I don't feel anything."

The Belgian had come closer to him. With an air of false concern, he asked, "Aren't you feeling well?"

Tom didn't answer. The Belgian looked at the puddle without comment.

"I don't know what that is," Tom said savagely, "but I'm not afraid. I swear to you, I'm not afraid."

The Belgian made no answer. Tom rose and went to the corner. He came back, buttoning his fly, and sat down, without a word. The Belgian was taking notes.

We were watching the doctor. Juan was watching him too. All three of us were watching him because he was alive. He had the gestures of a living person, the interests of a living person; he was shivering in this cellar the way living people shiver; he had an obedient, well-fed body. We, on the other hand, didn't feel our bodies any more—not the same way, in any case. I felt like touching my trousers, but I didn't dare to. I looked at the Belgian, well-planted on his two legs, master of his muscles—and able to plan for tomorrow. We were like three shadows deprived of blood; we were watching him and sucking his life like vampires.

Finally he came over to Juan. Was he going to lay his hand on the nape of Juan's neck for some professional reason, or had he obeyed a charitable impulse? If he had acted out of charity, it was the one and only time during the whole night. He fondled Juan's head and the nape of his neck. The kid let him do it, without taking his eyes off him. Then, suddenly, he took hold of the doctor's hand and looked at it in a funny way. He held the Belgian's hand between his own two hands and there was nothing pleasing about them, those two gray paws squeezing that fat red hand. I sensed what was going to happen and Tom must have sensed it, too. But all the Belgian saw was emotion, and he smiled paternally. After a moment, the kid lifted the big red paw to his mouth and started to bite it. The Belgian drew back quickly and stumbled toward the wall. For a second, he looked at us with horror. He must have suddenly understood that we were not men like himself. I began to laugh, and one of the guards started up. The other had fallen asleep with his eyes wide open, showing only the whites.

I felt tired and over-excited at the same time. I didn't want to think any more about what was going to happen at dawn—about death. It didn't make sense, and I never got beyond just words, or emptiness. But whenever I tried to think about something else I saw the barrels of rifles aimed at me. I must have lived through my execution twenty times in succession; one time I thought it was the real thing; I must have dozed off for a moment. They were dragging me toward the wall and I was resisting; I was imploring their pardon. I woke with a start and looked at the Belgian. I was afraid I had cried out in my sleep. But he was smoothing his mustache; he hadn't noticed anything. If I had wanted to, I believe I could have slept for a while. I had been awake for the last forty-eight hours, and I was worn out. But I didn't want to lose two hours of life. They would have had to come and wake me at dawn. I would have followed them, drunk with sleep, and I would have gone off without so much as "Gosh!" I didn't want it that way. I didn't want to die like an animal. I wanted to understand. Besides, I was afraid of having nightmares. I got up and began to walk up and down and, so as to think about something else, I began to think about my past life. Memories crowded in on me, helter-skelter. Some were good and some were bad—at least that was how I had thought of them *before*. There were faces and happenings. I saw the face of a little *novilero* who had gotten himself horned during the *Feria,* in Valencia. I saw the face of one of my uncles, of Ramon Gris. I remembered all kinds of things that had happened: how I had been on strike for three months in 1926, and had almost died of hunger. I recalled a night I had spent on a beach in Granada; I hadn't eaten for three days, I was nearly wild, I didn't want to give up the sponge. I had to smile. With what eagerness I had run after happiness, and women, and liberty! And to what end? I had wanted to liberate Spain, I admired Py Margall, I had belonged to the anarchist movement, I had spoken at public meetings. I took everything as seriously as if I had been immortal.

At that time I had the impression that I had my whole life before me, and I thought to myself, "It's all a god-damned lie." Now it wasn't worth anything because it was finished. I wondered how I had ever been able to go out and have a good time with girls. I wouldn't have lifted my little finger if I had ever imagined that I would die like this. I saw my life before me, finished, closed, like a bag, and yet what was inside was not finished. For a moment I tried to appraise it. I would have liked to say to myself, "It's been a good life." But it couldn't be appraised, it was only an outline. I had spent my time writing checks on eternity, and had understood nothing. Now, I didn't miss anything. There were a lot of things I might have missed: the taste of manzanilla, for instance, or the swims I used to take in summer in a little creek near Cadiz. But death had taken the charm out of everything.

Suddenly the Belgian had a wonderful idea.

"My friends," he said to us, "if you want me to—and providing the military authorities give their consent—I could undertake to deliver a word or some token from you to your loved ones. . . ."

Tom growled, "I haven't got anybody."

I didn't answer. Tom waited for a moment, then he looked at me with curiosity. "Aren't you going to send any message to Concha?"

"No."

I hated that sort of sentimental conspiracy. Of course, it was my fault, since I had mentioned Concha the night before, and I should have kept my mouth shut. I had been with her for a year. Even as late as last night, I would have cut my arm off with a hatchet just to see her again for five minutes. That was why I had mentioned her. I couldn't help it. Now I didn't care any more about seeing her. I hadn't anything more to say to her. I didn't even want to hold her in my arms. I loathed my body because it had turned gray and was sweating—and I wasn't even sure that I didn't loathe hers too. Concha would cry when she heard about my death; for months she would have no more interest in life. But still it was I who was going to die. I thought of her beautiful, loving eyes. When she looked at me something went from her to me. But I thought to myself that it was all over; if she looked at me *now* her gaze would not leave her eyes, it would not reach out to me. I was alone.

Tom too, was alone, but not the same way. He was seated astride his chair and had begun to look at the bench with a sort of smile, with surprise, even. He reached out his hand and touched the wood cautiously, as though he were afraid of breaking something, then he drew his hand back hurriedly, and shivered. I wouldn't have amused myself touching that bench, if I had been Tom, that was just some more Irish play-acting. But somehow it seemed to me too that the different objects had something funny about them. They seemed to have grown paler, less massive than before. I had only to look at the bench, the lamp or the pile of coal dust to feel I was going to die. Naturally, I couldn't think clearly about my death, but I saw it everywhere, even on the different objects, the way they had withdrawn and kept their distance, tactfully, like people talking at the bedside of a dying person. It was *his own death* Tom had just touched on the bench.

In the state I was in, if they had come and told me I could go home quietly, that my life would be saved, it would have left me cold. A few hours, or a few years of waiting are all the same, when you've lost the illusion of being eternal. Nothing mattered to me any more. In a way, I was calm. But it was a horrible kind of calm—because of my body. My body—I saw with its eyes and I heard with its ears, but it was no longer I. It sweat and trembled independently, and I didn't recognize it any longer. I was obliged to touch it and look at it to know what was happening to it, just as if it had been someone else's body. At times I still felt it, I felt a slipping, a sort of headlong plunging, as in a falling airplane, or else I heard my heart beating. But this didn't give me confidence. In fact, everything that came from my body had something damned dubious about it. Most of the time it was silent, it stayed put and I didn't feel anything other than a sort of heaviness, a loathsome presence against me. I had the impression of being bound to an enormous vermin.

The Belgian took out his watch and looked at it.

"It's half-past three," he said.

The son-of-a-bitch! He must have done it on purpose. Tom jumped up. We hadn't yet realized the time was passing. The night surrounded us like a formless, dark mass; I didn't even remember it had started.

Juan started to shout. Wringing his hands, he implored, "I don't want to die! I don't want to die!"

He ran the whole length of the cellar with his arms in the air, then he dropped down onto one of the mattresses, sobbing. Tom looked at him with dismal eyes and didn't even try to console him any more. The fact was, it was no use; the kid made more noise than we did, but he was less affected, really. He was like a sick person who defends himself against his malady with a high fever. When there's not even any fever left, it's much more serious.

He was crying. I could tell he felt sorry for himself; he was thinking about death. For one second, one single second, I too felt like crying, crying out of pity for myself. But just the contrary happened. I took one look at the kid, saw his thin, sobbing shoulders, and I felt I was inhuman. I couldn't feel pity either for these others or for myself. I said to myself, "I want to die decently."

Tom had gotten up and was standing just under the round opening looking out for the first signs of daylight. I was determined, I wanted to die decently, and I only thought about that. But underneath, ever since the doctor had told us the time, I felt time slipping, flowing by, one drop at a time.

It was still dark when I heard Tom's voice.

"Do you hear them?"

"Yes."

People were walking in the courtyard.

"What the hell are they doing? After all, they can't shoot in the dark."

After a moment, we didn't hear anything more. I said to Tom, "There's the daylight."

Pedro got up yawning, and came and blew out the lamp. He turned to the man beside him. "It's hellish cold."

The cellar had grown gray. We could hear shots at a distance.

"It's about to start," I said to Tom. "That must be in the back courtyard."

Tom asked the doctor to give him a cigarette. I didn't want any; I didn't want either cigarettes or alcohol. From that moment on, the shooting didn't stop.

"Can you take it in?" Tom said.

He started to add something, then he stopped and began to watch the door. The door opened and a lieutenant came in with four soldiers. Tom dropped his cigarette.

"Steinbock?"

Tom didn't answer. Pedro pointed him out.

"Juan Mirbal?"

"He's the one on the mattress."

"Stand up," said the Lieutenant.

Juan didn't move. Two soldiers took hold of him by the armpits and stood him up on his feet. But as soon as they let go of him he fell down.

The soldiers hesitated a moment.

"He's not the first one to get sick," said the Lieutenant. "You'll have to carry him, the two of you. We'll arrange things when we get there." He turned to Tom. "All right, come along."

Tom left between two soldiers. Two other soldiers followed, carrying the kid by his arms and legs. He was not unconscious; his eyes were wide open and tears were rolling down his cheeks. When I started to go out, the Lieutenant stopped me.

"Are you Ibbieta?"

"Yes."

"You wait here. They'll come and get you later on."

They left. The Belgian and the two jailers left too, and I was alone. I didn't understand what had happened to me, but I would have liked it better if they had ended it all right away. I heard the volleys at almost regular intervals; at each one, I shuddered. I felt like howling and tearing my hair. But instead, I gritted my teeth and pushed my hands deep into my pockets, because I wanted to stay decent.

An hour later, they came to fetch me and took me up to the first floor in a little room which smelt of cigar smoke and was so hot it seemed to me suffocating. Here there were two officers sitting in comfortable chairs, smoking, with papers spread out on their knees.

"Your name is Ibbieta?"

"Yes."

"Where is Ramon Gris?"

"I don't know."

The man who questioned me was small and stocky. He had hard eyes behind his glasses.

"Come nearer," he said to me.

I went nearer. He rose and took me by the arms, looking at me in a way calculated to make me go through the floor. At the same time he pinched my arms with all his might. He didn't mean to hurt me; it was quite a game; he wanted to dominate me. He also seemed to think it was necessary to blow his fetid breath right into my face. We stood like that for a moment, only I felt more like laughing than anything else. It takes a lot more than that to intimidate a man who's about to die: it didn't work. He pushed me away violently and sat down again.

"It's your life or his," he said. "You'll be allowed to go free if you tell us where he is."

After all, these two bedizened fellows with their riding crops and boots were just men who were going to die one day. A little later than I, perhaps, but not a great deal. And there they were, looking for names among their papers, running after other men in order to put them in prison or do away with them entirely. They had their opinions on the future of Spain and on other subjects. Their petty activities seemed to me to be offensive and ludicrous. I could no longer put myself in their place. I had the impression they were crazy.

The little fat fellow kept looking at me, tapping his boots with his riding crop. All his gestures were calculated to make him appear like a spirited, ferocious animal.

"Well? Do you understand?"

"I don't know where Gris is," I said. "I thought he was in Madrid."

The other officer lifted his pale hand indolently. This indolence was also calculated. I saw through all their little tricks, and I was dumbfounded that men should still exist who took pleasure in that kind of thing.

"You have fifteen minutes to think it over," he said slowly. "Take him to the linen-room, and bring him back here in fifteen minutes. If he continues to refuse, he'll be executed at once."

They knew what they were doing. I had spent the night waiting. After that, they had made me wait another hour in the cellar, while they shot Tom and Juan, and now they locked me in the linen-room. They must have arranged the whole thing the night before. They figured that sooner or later people's nerves wear out and they hoped to get me that way.

They made a big mistake. In the linen-room I sat down on a ladder because I felt very weak, and I began to think things over. Not their proposition, however. Naturally I knew where Gris was. He was hiding in his cousins' house, about two miles outside the city. I knew, too, that I would not reveal his hiding place, unless they tortured me (but they didn't seem to be considering that). All that was definitely settled and didn't interest me in the least. Only I would have liked to understand the reasons for my own conduct. I would rather die than betray Gris. Why? I no longer liked Ramon Gris. My friendship for him had died shortly before dawn along with my love for Concha, along with my own desire to live. Of course I still admired him—he was hard. But it was not for that reason that I was willing to die in his place; his life was no more valuable than mine. No life was of any value. A man was going to be stood up against a wall and fired at till he dropped dead. It didn't make any difference whether it was I or Gris or somebody else. I knew perfectly well he was more useful to the Spanish cause than I was, but I didn't give a God damn about Spain or anarchy, either; nothing had any importance now. And yet, there I was. I could save my skin by betraying Gris and I refused to do it. It seemed more ludicrous to me than anything else; it was stubbornness.

I thought to myself, "Am I hard-headed!" And I was seized with a strange sort of cheerfulness.

They came to fetch me and took me back to the two officers. A rat darted out under our feet and that amused me. I turned to one of the falangists and said to him, "Did you see that rat?"

He made no reply. He was gloomy, and took himself very seriously. As for me, I felt like laughing, but I restrained myself because I was afraid that if I started, I wouldn't be able to stop. The falangist wore mustaches. I kept after him, "You ought to cut off those mustaches, you fool."

I was amused by the fact that he let hair grow all over his face while he was still alive. He gave me a kind of half-hearted kick, and I shut up.

"Well," said the fat officer. "have you thought things over?"

I looked at them with curiosity, like insects of a very rare species.

"I know where he is," I said. "He's hiding in the cemetery. Either in one of the vaults, or in the gravediggers' shack."

I said that just to make fools of them. I wanted to see them get up and fasten their belts and bustle about giving orders.

They jumped to their feet.

"Fine. Moles, go ask Lieutenant Lopez for fifteen men. And as for you," the little fat fellow said to me, "if you've told the truth, I don't go back on my word. But you'll pay for this, if you're pulling our leg."

They left noisily and I waited in peace, still guarded by the falangists. From time to time I smiled at the thought of the face they were going to make. I felt dull and malicious. I could see them lifting up the gravestones, or opening the doors of the vaults one by one. I saw the whole situation as though I were another person: the prisoner determined to play the hero, the solemn falangists with their mustaches and the men in uniform running around among the graves. It was irresistibly funny.

After half an hour, the little fat fellow came back alone. I thought he had come to give the order to execute me. The others must have stayed in the cemetery.

The officer looked at me. He didn't look at all foolish.

"Take him out in the big courtyard with the others," he said. "When military operations are over, a regular tribunal will decide his case."

I thought I must have misunderstood.

"So they're not—they're not going to shoot me?" I asked.

"Not now, in any case. Afterwards, that doesn't concern me."

I still didn't understand.

"But why?" I said to him.

He shrugged his shoulders without replying, and the soldiers led me away. In the big courtyard there were a hundred or so prisoners, women, children and a few old men. I started to walk around the grass plot in the middle. I felt absolutely idiotic. At noon we were fed in the dining hall. Two or three fellows spoke to me. I must have known them, but I didn't answer. I didn't even know where I was.

Toward evening, about ten new prisoners were pushed into the courtyard. I recognized Garcia, the baker.

He said to me, "Lucky dog! I didn't expect to find you alive."

"They condemned me to death," I said, "and then they changed their minds. I don't know why."

"I was arrested at two o'clock," Garcia said.

"What for?"

Garcia took no part in politics.

"I don't know," he said. "They arrest everybody who doesn't think the way they do."

He lowered his voice.

"They got Gris."

I began to tremble.

"When?"

This morning. He acted like a damned fool. He left his cousins' house Tuesday because of a disagreement. There were any number of fellows who would have hidden him, but he didn't want to be indebted to anybody any more. He said, 'I would have hidden at Ibbieta's, but since they've got him, I'll go hide in the cemetery.' "

"In the cemetery?"

"Yes. It was the god-damnedest thing. Naturally, they passed by there this morning; that had to happen. They found him in the gravediggers' shack. They opened fire at him and they finished him off."

"In the cemetery!"

Everything went around in circles, and when I came to I was sitting on the ground. I laughed so hard the tears came to my eyes.

GRAHAM GREENE

The Hint of an Explanation

A long train journey on a late December evening, in this new version of peace, is a dreary experience. I suppose that my fellow traveller and I could consider ourselves lucky to have a compartment to ourselves, even though the heating apparatus was not working, even though the lights went out entirely in the frequent Pennine tunnels and were too dim anyway for us to read our books without straining our eyes, and though there was no restaurant car to give at least a change of scene. It was when we were trying simultaneously to chew the same kind of dry bun bought at the same station buffet that my companion and I came together. Before that we had sat at opposite ends of the carriage, both muffled to the chin in overcoats, both bent low over type we could barely make out, but as I threw the remains of my cake under the seat our eyes met, and he laid his book down.

By the time we were half-way to Bedwell Junction we had found an enormous range of subjects for discussion; starting with buns and the weather, we had gone on to politics, the government, foreign affairs, the atom bomb, and, by an inevitable progression, God. We had not, however, become either shrill or acid. My companion, who now sat opposite me, leaning a little forward, so that our knees nearly touched, gave such an impression of serenity that it would have been impossible to quarrel with him, however much our views differed, and differ they did profoundly.

I had soon realized I was speaking to a Catholic, to someone who believed—how do they put it?—in an omnipotent and omniscient Deity, while I was what is loosely called an Agnostic. I have a certain intuition (which I do not trust, founded as it may well be on childish experiences and needs) that a God exists, and I am surprised occasionally into belief by the extraordinary coincidences that beset our path like the traps set for leopards in the jungle, but intellectually I am revolted at the whole notion of such a God who can so abandon his creatures to the enormities of Free Will. I found myself expressing this view to my companion, who listened quietly and with respect. He made no attempt to interrupt: he showed none of the impatience or the intellectual arrogance I have grown to expect from Catholics; when the lights of a wayside station flashed across his face that had escaped hitherto the rays of the one globe working in the compartment, I caught a glimpse suddenly of—what? I stopped speaking, so strong was the impression. I was carried back ten years, to the other side of the great useless conflict, to a small town, Gisors in Normandy. I was again, for a moment, walking on the ancient battlements and looking down across the grey roofs, until my eyes for some reason lit on one grey stony "back" out of the many, where the face of a middle-aged man was pressed against a windowpane (I suppose that face has ceased to exist now, just as I believe the whole town with its medieval memories has been reduced to rubble). I remembered saying to myself with astonishment, "That man is happy—completely happy." I looked across the compartment at my fellow traveller, but his face was already again in shadow. I said weakly, "When you think what God—if there is a God—allows. It's not merely the physical agonies, but think of the corruption, even of children. . . ."

He said, "Our view is so limited," and I was disappointed at the conventionality of his reply. He must have been aware of my disappointment (it was as though our thoughts were huddled as closely as ourselves for warmth), for he went on, "Of course there is no answer here. We catch hints . . ." and then the train roared into another tunnel and the lights again went out. It was the longest tunnel yet; we went rocking down it, and the cold seemed to become more intense with the darkness like an icy fog (perhaps when one sense—of sight—is robbed of sensation, the others grow more sensitive). When we emerged into the mere grey of night and the globe lit up once more, I could see that my companion was leaning back on his seat.

I repeated his last words as a question, "Hints?"

"Oh, they mean very little in cold print—or cold speech," he said, shivering in his overcoat. "And they mean nothing at all to a human being other than the man who catches them. They are not scientific evidence—or evidence at all for that matter. Events that don't somehow, turn out as they were intended—by the human actors I mean, or by the thing behind the human actors."

"The thing?"

"The word Satan is so anthropomorphic."

I had to lean forward now: I wanted to hear what he had to say. I am—I really am, God knows—open to conviction.

He said, "One's words are so crude, but I sometimes feel pity for that thing. It is so continually finding the right weapon to use against its Enemy and the weapon breaks in its own breast. It sometimes seems to me so—powerless. You said something just now about the corruption of children. It reminded me of something in my own childhood. You are the first person—except for one—that I have thought of telling it to, perhaps because you are anonymous. It's not a very long story, and in a way it's relevant."

I said, "I'd like to hear it."

"You mustn't expect too much meaning. But to me there seems to be a hint. That's all. A hint."

He went slowly on, turning his face to the pane, though he could have seen nothing real in the whirling world outside except an occasional signal lamp, a light in a window, a small country station torn backwards by our rush, picking his words with precision. He said, "When I was a child they taught me to serve at Mass. The church was a small one, for there were very few Catholics where I lived. It was a market town in East Anglia, surrounded by flat, chalky fields and ditches—so many ditches. I don't suppose there were fifty Catholics all told, and for some reason there was a tradition of hostility to us. Perhaps it went back to the burning of a Protestant martyr in the sixteenth century—there was a stone marking the place near where the meat stalls stood on Wednesdays. I was only half aware of the enmity, though I know that my school nickname of Popey Martin had something to do with my religion, and I had heard that my father was nearly excluded from the Constitutional Club when he first came to the town.

"Every Sunday I had to dress up in my surplice and serve Mass. I hated it—I have always hated dressing up in any way (which is funny when you come to think of it), and I never ceased to be afraid of losing my place in the service and doing something which would put me to ridicule. Our services were at a different hour from the Anglican, and as our small, far-from-select band trudged out of the hideous chapel the whole of the townsfolk seemed to be on the way past to the proper church—I always thought of it as the proper church. We had to pass the parade of their eyes, indifferent, supercilious, mocking; you can't imagine how seriously religion can be taken in a small town, if only for social reasons.

"There was one man in particular; he was one of the two bakers in the town, the one my family did not patronize. I don't think any of the Catholics patronized him because he was called a free-thinker—an odd title, for poor man, no one's thoughts were less free than his. He was hemmed in by his hatred—his hatred of us. He was very ugly to look at, with one wall-eye and a head the shape of a turnip, with the hair gone on the crown, and he was unmarried. He had no interests, apparently, but his baking and his hatred, though now that I am older I begin to see other sides to his nature—it did contain, perhaps, a certain furtive love. One would come across him suddenly sometimes on a country walk, especially if one were alone and it was Sunday. It was as if he rose from the ditches, and the smear of chalk on his clothes reminded one of the flour on his working overalls. He would have a stick in his hand and stab at the hedges, and if his mood were very black he would call out after one strange abrupt words like a foreign tongue—I know the meaning of those words, of course, now. Once the police went to his house because of what a boy said he'd seen, but nothing came of it except that the hate shackled him closer. His name was Blacker and he terrified me.

"I think he had a particular hatred of my father—I don't know why. My father was manager of the Midland Bank, and it's possible that at some time Blacker may have had unsatisfactory dealings with the bank; my father was a very cautious man who suffered all his life from anxiety about money—his own and other people's. If I try and picture Blacker now I see him walking along a narrow path between high windowless walls, and at the end of the path stands a small boy of ten—me. I don't know whether it's a symbolic picture or the memory of one of our encounters—our encounters somehow got more and more frequent. You talked just now about the corruption of children. That poor man was preparing to revenge himself on everything he hated—my father, the Catholics, the God whom people persisted in crediting—and that by corrupting me. He had evolved a horrible and ingenious plan.

"I remember the first time I had a friendly word from him. I was passing his shop as rapidly as I could when I heard his voice call out with a kind of sly subservience as though he were an under servant. 'Master David,' he called, 'Master David,' and I hurried on. But the next time I passed that way he was at his door (he must have seen me coming) with one of those curly cakes in his hand that we called Chelsea buns. I didn't want to take it, but he made me, and then I couldn't be other than polite when he asked me to come into his parlour behind the shop and see something very special.

"It was a small electric railway—a rare sight in those days, and he insisted on showing me how it worked. He made me turn the switches and stop and start it, and he told me that I could come in any morning and have a game with it. He used the word 'game' as though it were something secret, and it's true that I never told my family of this invitation and of how, perhaps twice a week those holidays, the desire to control that little railway became overpowering, and looking up and down the street to see if I were observed, I would dive into the shop."

Our larger, dirtier, adult train drove into a tunnel and the light went out. We sat in darkness and silence, with the noise of the train blocking our ears like wax. When we were through we didn't speak at once and I had to prick him into continuing. "An elaborate seduction," I said.

"Don't think his plans were as simple as that," my companion said, "or as crude. There was much more hate than love, poor man, in his make-up. Can you hate something you don't believe in? And yet he called himself a free-thinker. What an impossible paradox, to be free and to be so obsessed. Day by day all through those holidays his obsession must have grown, but he kept a grip; he bided his time. Perhaps that thing I spoke of gave him the strength and the wisdom. It was only a week from the end of the holidays that he spoke to me on what concerned him so deeply.

"I heard him behind me as I knelt on the floor, coupling two coaches. He said, 'You won't be able to do this, Master David, when school starts.' It wasn't a sentence that needed any comment from me any more than the one that followed. 'You ought to have it for your own, you ought,' but how skilfully and unemphatically he had sowed the longing, the idea of a possibility. . . . I was coming to his parlour every day now; you see, I had to cram every opportunity in before the hated term started again, and I suppose I was becoming accustomed to Blacker, to that wall-eye, that turnip head, that nauseating subservience. The Pope, you know, describes himself as 'the servant of the servants of God,' and Blacker—I sometimes think that Blacker was 'the servant of the servants of. . . .' well, let it be.

"The very next day, standing in the doorway watching me play, he began to talk to me about religion. He said, with what untruth even I recognized, how much he admired the Catholics; he wished he could believe like that, but how could a baker believe? He accented 'a baker' as one might say a biologist, and the tiny train spun round the gauge 0 track. He said, 'I can bake the things you eat just as well as any Catholic can,' and disappeared into his shop. I hadn't the faintest idea what he meant. Presently he emerged again, holding in his hand a little wafer. 'Here,' he said, 'eat that and tell me. . . .' When I put it in my mouth I could tell that it was made in the same way as our wafers for communion—he had got the shape a little wrong, that was all—and I felt guilty and irrationally scared. 'Tell me,' he said, 'what's the difference?'

" 'Difference?' I asked.

" 'Isn't that just the same as you eat in church?'

"I said smugly, 'It hasn't been consecrated.'

"He said, 'Do you think, if I put the two of them under a microscope, you could tell the difference?'

"But even at ten I had the answer to that question. 'No,' I said, 'the—accidents don't change,' stumbling a little on the word 'accidents' which had suddenly conveyed to me the idea of death and wounds.

"Blacker said with sudden intensity, 'How I'd like to get one of your ones in my mouth—just to see. . . .'

"It may seem odd to you, but this was the first time that the idea of transsubstantiation really lodged in my mind. I had learned it all by rote; I had grown up with the idea. The Mass was as lifeless to me as the sentences in *De Bello Gallico;* communion a routine like drill in the school-yard, but here suddenly I was in the presence of a man who took it seriously, as seriously as the priest whom naturally one didn't count—it was his job. I felt more scared than ever.

"He said, 'It's all nonsense, but I'd just like to have it in my mouth.'

" 'You could if you were a Catholic,' I said naïvely.

"He gazed at me with his one good eye, like a Cyclops. He said, 'You serve at Mass, don't you? It would be easy for you to get at one of those things. I tell you what I'd do—I'd swap this electric train for one of your wafers—consecrated, mind. It's got to be consecrated.'

" 'I could get you one out of the box,' I said. I think I still imagined that his interest was a baker's interest—to see how they were made.

" 'Oh, no,' he said, 'I want to see what your God tastes like.'

" 'I couldn't do that.'

" 'Not for a whole electric train, just for yourself? You wouldn't have any trouble at home. I'd pack it up and put a label inside that your dad could see: "For my bank manager's little boy from a grateful client." He'd be pleased as punch with that.'

"Now that we are grown men it seems a trivial temptation, doesn't it? But try to think back to your own childhood. There was a whole circuit of rails there on the floor at our feet, straight rails and curved, and a little station with porters and passengers, a tunnel, a foot-bridge, a level crossing, two signals, buffers, of course—and, above all, a turntable. The tears of longing came into my eyes when I looked at the turntable. It was my favorite piece—it looked so ugly and practical and true. I said weakly, 'I wouldn't know how.'

"How carefully he had been studying the ground! He must have slipped several times into Mass at the back of the church. It would have been no good, you understand, in a little town like that, presenting himself for communion. Everybody there knew him for what he was. He said to me, 'When you've been given communion you could just put it under your tongue a moment. He serves you and the other boy first, and I saw you once go out behind the curtain straight afterwards. You'd forgotten one of those little bottles.'

" 'The cruet,' I said.

" 'Pepper and salt.' He grinned at me jovially, and I—well, I looked at the little railway which I could no longer come and play with when term started. I said, 'You'd just swallow it, wouldn't you?'

" 'Oh, yes,' he said. 'I'd just swallow it.'

"Somehow I didn't want to play with the train any more that day. I got up and made for the door, but he detained me, gripping my lapel. He said, 'This will be a secret between you and me. Tomorrow's Sunday. You come along here in the afternoon. Put it in an envelope and post it me. Monday morning the train will be delivered bright and early.'

" 'Not tomorrow,' I implored him.

" 'I'm not interested in any other Sunday,' he said. 'It's your only chance.' He shook me gently backwards and forwards. 'It will always have to be a secret between you and me,' he said. 'Why, if anyone knew they'd take away the train and there'd be me to reckon with. I'd bleed you something awful. You know how I'm always about on Sunday walks. You can't avoid a man like me. I crop up. You wouldn't ever be safe in your own house. I know ways to get into houses when people are asleep.' He pulled me into the shop after him and opened a drawer. In the drawer was an odd looking key and a cut-throat razor. He said, "That's a master key that opens all locks and that—that's what I bleed people with.' Then he patted my cheek with his plump floury fingers and said, 'Forget it. You and me are friends.'

"That Sunday Mass stays in my head, every detail of it, as though it had happened only a week ago. From the moment of the Confession to the moment of Consecration it had a terrible importance; only one other Mass has ever been so important to me—perhaps not even one, for this was a solitary Mass which would never happen again. It seemed as final as the last Sacrament when the priest bent down and put the wafer in my mouth where I knelt before the altar with my fellow server.

"I suppose I had made up my mind to commit this awful act—for, you know, to us it must always seem an awful act—from the moment when I saw Blacker watching from the back of the church. He had put on his best black Sunday clothes and, as though he could never quite escape the smear of his profession, he had a dab of dried talcum on his cheek, which he had presumably applied after using that cut-throat of his. He was watching me closely all the time, and I think it was fear—fear of that terrible undefined thing called bleeding—as much as covetousness that drove me to carry out my instructions.

"My fellow server got briskly up and, taking the paten, preceded Father Carey to the altar rail where the other communicants knelt. I had the Host lodged under my tongue: it felt like a blister. I got up and made for the curtain to get the cruet that I had purposely left in the sacristy. When I was there I looked quickly round for a hiding place and saw an old copy of the *Universe* lying on a chair. I took the Host from my mouth and inserted it between two sheets—a little damp mess of pulp. Then I thought: perhaps Father Carey has put out the paper for a particular purpose and he will find the Host before I have time to remove it, and the enormity of my act began to come home to me when I tried to imagine what punishment I should incur. Murder is sufficiently trivial to have its appropriate punishment, but for this act the mind boggled at the thought of any retribution at all. I tried to remove the Host, but it stuck clammily between the pages, and in desperation I tore out a piece of the newspaper and, screwing the whole thing up, stuck it in my trousers pocket. When I came back through the curtain carrying the cruet my eyes met Blacker's. He gave me a grin of encouragement and unhappiness—yes, I am sure, unhappiness. Was it perhaps that the poor man was all the time seeking something incorruptible?

"I can remember little more of that day. I think my mind was shocked and stunned, and I was caught up too in the family bustle of Sunday. Sunday in a provincial town is the day for relations. All the family are at home, and unfamiliar cousins and uncles are apt to arrive, packed in the back seats of other people's cars. I remember that some crowd of the kind descended on us and pushed Blacker temporarily out of the foreground of my mind. There was somebody called Aunt Lucy, with a loud hollow laugh that filled the house with mechanical merriment like the sound of recorded laughter from inside a hall of mirrors, and I had no opportunity to go out alone even if I had wished to. When six o'clock came and Aunt Lucy and the cousins departed and peace returned, it was too late to go to Blacker's, and at eight it was my own bed-time.

"I think I had half forgotten what I had in my pocket. As I emptied my pocket the little screw of newspaper brought quickly back the Mass, the priest bending over me, Blacker's grin. I laid the packet on the chair by my bed and tried to go to sleep, but I was haunted by the shadows on the wall where the curtains blew, the squeak of furniture, the rustle in the chimney, haunted by the presence of God there on the chair. The Host had always been to me—well, the Host. I knew theoretically, as I have said, what I had to believe, but suddenly, as someone whistled in the road outside, whistled secretively, knowingly, to me, I knew that this which I had beside my bed was something of infinite value—something a man would pay for with his whole peace of mind, something that was so hated one could love it as one loves an outcast or a bullied child. These are adult words, and it was a child of ten who lay scared in bed, listening to the whistle from the road, Blacker's whistle, but I think he felt fairly clearly what I am describing now. That is what I meant when I said this Thing, whatever it is, that seizes every possible weapon against God, is always, everywhere, disappointed at the moment of success. It must have felt as certain of me as Blacker did. It must have felt certain too of Blacker. But I wonder, if one knew what happened later to that poor man, whether one would not find again that the weapon had been turned against its own breast.

"At last I couldn't bear that whistle any more and got out of bed. I opened the curtains a little way, and there right under my window, the moonlight on his face, was Blacker. If I had stretched my hand down, his fingers reaching up could almost have touched mine. He looked up at me, flashing the one good eye, with hunger—I realize now that near-success must have developed his obsession almost to the point of madness. Desperation had driven him to the house. He whispered up at me. 'David, where is it?'

"I jerked my head back at the room. 'Give it me,' he said. 'Quick. You shall have the train in the morning.'

"I shook my head. He said, 'I've got the bleeder here, and the key. You'd better toss it down.'

" 'Go away,' I said, but I could hardly speak for fear.

" 'I'll bleed you first and then I'll have it just the same.'

" 'Oh, no, you won't,' I said. I went to the chair and picked it—Him—up. There was only one place where He was safe. I couldn't separate the Host from the paper, so I swallowed both. The newsprint stuck like a prune skin to the back of my throat, but I rinsed it down with water from the ewer. Then I went back to the window and looked down at Blacker. He began to wheedle me. 'What have you done with it, David? What's the fuss? It's only a bit of bread,' looking so longingly and pleadingly up at me that even as a child I wondered whether he could really think that, and yet desire it so much.

" 'I swallowed it,' I said.

" 'Swallowed it?'

" 'Yes,' I said. 'Go away.'

"Then something happened which seems to me now more terrible than his desire to corrupt or my thoughtless act: he began to weep—the tears ran lopsidedly out of the one good eye and his shoulders shook. I only saw his face for a moment before he bent his head and strode off, the bald turnip head shaking, into the dark. When I think of it now, it's almost as if I had seen that Thing weeping for its inevitable defeat. It had tried to use me as a weapon, and now I had broken in its hands and it wept its hopeless tears through one of Blacker's eyes."

The black furnaces of Bedwell Junction gathered around the line. The points switched and we were tossed from one set of rails to another. A spray of sparks, a signal light changing to red, tall chimneys jetting into the grey night sky, the fumes of steam from stationary engines—half the cold journey was over, and now remained the long wait for the slow cross-country train. I said, "It's an interesting story. I think I should have given Blacker what he wanted. I wonder what he would have done with it."

"I really believe," my companion said, "that he would first of all have put it under his microscope—before he did all the other things I expect he had planned."

"And the hints," I said. "I don't quite see what you mean by that."

"Oh, well," he said vaguely, "you know for me it was an odd beginning, that affair, when you come to think of it," but I never should have known what he meant had not his coat, when he rose to take the bag from the rack, come open and disclosed the collar of a priest.

I said, "I suppose you think you owe a lot to Blacker."

"Yes," he said, "you see, I am a very happy man."

2

CONFLICT

The first impulse of any reader of fiction is to ask, "What is the story about?" by which he usually means, "What happens in it?" The question betrays the feeling on the part of all fiction readers that a story, before it can be anything else, must be a narrative of something that happens to somebody. External action, so arranged and handled as to create curiosity, suspense, excitement, fear, or pity in one's audience, was the price that the first storyteller paid for attention. Aristotle's insistence that action was the center of all narrative, and that every story must have a beginning, a middle, and an end was simply a reaffirmation of the central place of action and plot in fiction or drama. In recent years, writer-critics like Sherwood Anderson have complained that the notion of "plot" has "poisoned" all storytelling, and experimental movie makers and avant-garde fiction writers have tried to create "plotless" stories, but their efforts, though sometimes interesting, are not fiction. For trying to write a story without some kind of narrative is analogous to trying to create a body without a skeleton.

But if most readers quite rightfully demand a narrative, they also are inclined either to exaggerate the importance of narrative in fiction or to ask of a narrative what its creator had no intention of providing. The influence of De Maupassant and Maugham and O. Henry, of TV westerns and Ian Fleming novels still heavily affect reading tastes, and external action is still *all* that many readers ask from fiction. But even the devotee of detective stories realizes that some stories, with comparatively little action, have somehow managed to interest him, and that others, with a great deal of action, have not. It is therefore necessary at the outset of a course in fiction, to consider some of the basic characteristics of narrative in fiction and some of the uses to which it can be put.

Until this century—or at least until writers like Chekhov began to experiment with and to modify existing story patterns and emphases—most narratives in fiction assumed a relatively fixed and formalized structure.

In this pattern, the action in stories was so arranged as to correspond to the divisions which Gustav Freytag found in five-act dramatic tragedies. In the "Freytag Pyramid" a plotted narrative proceeds through five distinct stages: (1) *exposition,* in which we are given all information necessary to our understanding of the story to follow; (2) *rising action, complication,* or *nouement* (tying up), in which conflict is initiated and developed; (3) a *climax, crisis,* or *turning point,* which leads to the resolution or unraveling of that conflict; (4) a period of *falling action;* and (5) a *denouement* (untying) or *resolution,* in which is provided not only the termination of the conflict but its significance, frequently through a "recognition scene."

Now Freytag was analyzing the plots of five-act dramas, and if his pyramid happens to describe the narrative arrangements of many novels and short stories, it does not describe them all. Particularly is this true of short stories, where extreme compression may obscure one or more of Freytag's divisions. If we have a story, the probability is that we can, though often only with considerable straining, find Freytag's pyramid in it, though the exposition may be buried in a single sentence and the recognition scene (the "epiphany" as James Joyce called it) may exist solely by implication. But because short fiction is in some respects radically different from fully developed drama, action and plot in fiction can be more meaningfully analyzed in simpler ways.

One such simplified approach was offered by E. M. Forster in his *Aspects of the Novel.* If, says Forster, a story can be defined "as a narrative of events arranged in their time-sequence," a plot can be defined as "a narrative of events, the emphasis falling on causality."

> "The king died and then the queen died" is a story. "The king died, and then the queen died of grief" is a plot. The time-sequence is preserved, but the sense of causality overshadows it. Or again: "The queen died, no one knew why, until is was discovered that it was through grief at the death of the king." This is a plot with a mystery in it, a form capable of high development. . . . Consider the death of the queen. If it is in a story we say "and then?" If it is in a plot we ask "why?"[1]

Forster's distinction between "story" and "plot" is a useful one. But in most cases, when we are dealing with short stories, we can understand more clearly this element of fiction by eliminating from our critical vocabulary the term *plot* and by substituting for it the term *conflict.* Plot, as we have seen, connotes a relatively inflexible story structure, and just as all poems do not consist of exactly fourteen lines, so all stories do not have a plot in the commonly accepted sense of the word. But all

[1] From *Aspects of the Novel* by E. M. Forster. Copyright, 1927 by Harcourt, Brace & World, Inc., renewed by E. M. Forster and used by permission of the publishers.

stories do have conflict at their core. The term *conflict* simply means that a story brings together two opposing forces which we call a *protagonist* (that is, one who struggles for) and an *antagonist* (that is, one who struggles against), and then develops and resolves the resultant conflict between these two forces. In most stories, these conflicts will assume one of two patterns: either they will be "accomplishment stories," in which the protagonist tries against opposition to achieve some goal, or they will be "decision stories," in which a protagonist is forced to choose between two things—two sets of values, say, or two courses of action.

Conflict, then, is a necessary element in fiction. Indeed it is the backbone of a story; it is conflict that provides us with pattern and direction and gives us the sense of a story going somewhere. But conflict must be handled in certain ways if it is to be convincing and effective. What, then, are the basic principles that writers consider when they want to arouse and maintain a reader's interest in a story?

The conflict in a story must first be *significant;* it must be of obvious importance to the characters involved. We can illustrate this by reference to experience. All of us face constant conflicts in our daily lives—whenever we cross a street, for example. Most of these are resolved easily. But we sometimes face conflicts which are not easily resolved. All of us experience from time to time conflicts which have some kind of a permanent effect upon us—which alter our basic values or our conception of human nature, or which modify our character, values, ideals, or concepts in some way. To mention only one case in point, there is that most common of human dilemmas, the choice between holding to a set of moral and ethical convictions or violating them in order to be accepted by our group. These are the kinds of conflicts which we find in fiction; and because they are of this nature, we call fictional conflicts *crisis situations.* We mean by this that as a result of a given conflict, the character or characters involved will never again be quite the same people that they were before the incident occurred.

One characteristic of conflict in fiction, then, is that some kind of change is effected in the character involved. A second characteristic is that the two forces which constitute the conflict must be reasonably equal in strength. In one way a skillful story is analogous to a prize fight, in which the outcome is in doubt until the final round. Hence, the skillful writer will balance his opposing forces so that the outcome of a story remains in *suspense* until the end. To put this in another way, conflict is *developed* in effective stories.

Third, a story must have *unity.* This is a comprehensive term; ultimately it means that everything—the conflict, the characters, the theme, the symbolism, the point of view, the incidental devices—must be interrelated, functional, and necessary to the achievement of a story's basic purpose or effect. In the narrower terms of conflict alone, unity means that each development in the conflict of a story must follow logically from a preceding development.

A writer may manage all this and still fail to convince, for his conflict may lack the most essential characteristic of fiction, that of *plausibility*—that inexplicable quality which makes us believe. Like unity, plausibility involves the *whole* story, not merely conflict. There is, however, one general principle on which plausibility rests: the most convincing story will be the one that most closely approximates life as the reader has experienced or observed it. This does not mean that the initial *situation* in a story must necessarily correspond to situations in our world; the skillful writer of fantasy, for example, can persuade us to accept a totally unfamiliar world. But it does mean that given a particular situation, the characters in a story will act and react according to familiar principles of human behavior. Or it means that the resolution of conflicts will adhere to basic facts of existence—that in a story as in life, for example, a stronger force will defeat a weaker force.

Given these necessary characteristics of effective fictional conflict, writers may employ other devices that are peculiarly associated with narrative handling. In story openings, for example, where a writer may have to establish time, place, character, or background before he can plunge us into his conflict, we may find *foreshadowing*—that is, giving the suggestion of conflict to follow. He may lure us into reading by *arousing curiosity.* He may intensify his conflict by employing *dilemma*—that is, he may place his character in a situation in which he is forced to choose between two equally undesirable alternatives. In these and other ways, writers can arouse and maintain interest in their conflict, intensify it, or otherwise increase its effectiveness.

The above may help us to understand how and why writers present action as they do; further, it may help us to understand why some stories, considered simply as *stories,* are more effective than others. But conflict is only one of several elements in fiction. And if conflict is the be-all and end-all of some stories, it is more frequently simply one way in which to achieve quite another end than just suspense. Hence, the most crucial questions we can ask about conflict are, "What is its *function* in a given story? To what use is it put?"

Since the relationship between all the elements in a story is the subject of this entire text, we cannot as yet discuss with any degree of completeness the function of conflict. But initially we can begin to see this relationship if we ask ourselves the following questions about a story's conflict.

1. Who is the protagonist? In most stories, the answer to this will be obvious. But in some it will not be. For example, is Henry or Nicky the protagonist in "The Facts of Life"? If it is Henry, the story says

one thing; if Nicky, it says another. In most stories, we can pinpoint the protagonist by asking ourselves, "On whom does this story have a maximum effect? For whom is it most genuinely a crisis?" And if, on occasion, we discover that a story has no clear protagonist, we have through that discovery taken a step toward determining what the story's purpose is and what function conflict plays in achieving that purpose.

2. What seems to be the emphasized element in a story? Is it conflict, or does conflict seem to be subordinated to some other element, such as characterization or description? Determining the dominant element is an important first step in discovering what a story's purpose is.

3. What is the focus of the conflict? In a story in which an ambitious company man is thwarted in his rise to the presidency by other ambitious men, the conflict is *external.* In a story in which that same company executive wants the presidency but not at the expense of making certain ethical compromises to obtain it, the conflict is *internal.* Ordinarily, a shift from external to internal conflict will change radically the purpose of a story.

4. How is the conflict resolved? A story in which a protagonist wins all says one thing. A story in which he loses all says another. A story in which he wins but finds the winning tainted with some dissatisfaction says a third. A story in which the conflict is never resolved says a fourth.

5. How is the conflict organized? Action may be organized in any of a number of ways, and frequently the function or purpose of the conflict is betrayed or at least suggested by this organization. If, for example, a writer wants to create suspense, he will organize his story chronologically, or at least will keep his resolution a secret until the end. But he may not be interested in creating suspense; he may want us to ask not "And then?" but "Why?" In this case, he may invert his organization, giving us the resolution before he gives us the developed conflict. A great many stories are not organized chronologically, and if we ask why the "normal" organization is abandoned, we often will find the answer a help in determining the function of conflict in a given story.

KAY BOYLE

Effigy of War

The barman at the big hotel on the sea front had been an officer in the Italian army during the last war, and somehow or other the rumor began to get around. Whether it was that he said too much to people who spoke his own language with him, saying late at night that the vines in Italy were like no other vines and the voices more musical and the soldiers as good as any others, no matter what history had to say about them, or whether it got around in some other way, it was impossible to know. But the story came to the director of the hotel (Cannes, it was, and the people just as gaudily dressed as other years, and the shops on the Croisette as fancy), and because of the feeling that ran high against the foreigner and against the name of Italy, the director stepped into the lounge bar about eleven one morning to tell the barman what he'd better do. He was a dressy, expensive-looking little man, the director, who could speak four languages with ease, and he had been a Russian once, a White Russian, so that France was the only country left to him now. He came into the bar at a quiet hour, just before the idle would begin wandering in out of the eternally springtime sun, and he jerked his cuffs inside his morning coat and screwed the soft, sagging folds of his throat from his collar wings and started speaking quietly over the mahogany-colored bar.

"Maestro," he said to the barman who had been ten years with them, "with all this trouble going on the management would quite understand your wanting to go back to Italy."

"Italy?" the barman said, and it might have been Siberia he was pronouncing as a destination and the look in his eyes was as startled. He stopped whatever it was he had been doing, setting the glasses straight or putting the ash trays out or the olives, and he looked at the director.

He was a slight, dark man and his face was as delicate-boned as a monkey's, and the hair was oiled down flat upon his monkey-fragile skull.

"A lot of Italians are going back," the director said, and he swung himself up onto the stool as elegantly and lightly as a dwarf dressed up for a public appearance, the flesh hairless and pink, and the hand on the wood of the bar as plump as a child's. "Give me a glass of milk," he said, and he went on saying in a lower voice: "In times like these everyone wants to avoid all the trouble they can. Everybody likes to feel he's in his own country." He said it with a slight Russian accent, and the barman waited while the director took the cigarette out of the silver case, and then the barman snapped the lighter open and held the flame to the end of the cigarette in his dark, monkey-nervous hand. "We're perfectly willing to discuss things with you," the director said, and as the first bluish breath of smoke drifted between them, their eyes met for a moment across it, and the director was the first to look away.

"Ah, if we should all go back to the places we belong to!" the barman said as he put the lighter into the pocket of his starched white coat. He turned aside to take the bottle of milk off the ice, and he went on saying in strangely poetic sorrow: "If we all returned to the waters of our own seas and the words of our own languages, France would be left a wilderness—"

"Of course, there are some national exceptions," the director added quickly. "There are some nationalities which cannot go back." He took a swallow of milk and looked rather severely at the barman. "In countries where there have been revolutions, economic upheavals," he went on, his hand with the cigarette in it making the vague, comprehensive gestures of unrest. "But with Italians," he said, and the barman suddenly leaned forward and laid his small bony hands down flat upon the bar.

"Well, me," he said, "I've been fifteen years in this country. I'm too old to go back now. For me, Mussolini was an economic upheaval," he said. He picked up the bottle of milk again and filled the director's glass, pouring it out a little too quickly. "I've never gone back, not since fifteen years," he said, the words spoken sharply and rapidly, almost breathlessly across the bar. "I'm like a refugee, like a political refugee," he said. "I haven't the right to go back."

"That can be taken care of," the director said, and he took out his folded handkerchief and dabbed at the drops of milk on his upper lip. "The management would advance you what you needed to get back, write you a good testimonial—"

"I haven't done military service for them," the barman said, and he was smiling in something like pain at the director, the grin pulled queer and ancient as a monkey's across his face. "I can't go back," he said. "This is my country by now. If I can't go on working here I can't work anywhere. I wouldn't leave this country no matter what anybody said to me or no matter what they did to me."

"You never did very much about getting any papers out," said the director. He was looking straight ahead at the small silk flags of all the nations and at his own immaculately preserved reflection in the glass. "You never did much about trying to change your nationality," he said, and he took another discreet swallow of milk. "You should have thought of that before."

"I might have been a Frenchman today if it hadn't been for my wife," the barman said, and his tongue ran eagerly out along his lip. "My wife—" he said, and he leaned closer, the starched sleeves, with the hairy, bony little wrists showing, laid on the bar. "I haven't seen her for fifteen years," he said, and the director looked at the glass of milk and shrugged his shoulders. "She's in Italy, and she wouldn't sign the papers. She wouldn't do that one thing," he said, the eyes dark and bright, and the face lit suddenly, like a poet's with eagerness and pain. "Not that she wanted me," he said. "It wasn't that. But women like that, Italian women, they're as soft and beautiful as flowers and as stubborn as weeds." He said it in abrupt poetic violence, and the director stirred a little uneasily and finished the milk in his glass.

"Now, you take a run up to the Italian Consul this afternoon and have a talk with him," he said, and he wiped his upper lip with his folded handkerchief again. "Tell him you're thinking of going back. Put Raymond on duty for the afternoon. And another thing, Maestro," he said as he got down off the bar stool, "Don't keep that *Corriere della Sera* out there where everybody can see it. Put it in your pocket and read it when you get home," he said.

It might have passed off quietly enough like that if the Dane hadn't come into it. He was a snub-nosed, sun-blacked, blond-headed little man who gave swimming lessons in one of the bathing establishments on the beach. He had been a long time there, walking season after season tough and cocky up and down the beach with his chest high and his thumbs hooked into the white belt of his bathing trunks. He wore a bright clean linen cap down to his yellow brows, and royal-blue swimming shorts, and the muscles in his shoulders and arms were as thick and smooth as taffy. But after the war came, he didn't parade up and down the esplanade in the same way in the sun, but stayed hour after hour in the water or else in a corner of the beach café. He still gave lessons, but he let the pupils seek him out in the shade of the café, as if the eyes of the mobilized and the uniformed and the envious could see him less distinctly there.

The one who started it all was the Greek waiter in the big hotel who had got his French naturalization papers eight months before and was leaving for training camp in a week or two. He'd lean over the diners—what was left of the English and the American colony, and the dukes and duchesses, and the Spanish who had got their jewels and their pelts and their money out of Spain—and he'd say:

"What nationality do you think I am, eh? What country would you say I come from?" showing his teeth in pride and pleasure at them as he slipped the dishes of *filets de soles bonne femme* or *champignons à la Reine d'Angleterre* down before them, provided the maître d'hôtel was looking the other way. Sometimes the guests would say he looked one thing, and sometimes another: Italian, Rumanian, or even Argentine, and he'd smile like a prima donna at them, leaning almost on their shoulders, with his eyes shining and the serviette flung rather wildly over his arm.

No, no, oh, *mon dieu,* no!" he'd say. "I'm pure French. What do you think of that? In another two or three months you'll see me coming in here with gold stripes on my sleeve, ordering everything like everybody else has to eat." And then he'd take out his mobilization order and show it to them, balancing the *homard à l'américaine* on its platter in the other hand as he opened out the stamped, signed paper. "I'm French," he'd say, with the garlic hanging on his breath. "I'm going right into the French army to fight. I'm going to fight for everybody sitting here having dinner tonight," he'd say, and he'd give the people at the next table their salad, holding his mobilization order open in his hand.

The Greek waiter had never liked the look of the Dane, and now that he had his military orders he couldn't so much as stand the sight of the cold-eyed, golden little man. In the hours he had off in the afternoons, he took the habit of walking out on the esplanade and stopping just above the bathing place to call the names down to him. There he would be, the Dane, with his white cap on and his royal-blue bathing trunks, talking half naked to the half naked girls or women on the beach, war or no war, and going on making money just the same.

"Sale étranger!" the Greek would call down, with a fine Greek accent to it, and *"Crepule!,"* with his voice ringing out like an opera singer's across the sand and the striped bathing houses and the sea. "France for the French!" he'd roar over the railing, and the little Dane in his bathing suit would go quietly on with his swimming lessons, or if he were alone he'd turn and go into the beach café and sit down out of sight in the shade. There was a week ahead still before the Greek waiter would go, and all those days in the afternoons he'd stand on the esplanade and call the names down. In the end he appealed to the French themselves, exhorting them to rise. "The French for the French!" he'd shout down through the funnel of his hands. "Don't employ foreigners! Give a Frenchman the job!"

The last night of the week the little Dane came into the lounge bar for a drink before he went to bed; coming late, in discretion, when no one else was there. The two of them were talking there together, the Dane sitting on the stool with the glass of beer before him, and the Italian on the other side with his starched jacket on and the wisps of his monkey hair slicked flat across his skull, and in a few minutes the barman would have taken the bottles down and locked the safes and turned the lights out, and then nothing would have occurred. But now the barman was leaning on the counter, speaking the French tongue in a low, rather grievous voice to the swimming teacher, his thin hand rocking from side to side like a little boat as he talked.

"Drinking has ceased," he was saying in faultless pentameter, "in the old way it has ceased. Even before September there was a difference, as if the thirst of man had been slaked at last. To any sensitive eye, the marks of death were to be seen for years on the façades of casinos, palace hotels, luxury restaurants, and on the terraces of country clubs and vast private estates. Even the life of the big bars has been dying," he said. "For years now that I can remember, the lounge bar has been passing through the agonies of death." He made a tragic and noble gesture toward the empty leather armchairs in the half-darkened room, and he said in a low, dreamy voice: "All this is finished. There is no more place in the hearts of men for this kind of thing. The race that insisted on this atmosphere of redundance for its pleasure, that demanded this futility, is vanishing, dying—"

"War levels the ranks," the Dane said quietly. His sun-blacked, sun-withered face under the bright light thatch of hair was as immobile as if carved from wood.

"Ah, before the war even," the barman said softly, and then he stopped, for the men had come into the bar. The Greek waiter walked a little ahead of the others, wearing a gray jersey and a cap pulled down, and they both of them knew him; it was the others behind him they had never seen before.

"Get that one, the one on the stool," the Greek waiter said, and one of the other men stepped past him and walked toward the bar. Just before he got there he lifted his right arm and hit the swimming teacher on the chin. The little, light-crowned head and the strong, small body rose clear of the stool an instant, like a piece of paper lifted and spun sidewise by the wind, and then it sailed into the corner and collapsed there, bent double, by the leather chair. "That's the kind of language he understands," the Greek said, and he crossed the length of thick, soft carpet, jerking his cap up on his forehead. He was smiling with delight when he kicked the swimming teacher's body into another shape. "Walking up and down out there on the beach," the Greek said, and he turned back to the others and the Italian barman behind the bar. "Giving lessons just like men weren't bleeding their guts out for him and people like him—"

"He volunteered. I tell you that man volunteered," the barman began saying, and his bones were shaking like a monkey's in his skin. "I've seen the paper he got. I know he volunteered to fight like anybody else would—" And when he jumped for the bell the Greek waiter reached over and took him by the collar and his starched white coat and dragged him out across the plates of potato chips and the empty beer bottle and the glass the Dane had been drinking and slung him across the elegant little glass-topped tables into the other corner of the room.

"Pick him up and take him along too," the Greek said. "I know all about him I need to know. He was an officer last war, officer in the Italian army, so you'll know what side he'll fight on this time. Take them both out," he said. "This country's not good enough for them, not good enough for either of them."

They did it by moonlight, taking the two men's clothes off on the sand and shingles by the Mediterranean water, and giving it to them in fiercely accelerating violence. They broke the swimming teacher's jaw, and they snapped the arms of the barman behind him like firewood, beating the breath and the life from them with whatever fell under their hands. The Greek carried over an armful of folding iron chairs from the bathing establishment's darkened, abandoned porch and, with these as weapons, they battered the two men's heads down and drove their mouths into the sand.

"So now repeat this after me, foreigners," the Greek began saying in wild holy passion as he kneeled beside them. He had taken the flag out of his jersey and was shaking out its folds. "So now repeat what I'm going to tell you," he said in violent religious fervor against the pulsing and murmuring of the water, and his hands were trembling as he laid the flag out where their mouths could bleed upon the tricolor emblem, the cotton stuff transformed now to the exigencies of a nation and a universe.

JAMES BALDWIN

This Morning, This Evening, So Soon

"You are full of nightmares," Harriet tells me. She is in her dressing gown and has cream all over her face. She and my older sister, Louisa, are going out to be girls together. I suppose they have many things to talk about—they have *me* to talk about, certainly—and they do not want my presence. I have been given a bachelor's evening. The director of the film which has brought us such incredible and troubling riches will be along later to take me out to dinner.

I watch her face. I know that it is quite impossible for her to be as untroubled as she seems. Her self-control is mainly for my benefit—my benefit, and Paul's. Harriet comes from orderly and progressive Sweden and has reacted against all the advanced doctrines to which she has been exposed by becoming steadily and beautifully old-fashioned. We never fought in front of Paul, not even when he was a baby. Harriet does not so much believe in protecting children as she does in helping them to build a foundation on which they can build and build again, each time life's high-flying steel ball knocks down everything they have built.

Whenever I become upset, Harriet becomes very cheerful and composed. I think she began to learn how to do this over eight years ago, when I returned from my only visit to America. Now, perhaps, it has become something she could not control if she wished to. This morning, at breakfast, when I yelled at Paul, she averted Paul's tears and my own guilt by looking up and saying, "My God, your father is cranky this morning, isn't he?"

Paul's attention was immediately distracted from his wounds, and the unjust inflicter of those wounds, to his mother's laughter. He watched her.

"It is because he is afraid they will not like his songs in New York. Your father is an *artiste, mon chou,* and they are very mysterious people, *les artistes.* Millions of people are waiting for him in New York, they are begging him to come, and they will give him a *lot* of money, but he is afraid they will not like him. Tell him he is wrong."

She succeeded in rekindling Paul's excitement about places he has never seen. I was also, at once, reinvested with all my glamour. I think it is sometimes extremely difficult for Paul to realize that the face he sees on record sleeves and in the newspapers and on the screen is nothing more or less than the face of his father—who sometimes yells at him. Of course, since he is only seven—going on eight, he will be eight years old this winter—he cannot know that I am baffled, too.

"Of course, you are wrong, you are silly," he said with passion—and caused me to smile. His English is strongly accented and is not, in fact, as good as his French, for he speaks French all day at school. French is really his first language, the first he ever heard. "You are the greatest singer in France"—sounding exactly as he must sound when he makes this pronouncement to his schoolmates—"the greatest *American* singer"—this concession was so gracefully made that it was not a concession at all, it added inches to my stature, America being only a glamorous word for Paul. It is the place from which his father came, and to which he now is going, a place which very few people have ever seen. But his aunt is one of them and he looked over at her. "Mme. Dumont says so, and she says he is a *great actor, too.*" Louisa nodded, smiling. "And she has seen *Les Fauves Nous Attendent*—five times." This clinched it, of course. Mme. Dumont is our concierge and she has known Paul all his life. I suppose he will not begin to doubt anything she says until he begins to doubt everything.

He looked over at me again. "So you are wrong to be afraid."

"I was wrong to yell at you, too. I won't yell at you any more today."

"All right." He was very grave.

Louisa poured more coffee. "He's going to knock them dead in New York. You'll see."

"Mais bien sur," said Paul, doubtfully. He does not quite know what "knock them dead" means, though he was sure, from her tone, that she must have been agreeing with him. He does not quite understand this aunt, whom he met for the first time two months ago, when she arrived to spend the summer with us. Her accent is entirely different from anything he has ever heard. He does not really understand why, since she is my sister and his aunt, she should be unable to speak French.

Harriet, Louisa, and I looked at each other and smiled. "Knock them dead," said Harriet, "means *d'avoir un succès fou.* But you will soon pick up all the American expressions." She looked at me and laughed. "So will I."

"That's what he's afraid of." Louisa grinned. "We have *got* some expressions, believe me. Don't let anybody ever tell you America hasn't got a culture. Our culture is as thick as clabber milk."

"Ah," Harriet answered, "I know. I know."

"I'm going to be practicing later," I told Paul.

His face lit up. *"Bon."* This meant that, later, he would come into my study and lie on the floor with his papers and crayons while I worked out with the piano and the tape recorder. He knew that I was offering this as an olive branch. All things considered, we get on pretty well, my son and I.

He looked over at Louisa again. She held a coffee cup in one hand and a cigarette in the other; and something about her baffled him. It was early, so she had not yet put on her face. Her short, thick, graying hair was rougher than usual, almost as rough as my own—later, she would be going to the hairdresser's; she is fairer than I, and better-looking; Louisa, in fact, caught all the looks in the family. Paul knows that she is my older sister and that she helped to raise me, though he does not, of course, know what this means. He knows that she is a schoolteacher in the *American* South, which is not, for some reason, the same place as South America. I could see him trying to fit all these exotic details together into a pattern which would explain her strangeness—strangeness of accent, strangeness of manner. In comparison with the people he has always known, Louisa must seem, for all her generosity and laughter and affection, peculiarly uncertain of herself, peculiarly hostile and embattled.

I wondered what he would think of his Uncle Norman, older and much blacker than I, who lives near the Alabama town in which we were born. Norman will meet us at the boat.

Now Harriet repeats, "Nightmares, nightmares. Nothing ever turns out as badly as you think it will—in fact," she adds laughing, "I am happy to say that that would scarcely be possible."

Her eyes seek mine in the mirror—dark-blue eyes, pale skin, black hair. I had always thought of Sweden as being populated entirely by blondes, and I thought that Harriet was abnormally dark for a Swedish girl. But when we visited Sweden, I found out differently. "It is all a great racial salad, Europe, that is why I am sure that I will never understand your country," Harriet said. That was in the days when we never imagined that we would be going to it.

I wonder what she is really thinking. Still, she is right, in two days we will be on a boat, and there is simply no point in carrying around my load of apprehension. I sit down on the bed, watching her fix her face. I realize that I am going to miss this old-fashioned bedroom. For years, we've talked about throwing out the old junk which came with the apartment and replacing it with less massive, modern furniture. But we never have.

"Oh, everything will probably work out," I say. "I've been in a bad mood all day long. I just can't sing any more." We both laugh. She reaches for a wad of tissues and begins wiping off the cream. "I wonder how Paul will like it, if he'll make friends—that's all."

"Paul will like any place where you are, where we are. Don't you worry about Paul."

Paul has never been called any names, so far. Only, once he asked us what the word *métis* meant and Harriet explained to him that it meant mixed blood, adding that the blood of just about everybody in the world was mixed by now. Mme. Dumont contributed bawdy and detailed corroboration from her own family tree, the roots of which were somewhere in Corsica; the moral of the story, as she told it, was that women were weak, men incorrigible, and *le bon Dieu* appallingly clever. Mme. Dumont's version is the version I prefer, but it may not be, for Paul, the most utilitarian.

Harriet rises from the dressing table and comes over to sit in my lap. I fall back with her on the bed, and she smiles down into my face.

"Now, don't worry," she tells me, "please try not to worry. Whatever is coming, we will manage it all very well, you will see. We have each other and we have our son and we know what we want. So, we are luckier than most people."

I kiss her on the chin. "I'm luckier than most men."

"I'm a very lucky woman, too."

And for a moment we are silent, alone in our room, which we have shared so long. The slight rise and fall of Harriet's breathing creates an intermittent pressure against my chest, and I think how, if I had never left America, I would never have met her and would never have established a life of my own, would never have entered my own life. For everyone's life begins on a level where races, armies, and churches stop. And yet everyone's life is always shaped by races, churches, and armies; races, churches, armies menace, and have taken, many lives. If Harriet had been born in America, it would have taken her a long time, perhaps forever, to look on me as a man like other men; if I had met her in America, I would never have been able to look on her as a woman like all other women. The habits of public rage and power would also have been our private compulsions, and would have blinded our eyes. We would never have been able to love each other. And Paul would never have been born.

Perhaps, if I had stayed in America, I would have found another woman and had another son. But that other woman, that other son are in the limbo of vanished possibilities. I might also have become something else, instead of an actor-singer, perhaps a lawyer, like my brother, or a teacher, like my sister. But no, I am what I have become and this woman beside me is my wife, and I love her. All the sons I might have had mean nothing, since I *have* a son, I named him, Paul, for my father, and I love him.

I think of all the things I have seen destroyed in America, all the things that I have lost there, all the threats it holds for me and mine.

I grin up at Harriet. "Do you love me?"

"Of course not. I simply have been madly plotting to get to America all these years."

"What a patient wench you are."

"The Swedes are very patient."

She kisses me again and stands up. Louisa comes in, also in a dressing gown.

"I hope you two aren't sitting in here yakking about the *subject.*" She looks at me. "My, you are the sorriest-looking celebrity I've ever seen. I've always wondered why people like you hired press agents. Now I know." She goes to Harriet's dressing table. "Honey, do you mind if I borrow some of the *mad* nail polish?"

Harriet goes over to the dressing table. "I'm not sure I know *which* mad nail polish you mean."

Harriet and Louisa, somewhat to my surprise, get on very well. Each seems to find the other full of the weirdest and most delightful surprises. Harriet has been teaching Louisa French and Swedish expressions, and Louisa has been teaching Harriet some of the saltier expressions of the black South. Whenever one of them is not playing straight man to the other's accent, they become involved in long speculations as to how a language reveals the history and the attitudes of a people. They discovered that all the European languages contain a phrase equivalent to "to work like a nigger." ("Of course," says Louisa, "they've had black men working for them for a long time.") "Language is experience and language is power," says Louisa, after regretting that she does not know any of the African dialects. "That's what I keep trying to tell those dicty bastards down South. They get their own experience into the language, we'll have a great language. But, no, they all want to talk like white folks." Then she leans forward, grasping Harriet by the knee. "I tell them, honey, white folks ain't saying *nothing*. Not a thing are they saying—and *some* of them know it, they *need* what you got, the whole world needs it." Then she leans back, in disgust. "You think they listen to me? Indeed they do not. They just go right on, trying to talk like white folks." She leans forward again, in tremendous indignation. "You know some of them folks are *ashamed* of Mahalia Jackson? *Ashamed* of her, one of the greatest singers alive! They think she's common." Then she looks about the room as though she held a bottle in her hand and were looking for a skull to crack.

I think it is because Louisa has never been able to talk like this to any white person before. All the white people she has ever met needed, in one way or another, to be reassured, consoled, to have their consciences pricked but not blasted; could not, could not afford to hear a truth which would shatter, irrevocably, their image of themselves. It is astonishing the lengths to which a person, or a people, will go in order to avoid a truthful mirror. But Harriet's necessity is precisely the opposite: it is of the utmost importance that she learn everything that Louisa can tell her, and then learn more, much more. Harriet is really trying to learn from Louisa how best to protect her husband and her son. This is why they are going out alone tonight. They will have, tonight, as it were, a final council of war. I may be moody, but they, thank God, are practical.

Now Louisa turns to me while Harriet rummages about on the dressing table. "What time is Vidal coming for you?"

"Oh, around seven-thirty, eight o'clock. He says he's reserved tables for us in some very chic place, but he won't say where." Louisa wriggles her shoulders, raises her eyebrows, and does a tiny bump and grind. I laugh. "That's right. And then I guess we'll go out and get drunk."

"I hope to God you do. You've been about as cheerful as a cemetery these last few days. And, that way, your hangover will keep you from bugging us tomorrow."

"What about *your* hangovers? I know the way you girls drink."

"Well, we'll be paying for our own drinks," says Harriet, "so I don't think we'll have that problem. But *you're* going to be feted, like an international movie star."

"You sure you don't want to change your mind and come out with Vidal and me?"

"We're sure," Louisa says. She looks down at me and gives a small, amused grunt. "An international movie star. And I used to change your diapers. I'll be damned." She is grave for a moment. "Mama'd be proud of you, you know that?" We look at each other and the air between us is charged with secrets which not even Harriet will ever know. "Now, get the hell out of here, so we can get dressed."

"I'll take Paul on down to Mme. Dumont's."

Paul is to have supper with her children and spend the night there.

"For the last time," says Mme. Dumont and she rubs her hand over Paul's violently curly black hair. *"Tu vas nous manquer, tu sais?"* Then she looks up at me and laughs. "He doesn't care. He is only interested in seeing the big ship and all the wonders of New York. Children are never sad to make journeys."

"I would be very sad to go," says Paul, "but my father must go to New York to work and he wants me to come with him."

Over his head, Mme. Dumont and I smile at each other. *"Il est malin, ton gosse!"* She looks down at him again. "And do you think, my little diplomat, that you will like New York?"

"We aren't only going to New York," Paul answers, "we are going to California, too."

"Well, do you think you will like California?"

Paul looks at me. "I don't know. If we don't like it, we'll come back."

"So simple. Just like that," says Mme. Dumont. She looks at me. "It is the best way to look at life. Do come back. You know, we feel that you belong to us, too, here in France."

"I hope you do," I say. "I hope you do. I have always felt—always felt at home here." I bend down and Paul and I kiss each other on the cheek. We have always done so—but will we be able to do so in America? American fathers never kiss American sons. I straighten, my hand on Paul's shoulder. "You be good. I'll pick you up for breakfast, or, if you get up first you come and pick me up and we can hang out together tomorrow, while your *Maman* and your Aunt Louisa finish packing. They won't want two men hanging around the house."

"*D'accord.* Where shall we hang out?" On the last two words he stumbles a little and imitates me.

"Maybe we can go to the zoo, I don't know. And I'll take you to lunch at the Eiffel Tower, would you like that?"

"Oh, yes," he says, "I'd love that." When he is pleased, he seems to glow. All the energy of his small, tough, concentrated being charges an unseen battery and adds an incredible luster to his eyes, which are large and dark brown—like mine—and to his skin, which always reminds me of the colors of honey and the fires of the sun.

"Ok, then." I shake hands with Mme. Dumont. *"Bonsoir, Madame,"* I ring for the elevator, staring at Paul. *"Ciao, Pauli."*

"Bonsoir, Papa."

And Mme. Dumont takes him inside.

Upstairs, Harriet and Louisa are finally powdered, perfumed, and jeweled, and ready to go: dry martinis at the Ritz, supper, "in some *very* expensive little place," says Harriet, and perhaps the Folies Bergère afterwards. "A real cornball, tourist evening," says Louisa. "I'm working on the theory that if I can get Harriet to act like an American now, she won't have so much trouble later."

"I very much doubt," Harriet says, "that I will be able to endure the Folies Bergère for three solid hours."

"Oh, then we'll duck across town to Harry's New York bar and drink mint juleps," says Louisa.

I realize that, quite apart from everything else, Louisa is having as much fun as she has ever had in her life. Perhaps she, too, will be sad to leave Paris, even though she has only known it for such a short time.

"Do people drink those in New York?" Harriet asks. I think she is making a list of the things people do or do not do in New York.

"*Some* people do." Louisa winks at me. "Do you realize that this Swedish chick's picked up an Alabama drawl?"

We laugh together. The elevator chugs to a landing.

"We'll stop and say goodnight to Paul," Harriet says. She kisses me. "Give our best to Vidal."

"Right. Have a good time. Don't let any Frenchmen run off with Louisa."

"I did not come to Paris to be protected, and if I had, this wild chick *you* married couldn't do it. I just *might* upset everybody and come home with a French count." She presses the elevator button and the cage goes down.

I walk back into our dismantled apartment. It stinks of departure. There are bags and crates in the hall which will be taken away tomorrow, there are no books in the bookcases, the kitchen looks as though we never cooked a meal there, never dawdled there, in the early morning or late at night, over coffee. Presently, I must shower and shave but now I pour myself a drink and light a cigarette and step out on our balcony. It is dusk, the brilliant light of Paris is beginning to fade, and the green of the trees is darkening.

I have lived in this city for twelve years. This apartment is on the top floor of a corner building. We look out over the trees and the roof tops of the Champ de Mars, where the Eiffel Tower stands. Beyond this field is the river, which I have crossed so often, in so many states of mind. I have crossed every bridge in Paris, I have walked along every *quai*. I know the river as one finally knows a friend, know it when it is black, guarding all the lights of Paris in its depths, and seeming, in its vast silence, to be communing with the dead who lie beneath it; when it is yellow, evil, and roaring, giving a rough time to tugboats and barges, and causing people to remember that it has been known to rise, it has been known to kill; when it is peaceful, a slick dark, dirty green, playing host to rowboats and *les bateaux mouches* and throwing up from time to time an extremely unhealthy fish. The men who stand along the *quais* all summer with their fishing lines gratefully accept the slimy object and throw it in a rusty can. I have always wondered who eats those fish.

And I walk up and down, up and down, glad to be alone.

It is August, the month when all Parisians desert Paris and one has to walk miles to find a barbershop or a laundry open in some tree-shadowed, silent side street. There is a single person on the avenue, a paratrooper walking toward École Militaire. He is also walking, almost certainly, and rather sooner than later, toward Algeria. I have a friend, a good-natured boy who was always hanging around the clubs in which I worked in the old days, who has just returned from Algeria, with a recurring, debilitating fever, and minus one eye. The government has set his pension at the sum, arbitrary if not occult, of fifty-three thousand francs every three months. Of course, it is quite impossible to live on this amount of money without working—but who will hire a half-blind invalid? This boy has been spoiled forever, long before his thirtieth birthday, and there are thousands like him all over France.

And there are fewer Algerians to be found on the streets of Paris now. The rug sellers, the peanut vendors, the postcard peddlers and money-changers have vanished. The boys I used to know during my first years in Paris are scattered—or corralled—the Lord knows where.

Most of them had no money. They lived three and four together in rooms with a single skylight, a single hard cot, or in buildings that seemed abandoned, with cardboard in the windows, with erratic plumbing in a wet, cobblestoned yard, in dark, dead-end alleys, or on the outer, chilling heights of Paris.

The Arab cafés are closed—those dark, acrid cafés in which I used to meet with them to drink tea, to get high on hashish, to listen to the obsessive, stringed music which has no relation to any beat, any time, that I have every known. I once thought of the North Africans as my brothers and that is why I went to their cafés. They were very friendly to me, perhaps one or two of them remained really fond of me even after I could no longer afford to smoke Lucky Strikes and after my collection of American sport shirts had vanished—mostly into their wardrobes. They seemed to feel that they had every right to them, since I could only have wrested these things from the world by cunning—it meant nothing to say that I had had no choice in the matter; perhaps I had wrested these things from the world by treason, by refusing to be identified with the misery of my people. Perhaps, indeed, I identified myself with those who were responsible for this misery.

And this was true. Their rage, the only note in all their music which I could not fail to recognize, to which I responded, yet had the effect of setting us more than ever at a division. They were perfectly prepared to drive all Frenchmen into the sea, and to level the city of Paris. But I could not hate the French, because they left me alone. And I love Paris, I will always love it, it is the city which saved my life. It saved my life by allowing me to find out who I am.

It was on a bridge, one tremendous, April morning, that I knew I had fallen in love. Harriet and I were walking hand in hand. The bridge was the Pont Royal, just before us was the great *horloge*, high and lifted up, saying ten to ten; beyond this, the golden statue of Joan of Arc, with her sword uplifted. Harriet and I were silent, for we had been quarreling about something. Now, when I look back, I think we had reached that state when an affair must either end or become something more than an affair.

I looked sideways at Harriet's face, which was still. Her dark-blue eyes were narrowed against the sun, and her full, pink lips were still slightly sulky, like a child's. In those days, she hardly ever wore make-up. I was in my shirt sleeves. Her face made me want to laugh and run my hand over her short dark hair. I wanted to pull her to me and say, *Baby, don't be mad at me,* and at that moment something tugged at my heart and made me catch my breath. There were millions of people all around us, but I was alone with Harriet. She was alone with me. Never, in all my life, until that moment, had I been alone with anyone. The world had always been with us, between us, defeating the quarrel we could not achieve, and making love impossible. During all the years of my life, until that moment, I had carried the menacing, the hostile, killing world with me everywhere. No matter what I was doing or saying or feeling, one eye had always been on the world—that world which I had learned to distrust almost as soon as I learned my name, that world on which I knew one could never turn one's back, the white man's world. And for the first time in my life I was free of it; it had not existed for me; I had been quarreling with my girl. It was our quarrel, it was entirely between us, it had nothing to do with anyone else in the world. For the first time in my life I had not been afraid of the patriotism of the mindless, in uniform or out, who would beat me up and treat the woman who was with me as though she were the lowest of untouchables. For the first time in my life I felt that no force jeopardized my right, my power, to possess and to protect a woman; for the first time, the first time, felt that the woman was not, in her own eyes or in the eyes of the world, degraded by my presence.

The sun fell over everything, like a blessing, people were moving all about us, I will never forget the feeling of Harriet's small hand in mine, dry and trusting, and I turned to her, slowing our pace. She looked up at me with her enormous, blue eyes, and she seemed to wait. I said, *Harriet. Harriet. Tu sais, il y a quelque chose de très grave qui m'est arrivé. Je t'aime. Je t'aime. Tu me comprends,* or shall I say it in English?"

This was eight years ago, shortly before my first and only visit home.

That was when my mother died. I stayed in America for three months. When I came back, Harriet thought that the change in me was due to my grief—I was very silent, very thin. But it had not been my mother's death which accounted for the change. I had known that my mother was going to die. I had not known what America would be like for me after nearly four years away.

I remember standing at the rail and watching the distance between myself and Le Havre increase. Hands fell, ceasing to wave, handkerchiefs ceased to flutter, people turned away, they mounted their bicycles or got into their cars and rode off. Soon, Le Havre was nothing but a blur. I thought of Harriet, already miles from me in Paris, and I pressed my lips tightly together in order not to cry.

Then, as Europe dropped below the water, as the days passed and passed, as we left behind us the skies of Europe and the eyes of everyone on the ship began, so to speak, to refocus, waiting for the first glimpse of America, my apprehension began to give way to a secret joy, a checked anticipation. I thought of such details as showers, which are rare in Paris, and I thought of such things as rich, cold, American milk and heavy, chocolate cake. I wondered about my friends, wondered if I had any left, and wondered if they would be glad to see me.

The Americans on the boat did not seem to be so bad, but I was fascinated, after such a long absence from it, by the nature of their friendliness. It was a friendliness which did not suggest, and was not intended to suggest, any possibility of friendship. Unlike Europeans, they dropped titles and used first names almost at once, leaving themselves, unlike the Europeans, with nowhere thereafter to go. Once one had become "Pete" or "Jane" or "Bill" all that could decently be known was known and any suggestion that there might be further depths, a person, so to speak, behind the name, was taken as a violation of that privacy which did not, paradoxically, since they trusted it so little, seem to exist among Americans. They apparently equated privacy with the unspeakable things they did in the bathroom or the bedroom, which they related only to the analyst, and then read about in the pages of best sellers. There was an eerie and unnerving irreality about everything they said and did, as though they were all members of the same team and were acting on orders from some invincibly cheerful and tirelessly inventive coach. I was fascinated by it. I found it oddly moving, but I cannot say that I was displeased. It had not occurred to me before that Americans, who had never treated me with any respect, had no respect for each other.

On the last night but one, there was a gala in the big ballroom and I sang. It had been a long time since I had sung before so many Americans. My audience had mainly been penniless French students, in the weird, Left Bank bistros I worked in those days. Still, I was a great hit with them and by this time I had become enough of a drawing card, in the Latin quarter and in St. Germain des Prés, to have attracted a couple of critics, to have had my picture in *France-soir*, and to have acquired a legal work permit which allowed me to make a little more money. Just the same, no matter how industrious and brilliant some of the musicians had been, or how devoted my audience, they did not know, they could not know, what my songs came out of. They did not know what was funny about it. It was impossible to translate: It damn well better be funny, or Laughing to keep from crying, or What did *I* do to be so black and blue?

The moment I stepped out on the floor, they began to smile, something opened in them, they were ready to be pleased. I found in their faces, as they watched me, smiling, waiting, an artless relief, a profound reassurance. Nothing was more familiar to them than the sight of a dark boy, singing, and there were few things on earth more necessary. It was under cover of darkness, my own darkness, that I could sing for them of the joys, passions, and terrors they smuggled about with them like steadily depreciating contraband. Under cover of the midnight fiction that I was unlike them because I was black, they could stealthily gaze at those treasures which they had been mysteriously forbidden to possess and were never permitted to declare.

I sang *I'm Coming, Virginia,* and *Take This Hammer,* and *Precious Lord.* They wouldn't let me go and I came back and sang a couple of the oldest blues I knew. Then someone asked me to sing *Swanee River,* and I did, astonished that I could, astonished that this song, which I had put down long ago, should have the power to move me. Then, if only, perhaps, to make the record complete, I wanted to sing *Strange Fruit,* but, on this number, no one can surpass the great, tormented Billie Holiday. So I finished with *Great Getting-Up Morning* and I guess I can say that if I didn't stop the show I certainly ended it. I got a big hand and I drank at a few tables and I danced with a few girls.

After one more day and one more night, the boat landed in New York. I woke up, I was bright awake at once, and I thought, *We're here.* I turned on all the lights in my small cabin and I stared into the mirror as though I were committing my face to memory. I took a shower and I took a long time shaving and I dressed myself very carefully. I walked the long ship corridors to the dining room, looking at the luggage piled high before the elevators and beside the steps. The dining room was nearly half empty and full of a quick and joyous excitement which depressed me even more. People ate quickly, chattering to each other, anxious to get upstairs and go on deck. Was it my imagination or was it true that they seemed to avoid my eyes? A few people waved and smiled, but let me pass; perhaps it would have made them uncomfortable, this morning, to try to share their excitement with me; perhaps they did not want to know whether or not it was possible for me to share it. I walked to my table and sat down. I munched toast as dry as paper and drank a pot of coffee. Then I tipped my waiter, who bowed and smiled and called me "sir" and said that he hoped to see me on the boat again. "I hope so, too," I said.

And was it true, or was it my imagination, that a flash of wondering comprehension, a flicker of wry sympathy, then appeared in the waiter's eyes? I walked upstairs to the deck.

There was a breeze from the water but the sun was hot and made me remember how ugly New York summers could be. All of the deck chairs had been taken away and people milled about in the space where the deck chairs had been, moved from one side of the ship to the other, clambered up and down the steps, crowded the rails, and they were busy taking photographs—of the harbor, of each other, of the sea, of the gulls. I walked slowly along the deck, and an impulse stronger than myself drove me to the rail. There it was, the great, unfinished city, with all its towers blazing in the sun. It came toward us slowly and patiently, like some enormous, cunning, and murderous beast, ready to devour, impossible to escape. I watched it come closer and I listened to the people around me, to their excitement and their pleasure. There was no doubt that it was real. I watched their shining faces and wondered if I were mad. For a moment I longed, with all my heart, to be able to feel whatever they were feeling, if only to know what such a feeling was like. As the boat moved slowly into the harbor, they were being moved into safety. It was only I who was being floated into danger. I turned my head, looking for Europe, but all that stretched behind me was the sky, thick with gulls. I moved away from the rail. A big, sandy-haired man held his daughter on his shoulders, showing her the Statue of Liberty. I would never know what this statue meant to others, she had always been an ugly joke for me. And the American flag was flying from the top of the ship, above my head. I had seen the French flag drive the French into the most unspeakable frenzies, I had seen the flag which was nominally mine used to dignify the vilest purposes: now I would never, as long as I lived, know what others saw when they saw a flag. "There's no place like home," said a voice close by, and I thought, *There damn sure isn't.* I decided to go back to my cabin and have a drink.

There was a cablegram from Harriet in my cabin. It said: Be good. Be quick. I'm waiting. I folded it carefully and put it in my breast pocket. Then I wondered if I would ever get back to her. How long would it take me to earn the money to get out of this land? Sweat broke out on my forehead and I poured myself some whiskey from my nearly empty bottle. I paced the tiny cabin. It was silent. There was no one down in the cabins now.

I was not sober when I faced the uniforms in the first-class lounge. There were two of them; they were not unfriendly. They looked at my passport, they looked at me. "You've been away a long time," said one of them.

"Yes," I said, "it's been a while."

"What did you do over there all that time?"—with a grin meant to hide more than it revealed, which hideously revealed more than it could hide.

I said, "I'm a singer," and the room seemed to rock around me. I held on to what I hoped was a calm, open smile. I had not had to deal with these faces in so long that I had forgotten how to do it. I had once known how to pitch my voice precisely between curtness and servility, and known what razor's edge of a pickaninny's smile would turn away wrath. But I had forgotten all the tricks on which my life had once depended. Once I had been an expert at baffling these people, at setting their teeth on edge, and dancing just outside the trap laid for me. But I was not an expert now. These faces were no longer merely the faces of two white men, who were my enemies. They were the faces of two white people whom I did not understand, and I could no longer plan my moves in accordance with what I knew of their cowardice and their needs and their strategy. That moment on the bridge had undone me forever.

"That's right," said one of them, "that's what it says, right here on the passport. Never heard of you, though." They looked up at me. "Did you do a lot of singing over there?"

"Some."

"What kind—concerts?"

"No." I wondered what I looked like, sounded like. I could tell nothing from their eyes. "I worked a few nightclubs."

"Nightclubs, eh? I guess they liked you over there."

"Yes," I said, "they seemed to like me all right."

"Well"—and my passport was stamped and handed back to me—"let's hope they like you over here."

"Thanks." They laughed—was it at me, or was it my imagination? and I picked up the one bag I was carrying and threw my trench coat over one shoulder and walked out of the first-class lounge. I stood in the slow-moving, murmuring line which led to the gangplank. I looked straight ahead and watched heads, smiling faces, step up to the shadow of the gangplank awning and then swiftly descend out of sight. I put my passport back in my breast pocket—*Be quick. I'm waiting*—and I held my landing card in my hand. Then, suddenly, there I was, standing on the edge of the boat, staring down the long ramp to the ground. At the end of the plank, on the ground, stood a heavy man in a uniform. His cap was pushed back from his gray hair and his face was red and wet. He looked up at me. This was the face I remembered, the face of my nightmares; perhaps hatred had caused me to know this face better than I would ever know the face of any lover. "Come on, boy," he cried, "come on, come on!"

And I almost smiled. I was home. I touched my breast pocket. I thought of a song I sometimes sang, *When will I ever get to be a man?* I came down the gangplank, stumbling a little, and gave the man my landing card.

Much later in the day, a customs inspector checked my baggage and waved me away. I picked up my bags and started walking down the long stretch which led to the gate, to the city.

And I heard someone call my name.

I looked up and saw Louisa running toward me. I dropped my bags and grabbed her in my arms and tears came to my eyes and rolled down my face. I did not know whether the tears were for joy at seeing her, or from rage, or both.

"How are you? How are you? You look wonderful, but, oh, haven't you lost weight? It's wonderful to see you again."

I wiped my eyes. "It's wonderful to see you, too, I bet you thought I was never coming back."

Louisa laughed. "I wouldn't have blamed you if you hadn't. These people are just as corny as ever, I swear I don't believe there's any hope for them. How's your French? Lord, when I think that it was I who studied French and now I can't speak a word. And you never went near it and you probably speak it like a native."

I grinned. *"Pas mal. Te me défends pas mal."* We started down the wide steps into the street. "My God," I said. "New York." I was not aware of its towers now. We were in the shadow of the elevated highway but the thing which most struck me was neither light nor shade, but noise. It came from a million things at once, from trucks and tires and clutches and brakes and doors; from machines shuttling and stamping and rolling and cutting and pressing; from the building of tunnels, the checking of gas mains, the laying of wires, the digging of foundations; from the chattering of rivets, the scream of the pile driver, the clanging of great shovels; from the battering down and the raising up of walls; from millions of radios and television sets and juke boxes. The human voices distinguished themselves from the roar only by their note of strain and hostility. Another fleshy man, uniformed and red faced, hailed a cab for us and touched his cap politely but could only manage a peremptory growl: "Right this way, miss. Step up, sir." He slammed the cab door behind us. Louisa directed the driver to the New Yorker Hotel.

"Do they take us there?"

She looked at me. "They got laws in New York, honey, it'd be the easiest thing in the world to spend all your time in court. But over at the New Yorker, I believe they've already got the message." She took my arm. "You see? In spite of all this chopping and booming, this place hasn't really changed very much. You still can't hear yourself talk."

And I thought to myself, Maybe that's the point.

Early the next morning we checked out of the hotel and took the plane for Alabama.

I am just stepping out of the shower when I hear the bell ring. I dry myself hurriedly and put on a bathrobe. It is Vidal, of course, and very elegant he is, too, with his bushy gray hair quite lustrous, his swarthy, cynical, gypsylike face shaved and lotioned. Usually he looks just any old way. But tonight his brief bulk is contained in a dark-blue suit and he has an ironical pearl stickpin in his blue tie.

"Come in, make yourself a drink. I'll be with you in a second."

"I am, *hélas!*, on time. I trust you will forgive me for my thoughtlessness."

But I am already back in the bathroom. Vidal puts on a record: Mahalia Jackson, singing *I'm Going to Live the Life I Sing About in My Song.*

When I am dressed, I find him sitting in a chair before the open window. The daylight is gone, but it is not exactly dark. The trees are black now against the darkening sky. The lights in windows and the lights of motorcars are yellow and ringed. The street lights have not yet been turned on. It is as though, out of deference to the departed day, Paris waited a decent interval before assigning her role to a more theatrical but inferior performer.

Vidal is drinking a whiskey and soda. I pour myself a drink. He watches me.

"Well. How are you, my friend? You are nearly gone. Are you happy to be leaving us?"

"No." I say this with more force than I had intended. Vidal raises his eyebrows, looking amused and distant. "I never really intended to go back there. I certainly never intended to raise my kid there—"

"*Mais, mon cher,*" Vidal says, calmly, "you are an intelligent man, you must have known that you would probably be returning one day." He pauses. "And, as for Pauli—did it never occur to you that he might wish one day to see the country in which his father and his father's fathers were born?"

"To do that, really, he'd have to go to Africa."

"America will always mean more to him than Africa, you know that."

"I don't know." I throw my drink down and pour myself another. "Why should he want to cross all that water just to be called a nigger? America never gave him anything."

"It gave him his father."

I look at him. "You mean, his father escaped."

Vidal throws back his head and laughs. If Vidal likes you, he is certain to laugh at you and his laughter can be very unnerving. But the look, the silence which follows this laughter can be very unnerving, too. And, now, in the silence, he asks me, "Do you really think that you have escaped anything? Come. I know you for a better man than that." He walks to the table which holds the liquor. "In that movie of ours which has made you so famous, and, as I now see, so troubled, what are you playing, after all? What is the tragedy of this half-breed troubadour if not, precisely, that he has taken all the possible roads to escape and that all these roads have failed him?" He pauses, with the bottle in one hand, and looks at me. "Do you remember the trouble I had to get a performance out of you? How you hated me, you sometimes looked as though you wanted to shoot me! And do you remember when the role of Chico began to come alive?" He pours his drink. "Think back, remember. I am a very great director, *mais pardon!* I could not have got such a performance out of anyone but you. And what were you thinking of, what was in your mind, what nightmare were you living with when you began, at last, to play the role—truthfully?" He walks back to his seat.

Chico, in the film, is the son of a Martinique woman and a French *colon* who hates both his mother and his father. He flees from the island to the capital, carrying his hatred with him. This hatred has now grown, naturally, to include all dark women and all white men, in a word, everyone. He descends into the underworld of Paris, where he dies. *Les fauves*—the wild beasts—refers to the life he has fled and to the life which engulfs him. When I agreed to do the role, I felt that I could probably achieve it by bearing in mind the North Africans I had watched in Paris for so long. But this did not please Vidal. The blowup came while we were rehearsing a fairly simple, straightforward scene. Chico goes into a sleazy Pigalle dance hall to beg the French owner for a particularly humiliating job. And this Frenchman reminds him of his father.

"You are playing this boy as though you thought of him as the noble savage," Vidal said, icily. *Ça vient d'où*—all these ghastly mannerisms you are using all the time?"

Everyone fell silent, for Vidal rarely spoke this way. This silence told me that everyone, the actor with whom I was playing the scene and all the people in the "dance hall," shared Vidal's opinion of my performance and were relieved that he was going to do something about it. I was humiliated and too angry to speak; but perhaps I also felt, at the very bottom of my heart, a certain relief, an unwilling respect.

"You are doing it all wrong," he said, more gently. Then, "Come, let us have a drink together."

We walked into his office. He took a bottle and two glasses out of his desk. "Forgive me, but you put me in mind of some of those English *lady* actresses who love to play *putain* as long as it is always absolutely clear to the audience that they are really ladies. So perhaps they read a book, not usually, *hélas!, Fanny Hill,* and they have their chauffeurs drive them through Soho once or twice—and they come to the stage with a performance so absolutely loaded with detail, every bit of it meaningless, that there can be no doubt that they are acting. It is what the British call a triumph." He poured two cognacs. "That is what you are doing. Why? Who do you think this boy is, what do you think he is feeling, when he asks for this job?" He watched me carefully and I bitterly resented his look. "You come from America. The situation is not so pretty there for boys like you. I know you may not have been as poor as—as some—but is it really impossible for you to understand what a boy like Chico feels? Have you never, yourself, been in a similar position?"

I hated him for asking the question because I knew he knew the answer to it. "I would have had to be a very lucky black man not to have been in such a position."

"You would have had to be a very lucky *man*."

"Oh, God," I said, "please don't give me any of this equality-in-anguish business."

"It is perfectly possible," he said, sharply, "that there is not another kind."

Then he was silent. He sat down behind his desk. He cut a cigar and lit it, puffing up clouds of smoke, as though to prevent us from seeing each other too clearly. "Consider this," he said. "I am a French director who has never seen your country. I have never done you any harm, except, perhaps, historically—I mean, because I am white—but I cannot be blamed for that—"

"But *I* can be," I said, "and I am! I've never understood why, if *I* have to pay for the history written in the color of my skin, *you* should get off scot-free!" But I was surprised at my vehemence, I had not known I was going to say these things, and by the fact that I was trembling and from the way he looked at me I knew that, from a professional point of view anyway, I was playing into his hands.

"What makes you think I *do?*" His face looked weary and stern. "I am a Frenchman. Look at France. You think that I—we—are not paying for our history?" He walked to the window, staring out at the rather grim little town in which the studio was located. "If it is revenge that you want, well, then, let me tell you, you will have it. You will probably have it, whether you want it or not, our stupidity will make it inevitable." He turned back into the room. "But I beg you not to confuse me with the happy people of your country, who scarcely know that there is such a thing as history and so, naturally, imagine that they can escape, as you put it, scot-free. That is what you are doing, that is what I was about to say. I was about to say that I am a French director and I have never been in your country and I have never done you any harm—but you are not talking to that man, in this room, now. You are not talking to Jean Luc Vidal, but to some other white man, whom you remember, who has nothing to do with me." He paused and went back to his desk. "Oh, most of the time you are not like this, I know. But it is there all the time, it must be, because when you are upset, this is what comes out. So you are not playing Chico truthfully, you are lying about him, and I will not let you do it. When you go back, now, and play this scene again, I want you to remember what has just happened in this room. You brought your past into this room. That is what Chico does when he walks into the dance hall. The Frenchman whom he begs for a job is not merely a Frenchman—he is the father who disowned and betrayed him and all the Frenchmen whom he hates." He smiled and poured me another cognac. "Ah! If it were not for *my* history, I would not have so much trouble to get the truth out of you." He looked into my face, half smiling. "And you, you are angry—are you not?—that I *ask* you for the truth. You think I have no right to ask." Then he said something which he knew would enrage me. "Who are you then, and what good has it done you to come to France, and how will you raise your son? Will you teach him never to tell the truth to anyone?" And he moved behind his desk and looked at me, as though from behind a barricade.

"You have no right to talk to me this way."

"Oh, yes, I do," he said. "I have a film to make and a reputation to maintain and I am going to get a performance out of you." He looked at his watch. "Let us go back to work."

I watch him now, sitting quietly in my living room, tough, cynical, crafty old Frenchman, and I wonder if he knows that the nightmare at the bottom of my mind, as I played the role of Chico, was all the possible fates of Paul. This is but another way of saying that I relived the disasters which had nearly undone me; but, because I was thinking of Paul, I discovered that I did not want my son ever to feel toward me as I had felt toward my own father. He had died when I was eleven, but I had watched the humiliations he had to bear, and I had pitied him. But was there not, in that pity, however painfully and unwillingly, also some contempt? For how could I *know* what he had borne? I knew only that I was his son. However he had loved me, whatever he had borne, I, his son, was despised. Even had he lived, he could have done nothing to prevent it, nothing to protect me. The best that he could hope to do was to prepare me for it; and even at that he had failed. How can one be prepared for the spittle in the face, all the tireless ingenuity which goes into the spite and fear of small, unutterably miserable people, whose greatest terror is the singular identity, whose joy, whose safety, is entirely dependent on the humiliation and anguish of others?

But for Paul, I swore it, such a day would never come. I would throw my life and my work between Paul and the nightmare of the world. I would make it impossible for the world to treat Paul as it had treated my father and me.

Mahalia's record ends. Vidal rises to turn it over. "Well?" He looks at me very affectionately. "Your nightmares, please!"

"Oh, I was thinking of that summer I spent in Alabama, when my mother died." I stop. "You know, but when we finally filmed that bar scene, I was thinking of New York. I was scared in Alabama, but I almost went crazy in New York. I was sure I'd never make it back here—back here to Harriet. And I knew if I didn't, it was going to be the end of me." Now Mahalia is singing *When the Saints Go Marching In*. "I got a job in the town as an elevator boy, in the town's big department store. It was a special favor, one of my father's white friends got it for me. For a long time, in the South, we all—depended—on the—*kindness*—of white friends." I take out a handkerchief and wipe my face. "But this man didn't like me. I guess I didn't seem grateful enough, wasn't enough like my father, what he thought my father was. And I couldn't get used to the town again, I'd been away too long, I hated it. It's a terrible town, anyway, the whole thing looks as though it's been built around a jailhouse. There's a room in the courthouse, a room where they beat you up. Maybe you're walking along the street one night, it's usually at night, but it happens in the daytime, too. And the police car comes up behind you and the cop says, 'Hey, boy. Come on over here.' So you go on over. He says, 'Boy, I believe you're drunk.' And, you see, if you say, 'No, no sir,' he'll beat you because you're calling him a liar. And if you say anything else, unless it's something to make him laugh, he'll take you in and beat you, just for fun. The trick is to think of some way for them to have their fun without beating you up."

The street lights of Paris click on and turn all the green leaves silver. "Or to go along with the ways *they* dream up. And they'll do anything, anything at all, to prove that you're no better than a dog and to make you feel like one. And they hated me because I'd been North and I'd been to Europe. People kept saying, I hope you didn't bring no foreign notions back here with you, boy. And I'd say, 'No sir,' or 'No ma'am,' but I never said it right. And there was a time, all of them remembered it, when I *had* said it right. But now they could tell that I despised them—I guess, no matter what, I wanted them to know that I despised them. But I didn't despise them any more than everyone else did, only the others never let it show. They knew how to keep the white folks happy, and it was easy—you just had to keep them feeling like they were God's favor to the universe. They'd walk around with great, big, foolish grins on their faces and the colored folks loved to see this, because they hated them so much. "Just look at So-and-So," somebody'd say. "His white is *on* him today." And when we didn't hate them, we pitied them. In America, that's usually what it means to have a white friend. You pity the poor bastard because he was born believing the world's a great place to be, and you know it's not, and you çan see that he's going to have a terrible time getting used to this idea, if he ever gets used to it."

Then I think of Paul again, those eyes which still imagine that I can do anything, that skin, the color of honey and fire, his jet-black, curly hair. I look out at Paris again, and I listen to Mahalia. "Maybe it's better to have the terrible times first. I don't know. Maybe, then, you can have, *if* you live, a better life, a real life, because you had to fight so hard to get it away—you know?—from the mad dog who held it in his teeth. But then your life has all those tooth marks, too, all those tatters, and all that blood." I walk to the bottle and raise it. "One for the road?"

"Thank you," says Vidal.

I pour us a drink, and he watches me. I have never talked so much before, not about those things anyway. I know that Vidal has nightmares, because he knows so much about them, but he has never told me what his are. I think that he probably does not talk about his nightmares any more. I know that the war cost him his wife and his son, and that he was in prison in Germany. He very rarely refers to it. He has a married daughter who lives in England, and he rarely speaks of her. He is like a man who has learned to live on what is left of an enormous fortune.

We are silent for a moment.

"Please go on," he says, with a smile. "I am curious about the reality behind the reality of your performance."

"My sister, Louisa, never married," I say, abruptly, "because, once, years ago, she and the boy she was going with and two friends of theirs were out driving in a car and the police stopped them. The girl who was with them was very fair and the police pretended not to believe her when she said she was colored. They made her get out and stand in front of the headlights of the car and pull down her pants and raise her dress—they said that was the only way they could be sure. And you can imagine what they said, and what they did—and they were lucky, at that, that it didn't go any further. But none of the men could do anything about it. Louisa couldn't face the boy again, and I guess he couldn't face her." Now it is really growing dark in the room and I cross to the light switch. "You know, I know what that boy felt, I've felt it. They want you to feel that you're not a man, maybe that's the only way they can feel like men, I don't know. I walked around New York with Harriet's cablegram in my pocket as though it were some atomic secret, in *code*, and they'd kill me if they ever found out what it meant. You know, there's something wrong with people like that. And thank God Harriet was here, she *proved* that the world was bigger than the world they wanted me to live in, I *had* to get back here, get to a place where people were too busy with their own lives, *their private lives,* to make fantasies about mine, to set up walls around mine." I look at him. The light in the room has made the night outside blue-black and golden and the great searchlight of the Eiffel Tower is turning in the sky. "That's what it's like in America, for me, anyway. I always feel that I don't exist there, except in someone else's—usually dirty—mind. I don't know if you know what that means, but I do, and I don't want to put Harriet through that and I don't want to raise Paul there."

"Well," he says at last, "you are not required to remain in America forever, are you? You will sing in that elegant club which apparently feels that it cannot, much longer, so much as open its doors without you, and you will probably accept the movie offer, you would be very foolish not to. You will make a lot of money. Then, one day, you will remember that airlines and steamship companies are still in business and that France still exists. *That* will certainly be cause for astonishment."

Vidal was a Gaullist before de Gaulle came to power. But he regrets the manner of de Gaulle's rise and he is worried about de Gaulle's regime. "It is not the fault of *mon général,*" he sometimes says, sadly. "Perhaps it is history's fault. I *suppose* it must be history which always arranges to bill a civilization at the very instant it is least prepared to pay."

Now he rises and walks out on the balcony, as though to reassure himself of the reality of Paris. Mahalia is singing *Didn't It Rain?* I walk out and stand beside him.

"You are a good boy—Chico," he says. I laugh. "You believe in love. You do not know all the things love cannot do, but"—he smiles—"love will teach you that."

We go, after dinner, to a Left Bank discothèque which can charge outrageous prices because Marlon Brando wandered in there one night. By accident, according to Vidal. "Do you know how many people in Paris are becoming rich—to say nothing of those, *hélas!,* who are going broke—on the off chance that Marlon Brando will lose his way again?"

He has not, presumably, lost his way tonight, but the discothèque is crowded with those strangely faceless people who are part of the night life of all great cities, and who always arrive, moments, hours, or decades late, on the spot made notorious by an event or a movement or a handful of personalities. So here are American boys, anything but beardless, scratching around for Hemingway; American girls, titillating themselves with Frenchmen and existentialism, while waiting for the American boys to shave off their beards; French painters, busily pursuing the revolution which ended thirty years ago; and the young, bored, perverted, American *arrivistes* who are buying their way into the art world via flattery and liquor, and the production of canvases as arid as their greedy little faces. Here are boys, of all nations, one step above the pimp, who are occasionally walked across a stage or trotted before a camera. And the girls, their enemies, whose faces are sometimes seen in ads, one of whom will surely have a tantrum before the evening is out.

In a corner, as usual, surrounded, as usual, by smiling young men, sits the drunken blonde woman who was once the mistress of a famous, dead painter. She is a figure of some importance in the art world, and so rarely has to pay for either her drinks or her lovers. An older Frenchman, who was once a famous director, is playing *quatre cent vingt-et-un* with the woman behind the cash register. He nods pleasantly to Vidal and me as we enter, but makes no move to join us, and I respect him for this. Vidal and I are obviously cast tonight in the role vacated by Brando: our entrance justifies the prices and sends a kind of shiver through the room. It is marvelous to watch the face of the waiter as he approaches, all smiles and deference and grace, not so much honored by our presence as achieving his reality from it; excellence, he seems to be saying, gravitates naturally toward excellence. We order two whiskey and sodas. I know why Vidal sometimes comes here. He is lonely. I do not think that he expects ever to love one woman again, and so he distracts himself with many.

Since this is a discothéque, jazz is blaring from the walls and record sleeves are scattered about with a devastating carelessness. Two of them are mine and no doubt, presently, someone will play the recording of the songs I sang in the film.

"I thought," says Vidal, with a malicious little smile, "that your farewell to Paris would not be complete without a brief exposure to the perils of fame. Perhaps it will help prepare you for America, where, I am told, the populace is yet more carnivorous than it is here."

I can see that one of the vacant models is preparing herself to come to our table and ask for an autograph, hoping, since she is pretty—she has, that is, the usual female equipment, dramatized in the usual, modern way—to be invited for a drink. Should the maneuver succeed, one of her boy friends or girl friends will contrive to come by the table, asking for a light or a pencil or a lipstick, and it will be extremely difficult not to invite this person to join us, too. Before the evening ends, we will be surrounded. I don't, now, know what I expected of fame, but I suppose it never occurred to me that the light could be just as dangerous, just as killing, as the dark.

"Well, let's make it brief," I tell him. "Sometimes I wish that you weren't quite so fond of me."

He laughs. "There are some very interesting people here tonight. Look."

Across the room from us, and now staring at our table, are a group of American Negro students, who are probably visiting Paris for the first time. There are four of them, two boys and two girls, and I suppose that they must be in their late teens or early twenties. One of the boys, a gleaming, curly-haired, golden-brown type—the color of his mother's fried chicken—is carrying a guitar. When they realize we have noticed them, they smile and wave—wave as though I were one of their possessions, as, indeed, I am. Golden-brown is a mime. He raises his guitar, drops his shoulders, and his face falls into the lugubrious lines of Chico's face as he approaches death. He strums a little of the film's theme music, and I laugh and the table laughs. It is as though we were all back home and had met for a moment, on a Sunday morning, say, before a church or a poolroom or a barbershop.

And they have created a sensation in the discothèque, naturally, having managed, with no effort whatever, to outwit all the gleaming boys and girls. Their table, which had been of no interest only a moment before, has now become the focus of a rather pathetic attention; their smiles have made it possible for the others to smile, and to nod in our direction.

"Oh," says Vidal, "he does that far better than you ever did, perhaps I will make him a star."

"Feel free, *m'sieu, le bon Dieu,* I got mine." But I can see that his attention has really been caught by one of the girls, slim, tense, and dark, who seems, though it is hard to know how one senses such things, to be treated by the others with a special respect. And, in fact, the table now seems to be having a council of war, to be demanding her opinion or her cooperation. She listens, frowning, laughing; the quality, the force of her intelligence causes her face to keep changing all the time, as though a light played on it. And, presently, with a gesture she might once have used to scatter feed to chickens, she scoops up from the floor one of those dangling rag bags women love to carry. She holds it loosely by the drawstrings, so that it is banging somewhere around her ankle, and walks over to our table. She has an honest, forthright walk, entirely unlike the calculated, pelvic workout by means of which most women get about. She is small, but sturdily, economically, put together.

As she reaches our table, Vidal and I rise, and this throws her for a second. (It has been a long time since I have seen such an attractive girl.)

Also, everyone, of course, is watching us. It is really a quite curious moment. They have put on the record of Chico singing a sad, angry Martinique ballad; my own voice is coming at us from the walls as the girl looks from Vidal to me, and smiles.

"I guess you know," she says, "we weren't *about* to let you get out of here without bugging you just a little bit. We've only been in Paris just a couple of days and we thought for sure that we wouldn't have a chance of running into you anywhere, because it's in all the papers that you're coming home."

"Yes," I say, "yes. I'm leaving the day after tomorrow."

"Oh!" She grins. "Then we really *are* lucky." I find that I have almost forgotten the urchin-like grin of a colored girl. "I guess, before I keep babbling on, I'd better introduce myself. My name is Ada Holmes."

We shake hands. "This is Monsieur Vidal, the director of the film."

"I'm very honored to meet you, sir."

"Will you join us for a moment? Won't you sit down?" And Vidal pulls a chair out for her.

But she frowns contritely. "I really ought to get back to my friends." She looks at me. "I really just came over to say, for myself and all the kids, that we've got your records and we've seen your movie, and it means so much to us"—and she laughs, breathlessly, nervously, it is somehow more moving than tears—"more than I can say. Much more. And we wanted to know if you and your friend"—she looks at Vidal—"your *director,* Monsieur Vidal, would allow us to buy you a drink? We'd be very honored if you would."

"It is we who are honored," says Vidal, promptly, "*and* grateful. We were getting terribly bored with one another, thank God you came along."

The three of us laugh, and we cross the room.

The three at the table rise, and Ada makes the introductions. The other girl, taller and paler than Ada, is named Ruth. One of the boys is named Talley—"short for Talliafero"—and Golden-brown's name is

Pete. "Man," he tells me, "I dig you the most. You tore me up, baby, tore me *up*."

"You tore up a lot of people," Talley says, cryptically, and he and Ruth laugh. Vidal does not know, but I do, that Talley is probably referring to white people.

They are from New Orleans and Tallahassee and North Carolina; are college students, and met on the boat. They have been in Europe all summer, in Italy and Spain, but are only just getting to Paris.

"We meant to come sooner," says Ada, "but we could never make up our minds to leave a place. I thought we'd never pry Ruth loose from Venice."

"I resigned myself," says Pete, "and just sat in the Piazza San Marco, drinking gin fizz and being photographed with the pigeons, while Ruth had herself driven *all* up and down the Grand Canal." He looks at Ruth. "Finally, thank heaven, it rained."

"She was working off her hostilities," says Ada, with a grin. "We thought we might as well let her do it in Venice, the opportunities in North Carolina are really terribly limited."

"There are some very upset people walking around down there," Ruth says, "and a couple of tours around the Grand Canal might do them a world of good."

Pete laughs. "Can't you just see Ruth escorting them to the edge of the water?"

"I haven't lifted my hand in anger yet," Ruth says, "but, oh Lord," and she laughs, clenching and unclenching her fists.

"You haven't been back for a long time, have you?" Talley asks me.

"Eight years. I haven't really lived there for twelve years."

Pete whistles. "I fear you are in for some surprises, my friend. There have been some changes made." Then, "Are you afraid?"

"A little."

"We all are," says Ada, "that's why I was so glad to get away for a little while."

"Then you haven't been back since Black Monday," Talley says. He laughs. "That's how it's gone down in Confederate history." He turns to Vidal. "What do people think about it here?"

Vidal smiles, delighted. "It seems extraordinarily infantile behavior, even for Americans, from whom, I must say, I have never expected very much in the way of maturity." Everyone at the table laughs. Vidal goes on. "But I cannot really talk about it, I do not understand it. I have never really understood Americans; I am an old man now, and I suppose I never will. There is something very nice about them, something very winning, but they seem so ignorant—so ignorant of life. Perhaps it is strange, but the only people from your country with whom I have ever made contact are black people—like my good friend, my discovery, here," and he slaps me on the shoulder. "Perhaps it is because we, in Europe, whatever else we do not know, or have forgotten, know about suffering. We have suffered here. You have suffered, too. But most Americans do not yet know what anguish is. It is too bad, because the life of the West is in their hands." He turns to Ada. "I cannot help saying that I think it is a scandal—and we may all pay very dearly for it—that a civilized nation should elect to represent it a man who is so simple that he thinks the world is simple." And silence falls at the table and the four young faces stare at him.

"Well," says Pete, at last, turning to me, "you won't be bored, man, when you get back there."

"It's much too nice a night," I say, "to stay cooped up in this place, where all I can hear is my own records." We laugh. "Why don't we get out of here and find a sidewalk café?" I tap Pete's guitar. "Maybe we can find out if you've got any talent."

"Oh, talent I've got," says Pete, "but character, man, I'm lacking."

So, after some confusion about the bill, for which Vidal has already made himself responsible, we walk out into the Paris night. It is very strange to feel that, very soon now, these boulevards will not exist for me. People will be walking up and down, as they are tonight, and lovers will be murmuring in the black shadows of the plane trees, and there will be these same still figures on the benches or in the parks—but they will not exist for me, I will not be here. For a long while Paris will no longer exist for me, except in my mind; and only in the minds of some people will I exist any longer for Paris. After departure, only invisible things are left, perhaps the life of the world is held together by invisible chains of memory and loss and love. So many things, so many people, depart! And we can only repossess them in our minds. Perhaps this is what the old folks meant, what my mother and my father meant, when they counseled us to keep the faith.

We have taken a table at the Deux Magots and Pete strums on his guitar and begins to play this song:

Preach the word, preach the word, preach the word!
If I never, never see you any more.
Preach the word, preach the word.
And I'll meet you on Canaan's shore.

He has a strong, clear, boyish voice, like a young preacher's, and he is smiling as he sings his song. Ada and I look at each other and grin, and Vidal is smiling. The waiter looks a little worried, for we are already beginning to attract a crowd, but it is a summer night, the gendarmes on the corner do not seem to mind, and there will be time, anyway, to stop us.

Pete was not there, none of us were, the first time this song was needed; and no one now alive can imagine what that time was like. But the song has come down the bloodstained ages. I suppose this to mean that the song is still needed, still has its work to do.

The others are all, visibly, very proud of Pete; and we all join him, and people stop to listen:

Testify! Testify!
If I never, never see you any more!
Testify! Testify!
I'll meet you on Canaan's shore!

In the crowd that has gathered to listen to us, I see a face I know, the face of a North African prize fighter, who is no longer in the ring. I used to know him well in the old days, but have not seen him for a long time. He looks quite well, his face is shining, he is quite decently dressed. And something about the way he holds himself, not quite looking at our table, tells me that he has seen me, but does not want to risk a rebuff. So I call him. "Boona!"

And he turns, smiling, and comes loping over to our table, his hands in his pockets. Pete is still singing and Ada and Vidal have taken off on a conversation of their own. Ruth and Talley look curiously, expectantly, at Boona. Now that I have called him over, I feel somewhat uneasy. I realize that I do not know what he is doing now, or how he will get along with any of these people, and I can see in his eyes that he is delighted to be in the presence of two young girls. There are virtually no North African women in Paris, and not even the dirty, rat-faced girls who live, apparently, in cafés are willing to go with an Arab. So Boona is always looking for a girl, and because he is so deprived and because he is not Western, his techniques can be very unsettling. I know he is relieved that the girls are not French and not white. He looks briefly at Vidal and Ada. Vidal, also, though for different reasons, is always looking for a girl.

But Boona has always been very nice to me. Perhaps I am sorry that I called him over, but I did not want to snub him.

He claps one hand to the side of my head, as is his habit. *"Comment vas-tu, mon frère?* I have not see you, oh, for long time." And he asks me, as in the old days, "You all right? Nobody bother you?" And he laughs. "Ah! *Tu as fait le chemin, toi!* Now you are *vedette,* big star—wonderful!" He looks around the table, made a little uncomfortable by the silence that has fallen, now that Pete has stopped singing. "I have seen you in the movies—you know?—and I tell everybody, I know *him!*"

He points to me, and laughs, and Ruth and Talley laugh with him. "That's right, man, you make me real proud, you make me cry!"

"Boona, I want you to meet some friends of mine." And I go round the table: "Ruth, Talley, Ada, Pete"—and he bows and shakes hands, his dark eyes gleaming with pleasure—*"et Monsieur Vidal, le metteur en scène du film qui t'a arraché des larmes."*

"Enchanté." But his attitude toward Vidal is colder, more distrustful. "Of course I have heard of Monsieur Vidal. He is the director of many films, many of them made me cry." This last statement is utterly, even insolently, insincere.

But Vidal, I think, is relieved that I will now be forced to speak to Boona and will leave him alone with Ada.

"Sit down," I say, "have a drink with us, let me have your news. What's been happening with you, what are you doing with yourself these days?"

"Ah," he sits down, "nothing very brilliant, my brother." He looks at me quickly, with a little smile. "You know, we have been having hard times here."

"Where are you from?" Ada asks him.

His brilliant eyes take her in entirely, but she does not flinch. "I am from Tunis." He says it proudly, with a little smile.

"From Tunis. I have never been to Africa, I would love to go one day."

He laughs. "Africa is a big place. Very big. There are many countries in Africa, many"—he looks briefly at Vidal—"different kinds of people, many colonies."

"But Tunis," she continues, in her innocence, "is free? Freedom is happening all over Africa. That's why I would like to go there."

"I have not been back for a long time," says Boona, "but all the news I get from Tunis, from my people, is not good."

"Wouldn't you like to go back?" Ruth asks.

Again he looks at Vidal. "That is not so easy."

Vidal smiles. "You know what I would like to do? There's a wonderful Spanish place not far from here, where we can listen to live music and dance a little." He turns to Ada. "Would you like that?"

He is leaving it up to me to get rid of Boona, and it is, of course, precisely for this reason that I cannot do it. Besides, it is no longer so simple.

"Oh, I'd love that," says Ada, and she turns to Boona. "Won't you come, too?"

"Thank you, mam'selle," he says, softly, and his tongue flicks briefly over his lower lip, and he smiles. He is very moved, people are not often nice to him.

In the Spanish place there are indeed a couple of Spanish guitars, drums, castanets, and a piano, but the uses to which these are being put carry one back, as Pete puts it, to the levee. "These are the wailingest Spanish cats I ever heard," says Ruth. "They didn't learn how to do this in Spain, no, they didn't, they been rambling. You ever hear anything like this going on in Spain?" Talley takes her out on the dance floor, which is already crowded. A very handsome Frenchwoman is dancing with an enormous, handsome black man, who seems to be her lover, who seems to have taught her how to dance. Apparently, they are known to the musicians, who egg them on with small cries of *"Olé!"* It is a very good-natured crowd, mostly foreigners, Spaniards, Swedes, Greeks. Boona takes Ada out on the dance floor while Vidal is answering some questions put to him by Pete on the entertainment situation in France. Vidal looks a little put out, and I am amused.

We are there for perhaps an hour, dancing, talking, and I am, at last, a little drunk. In spite of Boona, who is a very good and tireless dancer, Vidal continues his pursuit of Ada, and I begin to wonder if he will make it and I begin to wonder if I want him to.

I am still puzzling out my reaction when Pete, who has disappeared, comes in through the front door, catches my eye, and signals to me. I leave the table and follow him into the streets.

He looks very upset. "I don't want to bug you, man," he says, "but I fear your boy has goofed."

I know he is not joking. I think he is probably angry at Vidal because of Ada, and I wonder what I can do about it and why he should be telling me.

I stare at him, gravely, and he says, "It looks like he stole some money."

"Stole *money?* Who, Vidal?"

And then, of course, I get it, in the split second before he says, impatiently, "No, are you kidding? Your friend, the Tunisian."

I do not know what to say or what to do, and so I temporize with questions. All the time I am wondering if this can be true and what I can do about it if it is. The trouble is, I know that Boona steals, he would probably not be alive if he didn't, but I cannot say so to these children, who probably still imagine that everyone who steals is a thief. But he has never, to my knowledge, stolen from a friend. It seems unlike him. I have always thought of him as being better than that, and smarter than that. And so I cannot believe it, but neither can I doubt it. I do not know anything about Boona's life, these days. This causes me to realize that I do not really know much about Boona.

"Who did he steal it from?"

"From Ada. Out of her bag."

"How much?"

"Ten dollars. It's not an awful lot of money, but"—he grimaces—"none of us *have* an awful lot of money."

"I know." The dark side street on which we stand is nearly empty. The only sound on the street is the muffled music of the Spanish club. "How do you know it was Boona?"

He anticipates my own unspoken rejoinder. "Who else could it be? Besides—somebody *saw* him do it."

"Somebody saw him?"

"Yes."

I do not ask him who this person is, for fear that he will say it is Vidal.

"Well," I say, "I'll try to get it back." I think that I will take Boona aside and then replace the money myself. "Was it in dollars or in francs?"

"In francs."

I have no dollars and this makes it easier. I do not know how I can possibly face Boona and accuse him of stealing money from my friends. I would rather give him the benefit of even the faintest doubt. But, "Who saw him?" I ask.

"Talley. But we didn't want to make a thing about it—"

"Does Ada know it's gone?"

"Yes." He looks at me helplessly. "I know this makes you feel pretty bad, but we thought we'd better tell you, rather than"—lamely—"anybody else."

Now, Ada comes out of the club, carrying her ridiculous handbag, and with her face all knotted and sad. "Oh," she says, "I hate to cause all this trouble, it's not worth it, not for ten lousy dollars." I am astonished to see that she has been weeping, and tears come to her eyes now.

I put my arm around her shoulder. "Come on, now. You're not causing anybody any trouble and, anyway, it's nothing to cry about."

"It isn't your fault, Ada," Pete says, miserably.

"Oh, I ought to get a sensible handbag," she says, "like you're always telling me to do," and she laughs a little, then looks at me. "Please don't try to do anything about it. Let's just forget it."

"What's happening inside?" I ask her.

"Nothing. They're just talking. I think Mr. Vidal is dancing with Ruth. He's a great dancer, that little Frenchman."

"He's a great talker, too," Pete says.

"Oh, he doesn't mean anything," says Ada, "he's just having fun. He probably doesn't get a chance to talk to many American girls."

"He certainly made up for lost time tonight."

"Look," I say, "if Talley and Boona are alone, maybe you better go back in. We'll be in in a minute. Let's try to keep this as quiet as we can."

"Yeah," he says, "okay. We're going soon anyway, okay?"

"Yes," she tells him, "right away."

But as he turns away, Boona and Talley step out into the street, and it is clear that Talley feels that he has Boona under arrest. I almost laugh, the whole thing is beginning to resemble one of those mad French farces with people flying in and out of doors; but Boona comes straight to me.

"They say I stole money, my friend. You know me, you are the only one here who knows me, you know I would not do such a thing."

I look at him and I do not know what to say. Ada looks at him with her eyes full of tears and looks away. I take Boona's arm.

"We'll be back in a minute," I say. We walk a few paces up the dark, silent street.

"She say I take her money," he says. He, too, looks as though he is about to weep—but I do not know for which reason. "You know me, you know me almost twelve years, you think I do such a thing?"

Talley saw you, I want to say, but I cannot say it. Perhaps Talley only thought he saw him. Perhaps it is easy to see a boy who looks like Boona with his hand in an American girl's purse.

"If you not believe me," he says, "search me. Search me!" And he opens his arms wide, theatrically, and now there are tears standing in his eyes.

I do not know what his tears mean, but I certainly cannot search him. I want to say, I know you steal, I know you have to steal. Perhaps you took the money out of this girl's purse in order to eat tomorrow, in order not to be thrown into the streets tonight, in order to stay out of jail. This girl means nothing to you, after all, she is only an American, an American like me. Perhaps, I suddenly think, no girl means anything to you, or ever will again, they have beaten you too hard and kept you out in the gutter too long. And I also think, if you would steal from her, then of course you would lie to me, neither of us means anything to you; perhaps, in your eyes, we are simply luckier gangsters in a world which is run by gangsters. But I cannot say any of these things to Boona. I cannot say, Tell me the truth, nobody cares about the money any more.

So I say, "Of course I will not search you." And I realize that he knew I would not.

"I think it is that Frenchman who say I am a thief. They think we all are thieves." His eyes are bright and bitter. He looks over my shoulder. "They have all come out of the club now."

I look around and they are all there, in a little dark knot on the sidewalk.

"Don't worry," I say. "It doesn't matter."

"You believe me? My brother?" And his eyes look into mine with a terrible intensity.

"Yes," I force myself to say, "yes, of course, I believe you. Someone made a mistake, that's all."

"You know, the way American girls run around, they have their sack open all the time, she could have lost the money anywhere. Why she blame me? Because I come from Africa?" Tears are glittering on his face. "Here she come now."

And Ada comes up the street with her straight, determined walk. She walks straight to Boona and takes him hand. "I am sorry," she says, "for everything that happened. Please believe me. It isn't worth all this fuss. I'm sure you're a very nice person, and"—she falters—"I must have lost the money, I'm sure I lost it." She looks at him. "It isn't worth hurting your feelings, and I'm terribly sorry about it."

"I no take your money," he says. "Really, truly, I no take it. Ask him"—pointing to me, grabbing me by the arm, shaking me—"he know me for years, he will tell you that I never, never steal!"

"I'm sure," she says. "I'm sure."

I take Boona by the arm again. "Let's forget it. Let's forget it all. We're all going home now, and one of these days we'll have a drink again and we'll forget all about it, all right?"

"Yes," says Ada, "let us forget it." And she holds out her hand.

Boona takes it, wonderingly. His eyes take her in again. "You are a very nice girl. Really. A very nice girl."

"I'm sure you're a nice person, too." She pauses. "Goodnight."

"Goodnight," he says, after a long silence.

Then he kisses me on both cheeks. *"Au revoir, mon frère."*

"Au revoir, Boona."

After a moment we turn and walk away, leaving him standing there.

"Did he take it?" asks Vidal.

"I tell you, I *saw* him," says Talley.

"Well," I say, "it doesn't matter now." I look back and see Boona's stocky figure disappearing down the street.

"No," says Ada, "it doesn't matter." She looks up. "It's almost morning."

"I would gladly," says Vidal, stammering, "gladly—"

But she is herself again. "I wouldn't think of it. We had a wonderful time tonight, a wonderful time, and I wouldn't think of it." She turns to me with that urchin-like grin. "It was wonderful meeting you. I hope you won't have too much trouble getting used to the States again."

"Oh, I don't think I will," I say. And then, "I hope you won't."

"No," she says, "I don't think anything they can do will surprise me any more."

"Which way are we all going?" asks Vidal. "I hope someone will share my taxi with me."

But he lives in the sixteenth arrondissement, which is not in anyone's direction. We walk him to the line of cabs standing under the clock at Odéon.

And we look each other in the face, in the growing morning light. His face looks weary and lined and lonely. He puts both hands on my shoulders and then puts one hand on the nape of my neck. "Do not forget me, Chico," he says. "You must come back and see us, one of these days. Many of us depend on you for many things."

"I'll be back," I say. "I'll never forget you."

He raises his eyebrows and smiles. *"Alors, Adieu."*

"Adieu, Vidal."

"I was happy to meet all of you," he says. He looks at Ada. "Perhaps we will meet again before you leave."

"Perhaps," she says. "Goodby, Monsieur Vidal."

"Goodby."

Vidal's cab drives away. "I also leave you now," I say. "I must go home and wake up my son and prepare for our journey."

I leave them standing on the corner, under the clock, which points to six. They look very strange and lost and determined, the four of them. Just before my cab turns off the boulevard, I wave to them and they wave back.

Mme. Dumont is in the hall, mopping the floor.

"Did all my family get home?" I ask. I feel very cheerful, I do not know why.

"Yes," she says, "they are all here. Paul is still sleeping."

"May I go in and get him?"

She looks at me in surprise. "Of course."

So I walk into her apartment and walk into the room where Paul lies sleeping. I stand over his bed for a long time.

Perhaps my thoughts traveled—travel through to him. He opens his eyes and smiles up at me. He puts a fist to his eyes and raises his arms. *"Bonjour, Papa."*

I lift him up. *"Bonjour*. How do you feel today?"

"Oh, I don't know yet," he says.

I laugh. I put him on my shoulder and walk out into the hall. Mme. Dumont looks up at him with her radiant, aging face.

"Ah," she says, "you are going on a journey! How does it feel?"

"He doesn't know yet," I tell her. I walk to the elevator door and open it, dropping Paul down to the crook of my arm.

She laughs again. "He will know later. What a journey! *Jusqu'au nouveau monde!*"

I open the cage and we step inside. "Yes," I say, "all the way to the new world." I press the button and the cage, holding my son and me, goes up.

NADINE GORDIMER

Another Part of the Sky

Coming across the dark grass from the main building to his dark house at eleven o'clock on a Sunday night he stumbled against the edging of half-bricks. End up, all sunk into the earth at the same level, they formed a serrated border along every pathway and round every flower bed in the place. The young boys had laid them with all their race's peasant pleasure in simple repetitive patterns, some memory beneath their experience of rotting corrugated iron and hessian recalling to their hands the clean daub of white zigzag round a clay hut. That would come, he supposed with a smile: they would want whitewash for the bricks.

There were roses growing behind the bricks, tattering the darkness with blacker spangles of reaching foliage. The boys had planted those too. "The man who pulled down prison walls and grew geraniums in their place"—of course the papers had got it wrong. Wrong, all wrong. Whenever things are written down they go wrong. Mistakes are the least of it; by the time they are stamped in print, words have split meaning and whatever of truth they have managed to scoop up. Geraniums for roses; that was nothing: but "the man who pulled down prison walls and grew geraniums in their place"—that was a glib summing up that left everything out. As a fact it was true; in the nine years that he had been principal of the reformatory, he had taken down the six-foot walls with the broken bottles encrusted on the top, he had set the boys gardening, he had helped them build playing-fields, begged musical instruments for them. The photograph of him sitting at his desk, dipping a pen. The photograph of the boys sitting cross-legged in the garden, numbers on their khaki backs, gleams of sun on their heads cropped of wool. . . . When did that moment, the moment of the article, of all the articles that had been written about him, all the lectures that had been given in his honor—when did it exist?

As his feet sounded suddenly on gravel, he made a little sighing noise, casting off the bland unreality of it. It left out everything. What had it to do with now, the sleeping darkness of the reformatory behind him, the burning starts of red and flashes of print jittering his inner sight, the quiet of the night veld darkness; the worry that filled all the spaces of his body as his breath did.

This morning he had stood amidst the voices of the boys at church service, this afternoon he had written the draft of a penal reform pamphlet, after supper he had sat with a table full of reports. His nostrils were wide with a pause of concentration, his eyes did not see. His wife sewed at some garment in her lap without looking; he was conscious now and then of the quiet wink of her glasses as she watched him.

All the day, half the night; the worry had been with him all the time. Now the surface of the day had been rolled away, and he was left with the worry, he took it with him as he went up the three steps, over her door mat made of old tire-strips, through the door that gave to his thumb as though the latch had been waiting for his touch. For a moment the night stood in the doorway: the great hard polished winter sky that shone of itself—the nick of young moon was a minor brilliant amongst white sharp stars—without answer above the low heads of the kopjes; where in that humming space was the young boy with the neat head of a lizard? Then the door stood before night; and inside, the dry closed air of the house carried the unspoken question (Have you heard? Any news yet?), the shape of the telephone waited to ring. Here you could not escape the answer coming. . . . The telephone was a nerve, ready to jump.

Somewhere the boy who had lain in the clean discipline of a dormitory and learned so quickly the ritual of the hands and the bent head that made the day pass of itself in work, lay crouched in a hovel of smoke and bright eyes and the smell of breath and beer, and stared through hours at the sluggish possibilities of idleness, rising and writhing in half-discerned murk. Saw desire melt into violence . . . wanting into having. Sat in the cave of hunched faces painted with cosy fear by the light of a paraffin-tin fire, flickered with the torn filth of old newspapers stuffed in corners (newspapers that said stupidly, crime wave . . . robbery . . . old man knifed in the street): and was free. That was the boy's freedom; that was what he had run away to, a week ago.—It was easy . . . there were geraniums, no walls.—It happened a few times every year, always with this same twinge of peculiar pain to the principal: that was what they had to run away to, these young boys; to that; that troubled dreamlike existence of struggle and fear and horror which was what they knew, which to them was freedom. The governing board said consolingly: You mustn't get too discouraged when your system has occasional failures—it has justified itself magnificently in the long run, Collins. And he smiled at them, being accustomed to having patience with people whose understanding is limited to their own capabilities of feeling. Poor Collins, they said to each other—he was a dreamer, an idealist, after all—he's just like everyone else when he's proved wrong. Can't take the blow to his pride.

The boy had been gone now for a week and like others who had slipped from the cool bit of society tasting strange in their young hard mouths, he might have disappeared into the nameless faces of the native locations or he might have been brought back again to lower his head and watch himself watched. But yesterday the telephone had rung and the dutiful voice of the sergeant had said what he had been told to say: That boy that escaped from your place last week—there's been an old woman assaulted and robbed in Jeppe, and the description of the native that did it seems to fit the boy.—Yes, yes—The policeman read slowly through the description again.—Yes, that's right.—Well, that's all, we just wanted to tell you. There don't seem to be any fingerprints, unfortunately. But we should be able to get him. We just wanted to make sure we got the description right.—And the woman, is she badly hurt? —Fractured skull, ribs broken, the lot. He used an old dumbbell that was lying around the kitchen.

The boy with the neat, small head of the lizard, the long small deft hands. As the principal felt quietly along the passage to the bathroom, he saw again, for the thousandth time, the momentary reassurance of a flash of the boy's face, lifted from his desk as you walked in. Like a pain let go, relief came: that boy could never have done it.

He closed the bathroom door with a muted creak so that he could turn on the light without its pale square opening on the wall in the bedroom where his wife lay. The warm after-scent of a bath met him. He turned on the hot tap gently and the water was drawn like a soft skein over his hand. In the little mirror that sweated runnels of condensed steam from the bath, he saw his face with the nonrecognition of weariness in his eyes. There was a moment of childish comfort, as if, having worried so much, the whole thing was accounted for, expiated. The boy could not have done the thing; not this boy, and he knew boys, had studied thousands of them, every hour of his day, for nine years. It was all right. He had not done it. The description could be anybody, was anybody. It was only that the police happened to have the description of the boy on hand because he had escaped, and so they turned to it first. Whenever they did not have anything to go upon, they fell back on something easy like this; it made it sound as if they had done something, were getting somewhere. "The police are investigating and have the situation well in hand." He knew the police, too, after nine years. Thousands and thousands of faces, all brown, all brown eyes, all thick mouths. That was how the white people of the town saw the black: they were all the same, how could you tell one from another unless he had a scar, or a limp? So if a young boy escapes from a reformatory, and a young boy assaults a woman, it must be the same boy.—He washed his face under the running tap, trying not to make a noise, gasping at the water. And then he found the towel and dried his face, dried the day off his face and left his eyes burning, almost enjoying the relief of their own weariness. A muscle twitched relaxation in one lower lid.

Then he saw her stockings, washed and hung side by side on the towel rail.

As he saw them, the symbol of her routine, the orderly living out of the day which she maintained always, no matter what troubled her, what exile of worry she experienced beside him and with him—for sometimes he told her his worry, and sometimes he did not and she knew it just the same and suffered it quietly and kept her knowledge of it from him—he knew that she was awake in the bedroom. She was awake and worrying. Her hands did the things they had always done in an unconscious effort to keep one sane and quiet reassurance, the safety of commonplace. But the very fact of the reassurance proved the existence of the worry. He could feel her eyes open in the darkness of the next room, staring at a ceiling she could not see, and at once the comfort sucked away out of him and it seemed he had to breathe hard short breaths to relieve the weightiness of his chest. He stood there for a moment with his head jerking and sagging with the intake and release of this distressed breath, and it was all back again: Where was the boy? Had he done it? He had done it. Could he have done it? Was he the kind of boy to do it? With mechanical repetition he enacted the talk with the police sergeant, over and over again. Well, that's all, we just wanted to tell you. We just wanted to make sure we got the description right.—And the woman, is she badly hurt?—He used an old dumbbell that was lying around. We just wanted to tell you.—Yes, yes.—We just wanted to tell you. The cold of the concrete floor was hardening up through his feet as he stood dead still as though the worry were a pain that might pass if he let it, submitted to its spasm and did not give it the incentive of his own attempt to escape on which to tighten its clutch.

His feet were cold as he turned off the bathroom light before he opened the door (she would know from the very meticulousness of his care that he knew there was no sleep from which to awaken her) and felt across the passage into the bedroom. The soft slump of his clothes as he undressed moved like the darkness settling to itself; there was a pause before the long creak of his bed as he let his body down.

Across the strip of rug that separated his bed from hers he listened to her listening for him. She was so still, still with consciousness; stiller than sleep, that deepens and thins, floats and sinks, can ever be. Monday . . . Will it be tomorrow? They've found him. He did it. How can you fight against the time if it is coming, if it is to come; the time of hearing: he did it.

And though she would not let him hear her breathing because she did not want to give it away, the answering conviction of her fear slipped silently out with her soundless breath, and reached him. He did it. Oh did he do it?

But they did not speak. They would never speak. Somewhere below the face of the boy, a pang which had never yet found the right moment to claim attention lifted feebly like an eye of lightning that opens and shuts in another part of the sky. When would there be time to speak to her, to read the face of his wife as he struggled to read the suffering faces of the nameless, the dispossessed whom God made it incumbent upon him that he should spend his life reading?

The face lifted again from the desk. Brown eyes surrounded by a milky-blue rim, the flat flush ears, the sloping temples; the neat head of a lizard. . . . He studied the face, called it up again and again, searching.

The night was awake, listening to them.

They had both been asleep a short time when the knock came at the door. It dinned on sleep like thunder but at the instant of wakefulness it became a knock at the front door. The impact of dread, met at last! exploded his blood through his body like shot. His wife sat up for the light switch. The light blinded them both. His feet felt over the floor for his slippers and his arms went into his gown; the knocking was insistent but not loud, purposeful of the necessity to rouse, but considerate not to shock. His heart beat so slow and strong that every force of it seemed to swell his veins as if some painful object much too large for passage were being pushed through. He went through the house turning on light, acknowledged at last, behind him, and undid the latch of the door. It's all right, he was saying, Coming, coming. It was the voice that prisoners had heard in the condemned cell, the voice that came from somewhere, never failed him.

Ngubane, one of his assistants, stood there. With a thrill of recognition, he knew it, the lump in his blood ran fast and liquid and his heart torrented beats as drops of water fuse in the rush of a waterfall. He found his glasses in his hand and now he put them on and there was

Ngubane in his neat overcoat for it had been his Sunday off and he was dressed for leisure. His own shoulders shielded the light from Ngubane's face, but he saw the man's mouth parted forward in a kind of gasp as he pressed in.

Something terrible has happened, burst Ngubane as if the opening of the door had released the words, and as the principal fell back to let the man in and the light slipped past and lifted the face out of the dark, he saw the astonishing twitch of lost control from Ngubane's nose to lip, blisters of sweat along his eyebrows. It seemed that their panic rose and met, equal. In a trance they went along the passage together, through a door; swallowed; sat down. Their eyes held one another.

I—sir, sir . . . , said Ngubane.

I know, I know, he said passionately. The nostrils of his short strong nose were arched back, two cuts of sorrow held his mouth firm down the sides of his cheeks. His head was lifted in an unconscious gesture to bear. Ngubane, who had seen it before in him, flared his nostrils in sudden tears of gratitude for strength, the strength of Collins. My brother—he was shaking, shaking his head as if to rid himself of what he saw—my brother was killed on the road *now*. I was riding beside him and it happened . . . he was killed.

Your brother?

My brother who was out with me in Johannesburg. My brother Peter the teacher from Germiston. The one you knew—who came . . . The bus didn't see and he was riding on the outside. He was killed, I didn't even see how it happened, he was riding there with me and then he was gone. . . .

Your brother? Collins was leaning forward with his face screwed up with the curious look of questioning closely, almost as if he were irritated with not understanding what the other was trying to say.

Two strings jerked in Ngubane's neck. He nodded till he could speak again. Peter, my brother.

He was killed on the road you say? Killed on the road. . . . Collins was repeating it to himself as if it were some marvel; the room, Ngubane, his own voice rising so oddly, seemed to be sliding rapidly away from him. . . . His head searched a little for air, his hand lying on its side on the table jumped, relaxed, faltered.

I'm sorry, he said, Ngubane, I'm sorry. He spoke quickly. His face was burning hot. He stood up quickly and had his hand on the man's shoulder. Tell me about it, Ngubane, he said. Speak of it.

As a child waits for permission to weep, the man put his head down on his arms and with his nose flattened against the tweed, let his eyes, showing yellow-white as they twisted up to Collins' face, slowly fill with a man's hard sorrow.

When the assistant had gone (they had given him something to make him sleep, words of comfort, and the comfort of promised action in the assurance that tomorrow he must take the day off to make arrangements for the funeral) the principal and his wife sat and had a cup of tea in the kitchen. The gulp of tea down their throats was easy between them. Come on, he said, and she tried the kitchen window to see if it was locked and flattened her hands against her dressing gown a moment in a pause before she went back to bed. He pottered about, locking up again, turning lights off, picking things up in vague question of why they should have been left where they were for the night. Then he came into the bedroom and got into bed. The two of them sighed as they moved about under their covers, settling for warmth and sleep.

Then they were still.

For a moment, you know, she said suddenly, I thought he'd come to tell us bad news about the boy.

Well so did I, he said.

She made a little sound that might have meant she was going to say something, or might have been a little sound of sleep.

He lay and the darkness came up to him, the darkness spread out to the edges of his being, the darkness washed away the edges of his being as the sea melts the edges of the sand. But just as it was about to smooth out his head and wash down the pinnacles of his features like a sandcastle, a return of consciousness rose within him and swept it away.

So did I.

It came to him suddenly and it filled him with desolation as startling and wakeful as the thump at the door. It stiffened him from head to foot with failure more bitter and complete than he could ever have imagined. *I'm sorry. I'm sorry. Tell me about it.* The boy is alive so Ngubane is dead. The boy has not done it yet, so tea can be drunk. The boy has not done it so you may lie easy in the dark. A peace can take your mind while Ngubane goes home with his brother's death. If there is room for the boy, there is no room for Ngubane. This conscience like a hunger that made him want to answer for all the faces, all the imploring of the dispossessed—what could he do with it? What had he done with it? The man who pulled down prison walls and grew geraniums. He saw himself, standing up at a meeting, the flash of attention from his glasses as they looked up to him. The silence of his wife, going about her business whilst he worried, nine years he worried, turned from her to this problem or that. If you search one face, you turn your back on another.

He did not know how he would live through this moment of knowledge, and he closed his lids against the bitter juice that they seemed to crush out, burning, from his eyes.

3

CHARACTER

It was with considerable difficulty, and more artificiality, that our last discussion tried to consider fictional conflict without constantly relating it to other story elements. All elements in fiction are closely interrelated and constantly interact with and influence each other. This is particularly true of conflict and character, for a story does not merely happen, it happens to somebody. Indeed, in the effective short story the characters will in large part determine the nature, development, outcome, and effects of the conflict, a principle recognized by Henry James when he asked, rhetorically, "What is character but the determination of incident? What is incident but the illustration of character?"

Because character determines and controls conflict, we can argue that characterization is at least as essential to fiction as conflict. We can also argue that it is as interesting. Even the person who reads (he thinks) primarily for plot knows that his interest in and attitude toward what happens in a story largely is determined by the people to whom it happens. In a formula Western, for example, we feel one way when the villain meets with defeat; we would feel very different were the hero defeated.

If it is true that characterization is as important as conflict in fiction, it is also true that characterization places certain demands upon a reader which conflict may not. In order to understand the whats and the whys of these demands, let us briefly examine the basic nature of the reading process.

Most people think of reading as a passive process; the relationship between reader and writer is one in which the writer does most of the work and the reader receives most of the reward. In the handling of action as *action,* this may be true; if somebody *does* something in a story, the writer can simply tell us what he does, and all the reader has to do is to translate the words that symbolize that action into a concept. In other words, action in fiction is, for the most part, handled *directly*. But as soon as a writer goes beyond the simple narration of action, he must, if he wants to be completely effective, employ a different approach to communication. The other elements in a story cannot effectively be handled directly; they must rather be handled indirectly. Another way of putting this is to say that a writer shows rather than tells; he handles character, theme, and emotion by implication or suggestion. He does not tell us that a protagonist is selfish; he shows him acting selfishly. He does not try to communicate a theme by writing an essay; he presents a story from which we must deduce his theme. He does not command us to feel sad; he places a sympathetic character in the kind of a situation which will elicit sadness in us. The good writer knows that handling these elements in any other way will not work; it will fail to convince and it may even fail to communicate at all. To illustrate, let us look at the opening of a very primitive form of fiction, a "story" in a first-grade reader:

> This is Dick and Jane. Dick is nice. Jane is nice, too. Jane likes Dick. Dick likes Jane. Dick and Jane run and play. Oh, happy, happy Dick. Oh, happy, happy Jane.

Clearly, no adult reader in his right mind could derive any aesthetic pleasure from this passage because everything in it—what the characters are like, what they do, how they feel—is *told.* And if we contrast this passage to the opening of Kay Boyle's "Effigy of War," we will see the difference that implication makes in a story. In this opening we must, if we are to realize the characters of either the barman or the director, deduce them. We must deduce character traits from description, from dialogue, from metaphors supplied by the author. We must sense that the quiet, polite, understanding comments of the director mask callousness and selfishness, and that the reasonable replies of the barman mask a quite unreasonable fear. We must make something of the ironies in the passage (both these men are expatriates, both have fled from the same kind of a political phenomenon). The director jerks his cuffs into his morning coat and the barman lights the director's cigaret, and we must use these actions as clues to character or emotion. This entire process of deduction is similar to that of interpreting and appreciating a joke. And if we were to extend this comparison to include a range of stories from juveniles to stories in *The New Yorker,* we would discover that the more sophisticated the fiction, the more the writer will rely on implication in order to accomplish his purpose and effects.[1]

[1] I am of course aware that fiction writers employ two basic methods of characterization: the *expository* (in which the writer tells us directly about a character) and the *dramatic* (in which a character reveals himself through action, dialogue, and so on). But I know of no effective story in which exposition is the *sole* method used in characterization; it is always supported by dramatization, and it is in the

But dramatization is not enough; it is simply a *method* of presenting characters, and beyond it, characters in a story must be credible, must seem "real." Unless we believe in the people in a story, we cannot believe in what happens to them, and consequently we stop believing in the story.

Plausible characterization, like plausible conflict, defies complete analysis; it may depend on anything from motivated action to the employment of certain literary conventions that are peculiar to a given time in literary history. But again, one general principle underlies plausibility of characterization as it underlies plausibility in conflict; the most convincing fictional characters are those who most closely approximate persons we have observed in life.

This means, among other things, that fictional characters will be *consistent;* if a character is established as gentle, we expect him to behave gently throughout the story. On the surface, this may seem contradictory, for in actual life we have all known people to behave inconsistently. We accept this "acting out of character" because we observe it. But we also know that such inconsistency is the exception; in general, given a certain kind of person, we can count on him to behave in a certain, predictable way. And one important difference between fiction and life is that the behavior of people in stories imitates what people *usually* do, not what they *occasionally* do.

But how do we reconcile consistency with the principle of story as crisis, the principle that story involves some kind of character change? Here we meet with a second requirement, which is that the plausible character in fiction must be *motivated;* that is, a story is concerned not only with what a character is and does but with why he does it. A character in fiction may change provided we are shown a convincing reason for that change; such a character will still be consistent. This matter of motivation is perhaps peculiar to twentieth-century fiction, a fact we can appreciate when we realize the discomfort we sometimes experience on observing the unexplained and apparently inconsistent behavior patterns of characters in older fiction—the actions of Bret Harte characters, for example. For this century is dominated by scientific thought patterns, and the heart of scientific thinking is an acceptance of the principle of cause and effect. We also live in an age of psychology, in which the witch doctor or the priest has been replaced by the psychoanalyst. And the assumption that

---

dramatized portions of a story that the character usually becomes "real" for us. Indeed, the expository treatment of character is as often as not misleading; it is as often ironical as literal. "She was one of those pretty and charming girls" begins a famous De Maupassant story; but Mme. Loisel's subsequent actions betray the fact that though she may be pretty, she is not precisely charming. In other words, deduction is as frequently demanded of us in an expository as in a dramatized presentation of character.

all human behavior can be accounted for within some kind of cause-effect frame of reference may be as open to argument as the assumption that the universe is ruled by gods with human traits who intervene whimsically in human affairs. Nonetheless, literature is always a reflection of the culture from which it springs, and contemporary writers are saddled with the burden either of explaining a character's behavior or of having the reader reject that character as implausible.

This explains why other kinds of fictional characters no longer satisfy the modern reader. If we are to believe today in a fictional character, we must *know* him; we will not be happy with the *shadowy* character in a story. There may have been a time when the character who was nothing beyond a name on a page and a few physical traits was accepted by readers, but now we want to know what a character is like, we want some insight into what makes him tick. Similarly, the modern reader will find the *stock* character implausible; we can define the stock character as one who is borrowed from other fiction rather than drawn from observation, insight, imagination—the Madison Avenue advertising man in many contemporary novels of suburbia is an example. Sophisticated readers will reject the *oversimplified* or *flat* character—the character who is completely good or completely bad, or who is reduced to a single, one-dimensional character trait. There was a time when such a character was accepted by an audience, but the modern reader is not as naive as his ancestors who hissed villains, cheered heroes, and wept for chaste but bedeviled heroines; he is sophisticated enough to know that human beings are complex mixtures of good and evil, even, paradoxically, mixtures of apparently contradictory traits. Consequently, readers will in general find the *round* or relatively complex character more plausible than the flat or oversimplified character.[2]

If all stories were predominately character analyses, the above would perhaps be an adequate if elementary introduction to the subject of fictional characterization. But as with conflict, character is only one element in the total story. Hence, a reader must do more than accept a fictional character as "real"; he must also be able to perceive the function of a character in a story.

Again, we can offer no easy formula for understanding this function.

[2] This is, of course, a relative proposition and depends among other things on the nature of a story's conflict. A story which exploits a very brief conflict (in time) will probably have flatter characters than will a story which covers a long time span and which is consequently much longer. Here we will tend to accept relatively flat characters because people in actual life, when faced with such crises, will also tend to become oversimplified; one character trait will become dominant, other traits will tend temporarily to disappear. Moreover, readers will tend to accept oversimplified minor characters in a story where they will not accept oversimplified major characters.

But some of the questions we ask about conflict in a story can with equal validity be asked about character. How important is character in a story? Is it the dominant element, or is it subordinate to some other element? What *happens* to a character in a story? If the conflict changes him, how and why? If it teaches him something, what? If the conflict ends satisfactorily for the protagonist, why? If it does not, why not? Do you like, admire, or respect this or that character in a story? If so, why? The answers to such questions usually will provide significant clues as to a story's purpose or point.

The kind of character we have in a story can also help us to understand a story's purpose. In general, fictional characters will fall into one of three categories. Probably the majority of fictional characters are what we call *typical*. The human race is subject to division and subdivision; these groupings are determined by such things as our language, our race, our occupation, our position on a sociological ladder (upper, middle, or lower class), our ancestry, our age, our income, and so on. And because the human animal is a mimic, our personalities tend to be stamped by the groups to which we belong. Thus, a typical character in fiction can be defined as one who is representative of a group to which he belongs. No one can deny, for example, that one's occupation tends to determine much of one's character; public school teachers do not behave the same way, dress the same way, talk the same way, think the same way, subscribe to the same values, or follow the same mores as truck drivers. Hence, if we have a story about a school teacher, and if that teacher is characterized in such a way as to remind us of many teachers we have known, we can probably safely suspect that the story has something to say about teaching.

But in some stories, we find characters pushed beyond the typical to what can be called the *universal*. Regardless of whether we are black or white, old or young, rich or poor, we share with all members of the human race certain characteristics and instincts and values. The fact that all languages share certain abstractions like love, hate, pity, or selfishness attests to this. The fact that all human beings also share (or at least understand) many of the same desires—the desire for wealth or power, the desire for status, the desire to mate, the desire to live forever—further attests to it. Some stories concern themselves with human problems which are common to humanity as a whole, and some fictional characters share traits with all their brothers and sisters on the face of the earth. Clearly, the story with universal characters and universal conflicts or problems at its core will be saying something different from the story with typical characters in it. And sometimes universal characters will be pushed one step further into *allegorical* characters, who are not people, in the usual sense of the word, but symbols of abstract human traits—in which case we are probably dealing with a story which is very close to a kind of dramatized philosophical essay.

At the other extreme, characters in fiction may be *individual*. An individual character is one whose traits are so chosen as to separate him from his kind, traits which make him not representative but unique. The individual character is a comparative rarity in fiction, but he can be found in occasional stories, and usually his very uniqueness is a factor which can point us toward a discovery of a story's purpose or intention. Individuality, of course, is a relative matter. No writer, even the most imaginative creator of science-fiction, can create a completely individualized character, and even if he could, no reader would find either the character or the story comprehensible. But ordinarily the writer who is so characterizing will provide clues of his intention in his choice of minor characters; these will be used as *foils* (contrasts) to the individualized character. Thus, a story may contrast a nonmaterialistic American against a group of materialistic Americans, in which case we are probably dealing with a story which has something to say about materialistic values in our culture.

CAROLINE GORDON

Old Red

When the door had closed behind his daughter Mister Maury went to the window and stood a few moments looking out. The roses that had grown in a riot all along that side of the fence had died or been cleared away, but the sun lay across the garden in the same level lances of light that he remembered. He turned back into the room. The shadows had gathered until it was nearly all in gloom. The top of his minnow bucket just emerging from the duffel bag glinted in the last rays of the sun. He stood looking down at his traps all gathered neatly in a heap at the foot of the bed. He would leave them like that. Even if they came in here sweeping and cleaning up—it was only in hotels that a man was master of his own room—even if they came in here cleaning up, he would tell them to leave all his things exactly as they were. It was reassuring to see them all there together, ready to be taken up in the hand, to bc carried down and put into a car, to be driven off to some railroad station at a moment's notice.

As he moved toward the door, he spoke aloud, a habit that was growing on him:

"Anyhow I won't stay but a week. . . . I ain't going to stay but a week, no matter what they say. . . ."

Downstairs in the dining room they were already gathered at the supper table, his white-haired, shrunken mother-in-law, his tall sister-in-law who had the proud carriage of the head, the aquiline nose, but not the spirit of his dead wife, his lean, blond new son-in-law, his black-eyed daughter who, but that she was thin, looked so much like him, all of them gathered there waiting for him, Alexander Maury. It occurred to him that this was the first time he had sat down in the bosom of the family for some years. They were always writing saying that he must make a visit this summer or certainly next fall. ". . . all had a happy Christmas together but missed you. . . ." They had even made the pretext that he ought to come up to inspect his new son-in-law. As if he hadn't always known exactly the kind of young man Sarah would marry! What was the boy's name? Stephen, yes, Stephen. He must be sure and remember that.

He sat down, and shaking out his napkin spread it over his capacious paunch and tucked it well up under his chin in the way his wife had never allowed him to do. He let his eyes rove over the table and released a long sigh.

"Hot batter bread," he said, "and ham. Merry Point ham. I sure am glad to taste them one more time before I die."

The old lady was sending the little Negro girl scurrying back to the kitchen for a hot plate of batter bread. He pushed aside the cold plate and waited. She had bridled when he spoke of the batter bread and a faint flush had dawned on her withered cheeks. Vain she had always been as a peacock, of her housekeeping, her children, the animals on her place, anything that belonged to her. And she went on, even at her advanced age, making her batter bread, smoking her hams according to that old recipe she was so proud of; but who came here now to this old house to eat or to praise?

He helped himself to a generous slice of batter bread, buttered it, took the first mouthful and chewed it slowly. He shook his head.

"There ain't anything like it," he said. "There ain't anything else like it in this world."

His dark eyes roving the table fell on his son-in-law. "You like batter bread?" he inquired.

Stephen nodded, smiling. Mister Maury, still masticating slowly, regarded his face, measured the space between the eyes—his favorite test for man, horse, or dog. Yes, there was room enough for sense between the eyes. But how young the boy looked! And infected already with the fatal germ, the *cacoëthes scribendi.*[1] Well, their children would probably escape. It was like certain diseases of the eye, skipped every other generation. His own father had had it badly all his life. He could see him now sitting at the head of the table spouting his own poetry—or Shakespeare's—while the children watched the preserve dish to see if it was going around. He, Aleck Maury, had been lucky to be born in the generation he had. He had escaped that at least. A few translations from Heine in his courting days, a few fragments from the Greek, but no, he had kept clear of that on the whole. . . .

The eyes of his sister-in-law were fixed on him. She was smiling

[1] *Cacoëthes scribendi.* Itch for writing.

faintly. "You don't look much like dying, Aleck. Florida must agree with you."

The old lady spoke from the head of the table. "I can't see what you do with yourself all winter long. Doesn't time hang heavy on your hands?"

Time, he thought, time! They were always mouthing the word and what did they know about it? Nothing in God's world! He saw time suddenly, a dull, leaden-colored fabric depending from the old lady's hands, from the hands of all of them, a blanket that they pulled about, now this way, now that, trying to cover up their nakedness. Or they would cast it on the ground and creep in among the folds, finding one day a little more tightly rolled than another, but all of it everywhere the same dull gray substance. But time was a banner that whipped before him always in the wind. He stood on tiptoe to catch at the bright folds, to strain them to his bosom. They were bright and glittering. But they whipped by so fast and were whipping always ever faster. The tears came into his eyes. Where, for instance, had this year gone? He could swear he had not wasted a minute of it, for no man living, he thought, knew better how to make each day a pleasure to him. Not a minute wasted and yet here it was already May! If he lived to the Biblical three score and ten, which was all he ever allowed himself in his calculations, he had before him only nine more Mays. Only nine more Mays out of all eternity, and they wanted him to waste one of them sitting on the front porch at Merry Point!

The butter plate which had seemed to swim in a glittering mist was coming solidly to rest upon the white tablecloth. He winked his eyes rapidly and laying down his knife and fork squared himself about in his chair to address his mother-in-law:

"Well, ma'am, you know I'm a man that always likes to be learning something. Now this year I learned how to smell out fish." He glanced around the table, holding his head high and allowing his well-cut nostrils to flutter slightly with his indrawn breaths. "Yes, sir," he said, "I'm probably the only white man in this country knows how to smell out feesh."

There was a discreet smile on the faces of the others. Sarah was laughing outright. "Did you have to learn how or did it just come to you?" she asked.

"I learned it from an old nigger woman," her father said. He shook his head reminiscently. "It's wonderful how much you can learn from niggers. But you have to know how to handle them. I was half the winter wooing that old Fanny. . . ."

He waited until their laughter had died down. "We used to start off every morning from the same little cove and we'd drift in there together at night. I noticed how she always brought in a good string, so I says to her, 'Fanny, you just lemme go 'long with you.' But she wouldn't have nothing to do with me. I saw she was going to be a hard nut to crack, but I kept right on. Finally I began giving her presents. . . ."

Laura was regarding him fixedly, a queer look on her face.

"What sort of presents did you give her, Aleck?"

He made his tones hearty in answer. "I gave her a fine string of fish one day and I gave her fifty cents. And finally I made her a present of a Barlow knife. That was when she broke down. She took me with her that morning. . . ."

"Could she really smell fish?" the old lady asked curiously.

"You ought to 'a' seen her," Mister Maury said. "She'd sail over that lake like a hound on the scent. She'd row right along and then all of a sudden she'd stop rowing." He bent over, wrinkling his nose and peering into the depths of imaginary water. " 'Thar they are, White Folks, thar they are. Cain't you smell 'em?' "

Stephen was leaning forward, eyeing his father-in-law intently. "Could you?" he asked.

"I got so I could smell feesh," Mister Maury told him. "I could smell out the feesh, but I couldn't tell which kind they were. Now Fanny could row over a bed and tell just by the smell whether it was bass or bream. But she'd been at it all her life." He paused, sighing. "You can't just pick these things up. You have to give yourself to them. Who was it said 'Genius is an infinite capacity for taking pains'?"

Sarah was rising briskly. Her eyes sought her husband's across the table. She was still laughing. "Sir Izaak Walton," she said, "we'd better go in the other room. Mandy wants to clear the table."

The two older ladies remained in the dining room. Mister Maury walked across the hall to the sitting room, accompanied by Steve and Sarah. He lowered himself cautiously into the most solid looking of the rocking chairs that were drawn up around the fire. Steve was standing on the hearthrug, back to the fire, gazing abstractedly off across the room.

Mister Maury glanced up at him curiously. "What are you thinking about, feller?" he asked.

Steve looked down. He smiled, but his gaze was still contemplative. "I was thinking about the sonnet," he said, "in the form in which it first came to England."

Mister Maury shook his head, "Wyatt and Surrey," he said. "Hey, nonny, nonny. . . . You'll have hardening of the liver long before you're my age." He looked past Steve's shoulder at the picture that hung over the mantel shelf: Cupid and Psyche holding between them a fluttering veil and running along a rocky path toward the beholder. "Old Merry Point," he said; "it don't change much, does it?"

He settled himself more solidly in his chair. His mind veered from the old house to his own wanderings in brighter places. He regarded his daughter and son-in-law affably.

"Yes, sir," he said, "this winter in Florida was valuable to me just for the acquaintances I made. Take my friend, Jim Barbee. Just to live in the same hotel with that man is an education." He paused, smiling reminiscently into the fire. "I'll never forget the first time I saw him. He came up to me there in the lobby of the hotel. 'Professor Maury!' he says, 'You been hearin' about me for twenty years and I been hearin' about you for twenty years. And now we've done met!' "

Sarah had sat down in the little rocking chair by the fire. She leaned toward him now, laughing. "They ought to have put down a cloth of gold for the meeting," she said.

Mister Maury shook his head. "Nature does that in Florida," he said. "I knew right off the reel it was him. There were half a dozen men standing around. I made 'em witness. 'Jim Barbee,' I says, 'Jim Barbee of Maysville or I'll eat my hat!' "

"Why is he so famous?" Sarah asked.

Mister Maury took out his knife and cut a slice from a plug of tobacco. When he had offered a slice to his son-in-law and it had been refused, he put the plug back in his pocket. "He's a man of imagination," he said slowly. "There ain't many in this world."

He took a small tin box out of his pocket and set it on the little table that held the lamp. Removing the top he tilted the box so that they could see its contents: an artificial lure, a bug with a dark body and a red, bulbous head, a hook protruding from what might he considered its vitals.

"Look at her," he said, "ain't she a killer?"

Sarah leaned forward to look and Steve, still standing on the hearth-rug, bent above them. The three heads ringed the light.

Mister Maury disregarded Sarah and addressed himself to Steve. "She takes nine strips of rind," he said, "nine strips just thick enough." He marked off the width of the strips with his two fingers on the table, then picking up the lure and cupping it in his palm he moved it back and forth quickly so that the painted eyes caught the light.

"Look at her," he said, "look at the wicked way she sets forward."

Sarah was poking at the lure with the tip of her finger.

"Wanton," she said, "simply wanton. What does he call her?"

"This is his Devil Bug," Mister Maury said. "He's the only man in this country makes it. I myself had the idea thirty years ago and let it slip by me the way I do with so many of my ideas." He sighed, then elevating his tremendous bulk slightly above the table level and continuing to hold Stephen with his gaze he produced from his coat pocket the oilskin book that held his flies. He spread it open on the table and began to turn the pages. His eyes sought his son-in-law's as his hand paused before a gray, rather draggled-looking lure.

"Old Speck," he said. "I've had that fly for twenty years. I reckon she's taken five hundred pounds of fish in her day. . . ."

The fire burned lower. A fiery coal rolled from the grate and fell onto the hearthrug. Sarah scooped it up with a shovel and threw it among the ashes. In the circle of the lamplight the two men still bent over the table looking at the flies. Steve was absorbed in them but he spoke seldom. It was her father's voice that rising and falling filled the room. He talked a great deal, but he had a beautiful speaking voice. He was telling Steve now about Little West Fork, the first stream ever he put a fly in. "My first love," he kept calling it. It sounded rather pretty, she thought, in his mellow voice. "My first love . . ."

II

When Mister Maury came downstairs the next morning the dining room was empty except for his daughter, Sarah, who sat dawdling over a cup of coffee and a cigarette. Mister Maury sat down opposite her. To the little Negro girl who presented herself at his elbow he outlined his wants briefly. "A cup of coffee and some hot batter bread just like we had last night." He turned to his daughter. "Where's Steve?"

"He's working," she said, "he was up at eight and he's been working ever since."

Mister Maury accepted the cup of coffee from the little girl, poured half of it into his saucer, set it aside to cool. "Ain't it wonderful," he said, "the way a man can sit down and work day after day? When I think of all the work I've done in my time. . . . Can he work *every* morning?"

"He sits down at his desk every morning," she said, "but of course he gets more done some mornings than others."

Mister Maury picked up the saucer, found the coffee cool enough for his taste. He sipped it slowly, looking out of the window. His mind was already busy with his day's program. No water—no running water—nearer than West Fork three miles away. He couldn't drive a car and Steven was going to be busy writing all morning. There was nothing for it but a pond. The Willow Sink. It was not much but it was better than nothing. He pushed his chair back and rose.

"Well," he said, "I'd better be starting."

When he came downstairs with his rod a few minutes later the hall was still full of the sound of measured typing. Sarah sat in the dining room in the same position in which he had left her, smoking. Mister Maury paused in the doorway while he slung his canvas bag over his shoulders. "How you ever going to get anything done if you don't take advantage of the morning hours?" he asked. He glanced at the door opposite as if it had been the entrance to a sick chamber.

"What's he writing about?" he inquired in a whisper.

"It's an essay on John Skelton."

Mister Maury looked out at the new green leaves framed in the doorway. "John Skelton," he said. "God Almighty!"

He went through the hall and stepped down off the porch onto the ground that was still moist with spring rains. As he crossed the lower yard he looked up into the branches of the maples. Yes, the leaves were full grown already even on the late trees. The year, how swiftly, how steadily it advanced! He had come to the far corner of the yard. Grown up it was in pokeberry shoots and honeysuckle, but there was a place to get through. The top strand of wire had been pulled down and fastened to the others with a ragged piece of rope. He rested his weight on his good leg and swung himself over onto the game one. It gave him a good, sharp twinge when he came down on it. It was getting worse all the time, that leg, but on the other hand he was learning better all the time how to handle it. His mind flew back to a dark, startled moment, that day when the cramp first came on him. He had been sitting still in the boat all day long and that evening when he had stood up to get out his leg had failed him utterly. He had pitched forward among the reeds, had lain there a second, face downwards, before it came to him what had happened. With the realization came a sharp picture of his faraway youth: Uncle Quent lowering himself ponderously out of the saddle after a hard day's hunting had fallen forward in exactly the same way, into a knot of yowling little Negroes. He had got up and cursed them all out of the lot. It had scared the old boy to death, coming down like that. The black dog he had had on his shoulder all that fall. But he himself had never lost one day's fishing on account of his leg. He had known from the start how to handle it. It meant simply that he was slowed down that much. It hadn't really made much difference in fishing. He didn't do as much wading but he got around just about as well on the whole. Hunting, of course, had had to go. You couldn't walk all day shooting birds, dragging a game leg. He had just given it up right off the reel, though it was a shame when a man was as good a shot as he was. That day he was out with Tom Kensington last November, the only day he got out during the season. Nine shots he'd had and he'd bagged nine birds. Yes, it was a shame. But a man couldn't do everything. He had to limit himself. . . .

He was up over the little rise now. The field slanted straight down before him to where the pond lay, silver in the morning sun. A Negro cabin was perched halfway up the opposite slope. A woman was hanging out washing on a line stretched between two trees. From the open doorway little Negroes spilled down the path toward the pond. Mister Maury surveyed the scene, spoke aloud:

"Ain't it funny now? Niggers always live in the good places."

He stopped under a wild cherry tree to light his pipe. It had been hot crossing the field, but the sunlight here was agreeably tempered by the branches. And that pond down there was fringed with willows. His eyes sought the bright disk of the water, then rose to where the smoke from the cabin chimney lay in a soft plume along the crest of the hill.

When he stooped to pick up his rod again it was with a feeling of sudden, keen elation. An image had risen in his memory, an image that was familiar but came to him infrequently of late and that only in moments of elation: the wide field in front of his uncle's old house in Albermarle, on one side the dark line of undergrowth that marked the Rivanna River, on the other the blue of Peters' Mountain. They would be waiting there in that broad plain when they had the first sight of the fox. On that little rise by the river, loping steadily, not yet alarmed. The sun would glint on his bright coat, on his quick-turning head as he dove into the dark of the woods. There would be hullabaloo after that and shouting and riding. Sometimes there was the tailing of the fox—that time old Whisky was brought home on a mattress! All of that to come afterward, but none of it ever like that first sight of the fox there on the broad plain between the river and the mountain.

There was one fox, they grew to know him in time, to call him affectionately by name. Old Red it was who showed himself always like that there on the crest of the hill. "There he goes, the damn' impudent scoundrel!" . . . Uncle Quent would shout and slap his thigh and yell himself hoarse at Whisky and Mag and the pups, but they would have already settled to their work. They knew his course, every turn of it by heart. Through the woods and then down across the fields again to the river. Their hope was always to cut him off before he could circle back to the mountain. If he got in there among those old field pines it was all up. But he always made it. Lost 'em every time and then dodged through to his hole in Pinnacle Rock. . . . A smart fox, Old Red. . . .

He descended the slope and paused in the shade of a clump of willows. The little Negroes who squatted, dabbling in the water, watched him out of round eyes as he unslung his canvas bag and laid it on a stump. He looked down at them gravely.

"D'you ever see a white man that could conjure?" he asked.

The oldest boy laid the brick he was fashioning out of mud down on a plank. He ran the tip of his tongue over his lower lip to moisten it before he spoke. "Naw suh."

"I'm the man," Mister Maury told him. "You chillun better quit that playin' an dig me some worms."

He drew his rod out of the case, jointed it up and laid it down on a stump. Taking out his book of flies he turned the pages, considering. "Silver Spinner," he said aloud. "They ought to take that . . . in May. Naw, I'll just give Old Speck a chance. It's a long time now since we had her out."

The little Negroes had risen and were stepping quietly off along the path toward the cabin, the two little boys hand in hand, the little girl following, the baby astride her hip. They were pausing now before a dilapidated building that might long ago have been a hen-house. Mister Maury shouted at them. "Look under them old boards. That's the place for worms." The biggest boy was turning around. His treble "Yassuh" quavered over the water. Then their voices died away. There was no sound except the light turning of the willow boughs in the wind.

Mister Maury walked along the bank, rod in hand, humming: "Bangum's gone to the wild boar's den . . . *Bangum's* gone to the wild boar's den . . ." He stopped where a white, peeled log protruded six or seven feet into the water. The pond made a little turn here. Two lines of willows curving in framed the whole surface of the water. He stepped out squarely upon the log, still humming. The line rose smoothly, soared against the blue and curved sweetly back upon the still water. His quick ear caught the little whish that the fly made when it clove the surface, his eye followed the tiny ripples of its flight. He cast again, leaning a little backward as he did sometimes when the mood was on him. Again and again his line soared out over the water. His eye rested now and then on his wrist. He noted with detachment the expert play of the muscles, admired each time the accuracy of his aim. It occurred to him that it was four days now since he had wet a line. Four days. One whole day packing up, parts of two days on the train and yesterday wasted sitting there on that front porch with the family. But the abstinence had done him good. He had never cast better than he was casting this morning.

There was a rustling along the bank, a glimpse of blue through the trees. Mister Maury leaned forward and peered around the clump of willows. A hundred yards away Steve, hatless, in an old blue shirt and khaki pants, stood jointing up a rod.

Mister Maury backed off his log and advanced along the path. He called out cheerfully, "Well, feller, do any good?"

Steve looked up. His face had lightened for a moment, but the abstracted expression stole over it again when he spoke. "Oh, I fiddled with it," he said, "all morning, but I didn't do much good."

Mister Maury nodded sympathetically. *"Minerva invita erat,"*[2] he said; "you can do nothing unless Minerva perches on the rooftree. Why, I been castin' here all morning and not a strike. But there's a boat tied up over on the other side. What say we get in it and just drift around?" He paused, looked at the rod Steve had finished jointing up. "I brought another rod along," he said.

"You want to use it?"

Steve shook his head. "I'm used to this one."

An expression of relief came over Mister Maury's face. "That's right," he said, "a man always does better with his own rod."

The boat was only a quarter full of water. They heaved her over and dumped it out, then dragged her down to the bank. The little Negroes had come up, bringing a can of worms. Mister Maury threw them each a nickel and set the can in the bottom of the boat. "I always like to have a few worms handy," he told Steve, "ever since I was a boy." He lowered himself ponderously into the bow and Steve pushed off and dropped down behind him.

The little Negroes still stood on the bank staring. When the boat was a little distance out on the water the boldest of them spoke: "You reckon 'at ole jawnboat going to hold you up, Cap'm?"

Mister Maury turned his head to call over his shoulder. "Go 'way, boy, ain't I done tole you I's a conjure?"

The boat dipped ominously. Steve changed his position a little and she settled to the water. Sitting well forward Mister Maury made graceful casts, now to this side, now to that. Steve, in the stern, made occasional casts, but he laid his rod down every now and then to paddle, though there was really no use in it. The boat drifted well enough with the wind. At the end of half an hour seven sizable bass lay on the bottom of the boat. Mister Maury had caught five of them. He reflected that perhaps he really ought to change places with Steve. The man in the bow certainly had the best chance at the fish. "But no," he thought, "it don't make any difference. He don't hardly know where he is now."

He stole a glance over his shoulder at the young man's serious, abstracted face. It was like that of a person submerged. Steve seemed to float up to the surface every now and then, his expression would lighten, he would make some observation that showed he knew where he was, then he would sink again. If you asked him a question he answered punctiliously, two minutes later. Poor boy, dead to the world and would probably be that way the rest of his life! A pang of pity shot through Mister Maury, and on the heels of it a gust of that black fear that occasionally shook him. It was he, not Steve, that was the queer one! The world was full

[2] *Minerva invita erat.* Minerva was unwilling.

of people like this boy, all of them walking round with their heads so full of this and that they hardly knew where they were going. There was hardly anybody—there was *nobody* really in the whole world like him. . . .

Steve, coming out of his abstraction, spoke politely. He had heard that Mister Maury was a fine shot. Did he like to fish better than hunt?

Mister Maury reflected. "Well," he said, "they's something about a covey of birds rising up in front of you . . . they's something. And a good dog. Now they ain't anything in this world that I like better than a good bird dog." He stopped and sighed. "A man has got to come to himself early in life if he's going to amount to anything. Now I was smart, even as a boy. I could look around me and see all the men of my family, Uncle Jeems, Uncle Quent, my father, every one of 'em weighed two hundred by the time he was fifty. You get as heavy on your feet as all that and you can't do any good shooting. But a man can fish as long as he lives. . . . Why, one place I stayed last summer there was an old man ninety years old had himself carried down to the river every morning. . . . Yes, sir, a man can fish as long as he can get down to the water's edge. . . ."

There was a little plop to the right. He turned just in time to see the fish flash out of the water. He watched Steve take it off the hook and drop it on top of the pile in the bottom of the boat. Eight bass that made and two bream. The old lady would be pleased. "Aleck always catches me fish," she'd say.

The boat glided on over the still water. There was no wind at all now. The willows that fringed the bank might have been cut out of paper. The plume of smoke hung perfectly horizontal over the roof of the Negro cabin. Mister Maury watched it stream out in the little eddies and disappear into the bright blue.

He spoke softly: "Ain't it wonderful . . . ain't it wonderful now that a man of my gifts can content himself a whole morning on this here little old pond?"

III

Mister Maury woke with a start. He realized that he had been sleeping on his left side again. A bad idea. It always gave him palpitations of the heart. It must be that that had waked him up. He had gone to sleep almost immediately after his head hit the pillow. He rolled over, cautiously, as he always did since that bed in Leesburg had given down with him, and lying flat on his back stared at the opposite wall.

The moon rose late. It must be at its height now. That patch of light was so brilliant he could always discern the pattern of the wall paper. It hung there, wavering, bitten by the shadows into a semblance of a human figure, a man striding with bent head and swinging arms. All the shadows in the room seemed to be moving toward him. The protruding corner of the washstand was an arrow aimed at his heart, the clumsy old-fashioned dresser was a giant towering above him.

They had put him to sleep in this same room the night after his wife died. In the summer it had been, too, in June, and there must have been a full moon, for the same giant shadows had struggled there with the same towering monsters. It would be like that here on this wall every full moon, for the pieces of furniture would never change their position, had never been changed, probably, since the house was built.

He turned back on his side. The wall before him was dark, but he knew every flower in the pattern of the wall paper, interlacing pink roses with thrusting up between every third cluster the enormous, spreading fonds of ferns. The wall paper in the room across the hall was like that too. The old lady slept there, and in the room next to his own, Laura, his sister-in-law, and in the east bedroom downstairs the young couple. He and Mary had slept there when they were first married, when they were the young couple in the house.

He tried to remember Mary as she must have looked the day he first saw her, the day he arrived from Virginia to open his school in the old office that used to stand there in the corner of the yard. He could see Mister Allard plainly, sitting there under the sugar tree with his chair tilted back, could discern the old lady—young she had been then!—hospitably poised in the doorway, could hear her voice: "Well, here are two of your pupils to start with. . . ." He remembered Laura, a shy child of nine hiding her face in her mother's skirts, but Mary was only a shadow in the dark hall. He could not even remember how her voice had sounded. "Professor Maury," she would have said and her mother would have corrected her with "Cousin Aleck. . . ."

That day a year later when she was getting off her horse at the stile blocks. . . . She had turned as she walked across the lawn to look back at him. Her white sunbonnet had fallen back on her shoulders, her eyes meeting his had been wide and startled. He had gone on and had hitched both the horses before he leaped over the stile to join her. But he had known in that moment that she was the woman he was going to have. He could not remember all the rest of it, only that moment stood out. He had won her. She had become his wife, but the woman he had won was not the woman he had sought. It was as if he had had her only in that moment there on the lawn. As if she had paused there only for that one moment, and was ever after retreating before him down a devious, a dark way that he would never have chosen.

The death of the first baby had been the start of it, of course. It had been a relief when she took so definitely to religion. Before that there had been those sudden, unaccountable forays out of some dark lurking place that she had. Guerrilla warfare and trying to the nerves, but that had been only at the first. For many years they had been two enemies contending in the open. . . . Toward the last she had taken mightily to prayer. He would wake often to find her kneeling by the side of the bed in the dark. It had gone on for years. She had never given up hope. . . .

Ah, a stout-hearted one, Mary! She had never given up hope of changing him, of making him over into the man she thought he ought to be. Time and again she almost had him. And there were long periods, of course, during which he had been worn down by the conflict, one spring when he himself said, when she had told all the neighbors that he was too old now to go fishing any more. . . . But he had made a comeback. She had had to resort to stratagem. His lips curved in a smile, remembering the trick.

It had come over him suddenly, a general lassitude, an odd faintness in the mornings, the time when his spirits ordinarily were always at their highest. He had sat there looking out of the window at the woods glistening with spring rain; he had not even taken his gun down to shoot a squirrel.

Remembering Uncle Quent's last days, he had been alarmed, had decided finally that he must tell her so that they might begin preparations for the future—he had shuddered at the thought of eventual confinement, perhaps in some institution. She had looked up from her sewing, unable to repress a smile.

"You think it's your mind, Aleck. . . . It's coffee. . . . I've been giving you a coffee substitute every morning. . . ."

They had laughed together over her cleverness. He had not gone back to coffee, but the lassitude had worn off. She had gone back to the attack with redoubled vigor. In the afternoons she would stand on the porch calling after him as he slipped down to the creek, "Now, don't stay long enough to get that cramp. You remember how you suffered last time. . . ." He would have forgotten all about the cramp until that moment, but it would hang over him then through the whole afternoon's sport, and it would descend upon him inevitably when he left the river and started for the house.

Yes, he thought with pride. She was wearing him down—he didn't believe there was a man living who could withstand her a lifetime!—she was wearing him down and would have had him in another few months, another year certainly. But she had been struck down just as victory was in her grasp. The paralysis had come on her in the night. It was as if a curtain had descended, dividing their life sharply into two parts. In the bewildered year and a half that followed he had found himself forlornly trying to reconstruct the Mary he had known. The pressure she had so constantly exerted upon him had become for him a part of her personality. This new, calm Mary was not the woman he had loved all these years. She had lain there—heroically they all said—waiting for death. And lying there, waiting, all her faculties engaged now in defensive warfare, she had raised as it were her lifelong siege; she had lost interest in his comings and goings, had once even encouraged him to go out for an afternoon's sport. He felt a rushing of warm pity. Poor Mary! She must have realized toward the last that she had wasted herself in conflict; she had spent her arms and her strength against an inglorious foe when all the time the real, the invincible adversary waited. . . .

He turned over on his back again. The moonlight was waning, the contending shadows paler now and retreating toward the door. From across the hall came the sound of long, sibilant breaths, ending each one on a little upward groan. The old lady . . . she would maintain till her dying day that she did not snore. He fancied that he could hear from the next room Laura's light, regular breathing, and downstairs were the young couple asleep in each other's arms. . . .

All of them quiet and relaxed now, but they had been lively enough at dinner time! It had started with the talk about Aunt Sally Crenfew's funeral Tuesday. Living as he had for some years away from women of his family he had forgotten the need to be cautious. He had spoken up before he thought:

"But that's the day Steve and I were going to Barker's Mill. . . ."

Sarah had cried out at the idea. "Barker's Mill!" she had said, "right on the Crenfew land . . . well, if not on the very farm in the very next field." It would be a scandal if he, Professor Maury, known by everybody to be in the neighborhood, could not spare one afternoon, one insignificant summer afternoon from his fishing long enough to attend the funeral of his cousin, the cousin of all of them, the oldest lady in the whole family connection. . . .

She had got him rattled; he had fallen back upon technicalities:

"I'm not a Crenfew. I'm a Maury. Aunt Sally Crenfew is no more kin to me than a catfish. . . ."

An unlucky crack, that about the catfish. Glancing around the table he had caught the same look in every eye. He had felt a gust of the same fright that had shaken him there on the pond. That look! Sooner or later you met it in every human eye. The thing was to be up and ready, ready to run for your life at a moment's notice. Yes, it had always been like that. It always would be. His fear of them was shot through suddenly with contempt. It was as if Mary was there laughing at them with him. *She* knew that none of them could have survived what he had survived, could have paid the price for freedom that he had paid. . . .

Sarah had come to a full stop. He had to say something. He shook his head:

"You think we just go fishing to have a good time. The boy and I hold high converse on that pond. . . . I'm starved for intellectual companionship, I tell you. In Florida I never see anybody but niggers. . . ."

They had all laughed out at that. "As if you didn't *prefer* the society of niggers," Sarah said scornfully.

The old lady had been moved to anecdote:

"I remember when Aleck first came out here from Virginia, Cousin Sophy said: 'Professor Maury is so well educated. Now Cousin Cave Maynor is dead, who is there in this neighborhood for him to associate with?' 'Well,' I said, 'I don't know about that. He seems perfectly satisfied now with Ben Hooser. They're off to the creek together every evening soon as school is out.' "

Ben Hooser. . . . He could see now the wrinkled face, overlaid with that ashy pallor of the aged Negro, the shrewd, smiling eyes, the pendulous lower lip that dropping away showed always some of the rotten teeth. A fine nigger, Ben, and on to a lot of tricks, the only man really that he'd ever cared to take fishing with him. . . .

But the first real friend of his bosom had been old Uncle Teague, back in Virginia. Once a week, or more likely every ten days, he fed the hounds on the carcass of a calf that had had time to get pretty high. They would drive the spring wagon out into the lot, he, a boy of ten, beside Uncle Teague on the driver's seat. The hounds would come in a great rush and rear their slobbering jowls against the wagon wheels. Uncle Teague would wield his whip, chuckling while he threw the first hunk of meat to Old Mag, his favorite.

"Dey goin' run on dis," he'd say, "dey goin' run like a shadow. . . ."

He shifted his position again, cautiously. People, he thought . . . people . . . so bone ignorant, all of them. Not one person in a thousand realized that a fox hound remains at heart a wild beast and must kill and gorge, and then when he is ravenous kill and gorge again. . . . Or that the channel cat is a night feeder. . . . Or . . . his daughter had told him once that he ought to set all his knowledges down in a book. "Why?" he had asked. "So everybody else can know as much as I do?"

If he allowed his mind to get active, really active, he would never get any sleep. He was fighting an inclination now to get up and find a cigarette. He relaxed again upon his pillows, deliberately summoned pictures up before his mind's eye. Landscapes—and streams. He observed their outlines, watched one flow into another. The Black River into West Fork, that in turn into Spring Creek and Spring Creek into the Withlicoochee. Then they were all flowing together, merging into one broad plain. He watched it take form slowly: the wide field in front of Hawkwood, the Rivanna River on one side, on the other Peters' Mountain. They would be waiting there till the fox showed himself on that little rise by the river. The young men would hold back till Uncle Quent had wheeled Old Filly, then they would all be off pell-mell across the plain. He himself would be mounted on Jonesboro. Blind as a bat, but she would take anything you put her at. That first thicket on the edge of the woods. They would break there, one half of them going around, the other half streaking it through the woods. He was always of those going around to try to cut the fox off on the other side. No, he was down off his horse. He was coursing with the fox. He could hear the sharp, pointed feet padding on the dead leaves, see the quick head turned now and then over the shoulder.

The trees kept flashing by, one black trunk after another. And now it was a ragged mountain field and the sage grass running before them in waves to where a narrow stream curved in between the ridges. The fox's feet were light in the water. He ran steadily, head down. The hounds' baying was louder now. Old Mag knew the trick. She had stopped to give tongue by the big rock, and now they had all leaped the gulch and were scrambling up through the pines. But the fox's feet were already hard on the mountain path. He ran slowly now, past the big boulder, past the blasted pine to where the shadow of the Pinnacle Rock was black across the path. He ran on and the shadow rose and swayed to meet him. Its cool touch was on his hot tongue, his heaving flanks. He had slipped in under it. He was sinking down, panting, in black dark, on moist earth while the hounds' baying filled the bowl of the valley and reverberated from the mountainside.

JOHN CHEEVER

The Country Husband

To begin at the beginning, the airplane from Minneapolis in which Francis Weed was travelling East ran into heavy weather. The sky had been a hazy blue, with the clouds below the plane lying so close together that nothing could be seen of the earth. Then mist began to form outside the windows, and they flew into a white cloud of such density that it reflected the exhaust fires. The color of the cloud darkened to gray, and the plane began to rock. Francis had been in heavy weather before, but he had never been shaken up so much. The man in the seat beside him pulled a flask out of his pocket and took a drink. Francis smiled at his neighbor, but the man looked away; he wasn't sharing his painkiller with anyone. The plane had begun to drop and flounder wildly. A child was crying. The air in the cabin was overheated and stale, and Francis' left foot went to sleep. He read a little from a paper book that he had bought at the airport, but the violence of the storm divided his attention. It was black outside the ports. The exhaust fires blazed and shed sparks in the dark, and, inside, the shaded lights, the stuffiness, and the window curtains gave the cabin an atmosphere of intense and misplaced domesticity. Then the lights flickered and went out. "You know what I've always wanted to do?" the man beside Francis said suddenly. "I've always wanted to buy a farm in New Hampshire and raise beef cattle." The stewardess announced that they were going to make an emergency landing. All but the child saw in their minds the spreading wings of the Angel of Death. The pilot could be heard singing faintly, "I've got sixpence, jolly, jolly sixpence. I've got sixpence to last me all my life . . ." There was no other sound.

The loud groaning of the hydraulic valves swallowed up the pilot's song, and there was a shrieking high in the air, like automobile brakes, and the plane hit flat on its belly in a cornfield and shook them so violently that an old man up forward howled, "Me kidneys! Me kidneys!" The stewardess flung open the door, and someone opened an emergency door at the back, letting in the sweet noise of their continuing mortality—the idle splash and smell of a heavy rain. Anxious for their lives, they filed out of the doors and scattered over the cornfield in all directions, praying that the thread would hold. It did. Nothing happened. When it was clear that the plane would not burn or explode, the crew and the stewardess gathered the passengers together and led them to the shelter of a barn. They were not far from Philadelphia, and in a little while a string of taxis took them into the city. "It's just like the Marne," someone said, but there was surprisingly little relaxation of that suspiciousness with which many Americans regard their fellow-travellers.

In Philadelphia, Francis Weed got a train to New York. At the end of that journey, he crossed the city and caught, just as it was about to pull out, the commuting train that he took five nights a week to his home in Shady Hill.

He sat with Trace Bearden. "You know, I was in that plane that just crashed outside Philadelphia," he said. "We came down in a field . . ." He had travelled faster than the newspapers or the rain, and the weather in New York was sunny and mild. It was a day in late September, as fragrant and shapely as an apple. Trace listened to the story, but how could he get excited? Francis had no powers that would let him recreate a brush with death—particularly in the atmosphere of a commuting train, journeying through a sunny countryside where already, in the slum gardens, there were signs of harvest. Trace picked up his newspaper, and Francis was left alone with his thoughts. He said good night to Trace on the platform at Shady Hill and drove in his secondhand Volkswagen up to the Blenhollow neighborhood, where he lived.

The Weeds' Dutch Colonial house was larger than it appeared to be from the driveway. The living room was spacious and divided like Gaul into three parts. Around an ell to the left as one entered from the vestibule was the long table, laid for six, with candles and a bowl of fruit in the center. The sounds and smells that came from the open kitchen door were appetizing, for Julia Weed was a good cook. The largest part of the living room centered around a fireplace. On the right were some bookshelves and a piano. The room was polished and tranquil, and from the windows that opened to the west there was some late-summer sunlight, brilliant and as clear as water. Nothing here was neglected; nothing had not been burnished. It was not the kind of household where, after prying open a stuck cigarette box, you would find an old shirt button and a tarnished nickel. The hearth was swept, the roses on the piano were reflected in the polish of the broad top, and there was an album of Schubert waltzes on the rack. Louisa Weed, a pretty girl of nine, was looking out the western windows. Her younger brother Henry was standing beside her. Her still younger brother, Toby, was studying the figures of some tonsured monks drinking beer on the polished brass of the wood box. Francis, taking off his hat and putting down his paper, was not consciously pleased with the scene; he was not that reflective. It was his element, his creation, and he returned to it with that sense of lightness and strength with which any creature returns to its home. "Hi, everybody," he said. "The plane from Minneapolis . . ."

Nine times out of ten, Francis would be greeted with affection, but tonight the children are absorbed in their own antagonisms. Francis has not finished his sentence about the plane crash before Henry plants a kick in Louisa's behind. Louisa swings around, saying "*Damn* you!" Francis makes the mistake of scolding Louisa for bad language before he punishes Henry. Now Louisa turns on her father and accuses him of favoritism. Henry is always right; she is persecuted and lonely; her lot is hopeless. Francis turns to his son, but the boy has justification for the kick—she hit him first; she hit him on the ear, which is dangerous. Louisa agrees with this passionately. She hit him on the ear, and she *meant* to hit him on the ear, because he messed up her china collection. Henry says that this is a lie. Little Toby turns away from the wood box to throw in some evidence for Louisa. Henry claps his hand over little Toby's mouth. Francis separates the two boys but accidentally pushes Toby into the wood box. Toby begins to cry. Louisa is already crying. Just then, Julia Weed comes into that part of the room where the table is laid. She is a pretty, intelligent woman, and the white in her hair is premature. She does not seem to notice the fracas. "Hello, darling," she says serenely to Francis. "Wash your hands, everyone. Dinner is ready." She strikes a match and lights the six candles in this vale of tears.

This simple announcement, like the war cries of the Scottish chieftains, only refreshes the ferocity of the combatants. Louisa gives Henry a blow on the shoulder. Henry, although he seldom cries, has pitched nine innings and is tired. He bursts into tears. Little Toby discovers a splinter in his hand and begins to howl. Francis says loudly that he has been in a plane crash and that he is tired. Julia appears again, from the kitchen, and, still ignoring the chaos, asks Francis to go upstairs and tell Helen that everything is ready. Francis is happy to go; it is like getting back to headquarters company. He is planning to tell his oldest daughter about the airplane crash, but Helen is lying on her bed reading a *True Romance* magazine, and the first thing Francis does is to take the magazine from her hand and remind Helen that he has forbidden her to buy it.

She did not buy it, Helen replies. It was given to her by her best friend, Bessie Black. Everybody reads *True Romance*. Bessie Black's father reads *True Romance*. There isn't a girl in Helen's class who doesn't read *True Romance*. Francis expresses his detestation of the magazine and then tells her that dinner's ready—although from the sounds downstairs it doesn't seem so. Helen follows him down the stairs. Julia has seated herself in the candlelight and spread a napkin over her lap. Neither Louisa nor Henry has come to the table. Little Toby is still howling, lying face down on the floor. Francis speaks to him gently: "Daddy was in a plane crash this afternoon, Toby. Don't you want to hear about it?" Toby goes on crying. "If you don't come to the table now, Toby," Francis says, "I'll have to send you to bed without any supper." The little boy rises, gives him a cutting look, flies up the stairs to his bedroom, and slams the door. "Oh dear," Julia says, and starts to go after him. Francis says that she will spoil him. Julia says that Toby is ten pounds underweight and has to be encouraged to eat. Winter is coming, and he will spend the cold months in bed unless he has his dinner. Julia goes upstairs. Francis sits down at the table with Helen. Helen is suffering from the dismal feeling of having read too intently on a fine day and she gives her father and the room a jaded look. She doesn't understand about the plane crash, because there wasn't a drop of rain in Shady Hill.

Julia returns with Toby, and they all sit down and are served. "Do I have to look at that big, fat slob?" Henry says, of Louisa. Everybody but Toby enters into this skirmish, and it rages up and down the table for five minutes. Toward the end, Henry puts his napkin over his head and, trying to eat that way, spills spinach all over his shirt. Francis asks Julia if the children couldn't have their dinner earlier. Julia's guns are loaded for this. She can't cook two dinners and lay two tables. She paints with lightning strokes that panorama of drudgery in which her youth, her beauty, and her wit have been lost. Francis says that he must be understood; he was nearly killed in an airplane crash, and he doesn't like to come home every night to a battlefield. Now Julia is deeply committed. Her voice trembles. He doesn't come home every night to a battlefield. The accusation is stupid and mean. Everything was tranquil until he arrived. She stops speaking, puts down her knife and fork, and looks into her plate as if it is a gulf. She begins to cry. "Poor Mummy!" Toby says, and when Julia gets up from the table, drying her tears with a napkin, Toby goes to her side. "Poor Mummy," he says. "Poor Mummy!" And they climb the stairs together. The other children drift away from the battlefield, and Francis goes into the back garden for a cigarette and some air.

It was a pleasant garden, with walks and flower beds and places to sit. The sunset had nearly burned out, but there was still plenty of light. Put into a thoughtful mood by the crash and the battle, Francis listened to the evening sounds of Shady Hill. "Varmints! Rascals!" old Mr. Nixon shouted to the squirrels in his bird-feeding station. "Avaunt and quit my sight!" A door slammed. Someone was playing tennis on the Babcocks' court; someone was cutting grass. Then Donald Goslin, who lived at the corner, began to play the "Moonlight Sonata." He did this nearly every night. He threw the tempo out the window and played it *rubato* from beginning to end, like an outpouring of tearful petulance, lonesomeness, and self-pity—of everything it was Beethoven's greatness not to know. The music rang up and down the street beneath the trees like an appeal for love, for tenderness, aimed at some lonely housemaid—some fresh-faced, homesick girl from Galway, looking at old snapshots in her third-floor room. "Here, Jupiter, here, Jupiter," Francis called to the Mercers' retriever. Jupiter crashed through the tomato vines with the remains of a felt hat in his mouth.

Jupiter was an anomaly. His retrieving instincts and his high spirits were out of place in Shady Hill. He was as black as coal, with a long, alert, intelligent, rakehell face. His eyes gleamed wtih mischief, and he held his head high. It was the fierce, heavily collared dog's head that appears in heraldry, in tapestry, and that used to appear on umbrella handles and walking sticks. Jupiter went where he pleased, ransacking wastebaskets, clotheslines, garbage pails, and shoe bags. He broke up garden parties and tennis matches, and got mixed up in the processional at Christ's Church on Sunday, barking at the men in red dresses. He crashed through old Mr. Nixon's rose garden two or three times a day, cutting a wide swath through the Condesa de Sastagos, and as soon as Donald Goslin lighted his barbecue fire on Thursday nights, Jupiter would get the scent. Nothing the Goslins did could drive him away. Sticks and stones and rude commands only moved him to the edge of the terrace, where he remained, with his gallant and heraldic muzzle, waiting for Donald Goslin to turn his back and reach for the salt. Then he would spring onto the terrace, lift the steak lightly off the fire, and run away with the Goslins' dinner. Jupiter's days were numbered. The Wrightsons' German gardener or the Farquarsons' cook would soon poison him. Even old Mr. Nixon might put some arsenic in the garbage that Jupiter loved. "Here, Jupiter, Jupiter!" Francis called, but the dog pranced off, shaking the hat in his white teeth. Looking in at the windows of his house, Francis saw that Julia had come down and was blowing out the candles.

Julia and Francis Weed went out a great deal. Julia was well liked and gregarious, and her love of parties sprang from a most natural dread of chaos and loneliness. She went through her morning mail with real anxiety, looking for invitations, and she usually found some, but she was insatiable, and if she had gone out seven nights a week, it would not have cured her of a reflective look—the look of someone who hears distant music—for she would always suppose that there was a more brilliant party somewhere else. Francis limited her to two week-night parties, putting a flexible interpretation on Friday, and rode through the weekend like a dory in a gale. The day after the airplane crash, the Weeds were to have dinner with the Farquarsons.

Francis got home late from town, and Julia got the sitter while he dressed, and then hurried him out of the house. The party was small and pleasant, and Francis settled down to enjoy himself. A new maid passed the drinks. Her hair was dark, and her face was round and pale and seemed familiar to Francis. He had not developed his memory as a sentimental faculty. Wood smoke lilac, and other such perfumes did not stir him, and his memory was something like his appendix—a vestigial repository. It was not his limitation at all to be unable to escape the past; it was perhaps his limitation that he had escaped it so successfully. He might have seen the maid at other parties, he might have seen her taking a walk on Sunday afternoons, but in either case he would not be searching his memory now. Her face was, in a wonderful way, a moon face—Norman or Irish—but it was not beautiful enough to account for his feeling that he had seen her before, in circumstances that he ought to be able to remember. He asked Nellie Farquarson who she was. Nellie said that the maid had come through an agency, and that her home was Trenon, in Normandy—a small place with a church and a restaurant that Nellie had once visited. While Nellie talked on about her travels abroad, Francis realized where he had seen the woman before. It had been at the end of the war. He had left a replacement depot with some other men and taken a three-day pass in Trenon. On their second day, they had walked out to a crossroads to see the public chastisement of a young woman who had lived with the German commandant during the Occupation.

It was a cool morning in the fall. The sky was overcast, and poured down onto the dirt crossroads a very discouraging light. They were on high land and could see how like one another the shapes of the clouds and the hills were as they stretched off toward the sea. The prisoner arrived sitting on a three-legged stool in a farm cart. She stood by the cart while the mayor read the accusation and the sentence. Her head was bent and her face was set in that empty half smile behind which the whipped soul is suspended. When the mayor was finished, she undid her hair and let it fall across her back. A little man with a gray mustache cut off her hair with shears and dropped it on the ground. Then, with a bowl of soapy water and a straight razor, he shaved her skull clean. A woman approached and began to undo the fastenings of her clothes, but the prisoner pushed her aside and undressed herself. When she pulled her chemise over her head and threw it on the ground, she was naked. The woman jeered; the men were still. There was no change in the falseness or the plaintiveness of the prisoner's smile. The cold wind made her white skin rough and hardened the nipples of her breasts. The jeering ended gradually, put down by the recognition of their common humanity. One woman spat on her, but some inviolable grandeur in her nakedness lasted through the ordeal. When the crowd was quiet, she turned—she had begun to cry—and, with nothing on but a pair of worn black shoes and stockings, walked down the dirt road alone away from the village. The round white face had aged a little, but there was no question but that the maid who passed his cocktails and later served Francis his dinner was the woman who had been punished at the crossroads.

The war seemed now so distant and that world where the cost of partisanship had been death or torture so long ago. Francis had lost track of the men who had been with him in Vesey. He could not count on Julia's discretion. He could not tell anyone. And if he had told the story now, at the dinner table, it would have been a social as well as a human error. The people in the Farquarsons' living room seemed united in their tacit claim that there had been no past, no war—that there was no danger or trouble in the world. In the recorded history of human arrangements, this extraordinary meeting would have fallen into place, but the atmosphere of Shady Hill made the memory unseemly and impolite. The prisoner withdrew after passing the coffee, but the encounter left Francis feeling languid; it had opened his memory and his senses, and left them dilated. He and Julia drove home when the party ended, and Julia went into the house. Francis stayed in the car to take the sitter home.

Expecting to see Mrs. Henlein, the old lady who usually stayed with the children, he was surprised when a young girl opened the door and came out onto the lighted stoop. She stayed in the light to count her textbooks. She was frowning and beautiful. Now, the world is full of beautiful young girls, but Francis saw here the difference between beauty and perfection. All those endearing flaws, moles, birthmarks, and healed wounds were missing, and he experienced in his consciousness that moment when music breaks glass, and felt a pang of recognition as strange, deep, and wonderful as anything in his life. It hung from her frown, from an impalpable darkness in her face—a look that impressed him as a direct appeal for love. When she had counted her books, she came down the steps and opened the car door. In the light, he saw that her cheeks were wet. She got in and shut the door.

"You're new," Francis said.

"Yes. Mrs. Henlein is sick. I'm Anne Murchison."

"Did the children give you any trouble?"

"Oh, no, no." She turned and smiled at him unhappily in the dim dashboard light. Her light hair caught on the collar of her jacket, and she shook her head to set it loose.

"You've been crying."

"Yes."

"I hope it was nothing that happened in our house."

"No, no, it was nothing that happened in your house." Her voice was bleak. "It's no secret. Everybody in the village knows. Daddy's an alcoholic, and he just called me from some saloon and gave me a piece of his mind. He thinks I'm immoral. He called just before Mrs. Weed came back."

"I'm sorry."

"Oh, *Lord!*" She gasped and began to cry. She turned toward Francis, and he took her in his arms and let her cry on his shoulder. She shook in his embrace, and this movement accentuated his sense of the fineness of her flesh and bone. The layers of their clothing felt thin, and when her shuddering began to diminish, it was so much like a paroxysm of love that Francis lost his head and pulled her roughly against him. She drew away. "I live on Belleview Avenue," she said. "You go down Lansing Street to the railroad bridge."

"All right." He started the car.

"You turn left at that traffic light. . . . Now you turn right here and go straight on toward the tracks."

The road Francis took brought him out of his own neighborhood, across the tracks, and toward the river, to a street where the near-poor lived, in houses whose peaked gables and trimmings of wooden lace conveyed the purest feelings of pride and romance, although the houses themselves could not have offered much privacy or comfort, they were all so small. The street was dark, and, stirred by the grace and beauty of the troubled girl, he seemed, in turning in to it, to have come into the deepest part of some submerged memory. In the distance, he saw a porch light burning. It was the only one, and she said that the house with the light was where she lived. When he stopped the car, he could see beyond the porch light into a dimly-lighted hallway with an old-fashioned clothes tree. "Well, here we are," he said, conscious that a young man would have said something different.

She did not move her hands from the books, where they were folded, and she turned and faced him. There were tears of lust in his eyes. Determinedly—not sadly—he opened the door on his side and walked around to open hers. He took her free hand, letting his fingers in between hers, climbed at her side the two concrete steps, and went up a narrow walk through a front garden where dahlias, marigolds, and roses—things that had withstood the light frosts—still bloomed, and made a bittersweet smell in the night air. At the steps, she freed her hand and then turned and kissed him swiftly. Then she crossed the porch and shut the door. The porch light went out, then the light in the hall. A second later, a light went on upstairs at the side of the house, shining into a tree that was still covered with leaves. It took her only a few minutes to undress and get into bed, and then the house was dark.

Julia was asleep when Francis got home. He opened a second window and got into bed to shut his eyes on that night, but as soon as they were shut—as soon as he had dropped off to sleep—the girl entered his mind, moving with perfect freedom through its shut doors and filling chamber after chamber with her light, her perfume, and the music of her voice. He was crossing the Atlantic with her on the old Mauretania and, later, living with her in Paris. When he woke from this dream, he got up and smoked a cigarette at the open window. Getting back into bed, he cast around in his mind for something he desired to do that would injure no one, and he thought of skiing. Up through the dimness in his mind rose the image of a mountain deep in snow. It was late in the day. Wherever his eyes looked, he saw broad and heartening things. Over his shoulder, there was a snow-filled valley, rising into wooded hills where the trees dimmed the whiteness like a sparse coat of hair. The cold deadened all sound but the loud, iron clanking of the lift machinery. The light on the trails was blue, and it was harder than it had been a minute or two earlier to pick the turns, harder to judge—now that the snow was all deep blue—the crust, the ice, the bare spots, and the deep piles of dry powder. Down the mountain he swung, matching his speed against the contours of a slope that had been formed in the first ice age, seeking with ardor some simplicity of feeling and circumstance. Night fell then, and he drank a Martini with some old friend in a dirty country bar.

In the morning, Francis's snow-covered mountain was gone, and he was left with his vivid memories of Paris and the Mauretania. He had been bitten gravely. He washed his body, shaved his jaws, drank his coffee, and missed the seven-thirty-one. The train pulled out just as he brought his car to the station, and the longing he felt for the coaches as they drew stubbornly away from him reminded him of the humors of love. He waited for the eight-two, on what was now an empty platform. It was a clear morning; the morning seemed thrown like a gleaming bridge of light over his mixed affairs. His spirits were feverish and high. The image of the girl seemed to put him into a relationship to the world that was mysterious and enthralling. Cars were beginning to fill up the parking lot, and he noticed that those that had driven down from the high land above Shady Hill were white with hoarfrost. This first clear sign of autumn thrilled him. An express train—a night train from Buffalo or Albany—came down the tracks between the platforms, and he saw that the roofs of the foremost cars were covered with a skin of ice. Struck by the miraculous physicalness of everything, he smiled at the passengers in the dining car, who could be seen eating eggs and wiping their mouths with napkins as they travelled. The sleeping-car compartments, with their soiled bed linen, trailed through the fresh morning like a string of rooming-house windows. Then he saw an extraordinary thing; at one of the bedroom windows sat an unclothed woman of exceptional beauty, combing her golden hair. She passed like an apparition through Shady Hill, combing and combing her hair, and Francis followed her with his eyes until she was out of sight. Then old Mrs. Wrightson joined him on the platform and began to talk.

"Well, I guess you must be surprised to see me here the third morning in a row," she said, "but because of my window curtains I'm becoming a regular commuter. The curtains I bought on Monday I returned on Tuesday, and the curtains I bought Tuesday I'm returning today. On Monday, I got exactly what I wanted—it's a wool tapestry with roses and birds—but when I got them home, I found they were the wrong length. Well, I exchanged them yesterday, and when I got them home, I found they were still the wrong length. Now I'm praying to high Heaven that the decorator will have them in the right length, because you know my house, you *know* my living-room windows, and you can imagine what a problem they present. I don't know what to do with them."

"I know what to do with them," Francis said.

"What?"

"Paint them black on the inside, and shut up."

There was a gasp from Mrs. Wrightson, and Francis looked down at her to be sure that she knew he meant to be rude. She turned and walked away from him, so damaged in spirit that she limped. A wonderful feeling enveloped him, as if light were being shaken about him, and he thought again of Venus combing and combing her hair as she drifted through the Bronx. The realization of how many years had passed since he had enjoyed being deliberately impolite sobered him. Among his friends and neighbors, there were brilliant and gifted people—he saw that—but many of them, also, were bores and fools, and he had made the mistake of listening to them all with equal attention. He had confused a lack of discrimination with Christian love, and the confusion seemed general and destructive. He was grateful to the girl for this bracing sensation of independence. Birds were singing—cardinals and the last of the robins. The sky shone like enamel. Even the smell of ink from his morning paper honed his appetite for life, and the world that was spread out around him was plainly a paradise.

If Francis had believed in some hierarchy of love—in spirits armed with hunting bows, in the capriciousness of Venus and Eros—or even in magical potions, philtres, and stews, in scapulae and quarters of the moon, it might have explained his susceptibility and his feverish high spirits. The autumnal loves of middle age are well publicized, and he guessed that he was face to face with one of these, but there was not a trace of autumn in what he felt. He wanted to sport in the green woods, scratch where he itched, and drink from the same cup.

His secretary, Miss Rainery, was late that morning—she went to a psychiatrist three mornings a week—and when she came in, Francis wondered what advice a psychiatrist would have for him. But the girl promised to bring back into his life something like the sound of music. The realization that this music might lead him straight to a trial for statutory rape at the county courthouse collapsed his happiness. The photograph of his four children laughing into the camera on the beach at Gay Head reproached him. On the letterhead of his firm there was a drawing of the Laocoon, and the figure of the priest and his sons in the coils of the snake appeared to him to have the deepest meaning.

He had lunch with Pinky Trabert, who told him a couple of dirty stories. At the conversational level, the mores of his friends were robust and elastic, but he knew that the moral card house would come down on them all—on Julia and the children as well—if he got caught taking advantage of a babysitter. Looking back over the recent history of Shady Hill for some precedent, he found there was none. There was no turpitude; there had not been a divorce since he lived there; there had not even been a breath of scandal. Things seemed arranged with more propriety even than in the Kingdom of Heaven. After leaving Pinky, Francis went to a jeweller's and bought the girl a bracelet. How happy this clandestine purchase made him, how stuffy and comical the jeweller's clerks seemed, how sweet the women who passed at his back smelled! On Fifth Avenue, passing Atlas with his shoulders bent under the weight of the world, Francis thought of the strenuousness of containing his physicalness within the patterns he had chosen.

He did not know when he would see the girl next. He had the bracelet in his inside pocket when he got home. Opening the door of his house, he found her in the hall. Her back was to him, and she turned when she heard the door close. Her smile was open and loving. Her perfection stunned him like a fine day—a day after a thunderstorm. He seized her and covered her lips with his, and she struggled but she did not have to struggle for long, because just then little Gertrude Flannery appeared from somewhere and said, "Oh, Mr. Weed . . ."

Gertrude was a stray. She had been born with a taste for exploration, and she did not have it in her to center her life with her affectionate parents. People who did not know the Flannerys concluded from Gertrude's behavior that she was the child of a bitterly divided family, where drunken quarrels were the rule. This was not true. The fact that little Gertrude's clothing was ragged and thin was her own triumph over her mother's struggle to dress her warmly and neatly. Garrulous, skinny, and unwashed, she drifted from house to house around the Blenhollow neighborhood, forming and breaking alliances based on an attachment to babies, animals, children her own age, adolescents, and sometimes adults. Opening your front door in the morning, you would find Gertrude sitting on your stoop. Going into the bathroom to shave, you would find Gertrude using the toilet. Looking into your son's crib, you would find it empty, and, looking further, you would find that Gertrude had pushed him in his baby carriage into the next village. She was helpful, pervasive, honest, hungry, and loyal. She never went home of her own choice. When the time to go arrived, she was indifferent to all its signs. "Go home, Gertrude," people could be heard saying in one house or another, night after night. "Go home, Gertrude." "It's time for you to go home now, Gertrude." "You had better go home and get your supper, Gertrude." "I told you to go home twenty minutes ago, Gertrude." "Your mother will be worrying about you, Gertrude." "Go home, Gertrude, go home."

There are times when the lines around the human eye seem like shelves of eroded stone and when the staring eye itself strikes us with such a wilderness of animal feeling that we are at a loss. The look Francis gave the little girl was ugly and queer, and it frightened her. He reached into his pocket—his hands were shaking—and took out a quarter. "Go home, Gertrude, go home, and don't tell anyone, Gertrude. Don't—" He choked and ran into the living room as Julia called down to him from upstairs to hurry and dress.

The thought that he would drive Anne Murchison home later that night ran like a golden thread through the events of the party that Francis and Julia went to, and he laughed uproariously at dull jokes, dried a tear when Mabel Mercer told him about the death of her kitten, and stretched, yawned, sighed, and grunted like any other man with a rendezvous at the back of his mind. The bracelet was in his pocket. As he sat talking, the smell of grass was in his nose, and he was wondering where he would park the car. Nobody lived in the old Parker mansion, and the driveway was used as a lovers' lane. Townsend Street was a dead end, and he could park there, beyond the last house. The old lane that used to connect Elm Street to the riverbanks was overgrown, but he had walked there with his children, and he could drive his car deep enough into the brushwoods to be concealed.

The Weeds were the last to leave the party, and their host and hostess spoke of their own married happiness while they all four stood in the hallway saying good night. "She's my girl," their host said, squeezing his wife. "She's my blue sky. After sixteen years, I still bite her shoulders. She makes me feel like Hannibal crossing the Alps."

The Weeds drove home in silence. Francis brought the car up the driveway and sat still, with the motor running. "You can put the car in the garage," Julia said as she got out. "I told the Murchison girl she could leave at eleven. Someone drove her home." She shut the door, and Francis sat in the dark. He would be spared nothing then, it seemed, that a fool was not spared: ravening lewdness, jealousy, this hurt to his feelings that put tears in his eyes, even scorn—for he could see clearly the image he now presented, his arms spread over the steering wheel and his head buried in them for love.

Francis had been a dedicated Boy Scout when he was young, and, remembering the precepts of his youth, he left his office early the next afternoon and played some round-robin squash, but, with his body toned up by exercise and a shower, he realized that he might better have stayed at his desk. It was a frosty night when he got home. The air smelled sharply of change. When he stepped into the house, he sensed an unusual stir. The children were in their best clothes, and when Julia came down, she was wearing a lavender dress and her diamond sunburst. She explained the stir: Mr. Hubber was coming at seven to take their photograph for the Christmas card. She had put out Francis' blue suit and a tie with some color in it, because the picture was going to be in color this year. Julia was lighthearted at the thought of being photographed for Christmas. It was the kind of ceremony she enjoyed.

Francis went upstairs to change his clothes. He was tired from the day's work and tired with longing, and sitting on the edge of the bed had the effect of deepening his weariness. He thought of Anne Murchison, and the physical need to express himself, instead of being restrained by the pink lamps on Julia's dressing table, engulfed him. He went to Julia's desk, took a piece of writing paper, and began to write on it. "Dear Anne, I love you, I love you, I love you . . ." No one would see the letter, and he used no restraint. He used phrases like "heavenly bliss," and "love nest." He salivated, sighed, and trembled. When Julia called him to come down, the abyss between his fantasy and the practical world opened so wide that he felt it affect the muscles of his heart.

Julia and the children were on the stoop, and the photographer and his assistant had set up a double battery of floodlights to show the family and the architectural beauty of the entrance to their house. People who had come home on a late train slowed their cars to see the Weeds being photographed for their Christmas card. A few waved and called to the family. It took half an hour of smiling and wetting their lips before Mr. Hubber was satisfied. The heat of the lights made an unfresh smell in the frosty air, and when they were turned off, they lingered on the retina of Francis' eyes.

Later that night, while Francis and Julia were drinking their coffee in the living room, the doorbell rang. Julia answered the door and let in Clayton Thomas. He had come to pay her for some theatre tickets that she had given his mother some time ago, and that Helen Thomas had scrupulously insisted on paying for though Julia had asked her not to. Julia invited him in to have a cup of coffee. "I won't have any coffee," Clayton said, "but I will come in for a minute." He followed her into the living room, said good evening to Francis, and sat awkwardly in a chair.

Clayton's father had been killed in the war, and the young man's fatherlessness surrounded him like an element. This may have been conspicuous in Shady Hill because the Thomases were the only family that lacked a piece; all the other marriages were intact and productive. Clayton was in his second or third year of college, and he and his mother lived alone in a large house, which she hoped to sell. Clayton had once made some trouble. Years ago, he had stolen some money and run away; he had got to California before they caught up with him. He was tall and homely, wore horn-rimmed glasses, and spoke in a deep voice.

"When do you go back to college, Clayton?" Francis asked.

"I'm not going back," Clayton said. "Mother doesn't have the money, and there's no sense in all this pretense. I'm going to get a job, and if we sell the house, we'll take an apartment in New York."

"Won't you miss Shady Hill?" Julia asked.

"No," Clayton said. "I don't like it."

"Why not?" Francis asked.

"Well, there's a lot here I don't approve of," Clayton said gravely. "Things like the club dances. Last Saturday night, I looked in toward the end and saw Mr. Granner trying to put Mrs. Minot into the trophy case. They were both drunk. I disapprove of so much drinking."

"It was Saturday night," Francis said.

"And all the dovecotes are phony," Clayton said. "And the way people clutter up their lives. I've thought about it a lot, and what seems to me to be really wrong with Shady Hill is that it doesn't have any future. So much energy is spent in perpetuating the place—in keeping out undesirables, and so forth—that the only idea of the future anyone has is just more and more commuting trains and more parties. I don't think that's healthy. I think people ought to be able to dream big dreams about the future. I think people ought to be able to dream great dreams."

"It's too bad you couldn't continue with college," Julia said.

"I wanted to go to divinity school," Clayton said.

"What's your church?" Francis asked.

"Unitarian, Theosophist, Transcendentalist, Humanist," Clayton said.

"Wasn't Emerson a transcendentalist?" Julia asked.

"I mean the English transcendentalists," Clayton said. "All the American transcendentalists were goops."

"What kind of a job do you expect to get?" Francis asked.

"Well, I'd like to work for a publisher," Clayton said, "but everyone tells me there is nothing doing. But it's the kind of thing I'm interested in. I'm writing a long verse play about good and evil. Uncle Charlie might get me into a bank, and that would be good for me. I need the discipline. I have a long way to go in forming my character. I have some terrible habits. I talk too much. I think I ought to take vows of silence. I ought to try not to speak for a week, and discipline myself. I've thought of making a retreat at one of the Episcopalian monasteries, but I don't like Trinitarianism."

"Do you have any girl friends?" Francis asked.

"I'm engaged to be married," Clayton said. "Of course, I'm not old enough or rich enough to have my engagement observed or respected or anything, but I bought a simulated emerald for Anne Murchison with the money I made cutting lawns this summer. We're going to be married as soon as she finishes school."

Francis recoiled at the mention of the girl's name. Then a dingy light seemed to emanate from his spirit, showing everything—Julia, the boy, the chairs—in their true colorlessness. It was like a bitter turn of the weather.

"We're going to have a large family," Clayton said. "Her father's a terrible rummy, and I've had my hard times, and we want to have lots of children. Oh, she's wonderful, Mr. and Mrs. Weed, and we have so much in common. We like all the same things. We sent out the same Christmas card last year without planning it, and we both have an allergy to tomatoes, and our eyebrows grow together in the middle. Well, good night."

Julia went to the door with him. When she returned, Francis said that Clayton was lazy, irresponsible, affected, and smelly. Julia said that Francis seemed to be getting intolerant; the Thomas boy was young and should be given a chance. Julia had noticed other cases where Francis had been short-tempered. "Mrs. Wrightson has asked everyone in Shady Hill to her anniversay party but us," she said.

"I'm sorry, Julia."

"Do you know why they didn't ask us?"

"Why?"

"Because you insulted Mrs. Wrightson."

"Then you know about it?"

"June Masterson told me. She was standing behind you."

Julia walked in front of the sofa with a small step that expressed, Francis knew, a feeling of anger.

"I did insult Mrs. Wrightson, Julia, and I meant to. I've never liked her parties, and I'm glad she's dropped us."

"What about Helen?"

'How does Helen come into this?"

"Mrs. Wrightson's the one who decides who goes to the assemblies."

"You mean she can keep Helen from going to the dances?"

"Yes."

"I hadn't thought of that."

"Oh, I knew you hadn't thought of it," Julia cried, thrusting hilt-deep into this chink of his armor. "And it makes me furious to see this kind of stupid thoughtlessness wreck everyone's happiness."

"I don't think I've wrecked anyone's happiness."

"Mrs. Wrightson runs Shady Hill and has run it for the last forty years. I don't know what makes you think that in a community like this you can indulge every impulse you have to be insulting, vulgar, and offensive."

"I have very good manners," Francis said, trying to give the evening a turn toward the light.

"Damn you, Francis Weed!" Julia cried, and the spit of her words struck him in the face. "I've worked hard for the social position we enjoy in this place, and I won't stand by and see you wreck it. You must have understood when you settled here that you couldn't expect to live like a bear in a cave."

"I've got to express my likes and dislikes."

"You can conceal your dislikes. You don't have to meet everything head-on, like a child. Unless you're anxious to be a social leper. It's no accident that we get asked out a great deal. It's no accident that Helen has so many friends. How would you like to spend your Saturday nights at the movies? How would you like to spend your Sundays raking up dead leaves? How would you like it if your daughter spent the assembly nights sitting at her window, listening to the music from the club? How would you like it—" He did something then that was, after all, not so unaccountable, since her words seemed to raise up between them a wall so deadening that he gagged: He struck her full in the face. She staggered and then, a moment later, seemed composed. She went up the stairs to their room. She didn't slam the door. When Francis followed, a few minutes later, he found her packing a suitcase.

"Julia, I'm very sorry."

"It doesn't matter," she said. She was crying.

"Where do you think you're going?"

"I don't know. I just looked at a timetable. There's an eleven-sixteen into New York. I'll take that."

"You can't go, Julia."

"I can't stay. I know that."

"I'm sorry about Mrs. Wrightson, Julia, and I'm—"

"It doesn't matter about Mrs. Wrightson. That isn't the trouble."

"What is the trouble?"

"You don't love me."

"I do love you, Julia."

"No, you don't."

"Julia, I do love you, and I would like to be as we were—sweet and bawdy and dark—but now there are so many people."

"You hate me."

"I don't hate you, Julia."

"You have no idea of how much you hate me. I think it's subconscious. You don't realize the cruel things you've done."

"What cruel things, Julia?"

"The cruel acts your subconscious drives you to in order to express your hatred of me."

"What, Julia?"

"I've never complained."

"Tell me."

"You don't know what you're doing."

"Tell me."

"Your clothes."

"What do you mean?"

"I mean the way you leave your dirty clothes around in order to express your subconscious hatred of me."

"I don't understand."

"I mean your dirty socks and your dirty pajamas and your dirty underwear and your dirty shirts!" She rose from kneeling by the suitcase and faced him, her eyes blazing and her voice ringing with emotion. "I'm talking about the fact that you've never learned to hang up anything. You just leave your clothes all over the floor where they drop, in order to humiliate me. You do it on purpose!" She fell on the bed, sobbing.

"Julia, darling!" he said, but when she felt his hand on her shoulder she got up.

"Leave me alone," she said. "I have to go." She brushed past him to the closet and came back with a dress. "I'm not taking any of the things you've given me," she said. "I'm leaving my pearls and the fur jacket."

"Oh, Julia!" Her figure, so helpless in its self-deceptions, bent over the suitcase made him nearly sick with pity. She did not understand how desolate her life would be without him. She didn't understand the hours that working women have to keep. She didn't understand that most of her friendships existed within the framework of their marriage, and that without this she would find herself alone. She didn't understand about travel, about hotels, about money. "Julia, I can't let you go! What you don't understand, Julia, is that you've come to be dependent on me."

She tossed her head back and covered her face with her hands. "Did you say that *I* was dependent on *you?*" she asked. "Is that what you said? And who is it that tells you what time to get up in the morning and when to go to bed at night? Who is it that prepares your meals and picks up your dirty closet and invites your friends to dinner? If it weren't for me, your neckties would be greasy and your clothing would be full of moth holes. You were alone when I met you, Francis Weed, and you'll be alone when I leave. When Mother asked you for a list to send out invitations to our wedding, how many names did you have to give her? Fourteen!"

"Cleveland wasn't my home, Julia."

"And how many of your friends came to the church? Two!"

"Cleveland wasn't my home, Julia."

"Since I'm not taking the fur jacket," she said quietly, "you'd better put it back into storage. There's an insurance policy on the pearls that comes due in January. The name of the laundry and the maid's telephone number—all those things are in my desk. I hope you won't drink too much, Francis. I hope that nothing bad will happen to you. If you do get into serious trouble, you can call me."

"Oh my darling, I can't let you go!" Francis said, "I can't let you go, Julia!" He took her in his arms.

"I guess I'd better stay and take care of you for a little while longer," she said.

Riding to work in the morning, Francis saw the girl walk down the aisle of the coach. He was surprised; he hadn't realized that the school she went to was in the city, but she was carrying books, she seemed to be going to school. His surprise delayed his reaction, but then he got up clumsily and stepped into the aisle. Several people had come between them, but he could see her ahead of him, waiting for someone to open the car door, and then, as the train swerved, putting out her hand to support herself as she crossed the platform into the next car. He followed her through that car and halfway through another before calling her name—"Anne! Anne!"—but she didn't turn. He followed her into still another car, and she sat down in an aisle seat. Coming up to her, all his feelings warm and bent in her direction, he put his hand on the back of her seat—even this touch warmed him—and, leaning down to speak to her, he saw that it was not Anne. It was an older woman wearing glasses. He went on deliberately into another car, his face red with embarrassment and the much deeper feeling of having his good sense challenged; for if he couldn't tell one person from another, what evidence was there that his life with Julia and the children had as much reality as his dreams of iniquity in Paris or the litter, the grass smell, and the cave-shaped trees in Lovers' Lane.

Late that afternoon, Julia called to remind Francis that they were going out for dinner. A few minutes later, Trace Bearden called. "Look, fellar," Trace said. "I'm calling for Mrs. Thomas. You know? Clayton, that boy of hers, doesn't seem able to get a job, and I wondered if you could help. If you'd call Charlie Bell—I know he's indebted to you—and say a good word for the kid, I think Charlie would—"

"Trace, I hate to say this," Francis said, "but I don't feel that I can do anything for that boy. The kid's worthless. I know it's a harsh thing to say, but it's a fact. Any kindness done for him would backfire in everybody's face. He's just a worthless kid, Trace, and there's nothing to be done about it. Even if we got him a job, he wouldn't be able to keep it for a week. I know that to be a fact. It's an awful thing, Trace, and I know it is, but instead of recommending that kid, I'd feel obliged to warn people against him—people who knew his father and would naturally want to step in and do something. I'd feel obliged to warn them. He's a thief . . ."

The moment this conversation was finished, Miss Rainey came in and stood by his desk. "I'm not going to be able to work for you any more, Mr. Weed," she said. "I can stay until the seventeenth if you need me, but I've been offered a whirlwind of a job, and I'd like to leave as soon as possible."

She went out, leaving him to face alone the wickedness of what he had done to the Thomas boy. His children in their photograph laughed and laughed, glazed with all the bright colors of summer, and he remembered that they had met a bagpiper on the beach that day and he had paid the piper a dollar to play them a battle song of the Black Watch. The girls would be at the house when he got home. He would spend another evening among his kind neighbors, picking and choosing dead-end streets, cart tracks, and the driveways of abandoned houses. There was nothing to mitigate his feeling—nothing that laughter or a game of softball with the children would change—and, thinking back over the plane crash, the Farquarsons' new maid, and Anne Murchison's difficulties with her drunken father, he wondered how he could have avoided arriving at just where he was. He was in trouble. He had been lost once in his life, coming back from a trout stream in the north woods, and he had now the same bleak realization that no amount of cheerfulness or hopefulness or valor or perseverance could help him find, in the gathering dark, the path that he'd lost. He smelled the forest. The feeling of bleakness was intolerable, and he saw clearly that he had reached the point where he would have to make a choice.

He could go to a psychiatrist, like Miss Rainey; he could go to church and confess his lusts; he could go to a Danish massage parlor in the West Seventies that had been recommended by a salesman; he could rape the girl or trust that he would somehow be prevented from doing this; or he could get drunk. It was his life, his boat, and, like every other man, he was made to be the father of thousands, and what harm could there be in a tryst that would make them both feel more kindly toward the world? This was the wrong train of thought, and he came back to the first, the psychiatrist. He had the telephone number of Miss Rainey's doctor, and he called and asked for an immediate appointment. He was insistent with the doctor's secretary—it was his manner in business—and when she said that the doctor's schedule was full for the next few weeks, Francis demanded an appointment that day and was told to come at five.

The psychiatrist's office was in a building that was used mostly by doctors and dentists, and the hallways were filled with the candy smell of mouthwash and memories of pain. Francis' character had been formed upon a series of private resolves—resolves about cleanliness, about going off the high diving board or repeating any other feat that challenged his courage, about punctuality, honesty, and virtue. To abdicate the perfect loneliness in which he had made his most vital decisions shattered his concept of character and left him now in a condition that felt like shock. He was stupefied. The scene for his *miserere mei Deus* was, like the waiting room of so many doctors' offices, a crude token gesture toward the sweets of domestic bliss: a place arranged with antiques, coffee tables, potted plants, and etchings of snow-covered bridges and geese in flight, although there were no children, no marriage bed, no stove, even, in this travesty of a house, where no one had ever spent the night and where the curtained windows looked straight onto a dark air shaft. Francis gave his name and address to a secretary and then saw, at the side of the room, a policeman moving toward him. "Hold it, hold it," the policeman said. "Don't move. Keep your hands where they are."

"I think it's all right, Officer," the secretary began. "I think it will be—"

"Let's make sure," the policeman said, and he began to slap Francis' clothes, looking for what—pistols, knives, an icepick? Finding nothing, he went off, and the secretary began a nervous apology: "When you called on the telephone, Mr. Weed, you seemed very excited, and one of the doctor's patients has been threatening his life, and we have to be careful. If you want to go in now?" Francis pushed open a door connected to an electrical chime, and in the doctor's lair sat down heavily, blew his nose into a handkerchief, searched in his pockets for cigarettes, for matches, for something, and said hoarsely, with tears in his eyes, "I'm in love, Dr. Herzog."

It is a week or ten days later in Shady Hill. The seven-fourteen has come and gone, and here and there dinner is finished and the dishes are in the dishwashing machine. The village hangs, morally and economically, from a thread; but it hangs by its thread in the evening light. Donald Goslin has begun to worry the "Moonlight Sonata" again. *Marcato ma sempre pianissimo!* He seems to be wringing out a wet bath towel, but the housemaid does not heed him. She is writing a letter to Arthur Godfrey. In the cellar of his house, Francis Weed is building a coffee table. Dr. Herzog recommended woodwork as a therapy, and Francis finds some true consolation in the simple arithmetic involved and in the holy smell of new wood. Francis is happy. Upstairs, little Toby is crying, because he is tired. He puts off his cowboy hat, gloves, and fringed jacket, unbuckles the belt studded with gold and rubies, the silver bullets and holsters, slips off his suspenders, his checked shirt, and Levis, and sits on the edge of his bed to pull off his high boots. Leaving this equipment in a heap, he goes to the closet and takes his space suit off a nail. It is a struggle for him to get into the long tights, but he succeeds. He loops the magic cape over his shoulders and, climbing onto the footboard of his bed, he spreads his arms and flies the short distance to the floor, landing with a thump that is audible to everyone in the house but himself.

"Go home, Gertrude, go home," Mrs. Masterson says. "I told you to go home an hour ago, Gertrude. It's way past your suppertime, and your mother will be worried. Go home!" A door on the Babcocks' terrace flies open, and out comes Mrs. Babcock without any clothes on, pursued by her naked husband. (Their children are away at boarding school, and their terrace is screened by a hedge.) Over the terrace they go and in at the kitchen door, as passionate and handsome a nymph and satyr as you will find on any wall in Venice. Cutting the last of the roses in her garden, Julia hears old Mr. Nixon shouting at the squirrels in his bird-feeding station. "Rapscallions! Varmits! Avaunt and quit my sight!" A miserable cat wanders into the garden, sunk in spiritual and physical discomfort. Tied to its head is a small straw hat—a doll's hat—and it is securely buttoned into a doll's dress, from the skirts of which protrudes its long, hairy tail. As it walks, it shakes its feet, as if it had fallen into water.

"Here, pussy, pussy, pussy!" Julia calls.

"Here, pussy, here, poor pussy!" But the cat gives her a skeptical look and stumbles away in its skirts. The last to come is Jupiter. He prances through the tomato vines, holding in his generous mouth the remains of an evening slipper. Then it is dark; it is a night where kings in golden suits ride elephants over the mountains.

BERNARD MALAMUD

The Prison

Though he tried not to think of it, at twenty-nine Tommy Castelli's life was a screaming bore. It wasn't just Rosa or the store they tended for profits counted in pennies, or the unendurably slow hours and endless drivel that went with selling candy, cigarettes, and soda water; it was this sick-in-the-stomach feeling of being trapped in old mistakes, even some he had made before Rosa changed Tony into Tommy. He had been as Tony a kid of many dreams and schemes, especially getting out of this tenement-crowded, kid-squawking neighborhood, with its lousy poverty, but everything had fouled up against him before he could. When he was sixteen he quit the vocational school where they were making him into a shoemaker, and began to hang out with the gray-hatted, thick-soled-shoe boys, who had the spare time and the mazuma and showed it in fat wonderful rolls down in the cellar clubs to all who would look, and everybody did, popeyed. They were the ones who had bought the silver caffe espresso urn and later the television, and they arranged the pizza parties and had the girls down; but it was getting in with them and their cars, leading to the holdup of a liquor store, that had started all the present trouble. Lucky for him the coal-and-ice man who was their landlord knew the leader in the district, and they arranged something so nobody bothered him after that. Then before he knew what was going on—he had been frightened sick by the whole mess—there was his father cooking up a deal with Rosa Agnello's old man that Tony would marry her and the father-in-law would, out of his savings, open a candy store for him to make an honest living. He wouldn't spit on a candy store, and Rosa was too plain and lank a chick for his personal taste, so he beat it off to Texas and bummed around in too much space, and when he came back everybody said it was for Rosa and the candy store, and it was all arranged again and he, without saying no, was in it.

That was how he had landed on Prince Street in the Village, working from eight in the morning to almost midnight every day, except for an hour off each afternoon when he went upstairs to sleep, and on Tuesdays, when the store was closed and he slept some more and went at night alone to the movies. He was too tired always for schemes now, but once he tried to make a little cash on the side by secretly taking in punchboards some syndicate was distributing in the neighborhood, on which he collected a nice cut and in this way saved fifty-five bucks that Rosa didn't know about; but then the syndicate was written up by a newspaper, and the punchboards all disappeared. Another time, when Rosa was at her mother's house, he took a chance and let them put in a slot machine that could guarantee a nice piece of change if he kept it long enough. He knew of course he couldn't hide it from her, so when she came and screamed when she saw it, he was ready and patient, for once not yelling back when she yelled, and he explained it was not the same as gambling because anybody who played it got a roll of mints every time he put in a nickel. Also the machine would supply them a few extra dollars cash they could use to buy television so he could see the fights without going to a bar; but Rosa wouldn't let up screaming, and later her father came in shouting that he was a criminal and chopped the machine apart with a plumber's hammer. The next day the cops raided for slot machines and gave out summonses wherever they found them, and though Tommy's place was practically the only candy store in the neighborhood that didn't have one, he felt bad about the machine for a long time.

Mornings had been his best time of day because Rosa stayed upstairs cleaning, and since few people came into the store till noon, he could sit around alone, a toothpick in his teeth, looking over the *News* and *Mirror* on the fountain counter, or maybe gab with one of the old cellar-club guys who had happened to come by for a pack of butts, about a horse that was running that day or how the numbers were paying lately; or just sit there, drinking coffee and thinking how far away he could get on the fifty-five he had stashed away in the cellar. Generally the mornings were this way, but after the slot machine, usually the whole day stank and he along with it. Time rotted in him, and all he could think of the whole morning, was going to sleep in the afternoon, and he would wake up with the sour remembrance of the long night in the store ahead of him, while everybody else was doing as he damn pleased. He cursed the candy store and Rosa, and cursed, from its beginning, his unhappy life.

It was on one of these bad mornings that a ten-year-old girl from around the block came in and asked for two rolls of colored tissue paper, one red and one yellow. He wanted to tell her to go to hell and stop bothering, but instead went with bad grace to the rear, where Rosa, whose bright idea it was to keep the stuff, had put it. He went from force of habit, for the girl had been coming in every Monday since the summer for the same thing, because her rock-faced mother, who looked as if she arranged her own widowhood, took care of some small kids after school and gave them the paper to cut out dolls and such things. The girls, whose name he didn't know, resembled her mother, except her features were not quite so sharp and she had very light skin with dark eyes; but she was a plain kid and would be more so at twenty. He had noticed, when he went to get the paper, that she always hung back as if afraid to go where it was dark, though he kept the comics there and most of the other kids had to be slapped away from them; and that when he brought her the tissue paper her skin seemed to grow whiter and her eyes shone. She always handed him two hot dimes and went out without glancing back.

It happened that Rosa, who trusted nobody, had just hung a mirror on the back wall, and as Tommy opened the drawer to get the girl her paper this Monday morning that he felt so bad, he looked up and saw in the glass something that made it seem as if he were dreaming. The girl had disappeared, but he saw a white hand reach into the candy case for a chocolate bar and for another, then she came forth from behind the counter and stood there, innocently waiting for him. He felt at first like grabbing her by the neck and socking till she threw up, but he had been caught, as he sometimes was, by his thought of how his Uncle Dom, years ago before he went away, used to take with him Tony alone of all the kids, when he went crabbing to Sheepshead Bay. Once they went at night and threw the baited wire traps into the water and after a while pulled them up and they had this green lobster in one, and just then this fat-faced cop came along and said they had to throw it back unless it was nine inches. Dom said it was nine inches, but the cop said not to be a wise guy so Dom measured it and it was ten, and they laughed about that lobster all night. Then he remembered how he had felt after Dom was gone, and tears filled his eyes. He found himself thinking about the way his life had turned out, and then about this girl, moved that she was so young and a thief. He felt he ought to do something for her, warn her to cut it out before she got trapped and fouled up her life before it got started. His urge to do this was strong, but when he went forward she looked up frightened because he had taken so long. The fear in her eyes bothered him and he didn't say anything. She thrust out the dimes, grabbed at the tissue rolls and ran out of the store.

He had to sit down. He kept trying to make the desire to speak to her go away, but it came back stronger than ever. He asked himself what difference does it make if she swipes candy—so she swipes it; and the role of reformer was strange and distasteful to him, yet he could not convince himself that what he felt he must do was unimportant. But he worried he would not know what to say to her. Always he had trouble speaking right, stumbled over words, especially in new situations. He was afraid he would sound like a jerk and she would not take him seriously. He had to tell her in a sure way so that even if it scared her, she would understand he had done it to set her straight. He mentioned her to no one but often thought about her, always looking around whenever he went outside to raise the awning or wash the window, to see if any of the girls playing in the street was her, but they never were. The following Monday, an hour after opening the store he had smoked a full pack of butts. He thought he had found what he wanted to say but was afraid for some reason she wouldn't come in, or if she did, this time she would be afraid to take the candy. He wasn't sure he wanted that to happen until he had said what he had to say. But at about eleven, while he was reading the *News,* she appeared, asking for the tissue paper, her eyes shining so he had to look away. He knew she meant to steal. Going to the rear he slowly opened the drawer, keeping his head lowered as he sneaked a look into the glass and saw her slide behind the counter. His heart beat hard and his feet felt nailed to the floor. He tried to remember what he had intended to do, but his mind was like a dark, empty room so he let her, in the end, slip away and stood tongue-tied, the dimes burning his palm.

Afterwards, he told himself that he hadn't spoken to her because it was while she still had the candy on her, and she would have been scared worse than he wanted. When he went upstairs, instead of sleeping, he sat at the kitchen window, looking out into the back yard. He blamed himself for being too soft, too chicken, but then he thought, no there was a better way to do it. He would do it indirectly, slip her a hint he knew, and he was pretty sure that would stop her. Sometime after, he would explain to her why it was good she had stopped. So next time he cleaned out this candy platter she helped herself from, thinking she might get wise he was on to her, but she seemed not to, only hesitated with her hand before she took two candy bars from the next plate and dropped them into the black patent leather purse she always had with her. The time after that he cleaned out the whole top shelf, and still she was not suspicious, and reached down to the next and took something different. One Monday he put some loose change, nickels and dimes, on the candy plate, but she left them there, only taking the candy, which bothered him a little. Rosa asked him what he was mooning about so much and why was he eating chocolate lately. He didn't answer her, and she began to look suspiciously at the women who came in, not excluding the little girls; and he would have been glad to rap her in the teeth, but it didn't matter as long as she didn't know what he had on his mind.

At the same time he figured he would have to do something sure soon, or it would get harder for the girl to stop her stealing. He had to be strong about it. Then he thought of a plan that satisfied him. He would leave two bars on the plate and put in the wrapper of one a note she could read when she was alone. He tried out on paper many messages to her, and the one that seemed best he cleanly printed on a strip of cardboard and slipped it under the wrapper of one chocolate bar. It said, "Don't do this any more or you will suffer your whole life." He puzzled whether to sign it A Friend or Your Friend and finally chose Your Friend.

This was Friday, and he could not hold his impatience for Monday. But on Monday she did not appear. He waited for a long time, until Rosa came down, then he had to go up and the girl still hadn't come. He was greatly disappointed because she had never failed to come before. He lay on the bed, his shoes on, staring at the ceiling. He felt hurt, the sucker she had played him for and was now finished with because she probably had another on her hook. The more he thought about it the worse he felt. He worked up a splitting headache that kept him from sleeping, then he suddenly slept and woke without it. But he had awaked depressed, saddened. He thought about Dom getting out of jail and going away God knows where. He wondered whether he would ever meet up with him somewhere, if he took the fifty-five bucks and left. Then he remembered Dom was a pretty old guy now, and he might not know him if they did meet. He thought about life. You never really got what you wanted. No matter how hard you tried you made mistakes and couldn't get past them. You could never see the sky outside or the ocean because you were in a prison, except nobody called it a prison, and if you did they didn't know what you were talking about, or they said they didn't. A pall settled on him. He lay motionless, without thought or sympathy for himself or anybody.

But when he finally went downstairs, ironically amused that Rosa had allowed him so long a time without bitching, there were people in the store and he could hear her screeching. Shoving his way through the crowd he saw in one sickening look that she had caught the girl with the candy bars and was shaking her so hard the kid's head bounced back and forth like a balloon on a stick. With a curse he tore her away from the girl, whose sickly face showed the depth of her fright.

"Whatsamatter," he shouted at Rosa, "you want her blood?"

"She's a thief," cried Rosa.

"Shut your face."

To stop her yowling he slapped her across her mouth, but it was a harder crack than he had intended. Rosa fell back with a gasp. She did not cry but looked around dazedly at everybody, and tried to smile, and everybody there could see her teeth were flecked with blood.

"Go home," Tommy ordered the girl, but then there was a movement near the door and her mother came into the store.

"What happened?" she said.

"She stole my candy," Rosa cried.

"I let her take it," said Tommy.

Rosa stared at him as if she had been hit again, then with mouth distorted began to sob.

"One was for you, Mother," said the girl.

Her mother socked her hard across the face. "You little thief, this time you'll get your hands burned good."

She pawed at the girl, grabbed her arm and yanked it. The girl, like a grotesque dancer, half ran, half fell forward, but at the door she managed to turn her white face and thrust out at him her red tongue.

4

THEME

All stories have a conflict. All stories have characters. And all stories have themes. For most readers, the first two elements are relatively easy to grasp and explore. Most readers have been reading for "plot" much of their lives; and if a story is not too subtle or complex, or if the author has not handled his characterization in some unfamiliar frame of reference, most readers can grasp at least intuitively the nature of a character in a story. But theme in story is not so easily understood. For one thing, not even critics agree as to precisely what the term means. Some critics equate *theme* with *topic* or *subject;* the theme of this story, they will say, is love or ambition or totalitarianism. Other critics, aware that all stories have repetitive patterns which we call *motifs*, will make no distinction between motif and theme. Still others—though very rarely any more—think of theme as a kind of didactic *moral* or *lesson* of the kind which we find tacked onto an Aesop's fable. But most modern critics, including this one, mean by theme the application which the story has for the reader, the generalization we can derive from it, the comment which the story makes on some aspect of the human condition. In order to explain what we mean by this, we should consider some of the reasons that lead to the writing of a story.

One of man's impulses is to generalize about his experiences. We read in newspapers of crimes committed and criminals caught, and we conclude that crime does not pay. We meet men who have made a lot of money and who have ulcers, and we gather that acquiring wealth is not necessarily a formula for happiness. A friend dies in an automobile accident and we deduce that life is sometimes a matter of blind and cruel chance. Like the rest of us, the writer experiences and observes human existence, and like the rest of us he comes to certain generalizations about human beings and their problems, generalizations which he feels impelled to communicate to others. One way he can do this is by telling a story.

Theme, then, can be defined as the generalization, stated or implied, that lies behind the narration of a specific situation involving specific individuals. Theme exists in fiction because human beings live in the same world, share similar emotions, react in similar ways to similar stimuli, and face common problems. These generalizations tend to fall roughly into one of two categories.

Most "popular" or "commercial" fiction has at its core an interpretation of life which results from man's eternal impulse toward wishful thinking. We all *prefer* to believe that poetic justice is an operative principle in the universe; that good will prevail over evil; that life has purpose and order and direction; that virtue will somehow be rewarded; that for those who earn it, stories in life end happily. All of us, moreover, hold to certain prejudices and preconceptions which we like to think of as the "truth" about life. And escapist fiction will, in general, tell us what we want to hear. It will confirm our prejudices and endorse our opinions. It will present life as we wish it were, not necessarily as it is. And here we must point out that the themes in escapist fiction are not necessarily inaccurate interpretations of life. Any interpretation of life, no matter how platitudinous or naïve, is open to argument; it may be quite true that honesty is the best policy, that life does reward the virtuous, that God is in His Heaven and all's right in this best of all possible worlds. A critic does not dismiss stories with such themes because he disagrees with their premises; he dismisses them because of their presentation. For the escapist story will in general seem either to falsify or to oversimplify human life. If a story employs black-white characters, if it too easily and neatly solves what we know to be a difficult problem, if it wrenches character out of an established pattern, if it resolves a conflict implausibly, then we dismiss it as a false or oversimplified presentation of life as we know it. And if we cannot believe a story, we cannot take its theme seriously.

What therefore seems first to differentiate the serious story (by which we mean the story that can be taken seriously) from the hack story is a quality which we can call *intellectual honesty*. That honesty may assume a number of forms and directions. To begin with, the honest writer tends to approach life not with answers but with questions. Most of us view life through a haze of preconceived ideas, which we have garnered from parents or teachers or peers, or from what we have read in books, or from platitudes which through the sheer weight of repetition we have come to accept as truths; and regardless of how sharply or obviously experience seems to contradict these ideas, we persist in clinging to them. But the honest writer will more frequently challenge commonly held ideas than accept them. Further, the honest writer sees life as complex rather than simple, and his stories and themes will try to capture all the complexity and ambiguity which characterizes validity. It follows then that the honest and intelligent writer will be more concerned with truth than with agreement; he will interpret existence not as we may want him to but as he must. "A great enough writer," Hemingway once said, "seems to be born with an intelligence to accept or reject what is already presented as knowledge." Or again, "I found the greatest difficulty," he wrote, in "knowing truly what you really felt, rather than what you were supposed to feel, and had been taught to feel."

If themes in stories can be classified as valid or invalid, honest or dishonest, intelligent or naive, they can also be classified as either *topical* or *universal*. On the one hand, a writer lives in and observes a particular, immediate world, a world of this time and this place; in some ways this world is unique, and the writer may comment on it in such a way that his observations apply to no other time or place. On the other hand, there are many experiences or problems that man has faced from the beginning of time. All men are born and all men die. All men love and all men hate. Most men mate and reproduce. All men speculate about the existence or nature of God, about the kind of a universe we live in, about the distinction between good and evil. When a writer deals with such subjects, we say that his themes are universal. To a very limited extent, of course, all story themes combine the topical and the universal. A story is always about a specific character in a specific situation in a given place at a given time, and hence is a comment on now. At the same time, no story can comment on today without saying something about both yesterday and tomorrow. Nonetheless, the distinction between topical and universal themes can be useful not only in helping us to understand a story, but also in helping us to evaluate it. As a general rule, a story with a topical theme will be more immediately interesting; it will at first glance seem more pertinent. At the same time, a story with a universal theme is likely to have more endurance. A story which tells us, for example, that modern airports are inadequate, inefficient, and dangerous will be interesting exactly as long as airports need improvement and no longer. But a story which explores the theme that men who marry and have children give hostages to fortune will be interesting for as long as men mate and reproduce.

If all stories carried titles like "War Is Stupid," or if they always incorporated little essays which interpreted for us the meaning of the story, theme would probably not present the problems it does in fiction. But to an even greater degree than in characterization, theme in fiction is likely to be handled by implication. As with character, theme in most stories must be deduced, a process which sometimes can involve much the same kind of hard work as goes into the solving of a difficult problem in mathematics. For that process is likely to involve analysis of conflict and character, consideration of a story's point of view, definition of symbols, interpretation of style and tone, and recognition of allusions, to mention only some of the elements in fiction which can have bearing on meaning. Hence, one crucial question in regard to theme is this: When a reader is not told what a given story means but is instead expected to deduce that meaning, what are some of the things he looks for in order to arrive at that deduction?

This is not the place to try to answer this question with any degree of completeness. But our first step will be to determine what the story is *about.* Every story concerns itself with some subject—materialism or individuality or justice or death or good and evil. But the subject of a story is not its theme; a story will make some statement about death, say, or justice. To determine what that statement is, look next at the characters. For a story to have meaning, the people in it must have something in common (character traits, or attitudes, or concepts, or values) either with the reader or with people in the reader's world. Consider, therefore, in what ways the characters are representative of human beings outside that story.

As with character, so with situation; the situation in which fictional characters find themselves, the problem they face, will ordinarily parallel in some way situations in which we have found ourselves, problems which we have experienced or observed. Then, with character and situation analyzed, consider how the characters react to this situation and what happens to them as a result. From this analysis of the *specifics* in a story, it will be a short step to the generalization which, in effect, will suggest that *if* we have this kind of a character in this kind of a situation, and *if* he reacts thus, then this is what will happen to him.

This approach will not apply to all stories. Indeed, many modern stories employ other methods than character, situation, reaction, and outcome to arrive at theme—methods like symbol or allusion or point of view or irony or contrast or even style. But in exploring the theme of any story, these are the first factors to be considered. At the same time, we should know that in translating something specific into something general, we are always driving along a very treacherous road, and that it therefore behooves us to take into account the warning signs along the way. For example:

1. In the terms in which we have already defined it, the theme of a story should not be confused with a story's *subject;* theme is, rather, a statement about that subject. The subject of a story may be, say, marriage. But ten stories on that subject can say ten different things about marriage. Hence, one's "summary" of the theme of any story must be a complete statement—a sentence or a series of sentences. If, for example, we say that a story suggests that "love" in marriage is a quite different

proposition from "love" during courtship, we have put the statement of theme in its proper *form*.

2. A theme is always a generalization which applies not to the specific characters in a story but to people outside that story. Hence, in stating the theme of a story, make your statement move beyond the specific details. A story's theme does not tell us that Alan Jones, an ambitious actor, has, in achieving success, found that success is not worth the price he has had to pay for it. Rather, a story's theme will tell us that *many* ambitious and successful actors find that success is not worth the price. Indeed, the theme of such a story might be more general yet; it might suggest that success in any area of human endeavor can cost more than it is worth.

3. The idea of theme should not be equated with that of a "moral" or a "lesson." Frequently, readers think of fictional theme as some kind of an object lesson in ethics or behavior, but mature fiction is always more than simply sermon or fable. Although serious fiction can deal with ethical or moral values, many stories do not, and even those which do are often concerned with challenging—not reaffirming—moral axioms or platitudes. When, for example, Hemingway shows us a naturalistic world without moral purpose or order, he is obviously not offering us a didactic story. In short, good stories do not *teach,* they reveal; they do not *preach,* they *interpret*.

4. Further, in the intelligent story the theme cannot be reduced to a pat maxim like "honesty is the best policy." Human experience is complex, and the thoughtful story illustrates rather than minimizes that complexity. That complexity will be manifested in a number of ways. For one thing, no intelligent story will suggest that a given generalization is *always* true; it will only be true under certain circumstances. For another thing, the subjects and predicates of a story's theme will be constantly modified, or ambiguous, or ambivalent; good will never be totally good or evil completely evil. Finally, a story's theme (no matter how universal its characters or how common its situation) will never apply to *all* human beings at *all* times. And if we are to state a story's theme at all accurately, we must account in our summary for these modifications.

5. For this reason as well as others, we cannot approach a thematic story as we would a problem in physics, expecting to find only one correct interpretation. Art is not mathematics; a story will always mean *somewhat* different things to different readers, just as it will never mean to a reader quite what the author intended it to mean. This because the writer brings to a story one set of experiences and interests where the reader brings to that same story another set of experiences and interests. In some respects, these two backgrounds must be similar if the story is to communi-

cate any meaning at all, but though they may be similar, they will not be identical. Hence, no two interpretations of a story will ever be identical.

This does not mean that the search for meaning in fiction is some kind of a speculative free-for-all, an exercise in ingenuity or guess work; it does not mean that a story can mean *anything* we choose to make it mean. Behind every story lies a specific intent, and the skillful writer selects and arranges his material in a way that will enable a reader to recognize that intent. For this reason, a student, in his discussion of the meaning of a given story, should be prepared not only to define *what* he thinks the story says but to explain *why* he thinks it says this by relating *all* details to his conclusion. The phrase *all details* is crucial and should be marked. A good story is, among other things, a unified story; unity means that everything is there for a purpose, has bearing on a story's intent. Hence (given a good story, of course), if our interpretation of theme does not allow for the function of a certain character, or the significance of a certain turn of events, or the inclusion of a certain symbol, then we must question our interpretation. Or if some detail in the story contradicts our interpretation, then we must suspect our interpretation. Or if we must go outside the story for material to substantiate our thesis, then we are again off on a wrong track.

6. We have said that a story is, among other things, an interpretation of some aspect of the human condition. That interpretation is the essence of a story's theme. But regardless of how intelligent, how perceptive, how wise a writer is, a reader is under no obligation to *accept* a story's theme. Indeed, if he approaches fiction with the expectation of being convinced by every thesis he encounters, he is going to find himself very bewildered indeed. Assign ten writers a story and a theme, and you will get ten different and probably contradictory interpretations from them. One explores theme in story not to *learn* about life (though we can, of course) but to *think* about it. The story which prompts us to examine critically our world or our ideas about the nature of human nature or our concepts of self has done all that a story can be expected to do.

7. Above all else, we must constantly bear in mind that theme is only one of three basic elements in fiction; it is never the be-all or end-all of effective fiction nor can it by itself create an effective story. The elements of conflict and character are at least as important as that of theme, and the writer who fails to handle these elements skillfully will have written a poor story regardless of how profound or significant his meaning.

For the reader who thinks of fiction primarily as entertainment, this concept of its interpretative function will be a new one. Serious fiction does not exist merely to entertain; indeed, the most effective fiction might be defined as that which interprets honestly and intelligently a genuine human problem. One statement which we frequently hear is that "fact is stranger than fiction"; it is a statement that was fathered by an article writer, and it is true because the article writer deals with the unusual, the out-of-the-ordinary, the unique. To put this in another way, *factual* writing deals with what happens to one percent of the people one percent of the time. But the proper subject of fiction is the ordinary, the usual, the commonplace; fiction is concerned with what happens to ninety-nine percent of the people ninety-nine percent of the time. The basic distinction between fiction and life is that fiction *interprets* life. It is because fiction does interpret, and does so *emotionally,* by subjecting us vicariously to the ordered experience of the story, that the fiction writer can reply, "Fiction is stronger than fact." In a very large degree it is theme that is responsible for this strength.

PAUL BOWLES

A Distant Episode

The September sunsets were at their reddest the week the Professor decided to visit Aïn Tadouirt, which is in the warm country. He came down out of the high, flat region in the evening by bus, with two small overnight bags full of maps, sun lotions and medicines. Ten years ago he had been in the village for three days; long enough, however, to establish a fairly firm friendship with a café-keeper, who had written him several times during the first year after his visit, if never since. "Hassan Ramani," the Professor said over and over, as the bus bumped downward through ever warmer layers of air. Now facing the flaming sky in the west, and now facing the sharp mountains, the car followed the dusty trail down the canyons into air which began to smell of other things besides the endless ozone of the heights: orange blossoms, pepper, sun-baked excrement, burning olive oil, rotten fruit. He closed his eyes happily and lived for an instant in a purely olfactory world. The distant past returned—what part of it, he could not decide.

The chauffeur, whose seat the Professor shared, spoke to him without taking his eyes from the road. *"Vous êtes géologue?"*

A geologist? Ah, no! I'm a linguist."

"There are no languages here. Only dialects."

"Exactly. I'm making a survey of variations on Moghrebi."

The chauffeur was scornful. "Keep on going south," he said. "You'll find some language you never heard of before."

As they drove through the town gate, the usual swarm of urchins rose up out of the dust and ran screaming beside the bus. The Professor folded his dark glasses, put them in his pocket; and as soon as the vehicle had come to a standstill he jumped out, pushing his way through the indignant boys who clutched at his luggage in vain, and walked quickly into the Grand Hotel Saharien. Out of its eight rooms there were two available—one facing the market and the other, a smaller and cheaper one, giving onto a tiny yard full of refuse and barrels, where two gazelles wandered about. He took the smaller room, and pouring the entire pitcher of water into the tin basin, began to wash the grit from his face and ears. The afterglow was nearly gone from the sky, and the pinkness in objects was disappearing, almost as he watched. He lit the carbide lamp and winced at its odor.

After dinner the Professor walked slowly through the streets to Hassan Ramani's café, whose back room hung hazardously out above the river. The entrance was very low, and he had to bend down slightly to get in. A man was tending the fire. There was one guest sipping tea. The *qaouaji* tried to make him take a seat at the other table in the front room, but the Professor walked airily ahead into the back room and sat down. The moon was shining through the reed latticework and there was not a sound outside but the occasional distant bark of a dog. He changed tables so he could see the river. It was dry, but there was a pool here and there that reflected the bright night sky. The *qaouaji* came in and wiped off the table.

"Does this café still belong to Hassan Ramani?" he asked him in the Moghrebi he had taken four years to learn.

The man replied in bad French: "He is deceased."

"Deceased?" repeated the Professor, without noticing the absurdity of the word. "Really? When?"

"I don't know," said the *qaouaji*. "One tea?"

"Yes. But I don't understand . . ."

The man was already out of the room, fanning the fire. The Professor sat still, feeling lonely, and arguing with himself that to do so was ridiculous. Soon the *qaouaji* returned with the tea. He paid him and gave him an enormous tip, for which he received a grave bow.

"Tell me," he said, as the other started away. "Can one still get those little boxes made from camel udders?"

The man looked angry. "Sometimes the Reguibat bring in those things. We do not buy them here." Then insolently, in Arabic: "And why a camel-udder box?"

"Because I like them," retorted the Professor. And then because he was feeling a little exalted, he added, "I like them so much I want to make a collection of them, and I will pay you ten francs for every one you can get me."

"*Khamstache,*" said the *qaouaji,* opening his left hand rapidly three times in succession.

"Never. Ten."

"Not possible. But wait until later and come with me. You can give me what you like. And you will get camel-udder boxes if there are any."

He went out into the front room, leaving the Professor to drink his tea and listen to the growing chorus of dogs that barked and howled as the moon rose higher into the sky. A group of customers came into the front room and sat talking for an hour or so. When they had left, the *qaouaji* put out the fire and stood in the doorway putting on his burnous. "Come," he said.

Outside in the street there was very little movement. The booths were all closed and the only light came from the moon. An occasional pedestrian passed, and grunted a brief greeting to the *qaouaji*.

"Everyone knows you," said the Professor, to cut the silence between them.

"Yes."

"I wish everyone knew me," said the Professor, before he realized how infantile such a remark must sound.

"*No* one knows you," said his companion gruffly.

They had come to the other side of the town, on the promontory above the desert, and through a great rift in the wall the Professor saw the white endlessness, broken in the foreground by dark spots of oasis. They walked through the opening and followed a winding road between rocks, downward toward the nearest small forest of palms. The Professor thought: "He may cut my throat. But his café—he would surely be found out."

"Is it far?" he asked, casually.

"Are you tired?" countered the *qaouaji*.

"They are expecting me back at the Hotel Saharien," he lied.

"You can't be there and here," said the *qaouaji*.

The Professor laughed. He wondered if it sounded uneasy to the other.

"Have you owned Ramani's café long?"

"I work there for a friend." The reply made the Professor more unhappy than he had imagined it would.

"Oh. Will you work tomorrow?"

"That is impossible to say."

The Professor stumbled on a stone, and fell, scraping his hand. The *qaouaji* said: "Be careful."

The sweet black odor of rotten meat hung in the air suddenly.

"Agh!" said the Professor, choking. "What is it?"

The *qaouaji* had covered his face with his burnous and did not answer. Soon the stench had been left behind. They were on flat ground. Ahead the path was bordered on each side by a high mud wall. There was no breeze and the palms were quite still, but behind the walls was the sound of running water. Also, the odor of human excrement was almost constant as they walked between the walls.

The Professor waited until he thought it seemed logical for him to ask with a certain degree of annoyance: "But where are we going?"

"Soon," said the guide, pausing to gather some stones in the ditch.

"Pick up some stones," he advised. "Here are bad dogs."

"Where?" asked the Professor, but he stooped and got three large ones with pointed edges.

They continued very quietly. The walls came to an end and the bright desert lay ahead. Nearby was a ruined marabout, with its tiny dome only half standing, and the front wall entirely destroyed. Behind it were clumps of stunted, useless palms. A dog came running crazily toward them on three legs. Not until it got quite close did the Professor hear its steady low growl. The *qaouaji* let fly a large stone at it, striking it square in the muzzle. There was a strange snapping of jaws and the dog ran sideways in another direction, falling blindly against rocks and scrambling haphazardly about like an injured insect.

Turning off the road, they walked across the earth strewn with sharp stones, past the little ruin, through the trees, until they came to a place where the ground dropped abruptly away in front of them.

"It looks like a quarry," said the Professor, resorting to French for the word "quarry," whose Arabic equivalent he could not call to mind at the moment. The *qaouaji* did not answer. Instead he stood still and turned his head, as if listening. And indeed, from somewhere down below, but very far below, came the faint sound of a low flute. The *qaouaji* nodded his head slowly several times. Then he said: "The path begins here. You can see it well all the way. The rock is white and the moon is strong. So you can see well. I am going back now and sleep. It is late. You can give me what you like."

Standing there at the edge of the abyss which at each moment looked deeper, with the dark face of the *qaouaji* framed in its moonlit burnous close to his own face, the Professor asked himself exactly what he felt. Indignation, curiosity, fear, perhaps, but most of all relief and the hope that this was not a trick, the hope that the *qaouaji* would really leave him alone and turn back without him.

He stepped back a little from the edge, and fumbled in his pocket for a loose note, because he did not want to show his wallet. Fortunately there was a fifty-franc bill there, which he took out and handed to the man. He knew the *qaouaji* was pleased, and so he paid no attention when he heard him saying: "It is not enough. I have to walk a long way home and there are dogs. . . ."

"Thank you and good night," said the Professor, sitting down with his legs drawn up under him, and lighting a cigarette. He felt almost happy.

"Give me only one cigarette," pleaded the man.

"Of course," he said, a bit curtly, and he held up the pack.

The *qaouaji* squatted close beside him. His face was not pleasant to see. "What is it?" thought the Professor, terrified again, as he held out his lighted cigarette toward him.

The man's eyes were almost closed. It was the most obvious registering of concentrated scheming the Professor had ever seen. When the second cigarette was burning, he ventured to say to the still-squatting Arab: "What are you thinking about?"

The other drew on his cigarette deliberately, and seemed about to speak. Then his expression changed to one of satisfaction, but he did not speak. A cool wind had risen in the air, and the Professor shivered. The sound of the flute came up from the depths below at intervals, sometimes mingled with the scraping of nearby palm fronds one against the other. "These people are not primitives," the Professor found himself saying in his mind.

"Good," said the *qaouaji,* rising slowly. "Keep your money. Fifty francs is enough. It is an honor." Then he went back into French: *"Ti n'as qu' à discendre, to' droit."* He spat, chuckled (or was the Professor hysterical?), and strode away quickly.

The Professor was in a state of nerves. He lit another cigarette, and found his lips moving automatically. They were saying: "Is this a situation or a predicament? This is ridiculous." He sat very still for several minutes, waiting for a sense of reality to come to him. He stretched out on the hard, cold ground and looked up at the moon. It was almost like looking straight at the sun. If he shifted his gaze a little at a time, he could make a string of weaker moons across the sky. "Incredible," he whispered. Then he sat up quickly and looked about. There was no guarantee that the *qaouaji* really had gone back to town. He got to his feet and looked over the edge of the precipice. In the moonlight the bottom seemed miles away. And there was nothing to give it scale; not a tree, not a house, not a person. . . . He listened for the flute, and heard only the wind going by his ears. A sudden violent desire to run back to the road seized him, and he turned and looked in the direction the *qaouaji* had taken. At the same time he felt softly of his wallet in his breast pocket. Then he spat over the edge of the cliff. Then he made water over it, and listened intently, like a child. This gave him the impetus to start down the path into the abyss. Curiously enough, he was not dizzy. But prudently he kept from peering to his right, over the edge. It was a steady and steep downward climb. The monotony of it put him into a frame of mind not unlike that which had been induced by the bus ride. He was murmuring "Hassan Ramani" again, repeatedly and in rhythm. He stopped, furious with himself for the sinister overtones the name now suggested to him. He decided he was exhausted from the trip. "And the walk," he added.

He was now well down the gigantic cliff, but the moon, being directly overhead, gave as much light as ever. Only the wind was left behind, above, to wander among the trees, to blow through the dusty streets of Aïn Tadouirt, into the hall of the Grand Hotel Saharien, and under the door of his little room.

It occurred to him that he ought to ask himself why he was doing this irrational thing, but he was intelligent enough to know that since he was doing it, it was not so important to probe for explanations at that moment.

Suddenly the earth was flat beneath his feet. He had reached the bottom sooner than he had expected. He stepped ahead distrustfully still, as if he expected another treacherous drop. It was so hard to know in this uniform, dim brightness. Before he knew what had happened the dog was upon him, a heavy mass of fur trying to push him backwards, a sharp nail rubbing down his chest, a straining of muscles against him to get the teeth into his neck. The Professor thought: "I refuse to die this way." The dog fell back; it looked like an Eskimo dog. As it sprang again, he called out, very loud: "Ay!" It fell against him, there was a confusion of sensations and a pain somewhere. There was also the sound of voices very near to him, and he could not understand what they were saying. Something cold and metallic was pushed brutally against his spine as the dog still hung for a second by his teeth from a mass of clothing and perhaps flesh. The Professor knew it was a gun, and he raised his hands, shouting in Moghrebi: "Take away the dog!" But the gun merely pushed him forward, and since the dog, once it was back on the ground, did not leap again, he took a step ahead. The gun kept pushing; he kept taking steps. Again he heard voices, but the person directly behind him said nothing. People seemed to be running about; it sounded that way, at least. For his eyes, he discovered, were still shut tight against the dog's attack. He opened them. A group of men was advancing toward him. They were dressed in the black clothes of the Reguibat. "The Reguiba is a cloud across the face of the sun." "When the Reguiba appears the righteous man turns away." In how many shops and market-places he had heard these maxims uttered banteringly among friends. Never to a Reguiba, to be sure, for these men do not frequent towns. They send a representative in disguise, to arrange with shady elements there for the disposal of captured goods. "An opportunity," he thought quickly, "of testing the accuracy of such statements." He did not doubt for a moment that the adventure would prove to be a kind of warning against such foolishness on his part—a warning which in retrospect would be half sinister, half farcical.

Two snarling dogs came running from behind the oncoming men and threw themselves at his legs. He was scandalized to note that no one paid any attention to this breach of etiquette. The gun pushed him harder as he tried to sidestep the animals' noisy assault. Again he cried: "The dogs! Take them away!" The gun shoved him forward with great force and he fell, almost at the feet of the crowd of men facing him. The dogs were wrenching at his hands and arms. A boot kicked them aside, yelping, and then with increased vigor it kicked the Professor in the hip. Then came a chorus of kicks from different sides, and he was rolled violently about on the earth for a while. During this time he was conscious of hands reaching into his pockets and removing everything from them. He tried to say: "You have all my money; stop kicking me!" But his bruised facial muscles would not work; he felt himself pouting and that was all. Someone dealt him a terrific blow on the head, and he thought: "Now at least I shall lose consciousness, thank Heaven." Still he went on being aware of the guttural voices he could not understand, and of being bound tightly about the ankles and chest. Then there was black silence that opened like a wound from time to time, to let in the soft, deep notes of the flute playing the same succession of notes again and again. Suddenly he felt excruciating pain everywhere—pain and cold. "So I have been unconscious, after all," he thought. In spite of that, the present seemed only like a direct continuation of what had gone before.

It was growing faintly light. There were camels near where he was lying; he could hear their gurgling and their heavy breathing. He could not bring himself to attempt opening his eyes, just in case it should turn out to be impossible. However, when he heard someone approaching, he found that he had no difficulty in seeing.

The man looked at him dispassionately in the gray morning light. With one hand he pinched together the Professor's nostrils. When the Professor opened his mouth to breathe, the man swiftly seized his tongue and pulled on it with all his might. The Professor was gagging and catching his breath; he did not see what was happening. He could not distinguish the pain of the brutal yanking from that of the sharp knife. Then there was an endless choking and spitting that went on automatically, as though he were scarcely a part of it. The word "operation" kept going through his mind; it calmed his terror somewhat as he sank back into darkness.

The caravan left sometime toward midmorning. The Professor, not unconscious, but in a state of utter stupor, still gagging and drooling blood, was dumped doubled-up into a sack and tied at one side of a camel. The lower end of the enormous amphitheater contained a natural gate in the rocks. The camels, swift *mehara,* were lightly laden on this trip. They passed through single file, and slowly mounted the gentle slope that led up into the beginning of the desert. That night, at a stop behind some low hills, the men took him out, still in a state which permitted no thought, and over the dusty rags that remained of his clothing they fastened a serious of curious belts made of the bottoms of tin cans strung together. One after another of these bright girdles was wired about his torso, his arms and legs, even across his face, until he was entirely within a suit of armor that covered him with its circular metal scales. There was a good deal of merriment during this decking-out of the Professor. One man brought out a flute and a younger one did a not ungraceful caricature of an Ouled Naïl executing a cane dance. The Professor was no longer conscious; to be exact, he existed in the middle of the movements made by these other men. When they had finished dressing him the way they wished him to look, they stuffed some food under the tin bangles hanging over his face. Even though he chewed mechanically, most of it eventually fell out onto the ground. They put him back into the sack and left him there.

Two days later they arrived at one of their own encampments. There were women and children here in the tents, and the men had to drive away the snarling dogs they had left there to guard them. When they emptied the Professor out of his sack, there were screams of fright, and it took several hours to convince the last woman that he was harmless, although there had been no doubt from the start that he was a valuable possession. After a few days they began to move on again, taking everything with them, and traveling only at night as the terrain grew warmer.

Even when all his wounds had healed and he felt no more pain, the Professor did not begin to think again; he ate and defecated, and he danced when he was bidden, a senseless hopping up and down that delighted the children, principally because of the wonderful jangling racket it made. And he generally slept through the heat of the day, in among the camels.

Wending its way southeast, the caravan avoided all stationary civilization. In a few weeks they reached a new plateau, wholly wild and with a sparse vegetation. Here they pitched camp and remained, while the *mehara* were turned loose to graze. Everyone was happy here; the weather was cooler and there was a well only a few hours away on a seldom-frequented trail. It was here they conceived the idea of taking the Professor to Fogara and selling him to the Touareg.

It was a full year before they carried out this project. By this time the Professor was much better trained. He could do a handspring, make a series of fearful growling noises which had, nevertheless, a certain element of humor; and when the Reguibat removed the tin from his face they discovered he could grimace admirably while he danced. They also taught him a few basic obscene gestures which never failed to elicit delighted shrieks from the women. He was now brought forth only after especially abundant meals, when there was music and festivity. He easily fell in with their sense of ritual, and evolved an elementary sort of "program" to present when he was called for: dancing, rolling on the ground, imitating certain animals, and finally rushing toward the group in feigned anger, to see the resultant confusion and hilarity.

When three of the men set out for Fogara with him, they took four *mehara* with them, and he rode astride his quite naturally. No precautions were taken to guard him, save he was kept among them, one man always staying at the rear of the party. They came within sight of the walls at dawn, and they waited among the rocks all day. At dusk the youngest started out, and in three hours he returned with a friend who carried a stout cane. They tried to put the Professor through his routine then and there, but the man from Fogara was in a hurry to get back to town, so they all set out on the *mehara*.

In the town they went directly to the villager's home, where they had coffee in the courtyard sitting among the camels. Here the Professor went into his act again, and this time there was prolonged merriment and much rubbing together of hands. An agreement was reached, a sum of money paid, and the Reguibat withdrew, leaving the Professor in the house of the man with the cane, who did not delay in locking him into a tiny enclosure off the courtyard.

The next day was an important one in the Professor's life, for it was then that pain began to stir again in his being. A group of men came to the house, among whom was a venerable gentleman, better clothed than those others who spent their time flattering him, setting fervent kisses upon his hands and the edges of his garments. This person made a point of going into classical Arabic from time to time, to impress the others, who had not learned a word of the Koran. Thus his conversation would run more or less as follows: "Perhaps at In Salah. The French there are stupid. Celestial vengeance is approaching. Let us not hasten it. Praise the highest and cast thine anathema against idols. With paint on his face. In case the police wish to look close." The others listened and agreed, nodding their heads slowly and solemnly. And the Professor in his stall beside him listened, too. That is, he was *conscious* of the sound of the old man's Arabic. The words penetrated for the first time in many months. Noises, then: "Celestial vengeance is approaching." Then: "It is an honor. Fifty francs is enough. Keep your money. Good." And the *qaouaji* squatting near him at the edge of the precipice. Then "anathema against idols" and more gibberish. He turned over panting on the sand and forgot about it. But the pain had begun. It operated in a kind of delirium, because he had begun to enter into consciousness again. When the man opened the door and prodded him with his cane, he cried out in rage, and everyone laughed.

They got him into his feet, but he would not dance. He stood before them, staring at the ground, stubbornly refusing to move. The owner was furious, and so annoyed by the laughter of the others that he felt obliged to send them away, saying that he would await a more propitious time for exhibiting his property, because he dared not show his anger before the elder. However, when they had left he dealt the Professor a violent blow on the shoulder with his cane, called him various obscene things, and went out into the street, slamming the gate behind him. He walked straight to the street of the Ouled Naïl, because he was sure of finding the Reguibat there among the girls, spending the money. And there in a tent he found one of them still abed, while an Ouled Naïl washed the tea glasses. He walked in and almost decapitated the man before the latter had even attempted to sit up. Then he threw his razor on the bed and ran out.

The Ouled Naïl saw the blood, screamed, ran out of her tent into the next, and soon emerged from that with four girls who rushed together into the coffee house and told the *qaouaji* who had killed the Reguiba. It was only a matter of an hour before the French military police had caught him at a friend's house, and dragged him off to the barracks. That night the Professor had nothing to eat, and the next afternoon, in the slow sharpening of his consciousness caused by increasing hunger, he walked aimlessly about the courtyard and the rooms that gave onto it. There was no one. In one room a calendar hung on the wall. The Professor watched nervously, like a dog watching a fly in front of its nose. On the white paper were black objects that made sounds in his head. He heard them: *"Grande Epicerie du Sahel. Juin. Lundi, Mardi, Mercredi. . . ."*

The tiny inkmarks of which a symphony consists may have been made long ago, but when they are fulfilled in sound they become imminent and mighty. So a kind of music of feeling began to play in the Professor's head, increasing in volume as he looked at the mud wall, and he had the feeling that he was performing what had been written for him long ago. He felt like weeping; he felt like roaring through the little house, upsetting and smashing the few breakable objects. His emotion got no further than this one overwhelming desire. So, bellowing as loud as he could, he attacked the house and its belongings. Then he attacked the door into the street, which resisted for a while and finally broke. He climbed through the opening made by the boards he had ripped apart, and still bellowing and shaking his arms in the air to make as loud a jangling as possible, he began to gallop along the quiet street toward the gateway of the town. A few people looked at him with great curiosity. As he passed the garage, the last building before the high mud archway that framed the desert beyond, a French soldier saw him. *"Tiens,"* he said to himself, "a holy maniac."

Again, it was sunset time. The Professor ran beneath the arched gate, turned his face toward the red sky, and began to trot along the Piste d'In Salah, straight into the setting sun. Behind him, from the garage, the soldier took a pot shot at him for good luck. The bullet whistled dangerously near the Professor's head, and his yelling rose into an indignant lament as he waved his arms more wildly, and hopped high into the air at every few steps, in an access of terror.

The soldier watched a while, smiling, as the cavorting figure grew smaller in the oncoming evening darkness, and the rattling of the tin became a part of the great silence out there beyond the gate. The wall of the garage as he leaned against it still gave forth heat, left there by the sun, but even then the lunar chill was growing in the air.

STEPHEN CRANE

The Blue Hotel

The Palace Hotel at Fort Romper was painted a light blue, a shade that is on the legs of a kind of heron, causing the bird to declare its position against any background. The Palace Hotel, then, was always screaming and howling in a way that made the dazzling winter landscape of Nebraska seem only a gray swampish hush. It stood alone on the prairie, and when the snow was falling the town two hundred yards away was not visible. But when the traveler alighted at the railway station he was obliged to pass the Palace Hotel before he could come upon the company of low clapboard houses which composed Fort Romper, and it was not to be thought that any traveler could pass the Palace Hotel without looking at it. Pat Scully, the proprietor, had proved himself a master of strategy when he chose his paints. It is true that on clear days, when the great transcontinental expresses, long lines of swaying Pullmans, swept through Fort Romper, passengers were overcome at the sight, and the cult that knows the brown-reds and the subdivisions of the dark greens of the East expressed shame, pity, horror, in a laugh. But to the citizens of this prairie town and to the people who would naturally stop there, Pat Scully had performed a feat. With this opulence and splendor, these creeds, classes, egotisms, that streamed through Romper on the rails day after day, they had no color in common.

As if the displayed delights of such a blue hotel were not sufficiently enticing, it was Scully's habit to go every morning and evening to meet the leisurely trains that stopped at Romper and work his seductions upon any man that he might see wavering, gripsack in hand.

One morning, when a snow-crusted engine dragged its long string of freight cars and its one passenger coach to the station, Scully performed the marvel of catching three men. One was a shaky and quick-eyed Swede, with a great shining cheap valise; one was a tall bronzed cowboy, who was on his way to a ranch near the Dakota line; one was a little silent man from the East, who didn't look it, and didn't announce it. Scully practically made them prisoners. He was so nimble and merry and kindly that each probably felt it would be the height of brutality to try to escape. They trudged off over the creaking board sidewalks in the wake of the eager little Irishman. He wore a heavy fur cap squeezed tightly down on his head. It caused his two red ears to stick out stiffly, as if they were made of tin.

At last, Scully, elaborately, with boisterous hospitality, conducted them through the portals of the blue hotel. The room which they entered was small. It seemed to be merely a proper temple for an enormous stove, which, in the center, was humming with godlike violence. At various points on its surface the iron had become luminous and glowed yellow from the heat. Beside the stove Scully's son Johnnie was playing High-Five with an old farmer who had whiskers both gray and sandy. They were quarreling. Frequently the old farmer turned his face toward a box of sawdust—colored brown from tobacco juice—that was behind the stove, and spat with an air of great impatience and irritation. With a loud flourish of words Scully destroyed the game of cards, and bustled his son upstairs with part of the baggage of the new guests. He himself conducted them to three basins of the coldest water in the world. The cowboy and the Easterner burnished themselves fiery red with this water, until it seemed to be some kind of metal-polish. The Swede, however, merely dipped his fingers gingerly and with trepidation. It was notable that throughout this series of small ceremonies the three travelers were made to feel that Scully was very benevolent. He was conferring great favors upon them. He handed the towel from one to another with an air of philanthropic impulse.

Afterward they went to the first room, and, sitting about the stove, listened to Scully's officious clamor at his daughters, who were preparing the midday meal. They reflected in the silence of experienced men who tread carefully amid new people. Nevertheless, the old farmer, stationary, invincible in his chair near the warmest part of the stove, turned his face from the sawdust-box frequently and addressed a glowing commonplace to the strangers. Usually he was answered in short but adequate sentences by either the cowboy or the Easterner. The Swede said nothing. He seemed to be occupied in making furtive estimates of each man in the room. One might have thought that he had the sense of silly suspicion which comes to guilt. He resembled a badly frightened man.

Later, at dinner, he spoke a little, addressing his conversation entirely to Scully. He volunteered that he had come from New York, where for ten years he had worked as a tailor. These facts seemed to strike Scully as fascinating, and afterward he volunteered that he had lived at Romper for fourteen years. The Swede asked about the crops and the price of labor. He seemed barely to listen to Scully's extended replies. His eyes continued to rove from man to man.

Finally, with a laugh and a wink, he said that some of these Western communities were very dangerous; and after his statement he straightened his legs under the table, tilted his head, and laughed again, loudly. It was plain that the demonstration had no meaning to the others. They looked at him wondering and in silence.

II

As the men trooped heavily back into the front room, the two little windows presented views of a turmoiling sea of snow. The huge arms of the wind were making attempts—mighty, circular, futile—to embrace the flakes as they sped. A gate-post like a still man with a blanched face stood aghast amid this profligate fury. In a hearty voice Scully announced the presence of a blizzard. The guests of the blue hotel, lighting their pipes, assented with grunts of lazy masculine contentment. No island of the sea could be exempt in the degree of this little room with its humming stove. Johnnie, son of Scully, in a tone which defined his opinion of his ability as a card-player, challenged the old farmer of both gray and sandy whiskers to a game of High-Five. The farmer agreed with a contemptuous and bitter scoff. They sat close to the stove, and squared their knees under a wide board. The cowboy and the Easterner watched the game with interest. The Swede remained near the window, aloof, but with a countenance that showed signs of an inexplicable excitement.

The play of Johnnie and the gray-beard was suddenly ended by another quarrel. The old man arose while casting a look of heated scorn at his adversary. He slowly buttoned his coat, and then stalked with fabulous dignity from the room. In the discreet silence of all other men the Swede laughed. His laughter rang somehow childish. Men by this time had begun to look at him askance, as if they wished to inquire what ailed him.

A new game was formed jocosely. The cowboy volunteered to become the partner of Johnnie, and they all then turned to ask the Swede to throw in his lot with the little Easterner. He asked some questions about the game, and, learning that it wore many names, and that he had played it when it was under an alias, he accepted the invitation. He strode toward the men nervously, as if he expected to be assaulted. Finally, seated, he gazed from face to face and laughed shrilly. This laugh was so strange that the Easterner looked up quickly, the cowboy sat intent and with his mouth open, and Johnnie paused, holding the cards with still fingers.

Afterward there was a short silence. Then Johnnie said, "Well, let's get at it. Come on now!" They pulled their chairs forward until their knees were bunched under the board. They began to play, and their interest in the game caused the others to forget the manner of the Swede.

The cowboy was a board-whacker. Each time that he held superior cards he whanged them, one by one, with exceeding force, down upon the improvised table, and took the tricks with a glowing air of prowess and pride that sent thrills of indignation into the hearts of his opponents. A game with a board-whacker in it is sure to become intense. The countenances of the Easterner and the Swede were miserable whenever the cowboy thundered down his aces and kings, while Johnnie, his eyes gleaming with joy, chuckled and chuckled.

Because of the absorbing play none considered the strange ways of the Swede. They paid strict heed to the game. Finally, during a lull caused by a new deal, the Swede suddenly addressed Johnnie: "I suppose there have been a good many men killed in this room." The jaws of the others dropped and they looked at him.

"What in hell are you talking about?" said Johnnie.

The Swede laughed again his blatant laugh, full of a kind of false courage and defiance. "Oh, you know what I mean all right," he answered.

"I'm a liar if I do!" Johnnie protested. The card game was halted, and the men stared at the Swede. Johnnie evidently felt that as the son of the proprietor, he should make a direct inquiry. "Now, what might you be drivin' at, mister?" he asked. The Swede winked at him. It was a wink full of cunning. His fingers shook on the edge of the board. "Oh, maybe you think I have been to nowheres. Maybe you think I'm a tenderfoot?"

"I don't know nothin' about you," answered Johnnie, "and I don't give a damn where you've been. All I got to say is that I don't know what you're driving at. There hain't never been nobody killed in this room."

The cowboy, who had been steadily gazing at the Swede, then spoke: "What's wrong with you, mister?"

Apparently it seemed to the Swede that he was formidably menaced. He shivered and turned white near the corners of his mouth. He sent an appealing glance in the direction of the little Easterner. During these moments he did not forget to wear his air of advanced pot-valor. "They say they don't know what I mean," he remarked mockingly to the Easterner.

The latter answered after prolonged and cautious reflection. "I don't understand you," he said, impassively.

The Swede made a movement then which announced that he thought he had encountered treachery from the only quarter where he had expected sympathy, if not help. "Oh, I see you are all against me, I see—"

The cowboy was in a state of deep stupefaction. "Say," he cried, as he tumbled the deck violently down upon the board, "say, what are you gitting' at, hey?"

The Swede sprang up with the celerity of a man escaping from a snake on the floor. "I don't want to fight!" he shouted. "I don't want to fight!"

The cowboy stretched his long legs indolently and deliberately. His hands were in his pockets. He spat into the sawdust-box. "Well, who the hell thought you did?" he inquired.

The Swede backed rapidly toward a corner of the room. His hands were out protectingly in front of his chest, but he was making an obvious struggle to control his fright. "Gentlemen," he quavered, "I suppose I am going to be killed before I can leave this house! I suppose I am going to be killed before I can leave this house!" In his eyes was the dying-swan look. Through the windows could be seen the snow turning blue in the shadow of dusk. The wind tore at the house, and some loose thing beat regularly against the clapboards like a spirit tapping.

A door opened, and Scully himself entered. He paused in surprise as he noted the tragic attitude of the Swede. Then he said, "What's the matter here?"

The Swede answered him swiftly and eagerly: "These men are going to kill me."

"Kill you!" ejaculated Scully. "Kill you! What are you talkin'?"

The Swede made the gesture of a martyr.

Scully wheeled sternly upon his son. "What is this, Johnnie?"

The lad had grown sullen. "Damned if I know," he answered. "I can't make no sense to it." He began to shuffle the cards, fluttering them together with an angry snap. "He says a good many men have been killed in this room, or something like that. And he says he's goin' to be killed here too. I don't know what ails him. He's crazy, I shouldn't wonder."

Scully then looked for explanation to the cowboy, but the cowboy simply shrugged his shoulders.

"Kill you?" said Scully again to the Swede. "Kill you? Man, you're off your nut."

"Oh, I know," burst out the Swede. "I know what will happen. Yes, I'm crazy—yes. Yes, of course, I'm crazy—yes. But I know one thing—" There was a sort of sweat of misery and terror upon his face. "I know I won't get out of here alive."

The cowboy drew a deep breath, as if his mind was passing into the last stages of dissolution. "Well, I'm doggoned," he whispered to himself.

Scully wheeled suddenly and faced his son. "You've been troublin' this man!"

Johnnie's voice was loud with its burden of grievance. "Why, good Gawd, I ain't done nothin' to 'im."

The Swede broke in. "Gentlemen, do not disturb yourselves. I will leave this house. I will go away, because"—he accused them dramatically with his glance—"because I do not want to be killed."

Scully was furious with his son. "Will you tell me what is the matter, you young divil? What's the matter, anyhow? Speak out!"

"Blame it!" cried Johnnie in despair, "don't I tell you I don't know? He—he says we want to kill him, and that's all I know. I can't tell what ails him."

The Swede continued to repeat: "Never mind, Mr. Scully; never mind. I will leave this house. I will go away, because I do not wish to be killed. Yes, of course, I am crazy—yes. But I know one thing! I will go away. I will leave this house. Never mind, Mr. Scully; never mind. I will go away."

"You will not go 'way," said Scully. "You will not go 'way until I hear the reason of this business. If anybody has troubled you I will take care of him. This is my house. You are under my roof, and I will not allow any peaceable man to be troubled here." He cast a terrible eye upon Johnnie, the cowboy, and the Easterner.

"Never mind, Mr. Scully; never mind. I will go away. I do not wish to be killed." The Swede moved toward the door which opened upon the stairs. It was evidently his intention to go at once for his baggage.

"No, no," shouted Scully peremptorily; but the white-faced man slid by him and disappeared. "Now," said Scully severely, "what does this mane?"

Johnnie and the cowboy cried together: "Why, we didn't do nothin' to 'im!"

Scully's eyes were cold. "No," he said, "you didn't?"

Johnnie swore a deep oath. "Why, this is the wildest loon I ever see. We didn't do nothin' at all. We were jest sittin' here playin' cards, and he—"

The father suddenly spoke to the Easterner, "Mr. Blanc," he asked, "what has these boys been doin'?"

The Easterner reflected again. "I didn't see anything wrong at all," he said at last, slowly.

Scully began to howl. "But what does it mane?" He stared ferociously at his son. "I have a mind to lather you for this, me boy."

Johnnie was frantic. "Well, what have I done?" he bawled at his father.

III

"I think you are tongue-tied," said Scully finally to his son, the cowboy, and the Easterner; and at the end of this scornful sentence he left the room.

Upstairs the Swede was swiftly fastening the straps of his great valise.

Once his back happened to be half turned toward the door, and, hearing a noise there, he wheeled and sprang up, uttering a loud cry. Scully's wrinkled visage showed grimly in the light of the small lamp he carried. This yellow effulgence, streaming upward, colored only his prominent features, and left his eyes, for instance, in mysterious shadow. He resembled a murderer.

"Man! man!" he exclaimed, "have you gone daffy?"

"Oh, no! Oh, no!" rejoined the other. "There are people in this world who know pretty nearly as much as you do—understand?"

For a moment they stood gazing at each other. Upon the Swede's deathly pale cheeks were two spots brightly crimson and sharply edged, as if they had been carefully painted. Scully placed the light on the table and sat himself on the edge of the bed. He spoke ruminatively. "By cracky, I never heard of such a thing in my life. It's a complete muddle. I can't, for the soul of me, think how you ever got this idea into your head." Presently he lifted his eyes and asked: "And did you sure think they were going to kill you?"

The Swede scanned the old man as if he wished to see into his mind. "I did," he said at last. He obviously suspected that this answer might precipitate an outbreak. As he pulled on a strap his whole arm shook, the elbow wavering like a bit of paper.

Scully banged his hand impressively on the footboard of the bed. "Why, man, we're goin' to have a line of ilictric street-cars in this town next spring."

" 'A line of electric street-cars,' " repeated the Swede, stupidly.

"And," said Scully, "there's a new railroad goin' to be built down from Broken Arm to here. Not to mintion the four churches and the smashin' big brick schoolhouse. Then there's the big factory, too. Why, in two years Romper'll be a met-tro-*pol*-is."

Having finished the preparation of his baggage, the Swede straightened himself. "Mr. Scully," he said, with sudden hardihood, "how much do I owe you?"

"You don't owe me anythin'," said the old man, angrily.

"Yes, I do," retorted the Swede. He took seventy-five cents from his pocket and tendered it to Scully; but the latter snapped his fingers in disdainful refusal. However, it happened that they both stood gazing in a strange fashion at three silver pieces on the Swede's open palm.

"I'll not take your money," said Scully at last. "Not after what's been goin' on here." Then a plan seemed to strike him. "Here," he cried, picking up his lamp and moving toward the door. "Here! Come with me a minute."

"No," said the Swede, in overwhelming alarm.

"Yes," urged the old man. "Come on! I want you to come and see a picter—just across the hall—in my room."

The Swede must have concluded that his hour was come. His jaw dropped and his teeth showed like a dead man's. He ultimately followed Scully across the corridor, but he had the step of one hung in chains.

Scully flashed the light high on the wall of his own chamber. There was revealed a ridiculous photograph of a little girl. She was leaning against a balustrade of gorgeous decoration, and the formidable bang to her hair was prominent. The figure was as graceful as an upright sled-stake, and, withal, it was of the hue of lead. "There," said Scully, tenderly, "that's the picter of my little girl that died. Her name was Carrie. She had the purtiest hair you ever saw! I was that fond of her, she—"

Turning then, he saw that the Swede was not contemplating the picture at all, but, instead, was keeping keen watch on the gloom in the rear.

"Look, man!" cried Scully, heartily. "That's the picter of my little gal that died. Her name was Carrie. And then here's the picter of my oldest boy, Michael. He's a lawyer in Lincoln, an' doin' well. I gave that boy a grand eddication, and I'm glad for it now. He's a fine boy. Look at 'im now. Ain't he bold as blazes, him there in Lincoln, an honored an' respicted gintleman! An honored and respicted gintleman," concluded Scully with a flourish. And, so saying, he smote the Swede jovially on the back.

The Swede faintly smiled.

"Now," said the old man, "there's only one more thing." He dropped suddenly to the floor and thrust his head beneath the bed. The Swede could hear his muffled voice. "I'd keep it under me piller if it wasn't for that boy Johnnie. Then there's the old woman— Where is it now? I never put it twice in the same place. Ah, now come out with you!"

Presently he backed clumsily from under the bed, dragging with him an old coat rolled into a bundle. "I've fetched him," he muttered. Kneeling on the floor, he unrolled the coat and extracted from its heart a large yellow-brown whisky-bottle.

His first maneuver was to hold the bottle up to the light. Reassured, apparently, that nobody had been tampering with it, he thrust it with a generous movement toward the Swede.

The weak-kneed Swede was about to eagerly clutch this element of strength, but he suddenly jerked his hand away and cast a look of horror upon Scully.

"Drink," said the old man affectionately. He had risen to his feet, and now stood facing the Swede.

There was a silence. Then again Scully said: "Drink!"

The Swede laughed wildly. He grabbed the bottle, put it to his mouth; and as his lips curled absurdly around the opening and his throat worked, he kept his glance, burning with hatred, upon the old man's face.

IV

After the departure of Scully the three men, with the cardboard still upon their knees, preserved for a long time an astounded silence. Then Johnnie said: "That's the doddangedest Swede I ever see."

"He ain't no Swede," said the cowboy, scornfully.

"Well, what is he then?" cried Johnnie. "What is he then?"

"It's my opinion," replied the cowboy deliberately, "he's some kind of a Dutchman." It was a venerable custom of the country to entitle as Swedes all light-haired men who spoke with a heavy tongue. In consequence the idea of the cowboy was not without its daring. "Yes, sir," he repeated, "It's my opinion this fellow is some kind of a Dutchman."

"Well, he says he's a Swede, anyhow," muttered Johnnie, sulkily. He turned to the Easterner: "What do you think, Mr. Blanc?"

Oh, I don't know," replied the Easterner.

"Well, what do you think makes him act that way?" asked the cowboy.

"Why, he's frightened." The Easterner knocked his pipe against a rim of the stove. "He's clear frightened out of his boots."

"What at?" cried Johnnie and the cowboy together.

The Easterner reflected over his answer.

"What at?" cried the others again.

"Oh, I don't know, but it seems to me this man has been reading dime novels, and he thinks he's right out in the middle of it—the shootin' and stabbin' and all."

"But," said the cowboy, deeply scandalized, "this ain't Wyoming, ner none of them places. This is Nebrasker."

"Yes," added Johnnie, "an' why don't he wait till he gits *out West?"*

The traveled Easterner laughed. "It isn't different there even—not in these days. But he thinks he's right in the middle of hell."

Johnnie and the cowboy mused long.

"It's awful funny," remarked Johnnie at last.

"Yes," said the cowboy. "This is a queer game. I hope we don't git snowed in, because then we'd have to stand this here man bein' around with us all the time. That wouldn't be no good."

"I wish pop would throw him out," said Johnnie.

Presently they heard a loud stamping on the stairs, accompanied by ringing jokes in the voice of old Scully, and laughter, evidently from the Swede. The men around the stove stared vacantly at each other. "Gosh!" said the cowboy. The door flew open, and old Scully, flushed and anecdotal, came into the room. He was jabbering at the Swede, who followed him, laughing bravely. It was the entry of two roisterers from a banquet hall.

"Come now," said Scully sharply to the three seated men, "move up and give us a chance at the stove." The cowboy and the Easterner obediently sidled their chairs to make room for the new-comers. Johnnie, however, simply arranged himself in a more indolent attitude, and then remained motionless.

"Come! Git over, there," said Scully.

"Plenty of room on the other side of the stove," said Johnnie.

"Do you think we want to sit in the draught?" roared the father.

But the Swede here interposed with a grandeur of confidence. "No, no. Let the boy sit where he likes," he cried in a bullying voice to the father.

"All right! All right!" said Scully, deferentally. The cowboy and the Easterner exchanged glances of wonder.

The five chairs were formed in a crescent about one side of the stove. The Swede began to talk; he talked arrogantly, profanely, angrily. Johnnie, the cowboy, and the Easterner maintained a morose silence, while old Scully appeared to be receptive and eager, breaking in constantly with sympathetic ejaculations.

Finally the Swede announced that he was thirsty. He moved in his chair, and said that he would go for a drink of water.

"I'll git it for you," cried Scully at once.

"No," said the Swede, contemptuously. "I'll get it for myself." He arose and stalked with the air of an owner off into the executive parts of the hotel.

As soon as the Swede was out of hearing Scully sprang to his feet and whispered intensely to the others: "Upstairs he thought I was tryin' to poison 'im."

"Say," said Johnnie, "this makes me sick. Why don't you throw 'im out in the snow?".

"Why, he's all right now," declared Scully, "It was only that he was from the East, and he thought this was a tough place. That's all. He's all right now."

The cowboy looked with admiration upon the Easterner. "You were straight," he said. "You were on to that there Dutchman."

"Well," said Johnnie to his father, "he may be all right now, but I don't see it. Other time he was scared, but now he's too fresh."

Scully's speech was always a combination of Irish brogue and idiom, Western twang and idiom, and scraps of curiously formal diction taken from the story-books and newspapers. He now hurled a strange mass of language at the head of his son. "What do I keep? What do I keep? What do I keep?" he demanded, in a voice of thunder. He slapped his knee impressively, to indicate that he himself was going to make reply, and that all should heed. "I keep a hotel," he shouted. "A hotel, do you mind? A guest under my roof has sacred privileges. He is to be intimidated by none. Not one work shall he hear that would prijudice him in favor of goin' away. I'll not have it. There's no place in this here town where they can say they iver took in a guest of mine because he was afraid to stay here." He wheeled suddenly upon the cowboy and the Easterner. "Am I right?"

"Yes, Mr. Scully," said the cowboy, "I think you're right."

"Yes, Mr. Scully," said the Easterner, "I think you're right."

V

At six-o'clock supper, the Swede fizzed like a firewheel. He sometimes seemed on the point of bursting into riotous song, and in all his madness he was encouraged by old Scully. The Easterner was encased in reserve; the cowboy sat in wide-mouthed amazement, forgetting to eat, while Johnnie wrathily demolished great plates of food. The daughters of the house, when they were obliged to replenish the biscuits, approached as warily as Indians, and, having succeeded in their purpose, fled with ill-concealed trepidation. The Swede domineered the whole feast, and he gave it the appearance of a cruel bacchanal. He seemed to have grown suddenly taller; he gazed, brutally disdainful, into every face. His voice rang through the room. Once when he jabbed out harpoon-fashion with his fork to pinion a biscuit, the weapon nearly impaled the hand of the Easterner which had been stretched quietly out for the same biscuit.

After supper, as the men filed toward the other room, the Swede smote Scully ruthlessly on the shoulder. "Well, old boy, that was a good, square meal." Johnnie looked hopefully at his father; he knew that shoulder was tender from an old fall; and, indeed, it appeared for a moment Scully was going to flame out over the matter, but in the end he smiled a sickly smile and remained silent. The others understood from his manner that he was admitting his responsibility for the Swede's new viewpoint.

Johnnie, however, addressed his parent in an aside. "Why don't you license somebody to kick you downstairs?" Scully scowled darkly by way of reply.

When they were gathered about the stove, the Swede insisted on another game of High-Five. Scully gently deprecated the plan at first, but the Swede turned a wolfish glare upon him. The old man subsided, and the Swede canvassed the others. In his tone there was always a great threat. The cowboy and the Easterner both remarked indifferently that they would play. Scully said that he would presently have to go to meet the 6:58 train, and so the Swede turned menacingly upon Johnnie. For a moment their glances crossed like blades, and then Johnnie smiled and said, "Yes, I'll play."

They formed a square, with the little board on their knees. The Easterner and the Swede were again partners. As the play went on, it was noticeable that the cowboy was not board-whacking as usual. Meanwhile, Scully, near the lamp, had put on his spectacles and, with an appearance curiously like an old priest, was reading a newsaper. In time he went out to meet the 6:58 train, and, despite his precautions, a gust of polar wind whirled into the room as he opened the door. Besides scattering the cards, it chilled the players to the marrow. The Swede cursed frightfully. When Scully returned, his entrance disturbed a cozy and friendly scene. The Swede again cursed. But presently they were once more intent, their heads bent forward and their hands moving swiftly. The Swede had adopted the fashion of board-whacking.

Scully took up his paper and for a long time remained immersed in matters which were extraordinarily remote from him. The lamp burned badly, and once he stopped to adjust the wick. The newspaper, as he turned from page to page, rustled with a slow and comfortable sound. Then suddenly he heard three terrible words: "You are cheatin'!"

Such scenes often prove that there can be little of dramatic import in environment. Any room can present a tragic front; any room can be comic. This little den was now hideous as a torture-chamber. The new faces of the men themselves had changed it upon the instant. The Swede held a huge fist in front of Johnnie's face, while the latter looked steadily over it into the blazing orbs of his accuser. The Easterner had grown pallid; the cowboy's jaw had dropped in that expression of bovine amazement which was one of his important mannerisms. After the three words, the first sound in the room was made by Scully's paper as it floated forgotten to his feet. His spectacles had also fallen from his nose, but by a clutch he had saved them in air. His hand, grasping the spectacles, now remained poised awkwardly and near his shoulder. He stared at the card-players.

Probably the silence was while a second elapsed. Then, if the floor had been suddenly twitched out from under the men they could not have moved quicker. The five had projected themselves headlong toward a common point. It happened that Johnnie, in rising to hurl himself upon the Swede, had stumbled slightly because of his curiously instinctive care for the cards and the board. The loss of the moment allowed time for the arrival of Scully, and also allowed the cowboy time to give the Swede a great push which sent him staggering back. The men found tongue together, and hoarse shouts of rage, appeal, or fear burst from every throat. The cowboy pushed and jostled feverishly at the Swede, and the Easterner and Scully clung wildly to Johnnie; but through the smoky air, above the swaying bodies of the peace-compellers, the eyes of the two warriors ever sought each other in glances of challenge that were at once hot and steely.

Of course the board had been overturned, and now the whole company of cards was scattered over the floor, where the boots of the men trampled the fat and painted kings and queens as they gazed with their silly eyes at the war that was waging above them.

Scully's voice was dominating the yells. "Stop now! Stop, I say! Stop, now—"

Johnnie, as he struggled to burst through the rank formed by Scully and the Easterner, was crying, "Well, he says I cheated! He says I cheated! I won't allow no man to say I cheated! if he says I cheated, he's a ————!"

The cowboy was telling the Swede, "Quit now! Quit, d'ye hear—"

The screams of the Swede never ceased: "He did cheat! I saw him! I saw him—"

As for the Easterner, he was importuning in a voice that was not heeded: "Wait a moment, can't you? Oh, wait a moment. What's the good of a fight over a game of cards? Wait a moment—"

In this tumult no complete sentences were clear. "Cheat"—"Quit"—"He says"—these fragments pierced the uproar and rang out sharply. It was remarkable that, whereas Scully undoubtedly made the most noise, he was the least heard of any of the riotous band.

Then suddenly there was a great cessation. It was as if each man had paused for breath; and although the room was still lighted with the anger of men, it could be seen that there was no danger of immediate conflict, and at once Johnnie, shouldering his way forward, almost succeeded in confronting the Swede. "What did you say I cheated for? What did you say I cheated for? I don't cheat, and I won't let any man say I do!"

The Swede said, "I saw you! I saw you!"

"Well," cried Johnnie, "I'll fight any man what says I cheat!"

"No, you won't," said the cowboy. "Not here."

"Ah, be still, can't you?" said Scully, coming between them.

The quiet was sufficient to allow the Easterner's voice to be heard. He was repeating, "Oh, wait a moment, can't you? What's the good of a fight over a game of cards? Wait a moment!"

Johnnie, his red face appearing above his father's shoulder, hailed the Swede again. "Did you say I cheated?"

The Swede showed his teeth. "Yes."

"Then," said Johnnie, "we must fight."

"Yes, fight," roared the Swede. He was like a demoniac. "Yes, fight! I'll show you what kind of a man I am! I'll show you who you want to fight! Maybe you think I can't fight! Maybe you think I can't! I'll show you, you skin, you card-sharp! Yes, you cheated! You cheated! You cheated!"

"Well, let's go at it, then, mister," said Johnnie, coolly.

The cowboy's brow was beaded with sweat from his efforts in intercepting all sorts of raids. He turned in despair to Scully. "What are you goin' to do now?"

A change had come over the Celtic visage of the old man. He now seemed all eagerness; his eyes glowed.

"We'll let them fight," he answered, stalwartly. "I can't put up with it any longer. I've stood this damned Swede till I'm sick. We'll let them fight."

VI

The men prepared to go out of doors. The Easterner was so nervous that he had great difficulty in getting his arms into the sleeves of his new leather coat. As the cowboy drew his fur cap down over his ears his hands trembled. In fact, Johnnie and old Scully were the only ones who displayed no agitation. These preliminaries were conducted without words.

Scully threw open the door. "Well, come on," he said. Instantly a terrific wind caused the flame of the lamp to struggle at its wick, while a puff of black smoke sprang from the chimney-top. The stove was in mid-current of the blast, and its voice swelled to equal the roar of the storm. Some of the scarred and bedabbled cards were caught up from the floor and dashed helplessly against the farther wall. The men lowered their heads and plunged into the tempest as into a sea.

No snow was falling, but great whirls and clouds of flakes, swept up from the ground by the frantic winds, were streaming southward with the speed of bullets. The covered land was blue with the sheen of an unearthly satin, and there was no other hue save where, at the low, black railway station—which seemed incredibly distant—one light gleamed like a tiny jewel. As the men floundered into a thigh-deep drift, it was known that the Swede was bawling out something. Scully went to him, put a hand on his shoulder, and projected an ear. "What's that you say?" he shouted.

"I say," bawled the Swede again, "I won't stand much show against this gang. I know you'll all pitch on me."

Scully smote him reproachfully on the arm. "Tut, man!" he yelled. The wind tore the words from Scully's lips and scattered them far alee.

"You are all a gang of—" boomed the Swede, but the storm also seized the remainder of this sentence.

Immediately turning their backs upon the wind, the men had swung around a corner to the sheltered side of the hotel. It was the function of the little house to preserve here, amid this great devastation of snow, an irregular V-shape of heavily encrusted grass, which crackled beneath the feet. One could imagine the great drifts piled against the windward side. When the party reached the comparative peace of this spot it was found that the Swede was still bellowing.

"Oh, I know what kind of a thing this is! I know you'll all pitch on me. I can't lick you all!"

Scully turned upon him panther-fashion. "You'll not have to whip all of us. You'll have to whip my son Johnnie. An' the man what troubles you durin' that time will have me to dale with."

The arrangements were swiftly made. The two men faced each other, obedient to the harsh commands of Scully, whose face, in the subtly luminous gloom, could be seen set in the austere impersonal lines that are pictured on the countenances of the Roman veterans. The Easterner's teeth were chattering, and he was hopping up and down like a mechanical toy. The cowboy stood rock-like.

The contestants had not stripped off any clothing. Each was in his ordinary attire. Their fists were up, and they eyed each other in a calm that had the elements of leonine cruelty in it.

During this pause, the Easterner's mind, like a film, took lasting impressions of three men—the iron-nerved master of the ceremony; the Swede, pale, motionless, terrible; and Johnnie, serene yet ferocious, brutish yet heroic. The entire prelude had in it a tragedy greater than the tragedy of action, and this aspect was accentuated by the long, mellow cry of the blizzard, as it sped the tumbling and wailing flakes into the black abyss of the south.

"Now!" said Scully.

The two combatants leaped forward and crashed together like bullocks. There was heard the cushioned sound of blows, and of a curse squeezing out from between the tight teeth of one.

As for the spectators, the Easterner's pent-up breath exploded from him with a pop of relief, absolute relief from the tension of the preliminaries. The cowboy bounded into the air with a yowl. Scully was immovable as from supreme amazement and fear at the fury of the fight which he himself had permitted and arranged.

For a time the encounter in the darkness was such a perplexity of flying arms that it presented no more detail than would a swiftly revolving wheel. Occasionally a face, as if illumined by a flash of light, would shine out, ghastly and marked with pink spots. A moment later, the men might have been known as shadows, if it were not for the involuntary utterance of oaths that came from them in whispers.

Suddenly a holocaust of warlike desire caught the cowboy, and he bolted forward with the speed of a broncho. "Go it, Johnnie! go it! Kill him! Kill him!"

Scully confronted him. "Kape back," he said; and by his glance the cowboy could tell that this man was Johnnie's father.

To the Easterner there was a monotony of unchangeable fighting that was an abomination. This confused mingling was eternal to his sense, which was concentrated in a longing for the end, the priceless end. Once the fighters lurched near him, and as he scrambled hastily backward he heard them breathe like men on the rack.

"Kill him, Johnnie! Kill him! Kill him! Kill him!" The cowboy's face was contorted like one of those agony masks in museums.

"Keep still," said Scully, icily.

Then there was a sudden loud grunt, incomplete, cut short, and Johnnie's body swung away from the Swede and fell with sickening heaviness to the grass. The cowboy was barely in time to prevent the mad Swede from flinging himself upon his prone adversary. "No, you don't," said the cowboy, interposing an arm. "Wait a second."

Scully was at his son's side. "Johnnie! Johnnie, me boy!" His voice had a quality of melancholy tenderness. "Johnnie! Can you go on with it?" He looked anxiously down into the bloody, pulpy face of his son.

There was a moment of silence, and then Johnnie answered in his ordinary voice, "Yes, I—it—yes."

Assisted by his father he struggled to his feet. "Wait a bit now till you git your wind," said the old man.

A few paces away the cowboy was lecturing the Swede. "No, you don't! Wait a second!"

The Easterner was plucking at Scully's sleeve. "Oh, this is enough," he pleaded. "This is enough! Let it go as it stands. This is enough!"

"Bill," said Scully, "git out of the road." The cowboy stepped aside. "Now." The combatants were actuated by a new caution as they advanced toward collision. They glared at each other, and then the Swede aimed a lightning blow that carried with it his entire weight. Johnnie was evidently half stupid from weakness, but he miraculously dodged and his fist sent the over-balanced Swede sprawling.

The cowboy, Scully, and the Easterner burst into a cheer that was like a chorus of triumphant soldiery, but before its conclusion the Swede had scuffled agilely to his feet and come in berserk abandon at his foe.

There was another perplexity of flying arms, and Johnnie's body again swung away and fell, even as a bundle might fall from a roof. The Swede instantly staggered to a little wind-waved tree and leaned upon it, breathing like an engine, while his savage and flame-lit eyes roamed from face to face as the men bent over Johnnie. There was a splendor of isolation in his situation at this time which the Easterner felt once when, lifting his eyes from the man on the ground, he beheld that mysterious and lonely figure, waiting.

"Are you any good yet, Johnnie?" asked Scully in a broken voice.

The son gasped and opened his eyes languidly. After a moment he answered, "No—I ain't—any good—any—more." Then, from shame and bodily ill, he began to weep, the tears furrowing down through the bloodstains on his face. "He was too—too—too heavy for me."

Scully straightened and addressed the waiting figure. "Stranger," he said, evenly, "it's all up with our side." Then his voice changed into that vibrant huskiness which is commonly the tone of the most simple and deadly announcements. "Johnnie is whipped."

Without replying, the victor moved off on the route to the front door of the hotel.

The cowboy was formulating new and unspellable blasphemies. The Easterner was startled to find that they were out in a wind that seemed to come direct from the shadowed arctic floes. He heard again the wail of the snow as it was flung to its grave in the south. He knew now that all this time the cold had been sinking into him deeper and deeper, and he wondered that he had not perished. He felt indifferent to the condition of the vanquished man.

"Johnnie, can you walk?" asked Scully.

"Did I hurt—hurt him any?" asked the son.

"Can you walk, boy? Can you walk?"

Johnnie's voice was suddenly strong. There was a robust impatience in it. "I asked you whether I hurt him any!"

"Yes, yes, Johnnie," answered the cowboy, consolingly; "he's hurt a good deal."

They raised him from the ground, and as soon as he was on his feet he went tottering off, rebuffing all attempts at assistance. When the party rounded the corner they were fairly blinded by the pelting of the snow. It burned their faces like fire. The cowboy carried Johnnie through the drift to the door. As they entered, some cards again rose from the floor and beat against the wall.

The Easterner rushed to the stove. He was so profoundly chilled that he almost dared to embrace the glowing iron. The Swede was not in the room. Johnnie sank into a chair, and, folding his arms on his knees, buried his face in them. Scully, warming one foot and then the other at a rim of the stove, muttered to himself with Celtic mournfulness. The cowboy had removed his fur cap, and with a dazed and rueful air he was running one hand through his tousled locks. From overhead they could hear the creaking of boards, as the Swede tramped here and there in his room.

The sad quiet was broken by the sudden flinging open of a door that led toward the kitchen. It was instantly followed by an inrush of women. They precipitated themselves upon Johnnie amid a chorus of lamentation. Before they carried their prey off to the kitchen, there to be bathed and harangued with that mixture of sympathy and abuse which is a feat of their sex, the mother straightened herself and fixed old Scully with an eye of stern reproach. "Shame be upon you, Patrick Scully!" she cried. "Your own son, too. Shame be upon you!"

"There, now! Be quiet, now!" said the old man, weakly.

"Shame be upon you, Patrick Scully!" The girls, rallying to this slogan, sniffed disdainfully in the direction of those trembling accomplices, the cowboy and the Easterner. Presently they bore Johnnie away, and left the three men to dismal reflection.

VII

"I'd like to fight this here Dutchman myself," said the cowboy, breaking a long silence.

Scully wagged his head sadly. "No, that wouldn't do. It wouldn't be right. It wouldn't be right."

"Well, why wouldn't it?" argued the cowboy. "I don't see no harm in it."

"No,' answered Scully, with mournful heroism. "It wouldn't be right. It was Johnnie's fight, and now we mustn't whip the man just because he whipped Johnnie."

"Yes, that's true enough," said the cowboy; "but—he better not get fresh with me, because I couldn't stand no more of it."

"You'll not say a word to him," commanded Scully, and even then they heard the tread of the Swede on the stairs. His entrance was made theatric. He swept the door back with a bang and swaggered to the middle of the room. No one looked at him. "Well," he cried, insolently, at Scully, "I s'pose you'll tell me now how much I owe you?"

The old man remained stolid. "You don't owe me nothin'."

"Huh!" said the Swede, "huh! Don't owe 'im nothin'."

The cowboy addressed the Swede. "Stranger, I don't see how you come to be so gay around here."

Old Scully was instantly alert. "Stop!" he shouted, holding his hand forth, fingers upward. "Bill, you shut up!"

The cowboy spat carelessly into the sawdust-box. "I didn't say a word, did I?" he asked.

"Mr. Scully," called the Swede, "how much do I owe you?" It was seen that he was attired for departure, and that he had his valise in his hand.

"You don't owe me nothin' ," repeated Scully in the same imperturbable way.

"Huh!" said the Swede. "I guess you're right. I guess if it was any way at all, you'd owe me somethin.' That's what I guess." He turned to the cowboy. " 'Kill him! Kill him! Kill him!' " he mimicked, and then guffawed victoriously. " 'Kill him!' " He was convulsed with ironical humor.

But he might have been jeering the dead. The three men were immovable and silent, staring with glassy eyes at the stove.

The Swede opened the door and passed into the storm, giving one derisive glance backward at the still group.

As soon as the door was closed, Scully and the cowboy leaped to their feet and began to curse. They trampled to and fro, waving their arms and smashing into the air with their fists. "Oh, but that was a hard minute!" wailed Scully. "That was a hard minute! Him there leerin' and scoffin'! One bang at his nose was worth forty dollars to me that minute! How did you stand it, Bill?"

"How did I stand it?" cried the cowboy in a quivering voice. "How did I stand it? Oh!"

The old man burst into sudden brogue. "I'd loike to take that Swade," he wailed, "and hould 'im down on a shtone flure and bate 'im to a jelly wid a shtick!"

The cowboy groaned in sympathy. "I'd like to git him by the neck and ha-ammer him"—he brought his hand down on a chair with a noise like a pistol-shot—"hammer that there Dutchman until he couldn't tell himself from a dead coyote!"

"I'd bate 'im until he—"

"I'd show *him* some things—"

And then together they raised a yearning, fanatic cry—"Oh-o-o-oh! if we only could—"

"Yes!"

"Yes!"

"And then I'd—"

"O-o-oh!"

VIII

The Swede, tightly gripping his valise, tacked across the face of the storm as if he carried sails. He was following a line of little naked, gasping trees which, he knew, must mark the way of the road. His face, fresh from the pounding of Johnnie's fists, felt more pleasure than pain in the wind and the driving snow. A number of square shapes loomed upon him finally, and he knew them as the houses of the main body of the town. He found a street and made travel along it, leaning heavily upon the wind whenever, at a corner, a terrific blast caught him.

He might have been in a deserted village. We picture the world as thick with conquering and elate humanity, but here, with the bugles of the tempest pealing, it was hard to imagine a peopled earth. One viewed the existence of man then as a marvel, and conceded a glamour of wonder to these lice which were caused to cling to a whirling, fire-smitten, ice-locked, disease-stricken, space-lost bulb. The conceit of man was explained by this storm to be the very engine of life. One was a coxcomb not to die in it. However, the Swede found a saloon.

In front of it an indomitable red light was burning, and the snowflakes were made blood-color as they flew through the circumscribed territory of the lamp's shining. The Swede pushed open the door of the saloon and entered. A sanded expanse was before him, and at the end of it four men sat about a table drinking. Down one side of the room extended a radiant bar, and its guardian was leaning upon his elbows listening to the talk of the men at the table. The Swede dropped his valise upon the floor and, smiling fraternally upon the barkeeper, said, "Gimme some whisky, will you?" The man placed a bottle, a whisky-glass, and a glass of ice-thick water upon the bar. The Swede poured himself an abnormal portion of whisky and drank it in three gulps. "Pretty bad night," remarked the bartender, indifferently. He was making the pretension of blindness which is usually a distinction of his class; but it could have been seen that he was furtively studying the half-erased blood-stains on the face of the Swede. "Bad night," he said again.

"Oh, it's good enough for me," replied the Swede, hardily, as he poured himself some more whiskey. The barkeeper took his coin and maneuvered it through its reception by the highly nickeled cash-machine. A bell rang; a card labeled "20 cts." had appeared.

"No," continued the Swede, "this isn't too bad weather. It's good enough for me."

"So?" murmured the barkeeper, languidly.

The copious drams made the Swede's eyes swim, and he breathed a trifle heavier. "Yes, I like this weather. I like it. It suits me." It was apparently his design to impart a deep significance to these words.

"So?" murmured the bartender again. He turned to gaze dreamily at the scroll-like birds and bird-like scrolls which had been drawn with soap upon the mirrors in back of the bar.

"Well, I guess I'll take another drink," said the Swede, presently. "Have something?"

"No, thanks; I'm not drinkin'," answered the bartender. Afterward he asked, "How did you hurt your face?"

The Swede immediately began to boast loudly. "Why, in a fight. I thumped the soul out of a man down here at Scully's hotel."

The interest of the four men at the table was at last aroused.

"Who was it?" said one.

"Johnnie Scully," blustered the Swede. "Son of the man what runs it. He will be pretty near dead for some weeks, I can tell you. I made a nice thing of him, I did. He couldn't get up. They carried him in the house. Have a drink?"

Instantly the men in some subtle way encased themselves in reserve. "No, thanks," said one. The group was of curious formation. Two were prominent local business men; one was the district attorney; and one was a professional gambler of the kind known as "square." But a scrutiny of the group would not have enabled an observer to pick the gambler from the men of more reputable pursuits. He was, in fact, a man so delicate in manner, when among people of fair class, and so judicious in his choice of victims, that in the strictly masculine part of the town's life he had come to be explicitly trusted and admired. People called him a thoroughbred. The fear and contempt with which his craft was regarded were undoubtedly the reason why his quiet dignity shone conspicuous above the quiet dignity of men who might be merely hatters, billiard-markers, or grocery clerks. Beyond an occasional unwary traveler who came by rail, this gambler was supposed to prey solely upon reckless and senile farmers, who, when flush with good crops, drove into town in all the pride and confidence of an absolutely invulnerable stupidity. Hearing at times in circuitous fashion of the despoilment of such a farmer, the important men of Romper invariably laughed in contempt of the victim, and if they thought of the wolf at all, it was with a kind of pride at the knowledge that he would never dare think of attacking their wisdom and courage. Besides, it was popular that this gambler had a real wife and two real children in a neat cottage in a suburb, where he led an exemplary home life; and when anyone even suggested a discrepancy in his character, the crowd immediately vociferated descriptions of this virtuous family circle. Then men who led exemplary home lives, and men who did not lead exemplary home lives, all subsided in a bunch, remarking that there was nothing more to be said.

However, when a restriction was placed upon him—as, for instance, when a strong clique of members of the new Pollywog Club refused to permit him, even as a spectator, to appear in the rooms of the organization—the candor and gentleness with which he accepted the judgment disarmed many of his foes and made his friends more desperately partisan. He invariably distinguished between himself and a respectable Romper man so quickly and frankly that his manner actually appeared to be a continual broadcast compliment.

And one must not forget to declare the fundamental fact of his entire position in Romper. It is irrefutable that in all affairs outside his business, in all matters that occur eternally and commonly between man and man, this thieving card-player was so generous, so just, so moral, that, in a contest, he could have put to flight the consciences of nine tenths of the citizens of Romper.

And so it happened that he was seated in this saloon with the two prominent local merchants and the district attorney.

The Swede continued to drink raw whisky, meanwhile babbling at the barkeeper and trying to induce him to indulge in potations. "Come on. Have a drink. Come on. What—no? Well, have a little one, then. By gawd, I've whipped a man tonight, and I want to celebrate. I whipped him good, too. Gentlemen," the Swede cried to the men at the table, "have a drink?"

"Ssh!" said the barkeeper.

The group at the table, although furtively attentive, had been pretending to be deep in talk, but now a man lifted his eyes toward the Swede and said, shortly, "Thanks. We don't want any more."

At this reply the Swede ruffled out his chest like a rooster. "Well," he exploded, "it seems I can't get anybody to drink with me in this town. Seems so, don't it? Well!"

"Ssh!" said the barkeeper.

"Say," snarled the Swede, "don't you try to shut me up. I won't have it. I'm a gentleman, and I want people to drink with me. And I want 'em to drink with me now. *Now*—do you understand?" He rapped the bar with his knuckles.

Years of experience had calloused the bartender. He merely grew sulky. "I hear you," he answered.

"Well," cried the Swede, "listen hard then. See those men over there? Well, they're going to drink with me, and don't you forget it. Now you watch."

"Hi!" yelled the barkeeper, "this won't do!"

"Why won't it?" demanded the Swede. He stalked over to the table, and by chance laid his hand upon the shoulder of the gambler. "How about this?" he asked wrathfully. "I asked you to drink with me."

The gambler simply twisted his head and spoke over his shoulder. "My friend, I don't know you."

"Oh, hell!" answered the Swede, "come and have a drink."

"Now, my boy," advised the gambler, kindly, "take your hand off my shoulder and go 'way and mind your own business." He was a little, slim man, and it seemed strange to hear him use this tone of heroic patronage to the burly Swede. The other men at the table said nothing.

"What! You won't drink with me, you little dude? I'll make you, then! I'll make you!" The Swede had grasped the gambler frenziedly at the throat, and was dragging him from his chair. The other men sprang up. The barkeeper dashed around the corner of his bar. There was a great tumult, and then was seen a long blade in the hand of the gambler. It shot forward, and a human body, this citadel of virtue, wisdom, power, was pierced as easily as if it had been a melon. The Swede fell with a cry of supreme astonishment.

The prominent merchants and the district attorney must have at once tumbled out of the place backward. The bartender found himself hanging limply to the arm of a chair and gazing into the eyes of a murderer.

"Henry," said the latter, as he wiped his knife on one of the towels that hung beneath the bar rail, "you tell 'em where to find me. I'll be home, waiting for 'em." Then he vanished. A moment afterward the barkeeper was in the street dinning through the storm for help and, moreover, companionship.

The corpse of the Swede, alone in the saloon, had its eyes fixed upon a dreadful legend that dwelt atop of the cash-machine: "This registers the amount of your purchase."

IX

Months later, the cowboy was frying pork over the stove of a little ranch near the Dakota line, when there was a quick thud of hoofs outside, and presently the Easterner entered with the letters and the papers.

"Well," said the Easterner at once, "the chap that killed the Swede has got three years. Wasn't much, was it?"

"He has? Three years?" The cowboy poised his pan of pork, while he ruminated upon the news. "Three years. That ain't much."

"No. It was a light sentence," replied the Easterner as he unbuckled his spurs. "Seems there was a good deal of sympathy for him in Romper."

"If the bartender had been any good," observed the cowboy, thoughtfully, "he would have gone in and cracked that there Dutchman on the head with a bottle in the beginnin' of it and stopped all this here murderin'."

"Yes, a thousand things might have happened," said the Easterner, tartly.

The cowboy returned his pan of pork to the fire, but his philosophy continued. "It's funny, ain't it? If he hadn't said Johnnie was cheatin' he'd be alive this minute. He was an awful fool. Game played for fun, too. Not for money. I believe he was crazy."

"I feel sorry for that gambler," said the Easterner.

"Oh, so do I," said the cowboy. "He don't deserve none of it for killin' who he did."

"The Swede might not have been killed if everything had been square."

"Might not have been killed?" exclaimed the cowboy. "Everythin' square? Why, when he said that Johnnie was cheatin' and acted like such a jackass? And then in the saloon he fairly walked up to git hurt?" With these arguments the cowboy browbeat the Easterner and reduced him to rage.

"You're a fool!" cried the Easterner, viciously. "You're a bigger jackass than the Swede by a million majority. Now let me tell you one thing. Let me tell you something. Listen! Johnnie *was* cheating!"

" 'Johnnie,' " said the cowboy, blankly. There was a minute of silence, and then he said, robustly. "Why, no. The game was only for fun."

"Fun or not," said the Easterner, "Johnnie was cheating. I saw him. I know it. I saw him. And I refused to stand up and be a man. I let the Swede fight it out alone. And you—you were simply puffing around the place and wanting to fight. And then old Scully himself! We are all in it! This poor gambler isn't even a noun. He is kind of an adverb. Every sin is the result of a collaboration. We, five of us, have collaborated in the murder of this Swede. Usually there are from a dozen to forty women really involved in every murder, but in this case it seems to be only five men—you, I, Johnnie, old Scully; and that fool of an unfortunate gambler came merely as a culmination, the apex of a human movement, and gets all the punishment."

The cowboy, injured and rebellious, cried out blindly into this fog of mysterious theory: "Well, I didn't do anythin', did I?"

BERNARD MALAMUD

Take Pity

Davidov, the census-taker, opened the door without knocking, limped into the room and sat wearily down. Out came his notebook and he was on the job. Rosen, the ex-coffee salesman, wasted, eyes despairing, sat motionless, crosslegged, on his cot. The square, clean but cold room, lit by a dim globe, was sparsely furnished: the cot, a folding chair, small table, old unpainted chests—no closets but who needed them?—and a small sink with a rough piece of green, institutional soap on its holder—you could smell it across the room. The worn black shade over the single narrow window was drawn to the ledge, surprising Davidov.

"What's the matter you don't pull the shade up?" he remarked.

Rosen ultimately sighed. "Let it stay."

"Why? Outside is light."

"Who needs light?"

"What then you need?"

"Light I don't need," replied Rosen.

Davidov, sour-faced, flipped through the closely scrawled pages of his notebook until he found a clean one. He attempted to scratch in a word with his fountain pen but it had run dry, so he fished a pencil stub out of his vest pocket and sharpened it with a cracked razor blade. Rosen paid no attention to the feathery shavings falling to the floor. He looked restless, seemed to be listening to or for something, although Davidov was convinced there was absolutely nothing to listen to. It was only when the census-taker somewhat irritably and with increasing loudness repeated a question, that Rosen stirred and identified himself. He was about to furnish an address but caught himself and shrugged.

Davidov did not comment on the salesman's gesture. "So begin," he nodded.

"Who knows where to begin?" Rosen stared at the drawn shade. "Do they know here where to begin?"

"Philosophy we are not interested," said Davidov. "Start in how you met her."

"Who?" pretended Rosen.

"Her," he snapped.

"So if I got to begin, how you know about her already?" Rosen asked triumphantly.

Davidov spoke wearily, "You mentioned before."

Rosen remembered. They had questioned him upon his arrival and he now recalled blurting out her name. It was perhaps something in the air. It did not permit you to retain what you remembered. That was part of the cure, if you wanted a cure.

"Where I met her—?" Rosen murmured. "I met her where she always was—in the back room there in that hole in the wall that it was a waste of time for me I went there. Maybe I sold them a half a bag of coffee a month. This is not business."

"In business we are not interested."

"What then you are interested?" Rosen mimicked Davidov's tone.

Davidov clammed up coldly.

Rosen knew they had him where it hurt, so he went on: "The husband was maybe forty, Axel Kalish, a Polish refugee. He worked like a blind horse when he got to America, and saved maybe two—three thousand dollars that he bought with the money this pisher grocery in a dead neighborhood where he didn't have a chance. He called my company up for credit and they sent me I should see. I recommended okay because I felt sorry. He had a wife, Eva, you know already about her, and two darling girls, one five and one three, little dolls, Fega and Surale, that I didn't want them to suffer. So right away I told him, without tricks, 'Kiddo, this is a mistake. This place is a grave. Here they will bury you if you don't get out quick!' "

Rosen sighed deeply.

"So?" Davidov had thus far written nothing, irking the ex-salesman.

"So?—Nothing. He didn't get out. After a couple months he tried to sell but nobody bought, so he stayed and starved. They never made expenses. Every day they got poorer you couldn't look in their faces. 'Don't be a damn fool,' I told him, 'go in bankruptcy.' But he couldn't stand it to lose all his capital, and he was also afraid it would be hard to find a job. 'My God,' I said, 'do anything. Be a painter, a janitor, a junk man, but get out of here before everybody is a skeleton.'

"This he finally agreed with me, but before he could go in auction he dropped dead."

Davidov made a note. "How did he die?"

"On this I am not an expert," Rosen replied. "You know better than me."

"How did he die?" Davidov spoke impatiently. "Say in one word."

"From what he died?—he died, that's all."

"Answer, please, this question."

"Broke in him something. That's how."

"Broke what?"

"Broke what breaks. He was talking to me how bitter was his life, and he touched me on my sleeve to say something else, but the next minute his face got small and he fell down dead, the wife screaming, the little girls crying that it made in my heart pain. I am myself a sick man and when I saw him laying on the floor, I said to myself, 'Rosen, say goodbye, this guy is finished.' So I said it."

Rosen got up from the cot and strayed despondently around the room, avoiding the window. Davidov was occupying the only chair, so the ex-salesman was finally forced to sit on the edge of the bed again. This irritated him. He badly wanted a cigarette but disliked asking for one.

Davidov permitted him a short interval of silence, then leafed impatiently through his notebook. Rosen, to needle the census-taker, said nothing.

"So what happened?" Davidov finally demanded.

Rosen spoke with ashes in his mouth. "After the funeral—" he paused, tried to wet his lips, then went on, "He belonged to a society that they buried him, and he also left a thousand dollars insurance, but after the funeral I said to her, 'Eva, listen to me. Take the money and your children and run away from here. Let the creditors take the store. What will they get?—Nothing.'

"But she answered me. 'Where will I go, where, with my two orphans that their father left them to starve?'

" 'Go anywhere,' I said. 'Go to your relatives.'

"She laughed like laughs somebody who hasn't got no joy. 'My relatives Hitler took away from me.'

" 'What about Axel—surely an uncle somewheres?'

" 'Nobody,' she said. 'I will stay here like my Axel wanted. With the insurance I will buy new stock and fix up the store. Every week I will decorate the window, and in this way gradually will come in new customers—'

" 'Eva, my darling girl—'

" 'A millionaire I don't expect to be. All I want is I should make a little living and take care on my girls. We will live in the back here like before, and in this way I can work and watch them, too.'

" 'Eva,' I said, 'you are a nice-looking young woman, only thirty-eight years. Don't throw away your life here. Don't flush in the toilet—you should excuse me—the thousand poor dollars from your dead husband. Believe me, I know from such stores. After thirty-five years' experience I know a graveyard when I smell it. Go better some place and find a job. You're young yet. Sometime you will meet somebody and get married.'

" 'No, Rosen, not me,' she said. 'With marriage I am finished. Nobody wants a poor widow with two children.'

" 'This I don't believe it.'

" 'I know,' she said.

"Never in my life I saw so bitter a woman's face.

" 'No,' I said. 'No.'

" 'Yes, Rosen, yes. In my whole life I never had anything. In my whole life I always suffered. I don't expect better. This is my life.'

"I said no and she said yes. What could I do? I am a man with only one kidney, and worse than that, that I won't mention it. When I talked she didn't listen, so I stopped to talk. Who can argue with a widow?"

The ex-salesman glanced up at Davidov but the census-taker did not reply. "What happened then?" he asked.

"What happened?" mocked Rosen. "Happened what happens."

Davidov's face grew red.

"What happened, happened," Rosen said hastily. "She ordered from the wholesalers all kinds goods that she paid for them cash. All week she opened boxes and packed on the shelves cans, jars, packages. Also she cleaned, and she washed, and she mopped with oil the floor. With tissue paper she made new decorations in the window, everything should look nice—but who came in? Nobody except a few poor customers from the tenement around the corner. And when they came? When was closed the supermarkets and they needed some little item that they forgot to buy, like a quart milk, fifteen cents' cheese, a small can sardines for lunch. In a few months was again dusty the cans on the shelves, and her thousand was gone. Credit she couldn't get except from me, and from me she got because I paid out of my pocket the company. This she didn't know. She worked, she dressed clean, she waited that the store should get better. Little by little the shelves got empty, but where was the profit? They ate it up. When I looked on the little girls I knew what she didn't tell me. Their faces were white, they were thin, they were hungry. She kept the little food that was left, on the shelves. One night I brought in a nice piece sirloin, but I could see from her eyes that she didn't like that I did it. So what else could I do? I have a heart and I am human."

Here the ex-salesman wept.

Davidov pretended not to see though once he peeked.

Rosen blew his nose, then went on more calmly, "When the children were sleeping we sat in the dark there, in the back, and not once in four hours opened the door should come in a customer. 'Eva, for God-sakes, *run away,*' I said.

" 'I have no place to go,' she said.

" 'I will give you where you can go, and please don't say to me no. I am a bachelor, this you know. I got whatever I need and more besides. Let me help you and the children. Money don't interest me. Interests me good health, but I can't buy it. I'll tell you what I will do. Let this place go to the creditors and move into a two-family house that I own, which the top floor is now empty. Rent will cost you nothing. In the meantime you can go and find a job. I will also pay the downstairs lady to take care of the girls—God bless them—until you will come home. With your wages you will buy the food, if you need clothes, and also save a little. This you can use when you get married someday. What do you say?'

"She didn't answer me. She only looked on me in such a way, with such burning eyes, like I was small and ugly. For the first time I thought to myself, 'Rosen, this woman don't like you.'

" 'Thank you very kindly, my friend Mr. Rosen,' she answered me, 'but charity we are not needing. I got yet a paying business, and it will get better when times are better. Now is bad times. When comes again good times will get better the business.'

" 'Who charity?' I cried to her. 'What charity? Speaks to you your husband's a friend.'

" 'Mr. Rosen, my husband didn't have no friends.'

" 'Can't you see that I want to help the children?'

" 'The children have their mother.'

" 'Eva, what's the matter with you?' I said. 'Why do you make sound bad something that I mean it should be good?'

"This she didn't answer. I felt sick in my stomach, and was coming also a headache so I left.

"All night I didn't sleep, and then all of a sudden I figured out a reason why she was worried. She was worried I would ask for some kind payment except cash. She got the wrong man. Anyway, this made me think of something that I didn't think about before. I thought now to ask her to marry me. What did she have to lose? I could take care of myself without any trouble to them. Fega and Surale would have a father he could give them for the movies, or sometime to buy a little doll to play with, and when I died, would go to them my investments and insurance policies.

"The next day I spoke to her.

" 'For myself, Eva, I don't want a thing. Absolutely not a thing.

For you and your girls—everything. I am not a strong man, Eva. In fact, I am sick. I tell you this you should understand I don't expect to live long. But even for a few years would be nice to have a little family.'

"She was with her back to me and didn't speak.

"When she turned around again her face was white but the mouth was like iron.

" 'No, Mr. Rosen.'

" 'Why not, tell me?'

" 'I had enough with sick men.' She began to cry. 'Please, Mr. Rosen. Go home.'

"I didn't have strength I should argue with her, so I went home. I went home but hurt me my mind. All day long and all night I felt bad. My back pained me where was missing my kidney. Also too much smoking. I tried to understand this woman but I couldn't. Why should somebody that her two children were starving always say no to a man that he wanted to help her? What did I do to her bad? Am I maybe a murderer she should hate me so much? All that I felt in my heart was pity for her and the children, but I couldn't convince her. Then I went back and begged her she should let me help them, and once more she told me no.

" 'Eva,' I said, 'I don't blame you that you don't want a sick man. So come with me to a marriage broker and we will find you a strong, healthy husband that he will support you and your girls. I will give the dowry.'

"She screamed. 'On this I don't need your help, Rosen!'

"I didn't say no more. What more could I say? All day long, from early in the morning till late in the night she worked like an animal. All day she mopped, she washed with soap and a brush the shelves, the few cans she polished, but the store was still rotten. The little girls I was afraid to look at. I could see in their faces their bones. They were tired, they were weak. Little Surale held with her hand all the time the dress of Fega. Once when I saw them in the street I gave them some cakes, but when I tried the next day to give them something else, the mother shouldn't know, Fega answered me, 'We can't take, Momma says today is a fast day.'

"I went inside. I made my voice soft. 'Eva, on my bended knee I am a man with nothing in this world. Allow me that I should have a little pleasure before I die. Allow me that I should help you to stock up once more the store.'

"So what did she do? She cried, it was terrible to see. And after she cried, what did she say? She told me to go away and I shouldn't come back. I felt like to pick up a chair and break her head.

"In my house I was too weak to eat. For two days I took in my mouth nothing except maybe a spoon of chicken noodle soup, or maybe a glass tea without sugar. This wasn't good for me. My health felt bad.

"Then I made up a scheme that I was a friend of Axel's who lived in Jersey. I said I owed Axel seven hundred dollars that he lent me this money fifteen years ago, before he got married. I said I did not have the whole money now, but I would send her every week twenty dollars till it was paid up the debt. I put inside the letter two tens and gave it to a friend of mine, also a salesman, he should mail it in Newark so she would not be suspicious who wrote the letters."

To Rosen's surprise Davidov had stopped writing. The book was full, so he tossed it onto the table, yawned, but listened amiably. His curiosity had died.

Rosen got up and fingered the notebook. He tried to read the small distorted handwriting but could not make out a single word.

"It's not English and it's not Yiddish," he said. "Could it be in Hebrew?"

"No," answered Davidov. "It's an old-fashioned language that they don't use it nowadays."

"Oh?" Rosen returned to the cot. He saw no purpose to going on now that it was not required, but he felt he had to.

"Came back all the letters," he said dully. "The first she opened it, then pasted back again the envelope, but the rest she didn't even open."

" 'Here,' I said to myself, 'is a very strange thing—a person that you can never give her anything.—*But I will give.*'

"I went then to my lawyer and we made out a will that everything I had—all my investments, my two houses that I owned, also furniture, my car, the checking account—every cent would go to her, and when she died, the rest would be left for the two girls. The same with my insurance. They would be my beneficiaries. Then I signed and went home. In the kitchen I turned on the gas and put my head in the stove.

"Let her say now no."

Davidov, scratching his stubbled cheek, nodded. This was the part he already knew. He got up and before Rosen could cry no, idly raised the window shade.

It was twilight in space but a woman stood before the window.

Rosen with a bound was off his cot to see.

It was Eva, staring at him with haunted, beseeching eyes. She raised her arms to him.

Infuriated, the ex-salesman shook his fist.

"Whore, bastard, bitch," he shouted at her. "Go 'way from here. Go home to your children."

Davidov made no move to hinder him as Rosen rammed down the window shade.

5

IMPLICATION AND IRONY

In preceding discussions, we have repeatedly pointed out that perhaps the basic characteristic which differentiates fiction from nonfiction is its reliance upon implication; in this respect, the story is more closely related to the poem than to the essay. "Always show, never tell" was Chekhov's advice to fiction writers, and from Poe (who half a century earlier said much the same thing) to the present, writers have taken that as a general and essential principle. And as we have also suggested, communication through implication or suggestion places certain burdens on the reader. Hence, some of the inevitable questions which arise when a student is asked to "interpret" a story are these: Why do fiction writers handle characters or themes as they do? Why can't they just *say* what they mean? Why go to the trouble of burying a body only for the sake of forcing us to exhume it again?

We have already suggested one answer; the story which does not employ implication is less interesting than the one that does, a principle which is attested to by the fact that a story synopsis will inevitably be less interesting than the story itself. Indeed, we can put the generalization more forcefully: as one becomes an increasingly sophisticated reader, he will probably discover that a story's interest is in direct ratio to the extent to which it employs implication.[1]

But interest is only one reason for the employment of implication,

[1] Within limits, of course. Implication can be carried to a *reduction ad absurdum.* This is not the place, except in passing, to deal with the matter of what can be called obscurity for the sake of obscurity. Some avant-garde, "little magazine" stories do seem to have been written on the assumption that the first requirement for a "good" story is that it present the reader with a puzzle. The first requirement for a good story is, of course, that it tell a story as effectively as the skill, intelligence, and care of the writer can manage; and the genuinely good story will be only as difficult as it has to be in order to say what it wants to say. For this reason, we can dismiss the deliberately obscure story as readily as elsewhere we have dismissed the crassly commercial story.

and probably not the most important one. A second is to be discovered in the basic intent of fiction. Before it is anything else, a story is an attempt to communicate an experience. One ingredient of experience is emotion; experience may be in part intellectual, but it is also of necessity glandular. And in the communication of emotion, the writer *must* use indirection; T. S. Eliot's generalization that one cannot transmit emotion directly is as valid for fiction as for poetry. To be more specific: a writer cannot *tell* you that a character is sad and produce sadness in you; you may *understand* his feelings, but you will not *feel* anything. The reason is that the writer has used an abstraction in order to try to transmit something which is concrete; sadness is a vague and general term for a countless number of specific feelings, each of them the product of a specific set of circumstances. We feel "sad," for example, when a good friend falls sick; we feel "sad" when we fail an examination; we feel "sad" when we see the picture of an anonymous victim of cystic fibrosis in an advertisement. In no case, is any one of those feelings the same as any other. Hence, if a writer is going to make you feel "sad," he must work indirectly. He must, for one thing, provide you with a convincing character with whom you can, in some degree, identify. He must place that character in a situation in which a specific emotional reaction is inherent. Meanwhile, if he is to succeed, you, the reader, must also do something. You are not, of course, the character in a given story, nor, as you read the story, are you in the character's position. But the writer assumes that you have been in parallel situations and have experienced parallel emotions, and if he can make you recall such a situation, he can also evoke in you the emotions which attended it. And when he goes through this process, he is employing implication.

Or consider theme. Most generally, a writer handles theme indirectly because he distrusts the accuracy, the completeness, or the forcefulness of a generalization. A writer may quite humanly want to convince us that his interpretation of some aspect of the human condition is valid. To accomplish this, he can choose between two methods. On the one hand, he can appeal to his reader intellectually, through logic, reason, argument—that is, he can write an essay. On the other, he can appeal emotionally by subjecting his reader to an experience which seems to corroborate his thesis—that is, he can write a story. The first method will enable a reader to *understand* an abstract concept; the second can, with luck and skill, force him to *feel* the validity of that same concept.

The desire to transmit experience is perhaps the basic reason for the employment of implication in fiction. But there are other reasons, too. One is a writer's desire for *accuracy*. It may seem paradoxical, but a writer often can say most accurately what he wants to say by *not* saying it. In all studies of the process of communication, it is a truism that the more one relies on abstractions or generalizations in order to transmit meaning, the less effectively one communicates; conversely, the more specific one is, the more clearly he conveys what he means. That basic principle has been known to storytellers from the beginning. Does one want to evoke a feeling of excitement in an audience? There are as many different feelings which we can call excitement as there are experiences which evoke the feeling. Hence, if we are to capture a specific and exact feeling which might be termed excitement, we must present the experience that evokes it. And when we do so, we are again employing implication.

If implication is the only road a writer has to accuracy, it may also be the best road to *completeness.* To illustrate this, consider the use of symbol in story.[2] A symbol may be defined as a concrete object which suggests a complex of ideas or attitudes or feelings. Suppose that a writer wants to treat the subject of racism in a story. He will begin, of course, with a story, but any one that he chooses will probably be able to say only part of what he may want to say about racism. But in symbol a writer has a device that can say much more for him; by using, for instance, a fire hose or a hooded sheet or a police dog, he can suggest what he found it impossible to state. In effect, what symbol manages to do here is to persuade the reader to fill in a writer's gaps. And quite obviously, that use of symbol gives the writer an additional advantage; at the same time that it helps him to say more, it also enables him to say it with greater compression and economy than would any other method.

The advantages of implication to a fiction writer are, therefore, incalculable. But for most readers, the persistent question is not, "Why do writers employ implication?" Rather, it is, "What do I look for in a story in order not to miss its implications?"

In our discussions of conflict, character, and theme, we have already answered this in part—indeed, in very large part, for the basic implications of a story will almost always be found either in its characterization or in its development and resolution of conflict. And in future sections of this text, we will be discussing other elements and devices in fiction which play their part. Some of the implications of a given story can be discovered, for example, by carefully examining the story's point of view. Some can be discovered in a story's employment of such devices as symbol or allusion. Some can be deduced from the contrasts within a story. Some are even to be found in style: two simple declarative sentences, for example, can imply one thing; join them together, subordinating one to the other, and the same two clauses will imply quite another thing. But at this point, one other fictional device demands mention—that is the device of *irony.*

Irony may be defined as a contrast, a disparity between what actually is and what it ought to be, or between what is and what seems to be,

[2] For a more complete discussion of the use of symbol, see Section 7.

or between what is and what we could wish it to be. The heart of irony is incongruity, the linking together of opposites. So prevalent is it that one critic has gone so far as to insist that a story cannot exist without it; and it would indeed be difficult to find a modern story which does not contain at least one element of irony.

You will find irony assuming several forms. Easiest to recognize will be *verbal irony*; here a character or a writer will say one thing but clearly mean the opposite. Other forms of irony are both more important (to a story's theme or characterization or total effect) and more difficult to perceive. Irony, for example, may be inherent in a *situation*; a story in which a man spends a lifetime in the pursuit of money only to discover that the goal was not worth the struggle would be employing situational irony. Stories can employ what one critic has called irony of *attitude*; a story might present us with a John Bircher who thinks of himself as democratic but whom the reader sees as the opposite of democratic. Or a story can employ the subtlest of all types of irony, *tonal irony*; by choice of word or phrase, or by selection of detail, or simply by shrewd juxtaposition, writers can often suggest that what they seem to be saying should not be taken literally. The frequent use of *understatement* in fiction (stating the important as though it were trivial) or the somewhat less common use of *exaggeration* (stating the trivial as though it were important) are two examples of tonal irony.

Whatever form irony may assume, it is crucial that a reader be alert to it, for both a story's meaning and its effect may depend upon it. For as with other kinds of implication, irony is frequently a writer's main path to both accuracy and complexity. Through irony a writer can show his awareness of the fact that life is made up of contradictions and paradoxes, that no truth is ever the whole and absolute truth, that black is never wholly black nor white wholly white, that the problems inherent in the human condition should not be taken either with the seriousness or the literalness with which most of us are inclined to take them. To put this in another way, irony puts life in its proper perspective. Thus, though it might be possible to create a story without it, it is probably true that no intelligent story exists which does not have in it some element of irony.

MARK SCHORER

The Face Within the Face

"Don't!" Laura Newman said, too sharply for the occasion, and Robert, her husband, who had just begun to trace a light imaginary line along her smooth brown thigh, pulled his hand away and fell back on the sand. Laura did not move. In a white swimming suit, she lay stretched out on a white towel, as arranged and quiet as a statue, hair flowing back, eyes closed, lips a little parted, face and body gleaming, offering herself to the sun as supine marble figures on monuments coldly offer themselves to God.

On the sand beyond his father, staring out at the sea, sat David, their thirteen-year-old son, who looked over toward his mother speculatively now and asked, "Don't what?"

"She was talking to me," Robert said. He stretched out and, leaning on his elbow, looked gloomily down at his wife's ear—an object strange and perfect, as if wrought, like an artifact, by cautious, astonishing skill. He turned away, toward the boy. "Let's swim," he said.

Laura did not speak or move. *Burn, burn,* she was thinking, *burn, burn, burn,* in the rhythm of the small, lapping waves that endlessly, warmly buffeted the yellow shore. The perfect, paradoxical, immaculate pleasure as the hot sun burns and burns on the skin! The accumulated and clinging irritations and frustrations and dismal intensities of four wet and cold winter months seemed to dry upon her and fall away like scales, and she could almost feel herself emerging, with this hot balm, new and absolutely pure, and in her mind she likened the images, from a forgotton school poem, of fire and ice.

She could hear, high above her or far out over the blue cove, the distant, whimpering cry of gulls—shrill whispers—and behind her closed lids she pictured them wheeling in silvery arcs against the cool blue of the sky. Nearer, travelling along the sand to her ear, she heard the swishing sound of feet as Robert and David went down to the water. Then she heard them splashing. Then she thought, *Puberty*, and at once, with the thought, she shuddered, and her warm skin was chilled, as if the sun had gone under a cloud and a cold wind abruptly blew.

"You should take him South with you if you can manage," Mr. Lowell, the headmaster, had written. "He is well along toward puberty now, you know, growing a little too fast, and he needs some sun, needs to be built up. He's not a rugged boy by nature. Of course, we would be glad to keep him here at the school during the spring holiday—he's a most likable and tractable lad, and I'm confident that the arrangements could be made—but in his own interest we all feel that you should consider taking him with you." And so on, and, of course, there had been no question but that the headmaster was right, only there had been the somewhat irritating question of revising their plans, of cutting their three weeks to a little less than two. Yet here they were, their sixth gorgeous day, and she expressed her gratitude to the sun in a luxurious arching of her back and stretching of her toes, until her body was taut with pleasure. Into this momentary intense delight, voices broke. She relaxed and slowly turned, and raised her head and shoulders with her elbows under her.

Robert and David were still in the water, Robert swimming briskly out, David standing still, water to his knees, a bony little figure in the forefront of the vast expanse of empty sea. Turning her head, she saw that other people had come and were settling themselves on the sand at a barely reasonable distance behind her—a man and woman and two girls and a boy.

Laura swore softly. On their first day, the Newmans had wandered away from the big stretch of beach in front of their hotel and had found this quiet cove, where the surf broke far out and where almost no one ever came. They had enjoyed the empty sea from the small empty beach fringed with barren dunes, where there was no intrusion of strident voices, no gross intimacy with other bodies. Then who were these people disposing themselves now on the sand just behind her, already shouting and calling and shrilling, the mother to her scattering children, the husband to the wife? Not, Laura thought, guests of the hotel.

She stared at them. The man wore droopy flowered trunks. He had a long, skinny white body, with a scrawny patch of black hair on his white chest, and black forearms and legs, and a narrow head with too much black hair above his ears, and the white scalp showing through the thin hair on top. The wife was short and round, with a round head and, again, too much black, untidy hair. The children were like their mother—short and round, with round heads and faces, the girls with fuzzy black pigtails, the boy with a black shock that stood up in ragged thrusts. The man was pulling towels from a basket and spreading them on the sand, and when the wife had seated herself on one, she reached into the basket and brought out a tube, and Laura watched her spread a thick layer of white salve over her nose, under her eyes, and on her cheekbones, so that she suddenly gave the fantastic impression of wearing a white domino that had been cut in half. Then Laura saw that something was wrong with her right arm; it seemed, somehow, crippled, the fingers that applied the ointment knotted in a queer way and the elbow not quite free. And when, suddenly, she shouted to her children, who had run down to the water, her face, too, or the right side of it, showed some similar defect—a partial paralysis, which made her seem to leer. When she stopped shouting, her face settled into what was apparently its perpetual expression—a horrid, rigid simper.

Laura shuddered with distaste, turned around and sat up, and determinedly faced the sea. Two things she passionately claimed as belonging to her life, and she wanted them in no less than large ways. They were privacy and self-possession. At this moment, in a small way, this family had snatched the second with the first. As she watched Robert helping David with his crawl in the quiet water of the cove, she wondered irritably how people such as these could disturb her composure, until, in a sudden misery of recollection, she knew that it was because of their disgusting domesticity; somehow they gave the impression of having brought their entire household onto the immaculate beach, spilled out on the sand the whole steamy clutter of their lives, so that Laura thought of a cantankerous parrot in a parlor cage, some potted ferns before stiff lace curtains, a kitchen sink full of greasy dishes, and soiled bed linen, gray.

Laura sat stiffly on the sand in the abrupt and heavy grip of a life long since dead—of a sordid beach town in New Jersey, of a cheap, flimsily built cottage, a girl lying at night with her head under her pillow to shut out the sounds that came through the walls from the bedroom next to hers, and the girl in the day, seeking out some lonely place on the beach where she could lie in the sun for hours, unmolested, to purge herself. The people behind her, by their presence alone, had destroyed her careful peace, and through closed teeth she swore in anger, because now the sun was helpless.

The woman was screaming at the boy, who had walked down to the water and was watching Robert and David. "Lou-ee! Lou-ee!" she shrilled, and then some word that came to Laura as "Ny-ah! Ny-ah!"—like an abstraction from all negatives. Laura glanced over her shoulder at the distorted mouth under the white mask, and the stiff arm gesticulating, and then, turning back, lowered her head into her cupped hands, so that she sat with her fingers pressed over her ears. Yet she could hear the father, calling more gently, "Lou-ee, come!" The boy stared at his parents and, at last, laggingly, came back to where they sat. Laura heard his grunt as he flung himself on the sand behind her, saying, "What's the fun? What'd we come for?" The mother said, "Just wait," and the father said, "We'll go in soon."

Dripping, gleaming in the sun, Robert and David came out of the water, up the sand. "We have company," Laura said quietly when they stood before her. With identical indifferences in their eyes, they looked at the group behind her. "What's wrong with the woman's face and arm, Robert?" she asked with whispered irritation.

I don't know," Robert said. He dropped to the sand and sat cross-legged beside her towel, at her feet. David duplicated the position on her other side.

"Ny-ah, Ny-ah!" the woman called out to one of her little girls, who was digging in the sand and scattering it. Involuntarily, Laura glanced at her again.

"Some slight paralysis," Robert said, his face turned away, and Laura, watching the stiff arm stuck out with its twisted fingers, said "Ugh!" and turned away, too.

Briskly, Robert said, "Well, David's getting good," but even when he leaned over and slapped the boy lightly on the shoulder in congratulation, David continued to stare at the woman and then let his eyes move to the white-faced boy who sat near her, sifting sand through his fingers.

"Aren't you, David?" Robert said loudly.

"What?" the boy asked vaguely, blinking suddenly as he looked at his father.

"Your crawl. It's good."

"Oh."

The blank indifference in David's voice made Laura shift her gaze from the glinting sea to the boy's impassive face. Once more he was staring at the people behind her while his hands, too, idly sifted sand. Then, as she looked at him, she saw that some subtle difference had overtaken his features since she had last really studied them. He was on the way to becoming a different boy. Since his last holiday, she thought, his neck had visibly lengthened, and all the bones of his face had coarsened—the jaw longer, the cheekbones more prominent, the forehead higher. And yet he was still a little boy. It was almost as if, within the hairless, child's face, another face was pushing through. That was a man's face. It was—she glanced at her husband—it was, indeed, Robert's face. *Puberty,* she thought, staring at the boy with a kind of horror. She saw him lengthening out and broadening, the chest swelling, the arms swelling, nails thickening, hair—and her legs and arms were suddenly covered with goose flesh, shivering prickles sweeping her skin as, for the first time, she recognized in him the gross, inevitable thrust into manhood.

Then, behind her, the woman began noisily to scold, and Laura, who was clutching her arms to her sides, as if she were cold, lay back and tried to relax, closed her eyes once more, and sought to regain her private exchange with the sun, her perfect isolation in light. But she was too aware of everything around her to capture that pure sensation of complete and separate being. Even as her body warmed and her skin began to burn, she heard the people behind her moving about, preparing at last to go down to the water, and the sounds of running, sliding in the sand and their shifting cries told her when they went. Robert and David were talking together in low voices, and then she was aware of David's moving off a bit and beginning to dig in the sand. She heard the distant sound of splashing water, of voices laughing and shouting, of David's hands digging, slapping wet sand, scraping, and she felt Robert's eyes on her as he still sat at her feet.

Then he spoke. "What do you think of David?" he asked.

She lay completely quiet. "Think of him?"

"We haven't talked about him. How do you think he is?"

"I think he's fine. Don't you?"

"No. I think we should bring him home."

She sat up abruptly. "What did you say, Robert?" The sun seemed to blind her as she tried to see his face.

"The end of this term would be a good time to break. Bring him back to a school in the city."

"But why *break* from a good school to a less good one? There's no city school that—"

"The schooling isn't all that matters. He needs us. He needs a home."

"David? He's thirteen! He's been away for three years. What does he need with us now? I've just thought—he's—why, he's nearly a man. . . ."

"He's lonely."

"Lonely? David?"

"Lonely. Yes. It hurts me."

She looked at him with blind eyes, staring, and he said, "A man? He's nearly a *man?*"

With this question, the mad shimmering of the sun suddenly died, and she saw him clearly. He was *there,* thin and clear and brown and tractable. She said, "Yes. After all, only four or five more years . . . just now, I could see you in him, emerging. He's a big boy. He *needs* to be away from home. He shouldn't have to depend on us now. What can we do for him?"

"Everything we've never done," Robert said.

"I don't know what you're talking about."

"He doesn't seem to have any anchorage. Least of all in us. He's adrift—lost in himself some way."

She said curtly, "Nonsense."

He looked at her steadily before he spoke. "You're so beautiful," he said at last, almost as if he were meditating upon a theory, and then he went on quietly, "But something's wrong with our life. I don't know what it is, but. . . ."

"But?" she asked.

"But. . . ."

"Yes?"

He began to run his hands through the sand aimlessly, letting the grains sift slowly between his fingers. She watched him, and at last she said, "Well, that's gratitude!" She looked away from him to the running figures on the shore—the man and his wife and the three children, in and out of the water at the shallow edge of beach, shouting and ridiculously running. "I thought that we lived the way you wanted. I thought we had a—"

"We have," he said for her. "It's a beautiful, smooth, perfectly organized life. But what's missing?"

"Is anything?"

"Well, for example, whatever it is that David ought to feel about you."

"I don't know what you're talking about."

"Do you think you know him?"

"Of course."

"Look," Robert said. "Does he ever *talk* to you? Do you know what he's thinking about? Do you know what he's *like?*"

Laura looked at him. "It's you—I don't know what *you're* like," she said.

"Ahh!" he said, a long, disparaging denial, and turned away from her.

She lay back and began to cry. With a certain luxury, she felt the tears push up through her locked lids and run down and over her cheeks. They must be dropping on her towel! She said, "At last. I knew it would come sometime—it had to—and now it has. You—always so reservedly kind and unclaiming. Now, at last, you're using your position that until now you've hardly ever admitted. Now you tell me that I've failed—from *my* position!"

"Position?" he cried. "Oh, my God!"

She felt her tears burning on her skin, and, eyes still closed, she said, "Don't exclaim. I know it's true. I've always waited. I knew it would come someday. My inadequacy. So now it's come." Then, roughly brushing her cheeks with her fingers, she sat up. She tossed her hair back and cried, "But why today? Why, on the day that. . . ." She looked to the water's edge, where the other family, gathered in a group, was starting back up the beach. "Why today, with those people here?"

He glanced at them. "What of them? What have they got to do with anything?" And, looking back at her, he cried, "Oh, look, don't be a fool!" Then he came through the sand on his knees and seized her hands. He held them and rubbed them and looked at her blurred brown eyes. "Laura, don't be a fool," he said, and hearing the protestation of love in these unlikely words, she looked away from him and down at the sand. She detached her hands. She felt the sun blessedly burn away the dampness around her eyelids. She looked out to the sea—the miles of blue, endless blue, nothing but blue, and over it the interminable reaches of cool blue sky—and she looked back at Robert, anxious beside her, and said with slow ease, "I'm sorry."

"I am, too."

"But you agree, don't you, that David shouldn't be taken from his school?"

Robert looked past her face and said, "David's heard. Perhaps all of it," and when Laura turned, she saw that, yes, there he was, only twelve of fifteen feet away from them, his hands deep in the bowels of a sand castle, stopped there for Lord knew how long, and his face turned toward them, his eyes wide and watchful. She could think of nothing to say except "They're coming back."

The others were just passing David. They had walked in a group from the shore, the mother in the lead, her foolish round face, encumbered with its unintended grin and its ridiculous swath of white ointment, lifted as she led her throng, her tribe. Behind her was the skinny, hairy, fish-white husband, behind him the homely little girls and, lagging now at David's castle, the boy. He stopped there and watched while the others went on, until David made some gesture of invitation, and then he dropped to his knees and both began silently to dig. The rest of the family settled itself again in its place, and when the little girls began a tentative movement toward the boys, the mother said sharply, "Ny-ah! Esther! Mir!" Reluctantly, they turned back and sat on the sand beside her.

Laura looked away from her. "What mad possessiveness!" she said.

The two boys were standing over the castle now, facing the sea, and the strange boy asked David a question, which he answered by ducking his head, hunching his shoulders, and moving his arms in the motion of a crawl. The other boy imitated them. Then, talking, they moved down to the water, and both ran in. David swam and the other boy watched, but only for a moment. Then the boy's mother was on her feet and screaming again, "Ny-ah! Ny-ah! Lou-ee! Come!" Her right cheek was distorted in her excitement, and her injured arm flailed grotesquely at the air.

The boy turned slowly and looked at her. Now, at last, he was outraged. Over the bright distance, Laura could see the fury in his tense, white face. He did not look back at David but came walking with slow deliberation up the beach, past the Newmans, whose heads turned as he walked, to his mother, who was still shaking her hand at him. Then, standing perhaps six feet before her, his arms flailing too, but in a rage, he yelled at her, "Ny-ah! Ny-ah! Ny-ah!"

She looked at him in amazement for a moment and then seemed to wilt. All the perky animation left her round body as she turned slowly and settled saggingly on her towel and, at last, sinking prone, with her face pressed into its folds, wept. Her husband hurried to her, and Laura looked back to the sea. She saw David standing in the shallow water, watching intently, and then, glancing at his lifted hand, move his fingers experimentally. Then he started back to them.

The husband, kneeling beside his wife with his arm over her shoulders, murmured consolingly to her, and her sobs began to subside. The boy, quiet now, with a kind of shamed determination on his face, stood stiffly on the spot where he had faced her. Then the father summoned him with an uncompromising gesture, until the boy moved reluctantly to her. There were words that the Newmans could not hear, but the boy presently knelt beside his mother, where his father had been, and spoke softly to her. Then the mother swiftly twisted to a sitting position, her contorted face red, and, seizing the boy in her arms, she broke again into sobs as she embraced him in a convulsion of love.

"My God! Let's go," Laura said, and leaped up. Hastily, Robert helped her put their belongings in their beach basket and, without looking at the other family again, they walked away as rapidly as the loose sand allowed. Only David, lagging behind his parents, kept looking back, until the dunes cut off his view.

On the way to the hotel, the Newmans did not talk much, and they did not mention the other family, but a few hours later, when Laura was brushing her hair before a tall triple mirror in the dressing-room alcove off her bedroom, she suddenly exclaimed, "I can't get them out of my mind!"

Robert was sitting on the edge of her bed, leafing through a magazine and he looked up and asked, "Who?"

"That awful family—that woman."

"Oh."

David, who was lying on his back on a chaise lounge, his legs flung out in masculine abandon, was doing something with his hands, which he held close before his face. Apparently preoccupied with his fingers and oblivious of his parents, he nevertheless now said quietly, "They weren't bad."

"That man's—*drawers!* That's all you can call them."

Robert laughed, but David asked in an innocent tone, "Just ordinary trunks, weren't they?" He rolled over on his stomach, as if to study his hands more closely.

Laura said, "You could hardly blame the boy for screaming back at her."

David said, "The boy was O.K. I like him."

Laura watched him in the glass. "What are you doing, David?"

He stood up lazily. "Nothing," he said. He walked to a window and leaned against the frame, and then he was fooling with his fingers again.

Suddenly, Laura saw what he was doing. "Stop it, David!" she said sharply.

Robert looked up again. "What's the matter?"

She watched David closely. He was standing by the window in such a way that the late-afternoon sunlight made a nimbus of the down on one cheek and along his chin. She thought of that down as a precursor to coarse stubble, and she said, "David, get out of here, will you? You make me nervous. Go wash your face."

"It's clean," he said as he started toward the door. He watched her with empty eyes as he sidled away.

Robert moved, and presently he was standing behind her. She looked up in the central mirror and met his sad, inquiring, forgiving eyes. "What was he doing?" Robert asked.

"I think he was trying to make his fingers look paralyzed, like that grotesque woman's."

Robert laughed uneasily. "Curiosity, probably. You know boys—they're interested in oddity. Probably not at all grotesque to him. Perhaps the contrary. Rather fascinating."

Laura brushed her hair with renewed vigor, until she had counted ten, twenty, thirty strokes. "He practically said he liked them."

"Well," Robert allowed, "perhaps he did."

Her brush paused in her hair. "Is it time for a drink?"

"I'll get you one." But he did not go. He put his hands on her shoulders and stroked her upper arms. "You are beautiful," he said.

For a moment or two, she sat immobile, unprotesting, under his hand. Then she said, "What about that drink?" She watched his reflection move away, and when he was out of the room, she leaned toward the mirror, toward her reflection. Her face cleared, as if shadows were passing from it, as if shadows had vanished from the shadows of her mind, and she smiled.

She opened a drawer of the dressing table and took out two gold bracelets—one with square chunks of jewels held in heavy links, and one with coins the size of half dollars—and put one on each wrist. Late sunlight shone upon her and flashed off the chains and the jewels in darting angles on the glass surfaces around her. Then, in the triple mirror, she caught sight of a figure moving. It was David again—moving, stopping. She watched his reflection. He was looking not at her but at his right hand, as he held it before him and forced his fingers into an imitation of gnarled paralysis.

"David," she said quietly, "please don't do that. Why do you keep doing that?"

He looked up and met her eyes in the mirror. "I just want to know how it feels," he said. "That woman—how she feels."

"If her hand is paralyzed, she probably doesn't feel anything. And why should you want to know how *she* feels?"

"I kind of liked her." He looked at Laura blandly.

"She was so loud—screaming all the time."

"They just weren't used to a beach, that was all. She was worried."

Laura lifted her hands to fasten a gold barrette in her brushed hair so that one ear would show, but she still watched David manipulating his fingers.

Suddenly, his face brightened. At last, he had duplicated the crippled arm. "This is the way it feels!"

Her eyes searched the mirror until his glance met hers. Then she grimaced in disgust and said with sharp finality, "Don't be perverse! She was—ugly!"

David was standing rigid behind her. His arm rose until it pointed out at her with a stiff, accusing crook at the elbow and in the clumsy-knuckled fingers. His drawn face was stiff with revulsion, only his eyes alive, glimmering upon her. "Says who?" he asked in a dead voice, and as his wild, unhappy eyes held and held hers, her bracelets clanked down on the mirrored top of the dressing table with a metallic chorus, and the mirrors flashed.

GRAHAM GREENE

Brother

The Communists were the first to appear. They walked quickly, a group of about a dozen, up the boulevard which runs from Combat to Ménilmontant; a young man and a girl lagged a little way behind because the man's leg was hurt and the girl was helping him along. They looked impatient, harassed, hopeless, as if they were trying to catch a train which they knew already in their hearts they were too late to catch.

The proprietor of the café saw them coming when they were still a long way off; the lamps at that time were still alight (it was later that the bullets broke the bulbs and dropped darkness all over that quarter of Paris), and the group showed up plainly in the wide barren boulevard. Since sunset only one customer had entered the café, and very soon after sunset firing could be heard from the direction of Combat; the Métro station had closed hours ago. And yet something obstinate and undefeatable in the proprietor's character prevented him from putting up the shutters; it might have been avarice; he could not himself have told what it was as he pressed his broad yellow forehead against the glass and stared this way and that, up the boulevard and down the boulevard.

But when he saw the group and their air of hurry he began immediately to close his café. First he went and warned his only customer, who was practising billiard shots, walking round and round the table, frowning and stroking a thin moustache between shots, a little green in the face under the low diffused lights.

"The Reds are coming," the proprietor said, "you'd better be off. I'm putting up the shutters."

"Don't interrupt. They won't harm me," the customer said. "This is a tricky shot. Reds in baulk. Off the cushion. Screw on spot." He shot his ball straight into a pocket.

"I knew you couldn't do anything with that," the proprietor said, nodding his bald head. "You might just as well go home. Give me a hand with the shutters first. I've sent my wife away." The customer turned on him maliciously, rattling the cue between his fingers. "It was your talking that spoilt the shot. You've cause to be frightened, I dare say. But I'm a poor man. I'm safe. I'm not going to stir." He went across to his coat and took out a dry cigar. "Bring me a bock." He walked round the table on his toes and the balls clicked and the proprietor padded back into the bar, elderly and irritated. He did not fetch the beer but began to close the shutters; every move he made was slow and clumsy. Long before he had finished the group of Communists was outside.

He stopped what he was doing and watched them with furtive dislike. He was afraid that the rattle of the shutters would attract their attention. If I am very quiet and still, he thought, they may go on, and he remembered with malicious pleasure the police barricade across the Place de la République. That will finish them. In the meanwhile I must be very quiet, very still, and he felt a kind of warm satisfaction at the idea that worldly wisdom dictated the very attitude most suited to his nature. So he stared through the edge of a shutter, yellow, plump, cautious, hearing the billiard balls crackle in the other room, seeing the young man come limping up the pavement on the girl's arm, watching them stand and stare with dubious faces up the boulevard towards Combat.

But when they came into the café he was already behind the bar, smiling and bowing and missing nothing, noticing how they had divided forces, how six of them had begun to run back the way they had come.

The young man sat down in a dark corner above the cellar stairs and the others stood round the door waiting for something to happen. It gave the proprietor an odd feeling that they should stand there in his café not asking for a drink, knowing what to expect, when he, the owner, knew nothing, understood nothing. At last the girl said "Cognac," leaving the others and coming to the bar, but when he had poured it out for her, very careful to give a fair and not a generous measure, she simply took it to the man sitting in the dark and held it to his mouth.

"Three francs," the proprietor said. She took the glass and sipped a little and turned it so that the man's lips might touch the same spot. Then she knelt down and rested her forehead against the man's forehead and so they stayed.

"Three francs," the proprietor said, but he could not make his voice bold. The man was no longer visible in his corner, only the girl's back, thin and shabby in a black cotton frock, as she knelt, leaning forward to find the man's face. The proprietor was daunted by the four men at the door, by the knowledge that they were Reds who had no respect for private property, who would drink his wine and go away without paying, who would rape his women (but there was only his wife, and she was not there), who would rob his bank, who would murder him as soon as look at him. So with fear in his heart he gave up the three francs as lost rather than attract any more attention.

Then the worst that he contemplated happened.

One of the men at the door came up to the bar and told him to pour out four glasses of cognac. "Yes, yes," the proprietor said, fumbling with the cork, praying secretly to the Virgin to send an angel, to send the police, to send the Gardes Mobiles, now, immediately, before the cork came out, "that will be twelve francs."

"Oh, no," the man said, "we are all comrades here. Share and share alike. Listen," he said, with earnest mockery, leaning across the bar, "all we have is yours just as much as it's ours, comrade," and stepping back a pace he presented himself to the proprietor, so that he might take his choice of stringy tie, of threadbare trousers, of starved features. "And it follows from that, comrade, that all you have is ours. So four cognacs. Share and share alike."

"Of course," the proprietor said, "I was only joking." Then he stood with bottle poised, and the four glasses tingled upon the counter. "A machine-gun," he said, "up by Combat," and smiled to see how for the moment the men forgot their brandy as they fidgeted near the door. Very soon now, he thought, and I shall be quit of them.

"A machine-gun," the Red said incredulously, "they're using machine-guns?"

"Well," the proprietor said, encouraged by this sign that the Gardes Mobiles were not very far away, "you can't pretend that you aren't armed yourselves." He leant across the bar in a way that was almost paternal. "After all, you know, your ideas—they wouldn't do in France. Free love."

"Who's talking of free love?" the Red said.

The proprietor shrugged and smiled and nodded at the corner. The girl knelt with her head on the man's shoulder, her back to the room. They were quite silent and the glass of brandy stood on the floor beside them. The girl's beret was pushed back on her head and one stocking was laddered and darned from knee to ankle.

"What, those two? They aren't lovers."

"I," the proprietor said, "with my bourgeois notions would have thought . . ."

"He's her brother," the Red said.

The men came clustering round the bar and laughed at him, but softly as if a sleeper or a sick person were in the house. All the time they were listening for something. Between their shoulders the proprietor could look out across the boulevard; he could see the corner of the Faubourg du Temple.

"What are you waiting for?"

"For friends," the Red said. He made a gesture with open palm as if to say, You see, we share and share alike. We have no secrets.

Something moved at the corner of the Faubourg du Temple.

"Four more cognacs," the Red said.

"What about those two?" the proprietor asked.

"Leave them alone. They'll look after themselves. They're tired."

How tired they were. No walk up the boulevard from Ménilmontant could explain the tiredness. They seemed to have come farther and fared a great deal worse than their companions. They were more starved; they were infinitely more hopeless, sitting in their dark corner away from the friendly gossip, the amicable desperate voices which now confused the proprietor's brain, until for a moment he believed himself to be a host entertaining friends.

He laughed and made a broad joke directed at the two of them; but they made no sign of understanding. Perhaps they were to be pitied, cut off from the camaraderie round the counter; perhaps they were to be envied for their deeper comradeship. The proprietor thought for no reason at all of the bare grey trees of the Tuileries like a series of exclamation marks drawn against the winter sky. Puzzled, disintegrated, with all his bearings lost, he stared out through the door towards the Faubourg.

It was as if they had not seen each other for a long while and would soon again be saying good-bye. Hardly aware of what he was doing he filled the four glasses with brandy. They stretched out worn blunted fingers for them.

"Wait," he said. "I've got something better than this"; then paused, conscious of what was happening across the boulevard. The lamplight splashed down on blue steel helmets; the Gardes Mobiles were lining out across the entrance to the Faubourg, and a machine-gun pointed directly at the café windows.

So, the proprietor thought, my prayers are answered. Now I must do my part, not look, not warn them, save myself. Have they covered the side door? I will get the other bottle. Real Napoleon brandy. Share and share alike.

He felt a curious lack of triumph as he opened the trap of the bar and came out. He tried not to walk quickly back towards the billiard room. Nothing that he did must warn these men; he tried to spur himself with the thought that every slow casual step he took was a blow for France, for his café, for his savings. He had to step over the girl's feet to pass her; she was asleep. He noted the sharp shoulder blades thrusting through the cotton, and raised his eyes and met her brother's, filled with pain and despair.

He stopped. He found he could not pass without a word. It was as if he needed to explain something, as if he belonged to the wrong party. With false bonhomie he waved the corkscrew he carried in the other's face. "Another cognac, eh?"

"It's no good talking to them," the Red said. "They're German. They don't understand a word."

"German?"

"That's what's wrong with his leg. A concentration camp."

The proprietor told himself that he must be quick, that he must put a door between him and them, that the end was very close, but he was bewildered by the hopelessness in the man's gaze. "What's he doing here?" Nobody answered him. It was as if his question were too foolish to need a reply. With his head sunk upon his breast the proprietor went past, and the girl slept on. He was like a stranger leaving a room where all the rest are friends. A German. They don't understand a word; and up, up through the heavy darkness of his mind, through the avarice and the dubious triumph, a few German words remembered from very old days climbed like spies into the light: a line from the *Lorelei* learnt at school, *Kamerad* with its war-time suggestion of fear and surrender, and oddly from nowhere the phrase *mein Bruder*. He opened the door of the billiard room and closed it behind him and softly turned the key.

"Spot in baulk," the customer explained and leant across the great green table, but while he took aim, wrinkling his narrow peevish eyes, the firing started. It came in two bursts with a rip of glass between. The girl cried out something, but it was not one of the words he knew. Then feet ran across the floor, the trap of the bar slammed. The proprietor sat back against the table and listened and listened for any further sound; but silence came in under the door and silence through the keyhole.

"The cloth. My God, the cloth," the customer said, and the proprietor looked down at his own hand which was working the corkscrew into the table.

"Will this absurdity ever end?" the customer said. "I shall go home."

"Wait," the proprietor said. "Wait." He was listening to voices and footsteps in the other room. These were voices he did not recognize. Then a car drove up and presently drove away again. Somebody rattled the handle of the door.

"Who is it?" the proprietor called.

"Who are you? Open that door."

"Ah," the customer said with relief, "the police. Where was I now? Spot in baulk." He began to chalk his cue. The proprietor opened the door. Yes, the Gardes Mobiles had arrived; he was safe again, though his windows were smashed. The Reds had vanished as if they had never been. He looked at the raised trap, at the smashed electric bulbs, at the broken bottle which dripped behind the bar. The café was full of men, and he remembered with odd relief that he had not had time to lock the side door.

"Are you the owner?" the officer asked. "A bock for each of these men and a cognac for myself. Be quick about it."

The proprietor calculated: "Nine francs fifty," and watched closely with bent head the coins rattle down upon the counter.

"You see," the officer said with significance, "we pay." He nodded towards the side door. "Those others: did they pay?"

No, the proprietor admitted, they had not paid, but as he counted the coins and slipped them into the till, he caught himself silently repeating the officer's order—"A bock for each of these men." Those others, he thought, one's got to say that for them, they weren't mean about the drink. It was four cognacs with them. But, of course, they did not pay. "And my windows," he complained aloud with sudden asperity, "what about my windows?"

"Never you mind," the officer said, "the government will pay. You have only to send in your bill. Hurry up now with my cognac. I have no time for gossip."

"You can see for yourself," the proprietor said, "how the bottles have been broken. Who will pay for that?"

"Everything will be paid for," the officer said.

"And now I must go to the cellar to fetch more."

He was angry at the reiteration of the word pay. They enter my café, he thought, they smash my windows, they order me about and think that all is well if they pay, pay, pay. It occurred to him that these men were intruders.

"Step to it," the officer said and turned and rebuked one of the men who had leant his rifle against the bar.

At the top of the cellar stairs the proprietor stopped. They were in darkness, but by the light from the bar he could just make out a body half-way down. He began to tremble violently, and it was some seconds before he could strike a match. The young German lay head downwards, and the blood from his head had dropped on to the step below. His eyes were open and stared back at the proprietor with the old despairing expression of life. The proprietor would not believe that he was dead. "Kamerad," he said bending down, while the match singed his fingers and went out, trying to recall some phrase in German, but he could only remember, as he bent lower still, "mein Bruder." Then suddenly he turned and ran up the steps, waved the match-box in the officer's face, and called out in a low hysterical voice to him and his men and to the customer stooping under the low green shade, "Cochons. Cochons."

"What was that? What was that?" the officer exclaimed. "Did you say that he was your brother? It's impossible," and he frowned incredulously at the proprietor and rattled the coins in his pocket.

ALBERT CAMUS

The Guest

The schoolmaster was watching the two men climb toward him. One was on horseback, the other on foot. They had not yet tackled the abrupt rise leading to the schoolhouse built on the hillside. They were toiling onward, making slow progress in the snow, among the stones, on the vast expanse of the high, deserted plateau. From time to time the horse stumbled. Without hearing anything yet, he could see the breath issuing from the horse's nostrils. One of the men, at least, knew the region. They were following the trail although it had disappeared days ago under a layer of dirty white snow. The schoolmaster calculated that it would take them half an hour to get onto the hill. It was cold; he went back into the school to get a sweater.

He crossed the empty, frigid classroom. On the blackboard the four rivers of France, drawn with four different colored chalks, had been flowing toward their estuaries for the past three days. Snow had suddenly fallen in mid-October after eight months of drought without the transition of rain, and the twenty pupils, more or less, who lived in the villages scattered over the plateau had stopped coming. With fair weather they would return. Daru now heated only the single room that was his lodging, adjoining the classroom and giving also onto the plateau to the east. Like the class windows, his window looked to the south too. On that side the school was a few kilometers from the point where the plateau began to slope toward the south. In clear weather could be seen the purple mass of the mountain range where the gap opened onto the desert.

Somewhat warmed, Daru returned to the window from which he had first seen the two men. They were no longer visible. Hence they must have tackled the rise. The sky was not so dark, for the snow had stopped falling during the night. The morning had opened with a dirty light which had scarcely become brighter as the ceiling of clouds lifted. At two in the afternoon it seemed as if the day were merely beginning. But still this was better than those three days when the thick snow was falling amidst unbroken darkness with little gusts of wind that rattled the double door of the classroom. Then Daru had spent long hours in his room, leaving it only to go to the shed and feed the chickens or get some coal. Fortunately the delivery truck from Tadjid, the nearest village to the north, had brought his supplies two days before the blizzard. It would return in forty-eight hours.

Besides, he had enough to resist a siege, for the little room was cluttered with bags of wheat that the administration left as a stock to distribute to those of his pupils whose families had suffered from the drought. Actually they had all been victims because they were all poor. Every day Daru would distribute a ration to the children. They had missed it, he knew, during these bad days. Possibly one of the fathers or big brothers would come this afternoon and he could supply them with grain. It was just a matter of carrying them over to the next harvest. Now shiploads of wheat were arriving from France and the worst was over. But it would be hard to forget that poverty, that army of ragged ghosts wandering in the sunlight, the plateaus burned to a cinder month after month, the earth shriveled up little by little, literally scorched, every stone bursting into dust under one's foot. The sheep had died then by thousands and even a few men, here and there, sometimes without anyone's knowing.

In contrast with such poverty, he who lived almost like a monk in his remote schoolhouse, nonetheless satisfied with the little he had and with the rough life, had felt like a lord with his whitewashed walls, his narrow couch, his unpainted shelves, his well, and his weekly provision of water and food. And suddenly this snow, without warning, without the foretaste of rain. This is the way the region was, cruel to live in, even without men—who didn't help matters either. But Daru had been born here. Everywhere else, he felt exiled.

He stepped out onto the terrace in front of the schoolhouse. The two men were now halfway up the slope. He recognized the horseman as Balducci, the old gendarme he had known for a long time. Balducci was holding on the end of a rope an Arab who was walking behind him with hands bound and head lowered. The gendarme waved a greeting to which Daru did not reply, lost as he was in contemplation of the Arab dressed in a faded blue jellaba, his feet in sandals but covered with socks of heavy raw wool, his head surmounted by a narrow, short *chèche.*[1] They were approaching. Balducci was holding back his horse in order not to hurt the Arab, and the group was advancing slowly.

Within earshot, Balducci shouted: "One hour to do the three kilo-

[1] *chèche:* a cloth cap.

meters from El Ameur!" Daru did not answer. Short and square in his thick sweater, he watched them climb. Not once had the Arab raised his head. "Hello," said Daru when they got up onto the terrace. "Come in and warm up." Balducci painfully got down from his horse without letting go the rope. From under his bristling mustache he smiled at the schoolmaster. His little dark eyes, deep-set under a tanned forehead, and his mouth surrounded with wrinkles made him look attentive and studious. Daru took the bridle, led the horse to the shed, and came back to the two men, who were now waiting for him in the school. He led them into his room. "I am going to heat up the classroom," he said. "We'll be more comfortable there." When he entered the room again, Balducci was on the couch. He had undone the rope tying him to the Arab, who had squatted near the stove. His hands still bound, the *chèche* pushed back on his head, he was looking toward the window. At first Daru noticed only his huge lips, fat, smooth, almost Negroid; yet his nose was straight, his eyes were dark and full of fever. The *chèche* revealed an obstinate forehead and, under the weathered skin now rather discolored by the cold, the whole face had a restless and rebellious look that struck Daru when the Arab, turning his face toward him, looked him straight in the eyes. "Go into the other room," said the schoolmaster, "and I'll make you some mint tea." "Thanks," Balducci said. "What a chore! How I long for retirement." And addressing his prisoner in Arabic: "Come on, you." The Arab got up and, slowly, holding his bound wrists in front of him, went into the classroom.

With the tea, Daru brought a chair. But Balducci was already enthroned on the nearest pupil's desk and the Arab had squatted against the teacher's platform facing the stove, which stood between the desk and the window. When he held out the glass of tea to the prisoner, Daru hesitated at the sight of his bound hands. "He might perhaps be untied." "Sure," said Balducci. "That was for the trip." He started to get to his feet. But Daru, setting the glass on the floor, had knelt beside the Arab. Without saying anything, the Arab watched him with his feverish eyes. Once his hands were free, he rubbed his swollen wrists against each other, took the glass of tea, and sucked up the burning liquid in swift little sips.

"Good," said Daru. "And where are you headed?"

Balducci withdrew his mustache from the tea. "Here, son."

"Odd pupils! And you're spending the night?"

"No. I'm going back to El Ameur. And you will deliver this fellow to Tinguit. He is expected at police headquarters."

Balducci was looking at Daru with a friendly little smile.

"What's this story?" asked the schoolmaster. "Are you pulling my leg?"

"No, son. Those are the orders."

"The orders? I'm not . . ." Daru hesitated, not wanting to hurt the old Corsican. "I mean, that's not my job."

"What! What's the meaning of that? In wartime people do all kinds of jobs."

"Then I'll wait for the declaration of war!"

Balducci nodded.

"O.K. But the orders exist and they concern you too. Things are brewing, it appears. There is talk of a forthcoming revolt. We are mobilized, in a way."

Daru still had his obstinate look.

"Listen, son," Balducci said. "I like you and you must understand. There's only a dozen of us at El Ameur to patrol throughout the whole territory of a small department and I must get back in a hurry. I was told to hand this guy over to you and return without delay. He couldn't be kept there. His village was beginning to stir; they wanted to take him back. You must take him to Tinguit tomorrow before the day is over. Twenty kilometers shouldn't faze a husky fellow like you. After that, all will be over. You'll come back to your pupils and your comfortable life."

Behind the wall the horse could be heard snorting and pawing the earth. Daru was looking out the window. Decidedly, the weather was clearing and the light was increasing over the snowy plateau. When all the snow was melted, the sun would take over again and once more would burn the fields of stone. For days, still, the unchanging sky would shed its dry light on the solitary expanse where nothing had any connection with man.

"After all," he said, turning around toward Balducci, "what did he do?" And, before the gendarme had opened his mouth, he asked: "Does he speak French?"

"No, not a word. We had been looking for him for a month, but they were hiding him. He killed his cousin."

"Is he against us?"

"I don't think so. But you can never be sure."

"Why did he kill?"

"A family squabble, I think. One owed the other grain, it seems. It's not at all clear. In short, he killed his cousin with a billhook. You know, like a sheep, *kreezk!*"

Balducci made the gesture of drawing a blade across his throat and the Arab, his attention attracted, watched him with a sort of anxiety. Daru felt a sudden wrath against the man, against all men with their rotten spite, their tireless hates, their blood lust.

But the kettle was singing on the stove. He served Balducci more tea, hesitated, then served the Arab again, who, a second time, drank avidly. His raised arms made the jellaba fall open and the schoolmaster saw his thin, muscular chest.

"Thanks, kid," Balducci said. "And now, I'm off."

He got up and went toward the Arab, taking a small rope from his pocket.

"What are you doing?" Daru asked dryly.

Balducci, disconcerted, showed him the rope.

"Don't bother."

The old gendarme hesitated. "It's up to you. Of course, you are armed?"

"I have my shotgun."

"Where?"

"In the trunk."

"You ought to have it near your bed."

"Why? I have nothing to fear."

"You're crazy, son. If there's an uprising, no one is safe, we're all in the same boat."

"I'll defend myself. I'll have time to see them coming."

Balducci began to laugh, then suddenly the mustache covered the white teeth.

"You'll have time? O.K. That's just what I was saying. You have always been a little cracked. That's why I like you, my son was like that."

At the same time he took out his revolver and put it on the desk.

"Keep it; I don't need two weapons from here to El Ameur."

The revolver shone against the black paint of the table. When the gendarme turned toward him, the schoolmaster caught the smell of leather and horseflesh.

"Listen, Balducci," Daru said suddenly, "every bit of this disgusts me, and first of all your fellow here. But I won't hand him over. Fight, yes, if I have to. But not that."

The old gendarme stood in front of him and looked at him severely.

"You're being a fool," he said slowly. "I don't like it either. You don't get used to putting a rope on a man even after years of it, and you're even ashamed—yes, ashamed. But you can't let them have their way."

"I won't hand him over," Daru said again.

"It's an order, son, and I repeat it."

"That's right. Repeat to them what I've said to you: I won't hand him over."

Balducci made a visible effort to reflect. He looked at the Arab and at Daru. At last he decided.

"No, I won't tell them anything. If you want to drop us, go ahead; I'll not denounce you. I have an order to deliver the prisoner and I'm doing so. And now you'll just sign this paper for me."

"There's no need. I'll not deny that you left him with me."

"Don't be mean with me. I know you'll tell the truth. You're from hereabouts and you are a man. But you must sign, that's the rule."

Daru opened his drawer, took out a little square bottle of purple ink, the red wooden penholder with the "sergeant-major" pen he used for making models of penmanship, and signed. The gendarme carefully folded the paper and put it into his wallet. Then he moved toward the door.

"I'll see you off," Daru said.

"No," said Balducci. "There's no use being polite. You insulted me."

He looked at the Arab, motionless in the same spot, sniffed peevishly, and turned away toward the door. "Good-by son," he said. The door shut behind him. Balducci appeared suddenly outside the window and then disappeared. His footsteps were muffled by the snow. The horse stirred on the other side of the wall and several chickens fluttered in fright. A moment later Balducci reappeared outside the window leading the horse by the bridle. He walked toward the little rise without turning around and disappeared from sight with the horse following him. A big stone could be heard bouncing down. Daru walked back toward the prisoner, who, without stirring, never took his eyes off him. "Wait," the schoolmaster said in Arabic and went toward the bedroom. As he was going through the door, he had a second thought, went to the desk, took the revolver, and stuck it in his pocket. Then, without looking back, he went into his room.

For some time he lay on his couch watching the sky gradually close over, listening to the silence. It was this silence that had seemed painful to him during the first days here, after the war. He had requested a post in the little town at the base of the foothills separating the upper plateaus from the desert. There, rocky walls, green and black to the north, pink and lavender to the south, marked the frontier of eternal summer. He had been named to a post farther north, on the plateau itself. In the beginning, the solitude and the silence had been hard for him on these wastelands peopled only by stones. Occasionally, furrows suggested cultivation, but they had been dug to uncover a certain kind of stone good for building. The only plowing here was to harvest rocks. Elsewhere a thin layer of soil accumulated in the hollows would be scraped out to enrich paltry village gardens. This is the way it was: bare rock covered three quarters of the region. Towns sprang up, flourished, then disappeared; men came by, loved one another or fought bitterly, then died. No one in this desert, neither he nor his guest, mattered. And yet, outside this desert neither of them, Daru know, could have really lived.

When he got up, no noise came from the classroom. He was amazed at the unmixed joy he derived from the mere thought that the Arab might have fled and that he would be alone with no decision to make. But the prisoner was there. He had merely stretched out between the stove and the desk. With eyes open, he was staring at the ceiling. In that position, his thick lips were particularly noticeable, giving him a pouting look. "Come," said Daru. The Arab got up and followed him. In the bedroom, the schoolmaster pointed to a chair near the table under the window. The Arab sat down without taking his eyes off Daru.

"Are you hungry?"

"Yes," the prisoner said.

Daru set the table for two. He took flour and oil, shaped a cake in a frying-pan, and lighted the little stove that functioned on bottled gas. While the cake was cooking, he went out to the shed to get cheese, eggs, dates, and condensed milk. When the cake was done he set it on the window sill to cool, heated some condensed milk diluted with water, and beat up the eggs into an omelette. In one of his motions he knocked against the revolver stuck in his right pocket. He set the bowl down, went into the classroom, and put the revolver in his desk drawer. When he came back to the room, night was falling. He put on the light and served the Arab. "Eat," he said. The Arab took a piece of the cake, lifted it eagerly to his mouth, and stopped short.

"And you?" he asked.

"After you. I'll eat too."

The thick lips opened slightly. The Arab hesitated, then bit into the cake determinedly.

The meal over, the Arab looked at the schoolmaster. "Are you the judge?"

"No, I'm simply keeping you until tomorrow."

"Why do you eat with me?"

"I'm hungry."

The Arab fell silent. Daru got up and went out. He brought back a folding bed from the shed, set it up between the table and the stove, perpendicular to his own bed. From a large suitcase which, upright in a corner, served as a shelf for papers, he took two blankets and arranged them on the camp bed. Then he stopped, felt useless, and sat down on his bed. There was nothing more to do or to get ready. He had to look at this man. He looked at him, therefore, trying to imagine his face bursting with rage. He couldn't do so. He could see nothing but the dark yet shining eyes and the animal mouth.

"Why did you kill him?" he asked in a voice whose hostile tone surprised him.

The Arab looked away.

"He ran away. I ran after him."

He raised his eyes to Daru again and they were full of a sort of woeful interrogation. "Now what will they do to me?'"

"Are you afraid?'"

He stiffened, turning his eyes away.

"Are you sorry?"

The Arab stared at him openmouthed. Obviously he did not understand. Daru's annoyance was growing. At the same time he felt awkward and self-conscious with his big body wedged between the two beds.

"Lie down there," he said impatiently. "That's your bed."

The Arab didn't move. He called to Daru:

"Tell me!"

The schoolmaster looked at him.

"Is the gendarme coming back tomorrow?"

"I don't know."

"Are you coming with us?"

"I don't know. Why?"

The prisoner got up and stretched out on top of the blankets, his feet toward the window. The light from the electric bulb shone straight into his eyes and he closed them at once.

"Why?" Daru repeated, standing beside the bed.

The Arab opened his eyes under the blinding light and looked at him, trying not to blink.

"Come with us," he said.

In the middle of the night, Daru was still not asleep. He had gone to bed after undressing completely; he generally slept naked. But when he suddenly realized that he had nothing on, he hesitated. He felt vulnerable and the temptation came to him to put his clothes back on. Then he shrugged his shoulders; after all, he wasn't a child and, if need be, he could break his adversary in two. From his bed he could observe him, lying on his back, still motionless with his eyes closed under the harsh light. When Daru turned out the light, the darkness seemed to coagulate all of a sudden. Little by little, the night came back to life in the window where the starless sky was stirring gently. The schoolmaster soon made out the body lying at his feet. The Arab still did not move, but his eyes seemed open. A faint wind was prowling around the schoolhouse. Perhaps it would drive away the clouds and the sun would reappear.

During the night the wind increased. The hens fluttered a little and then were silent. The Arab turned over on his side with his back to Daru, who thought he heard him moan. Then he listened for his guest's breathing, become heavier and more regular. He listened to that breath so close to him and mused without being able to go to sleep. In this room where he had been sleeping alone for a year, this presence bothered him. But it bothered him also by imposing on him a sort of brotherhood he knew well but refused to accept in the present circumstances. Men who share the same rooms, soldiers or prisoners, develop a strange alliance as if, having cast off their armor with their clothing, they fraternized every evening, over and above their differences, in the ancient community of dream and fatigue. But Daru shook himself; he didn't like such musings, and it was essential to sleep.

A little later, however, when the Arab stirred slightly, the schoolmaster was still not asleep. When the prisoner made a second move, he stiffened, on the alert. The Arab was lifting himself slowly on his arms with almost the motion of a sleepwalker. Seated upright in bed, he waited motionless without turning his head toward Daru, as if he were listening attentively. Daru did not stir; it had just occurred to him that the revolver was still in the drawer of his desk. It was better to act at once. Yet he continued to observe the prisoner, who, with the same slithery motion, put his feet on the ground, waited again, then began to stand up slowly. Daru was about to call out to him when the Arab began to walk, in a quite natural but extraordinarily silent way. He was heading toward the door at the end of the room that opened into the shed. He lifted the latch with precaution and went out, pushing the door behind him but without shutting it. Daru had not stirred. "He is running away," he merely thought. "Good riddance!" Yet he listened attentively. The hens were not fluttering; the guest must be on the plateau. A faint sound of water reached him, and he didn't know what it was until the Arab again stood framed in the doorway, closed the door carefully, and came back to bed without a sound. Then Daru turned his back on him and fell asleep. Still later he seemed, from the depths of his sleep, to hear furtive steps around the schoolhouse. "I'm dreaming! I'm dreaming!" he repeated to himself. And he went on sleeping.

When he awoke, the sky was clear; the loose window let in a cold, pure air. The Arab was asleep, hunched up under the blankets now, his mouth open, utterly relaxed. But when Daru shook him, he started dreadfully, staring at Daru with wild eyes as if he had never seen him and such a frightened expression that the schoolmaster stepped back. "Don't be afraid. It's me. You must eat." The Arab nodded his head and said yes. Calm had returned to his face, but his expression was vacant and listless.

The coffee was ready. They drank it seated together on the folding bed as they munched their pieces of the cake. Then Daru led the Arab under the shed and showed him the faucet where he washed. He went back into the room, folded the blankets and the bed, made his own bed and put the room in order. Then he went through the classroom and out onto the terrace. The sun was already rising in the blue sky; a soft, bright light was bathing the deserted plateau. On the ridge the snow was melting in spots. The stones were about to reappear. Crouched on the edge of the plateau, the schoolmaster looked at the deserted expanse. He thought of Balducci. He had hurt him, for he had sent him off in a way as if he didn't want to be associated with him. He could still hear the gendarme's farewell and, without knowing why, he felt strangely empty and vulnerable. At that moment, from the other side of the schoolhouse, the prisoner coughed. Daru listened to him almost despite himself and then, furious, threw a pebble that whistled through the air before sinking into the snow. That man's stupid crime revolted him, but to hand him over was contrary to honor. Merely thinking of it made him smart with humiliation. And he cursed at one and the same time his own people who had sent him this Arab and the Arab too who had dared to kill and not managed to get away. Daru got up, walked in a circle on the terrace, waited motionless, and then went back into the schoolhouse.

The Arab, leaning over the cement floor of the shed, was washing his teeth with two fingers. Daru looked at him and said: "Come." He went back into the room ahead of the prisoner. He slipped a hunting-jacket on over his sweater and put on walking-shoes. Standing, he waited until the Arab had put on his *chèche* and sandals. They went into the classroom and the schoolmaster pointed to the exit, saying: "Go ahead." The fellow didn't budge. "I'm coming," said Daru. The Arab went out. Daru went back into the room and made a package of pieces of rusk, dates, and sugar. In the classroom, before going out, he hesitated a second in front of his desk, then crossed the threshold and locked the door. "That's the way," he said. He started toward the east, followed by the prisoner. But, a short distance from the schoolhouse, he thought he heard a slight sound behind them. He retraced his steps and examined the surroundings of the house; there was no one there. The Arab watched him without seeming to understand. "Come on," said Daru.

They walked for an hour and rested beside a sharp peak of limestone. The snow was melting faster and faster and the sun was drinking up the puddles at once, rapidly cleaning the plateau, which gradually dried and vibrated like the air itself. When they resumed walking, the ground rang under their feet. From time to time a bird rent the space in front of them with a joyful cry. Daru breathed in deeply the fresh morning light. He felt a sort of rapture before the vast familiar expanse, now almost entirely yellow under its dome of blue sky. They walked an hour more, descending toward the south. They reached a level height made up of crumbly rocks. From there on, the plateau sloped down, eastward, toward a low plain where there were a few spindly trees and, to the south, toward outcroppings of rock that gave the landscape a chaotic look.

Daru surveyed the two directions. There was nothing but the sky on the horizon. Not a man could be seen. He turned toward the Arab, who was looking at him blankly. Daru held out the package to him. "Take it," he said. "There are dates, bread, and sugar. You can hold out for two days. Here are a thousand francs too." The Arab took the package and the money but kept his full hands at chest level as if he didn't know what to do with what was being given him. "Now look," the schoolmaster said as he pointed in the direction of the east, "there's the way to Tinguit. You have a two-hour walk. At Tinguit you'll find the administration and the police. They are expecting you." The Arab looked toward the east, still holding the package and the money against his chest. Daru took his elbow and turned him rather roughly toward the south. At the foot of the height on which they stood could be seen a faint path. "That's the trail across the plateau. In a day's walk from here you'll find pasturelands and the first nomads. They'll take you in and shelter you according to their law." The Arab had now turned toward Daru and a sort of panic was visible in his expression. "Listen," he said. Daru shook his head: "No, be quiet. Now I'm leaving you." He turned his back on him, took two long steps in the direction of the school, looked hesitantly at the motionless Arab, and started off again. For a few minutes he heard nothing but his own step resounding on the cold ground and did not turn his head. A moment later, however, he turned around. The Arab was still there on the edge of the hill, his arms hanging now, and he was looking at the schoolmaster. Daru felt something rise in his throat. But he swore with impatience, waved vaguely, and started off again. He had already gone some distance when he again stopped and looked. There was no longer anyone on the hill.

Daru hesitated. The sun was now rather high in the sky and was beginning to beat down on his head. The schoolmaster retraced his steps, at first somewhat uncertainly, then with decision. When he reached the little hill, he was bathed in sweat. He climbed it as fast as he could and stopped, out of breath, at the top. The rock-fields to the south stood out sharply against the blue sky, but on the plain to the east a steamy heat was already rising. And in that slight haze, Daru, with heavy heart, made out the Arab walking slowly on the road to prison.

A little later, standing before the window of the classroom, the schoolmaster was watching the clear light bathing the whole surface of the plateau, but he hardly saw it. Behind him on the blackboard, among the winding French rivers, sprawled the clumsily chalked-up words he had just read: "You handed over our brother. You will pay for this." Daru looked at the sky, the plateau, and, beyond, the invisible lands stretching all the way to the sea. In this vast landscape he had loved so much, he was alone.

6

POINT OF VIEW

The basic methods of contemporary writers are still those of the first storytellers: the use of the five tools of action, dialogue, description, thoughts, and exposition put to the developing and resolving of a conflict, the portraying of characters, and the realizing of a theme. But in the development of modern fiction another facet of fictional technique has come to assume such importance that it can almost be said to constitute a sixth tool. This facet is called *point of view*.

The term *point of view* as it applies to fiction is a severely technical one, and determining the point of view of any story involves answering these questions: first, "Who tells the story?" and "What is the relationship of that person to the story?" or "What is the position from which the story gets told?" Most analyses of fictional point of view attempt a division and subdivision by considering these questions simultaneously; further, most analyses employ different terminology for what is usually the same phenomenon. One such analysis, for example, divides all narrative points of view into two types: the participant (or first person) and the omniscient (or third person). A second finds four possible points of view in stories: the point of view of the "real" author, the "implied" author, the narrator, or the protagonist. Still a third identifies possible points of view as first-person omniscient, first-person restrictive, third-person omniscient, and third-person restrictive. Yet another finds three points of view in fiction: the editorial omniscient, the neutral omniscient, and the limited omniscient. A fifth suggests that points of view are either "outside" or "inside"; the outside point of view can be further subdivided into the privileged narrator and the effaced narrator, and the inside point of view can be subdivided into the dramatized narrator and the restricted narrator. A sixth identifies the four possible points of view as first-person narrator, omniscient narrator, concealed narrator, and "the method of the central intelligence." Finally, the most commonly accepted division is (1) omniscient; (2)

limited omniscient (either major or minor character); (3) first person (either major or minor character); and (4) objective. Most of these analyses represent not differing principles but differing terminology; what one critic, for example, will call the "neutral omniscient" point of view another will call the "objective" point of view. At the same time, most analyses do try to answer the two questions—"Who tells the story?" and "What is the position from which the story gets told?"—simultaneously, with results that are, at best, complicated and, at worst, confusing. Hence, for purposes of simplification, the following discussion will treat these two aspects of point of view (*position* and *choice* of narrator) separately.

To begin with, a writer has two choices of narrator: he may employ first person ("I") or third person ("he"). Obviously, the story that is told in first person will differ radically—in style, vocabulary, even structure or content—from the story that is told in third person. We can illustrate this by reference to a possible story situation. Suppose that a writer chooses war as a story subject; suppose too that this writer hates war. He may, on the one hand, choose to allow his protagonist to tell his own story. Now suppose that his protagonist has a limited education, is provincial, and enjoys killing. Obviously, both the style of this story and the content will here be determined by the character of the protagonist; and whatever *negative* reaction toward war the writer wants from us must be accomplished by implication—by the use of irony, say, or by the shrewd selection or juxtaposition of detail. In other words, when a writer chooses to use the first person narrator, he in effect secedes from his own story; he commits himself to the style, background, and character of his narrator. But suppose that this same writer chooses to tell this man's story in third person. Now, since the writer has interposed himself between his reader and his protagonist, the language and style will change; they will become the writer's language and style. Beyond that, even the content can change, for now the writer's attitude toward war can quite legitimately seep into his story.

Choice of narrator, then, has a great deal to do with the content, style, and effect of a story. The matter of position, of the relationship of the narrator to the story, plays an even more important part. Here we meet with the possibility of almost infinite variation, gradation, or combination. Narrative positions in stories can range from that extreme which Robert Penn Warren calls the *panoramic,* in which a story is viewed from a constantly shifting position, to that which he calls *strict focus,* a severely restricted position that is usually found only in the well-handled first-person narrative. If we allow for all these variations and gradations, we can say that basically there are four positions from which a story can be told: the omniscient point of view, the central point of view, the peripheral point of view, and the objective point of view.

The omniscient point of view might also be called the shifting or multiple or panoramic point of view. It is the oldest point of view in fiction, but for a number of reasons it is infrequently employed in modern fiction. With this point of view, the writer assumes the freedom to move at will from one point in his story to another. He may, for example, tell one part of his story through the eyes and mind of one character, another part through the eyes and mind of a second character. He may, at any point, shift from a character's position to his own, a shift known as author intrusion; or he may handle part of his material subjectively (that is, from the inside, from someone's mind), another part objectively (that is, from the outside, as drama is handled). The omniscient point of view obviously offers a writer maximum scope and flexibility. But in the hands of an unskillful writer, no point of view is so subject to abuse: such a writer will shift his point of view needlessly and create confusions in pattern or direction or focus; or he will come between his reader and his story; or he will use this point of view as an easy excuse for not handling his theme or characterization or emotion indirectly. For these and other reasons most writers prefer other points of view.

Of these, the central or limited omniscient point of view is the one used in most modern short stories. Here the story is told from the point of view of the central character; the writer allows himself access to the mind of this character but not to the minds of any other characters in his story. It is the most popular of all fictional points of view because the purpose of most stories is centered in the experiences, reactions, or changes of the central character; what the protagonist comes to understand or experience is essentially what the author intends the reader to understand or experience (though, as we shall see in a moment, this last generalization is subject to very careful modification).

In many stories, however, the author's purpose can best be accomplished by telling the story through the eyes of a minor character rather than the central one. We call this point of view *peripheral* because the story is told from the edge, so to speak, instead of from the center. Given a certain kind of story, this point of view offers a writer a number of advantages. For example, the author may want to incorporate interpretations or attitudes which, if assigned to the main character, would destroy plausibility or consistency, and if assigned to himself, to the writer, would constitute author intrusion. But if the writer chooses to approach his story from the position of a minor character, he can incorporate these comments without destroying other effects such as emotional unity. And in numerous other ways the peripheral point of view can achieve irony or thematic modification or depth of characterization or other effects that would be impossible if the story were approached from any other position.

The most recent development in fiction is that of the objective point of view, which approaches a story completely from the outside. Perhaps the best way to describe it is to imagine that you are not *participating* in a story but are rather *watching* it from a seat in a theater. Indeed, the objective point of view is in part a result of the very strong influence of drama on modern fiction; and like drama, it does not permit us to enter, except indirectly by inference, into the minds or inner feelings of *any* character. Everything, in short, is viewed from the outside; the story accomplishes everything through the external actions, speech, or appearance of the characters, or through description of setting.

Where the omniscient point of view is at once the easiest point of view and the one most subject to abuse, the objective point of view is the most difficult to handle but the one least subject to abuse. However, it works best with only certain kinds of material. It is the point of view, for example, of the so-called slice of life story, which accomplishes its purpose best when it is allowed to speak completely for itself, without author or character comment. It is also found in stories that deal not with a single protagonist but rather with a relationship—in a story dealing with marriage, for example, in which neither husband nor wife is the protagonist, we might expect to find this point of view employed.

Now it is as important for us to be aware of a story's point of view as it is to follow that story's conflict, assess its characters, interpret its theme, or grasp its implications. Indeed, we frequently cannot do any of these other things until we have considered the teller of the story—who he is, what his limitations are, what his involvement in or distance from the story is. In this regard, our first step is to identify the narrative point of view and to try to decide why the author chose one point of view over another. Definition, however, is only the first step and perhaps the simplest; it can, in fact, be done mechanically, simply by asking ourselves whose mind we are allowed access to in the story. The second step can be somewhat more delicate. In *The Rhetoric of Fiction,* Wayne Booth discusses what he calls the *authority* of a story's narrator, and this is as subject to variations as the possible positions from which a story can be approached. Every story is told by or through someone—an author, an "implied" author, a central character, a minor character, an anonymous and unidentified character, a number of characters—and what we make of the story is going to be determined in part by the reliability of that someone. Even the term *reliability* or *authority* has a special connotation; what we mean by it is how closely the *narrator's* attitudes toward, or feelings about, or interpretation of an experience approximates the *writer's* attitudes, feelings, or interpretation. As we have seen, behind every honest story is a writer who has certain views about life and who wants to communicate these to a reader. In doing so, he may choose any of a number of ways to get his "point" across. Ordinarily, if the story employs the omniscient point of view—that is, if the writer interprets his own story as he tells it—we can assume that the narrator is reliable. If the story is "objective," we can usually make the same assumption, though here an "implied narrator" may or may not represent the writer. But as soon as a writer chooses to tell a story through the eyes of someone other than himself, we can no longer assume the reliability of the narrator. He *may* speak for the writer but much more frequently he does not. Marlowe, for example, the narrator in some of Conrad's stories, *seems* to be reasonably reliable. At the other extreme, most narrators in Ring Lardner's stories are clearly unreliable, and instead of accepting their interpretation we accept an opposite one. Between these two extremes, we can have an infinite number of variations and gradations. Thus, when we read a story told through a child's eyes, or through the eyes of a clearly stupid narrator, or through the eyes of a narrator who is presented sympathetically but whose understanding of the situation is incomplete, we must obviously make allowances for the narrator before we can hope to understand what the author wants to say to us.

KATHERINE ANNE PORTER

Theft

She had the purse in her hand when she came in. Standing in the middle of the floor, holding her bathrobe around her and trailing a damp towel in one hand, she surveyed the immediate past and remembered everything clearly. Yes, she had opened the flap and spread it out on the bench after she had dried the purse with her handkerchief.

She had intended to take the Elevated, and naturally she looked in her purse to make certain she had the fare, and was pleased to find forty cents in the coin envelope. She was going to pay her own fare, too, even if Camilo did have the habit of seeing her up the steps and dropping a nickel in the machine before he gave the turnstile a little push and sent her through it with a bow. Camilo by a series of compromises had managed to make effective a fairly complete set of smaller courtesies, ignoring the larger and more troublesome ones. She had walked with him to the station in pouring rain, because she knew he was almost as poor as she was, and when he insisted on a taxi, she was firm and said, "You know it simply will not do." He was wearing a new hat of a pretty biscuit shade, for it never occurred to him to buy anything of a practical color; he had put it on for the first time and the rain was spoiling it. She kept thinking, "But this is dreadful, where will he get another?" She compared it with Eddie's hats that always seemed to be precisely seven years old and as if they had been quite purposely left out in the rain, and yet they sat with a careless and incidental rightness on Eddie. But Camilo was far different; if he wore a shabby hat it would be merely shabby on him, and he would lose his spirits over it. If she had not feared Camilo would take it badly, for he insisted on the practice of his little ceremonies up to the point he had fixed for them, she would have said to him as they left Thora's house, "Do go home. I can surely reach the station by myself."

"It is written that we must be rained upon tonight," said Camilo, "so let it be together."

At the foot of the platform stairway she staggered slightly—they were both nicely set up on Thora's cocktails—and said: "At least, Camilo, do me the favor not to climb these stairs in your present state, since for you it is only a matter of coming down again at once, and you'll certainly break your neck."

He made three quick bows, he was Spanish, and leaped off through the rainy darkness. She stood watching him, for he was a very graceful young man, thinking that tomorrow morning he would gaze soberly at his spoiled hat and soggy shoes and possibly associate her with his misery. As she watched, he stopped at the far corner and took off his hat and hid it under his overcoat. She felt she had betrayed him by seeing, because he would have been humiliated if he thought she even suspected him of trying to save his hat.

Roger's voice sounded over her shoulder above the clang of the rain falling on the stairway shed, wanting to know what she was doing out in the rain at this time of night, and did she take herself for a duck? His long, imperturbable face was streaming with water, and he tapped a bulging spot on the breast of his buttoned-up overcoat: "Hat," he said. "Come on, let's take a taxi."

She settled back against Roger's arm which he laid around her shoulders, and with the gesture they exchanged a glance full of long amiable associations, then she looked through the window of the rain changing the shapes of everything, and the colors. The taxi dodged in and out between the pillars of the Elevated, skidding slightly on every curve, and she said: "The more it skids the calmer I feel, so I really must be drunk."

"You must be," said Roger. "This bird is a homicidal maniac, and I could do with a cocktail myself this minute."

They waited on the traffic at Fortieth Street and Sixth Avenue, and three boys walked before the nose of the taxi. Under the globes of light they were cheerful scarecrows, all very thin and all wearing very seedy snappy-cut suits and gay neckties. They were not very sober either, and they stood for a moment wobbling in front of the car, and there was an argument going on among them. They leaned toward each other as if they were getting ready to sing, and the first one said: "When I get married it won't be jus' for getting married, I'm gonna marry for *love,* see?" and the second one said, "Aw, gwan and tell that stuff to *her,* why n't yuh?" and the third one gave a kind of hoot, and said, "Hell, dis guy? Wot the hell's he got?" and the first one said: "Aaah, shurrup yuh mush, I got plenty." Then they all squealed and scrambled across the street beating the first one on the back and pushing him around.

"Nuts," commented Roger, "pure nuts."

Two girls went skittering by in short transparent raincoats, one green, one red, their heads tucked against the drive of the rain. One of them was saying to the other, "Yes, I know all about *that*. But what about me? You're always so sorry for *him* . . ." and they ran on with their little pelican legs flashing back and forth.

The taxi backed up suddenly and leaped forward again, and after a while Roger said: "I had a letter from Stella today, and she'll be home on the twenty-sixth, so I suppose she's made up her mind and it's all settled."

"I had a sort of letter today too," she said, "making up my mind for me. I think it is time for you and Stella to do something definite."

When the taxi stopped on the corner of West Fifty-third Street, Roger said, "I've just enough if you'll add ten cents," so she opened her purse and gave him a dime, and he said, "That's beautiful, that purse."

"It's a birthday present," she told him, "and I like it. How's your show coming?"

"Oh, still hanging on, I guess. I don't go near the place. Nothing sold yet. I mean to keep right on the way I'm going and they can take it or leave it. I'm through with the argument."

"It's absolutely a matter of holding out, isn't it?"

"Holding out's the tough part."

"Good night, Roger."

"Good night, you should take aspirin and push yourself into a tub of hot water, you look as though you're catching cold."

"I will."

With the purse under her arm she went upstairs, and on the first landing Bill heard her step and poked his head out with his hair tumbled and his eyes red, and he said: "For Christ's sake, come in and have a drink with me. I've had some bad news."

"You're perfectly sopping," said Bill, looking at her drenched feet. They had two drinks, while Bill told how the director had thrown his play out after the cast had been picked over twice, and had gone through three rehearsals. "I said to him, 'I didn't say it was a masterpiece, I said it would make a good show.' And he said, 'It just doesn't *play,* do you see? It needs a doctor.' So I'm stuck, absolutely stuck," said Bill, on the edge of weeping again. "I've been crying," he told her, "in my cups." And he went on to ask her if she realized his wife was ruining him with her extravagance. "I send her ten dollars every week of my unhappy life, and I don't really have to. She threatens to jail me if I don't, but she can't do it. God, let her try it after the way she treated me! She's no right to alimony and she knows it. She keeps on saying she's got to have it for the baby and I keep on sending it because I can't bear to see anybody suffer. So I'm way behind on the piano and the victrola, but—"

"Well, this is a pretty rug, anyhow," she said.

Bill stared at it and blew his nose. "I got it at Ricci's for ninety-five dollars," he said. "Ricci told me it once belonged to Marie Dressler, and cost fifteen hundred dollars, but there's a burnt place on it, under the divan. Can you beat that?"

"No," she said. She was thinking about her empty purse and that she could not possibly expect a check for her latest review for another three days, and her arrangement with the basement restaurant could not last much longer if she did not pay something on account. "It's no time to speak of it," she said, "but I've been hoping you would have by now that fifty dollars you promised for my scene in the third act. Even if it doesn't play. You were to pay me for the work anyhow out of your advance."

"Weeping Jesus," said Bill, "you, too?" He gave a loud sob, or hiccough, in his moist handkerchief. "Your stuff was no better than mine, after all. Think of that."

"But you got something for it," she said. "Seven hundred dollars."

Bill said, "Do me a favor, will you? Have another drink and forget about it. I can't, you know I can't, I would if I could, but you know the fix I'm in."

"Let it go, then," she found herself saying almost in spite of herself. She had meant to be quite firm about it. They drank again without speaking, and she went to her apartment on the floor above.

There, she now remembered distinctly, she had taken the letter out of the purse before she spread the purse out to dry.

She had sat down and read the letter over again: but there were phrases that insisted on being read many times, they had a life of their own separate from the others, and when she tried to read past and around them, they moved with the movement of her eyes, and she could not escape them . . . "thinking about you more than I mean to . . . yes, I even talk about you . . . why were you so anxious to destroy . . . even if I could see you now I would not . . . not worth all this abominable . . . the end . . ."

Carefully she tore the letter into narrow strips and touched a lighted match to them in the coal grate.

Early the next morning she was in the bathtub when the janitress knocked and then came in, calling out that she wished to examine the radiators before she started the furnace going for the winter. After moving about the room for a few minutes, the janitress went out, closing the door very sharply.

She came out of the bathroom to get a cigarette from the package in the purse. The purse was gone. She dressed and made coffee, and sat by the window while she drank it. Certainly the janitress had taken the purse, and certainly it would be impossible to get it back without a great deal of ridiculous excitement. Then let it go. With this decision of her mind, there rose coincidentally in her blood a deep almost murderous anger. She set the cup carefully in the center of the table, and walked steadily downstairs, three long flights and a short hall and a steep short flight into the basement, where the janitress, her face streaked with coal dust, was shaking up the furnace. "Will you please give me back my purse? There isn't any money in it. It was a present, and I don't want to lose it."

The janitress turned without straightening up and peered at her with hot flickering eyes, a red light from the furnace reflected in them. "What do you mean, your purse?"

"The gold cloth purse you took from the wooden bench in my room," she said. "I must have it back."

"Before God I never laid eyes on your purse, and that's the holy truth," said the janitress.

"Oh, well then, keep it," she said, but in a very bitter voice; "keep it if you want it so much." And she walked away.

She remembered how she had never locked a door in her life, on some principle of rejection in her that made her uncomfortable in the ownership of things, and her paradoxical boast before the warnings of her friends, that she had never lost a penny by theft; and she had been pleased with the bleak humility of this concrete example designed to illustrate and justify a certain fixed, otherwise baseless and general faith which ordered the movements of her life without regard to her will in the matter.

In this moment she felt that she had been robbed of an enormous number of valuable things, whether material or intangible: things lost or broken by her own fault, things she had forgotten and left in houses when she moved: books borrowed from her and not returned, journeys she had planned and had not made, words she had waited to hear spoken to her and had not heard, and the words she had meant to answer with; bitter alternatives and intolerable substitutes worse than nothing, and yet inescapable: the long patient suffering of dying friendships and the dark inexplicable death of love—all that she had had, and all that she had missed, were lost together, and were twice lost in this landslide of remembered losses.

The janitress was following her upstairs with the purse in her hand and the same deep red fire flickering in her eyes. The janitress thrust the purse towards her while they were still a half dozen steps apart, and said: "Don't never tell on me. I musta been crazy. I get crazy in the head sometimes, I swear I do. My son can tell you."

She took the purse after a moment, and the janitress went on: "I got a niece who is going on seventeen, and she's a nice girl and I thought I'd give it to her. She needs a pretty purse. I musta been crazy; I thought maybe you wouldn't mind, you leave things around and don't seem to notice much."

She said: "I missed this because it was a present to me from someone . . ."

The janitress said: "He'd get you another if you lost this one. My niece is young and needs pretty things, we oughta give the young ones a chance. She's got young men after her maybe will want to marry her. She oughta have nice things. She needs them bad right now. You're a grown woman, you've had your chance, you ought to know how it is!"

She held the purse out to the janitress saying: "You don't know what you're talking about. Here, take it, I've changed my mind. I really don't want it."

The janitress looked up at her with hatred and said: "I don't want it either now. My niece is young and pretty, she don't need fixin' up to be pretty, she's young and pretty anyhow! I guess you need it worse than she does!"

"It wasn't really yours in the first place," she said, turning away. "You mustn't talk as if I had stolen it from you."

"It's not from me, it's from her you're stealing it," said the janitress, and went back downstairs.

She laid the purse on the table and sat down with the cup of chilled coffee, and thought: I was right not to be afraid of any thief but myself, who will end by leaving me nothing.

D. H. LAWRENCE

Tickets, Please

There is in the midlands a single-line tramway system which boldly leaves the county town and plunges off into the black, industrial countryside, up hill and down dale, through the long ugly villages of workmen's houses, over canals and railways, past churches perched high and nobly over the smoke and shadows, through stark, grimy, cold little market-places, tilting away in a rush past cinemas and shops down to the hollow where the collieries are, then up again, past a little rural church, under the ash trees, on in a rush to the terminus, the last little ugly place of industry, the cold little town that shivers on the edge of the wild, gloomy country beyond. There the green and creamy coloured tram-car seems to pause and purr with curious satisfaction. But in a few minutes—the clock on the turret of the Co-operative Wholesale Society's Shops gives the time—away it starts once more on the adventure. Again there are the reckless swoops downhill, bouncing the loops: again the chilly wait in the hill-top market-place: again the breathless slithering round the precipitous drop under the church: again the patient halts at the loops, waiting for the outcoming car: so on and on, for two long hours, till at last the city looms beyond the fat gas-works, the narrow factories draw near, we are in the sordid streets of the great town, once more we sidle to a standstill at our terminus, abashed by the great crimson and cream-coloured city cars, but still perky, jaunty, somewhat dare-devil, green as a jaunty sprig of parsley out of a black colliery garden.

To ride on these cars is always an adventure. Since we are in war-time, the drivers are men unfit for active service: cripples and hunchbacks. So they have the spirit of the devil in them. The ride becomes a steeple-chase. Hurray! we have leapt in a clear jump over the canal bridges—now for the four-lane corner. With a shriek and a trail of sparks we are clear again. To be sure, a tram often leaps the rails—but what matter! It sits in a ditch till other trams come to haul it out. It is quite common for a car, packed with one solid mass of living people, to come to a dead halt in the midst of unbroken blackness, the heart of nowhere on a dark night, and for the driver and the girl conductor to call, "All get off—car's on fire!" Instead, however, of rushing out in a panic, the passengers stolidly reply: "Get on—get on! We're not coming out. We're stopping where we are. Push on, George." So till flames actually appear.

The reason for this reluctance to dismount is that the nights are howlingly cold, black, and windswept, and a car is a haven of refuge. From village to village the miners travel, for a change of cinema, of girl, of pub. The trams are desperately packed. Who is going to risk himself in the black gulf outside, to wait perhaps an hour for another tram, then to see the forlorn notice "Depot Only," because there is something wrong! Or to greet a unit of three bright cars all so tight with people that they sail past with a howl of derision. Trams that pass in the night.

This, the most dangerous tram-service in England, as the authorities themselves declare, with pride, is entirely conducted by girls, and driven by rash young men, a little crippled, or by delicate young men, who creep forward in terror. The girls are fearless young hussies. In their ugly blue uniform, skirts up to their knees, shapeless old peaked caps in their heads, they have all the *sang-froid* of an old noncommissioned officer. With a tram packed with howling colliers, roaring hymns downstairs and a sort of antiphony of obscenities upstairs, the lasses are perfectly at their ease. They pounce on the youths who try to evade their ticket-machine. They push off the men at the end of their distance. They are not going to be done in the eye—not they. They fear nobody—and everybody fears them.

"Hello, Annie!"

"Hello, Ted!"

"Oh, mind my corn, Miss Stone. It's my belief you've got a heart of stone, for you've trod on it again."

"You should keep it in your pocket," replies Miss Stone, and she goes sturdily upstairs in her high boots.

"Tickets, please."

She is peremptory, suspicious, and ready to hit first. She can hold her own against ten thousand. The step of that tram-car is her Thermopylae.

Therefore, there is a certain wild romance aboard these cars—and in the sturdy bosom of Annie herself. The time for soft romance is in the morning, between ten o'clock and one, when things are rather slack: that is, except market-day and Saturday. Thus Annie has time to look about her. Then she often hops off her car and into a shop where she has spied something, while the driver chats in the main road. There is very good feeling between the girls and the drivers. Are they not companions in peril, shipments aboard this careering vessel of a tram-car, for ever rocking on the waves of a stormy land.

Then, also, during the easy hours, the inspectors are most in evidence. For some reason, everybody employed in this tram-service is young: there are no grey heads. It would not do. Therefore the inspectors are of the right age, and one, the chief, is also good-looking. See him stand on a wet, gloomy morning, in his long oilskin, his peaked cap well down over his eyes, waiting to board a car. His face is ruddy, his small brown moustache is weathered, he has a faint impudent smile. Fairly tall and agile, even in his waterproof, he springs aboard a car and greets Annie.

"Hello, Annie! Keeping the wet out?"

"Trying to."

There are only two people in the car. Inspecting is soon over. Then for a long and impudent chat on the foot-board, a good, easy, twelve-mile chat.

The inspector's name is John Thomas Raynor—always called John Thomas, except sometimes, in malice, Coddy. His face sets in fury when he is addressed, from a distance, with this abbreviation. There is considerable scandal about John Thomas in half a dozen villages. He flirts with the girl conductors in the morning and walks out with them in the dark night, when they leave their tram-car at the depot. Of course, the girls quit the service frequently. Then he flirts and walks out with the newcomer: always providing she is sufficiently attractive, and that she will consent to walk. It is remarkable, however, that most of the girls are quite comely, they are all young, and this roving life aboard the car gives them a sailor's dash and recklessness. What matter how they behave when the ship is in port? To-morrow they will be aboard again.

Annie, however, was something of a Tartar, and her sharp tongue had kept John Thomas at arm's length for many months. Perhaps, therefore, she liked him all the more: for he always came up smiling, with impudence. She watched him vanquish one girl, then another. She could tell by the movement of his mouth and eyes, when he flirted with her in the morning, that he had been walking out with this lass, or the other, the night before. A fine cock-of-the-walk he was. She could sum him up pretty well.

In this subtle antagonism they knew each other like old friends, they were as shrewd with one another almost as man and wife. But Annie had always kept him sufficiently at arm's length. Besides, she had a boy of her own.

The Statutes fair, however, came in November, at Bestwood. It happened that Annie had the Monday night off. It was a drizzling ugly night, yet she dressed herself up and went to the fair ground. She was alone, but she expected soon to find a pal of some sort.

The roundabouts were veering round and grinding out their music, the side-shows were making as much commotion as possible. In the coco-nut shies there were no coconuts, but artificial wartime substitutes, which the lads declared were fastened into the irons. There was a sad decline in brilliance and luxury. None the less, the ground was muddy as ever, there was the same crush, the press of faces lighted up by the flares and the electric lights, the same smell of naphtha and a few fried potatoes, and of electricity.

Who should be the first to greet Miss Annie, on the show-ground but John Thomas. He had a black overcoat buttoned up to his chin, and a tweed cap pulled down over his brows, his face between was ruddy and smiling and handy as ever. She knew so well the way his mouth moved.

She was very glad to have a "boy." To be at the Statutes without a fellow was no fun. Instantly, like the gallant he was, he took her on the Dragons, grim-toothed, roundabout switchbacks. It was not nearly so exciting as a tram-car actually. But, then, to be seated in a shaking, green dragon, uplifted above the sea of bubble faces, careering in a rickety fashion in the lower heavens, whilst John Thomas leaned over her, his cigarette in his mouth, was after all the right style. She was a plump, quick, alive little creature. So she was quite excited and happy.

John Thomas made her stay on for the next round. And therefore she could hardly for shame repulse him when he put his arm round her and drew her a little nearer to him, in a very warm and cuddly manner. Besides, he was fairly discreet, he kept his movement as hidden as possible. She looked down and saw that his red, clean hand was out of sight of the crowd. And they knew each other so well. So they warmed up to the fair.

After the dragons they went on the horses. John Thomas paid each time, so she could but be complaisant. He, of course, sat astride on the outer horse—named "Black Bess"—and she sat sideways, towards him, on the inner horse—named "Wildfire." But of course John Thomas was not going to sit discreetly on "Black Bess," holding the brass bar. Round they spun and heaved, in the light. And round he swung on his wooden steed, flinging one leg across her mount, and perilously tipping up and down, across the space, half lying back, laughing at her. He was perfectly happy; she was afraid her hat was on one side, but she was excited.

He threw quoits on a table and won for her two large, pale blue hat-pins. And then, hearing the noise of the cinemas, announcing another performance, they climbed the board and went in.

Of course, during these performances pitch darkness falls from time to time, when the machine goes wrong. Then there is a wild whooping, and a loud smacking of simulated kisses. In these moments John Thomas drew Annie towards him. After all, he had a wonderfully warm, cosy way of holding a girl with his arm, he seemed to make such a nice fit. And after all, it was pleasant to be so held: so very comforting and cosy and nice. He leaned over her and she felt his breath on her hair; she knew he wanted to kiss her on the lips. And after all, he was so warm and she fitted in to him so softly. After all, she wanted him to touch her lips.

But the light sprang up; she also started electrically, and put her hat straight. He left his arm lying nonchalantly behind her. Well, it was fun, it was exciting to be at the Statutes with John Thomas.

When the cinema was over they went for a walk across the dark, damp fields. He had all the arts of love-making. He was especially good at holding a girl, when he sat with her on a stile in the black, drizzling darkness. He seemed to be holding her in space, against his own warmth and gratification. And his kisses were soft and slow and searching.

So Annie walked out with John Thomas, though she kept her own boy dangling in the distance. Some of the tram-girls chose to be huffy. But there, you must take things as you find them, in this life.

There was no mistake about it, Annie liked John Thomas a good deal. She felt so rich and warm in herself whenever he was near. And John Thomas really liked Annie, more than usual. The soft, melting way in which she could flow into a fellow, as if she melted into his very bones, was something rare and good. He fully appreciated this.

But with a developing acquaintance there began a developing intimacy. Annie wanted to consider him a person, a man; she wanted to take an intelligent interest in him, and to have an intelligent response. She did not want a mere nocturnal presence, which was what he was so far. And she prided herself that he could not leave her.

Here she made a mistake. John Thomas intended to remain a nocturnal presence; he had no idea of becoming an all-round individual to her. When she started to take an intelligent interest in him and his life and his character, he sheered off. He hated intelligent interest. And he knew that the only way to stop it was to avoid it. The possessive female was aroused in Annie. So he left her.

It is no use saying she was not surprised. She was at first startled, thrown out of her count. For she had been so *very* sure of holding him. For a while she was staggered, and everything became uncertain to her. Then she wept with fury, indignation, desolation, and misery. Then she had a spasm of despair. And then, when he came, still impudently, on to her car, still familiar, but letting her see by the movement of his head that he had gone away to somebody else for the time being and was enjoying pastures new, then she determined to have her own back.

She had a very shrewd idea what girls John Thomas had taken out. She went to Nora Purdy. Nora was a tall, rather pale, but well-built girl, with beautiful yellow hair. She was rather secretive.

"Hey!" said Annie, accosting her; then softly, "Who's John Thomas on with now?"

"I don't know," said Nora.

"Why tha does," said Annie, ironically lapsing into dialect. "Tha knows as well as I do."

"Well, I do, then," said Nora. "It isn't me, so don't bother."

"It's Cissy Meakin, isn't it?"

"It is, for all I know."

"Hasn't he got a face on him!" said Annie. "I don't half like his cheek. I could knock him off the foot-board when he comes round at me."

"He'll get dropped on one of these days," said Nora.

"Ay, he will when somebody makes up their mind to drop it on him. I should like to see him taken down a peg or two, shouldn't you?"

"I shouldn't mind," said Nora.

"You've got a quite as much cause to as I have," said Annie. "But we'll drop on him one of these days, my girl. What? Don't you want to?"

"I shouldn't mind," said Nora.

But as a matter of fact, Nora was much more vindictive than Annie.

One by one Annie went the round of the old flames. It so happened that Cissy Meakin left the tramway service in quite a short time. Her mother made her leave. Then John Thomas was on the *qui vive*. He cast his eyes over his old flock. And his eyes lighted on Annie. He thought she would be safe now. Besides, he liked her.

She arranged to walk home with him on Sunday night. It so happened that her car would be in the depot at half-past nine: the last car would come in at 10.15. So John Thomas was to wait for her there.

At the depot the girls had a little waiting-room of their own. It was quite rough, but cosy, with a fire and an oven and a mirror, and table and wooden chairs. The half dozen girls who knew John Thomas only too well had arranged to take service this Sunday afternoon. So, as the cars began to come in, early, the girls dropped into the waiting-room. And instead of hurrying off home, they sat around the fire and had a cup of tea. Outside was the darkness and lawlessness of wartime.

John Thomas came on the car after Annie, at about a quarter to ten. He poked his head easily into the girls' waiting-room.

"Prayer-meeting?" he asked.

"Ay," said Laura Sharp. "Ladies only."

"That's me!" said John Thomas. It was one of his favourite exclamations.

"Shut the door, boy," said Muriel Baggaley.

"On which side of me?" said John Thomas.

"Which tha likes," said Polly Birkin.

He had come in and closed the door behind him. The girls moved in their circle, to make a place for him near the fire. He took off his great-coat and pushed back his hat.

"Who handles the teapot?" he said.

Nora Purdy silently poured him out a cup of tea.

"Want a bit o' my bread and drippin'?" said Muriel Baggaley to him.

"Ay, give us a bit."

And he began to eat his piece of bread.

"There's no place like home, girls," he said.

They all looked at him as he uttered this piece of impudence. He seemed to be sunning himself in the presence of so many damsels.

"Especially if you're not afriad to go home in the dark," said Laura Sharp.

"Me! By myself I am."

They sat till they heard the last tram come in. In a few minutes Emma Houselay entered.

"Come on, my old duck!'" cried Polly Birkin.

"It *is* perishing," said Emma, holding her fingers to the fire.

"But—I'm afraid to, go home in, the dark," sang Laura Sharp, the tune having got into her mind.

"Who're you going with tonight, John Thomas?" asked Muriel Baggaley, coolly.

"Tonight?" said John Thomas. "Oh, I'm going home by myself tonight—all on my lonely-o."

"That's me!" said Nora Purdy, using his own ejaculation.

The girls laughed shrilly.

"Me as well, Nora," said John Thomas.

"Don't know what you mean," said Laura.

"Yes, I'm toddling," said he, rising and reaching for his overcoat.

"Nay," said Polly. "We're all here waiting for you."

"We've got to be up in good time in the morning," he said in the benevolent official manner.

They all laughed.

"Nay," said Muriel. "Don't leave us all lonely, John Thomas. Take one!"

"I'll take the lot, if you like," he responded gallantly.

"That you won't, either," said Muriel. "Two's company; seven's too much of a good thing."

"Nay—take one," said Laura. "Fair and square, all above board and say which."

"Ay," cried Annie, speaking for the first time. "Pick, John Thomas; let's hear thee."

"Nay," he said. "I'm going home quiet tonight. Feeling good, for once."

"Whereabouts?" said Annie. "Take a good un, then. But tha's got to take one of us!"

"Nay, how can I take one," he said, laughing uneasily. "I don't want to make enemies."

"You'd only make *one*," said Annie.

"The chosen *one*," added Laura.

"Oh, my! Who said girls!" exclaimed John Thomas, again turning, as if to escape. "Well—good-night."

"Nay, you've got to make your pick," said Muriel. "Turn your face to the wall and say which one touches you. Go on—we shall only just touch your back—one of us. Go on—turn your face to the wall, and don't look, and say which one touches you."

He was uneasy, mistrusting them. Yet he had not the courage to break away. They pushed him to a wall and stood him there with his face to it. Behind his back they all grimaced, tittering. He looked so comical. He looked around uneasily.

"Go on!" he cried.

"You're looking—you're looking!" they shouted.

He turned his head away. And suddenly, with a movement like a swift cat, Annie went forward and fetched him a box on the side of the head that set his cap flying, and himself staggering. He started round.

But at Annie's signal they all flew at him, slapping him, pinching him, pulling his hair, though more in fun than in spite or anger. He, however, saw red. His blue eyes flamed with strange fear as well as fury, and he butted through the girls to the door. It was locked. He wrenched at it. Roused, alert, the girls stood round and looked at him. He faced them, at bay. At that moment they were rather horrifying to him, as they stood in their short uniforms. He was distinctly afraid.

"Come on, John Thomas! Come on! Choose!" said Annie.

"What are you after? Open the door," he said.

"We sha'n't—not till you've chosen!" said Muriel.

"Chosen what?" he said.

"Chosen the one you're going to marry," she replied.

He hesitated a moment.

"Open the blasted door," he said, "and get back to your senses." He spoke with official authority.

"You've got to choose!" cried the girls.

"Come on!" cried Annie, looking him in the eye. "Come on! Come on!"

He went forward, rather vaguely. She had taken off her belt, and swinging it, she fetched him a sharp blow over the head with the buckle end. He sprang and seized her. But immediately the other girls rushed upon him, pulling and tearing and beating him. Their blood was now thoroughly up. He was their sport now. They were going to have their own back, out of him. Strange, wild creatures, they hung on him and rushed at him to bear him down. His tunic was torn right up the back, Nora had hold at the back of his collar, and was actually strangling him. Luckily the button burst. He struggled in a wild frenzy of fury and terror, almost mad terror. His tunic was simply torn off his back, his shirt-sleeves were torn away, his arms were naked. The girls rushed at him, clenched their hands on him and pulled at him: or they rushed at him and pushed him, butted him with all their might: or they struck him wild blows. He ducked and cringed and struck sideways. They became more intense.

At last he was down. They rushed on him, kneeling on him. He had neither breath nor strength to move. His face was bleeding with a long scratch, his brow was bruised.

Annie knelt on him, the other girls knelt and hung on to him. Their faces were flushed, their hair wild, their eyes were all glittering strangely. He lay at last quite still, with face averted, as an animal lies when it is defeated and at the mercy of the captor. Sometimes his eye glanced back at the wild faces of the girls. His breast rose heavily, his wrists were torn.

"Now, then, my fellow!" gasped Annie at length. "Now then—now—"

At the sound of her terrifying cold triumph, he suddenly started to struggle as an animal might, but the girls threw themselves upon him with unnatural strength and power, forcing him down.

"Yes—now, then!" gasped Annie at length.

And there was a dead silence, in which the thud of heart-beating was to be heard. It was a suspense of pure silence in every soul.

"Now you know where you are," said Annie.

The sight of his white, bare arm maddened the girls. He lay in a kind of trance of fear and antagonism. They felt themselves filled with supernatural strength.

Suddenly Polly started to laugh—to giggle wildly—helplessly—and Emma and Muriel joined in. But Annie and Nora and Laura remained the same, tense, watchful, with gleaming eyes. He winced away from these eyes.

"Yes," said Annie, in a curious low tone, secret and deadly. "Yes! You've got it now! You know what you've done, don't you? You know what you've done."

He made no sound nor sign, but lay with bright, averted eyes, and averted, bleeding face.

"You ought to be *killed,* that's what you ought," said Annie tensely. "You ought to be *killed.*" And there was a terrifying lust in her voice.

Polly was ceasing to laugh, and giving long-drawn Oh-h-hs and sighs as she came to herself.

"He's got to choose," she said vaguely.

"Oh, yes, he has," said Laura, with vindictive decision.

"Do you hear—do you hear?" said Annie. And with a sharp movement that made him wince, she turned his face to her.

"Do you hear?" she repeated, shaking him.

But he was quite dumb. She fetched him a sharp slap on the face. He started, and his eyes widened. Then his face darkened with defiance, after all.

"Do you hear?" she repeated.

He only looked at her with hostile eyes.

"Speak!" she said, putting her face devilishly near his.

"What?" he said, almost overcome.

'You've got to *choose!*" she cried, as if it were some terrible menace, and as if it hurt her that she could not exact more.

"What?" he said in fear.

"Choose your girl, Coddy. You've got to choose her now. And you'll get your neck broken if you play any more of your tricks, my boy. You're settled now."

There was a pause. Again he averted his face. He was cunning in his overthrow. He did not give in to them really—no, not if they tore him to bits.

"All right, then," he said, "I choose Annie." His voice was strange and full of malice. Annie let go of him as if he had been a hot coal.

"He's chosen Annie!" said the girls in chorus.

"Me!" cried Annie. She was still kneeling, but away from him. He was still lying prostate, with averted face. The girls grouped uneasily around.

"Me!" repeated Annie, with a terrible bitter accent.

Then she got up, drawing away from him with strange disgust and bitterness.

"I wouldn't touch him," she said.

But her face quivered with a kind of agony, she seemed as if she would fall. The other girls turned aside. He remained lying on the floor, with his torn clothes and bleeding, averted face.

"Oh, if he's choosen—" said Polly.

"I don't want him—he can choose again," said Annie, with the same rather bitter hopelessness.

"Get up," said Polly, lifting his shoulder. "Get up."

He rose slowly, a strange, ragged, dazed creature. The girls eyed him from a distance, curiously, furtively, dangerously.

"Who wants him?" cried Laura roughly.

"Nobody," they answered with contempt. Yet each one of them waited for him to look at her, hoped he would look at her. All except Annie, and something was broken in her.

He, however, kept his face closed and averted from them all. There was a silence of the end. He picked up the torn pieces of his tunic, without knowing what to do with them. The girls stood about uneasily, flushed, panting, tidying their hair and their dress unconsciously, and watching him. He looked at none of them. He espied his cap in a corner and went and picked it up. He put it on his head, and one of the girls burst into a shrill, hysteric laugh at the sight he presented. He, however, took no heed but went straight to where his overcoat hung on a peg. The girls moved away from contact with him as if he had been an electric wire. He put on his coat and buttoned it down. Then he rolled his tunic-rags into a bundle, and stood before the locked door, dumbly.

"Open the door, somebody," said Laura.

"Annie's got the key," said one.

Annie silently offered the key to the girls. Nora unlocked the door.

"Tit for tat, old man," she said. "Show yourself a man, and don't bear a grudge."

But without a word or sign he had opened the door and gone, his face closed, his head dropped.

"That'll learn him," said Laura.

"Coddy!" said Nora.

"Shut up, for God's sake!" cried Annie fiercely, as if in torture.

"Well, I'm about ready to go, Polly. Look sharp!" said Muriel.

The girls were all anxious to be off. They were tidying themselves hurriedly, with mute, stupefied faces.

WILLIAM FAULKNER

Red Leaves

I

The two Indians crossed the plantation toward the slave quarters. Neat with the whitewash, of baked soft brick, the two rows of houses in which lived the slaves belonging to the clan, faced one another across the mild shade of the lane marked and scored with naked feet and with a few homemade toys mute in the dust. There was no sign of life.

"I know what we will find," the first Indian said.

"What we will not find," the second said. Although it was noon, the lane was vacant, the doors of the cabins empty and quiet; no cooking smoke rose from any of the chinked and plastered chimneys.

"Yes. It happened like this when the father of him who is now the Man died."

"You mean, of him who was the Man."

"Yao."

The first Indian's name was Three Basket. He was perhaps sixty. They were both squat men, a little solid, burgherlike; paunchy, with big heads, big, broad, dust-colored faces of a certain blurred serenity like carved heads on a ruined wall in Siam or Sumatra, looming out of a mist. The sun had done it, the violent sun, the violent shade. Their hair looked like sedge grass on burnt-over land. Clamped through one ear Three Basket wore an enameled snuffbox.

"I have said all the time that this is not the good way. In the old days there were no quarters, no Negroes. A man's time was his own then. He had time. Now he must spend most of it finding work for them who prefer sweating to do."

"They are like horses and dogs."

"They are like nothing in this sensible world. Nothing contents them save sweat. They are worse than the white people."

"It is not as though the Man himself had to find work for them to do."

"You said it. I do not like slavery. It is not the good way. In the old days, there was the good way. But not now."

"You do not remember the old way either."

"I have listened to them who do. And I have tried this way. Man was not made to sweat."

"That's so. See what it has done to their flesh."

"Yes. Black. It has a bitter taste, too."

"You have eaten of it?"

"Once. I was young then, and more hardy in the appetite than now. Now it is different with me."

"Yes. They are too valuable to eat now."

"There is a bitter taste to the flesh which I do not like."

"They are too valuable to eat, anyway, when the white men will give horses for them."

They entered the lane. The mute, meager toys—the fetish-shaped objects made of wood and rags and feathers—lay in the dust about the patinaed doorsteps, among bones and broken gourd dishes. But there was no sound from any cabin, no face in any door; had not been since yesterday, when Issetibbeha died. But they already knew what they would find.

It was in the central cabin, a house a little larger than the others, where at certain phases of the moon the Negroes would gather to begin their ceremonies before removing after nightfall to the creek bottom, where they kept the drums. In this room they kept the minor accessories, the cryptic ornaments, the ceremonial records which consisted of sticks daubed with red clay in symbols. It had a hearth in the center of the floor, beneath a hole in the roof, with a few cold wood ashes and a suspended iron pot. The window shutters were closed; when the two Indians entered, after the abashless sunlight they could distinguish nothing with the eyes save a movement, shadow, out of which eyeballs rolled, so that the place appeared to be full of Negroes. The two Indians stood in the door.

"Yao," Basket said. "I said this is not the good way."

"I don't think I want to be here," the second said.

"That is black man's fear which you smell. It does not smell as ours does."

"I don't think I want to be here."

"Your fear has an odor too."

"Maybe it is Issetibbeha which we smell."

"Yao. He knows. He knows what we will find here. He knew when he died what we should find here today." Out of the rank twilight of the room the eyes, the smell, of Negroes rolled about them. "I am Three

Basket, whom you know," Basket said into the room. "We are come from the Man. He whom we seek is gone?" The Negroes said nothing. The smell of them, of their bodies, seemed to ebb and flux in the still hot air. They seemed to be musing as one upon something remote, inscrutable. They were like a single octopus. They were like the roots of a huge tree uncovered, the earth broken momentarily upon the writhen, thick, fetid tangle of its lightless and outraged life. "Come," Basket said. "You know our errand. Is he whom we seek gone?"

"They are thinking something," the second said. "I do not want to be here."

"They are knowing something," Basket said.

"They are hiding him, you think?"

"No. He is gone. He has been gone since last night. It happened like this before, when the grandfather of him who is now the Man died. It took us three days to catch him. For three days Doom lay above the ground, saying, 'I see my horse and my dog. But I do not see my slave. What have you done with him that you will not permit me to lie quiet?' "

"They do not like to die."

"Yao. They cling. It makes trouble for us, always. A people without honor and without decorum. Always a trouble."

"I do not like it here."

"Nor do I. But then, they are savages; they cannot be expected to regard usage. That is why I say that this way is a bad way."

"Yao. They cling. They would even rather work in the sun than to enter the earth with a chief. But he is gone."

The Negroes had said nothing, made no sound. The white eyeballs rolled, wild, subdued; the smell was rank, violent. "Yes, they fear," the second said. "What shall we do now?"

"Let us go and talk with the Man."

"Will Moketubbe listen?"

"What can he do? He will not like to. But he is the Man now."

"Yao. He is the Man. He can wear the shoes with the red heels all the time now." They turned and went out. There was no door in the door frame. There were no doors in any of the cabins.

"He did that anyway," Basket said.

"Behind Issetibbeha's back. But now they are his shoes, since he is the Man."

"Yao. Issetibbeha did not like it. I have heard. I know that he said to Moketubbe: 'When you are the Man, the shoes will be yours. But until then, they are my shoes.' But now Moketubbe is the Man; he can wear them."

"Yao," the second said. "He is the Man now. He used to wear the shoes behind Issetibbeha's back, and it was not known if Issetibbeha knew this or not. And then Issetibbeha became dead, who was not old, and the shoes are Moketubbe's, since he is the Man now. What do you think of that?"

"I don't think about it," Basket said. "Do you?"

"No," the second said.

"Good," Basket said. "You are wise."

II

The house sat on a knoll, surrounded by oak trees. The front of it was one story in height, composed of the deck house of a steamboat which had gone ashore and which Doom, Issetibbeha's father, had dismantled with his slaves and hauled on cypress rollers twelve miles home overland. It took them five months. His house consisted at the time of one brick wall. He set the steamboat broadside on to the wall, where now the chipped and flaked gliding of the rococo cornices arched in faint splendor above the gilt lettering of the stateroom names above the jalousied doors.

Doom had been born merely a subchief, a Mingo, one of three children on the mother's side of the family. He made a journey—he was a young man then and New Orleans was a European city—from north Mississippi to New Orleans by keel boat, where he met the Chevalier Soeur Blonde de Vitry, a man whose social position, on its face, was as equivocal as Doom's own. In New Orleans, among the gamblers and cutthroats of the river front, Doom, under the tutelage of his patron, passed as the chief, the Man, the hereditary owner of that land which belonged to the male side of the family; it was the Chevalier de Vitry who spoke of him as *l'Homme* or *de l'Homme,* and hence Doom.

They were seen everywhere together—the Indian, the squat man with a bold, inscrutable, underbred face, and the Parisian, the expatriate, the friend, it was said, of Carondelet and the intimate of General Wilkinson. Then they disappeared, the two of them, vanishing from their old equivocal haunts and leaving behind them the legend of the sums which Doom was believed to have won, and some tale about a young woman, daughter of a fairly well-to-do West Indian family, the son and brother of whom sought Doom with a pistol about his old haunts for some time after his disappearance.

Six months later the young woman herself disappeared, boarding the Saint Louis packet, which put in one night at a wood landing on the north Mississippi side, where the woman, accompanied by a Negro maid, got off. Four Indians met her with a horse and wagon, and they traveled for three days, slowly, since she was already big with child, to the plantation, where she found that Doom was now chief. He never told her how he accomplished it, save that his uncle and his cousin had died suddenly. Before that time the house had consisted of a brick wall built by shiftless slaves, against which was propped a thatched lean-to divided into rooms and littered with bones and refuse, set in the center of ten thousand acres of matchless parklike forest where deer grazed like domestic cattle. Doom and the woman were married there a short time before Issetibbeha was born, by a combination itinerant minister and slave trader who arrived on a mule, to the saddle of which was lashed a cotton umbrella and a three-gallon demijohn of whiskey. After that, Doom began to acquire more slaves and to cultivate some of his land, as the white people did. But he never had enough for them to do. In utter idleness the majority of them led lives transplanted whole out of African jungles, save on the occasions when, entertaining guests, Doom coursed them with dogs.

When Doom died, Issetibbeha, his son, was nineteen. He became proprietor of the land and of the quintupled herd of blacks for which he had no use at all. Though the title of Man rested with him, there was a hierarchy of cousins and uncles who ruled the clan and who finally gathered in squatting conclave over the Negro question, squatting profoundly beneath the golden names above the doors of the steamboat.

"We cannot eat them," one said.

"Why not?"

"There are too many of them."

"That's true," a third said. "Once we started, we should have to eat them all. And that much flesh diet is not good for man."

"Perhaps they will be like deer flesh. That cannot hurt you."

"We might kill a few of them and not eat them," Issetibbeha said.

They looked at him for a while. "What for?" one said.

"That is true," a second said. "We cannot do that. They are too valuable; remember all the bother they have caused us, finding things for them to do. We must do as the white men do."

"How is that?" Issetibbeha said.

"Raise more Negroes by clearing more land to make corn to feed them, then sell them. We will clear the land and plant it with food and raise Negroes and sell them to the white men for money."

"But what will we do with this money?" a third said.

They thought for a while.

"We will see," the first said. They squatted, profound, grave.

"It means work," the third said.

"Let the Negroes do it," the first said.

"Yao. Let them. To sweat is bad. It is damp. It opens the pores."

"And then the night air enters."

"Yao. Let the Negroes do it. They appear to like sweating."

So they cleared the land with the Negroes and planted it in grain. Up to that time the slaves had lived in a huge pen with a lean-to roof over one corner, like a pen for pigs. But now they began to build quarters, cabins, putting the young Negroes in the cabins in pairs to mate; five years later Issetibbeha sold forty head to a Memphis trader, and he took the money and went abroad upon it, his maternal uncle from New Orleans conducting the trip. At that time the Chevalier Soeur Blonde de Vitry was an old man in Paris, in a toupee and a corset and a careful, toothless old face fixed in a grimace quizzical and profoundly tragic. He borrowed three hundred dollars from Issetibbeha and in return he introduced him into certain circles; a year later Issetibbeha returned home with a gilt bed, a pair of girandoles by whose light it was said that Pompadour arranged her hair while Louis smirked at his mirrored face across her powdered shoulder, and a pair of slippers with red heels. They were too small for him, since he had not worn shoes at all until he reached New Orleans on his way abroad.

He brought the slippers home in tissue paper and kept them in the remaining pocket of a pair of saddlebags filled with cedar shavings, save when he took them out on occasion for his son, Moketubbe, to play with. At three years of age Moketubbe had a broad, flat, Mongolian face that appeared to exist in a complete and unfathomable lethargy, until confronted by the slippers.

Moketubbe's mother was a comely girl whom Issetibbeha had seen one day working in her shift in a melon patch. He stopped and watched her for a while—the broad, solid thighs, the sound back, the serene face. He was on his way to the creek to fish that day, but he didn't go any farther; perhaps while he stood there watching the unaware girl he may have remembered his own mother, the city woman, the fugitive with her fans and laces and her Negro blood, and all the tawdry shabbiness of that sorry affair. Within the year Moketubbe was born; even at three he could not get his feet into the slippers. Watching him in the still, hot afternoons as he struggled with the slippers with a certain monstrous repudiation of fact, Issetibbeha laughed quietly to himself. He laughed at Moketubbe's antics with the shoes for several years, because Moketubbe did not give up trying to put them on until he was sixteen. Then he quit. Or Issetibbeha thought he had. But he had merely quit trying in Issetibbeha's presence. Issetibbeha's newest wife told him that Moketubbe had stolen and hidden the shoes. Issetibbeha quit laughing then, and he sent the woman away, so that he was alone. "Yao," he said. "I too like being alive, it seems." He sent for Moketubbe. "I give them to you," he said.

Moketubbe was twenty-five then, unmarried. Issetibbeha was not tall, but he was taller by six inches than his son and almost a hundred pounds lighter. Moketubbe was already diseased with flesh, with a pale, broad, inert face and dropsical hands and feet. "They are yours now," Issetibbeha said, watching him. Moketubbe had looked at him once when he entered, a glance brief, discreet, veiled.

"Thanks," he said.

Issetibbeha looked at him. He could never tell if Moketubbe saw anything, looked at anything. "Why will it not be the same if I give the slippers to you?"

"Thanks," Moketubbe said. Issetibbeha was using snuff at the time; a white man had shown him how to put the powder into his lip and scour it against his teeth with a twig of gum or of alphea.

"Well," he said, "a man cannot live forever." He looked at his son, then his gaze went blank in turn, unseeing, and he mused for an instant. You could not tell what he was thinking, save that he said half aloud: "Yao. But Doom's uncle had no shoes with red heels." He looked at his son again, fat, inert. "Beneath all that, a man might think of doing anything and it not be known until too late." He sat in a splint chair hammocked with deer thongs. "He cannot even get them on; he and I are both frustrated by the same gross meat which he wears. He cannot even get them on. But is that my fault?"

He lived for five years longer, then he died. He was sick one night, and though the doctor came in a skunk-skin vest and burned sticks, Issetibbeha died before noon.

That was yesterday; the grave was dug, and for twelve hours now the People had been coming in wagons and carriages and on horseback and afoot, to eat the baked dog and the succotash and the yams cooked in ashes and to attend the funeral.

III

"It will be three days," Basket said, as he and the other Indian returned to the house. "It will be three days and the food will not be enough; I have seen it before."

The second Indian's name was Louis Berry. "He will smell too, in this weather."

"Yao. They are nothing but a trouble and a care."

"Maybe it will not take three days."

"They run far. Yao. We will smell this Man before he enters the earth. You watch and see if I am not right."

They approached the house.

"He can wear the shoes now," Berry said. "He can wear them now in man's sight."

"He cannot wear them for a while yet," Basket said. Berry looked at him. "He will lead the hunt."

"Moketubbe?" Berry said. "Do you think he will? A man to whom even talking is travail?"

"What else can he do? It is his own father who will soon begin to smell."

"That is true," Berry said. "There is even yet a price he must pay for the shoes. Yao. He has truly bought them. What do you think?"

"What do you think?"

"What do you think?"

"I think nothing."

"Nor do I. Issetibbeha will not need the shoes now. Let Moketubbe have them; Issetibbeha will not care."

"Yao. Man must die."

"Yao. Let him; there is still the Man."

The bark roof of the porch was supported by peeled cypress poles, high above the texas of the steamboat, shading an unfloored banquette where on the trodden earth mules and horses were tethered in bad weather. On the forward end of the steamboat's deck sat an old man and two women. One of the women was dressing a fowl, the other was shelling corn. The old man was talking. He was barefoot, in a long linen frock coat and a beaver hat.

"This world is going to the dogs," he said. "It is being ruined by white men. We got along fine for years and years, before the white men foisted their Negroes upon us. In the old days the old men sat in the shade and ate stewed deer's flesh and corn and smoked tobacco and talked of honor and grave affairs; now what do we do? Even the old wear themselves into the grave taking care of them that like sweating." When Basket and Berry crossed the deck he ceased and looked up at them. His eyes were querulous, bleared; his face was myriad with tiny wrinkles. "He is fled also," he said.

"Yes," Berry said, "he is gone."

"I knew it. I told them so. It will take three weeks, like when Doom died. You watch and see."

"It was three days, not three weeks," Berry said.

"Were you there?"

"No," Berry said. "But I have heard."

"Well, I was there," the old man said. "For three whole weeks, through the swamps and the briers—" They went on and left him talking.

What had been the saloon of the steamboat was now a shell, rotting slowly; the polished mahogany, the carving glinting momentarily and fading through the mold in figures cabalistic and profound; the gutted windows were like cataracted eyes. It contained a few sacks of seed or grain, and the fore part of the running gear of a barouche, to the axle of which two C-springs rusted in graceful curves, supporting nothing. In one corner a fox cub ran steadily and soundlessly up and down a willow cage; three scrawny gamecocks moved in the dust, and the place was pocked and marked with their dried droppings.

They passed through the brick wall and entered a big room of chinked logs. It contained the hinder part of the barouche, and the dismantled body lying on its side, the window slatted over with willow withes, through which protruded the heads, the still, beady, outraged eyes and frayed combs of still more game chickens. It was floored with packed clay; in one corner leaned a crude plow and two hand-hewn boat paddles. From the ceiling, suspended by four deer thongs, hung the gilt bed which Issetibbeha had fetched from Paris. It had neither mattress nor springs, the frame crisscrossed now by a neat hammocking of thongs.

Issetibbeha had tried to have his newest wife, the young one, sleep in the bed. He was congenitally short of breath himself, and he passed the nights half reclining in his splint chair. He would see her to bed and, later, wakeful, sleeping as he did but three or four hours a night, he would sit in the darkness and simulate slumber and listen to her sneak infinitesimally from the gilt and ribboned bed, to lie on a quilt pallet on the floor until just before daylight. Then she would enter the bed quietly again and in turn simulate slumber, while in the darkness beside her Issetibbeha quietly laughed and laughed.

The girandoles were lashed by thongs to two sticks propped in a corner where a ten-gallon whiskey keg lay also. There was a clay hearth; facing it, in the splint chair, Moketubbe sat. He was maybe an inch better than five feet tall, and he weighed two hundred and fifty pounds. He wore a broadcloth coat and no shirt, his round, smooth copper balloon of belly swelling above the bottom piece of a suit of linen underwear. On his feet were the slippers with the red heels. Behind his chair stood a stripling with a punkah-like fan made of fringed paper. Moketubbe sat motionless, with his broad, yellow face with its closed eyes and flat nostrils, his flipperlike arms extended. On his face was an expression profound, tragic, and inert. He did not open his eyes when Basket and Berry came in.

"He has worn them since daylight?" Basket said.

"Since daylight," the stripling said. The fan did not cease. "You can see."

"Yao," Basket said. "We can see." Moketubbe did not move. He looked like an effigy, like a Malay god in frock coat, drawers, naked chest, the trivial scarlet-heeled shoes.

"I wouldn't disturb him, if I were you," the stripling said.

"Not if I were you," Basket said. He and Berry squatted. The stripling moved the fan steadily. "O Man," Basket said, "listen." Moketubbe did not move. "He is gone," Basket said.

"I told you so," the stripling said. "I knew he would flee. I told you."

"Yao," Basket said. "You are not the first to tell us afterward what we should have known before. Why is it that some of you wise men took no steps yesterday to prevent this?"

"He does not wish to die," Berry said.

"Why should he not wish it?" Basket said.

"Because he must die some day is no reason," the strippling said. "That would not convince me either, old man."

"Hold your tongue," Berry said.

"For twenty years," Basket said, "while others of his race sweat in the fields, he served the Man in the shade. Why should he not wish to die, since he did not wish to sweat?"

"And it will be quick," Berry said. "It will not take long."

"Catch him and tell him that," the stripling said.

"Hush," Berry said. They squatted, watching Moketubbe's face. He might have been dead himself. It was as though he were cased so in flesh that even breathing took place too deep within him to show.

"Listen, O Man," Basket said. "Issetibbeha is dead. He waits. His dog and his horse we have. But his slave has fled. The one who held the pot for him, who ate of his food, from his dish, is fled. Issetibbeha waits."

"Yao," Berry said,

"This is not the first time," Basket said. "This happened when Doom, thy grandfather, lay waiting at the door of the earth. He lay waiting three days, saying, 'Where is my Negro?' And Issetibbeha, thy father, answered, 'I will find him. Rest; I will bring him to you so that you may begin the journey.' "

"Yao," Berry said.

Moketubbe had not moved, had not opened his eyes.

"For three days Issetibbeha hunted in the bottom," Basket said. "He did not even return home for food, until the Negro was with him; then he said to Doom, his father, 'Here is thy dog, thy horse, thy Negro; rest.' Issetibbeha, who is dead since yesterday, said it. And now Issetibbeha's Negro is fled. His horse and his dog wait with him, but his Negro is fled."

"Yao," Berry said.

Moketubbe had not moved. His eyes were closed; upon his supine monstrous shape there was a colossal inertia, something profoundly immobile, beyond and impervious to flesh. They watched his face, squatting.

"When thy father was newly the Man, this happened," Basket said. "And it was Issetibbeha who brought back the slave to where his father waited to enter the earth." Moketubbe's face had not moved, his eyes had not moved. After a while Basket said, "Remove the shoes."

The stripling removed the shoes. Moketubbe began to pant, his bare chest moving deep, as though he were rising from beyond his unfathomed flesh back into life, like up from the water, the sea. But his eyes had not opened yet.

Berry said, "He will lead the hunt."

"Yao," Basket said. "He is the Man. He will lead the hunt."

IV

All that day the Negro, Issetibbeha's body servant, hidden in the barn, watched Issetibbeha's dying. He was forty, a Guinea man. He had a flat nose, a close, small head; the inside corners of his eyes showed red a little, and his prominent gums were a pale bluish red above his square, broad teeth. He had been taken at fourteen by a trader off Kamerun, before his teeth had been filed. He had been Issetibbeha's body servant for twenty-three years.

On the day before, the day on which Issetibbeha lay sick, he returned to the quarters at dusk. In that unhurried hour the smoke of the cooking fires blew slowly across the street from door to door, carrying into the opposite one the smell of the identical meat and bread. The women tended them; the men were gathered at the head of the lane, watching him as he came down the slope from the house, putting his naked feet down carefully in a strange dusk. To the waiting men his eyeballs were a little luminous.

"Issetibbeha is not dead yet," the headman said.

"Not dead," the body servant said. "Who not dead?"

In the dusk they had faces like his, the different ages, the thoughts sealed inscrutable behind faces like the death masks of apes. The smell of the fires, the cooking, blew sharp and slow across the strange dusk, as from another world, above the lane and the pickanninies naked in the dust.

"If he lives past sundown he will live until daybreak," one said.

"Who says?"

"Talk says."

"Yao. Talk says. We know but one thing." They looked at the body servant as he stood among them, his eyeballs a little luminous. He was breathing slow and deep. His chest was bare; he was sweating a little. "He knows. He knows it."

"Let us let the drums talk."

"Yao. Let the drums tell it."

The drums began after dark. They kept them hidden in the creek bottom. They were made of hollowed cypress knees, and the Negroes kept them hidden; why, none knew. They were buried in the mud on the bank of a slough; a lad of fourteen guarded them. He was undersized, and a mute; he squatted in the mud there all day, clouded over with mosquitos, naked save for the mud with which he coated himself against the mosquitoes, and about his neck a fiber bag containing a pig's rib to which black shreds of flesh still adhered, and two scaly barks on a wire. He slobbered onto his clutched knees, drooling; now and then Indians came noiselessly out of the bushes behind him and stood there and contemplated him for a while and went away, and he never knew it.

From the loft of the stable where he lay hidden until dark and after, the Negro could hear the drums. They were three miles away, but he could hear them as though they were in the barn itself below him, thudding and thudding. It was as though he could see the fire too, and the black limbs turning into and out of the flames in copper gleams. Only there would be no fire. There would be no more light there than where he lay in the dusty loft, with the whispering arpeggios of rat feet along the warm and immemorial ax-squared rafters. The only fire there would be the smudge against mosquitoes where the women with nursing children crouched, their heavy, sluggish breasts nippled full and smooth into the mouths of men children; contemplative, oblivious of the drumming, since a fire would signify life.

There was a fire in the steamboat, where Issetibbeha lay dying among his wives, beneath the lashed girandoles and the suspended bed. He could see the smoke, and just before sunset he saw the doctor come out, in a waistcoat made of skunk skins, and set fire to two clay-daubed sticks at the bows of the boat deck. "So he is not dead yet," the Negro said into the whispering gloom of the loft, answering himself; he could hear the two voices, himself and himself:

"Who not dead?"

"You are dead."

"Yao, I am dead," he said quietly. He wished to be where the drums were. He imagined himself springing out of the bushes, leaping among the drums on his bare, lean, greasy, invisible limbs. But he could not do that, because man leaped past life, into where death was; he dashed into death and did not die because when death took a man, it took him just this side of the end of living. It was when death overran him from behind, still in life. The thin whisper of rat feet died in fainting gusts along the rafters. Once he had eaten rat. He was a boy then, but just come to America. They had lived ninety days in a three-foot-high 'tween deck in tropic latitudes, hearing from topside the drunken New England captain intoning aloud from a book which he did not recognize for ten years afterward to be the Bible. Squatting in the stable so, he had watched the rat, civilized, by association with man reft of its inherent cunning of limb and eye; he had caught it without difficulty, with scarce a movement of his hand, and he ate it slowly, wondering how any of the rats had escaped so long. At that time he was still wearing the single white garment which the trader, a deacon in the Unitarian church, had given him, and he spoke then only his native tongue.

He was naked now, save for a pair of dungaree pants bought by Indians from white men, and an amulet slung on a thong about his hips. The amulet consisted of one half of a mother-of-pearl lorgnon which Issetibbeha had brought back from Paris, and the skull of a cottonmouth moccasin. He had killed the snake himself and eaten it, save the poison head. He lay in the loft, watching the house, the steamboat, listening to the drums, thinking of himself among the drums.

He lay there all night. The next morning he saw the doctor come out, in his skunk vest, and get on his mule and ride away, and he became quite still and watched the final dust from beneath the mule's delicate feet die away, and then he found that he was still breathing and it seemed strange to him that he still breathed air, still needed air. Then he lay and watched quietly, waiting to move, his eyeballs a little luminous, but with a quiet light, and his breathing light and regular, and saw Louis Berry come out and look at the sky. It was good light then, and already five Indians squatted in their Sunday clothes along the steamboat deck; by noon there were twenty-five there. That afternoon they dug the trench in which the meat would be baked, and the yams; by that time there were almost a hundred guests—decorous, quiet, patient in their stiff European finery—and he watched Berry lead Issetibbeha's mare from the stable and tie her to a tree, and then he watched Berry emerge from the house with the old hound which lay beside Issetibbeha's chair. He tied the hound to the tree too, and it sat there, looking gravely about at the faces. Then it began to howl. It was still howling at sundown, when the Negro climbed down the back wall of the barn and entered the spring branch, where it was already dusk. He began to run then. He could hear the hound howling behind him, and near the spring, already running, he passed another Negro. The two men, the one motionless and the other running, looked for an instant at each other as though across an actual boundary between two different worlds. He ran on into full darkness, mouth closed, fists doubled, his broad nostrils bellowing steadily.

He ran on in the darkness. He knew the country well, because he had hunted it often with Issetibbeha, following on his mule the course of the fox or the cat beside Issetibbeha's mare; he knew it as well as did the men who would pursue him. He saw them for the first time shortly before sunset of the second day. He had run thirty miles then, up the creek bottom, before doubling back; lying in a pawpaw thicket he saw the pursuit for the first time. There were two of them, in shirts and straw hats, carrying their neatly rolled trousers under their arms, and they had no weapons. They were middle-aged, paunchy, and they could not have moved very fast anyway; it would be twelve hours before they could return to where he lay watching them. "So I will have until midnight to rest," he said. He was near enough to the plantation to smell the cooking fires, and he thought how he ought to be hungry, since he had not eaten in thirty hours. "But it is more important to rest," he told himself. He continued to tell himself that, lying in the pawpaw thicket, because the effort of resting, the need and the haste to rest, made his heart thud the same as the running had done. It was as though he had forgot how to rest, as though the six hours were not long enough to do it in, to remember again how to do it.

As soon as dark came he moved again. He had thought to keep going steadily and quietly through the night, since there was nowhere for him to go, but as soon as he moved he began to run at top speed, breasting his panting chest, his broad-flaring nostrils through the choked and whipping darkness. He ran for an hour, lost by then, without direction, when suddenly he stopped, and after a time his thudding heart unraveled from the sound of the drums. By the sound they were not two miles away; he followed the sound until he could smell the smudge fire and taste the acrid smoke. When he stood among them the drums did not cease; only the headman came to him where he stood in the drifting smudge, panting, his nostrils flaring and pulsing, the hushed glare of his ceaseless eyeballs in his mud-daubed face as though they were worked from lungs.

"We have expected thee," the headman said. "Go, now."

"Go?"

"Eat, and go. The dead may not consort with the living; thou knowest that."

"Yao. I know that." They did not look at one another. The drums had not ceased.

"Wilt thou eat?" the headman said.

"I am not hungry. I caught a rabbit this afternoon, and ate while I lay hidden."

"Take some cooked meat with thee, then."

He accepted the cooked meat, wrapped in leaves, and entered the creek bottom again; after a while the sound of the drums ceased. He walked steadily until daybreak. "I have twelve hours," he said. "Maybe more, since the trail was followed by night." He squatted and ate the meat and wiped his hands on his thighs. Then he rose and removed the dungaree pants and squatted again beside a slough and coated himself with mud—face, arms, body and legs—and squatted again, clasping his knees, his head bowed. When it was light enough to see, he moved back into the swamp and squatted again and went to sleep so. He did not dream at all. It was well that he moved, for, waking suddenly in broad daylight and the high sun, he saw the two Indians. They still carried their neatly rolled trousers; they stood opposite the place where he lay hidden, paunchy, thick, soft-looking, a little ludicrous in their straw hats and shirt tails.

"This is wearying work," one said.

"I'd rather be at home in the shade myself," the other said. "But there is the Man waiting at the door to the earth."

"Yao." They looked quietly about; stooping, one of them removed from his shirt tail a clot of cockleburs. "Damn that Negro," he said.

"Yao. When have they ever been anything but a trial and a care to us?"

In the early afternoon, from the top of a tree, the Negro looked down into the plantation. He could see Issetibbeha's body in a hammock between the two trees where the horse and the dog were tethered, and the concourse about the steamboat was filled with wagons and horses and mules, with carts and saddle-horses, while in bright clumps the women and the smaller children and the old men squatted about the long trench where the smoke from the barbecuing meat blew slow and thick. The men and the big boys would all be down there in the creek bottom behind him, on the trail, their Sunday clothes rolled carefully up and wedged into tree crotches. There was a clump of men near the door to the house, to the saloon of the steamboat, though, and he watched them, and after a while he saw them bring Moketubbe out in a litter made of buckskin and persimmon poles; high hidden in his leafted nook the Negro, the quarry, looked quietly down upon his irrevocable doom with an expression as profound as Moketubbe's own. "Yao," he said quietly. "He will go then. That man whose body has been dead for fifteen years, he will go also."

In the middle of the afternoon he came face to face with an Indian. They were both on a footlog across a slough—the Negro gaunt, lean, hard, tireless and desperate; the Indian thick, soft-looking, the apparent embodiment of the ultimate and the supreme reluctance and inertia. The Indian made no move, no sound; he stood on the log and watched the Negro plunge into the slough and swim ashore and crash away into the undergrowth.

Just before sunset he lay behind a down log. Up the log in slow procession moved a line of ants. He caught them and ate them slowly, with a kind of detachment, like that of a dinner guest eating salted nuts from a dish. They too had a salt taste, engendering a salivary reaction out of all proportion. He ate them slowly, watching the unbroken line move up the log and into oblivious doom with a steady and terrific undeviation. He had eaten nothing else all day; in his caked mud mask his eyes rolled in reddened rims. At sunset, creeping along the creek bank toward where he had spotted a frog, a cottonmouth moccasin slashed him suddenly across the forearm with a thick, sluggish blow. It struck clumsily, leaving two long slashes across his arm like two razor slashes, and half sprawled with its own momentum and rage, it appeared for the moment utterly helpless with its own awkwardness and choleric anger. "Olé, Grandfather," the Negro said. He touched its head and watched it slash him again across his arm, and again, with thick, raking, awkward blows. "It's that I do not wish to die," he said. Then he said it again—"It's that I do not wish to die"—in a quiet tone, of slow and low amaze, as though it were something that, until the words had said themselves, he found that he had not known, or had not known the depth and extent of his desire.

V

Moketubbe took the slippers with him. He could not wear them very long while in motion, not even in the litter where he was slung reclining, so they rested upon a square of fawnskin upon his lap—the cracked, frail slippers a little shapeless now with their scaled patent-leather surface and buckleless tongues and scarlet heels, lying upon the supine, obese shape just barely alive, carried through swamp and brier by swinging relays of men who bore steadily all day long the crime and its object, on the business of the slain. To Moketubbe it must have been as though, himself immortal, he were being carried rapidly through hell by doomed spirits which, alive, had contemplated his disaster, and, dead, were oblivious partners to his damnation.

After resting for a while, the litter propped in the center of the squatting circle and Moketubbe motionless in it, with closed eyes and his face at once peaceful for the instant and filled with inescapable foreknowledge, he could wear the slippers for a while. The stripling put them on him, forcing his big, tender, dropsical feet into them; whereupon into his face came again that expression, tragic, passive, and profoundly attentive, which dyspeptics wear. Then they went on. He made no move, no sound, inert in the rhythmic litter out of some reserve of inertia, or maybe of some kingly virtue such as courage or fortitude. After a time they set the litter down and looked at him, at the yellow face like that of an idol, beaded over with sweat. Then Three Basket or Louis Berry would say: "Take them off. Honor has been served." They would remove the shoes. Moketubbe's face would not alter, but only then would his breathing become perceptible, going in and out of his pale lips with a faint ah-ah-ah sound, and they should squat again while the couriers and the runners came up.

"Not yet?"

"Not yet. He is going east. By sunset he will reach Mouth of Tippah. Then he will turn back. We may take him tomorrow."

"Let us hope so. It will not be too soon."

"Yao. It has been three days now."

"When Doom died, it took only three days."

"But that was an old man. This one is young."

"Yao. A good race. If he is taken tomorrow, I will win a horse."

"May you win it."

"Yao. This work is not pleasant."

That was the day on which the food gave out at the plantation. The guests returned home and came back the next day with more food, enough for a week longer. On that day Issetibbeha began to smell; they could smell him for a long way up and down the bottom when it got hot toward noon and the wind blew. But they didn't capture the Negro on that day, nor on the next. It was about dusk on the sixth day when the couriers came up to the litter; they had found blood. "He has injured himself."

"Not bad, I hope," Basket said. "We cannot send with Issetibbeha one who will be of no service to him."

"Nor whom Issetibbeha himself will have to nurse and care for," Berry said.

"We do not know," the courier said. "He has hidden himself. He has crept back into the swamp. We have left pickets."

They trotted with the litter now. The place where the Negro had crept into the swamp was an hour away. In the hurry and excitement they had forgotten that Moketubbe still wore the slippers; when they reached the place Moketubbe had fainted. They removed the slippers and brought him to.

With dark, they formed a circle about the swamp. They squatted, clouded over with gnats and mosquitoes; the evening star burned low and close down the west, and the constellations began to wheel overhead. "We will give him time," they said. "Tomorrow is just another name for today."

"Yao. Let him have time." Then they ceased, and gazed as one into the darkness where the swamp lay. After a while the noise ceased, and soon the courier came out of the darkness.

"He tried to break out."

"But you turned him back?"

"He turned back. We feared for a moment, the three of us. We could smell him creeping in the darkness, and we could smell something else, which we did not know. That was why we feared, until he told us. He said to slay him there, since it would be dark and he would not have to see the face when it came. But it was not that which we smelled; he told us what it was. A snake had struck him. That was two days ago. The arm swelled, and it smelled bad. But it was not that which we smelled then, because the swelling had gone down and his arm was no larger than that of a child. He showed us. We felt the arm, all of us did; it was no larger than that of a child. He said to give him a hatchet so he could chop the arm off. But tomorrow is today also."

"Yao. Tomorrow is today."

"We feared for a while. Then he went back into the swamp."

"That is good."

"Yao. We feared. Shall I tell the Man?"

"I will see," Basket said. He went away. The courier squatted, telling again about the Negro. Basket returned. "The Man says that it is good. Return to your post."

The courier crept away. They squatted about the litter; now and then they slept. Sometime after midnight the Negro waked them. He began to shout and talk to himself, his voice coming sharp and sudden out of the darkness, then he fell silent. Dawn came; a white crane flapped slowly across the jonquil sky. Basket was awake. "Let us go now," he said. "It is today."

Two Indians entered the swamp, their movements noisy. Before they reached the Negro they stopped, because he began to sing. They could see him, naked and mud-caked, sitting on a log, singing. They squatted silently a short distance away, until he finished. He was chanting something in his own language, his face lifted to the rising sun. His voice was clear, full, with a quality wild and sad. "Let him have time," the Indians said squatting, patient, waiting. He ceased and they approached. He looked back and up at them through the cracked mud mask. His eyes were bloodshot, his lips cracked upon his square short teeth. The mask of mud appeared to be loose on his face, as if he might have lost flesh since he put it there; he held his left arm close to his breast. From the elbow down it was caked and shapeless with black mud. They could smell him, a rank smell. He watched them quietly until one touched him on the arm. "Come," the Indian said. "You ran well. Do not be ashamed."

VI

As they neared the plantation in the tainted bright morning, the Negro's eyes began to roll a little, like those of a horse. The smoke from the cooking pit blew low along the earth and upon the squatting and waiting guests about the yard and upon the steamboat deck, in their bright, stiff, harsh finery; the women, the children, the old men. They had sent couriers along the bottom, and another on ahead, and Issetibbeha's body had already been removed to where the grave waited, along with the horse and the dog, though they could still smell him in death about the house where he had lived in life. The guests were beginning to move toward the grave when the bearers of Moketubbe's litter mounted the slope.

The Negro was the tallest there, his high, close, mud-caked head looming above them all. He was breathing hard, as though the desperate effort of the six suspended and desperate days had capitulated upon him at once; although they walked slowly, his naked scarred chest rose and fell above the close-clutched left arm. He looked this way and that continuously, as if he were not seeing, as though sight never quite caught up with the looking. His mouth was open a little upon his big white teeth; he began to pant. The already moving guests halted, pausing, looking back, some with pieces of meat in their hands, as the Negro looked about at their faces with his wild, restrained, unceasing eyes.

"Will you eat first?" Basket said. He had to say it twice.

"Yes," the Negro said. "That's it. I want to eat."

The throng had begun to press back toward the center; the word passed to the outermost: "He will eat first."

They reached the steamboat. "Sit down," Basket said. The Negro sat on the edge of the deck. He was still panting, his chest rising and falling, his head ceaseless with its white eyballs, turning from side to side. It was as if the inability to see came from within, from hopelessness, not from absence of vision. They brought food and watched quietly as he tried to eat it. He put the food into his mouth and chewed it, but chewing, the half-masticated matter began to merge from the corners of his mouth and to drool down his chin, onto his chest, and after a while he stopped chewing and sat there, naked, covered with dried mud, the plate on his knees, and his mouth filled with a mass of chewed food, open, his eyes wide and unceasing, panting and panting. They watched him, patient, implacable, waiting.

"Come," Basket said at last.

"It's water I want," the Negro said. "I want water."

The well was a little way down the slope toward the quarters. The slope lay dappled with the shadows of noon, of that peaceful hour when, Issetibbeha napping in his chair and waiting for the noon meal and the long afternoon to sleep in, the Negro, the body servant, would be free. He would sit in the kitchen door then, talking with the women that prepared the food. Beyond the kitchen the lane between the quarters would be quiet, peaceful, with the women talking to one another across the lane and the smoke of the dinner fires blowing upon the pickaninnies like ebony toys in the dust.

"Come," Basket said.

The Negro walked among them, taller than any. The guests were moving on toward where Issetibbeha and the horse and the dog waited. The Negro walked with his high ceaseless head, his panting chest. "Come," Basket said. "You wanted water."

"Yes," the Negro said. "Yes." He looked back at the house, then down to the quarters, where today no fire burned, no face showed in any door, no pickaninny in the dust, panting. "It struck me here, raking me across this arm; once, twice, three times. I said, 'Olé, Grandfather.' "

"Come now," Basket said. The Negro was still going through the motion of walking, his knee action high, his head high, as though he were on a treadmill. His eyeballs had a wild, restrained glare, like those of a horse. "You wanted water," Basket said. "Here it is."

There was a gourd in the well. They dipped it full and gave it to the Negro, and they watched him try to drink. His eyes had not ceased rolling as he tilted the gourd slowly against his caked face. They could watch his throat working and the bright water cascading from either side of the gourd, down his chin and breast. Then the water stopped. "Come," Basket said.

"Wait," the Negro said. He dipped the gourd again and tilted it against his face, beneath his ceaseless eyes. Again they watched his throat working and the unswallowed water sheathing broken and myriad down his chin, channeling his caked chest. They waited, patient, grave, decorous, implacable; clansman and guest and kin. Then the water ceased, though still the empty gourd tilted higher and higher, and still his black throat aped the vain motion of his frustrated swallowing. A piece of water-loosened mud carried away from his chest and broke at his muddy feet, and in the empty gourd they could hear his breath: ah-ah-ah.

"Come," Basket said, taking the gourd from the Negro and hanging it back in the well.

SHIRLEY JACKSON

Seven Types of Ambiguity

The basement room of the bookstore seemed to be enormous; it stretched in long rows of books off into dimness at either end, with books lined in tall bookcases along the walls, and books standing in piles on the floor. At the foor of the spiral staircase winding down from the neat small store upstairs, Mr. Harris, owner and sales-clerk of the bookstore, had a small desk, cluttered with catalogues, lighted by one dirty overhead lamp. The same lamp served to light the shelves which crowded heavily around Mr. Harris' desk; farther away, along the lines of book tables, there were other dirty overhead lamps, to be lighted by pulling a string and turned off by the customer when he was ready to grope his way back to Mr. Harris' desk, pay for his purchases and have them wrapped. Mr. Harris, who knew the position of any author or any title in all the heavy shelves, had one customer at the moment, a boy of about eighteen, who was standing far down the long room directly under one of the lamps, leafing through a book he had selected from the shelves. It was cold in the big basement room; both Mr. Harris and the boy had their coats on. Occasionally Mr. Harris got up from his desk to put a meagre shovelful of coal on a small iron stove which stood in the curve of the staircase. Except when Mr. Harris got up, or the boy turned to put a book back into the shelves and take out another, the room was quiet, the books standing silent in the dim light.

Then the silence was broken by the sound of the door opening in the little upstairs bookshop where Mr. Harris kept his best-sellers and art books on display. There was the sound of voices, while both Mr. Harris and the boy listened, and then the girl who took care of the upstairs bookshop said, "Right on down the stairs. Mr. Harris will help you."

Mr. Harris got up and walked around to the foot of the stairs, turning on another of the overhead lamps so that his new customer would be able to see his way down. The boy put his book back in the shelves and stood with his hand on the back of it, still listening.

When Mr. Harris saw that it was a woman coming down the stairs he stood back politely and said, "Watch the bottom step. There's one more than people think." The woman stepped carefully down and stood looking around. While she stood there a man came carefully around the turn in the staircase, ducking his head so his hat would clear the low ceiling. "Watch the bottom step," the woman said in a soft clear voice. The man came down beside her and raised his head to look around as she had.

"Quite a lot of books you have here," he said.

Mr. Harris smiled his professional smile. "Can I help you?"

The woman looked at the man, and he hesitated a minute and then said, "We want to get some books. Quite a few of them." He waved his hand inclusively. "Sets of books."

"Well, if it's books you want," Mr. Harris said, and smiled again. "Maybe the lady would like to come over and sit down?" He led the way around to his desk, the woman following him and the man walking uneasily between the tables of books, his hands close to his sides as though he were afraid of breaking something. Mr. Harris gave the lady his desk chair and then sat down on the edge of his desk, shoving aside a pile of catalogues.

"This is a very interesting place," the lady said, in the same soft voice she had used when she spoke before. She was middle-aged and nicely dressed; all her clothes were fairly new, but quiet and well planned for her age and air of shyness. The man was big and hearty-looking, his face reddened by the cold air and his big hands holding a pair of wool gloves uneasily.

"We'd like to buy some of your books," the man said. "Some good books."

"Anything in particular?" Mr. Harris asked.

The man laughed loudly, but with embarrassment. "Tell the truth," he said, "I sound sort of foolish, now. But I don't know much about these things, like books." In the large quiet store his voice seemed to echo, after his wife's soft voice and Mr. Harris'. "We were sort of hoping you'd be able to tell *us,*" he said. "None of this trash they turn out nowadays." He cleared his throat. "Something like Dickens," he said.

"Dickens," Mr. Harris said.

"I used to read Dickens when I was a kid," the man said. "Books like that, now, good books." He looked up as the boy who had been standing off among the books came over to them. "I'd like to read Dickens again," the big man said.

"Mr. Harris," the boy asked quietly.

Mr. Harris looked up. "Yes, Mr. Clark?" he said.

The boy came closer to the desk, as though unwilling to interrupt Mr. Harris with his customers. "I'd like to take another look at the Empson," he said.

Mr. Harris turned to the glass-doored bookcase immediately behind his desk and selected a book. "Here it is," he said, "you'll have it read through before you buy it at this rate." He smiled at the big man and his wife. "Some day he's going to come in and buy that book," he said, "and I'm going to go out of business from shock."

The boy turned away, holding the book, and the big man leaned forward to Mr. Harris. "I figure I'd like two good sets, big, like Dickens," he said, "and then a couple of smaller sets."

"And a copy of *Jane Eyre*," his wife said, in her soft voice. "I used to love that book," she said to Mr. Harris.

"I can let you have a very nice set of the Brontës," Mr. Harris said. "Beautiful binding."

"I want them to look nice," the man said, "but solid, for reading. I'm going to read through all of Dickens again."

The boy came back to the desk, holding the book out to Mr. Harris. "It still looks good," he said.

"It's right here when you want it." Mr. Harris said, turning back to the bookcase with the book. "It's pretty scarce, that book."

"I guess it'll be here a while longer," the boy said.

"What's the name of this book?" the big man asked curiously.

"Seven Types of Ambiguity," the boy said. "It's quite a good book."

"There's a fine name for a book," the big man said to Mr. Harris. "Pretty smart fellow, reading books with names like that."

"It's a good book," the boy repeated.

"I'm trying to buy some books myself," the big man said to the boy. "I want to catch up on a few I've missed. Dickens, I've always liked his books."

"Meredith is good," the boy said. "You ever try reading Meredith?"

"Meredith," the big man said. "Let's see a few of your books," he said to Mr. Harris. "I'd sort of like to pick out a few I want."

"Can I take the gentleman down there?" the boy said to Mr. Harris. "I've got to go back anyway to get my hat."

"I'll go with the young man and look at the books, Mother," the big man said to his wife. "You stay here and keep warm."

"Fine," Mr. Harris said. "He knows where the books are as well as I do," he said to the big man.

The boy started off down the aisle between the book tables, and the big man followed, still walking carefully, trying not to touch anything. They went down past the lamp still burning where the boy had left his hat and gloves, and the boy turned to another lamp further down. "Mr. Harris keeps most of his sets around here," the boy said. "Let's see what we can find." He squatted down in front of the bookcases, touching the backs of the rows of books lightly with his fingers. "How do you feel about the prices?" he asked.

"I'm willing to pay a reasonable amount for the books I have in mind," the big man said. He touched the book in front of him experimentally, with one finger. "A hundred and fifty, two hundred dollars altogether."

The boy looked up at him and laughed. "That ought to get you some nice books," he said.

"Never saw so many books in my life," the big man said. "I never thought I'd see the day when I'd just walk into a bookstore and buy up all the books I always wanted to read."

"It's a good feeling."

"I never got a chance to read much," the man said. "Went right into the machine-shop where my father worked when I was much younger than you, and worked ever since. Now all of a sudden I find I have a little more money than I used to, and Mother and I decided we'd like to get ourselves a few things we always wanted."

"Your wife was interested in the Brontës," the boy said. "Here's a very good set."

The man leaned down to look at the books the boy pointed out. "I don't know much about these things," he said. "They look nice, all alike. What's the next set?"

"Carlyle," the boy said. "You can skip him. He's not quite what you're looking for. Meredith is good. And Thackeray. I think you'd want Thackeray; he's a great writer."

The man took one of the books the boy handed him and opened it carefully, using only two fingers from each of his big hands. "This looks fine," he said.

"I'll write them down," the boy said. He took a pencil and a pocket memorandum from his coat pocket. "Brontës," he said, "Dickens, Meredith, Thackeray." He ran his hand along each of the sets as he read them off.

The big man narrowed his eyes. "I ought to take one more," he said. "These won't quite fill up the bookcase I got for them."

"Jane Austen," the boy said. "Your wife would be pleased with that."

"You read all these books?" the man asked.

"Most of them," the boy said.

The man was quiet for a minute and then he went on, "I never got much of a chance to read anything, going to work so early. I've got a lot to catch up on."

"You're going to have a fine time," the boy said.

"That book you had a while back," the man said. "What was that book?"

"It's aesthetics," the boy said. "About literature. It's very scarce. I've been trying to buy it for quite a while and haven't had the money."

"You go to college?" the man asked.

"Yes."

"Here's one I ought to read again," the man said. "Mark Twain. I read a couple of his books when I was a kid. But I guess I have enough to start on." He stood up.

The boy rose too, smiling. "You're going to have to do a lot of reading."

"I like to read," the man said. "I really like to read."

He started back down the aisles, going straight for Mr. Harris' desk. The boy turned off the lamps and followed, stopping to get his hat and gloves. When the big man reached Mr. Harris' desk he said to his wife "That's sure a smart kid. He knows those books right and left."

"Did you pick out what you want?" his wife asked.

"The kid has a fine list for me." He turned to Mr. Harris and went on, "It's quite an experience seeing a kid like that liking books the way he does. When I was his age I was working for four or five years."

The boy came up with the slip of paper in his hand. "These ought to hold him for a while," he said to Mr. Harris.

Mr. Harris glanced at the list and nodded. "That Thackeray's a nice set of books," he said.

The boy had put his hat on and was standing at the foot of the stairs. "Hope you enjoy them," he said. "I'll be back for another look at that Empson, Mr. Harris."

"I'll try to keep it around for you," Mr. Harris said. "I can't promise to hold it, you know."

"I'll just count on it's being here," the boy said.

"Thanks, son," the big man called out as the boy started up the stairs. "Appreciate your helping me."

"That's all right," the boy said.

"He's sure a smart kid," the man said to Mr. Harris. "He's got a great chance, with an education like that."

"He's a nice young fellow," Mr. Harris said, "and he sure wants that book."

"You think he'll ever buy it?" the big man asked.

"I doubt it," Mr. Harris said. "If you'll just write down your name and address, I'll add these prices."

Mr. Harris began to note down the prices of the books, copying from the boy's neat list. After the big man had written his name and address, he stood for a minute drumming his fingers on the desk, and then he said, "Can I have another look at that book?"

"The Empson?" Mr. Harris said, looking up.

"The one the boy was so interested in." Mr. Harris reached around to the bookcase in back of him and took out the book. The big man held it delicately, as he had held the others, and he frowned as he turned the pages. Then he put the book down on Mr. Harris' desk.

"If he isn't going to buy it, will it be all right if I put this in with the rest?" he asked.

Mr. Harris looked up from his figures for a minute, and then he made the entry on his list. He added quickly, wrote down the total, and then pushed the paper across the desk to the big man. While the man checked over the figures Mr. Harris turned to the woman and said, "Your husband has bought a lot of very pleasant reading."

"I'm glad to hear it," she said. "We've been looking forward to it for a long time."

The big man counted out the money carefully, handing the bills to Mr. Harris. Mr. Harris put the money in the top drawer of his desk and said, "We can have these delivered to you by the end of the week, if that will be all right."

"Fine," the big man said. "Ready, Mother?"

The woman rose, and the big man stood back to let her go ahead of him. Mr. Harris followed, stopping near the stairs to say to the woman, "Watch the bottom step."

They started up the stairs and Mr. Harris stood watching them until they got to the turn. Then he switched off the dirty overhead lamp and went back to his desk.

7

SYMBOL AND ALLUSION

In earlier sections of this text, we have suggested that most stories gain their effects and meaning *primarily* through the interaction of character and situation. But in most stories we also find other details, other juxtapositions, other emphases which *add* to meaning or effect. For example, certain descriptive passages in "Old Red" or "The Blue Hotel" may have little to do with either characterization or conflict development; yet to omit these passages or details is to alter the story in certain significant ways. In other words, many things in fiction other than what happens to whom can play their part in enabling a story to achieve its purpose. Two of these—the devices of irony and of point of view—we have already considered. Two other such devices used extensively by writers to help communicate effect or meaning are *symbol* and *allusion*.

You have already been prepared in part for the way these devices work in fiction by observing the way other fictional elements operate. From the beginning we have emphasized that stories operate on more than one level of meaning. There is, to begin with, the *literal* level; a story is always about a *specific* character or group of characters caught up in a *specific* situation, the development and resolution of which constitutes the primary level of the story. But we have also seen that fictional characters are in some ways representative of real people, and that story situations can suggest situations which we have experienced or observed, and that from fictional specifics we can therefore derive certain implied (or even stated) generalizations. In this reasoning process of moving from the specific to the general, from the concrete to the abstract, we are *extending* the meaning or implications of a story.

Both symbols and allusions are devices which can contribute to this process of extension. In its simplest form a symbol is something (usually concrete) that stands for something else (usually abstract). Our world is full of such symbols: a skull and crossbones on a medicine bottle symbolizes poison, a red octagonal sign at a crossroads signals a command to stop, a name on an office door symbolizes a person. If we have been taught the correct (that is, agreed upon) meaning for these symbols, they present us with few problems, for in such objects as name plates what we have is a concrete object which stands for a concrete object, a specific something which stands for a specific something. But most symbols are not precisely of this nature. The human mind works most comfortably on a concrete rather than an abstract level; hence one human impulse is to translate abstractions into concrete terms, to use concrete objects as substitutes for whole complexes of ideas or feelings. The American flag is one such symbol, the Cross is another; and because such substitutions are different in kind from those which have a specific one-for-one relationship, semanticists ordinarily call such symbols as name plates *signs* and such symbols as flags *symbols*.

In the stories you have already read, you have doubtless been aware of the use of symbol. To cite only one example, you may have suspected that Crane's blue hotel or the pack of playing cards did not stand *only* for a hotel or a pack of cards. If so, you have also been confronted with the two peculiar difficulties which symbols present to a reader of fiction. For one thing, you have not been taught the definition of this symbol or that one in a story. Indeed, you cannot be taught this, for symbol in fiction derives its meaning largely from context, and that context differs from story to story. In other words, just as with character or theme, a reader must deduce the meaning of a symbol from the story in which it appears. As soon as you embark on such a deductive process, you will probably discover a second difficulty: because fictional symbols do stand for complex abstractions, they can seldom be defined with absolute and certain precision. In other words, there is no one "right" answer for what Crane's blue hotel stands for, just as there is no one "right" answer for what the Cross suggests.

Nonetheless, we can make a number of generalizations about fictional symbols which can help us both to understand their function in stories and to define them with a reasonable degree of accuracy. To begin with, we can distinquish between two kinds of stories, those which are essentially *literal* and should be read thus, and those which are essentially *symbolic* and cannot be understood unless we understand their symbols. A literal story may have symbols in it, but we can understand it without recognizing their presence because the story's meaning and effect will depend primarily on its development of a situation. But in some stories, symbol is the primary method of communication, and without a translation of its symbols, the story will be without meaning.

Stories which operate primarily on a symbolic level can further be divided into *allegorical* and *symbolic* categories. The distinction between these has perhaps been put most shrewdly by Hollander and Lind in

The Art of the Story. "The functional difference between allegory and symbolism," they point out, "is that whereas symbolism always means what it says *and also* something else, allegory primarily means something else."[1] Or, if we discuss this from the point of view of writing a story, rather than reading it, we can say that allegory begins with an idea, and the author then creates an object (frequently a character) which stands for that idea; symbol, in contrast, begins with an object which then comes to suggest an idea. A story like *Pilgrim's Progress*, where Vanity Fair or the protagonist, Christian, are chosen simply to represent an abstraction, not to be taken on a literal level as an actual place or an actual person, is an allegory. A story like "A Clean Well-Lighted Place," where the café is at once a *real* café and at the same time suggestive of something else, is symbolical.

In symbolic stories, one may further distinquish between what we can call *established* symbols and what we can call *private* or *created* symbols. In some stories the symbols derive their meaning, at least in part, not from within the context of the story itself but from without it. If, for example, a writer uses a star in a story, and if it seems that the writer intends the star to be taken as a symbol, we could legitimately suspect that the star stood for hope or aspiration. We could assume this not because the story pointed us to this interpretation but because we have somewhere been taught to associate stars and hope. Many symbols in stories—water, or fire, or certain colors like black or white, or seasons of the year, or the time of day, or journeys, or symbols taken from myth or Christian traditions or Freudian psychology—are of this established nature, though we must always be alert to the possibility that in a given story such symbols may have their meaning modified or even reversed—as in Eudora Welty's "Death of a Traveling Saleman," for example, water seems to symbolize not life but death. But other symbols can be private—that is, definable only by and within the context of the story. If, for example, we were asked, without reference to any particular story, what a café might symbolize, we could not answer; but if we were asked what it symbolizes in "A Clean Well-Lighted Place," we could derive a definition from the story.

In contemporary fiction, the use of another device, that of the literary allusion, has become almost as common as the use of symbol. The allusion is a reference in one piece of literature to another piece of literature, and it is, of course, almost as old as literature itself. Nor has its usefulness as a device for both compression and enrichment changed greatly. If a Renaissance sonneteer, for example, quotes from an Horatian ode, he manages to add to his sonnet all of the implications, effects, or ideas

[1] Robert Hollander and Sidney Lind, *The Art of the Story* (New York: American Book Company, 1968), p. 30.

of another poem. But in contemporary literature the allusion can create problems which it did not create in the past, primarily the problem of recognition. In Shakespeare's day, readers tended to bring to a given poem or play or essay a common reading background; hence, Shakespeare could assume that allusions to Horace or Virgil would be recognized by his audience. The contemporary writer can make no such assumption; even the most obvious allusion can pass by a reader unrecognized. But when allusions in a story are recognized, you will discover that as with symbol they enrich the meaning or effect of a story.

So much for definition. But definition fails to answer some persistent questions raised by students who are first introduced to the use of symbol or allusion. Why, students ask, do writers use such devices? Why, apparently, do they go out of their way to make their meaning difficult or obscure? Does not the employment of symbol or allusion turn the reading of fiction into an intellectual game instead of the simple enjoyment of vicarious experience?

The most obvious reply to this is that writers use symbols (if not allusions) because the human mind works instinctively in terms of symbol. That can be substantiated in any number of ways—by the reliance of language upon simile and metaphor, for example, or by the persistence of symbol in proverbs and adages, or by the obvious abundance of symbol in our day-to-day lives. Beyond this, writers most often use symbol because they cannot say what they want to say in any other way. What, for example, does the butcher bird in Stegner's story stand for, or the statue in Flannery O'Conner's "The Artificial Nigger"? You will discover, when you read these stories, that you know what the authors intended these symbols to suggest, but you will also discover that when you try to translate them into abstractions, the result will be partial or inadequate or unclear.

Moreover, we must remember that any story is trying to do a great many things—explain character, develop conflict, communicate emotion, suggest theme—and it is trying to do all these things simultaneously. Here symbol serves what is probably its most important function. For symbol in fiction will usually be found to be working double, triple, even quadruple duty. It is, as is allusion, a device which enables a writer to achieve *compression* and *complexity* at one and the same time.

Useful and effective as these devices can be, however, a reader should approach them with certain cautions in mind. In this century writers have used both symbol and allusion so extensively, and teachers have so emphasized them in their approach to literature, that a reader can emerge from a "study" of literature with some serious misconceptions. Hence, we conclude this discussion with a few warnings and admonitions.

1. Occasionally, one meets with a reader who insists on reading a story *only* on a literal level, who refuses to admit to the existence

of symbol in fiction, and who either betrays this attitude with the question, "Do writers really think of these things when they write stories?" or who argues that to discuss a symbol is to "read into" a story what is not there. We have already noted that the strictly literal approach to story will make some stories incomprehensible. But even with those stories in which symbol is incidental rather than basic, such a literal approach can seriously limit the meaning, implications, or effect of many stories.

2. At the opposite extreme is the reader who brings to his reading the assumption that all objects in all stories must be given symbolic value, and that the art of reading is principally the art of "symbol hunting"; or, if there is any other legitimate subject for literary discussion, it is the identification of allusions, or "sources," or "parallels," or "echoes." For such readers we must emphasize the fact that symbol and allusion are *devices;* like other fictional devices they are never something that the good writer employs for their own sake, and the writer who incorporates symbols or allusions for this reason is guilty of bad writing just as the reader who finds symbols where none are intended is guilty of bad reading. We must also remember that symbol and allusion are only two of many fictional devices. The point of reading and discussing fiction is not to display one's ingenuity or to show off the breadth of one's reading background. Above all, we must remember that all writers do not employ symbol and that probably a minority of them employ allusion; hence, we must resist the temptation to make every concrete object in every story stand for something other than what it is. Even in Hemingway, who probably used symbol as extensively as any writer in this century, we can find objects which can legitimately be taken only literally. As Saul Bellow has put it, a railway schedule in a story does not *always* suggest a leitmotif, a journey does not *always* stand for life, soda crackers do not *always* suggest the Host or wood shavings the Cross. *Sometimes* a railway time schedule is just a time schedule, a journey just a journey; sometimes readers must let soda crackers or wood shavings simply be soda crackers or wood shavings.

3. From this it follows that objects in stories are to be treated as symbols only if there are clues that the author intended them to be so taken. And good stories will provide such clues. They will do so in a number of ways—by position, by repetition, by more than routine emphasis, by shrewd juxtapositioning. If, before we leap to a symbolic interpretation of an object, we first ask ourselves how we know that the object is to be taken symbolically, and if secondly we ask ourselves how comfortably it fits as symbol into the total context of the story, we will avoid the temptation of turning every simile into a symbol.

4. Once we have determined that an object is to be given symbolic value, we must then be careful of how we define it. Here we can take

either one of two wrong turns. Among readers who have been newly introduced to symbol, the common fault is to think of definition as some kind of free association in which a symbol can mean anything one chooses to make it. For this reader, we must emphasize that any definition is going to be limited in a number of ways by the context of the story in which a symbol appears. But an equally serious fault is to define a symbol not too broadly—outside of its frame of reference, so to speak—but too narrowly. This is a fault prevalent among modern professional critics; one literary critic, familiar with Freudian psychology, will somehow force sexual meaning on almost any fictional symbol; another, interested in myth or comparative religion, will give the same symbol a mythological definition. Both critics will tend to disregard or distort the total context and intent of the story under consideration.

WALLACE STEGNER

Butcher Bird

That summer the boy was alone on the farm except for his parents. His brother was working at Orullian's Grocery in town, and there was no one to run the trap line with or swim in the dark, weed-smelling reservoir where garter snakes made straight rapid lines in the water and the skaters rowed close to shore. So every excursion was an adventure, even if it was only a trip across the three miles of prairie to Larsen's to get mail or groceries. He was excited at the visit to Garfield's as he was excited by everything unusual. The hot midsummer afternoon was still and breathless, the air harder to breathe than usual. He knew there was a change in weather coming because the gingersnaps in their tall cardboard box were soft and bendable when he snitched two to stick in his pocket. He could tell too by his father's grumpiness accumulated through two weeks of drought, his habit of looking off into the southwest, from which either rain or hot winds might come, that something was brewing. If it was rain everything would be fine, his father would hum under his breath getting breakfast, maybe let him drive the stoneboat or ride the mare down to Larsen's for mail. If it was hot wind they'd have to walk soft and speak softer, and it wouldn't be any fun.

They didn't know the Garfields, who had moved in only the fall before, but people said they had a good big house and a bigger barn and that Mr. Garfield was an Englishman and a little funny talking about scientific farming and making the desert blossom like the rose. The boy's father hadn't wanted to go, but his mother thought it was unneighborly not to call at least once in a whole year when people lived only four miles away. She was, the boy knew, as anxious for a change, as eager to get out of that atmosphere of waiting to see what the weather would do—that tense and teeth-gritting expectancy—as he was.

He found more than he looked for at Garfield's. Mr. Garfield was tall and bald with a big nose, and talked very softly and politely. The boy's father was determined not to like him right from the start.

When Mr. Garfield said, "Dear, I think we might have a glass of lemonade, don't you?", the boy saw his parents look at each other, saw the beginning of a contemptuous smile on his father's face, saw his mother purse her lips and shake her head ever so little. And when Mrs. Garfield, prim and spectacled, with a habit of tucking her head back and to one side while she listened to anyone talk, brought in the lemonade, the boy saw his father taste his and make a little face behind the glass. He hated any summer drink without ice in it, and had spent two whole weeks digging a dugout icehouse just so that he could have ice water and cold beer when the hot weather came.

But Mr. and Mrs. Garfield were nice people. They sat down in their new parlor and showed the boy's mother the rug and the gramophone. When the boy came up curiously to inspect the little box with the petunia-shaped horn and the little china dog with "His Master's Voice" on it, and the Garfields found that he had never seen or heard a gramophone, they put on a cylinder like a big spool of tightly wound black thread and lowered a needle on it, and out came a man's voice singing in Scotch brogue, and his mother smiled and nodded and said, "My land, Harry Lauder! I heard him once a long time ago. Isn't it wonderful, Sonny?"

It was wonderful all right. He inspected it, reached out his fingers to touch things, wiggled the big horn to see if it was loose or screwed in. His father warned him sharply to keep his hands off, but then Mr. Garfield smiled and said, "Oh, he can't hurt it. Let's play something else," and found a record about the saucy little bird on Nelly's hat that had them all laughing. They let him wind the machine and play the record over again, all by himself, and he was very careful. It was a fine machine. He wished he had one.

About the time he had finished playing his sixth or seventh record, and George M. Cohan was singing "She's a grand old flag, she's a high-flying flag, and forever in peace may she wave," he glanced at his father and discovered that he was grouchy about something. He wasn't taking any part in the conversation but was sitting with his chin in his hand staring out of the window. Mr. Garfield was looking at him a little helplessly. His eyes met the boy's and he motioned him over.

"What do you find to do all summer? Only child, are you?"

"No, sir. My brother's in Whitemud. He's twelve. He's got a job."

"So you come out on the farm to help," said Mr. Garfield. He had his hand on the boy's shoulder and his voice was so kind that the boy lost his shyness and felt no embarrassment at all in being out there in the middle of the parlor with all of them watching.

"I don't help much," he said. "I'm too little to do anything but drive the stoneboat, Pa says. When I'm twelve he's going to get me a gun and then I can go hunting."

"Hunting?" Mr. Garfield said. "What do you hunt?"

"Oh, gophers and weasels. I got a pet weasel. His name's Lucifer."

"Well," said Mr. Garfield. "You seem to be a pretty manly little chap. What do you feed your weasel?"

"Gophers." The boy thought it best not to say that the gophers were live ones he threw into the weasel's cage. He thought probably Mr. Garfield would be a little shocked at that.

Mr. Garfield straightened up and looked round at the grown folks. "Isn't it a shame," he said," "that there are so many predatory animals and pests in this country that we have to spend our time destroying them? I hate killing things."

"I hate weasels," the boy said. "I'm just saving this one till he turns into an ermine, and then I'm going to skin him. Once I speared a weasel with the pitchfork in the chicken coop and he dropped right off the tine and ran up my leg and bit me after he was speared clean through."

He finished breathlessly, and his mother smiled at him, motioning him not to talk so much. But Mr. Garfield was still looking at him kindly. "So you want to make war on the cruel things, the weasels and hawks," he said.

"Yes, sir," the boy said. He looked at his mother and it was all right. He hadn't spoiled anything by telling about the weasels.

"Now that reminds me," Mr. Garfield said, rising. "Maybe I've got something you'd find useful."

He went into another room and came back with a .22 in his hand. "Could you use this?"

"I . . . yes, *sir!*" the boy said. He had almost, in his excitement, said "I hope to whisk in your piskers," because that was what his father always said when he meant anything real hard.

"If your parents want you to have it," Mr. Garfield said and raised his eyebrows at the boy's mother. He didn't look at the father, but the boy did.

"Can I, Pa?"

"I guess so," his father said. "Sure."

"Thank Mr. Garfield nicely," said his mother.

"Gee," the boy breathed. "Thanks, Mr. Garfield, ever so much."

"There's a promise goes with it," Mr. Garfield said. "I'd like you to promise never to shoot anything with it but the bloodthirsty animals—the cruel ones like weasels and hawks. Never anything like birds or prairie dogs."

"How about butcher birds?"

"Butcher birds?" Mr. Garfield said.

"Shrikes," said the boy's mother. "We've got some over by our place. They kill all sorts of things, snakes and gophers and other birds. They're worse than the hawks because they just kill for the fun of it."

"By all means," said Mr. Garfield. "Shoot all the shrikes you see. A thing that kills for the fun of it . . ." He shook his head and his voice got solemn, almost like the voice of Mr. McGregor, the Sunday School Superintendent in town, when he was asking the benediction. "There's something about the way the war drags on, or maybe just this country," he said, "that makes me hate killing. I just can't bear to shoot anything any more, even a weasel."

The boy's father turned cold eyes away from Mr. Garfield and looked out of the window. One big brown hand, a little dirty from the wheel of the car, rubbed against the day-old bristles on his jaws. Then he stood up and stretched. "Well, we got to be going," he said.

"Oh, stay a little while," Mr. Garfield said. "You just came. I wanted to show you my trees."

The boy's mother stared at him. "Trees?"

He smiled. "Sounds a bit odd out here, doesn't it? But I think trees will grow. I've made some plantings down below."

"I'd love to see them," she said. "Sometimes I'd give almost anything to get into a good deep shady woods. Just to smell it, and feel how cool . . ."

"There's a little story connected with these," Mr. Garfield said. He spoke to the mother alone, warmly. "When we first decided to come out here I said to Martha that if trees wouldn't grow we shouldn't stick it. That's just what I said, 'If trees won't grow we shan't stick it.' Trees are almost the breath of life to me."

The boy's father was shaken by a sudden spell of coughing, and the mother shot a quick look at him and looked back at Mr. Garfield with a light flush on her cheekbones. "I'd love to see them," she said. "I was raised in Minnesota, and I never will get used to a place as barren as this."

"When I think of the beeches back home in England," Mr. Garfield said, and shook his head with a puckering smile round his eyes.

The father lifted himself heavily out of his chair and followed the rest of them out to the coulee edge. Below them willows grew profusely along the almost-dry creek, and farther back from the water there was a grove of perhaps twenty trees about a dozen feet high.

"I'm trying cottonwoods first because they can stand dry weather," Mr. Garfield said.

The mother was looking down with all her longings suddenly plain and naked in her eyes. "It's wonderful," she said. "I'd give almost anything to have some on our place."

"I found the willows close by here," said Mr. Garfield. "Just at the south end of the hills they call Old-Man-on-His-Back, where the stream comes down."

"Stream?" the boy's father said. "You mean that trickle?"

"It's not much of a stream," Mr. Garfield said apologetically. "But . . ."

"Are there any more there?" the mother said.

"Oh, yes. You could get some. Cut them diagonally and push them into any damp ground. They'll grow."

"They'll grow about six feet high," the father said.

"Yes," said Mr. Garfield. "They're not, properly speaking, trees. Still . . ."

"It's getting pretty smothery," the father said rather loudly. "We better be getting on."

This time Mr. Garfield didn't object, and they went back to the car exchanging promises of visits. The father jerked the crank and climbed into the Ford, where the boy was sighting along his gun. "Put that down," his father said. "Don't you know any better than to point a gun around people?"

"It isn't loaded."

"They never are," his father said. "Put it down now."

The Garfields were standing with their arms round each other's waists, waiting to wave good-by. Mr. Garfield reached over and picked something from his wife's dress.

"What was it, Alfred?" she said peering.

"Nothing. Just a bit of fluff."

The boy's father coughed violently and the car started with a jerk. With his head down almost to the wheel, still coughing, he waved, and the mother and the boy waved as they went down along the badly set cedar posts of the pasture fence. They were almost a quarter of a mile away before the boy, with a last wave of the gun, turned around again and saw that his father was purple with laughter. He rocked the car with his joy, and when his wife said, "Oh, Harry, you big fool," he pointed helplessly to his shoulder. "Would you mind," he said. "Would you mind brushing that bit o' fluff off me showldah?" He roared again, pounding the wheel. "I shawn't stick it," he said. "I bloody well shawn't stick it, you knaow!"

"It isn't fair to laugh at him," she said. "He can't help being English."

"He can't help being a sanctimonious old mudhen either, braying about his luv-ly luv-ly trees. They'll freeze out the first winter."

"How do you know? Maybe it's like he says—if they get a start they'll grow here as well as anywhere."

"Maybe there's a gold mine in our back yard too, but I'm not gonna dig to see. I couldn't stick it."

"Oh, you're just being stubborn," she said. "Just because you didn't like Mr. Garfield . . ."

He turned on her in heavy amazement. "Well, my God! Did you?"

"I thought he was very nice," she said, and sat straighter in the back seat, speaking loudly above the creak of the springs and cough of the motor. "They're trying to make a home, not just a wheat crop. I liked them."

"Uh, huh." He was not laughing any more now. Sitting beside him, the boy could see that his face had hardened and the cold look had come into his eye again. "So I should start talking like I had a mouthful of bran, and planting trees around the house that'll look like clothesline poles in two months."

"I didn't say that."

"You thought it though." He looked irritably at the sky, misted with the same delusive film of cloud that had fooled him for three days, and spat at the roadside. "You thought it all the time we were there. 'Why aren't you more like Mr. Garfield, he's such a nice man.' " With mincing savagery he swung around and mocked her. "Shall I make it a walnut grove? Or a big maple sugar bush? Or maybe you'd like an orange orchard."

The boy was looking down at his gun, trying not to hear them quarrel, but he knew what his mother's face would be like—hurt and a little flushed, her chin trembling into stubbornness. "I don't suppose you could bear to have a rug on the floor, or a gramophone?" she said.

He smacked the wheel hard. "Of course I could bear it if we could afford it. But I sure as hell would rather do without than be like that old sandhill crane."

"I don't suppose you'd like to take me over to the Old-Man-on-His-Back some day to get some willow slips either."

"What for?"

"To plant down in the coulee, by the dam."

"That dam dries up every August. Your willows wouldn't live till snow flies."

"Well, would it do any harm to try?"

"Oh, shut up!" he said. "Just thinking about that guy and his fluff and his trees gives me the pleefer."

The topless Ford lurched, one wheel at a time, through the deep burnout by their pasture corner, and the boy clambered out with his gun in his hand to slip the loop from the three-strand gate. It was then that he saw the snake, a striped limp ribbon, dangling on the fence, and a moment later the sparrow, neatly butchered and hung by the throat from the barbed wire. He pointed the gun at them. "Lookit!" he said. "Lookit what the butcher bird's been doing."

His father's violent hand waved at him from the seat. "Come on! Get the wire out of the way!"

The boy dragged the gate through the dust, and the Ford went through and up behind the house, perched on the bare edge of the coulee in the midst of its baked yard and framed by the dark fireguard overgrown with Russian thistle. Walking across that yard a few minutes later, the boy felt its hard heat under his sneakers. There was hardly a spear of grass within the fireguard. It was one of his father's prides that the dooryard should be like cement. "Pour your wash water out long enough," he said, "and you'll have a surface so hard it won't even make mud." Religiously he threw his water out three times a day, carrying it sometimes a dozen steps to dump it on a dusty or grassy spot.

The mother had objected at first, asking why they had to live in the middle of an alkali flat, and why they couldn't let grass grow up to the door. But he snorted her down. Everything round the house ought to be bare as a bone. Get a good prairie fire going and it'd jump that guard like nothing, and if they had grass to the door where'd they be? She said why not plow a wider fireguard then, one a fire couldn't jump, but he said he had other things to do besides plowing fifty-foot fireguards.

They were arguing inside when the boy came up on the step to sit down and aim his empty .22 at a fencepost. Apparently his mother had been persistent, and persistence when he was not in a mood for it angered the father worse than anything else. Their talk came vaguely through his concentration, but he shut his ears on it. If that spot on the fencepost was a coyote now, and he held the sight steady, right on it, and pulled the trigger, that old coyote would jump about eighty feet in the air and come down dead as a mackerel, and he could tack his hide on the barn the way Mr. Larsen had one, only the dogs had jumped and torn the tail and hind legs off Mr. Larsen's pelt, and he wouldn't get more than the three-dollar bounty out of it. But then Mr. Larsen had shot his with a shotgun anyway, and the hide wasn't worth much even before the dogs tore it. . . .

"I can't for the life of me see why not," his mother said inside. "We could do it now. We're not doing anything else."

"I tell you they wouldn't grow!" said his father with emphasis on every word. "Why should we run our tongues out doing everything that mealymouthed fool does?"

"I don't want anything but the willows. They're easy."

He made his special sound of contempt, his half-snort, half-grunt. After a silence she tried again. "They might even have pussies on them in the spring. Mr. Garfield thinks they'd grow, and he used to work in a greenhouse, his wife told me."

"This isn't a greenhouse, for Chrissake."

"Oh, let it go," she said. "I've stood it this long without any green things around. I guess I can stand it some more."

The boy, aiming now toward the gate where the butcher bird, coming back to his prey, would in just a minute fly right into Deadeye's unerring bullet, heard his father stand up suddenly.

"Abused, aren't you?" he said.

The mother's voice rose. "No, I'm not abused! Only I can't see why it would be so awful to get some willows. Just because Mr. Garfield gave me the idea, and you didn't like him . . ."

"You're right I didn't like Mr. Garfield," the father said. "He gave me a pain right under the crupper."

"Because," the mother's voice said bitterly, "he calls his wife 'dear' and puts his arm around her and likes trees. It wouldn't occur to you to put your arm around your wife, would it?"

The boy aimed and held his breath. His mother ought to keep still, because if she didn't she'd get him real mad and then they'd both have to tiptoe around the rest of the day. He heard his father's breath whistle through his teeth, and his voice, mincing, nasty. "Would you like me to kiss you now, *dear?*"

"I wouldn't let you touch me with a ten-foot pole," his mother said. She sounded just as mad as he did, and it wasn't often she let herself get that way. The boy squirmed over when he heard the quick hard steps come up behind him and pause. Then his father's big hand, brown and meaty and felted with fine black hair, reached down over his shoulder and took the .22.

"Let's see this cannon old Scissor-bill gave you," he said.

It was a single-shot, bolt-action Savage, a little rusty on the barrel, the bolt sticky with hardened grease when the father removed it. Sighting up through the barrel, he grunted. "Takes care of a gun like he takes care of his farm. Probably used it to cultivate his luv-ly trees."

He went out into the sleeping porch, and after a minute came back with a rag and a can of machine oil. Hunching the boy over on the step, he sat down and began rubbing the bolt with the oil-soaked rag.

"I just can't bear to shoot anything any more," he said, and laughed suddenly. "I just cawn't stick it, little man." He leered at the boy, who grinned back uncertainly. Squinting through the barrel again, the father breathed through his nose and clamped his lips together, shaking his head.

The sun lay heavy on the baked yard. Out over the corner of the pasture a soaring hawk caught wind and sun at the same time, so that his light breast feathers flashed as he banked and rose. Just wait, the boy thought. Wait till I get my gun working and I'll fix you, you hen-robber. He thought of the three chicks a hawk had struck earlier in the summer, the three balls of yellow with the barred mature plumage just coming through. Two of them dead when he got there and chased the hawk away, the other grasping with its crop slashed wide open and the wheat spilling from it on the ground. His mother had sewed up the crop, and the chicken had lived, but it always looked droopy, like a plant in drought time, and sometimes it would stand and work its bill as if it were choking.

By golly, he thought, I'll shoot every hawk and butcher bird in twenty miles. I'll . . .

"Rustle around and find me a piece of baling wire," his father said. "This barrel looks like a henroost."

Behind the house he found a piece of rusty wire, brought it back and watched his father straighten it, wind a bit of rag round the end, ram it up and down through the barrel, and peer through again. "He's leaded her on so you can hardly see the grooves," he said. "But maybe she'll shoot. We'll fill her with vinegar and cork her up to-night."

The mother was behind them, leaning against the jamb and watching. She reached down and rumpled the father's black hair. "The minute you get a gun in your hand you start feeling better," she said. "It's just a shame you weren't born fifty years sooner."

"A gun's a good tool," he said. "It hadn't ought to be misused. Gun like this is enough to make a guy cry."

"Well, you've got to admit it was nice of Mr. Garfield to give it to Sonny," she said. It was the wrong thing to say. The boy had a feeling somehow that she knew it was the wrong thing to say, that she said it just to have one tiny triumph over him. He knew it would make him boiling mad again, even before he heard his father's answer.

"Oh, sure, Mr. Garfield's a fine man. He can preach a better sermon than any homesteader in Saskatchewan. God Almighty! everything he does is better than what I do. All right. All right, *all right!* Why the hell don't you move over there if you like it so well!"

"If you weren't so blind . . ."

He rose with the .22 in his hand and pushed past her into the house. "I'm not so blind," he said heavily in passing. "You've been throwing that bastard up to me for two hours. It don't take very good eyes to see what that means."

His mother started to say, "All because I want a few little . . ." but the boy cut in on her, anxious to help the situation somehow. "Will it shoot now?" he said.

His father said nothing. His mother looked down at him, shrugged, sighed, smiled bleakly with a tight mouth. She moved aside when the father came back with a box of cartridges in his hand. He ignored his wife, speaking to the boy alone in the particular half-jocular tone he always used with him or the dog when he wasn't mad or exasperated.

"Thought I had these around," he said. "Now we'll see what this smokepole will do."

He slipped a cartridge in and locked the bolt, looking round for something to shoot at. Behind him the mother's feet moved on the floor, and her voice came purposefully. "I can't see why you have to act this way," she said. "I'm going over and get some slips myself."

There was a long silence. The angled shade lay sharp as a knife across the baked front yard. The father's cheek was pressed against the stock of the gun, his arms and hands as steady as stone.

"How'll you get there?" he said, whispering down the barrel.

"I'll walk."

"Five miles and back."

"Yes, five miles and back. Or fifty miles and back. If there was any earthly reason why you should mind . . ."

"I don't mind," he said, and his voice was soft as silk. "Go ahead."

Close to his mother's long skirts in the doorway, the boy felt her stiffen as if she had been slapped. He squirmed anxiously, but his desperation could find only the question he had asked before. His voice squeaked on it: "Will it shoot now?"

"See that sparrow out there?" his father said, still whispering. "Right out by that cactus?"

"Harry!" the mother said. "If you shoot that harmless little bird!"

Fascinated, the boy watched his father's dark face against the rifle stock, the locked, immovable left arm, the thick finger crooked inside the trigger guard almost too small to hold it. He saw the sparrow, gray, white-breasted, hopping obliviously in search of bugs, fifty feet out on the gray earth. "I just . . . can't . . . bear . . . to . . . shoot . . . anything," the father said, his face like dark stone, his lips hardly moving. "I just . . . can't . . . stick it!"

"Harry!" his wife screamed.

The boy's mouth opened, a dark wash of terror shadowed his vision of the baked yard cut by its sharp angle of shade.

"Don't pa!"

The rocklike figure of his father never moved. The thick finger squeezed slowly down on the trigger, there was a thin, sharp report, and the sparrow jerked and collapsed into a shapeless wad on the ground. It was as if, in the instant of the shot, all its clean outlines vanished. Head, feet, the white breast, the perceptible outlines of the folded wings, disappeared all at once, were crumpled together and lost, and the boy sat beside his father on the step with the echo of the shot still in his ears.

He did not look at either of his parents. He looked only at the crumpled sparrow. Step by step, unable to keep away, he went to it, stopped, and picked it up. Blood stained his fingers, and he held the bird by the tail while he wiped the smeared hand on his overalls. He heard the click as the bolt was shot and the empty cartridge ejected, and he saw his mother come swiftly out of the house past his father, who sat still on the step. Her hands were clenched, and she walked with her head down, as if fighting tears.

"Ma!" the boy said dully. "Ma, what'll I do with it?"

She stopped and turned, and for a moment they faced each other. He saw the dead pallor of her face, the burning eyes, the not-quite-controllable quiver of her lips. But her words, when they came, were flat and level, almost casual.

"Leave it right there," she said. "After a while your father will want to hang it on the barbed wire."

TRUMAN CAPOTE

The Headless Hawk

They are of those that rebel against the light; they know not the ways thereof, nor abide in the paths thereof. In the dark they dig through houses, which they had marked for themselves in the day-time: they know not the light. For the morning is to them as the shadow of death: if one know them, they are in the terrors of the shadow of death. —JOB 24: 13, 16, 17

Vincent switched off the lights in the gallery. Outside, after locking the door, he smoothed the brim of an elegant Panama, and started toward Third Avenue, his umbrella-cane tap-tap-tapping along the pavement. A promise of rain had darkened the day since dawn, and a sky of bloated clouds blurred the five o'clock sun; it was hot, though, humid as tropical mist, and voices, sounding along the gray July street, sounding muffled and strange, carried a fretful undertone. Vincent felt as though he moved below the sea. Buses, cruising crosstown through Fifty-seventh Street, seemed like green-bellied fish, and faces loomed and rocked like wave-riding masks. He studied each passer-by, hunting one, and presently he saw her, a girl in a green raincoat. She was standing on the downtown corner of Fifty-seventh and Third, just standing there smoking a cigarette, and giving somehow the impression she hummed a tune. The raincoat was transparent. She wore dark slacks, no socks, a pair of huaraches, a man's white shirt. Her hair was fawn-colored, and cut like a boy's. When she noticed Vincent crossing toward her, she dropped the cigarette and hurried down the block to the doorway of an antique store.

Vincent slowed his step. He pulled out a handkerchief and dabbed his forehead; if only he could get away, go up to the Cape, lie in the sun. He bought an afternoon paper, and fumbled his change. It rolled in the gutter, dropped silently out of sight down a sewer grating. "Ain't but a nickel, bub," said the news-dealer, for Vincent, though actually unaware of his loss, looked heartbroken. And it was like that often now, never quite in contact, never sure whether a step would take him backward or forward, up or down. Very casually, with the handle of the umbrella hooked over an arm, and his eyes concentrated on the paper's headlines—but what did the damn thing say?—he continued downtown. A swarthy woman carrying a shopping bag jostled him, glared, muttered in coarsely vehement Italian. The ragged cut of her voice seemed to come through layers of wool. As he approached the antique store where the girl in the green raincoat waited, he walked slower still, counting one, two, three, four, five, six—at six he halted before the window.

The window was like a corner of an attic; a lifetime's discardings rose in a pyramid of no particular worth: vacant picture frames, a lavender wig, Gothic shaving mugs, beaded lamps. There was an oriental mask suspended on a ceiling cord, and wind from an electric fan whirling inside the shop revolved it slowly round and round. Vincent, by degrees, lifted his gaze, and looked at the girl directly. She was hovering in the doorway so that he saw her greenness distorted wavy through double glass; the elevated pounded overhead and the window trembled. Her image spread like a reflection on silverware, then gradually hardened again: she was watching him.

He hung an Old Gold between his lips, rummaged for a match and, finding none, sighed. The girl stepped from the doorway. She held out a cheap little lighter; as the flame pulsed up, her eyes, pale, shallow cat-green, fixed him with alarming intensity. Her eyes had an astonished, a shocked look, as though, having at one time witnessed a terrible incident, they'd locked wide open. Carefree bangs fringed her forehead; this boy haircut emphasized the childish and rather poetic quality of her narrow, hollow-cheeked face. It was the kind of face one sometimes sees in paintings of medieval youths.

Letting the smoke pour out his nose, Vincent, knowing it was useless to ask, wondered, as always, what she was living on, and where. He flipped away the cigarette, for he had not wanted it to begin with, and then, pivoting, crossed rapidly under the El; as he approached the curb he heard a crash of brakes, and suddenly, as if cotton plugs had been blasted from his ears, city noises crowded in. A cab driver hollered: "Fa crissake, sistuh, get the lead outa yuh pants!" but the girl did not even bother turning her head; trance-eyed, undisturbed as a sleepwalker, and staring straight at Vincent, who watched dumbly, she moved across the street. A colored boy wearing a jazzy purple suit took her elbow. "You sick, Miss?" he said, guiding her forward, and she did not answer.

"You look mighty funny, Miss. If you sick, I . . ." then, following the direction of her eyes, he released his hold. There was something here which made him all still inside. "Uh—yeah," he muttered, backing off with a grinning display of tartar-coated teeth.

So Vincent began walking in earnest, and his umbrella tapped code-like block after block. His shirt was soaked through with itchy sweat, and the noises, now so harsh, banged in his head: a trick car horn hooting "My Country, 'Tis of Thee," electric spray of sparks crackling bluely off thundering rails, whiskey laughter hiccuping through gaunt doors of beer-stale bars where orchid juke machines manufactured U.S.A. music—"I got spurs that jingle jangle jingle. . . ." Occasionally he caught a glimpse of her, once mirrored in the window of Paul's Seafood Palace where scarlet lobsters basked on a beach of flaked ice. She followed close with her hands shoved into the pockets of her raincoat. The brassy lights of a movie marquee blinked, and he remembered how she loved movies: murder films, spy chillers, Wild West shows. He turned into a side street leading toward the East River; it was quiet here, hushed like Sunday: a sailor-stroller munching an Eskimo pie, energetic twins skipping rope, an old velvety lady with gardenia-white hair lifting aside lace curtains and peering listlessly into rain-dark space—a city landscape in July. And behind him the soft insistent slap of sandals. Traffic lights on Second Avenue turned red; at the corner a bearded midget, Ruby the Popcorn Man, wailed, "Hot buttered popcorn, big bag, yah?" Vincent shook his head, and the midget looked very put out, then: "Yuh see?" he jeered, pushing a shovel inside of the candlelit cage where bursting kernels bounced like crazy moths. "Yuh see, de girlie knows popcorn's nourishin'." She bought a dime's worth, and it was in a green sack matching her raincoat, matching her eyes.

This is my neighborhood, my street, the house with the gateway is where I live. To remind himself of this was necessary, inasmuch as he'd substituted for a sense of reality a knowledge of time, and place. He glanced gratefully at sourfaced, faded ladies, at the pipe-puffing males squatting on the surrounding steps of brownstone stoops. Nine pale little girls shrieked round a corner flower cart begging daisies to pin in their hair, but the peddler said, "Shoo!" and, fleeing like beads of a broken bracelets, they circled in the street, the wild ones leaping with laughter, and the shy ones, silent and isolated, lifting summer-wilted faces skyward: the rain, would it never come?

Vincent, who lived in a basement apartment, descended several steps and took out his keycase; then, pausing behind the hallway door, he looked back through a peephole in the paneling. The girl was waiting on the sidewalk above; she leaned against a brownstone banister, and her arms fell limp—and popcorn spilled snowlike round her feet. A grimy little boy crept slyly up to pick among it like a squirrel.

II

For Vincent it was a holiday. No one had come by the gallery all morning, which, considering the arctic weather, was not unusual. He sat at his desk devouring tangerines, and enjoying immensely a Thurber story in an old *New Yorker.* Laughing loudly, he did not hear the girl enter, see her cross the dark carpet, notice her at all, in fact, until the telephone rang. "Garland Gallery, hello." She was odd, most certainly, that indecent haircut, those depthless eyes—"Oh, Paul, *Comme ci, comme ça,* and you?"—and dressed like a freak: no coat, just a lumberjack's shirt, navy-blue slacks and—was it a joke?—pink ankle socks, a pair of huaraches. "The ballet? Who's dancing? Oh, her!" Under an arm she carried a flat parcel wrapped in sheets of funny-paper—"Look, Paul, what say I call back? There's someone here . . ." and, anchoring the receiver, assuming a commercial smile, he stood up. "Yes?"

Her lips, crusty with chap, trembled with unrealized words as though she had possibly a defect of speech, and her eyes rolled in their sockets like loose marbles. It was the kind of disturbed shyness one associates with children. "I've a picture," she said. "You buy pictures?"

At this, Vincent's smile became fixed. "We exhibit."

"I painted it myself," she said, and her voice, hoarse and slurred, was Southern. "My picture—I painted it. A lady told me there were places around here that bought pictures."

Vincent said, "Yes, of course, but the truth is"—and he made a helpless gesture—"the truth is I've no authority whatever. Mr. Garland—this is his gallery, you know—is out of town." Standing there on the expanse of fine carpet, her body sagging sideways with the weight of her package, she looked like a sad rag doll. "Maybe," he began, "maybe Henry Krueger up the street at Sixty-five . . ." but she was not listening.

"I did it myself," she insisted softly. "Tuesdays and Thursdays were our painting days, and a whole year I worked. The others, they kept messing it up, and Mr. Destronelli . . ." Suddenly, as though aware of an indiscretion, she stopped and bit her lip. Her eyes narrowed. "He's not a friend of yours?"

"Who?" said Vincent, confused.

"Mr. Destronelli."

He shook his head, and wondered why it was that eccentricity always excited in him such curious admiration. It was the feeling he'd had as a child toward carnival freaks. And it was true that about those whom he'd loved there was always a little something wrong, broken. Strange, though, that this quality, having stimulated an attraction, should, in his case, regularly end it by destroying it. "Of course I haven't any authority," he repeated, sweeping tangerine hulls into a wastebasket, "but, if you like, I suppose I could look at your work."

A pause; then, kneeling on the floor, she commenced stripping off the funny-paper wrappings. It originally had been, Vincent noticed, part of the New Orleans *Times-Picayune*. "From the South, aren't you?" he said. She did not look up, but he saw her shoulders stiffen. "No," she said. Smiling, he considered a moment, decided it would be tactless to challenge so transparent a lie. Or could she have misunderstood? And all at once he felt an intense longing to touch her head, finger her boyish hair. He shoved his hands in his pockets and glanced at the window. It was spangled with February frost, and some passer-by had scratched on the glass an obscenity.

"There," she said.

A headless figure in a monklike robe reclined complacently on top a tacky vaudeville trunk; in one hand she held a fuming blue candle, in the other a miniature gold cage, and her severed head lay bleeding at her feet: it was the girl's, this head, but here her hair was long, very long, and a snowball kitten with crystal spitfire eyes playfully pawed, as it would a spool of yarn, the sprawling ends. The wings of a hawk, headless, scarlet-breasted, copper-clawed, curtained the background like a nightfall sky. It was a crude painting, the hard pure colors molded with male brutality, and, while there was not technical merit evident, it had that power often seen in something deeply felt, though primitively conveyed. Vincent reacted as he did when occasionally a phrase of music surprised a note of inward recognition, or a cluster of words in a poem revealed to him a secret concerning himself: he felt a powerful chill of pleasure run down his spine. "Mr. Garland is in Florida," he said cautiously, "but I think he should see it; you couldn't leave it for, say, a week?"

"I had a ring and I sold it," she said, and he had the feeling she was talking in a trance. "It was a nice ring, a wedding ring—not mine—with writing on it. I had an overcoat, too." She twisted one of her shirt buttons, pulled till it popped off and rolled on the carpet like a pearl eye. "I don't want much—fifty dollars; is that unfair?"

"Too much," said Vincent, more curtly than he intended. Now he wanted her painting, not for the gallery, but for himself. There are certain works of art which excite more interest in their creators than in what they have created, usually because in this kind of work one is able to identify something which has until that instant seemed a private inexpressible perception, and you wonder: who is this that knows me, and how? "I'll give thirty."

For a moment she gaped at him stupidly, and then, sucking her breath, held out her hand, palm up. This directness, too innocent to be offensive, caught him off guard. Somewhat embarrassed, he said, "I'm most awfully afraid I'll have to mail a check. Could you . . . ?" The telephone interrupted, and, as he went to answer, she followed, her hand outstretched, a frantic look pinching her face. "Oh, Paul, may I call back? Oh, I see. Well, hold on a sec." Cupping the mouthpiece against his shoulder, he pushed a pad and pencil across the desk. "Here, write your name and address."

But she shook her head, the dazed, anxious expression deepening.

"Check," said Vincent, "I have to mail a check. Please, your name and address." He grinned encouragingly when at last she began to write.

"Sorry, Paul . . . Whose party? Why, the little bitch, she didn't invite . . . Hey!" he called, for the girl was moving toward the door. "Please, hey!" Cold air chilled the gallery, and the door slammed with a glassy rattle. Hellohellohello. Vincent did not answer; he stood puzzling over the curious information she'd left printed on his pad: D. J.—Y.W.C.A. Hellohellohello.

It hung above his mantel, the painting, and on those nights when he could not sleep he would pour a glass of whiskey and talk to the headless hawk, tell it the stuff of his life: he was, he said, a poet who had never written poetry, a painter who had never painted, a lover who had never loved (absolutely)—someone, in short, without direction, and quite headless. Oh, it wasn't that he hadn't tried—good beginnings, always, bad endings, always. Vincent, white, male, age 36, college graduate: a man in the sea, fifty miles from shore; a victim, born to be murdered, either by himself or another; an actor unemployed. It was there, all of it, in the painting, everything disconnected and cockeyed, and who was she that she should know so much? Inquiries, those he'd made, had led nowhere, not another dealer knew of her, and to search for a D. J. living in, presumably, a Y.W.C.A. seemed absurd. Then, too, he'd quite expected she would reappear, but February passed, and March. One evening, crossing the square which fronts the Plaza, he had a queer thing happen. The archaic hansom drivers who line that location were lighting their carriage lamps, for it was dusk, and lamplight traced through moving leaves. A hansom pulled from the curb and rolled past in the twilight. There was a single occupant, and this passenger, whose face he could not see, was a girl with chopped fawn-colored hair. So he settled on a bench, and whiled away time talking with a soldier, and a fairy colored boy who quoted poetry, and a man out airing a dachshund: night characters with whom he waited—but the carriage, with the one for whom he waited, never came back. Again he saw her (or supposed he did) descending subway stairs, and this time lost her in the tiled tunnels of painted arrows and Spearmint machines. It was as if her face were imposèd upon his mind; he could no more dispossess it than could, for example, a dead man rid his legendary eyes of the last image seen. Around the middle of April he went up to Connecticut to spend a weekend with his married sister; keyed-up, caustic, he wasn't, as she complained, at all like himself. "What is it, Vinny, darling—if you need money . . ." "Oh, shut up!" he said. "Must be love," teased his brother-in-law. "Come on, Vinny, 'fess up; what's she like?" And all this so annoyed him he caught the next train home. From a booth in Grand Central he called to apologize, but a sick nervousness hummed inside him, and he hung up while the operator was still trying to make a connection. He wanted a drink. At the Commodore Bar he spent an hour or so drowning four daiquiris—it was Saturday, it was nine, there was nothing to do unless he did it alone, he was feeling sad for himself. Now in the park behind the Public Library sweethearts moved whisperingly under trees, and drinking-fountain water bubbled softly, like their voices, but for all the white April evening meant to him, Vincent, drunk a little and wandering, might as well have been old, like the old bench-sitters rasping phlegm.

In the country, spring is a time of small happenings happening quietly, hyacinth shoots thrusting in a garden, willows burning with a sudden frosty fire of green, lengthening afternoons of long flowing dusk, and midnight rain opening lilac; but in the city there is the fanfare of organ-grinders, and odors, undiluted by winter wind, clog the air; windows long closed go up, and conversation, drifting beyond a room, collides with the jangle of a peddler's bell. It is the crazy season of toy balloons and roller skates, of courtyard baritones and men of freakish enterprise, like the one who jumped up now like a jack-in-the-box. He was old, he had a telescope and a sign: 25¢ See the Moon! See the Stars! 25¢! No stars could penetrate a city's glare, but Vincent saw the moon, a round, shadowed whiteness, and then a blaze of electric bulbs: Four Roses, Bing Cro—— he was moving through caramel-scented staleness, swimming through oceans of cheese-pale faces, neon, and darkness. Above the blasting of a jukebox, bulletfire boomed, a cardboard duck fell plop, and somebody screeched: "Yay Iggy!" It was a Broadway funhouse, a penny arcade, and jammed from wall to wall with Saturday splurgers. He watched a penny movie (*What The Bootblack Saw*), and had his fortune told by a wax witch leering behind glass: "Yours is an affectionate nature" . . . but he read no further, for up near the jukebox there was an attractive commotion. A crowd of kids, clapping in time to jazz music, had formed a circle around two dancers. These dancers were both colored, both girls. They swayed together slow and easy, like lovers, rocked and stamped and rolled serious savage eyes, their muscles rhythmically attuned to the ripple of a clarinet, the rising harangue of a drum. Vincent's gaze traveled round the audience, and when he saw her a bright shiver went through him, for something of the dance's violence was reflected in her face. Standing there beside a tall ugly boy, it was as if she were the sleeper and the Negroes a dream. Trumpet-drum-piano, bawling on behind a black girl's froggy voice, wailed toward a rocking finale. The clapping ended, the dancers parted. She was alone now; though Vincent's instinct was to leave before she noticed, he advanced, and, as one would gently waken a sleeper, lightly touched her shoulder. "Hello," he said, his voice too loud. Turning, she stared at him, and her eyes were clear-blank. First terror, then puzzlement replaced the dead lost look. She took a step backward, and, just as the jukebox commenced hollering again, he seized her wrist: "You remember me," he prompted, "the gallery? Your painting?" She blinked, let the lids sink sleepily over those eyes, and he could feel the slow relaxing of tension in her arm. She was thinner than he recalled, prettier, too, and her hair, grown out somewhat, hung in casual disorder. A little silver Christmas ribbon dangled sadly from a stray lock. He started to say, "Can I buy you a drink?" but she leaned against him, her head resting on his chest like a child's, and he said: "Will you come home with me?" She lifted her face; the answer, when it came, was a breath, a whisper: "Please," she said.

Vincent stripped off his clothes, arranged them neatly in the closet, and admired his nakedness before a mirrored door. He was not so handsome as he supposed, but handsome all the same. For his moderate height he was excellently proportioned; his hair was dark yellow, and his delicate, rather snub-nosed face had a fine, ruddy coloring. The rumble of running water broke the quiet; she was in the bathroom preparing to bathe. He dressed in loose-fitting flannel pajamas, lit a cigarette, said, "Everything all right?" The water went off, a long silence, then: "Yes, thank you." On the way home in a cab he'd made an attempt at conversation, but she had said nothing, not even when they entered the apartment—and this last offended him, for, taking rather female pride in his quarters, he'd expected a complimentary remark. It was one enormously high-ceilinged room, a bath and kitchenette, a backyard garden. In the furnishings he'd combined modern with antique and produced a distinguished result. Decorating the walls were a trio of Toulouse-Lautrec prints, a framed circus poster, D. J.'s painting, photographs of Rilke, Nijinsky and Duse. A candelabra of lean blue candles burned on a desk; the room, washed in their delirious light, wavered. French doors led into the yard. He never used it much, for it was a place impossible to keep clean. There were a few dead tulip stalks dark in the moonshine, a puny heaven tree, and an old weather-worn chair left by the last tenant. He paced back and forth over the cold flagstones, hoping that in the cool air the drugged drunk sensation he felt would wear off. Nearby a piano was being badly mauled, and in a window above there was a child's face. He was thumbing a blade of grass when her shadow fell long across the yard. She was in the doorway. "You mustn't come out," he said, moving toward her. "It's turned a little cold."

There was about her now an appealing softness; she seemed somehow less angular, less out of tune with the average, and Vincent, offering a glass of sherry, was delighted at the delicacy with which she touched it to her lips. She was wearing his terry-cloth robe; it was by yards too large. Her feet were bare, and she tucked them up beside her on the couch. "It's like Glass Hill, the candlelight," she said, and smiled. "My Granny lived at Glass Hill. We had lovely times, sometimes; do you know what she used to say? She used to say, 'Candles are magic wands; light one and the world is a story book.' "

"What a dreary old lady she must've been," said Vincent, quite drunk. "We should probably have hated each other."

"Granny would've loved you," she said. "She loved any kind of man, every man she ever met, even Mr. Destronelli."

"Destronelli?" It was a name he'd heard before.

Her eyes slid slyly sideways, and this look seemed to say: There must be no subterfuge between us, we who understand each other have no need of it. "Oh, you know," she said with a conviction that, under more commonplace circumstances, would have been surprising. It was, however, as if he'd abandoned temporarily the faculty of surprise. "Everybody knows him."

He curved an arm around her, and brought her nearer. "Not me, I don't," he said, kissing her mouth, neck; she was not responsive especially, but he said—and his voice had gone adolescently shaky—"Never met Mr. Whoozits." He slipped a hand inside her robe, loosening it away from her shoulders. Above one breast she had a birthmark, small and star-shaped. He glanced at the mirrored door where uncertain light rippled their reflections, made them pale and incomplete. She was smiling. "Mr. Whoozits," he said, "what does he look like?" The suggestion of a smile faded, a small monkey-like frown flickered on her face. She looked above the mantel at her painting, and he realized that this was the first notice she'd shown it; she appeared to study in the picture a particular object, but whether hawk or head he could not say. "Well," she said quietly, pressing closer to him, "he looks like you, like me, like most anybody."

It was raining; in the wet noon light two nubs of candle still burned, and at an open window gray curtains tossed forlornly. Vincent extricated his arm; it was numb from the weight of her body. Careful not to make a noise, he eased out of bed, blew out the candles, tiptoed into the bathroom, and doused his face with cold water. On the way to the kitchenette he flexed his arms, feeling, as he hadn't for a long time, an intensely male pleasure in his strength, a healthy wholeness of person. He made and put on a tray orange juice, raisin-bread toast, a pot of tea; then, so inexpertly that everything on the tray rattled, he brought the breakfast in and placed it on a table beside the bed.

She had not moved; her ruffled hair spread fanwise across the pillow, and one hand rested in the hollow where his head had lain. He leaned over and kissed her lips, and her eyelids, blue with sleep, trembled. "Yes, yes, I'm awake," she murmured, and rain, lifting in the wind, sprayed against the window like surf. He somehow knew that with her there would be none of the usual artifice; no avoidance of eyes, no shamefaced, accusing pause. She raised herself on her elbow; she looked at him, Vincent thought, as if he were her husband, and, handing her the orange juice, he smiled his gratitude.

"What is today?"

"Sunday," he told her, bundling under the quilt, and settling the tray across his legs.

"But there are no church bells," she said. "And it's raining."

Vincent divided a piece of toast. "You don't mind that, do you? Rain—such a peaceful sound." He poured tea. "Sugar? Cream?"

She disregarded this, and said, "Today is Sunday what? What month, I mean?"

"Where have you been living, in the subway?" he said, grinning. And it puzzled him to think she was serious. "Oh, April . . . April something-or-other." . .

"April," she repeated. "Have I been here long?"

"Only since last night."

"Oh."

Vincent stirred his tea, the spoon tinkling in the cup like a bell. Toast crumbs spilled among the sheets, and he thought of the *Tribune* and the *Times* waiting outside the door, but they, this morning, held no charms; it was best lying there beside her in the warm bed, sipping tea, listening to the rain. Odd, when you stopped to consider, certainly very odd. She did not know his name, nor he hers. And so he said, "I still owe you thirty dollars, do you realize that? Your own fault, of course—leaving such a damn fool address. And D. J., what is that supposed to mean?"

"I don't think I'd better tell you my name," she said. "I could make up one easy enough: Dorothy Jordan, Delilah Johnson; see? There are all kinds of names I could make up, and if it wasn't for him I'd tell you right."

Vincent lowered the tray to the floor. He rolled over on his side, and, facing her, his heartbeat quickened. "Who's him?" Though her expression was calm, anger muddied her voice when she said, "If you don't know him, then tell me, why am I here?"

Silence, and outside the rain seemed suddenly suspended. A ship's horn moaned in the river. Holding her close, he combed his fingers through her hair, and, wanting so much to be believed, said, "Because I love you."

She closed her eyes. "What became of them?"

"Who?"

"The others you've said that to."

It commenced again, the rain spattering grayly at the window, falling on hushed Sunday streets; listening, Vincent remembered. He remembered his cousin, Lucille, poor, beautiful, stupid Lucille who sat all day embroidering silk flowers on scraps of linen. And Allen T. Baker—there was the winter they'd spent in Havana, the house they'd lived in, crumbling rooms of rose-colored rock; poor Allen, he'd thought it was to be forever. Gordon, too. Gordon, with the kinky yellow hair, and a head full of old Elizabethan ballads. Was it true he'd shot himself? And Connie Silver, the deaf girl, the one who had wanted to be an actress—what had become of her? Or Helen, Louise, Laura? "There was just one," he said, and to his own ears, this had a truthful ring. "Only one, and she's dead."

Tenderly, as if in sympathy, she touched his cheek. "I suppose he killed her," she said, her eyes so close he could see the outline of his face imprisoned in their greenness. "He killed Miss Hall, you know. The dearest woman in the world, Miss Hall, and so pretty your breath went away. I had piano lessons with her, and when she played the piano, when she said hello and when she said good-bye—it was like my heart would stop." Her voice had taken on an impersonal tone, as though she were talking of matters belonging to another age, and in which she was not concerned directly. "It was the end of summer when she married him—September, I think. She went to Atlanta, and they were married there, and she never came back. It was just that sudden." She snapped her fingers. "Just like that. I saw a picture of him in the paper. Sometimes I think if she'd known how much I loved her—why are there some you can't ever tell?—I think maybe she wouldn't have married; maybe it would've all been different, like I wanted it." She turned her face into the pillow, and if she cried there was no sound.

On May twentieth she was eighteen; it seemed incredible—Vincent had thought her many years older. He wanted to introduce her at a surprise party, but had finally to admit that this was an unsuitable plan. First off, though the subject was always there on the tip of his tongue, not once had he ever mentioned D. J. to any of his friends; secondly, he could visualize discouragingly well the entertainment provided them at meeting a girl about whom, while they openly shared an apartment, he knew nothing, not even her name. Still the birthday called for some kind of treat. Dinner and the theater were hopeless. She hadn't, through no fault of his, a dress of any sort. He'd given her forty-odd dollars to buy clothes, and here is what she spent it on: a leather windbreaker, a set of military brushes, a raincoat, a cigarette lighter. Also, her suitcase, which she'd brought to the apartment, had contained nothing but hotel soap, a pair of scissors she used for pruning her hair, two Bibles, and an appalling color-tinted photograph. The photograph showed a simpering middle-aged woman with dumpy features. There was an inscription: Best Wishes and Good Luck from Martha Lovejoy Hall.

Because she could not cook they had their meals out; his salary and the limitations of her wardrobe confined them mostly to the Automat—her favorite: the macaroni was so delicious!—or one of the bar-grills along Third. And so the birthday dinner was eaten in an Automat. She'd scrubbed her face until the skin shone red, trimmed and shampooed her hair, and with the messy skill of a six-year-old playing grownup, varnished her nails. She wore the leather windbreaker, and on it pinned a sheaf of violets he'd given her; it must have looked amusing, for two rowdy girls sharing their table giggled frantically. Vincent said if they didn't shut up . . .

"Oh, yeah, who do you think you are?"

"Superman. Jerk thinks he's superman."

It was too much, and Vincent lost his temper. He shoved back from the table, upsetting a ketchup jar. "Let's get the hell out of here," he said, but D. J., who had paid the fracas no attention whatever, went right on spooning blackberry cobbler; furious as he was, he waited quietly until she finished, for he respected her remoteness, and yet wondered in what period of time she lived. It was futile, he'd discovered, to question her past; still, she seemed only now and then aware of the present, and it was likely the future didn't mean much to her. Her mind was like a mirror reflecting blue space in a barren room.

"What would you like now?" he said, as they came into the street. "We could ride in a cab through the park."

She wiped off with her jacket-cuff flecks of blackberry staining the corners of her mouth, and said, "I want to go to a picture show."

The movies. Again. In the last month he'd seen so many films, snatches of Hollywood dialogue rumbled in his dreams. One Saturday at her insistence they'd bought tickets to three different theaters, cheap places where smells of latrine disinfectant poisoned the air. And each morning before leaving for work he left on the mantel fifty cents—rain or shine, she went to a picture show. But Vincent was sensitive enough to see why: there had been in his own life a certain time of limbo when he'd gone to movies every day, often sitting through several repeats of the same film; it was in its way like religion, for there, watching the shifting patterns of black and white, he knew a release of conscience similar to the kind a man must find confessing to his father.

"Handcuffs," she said, referring to an incident in *The Thirty-Nine Steps,* which they'd seen at the Beverly in a program of Hitchcock revivals. "That blonde woman and the man handcuffed together—well, it made me think of something else." She stepped into a pair of his pajamas, pinned the corsage of violets to the edge of her pillow, and folded up on the bed. "People getting caught like that, locked together."

Vincent yawned. "Uh huh," he said, and turned off the lights. "Again, happy birthday darling, it was a happy birthday?"

She said, "Once I was in this place, and there were two girls dancing; they were so free—there was just them and nobody else, and it was beautiful like a sunset." She was silent a long while; then, her slow Southern voice dragging over the words: "It was mighty nice of you to bring me violets."

"Glad—like them," he answered sleepily.

"It's a shame they have to die."

"Yes, well, good night."

"Good night."

Close-up. Oh, but John, it isn't for my sake after all we've the children to consider a divorce would ruin their lives! Fadeout. The screen trembles; rattle of drums, flourish of trumpets: R.K.O. PRESENTS . . .

Here is a hall without exit, a tunnel without end. Overhead, chandeliers sparkle, and wind-bent candles float on currents of air. Before him is an old man rocking in a rocking chair, an old man with yellow-dyed hair, powdered cheeks, kewpie-doll lips: Vincent recognizes Vincent. Go away, screams Vincent, the young and handsome, but Vincent, the old and horrid, creeps forward on all fours, and climbs spiderlike onto his back. Threats, pleas, blows, nothing will dislodge him. And so he races with his shadow, his rider jogging up and down. A serpent of lightning blazes, and all at once the tunnel seethes with men wearing white tie and tails, women costumed in brocaded gowns. He is humiliated; how gauche they must think him appearing at so elegant a gathering carrying on his back, like Sinbad, a sordid old man. The guests stand about in petrified pairs, and there is no conversation. He notices then that many are also saddled with malevolent semblances of themselves, outward embodiments of inner decay. Just beside him a lizard-like man rides an albino-eyed Negro. A man is coming toward him, the host; short, florid, bald, he steps lightly, precisely in glacé shoes; one arm, held stiffly crooked, supports a massive headless hawk whose talons, latched to the wrist, draw blood. The hawk's wings unfurl as its master struts by. On a pedestal there is perched an old-time phonograph. Winding the handle, the host supplies a record: a tinny worn-out waltz vibrates the morning-glory horn. He lifts a hand, and in a soprano voice announces: "Attention! The dancing will commence." The host with his hawk weaves in and out as round and round they dip, they turn. The walls widen, the ceiling grows tall. A girl glides into Vincent's arms, and a cracked, cruel imitation of his voice says: "Lucille, how divine; that exquisite scent, is it violet?" This is Cousin Lucille, and then, as they circle the room, her face changes. Now he waltzes with another. "Why, Connie, Connie Silver! How marvelous to see you," shrieks the voice, for Connie is quite deaf. Suddenly a gentleman with a bullet-bashed head cuts in: "Gordon, forgive me, I never meant . . ." but they are gone, Gordon and Connie, dancing together. Again, a new partner. It is D. J., and she too has a figure barnacled to her back, an enchanting auburn-haired child; like an emblem of innocence, the child cuddles to her chest a snowball kitten. "I am heavier than I look," says the child, and the terrible voice retorts, "But I am heaviest of all." The instant their hands meet he begins to feel the weight upon him diminish; the old Vincent is fading. His feet lift off the floor, he floats upward from her embrace. The victrola grinds away loud as ever, but he is rising high, and the white receding faces gleam below like mushrooms on a dark meadow.

The host releases his hawk, sends it soaring. Vincent thinks, no matter, it is a blind thing, and the wicked are safe among the blind. But the hawk wheels above him, swoops down, claws foremost; at last he knows there is to be no freedom.

And the blackness of the room filled his eyes. One arm lolled over the bed's edge, his pillow had fallen to the floor. Instinctively he reached out, asking mother-comfort of the girl beside him. Sheets smooth and cold; emptiness, and the tawdry fragrance of drying violets. He snapped up straight: "You, where are you?"

The French doors were open. An ashy trace of moon swayed on the threshold, for it was not yet light, and in the kitchen the refrigerator purred like a giant cat. A stack of papers rustled on the desk. Vincent called again, softly this time, as if he wished himself unheard. Rising, he stumbled forward on dizzy legs, and looked into the yard. She was there, leaning, half-kneeling, against the heaven tree. "What?" and she whirled around. He could not see her well, only a dark substantial shape. She came closer. A finger pressed her lips.

"What is it?" he whispered.

She rose on tiptoe, and her breath tingled in his ear. "I warn you, go inside."

"Stop this foolishness," he said in a normal voice. "Out here barefooted, you'll catch . . ." but she clamped a hand over his mouth.

"I saw him," she whispered. "He's here."

Vincent knocked her hand away. It was hard not to slap her. "Him! Him! Him! What's the matter with you? Are you—" he tried too late to prevent the word—"crazy?" There, the acknowledgment of something he'd known, but had not allowed his conscious mind to crystallize. And he thought: Why should this make a difference? A man cannot be held to account for those he loves. Untrue. Feeble-witted Lucille weaving mosaics on silk, embroidering his name on scarves; Connie, in her hushed deaf world, listening for his footstep, a sound she would surely hear; Allen T. Baker thumbing his photograph, still needing love, but old now, and lost—all betrayed. And he'd betrayed himself with talents unexploited, voyages never taken, promises unfulfilled. There had seemed nothing left him until—oh, why in his lovers must he always find the broken image of himself? Now, as he looked at her in the aging dawn, his heart was cold with the death of love.

She moved away, and under the tree. "Leave me here," she said, her eyes scanning tenement windows. "Only a moment."

Vincent waited, waited. On all sides windows looked down like the doors of dreams, and overhead, four flights up, a family's laundry whipped a washline. The setting moon was like the early moon of dusk, a vaporish cartwheel, and the sky, draining of dark, was washed with gray. Sunrise wind shook the leaves of the heaven tree, and in the paling light the yard assumed a pattern, objects a position, and from the roofs came the throaty morning rumble of pigeons. A light went on. Another.

And at last she lowered her head; whatever she was looking for, she had not found it. Or, he wondered as she turned to him with tilted lips, had she?

"Well, you're home kinda early, aren't you, Mr. Waters?" It was Mrs. Brennan, the super's bowlegged wife. "And, well, Mr. Waters—lovely weather, ain't it?—you and me got sumpin' to talk about."

"Mrs. Brennan—" how hard it was to breathe, to speak; the words grated his hurting throat, sounded loud as thunderclaps—"I'm rather ill, so if you don't mind . . ." and he tried to brush past her.

"Say, that's a pity. Ptomaine, must be ptomaine. Yessir, I tell you a person can't be too careful. It's them Jews, you know. They run all them delicatessens. Uh uh, none of that Jew food for me." She stepped before the gate, blocking his path, and pointed an admonishing finger: "Trouble with you, Mr. Waters, is that you don't lead no kinda *normal* life."

A knot of pain was set like a malignant jewel in the core of his head; each aching motion made jeweled pinpoints of color flare out. The super's wife blabbed on, but there were blank moments when, fortunately, he could not hear at all. It was like a radio—the volume turned low, then full blast. "Now I know she's a decent Christian lady, Mr. Waters, or else what would a gentleman like you be doing with—hm. Still, the fact is, Mr. Cooper don't tell lies, and he's a real calm man, besides. Been gas meter man for this district I don't know how long." A truck rolled down the street spraying water, and her voice, submerged below its roar, came up again like a shark. "Mr. Cooper had every reason to believe she meant to kill him—well, you can imagine, her standin' there with them scissors, and shoutin'. She called him an Eyetalian name. Now all you got to do is look at Mr. Cooper to know he ain't no Eyetalian. Well, you can see, Mr. Waters, such carryings-on are bound to give the house a bad . . ."

Brittle sunshine plundering the depths of his eyes made tears, and the super's wife, wagging her finger, seemed to break into separate pieces: a nose, a chin, a red, red eye. "Mr. Destronelli," he said. "Excuse me, Mrs. Brennan, I mean excuse me." She thinks I'm drunk, and I'm sick, and can't she see I'm sick? "My guest is leaving. She's leaving today, and she won't be back."

"Well, now, you don't say," said Mrs. Brennan, clucking her tongue. "Looks like she needs a rest, poor little thing. So pale, sorta. Course I don't want no more to do with them Eyetalians than the next one, but imagine thinking Mr. Cooper was an Eyetalian. Why, he's white as you or me." She tapped his shoulder solicitously. "Sorry you feel so sick, Mr. Waters; ptomaine, I tell you. A person can't be too care . . ."

The hall smelled of cooking and incinerator ashes. There was a stairway which he never used, his apartment being on the first floor, straight ahead. A match snapped fire, and Vincent, groping his way, saw a small boy—he was not more than three or four—squatting under the stairwell; he was playing with a big box of kitchen matches, and Vincent's presence appeared not to interest him. He simply struck another match. Vincent could not make his mind work well enough to phrase a reprimand, and as he waited there, tongue-tied, a door, his door, opened.

Hide. For if she saw him she would know something was wrong, suspect something. And if she spoke, if their eyes met, then he would never be able to go through with it. So he pressed into a dark corner was gone. The little boy sank back on the floor. "Whatcha doin', Mister?" She was coming—he heard the slap of her sandals, the green whisper of her raincoat. "Whatcha doin', Mister?" Quickly, his heart banging in his chest, Vincent stooped and, squeezing the child against him, pressed his hand over its mouth so it could not make a sound. He did not see her pass; it was later, after the front door clicked, that he realized she was gone. The little boy sank back on the floor. "Whatcha doin', Mister?"

Four aspirins, one right after the other, and he came back into the room; the bed had not been tidied for a week, a spilt ash tray messed the floor, odds and ends of clothing decorated improbable places, lampshades and such. But tomorrow, if he felt better, there would be a general cleaning; perhaps he'd have the walls repainted, maybe fix up the yard. Tomorrow he could begin thinking about his friends again, accept invitations, entertain. And yet this prospect, tasted in advance, was without flavor: all he'd known before seemed to him now sterile and spurious. Footsteps in the hall; could she return this soon, the movie over, the afternoon gone? Fever can make time pass so queerly, and for an instant he felt as though his bones were floating loose inside him. Clopclop, a child's sloppy shoefall, the footsteps passed up the stairs, and Vincent moved, floated toward the mirrored closet. He longed to hurry, knowing he must, but the air seemed thick with gummy fluid. He brought her suitcase from the closet, and put it on the bed, a sad cheap suitcase with rusty locks and a warped hide. He eyed it with guilt. Where would she go? How would she live? When he'd broken with Connie, Gordon, all the others, there had been about it at least a certain dignity. Really, though—and he'd thought it out—there was no other way. So he gathered her belongings. Miss Martha Lovejoy Hall peeked out from under the leather windbreaker, her music-teacher's face smiling an oblique reproach. Vincent turned her over, face down, and tucked in the frame an envelope containing twenty dollars. That would buy a ticket back to Glass Hill, or wherever it was she came from. Now he tried to close the case, and, too weak with fever, collapsed on the bed. Quick yellow wings glided through the window. A butterfly. He'd never seen a butterfly in this city, and it was like a floating mysterious flower, like a sign of some sort, and he watched with a kind of horror as it waltzed in the air. Outside, somewhere, the razzle-dazzle of a beggar's grind-organ started up; it sounded like a broken-down pianola, and it played *La Marseillaise*. The butterfly lighted on her painting, crept across crystal eyes, and flattened its wings like a ribbon bow over the loose head. He fished about in the suitcase until he found her scissors. He first purposed to slash the butterfly's wings, but it spiraled to the ceiling and hung there like a star. The scissors stabbed the hawk's heart, ate through canvas like a ravening steel mouth, scraps of picture flaking the floor like cuttings of stiff hair. He went on his knees, pushed the pieces into a pile, put them in the suitcase, and slammed the lid shut. He was crying. And through the tears the butterfly magnified on the ceiling, huge as a bird, and there was more: a flock of lilting, winking yellow; whispering lonesomely, like surf sucking a shore. The wind from their wings blew the room into space. He heaved forward, the suitcase banging his leg, and threw open the door. A match flared. The little boy said: "Whatcha doin', Mister?" And Vincent, setting the suitcase in the hall, grinned sheepishly. He closed the door like a thief, bolted the safety lock and, pulling up a chair, tilted it under the knob. In the still room there was only the subtlety of shifting sunlight and a crawling butterfly; it drifted downward like a tricky scrap of crayon paper, and landed on a candlestick. *Sometimes he is not a man at all*—she'd told him that, huddling here on the bed, talking swiftly in the minutes before dawn—*sometimes he is something very different: a hawk, a child, a butterfly.* And then she'd said: *At the place where they took me there were hundreds of old ladies, and young men, and one of the young men said he was a pirate, and one of the old ladies—she was near ninety—used to make me feel her stomach. "Feel," she'd say, "feel how strong he kicks?" This old lady took painting class, too, and her paintings looked like crazy quilts. And naturally he was in this place. Mr. Destronelli. Only he called himself Gum. Doctor Gum. Oh, he didn't fool me, even though he wore a gray wig, and made himself up to look real old and kind, I knew. And then one day I left, ran clear away, and hid under a lilac bush, and a man came along in a little red car, and he had a little mouse-haired mustache, and little cruel eyes. But it was him. And when I told him who he was he made me get out of his car. And then another man, that was in Philadelphia, picked me up in a café and took me into an alley. He talked Italian, and had tattoo pictures all over. But it was him. And the next man, he was the one who painted his toenails, sat down beside me in a movie because he thought I was a boy, and when he found out I wasn't he didn't get mad but let me live in his room, and cooked pretty things for me to eat. But he wore a silver locket and one day I looked inside and there was a picture of Miss Hall. So I knew it was him, so I had this feeling she was dead, so I knew he was going to murder me. And he will. He will."* Dusk, and nightfall, and the fibers of sound called silence wove a shiny blue mask. Waking, he peered through eyeslits, heard the frenzied pulse-beat of his watch, the scratch of a key in a lock. Somewhere in this dusk a murderer separates himself from shadow and with a rope follows the flash of silk legs up doomed stairs. And here the dreamer staring through his mask dreams of deceit. Without investigating he knows the suitcase is missing, that she has come, that she has gone; why, then, does he feel so little the pleasure of safety, and only cheated, and small—small as the night when he searched the moon through an old man's telescope?

III

Like fragments of an old letter, scattered popcorn lay trampled flat, and she, leaning back in a watchmen's attitude, allowed her gaze to hunt among it, as if deciphering here and there a word, an answer. Her eyes shifted discreetly to the man mounting the steps, Vincent. There was about him the freshness of a shower, shave, cologne, but dreary blue circled his eyes, and the crisp seersucker into which he'd changed had been made for a heavier man: a long month of pneumonia, and wakeful burning nights had lightened his weight a dozen pounds, and more. Each morning, evening, meeting her here at his gate, or near the gallery, or outside the restaurant where he lunched, a nameless disorder took hold, a paralysis of time and identity. The wordless pantomime of her pursuit contracted his heart, and there were coma-like days when she seemed not one, but all a multiple person, and her shadow in the street every shadow, following and followed. And once they'd been alone together in an automatic elevator, and he'd screamed: "I am not him! Only me, only me!" But she smiled as she'd smiled telling of the man with painted toenails, because, after all, she knew.

It was suppertime, and, not knowing where to eat, he paused under a street lamp that, blooming abruptly, fanned complex light over stone; while he waited there came a clap of thunder, and all along the street every face but two, his and the girl's, tilted upward. A blast of river breeze tossed the children's laughter as they, linking arms, pranced like carousel ponies, and carried the mama's voice who, leaning from a window, howled: rain, Rachel, rain—gonna rain gonna rain! And the gladiola, ivy-filled flower cart jerked crazily as the peddler, one eye slanted skyward, raced for shelter. A potted geranium fell off, and the little girls gathered the blooms and tucked them behind their ears. The blending spatter of running feet and raindrops tinkled on the xylophone sidewalks—the slamming of doors, the lowering of windows, then nothing but silence, and rain. Presently, with slow scraping steps, she came below the lamp to stand beside him, and it was as if the sky were a thunder-cracked mirror, for the rain fell between them like a curtain of splintered glass.

ERNEST HEMINGWAY

A Clean, Well-Lighted Place

It was late and every one had left the café except an old man who sat in the shadow the leaves of the tree made against the electric light. In the day time the street was dusty, but at night the dew settled the dust and the old man liked to sit late because he was deaf and now at night it was quiet and he felt the difference. The two waiters inside the café knew that the old man was a little drunk, and while he was a good client they knew that if he became too drunk he would leave without paying, so they kept watch on him.

"Last week he tried to commit suicide," one waiter said.

"Why?"

"He was in despair."

"What about?"

"Nothing."

"How do you know it was nothing?"

"He has plenty of money."

They sat together at a table that was close against the wall near the door of the café and looked at the terrace where the tables were all empty except where the old man sat in the shadow of the leaves of the tree that moved slightly in the wind. A girl and a soldier went by in the street. The street light shone on the brass number on his collar. The girl wore no head covering and hurried beside him.

"The guard will pick him up," one waiter said.

"What does it matter if he gets what he's after?"

"He had better get off the street now. The guard will get him. They went by five minutes ago."

The old man sitting in the shadow rapped on his saucer with his glass. The younger waiter went over to him.

"What do you want?"

The old man looked at him. "Another brandy," he said.

"You'll be drunk," the waiter said. The old man looked at him. The waiter went away.

"He'll stay all night," he said to his colleague. "I'm sleepy now. I never get into bed before three o'clock. He should have killed himself last week."

The waiter took the brandy bottle and another saucer from the counter inside the café and marched out to the old man's table. He put down the saucer and poured the glass full of brandy.

"You should have killed yourself last week," he said to the deaf man. The old man motioned with his finger. "A little more," he said. The waiter poured on into the glass so that the brandy slopped over and ran down the stem into the top saucer of the pile. "Thank you," the old man said. The waiter took the bottle back inside the café. He sat down at the table with his colleague again.

"He's drunk now," he said.

"He's drunk every night."

"What did he want to kill himself for?"

"How should I know."

"How did he do it?"

"He hung himself with a rope."

"Who cut him down?"

"His niece."

"Why did they do it?"

"Fear for his soul."

"How much money has he got?"

"He's got plenty."

"He must be eighty years old."

"Anyway I should say he was eighty."

"I wish he would go home. I never get to bed before three o'clock. What kind of hour is that to go to bed?"

"He stays up because he likes it."

"He's lonely. I'm not lonely. I have a wife waiting in bed for me."

"He had a wife once too."

"A wife would be no good to him now."

"You can't tell. He might be better with a wife."

"His niece looks after him. You said she cut him down."

"I know."

"I wouldn't want to be that old. An old man is a nasty thing."

"Not always. This old man is clean. He drinks without spilling. Even now, drunk. Look at him."

"I don't want to look at him. I wish he would go home. He has no regard for those who must work."

The old man looked from his glass across the square, then over at the waiters.

"Another brandy," he said, pointing to his glass. The waiter who was in a hurry came over.

"Finished," he said, speaking with that omission of syntax stupid people employ when talking to drunken people or foreigners. "No more tonight. Close now."

"Another," said the old man.

"No. Finished." The waiter wiped the edge of the table with a towel and shook his head.

The old man stood up, slowly counted the saucers, took a leather coin purse from his pocket and paid for the drinks, leaving half a peseta tip.

The waiter watched him go down the street, a very old man walking unsteadily but with dignity.

"Why didn't you let him stay and drink?" the unhurried waiter asked. They were putting up the shutters. "It is not half-past two."

"I want to go home to bed."

"What is an hour?"

"More to me than to him."

"An hour is the same."

"You talk like an old man yourself. He can buy a bottle and drink at home."

"It's not the same."

"No, it is not," agreed the waiter with a wife. He did not wish to be unjust. He was only in a hurry.

"And you? You have no fear of going home before your usual hour?"

"Are you trying to insult me?"

"No, hombre, only to make a joke."

"No," the waiter who was in a hurry said, rising from pulling down the metal shutters. "I have confidence. I am all confidence."

"You have youth, confidence, and a job," the older waiter said. "You have everything."

"And what do you lack?"

"Everything but work."

"You have everything I have."

"No. I have never had confidence and I am not young."

"Come on. Stop talking nonsense and lock up."

"I am of those who like to stay late at the café," the older waiter said. "With all those who do not want to go to bed. With all those who need a light for the night."

"I want to go home and into bed."

"We are of two different kinds," the older waiter said. He was now dressed to go home. "It is not only a question of youth and confidence although those things are very beautiful. Each night I am reluctant to close up because there may be some one who needs the café."

"Hombre, there are bodegas open all night long."

"You do not understand. This is a clean and pleasant café. It is well lighted. The light is very good and also, now, there are shadows of the leaves."

"Good night," said the younger waiter.

"Good night," the other said. Turning off the electric light he continued the conversation with himself. It is the light of course but it is necessary that the place be clean and pleasant. You do not want music. Certainly you do not want music. Nor can you stand before a bar with dignity although that is all that is provided for these hours. What did he fear? It was not fear or dread. It was nothing that he knew too well. It was all a nothing and a man was nothing too. It was only that and light was all it needed and a certain cleanness and order. Some lived in it and never felt it but he knew it all was nada y pues nada y nada y pues nada. Our nada who art in nada, nada be thy name thy kingdom nada thy will be nada in nada as it is in nada. Give us this nada our daily nada and nada us our nada as we nada our nadas and nada us not into nada but deliver us from nada; pues nada. Hail nothing full of nothing, nothing is with thee. He smiled and stood before a bar with a shining steam pressure coffee machine.

"What's yours?" asked the barman.

"Nada."

"Otro loco mas," said the barman and turned away.

"A little cup," said the waiter.

The barman poured it for him.

"The light is very bright and pleasant but the bar is unpolished," the waiter said.

The barman looked at him but did not answer. It was too late at night for conversation.

"You want another copita?" the barman asked.

"No, thank you," said the waiter and went out. He disliked bars and bodegas. A clean, well-lighted café was a very different thing. Now, without thinking further, he would go home to his room. He would lie in the bed and finally, with daylight, he would go to sleep. After all, he said to himself, it is probably only insomnia. Many must have it.

FLANNERY O'CONNOR

A Good Man Is Hard to Find

The Grandmother didn't want to go to Florida. She wanted to visit some of her connections in east Tennessee and she was seizing at every chance to change Bailey's mind. Bailey was the son she lived with, her only boy. He was sitting on the edge of his chair at the table, bent over the orange sports section of the *Journal*. "Now look here, Bailey," she said, "see here, read this," and she stood with one hand on her thin hip and the other rattling the newspaper at his bald head. "Here this fellow that calls himself The Misfit is aloose from the Federal Pen and headed toward Florida and you read here what it says he did to these people. Just you read it. I wouldn't take my children in any direction with a criminal like that aloose in it. I couldn't answer to my conscience if I did."

Bailey didn't look up from his reading so she wheeled around then and faced the children's mother; a young woman in slacks, whose face was as broad and innocent as a cabbage and was tied around with a green headkerchief that had two points on the top like rabbit's ears. She was sitting on the sofa, feeding the baby his apricots out of a jar. "The children have been to Florida before," the old lady said. "You all ought to take them somewhere else for a change so they would see different parts of the world and be broad. They never have been to east Tennessee."

The children's mother didn't seem to hear her but the eight-year-old boy, John Wesley, a stocky child with glasses, said, "If you don't want to go to Florida, why dontcha stay at home?" He and the little girl, June Star, were reading the funny papers on the floor.

"She wouldn't stay at home to be queen for a day," June Star said without raising her yellow head.

"Yes and what would you do if this fellow, The Misfit, caught you?" the grandmother asked.

"I'd smack his face," John Wesley said.

"She wouldn't stay at home for a million bucks," June Star said. "Afraid she'd miss something. She has to go everywhere we go."

"All right, Miss," the grandmother said. "Just remember that the next time you want me to curl your hair."

June Star said her hair was naturally curly.

The next morning the grandmother was the first one in the car, ready to go. She had her big black valise that looked like the head of a hippopotamus in one corner, and underneath it she was hiding a basket with Pitty Sing, the cat, in it. She didn't intend for the cat to be left alone in the house for three days because he would miss her too much and she was afraid he might brush against one of the gas burners and accidentally asphyxiate himself. Her son, Bailey, didn't like to arrive at a motel with a cat.

She sat in the middle of the back seat with John Wesley and June Star on either side of her. Bailey and the children's mother and the baby sat in the front and they left Atlanta at eight forty-five with the mileage on the car at 55890. The grandmother wrote this down because she thought it would be interesting to say how many miles they had been when they got back. It took them twenty minutes to reach the outskirts of the city.

The old lady settled herself comfortably, removing her white cotton gloves and putting them up with her purse on the shelf in front of the back window. The children's mother still had on slacks and still had her head tied up in a green kerchief, but the grandmother had on a navy blue straw sailor hat with a bunch of white violets on the brim and a navy blue dress with a small white dot in the print. Her collar and cuffs were white organdy trimmed with lace and at her neckline she had pinned a purple spray of cloth violets containing a sachet. In case of an accident, anyone seeing her dead on the highway would know at once that she was a lady.

She said she thought it was going to be a good day for driving, neither too hot nor too cold, and she cautioned Bailey that the speed limit was fifty-five miles an hour and that the patrolmen hid themselves behind billboards and small clumps of trees and sped out after you before you had a chance to slow down. She pointed out interesting details of the scenery: Stone Mountain; the blue granite that in some places came up to both sides of the highway; the brilliant red clay banks slightly streaked with purple; and the various crops that made rows of green lace-work on the ground. The trees were full of silver-white sunlight and the meanest of them sparkled. The children were reading comic magazines and their mother had gone back to sleep.

"Let's go through Georgia fast so we don't have to look at it much," John Wesley said.

"If I were a little boy," said the grandmother, "I wouldn't talk about my native state that way. Tennessee has the mountains and Georgia has the hills."

"Tennessee is just a hillbilly dumping ground," John Wesley said, "and Georgia is a lousy state too."

"You said it," June Star said.

"In my time," said the grandmother, folding her thin veined fingers, "children were more respectful of their native states and their parents and everything else. People did right then. Oh look at the cute little pickaninny!" she said and pointed to a Negro child standing in the door of a shack. "Wouldn't that make a picture, now?" she asked and they all turned and looked at the little Negro out of the back window. He waved.

"He didn't have any britches on," June Star said.

"He probably didn't have any," the grandmother explained. "Little niggers in the country don't have things like we do. If I could paint, I'd paint that picture," she said.

The children exchanged comic books.

The grandmother offered to hold the baby and the children's mother passed him over the front seat to her. She set him on her knee and bounced him and told him about the things they were passing. She rolled her eyes and screwed up her mouth and stuck her leathery thin face into his smooth bland one. Occasionally he gave her a faraway smile. They passed a large cotton field with five or six graves fenced in the middle of it, like a small island. "Look at the graveyard!" the grandmother said, pointing it out. "That was the old family burying ground. That belonged to the plantation."

"Where's the plantation?" John Wesley asked.

"Gone With the Wind," said the grandmother. "Ha. Ha."

When the children finished all the comic books they had brought, they opened the lunch and ate it. The grandmother ate a peanut butter sandwich and an olive and would not let the children throw the box and the paper napkins out the window. When there was nothing else to do they played a game by choosing a cloud and making the other two guess what shape it suggested. John Wesley took one the shape of a cow and June Star guessed a cow and John Wesley said, no, an automobile, and June Star said he didn't play fair, and they began to slap each other over the grandmother.

The grandmother said she would tell them a story if they would keep quiet. When she told a story, she rolled her eyes and waved her head and was very dramatic. She said once when she was a maiden lady she had been courted by a Mr. Edgar Atkins Teagarden from Jasper, Georgia. She said he was a very good-looking man and a gentleman and that he brought her a watermelon every Saturday afternoon with his initials cut in it, E.A.T. Well, one Saturday, she said, Mr. Teagarden brought the watermelon and there was nobody at home and he left it on the front porch and returned in his buggy to Jasper, but she never got the watermelon, she said, because a nigger boy ate it when he saw the initials, E. A. T.! This story tickled John Wesley's funny bone and he giggled and giggled but June Star didn't think it was any good. She said she wouldn't marry a man that just brought her a watermelon on Saturday. The grandmother said she would have done well to marry Mr. Teagarden because he was a gentleman and had bought Coco-Cola stock when it first came out and that he had died only a few years ago, a very wealthy man.

They stopped at The Tower for barbecued sandwiches. The Tower was a part stucco and part wood filling station and dance hall set in a clearing outside of Timothy. A fat man named Red Sammy Butts ran it and there were signs stuck here and there on the building and for miles up and down the highway saying, TRY RED SAMMY'S FAMOUS BARBECUE. NONE LIKE FAMOUS RED SAMMY'S! RED SAM! THE FAT BOY WITH THE HAPPY LAUGH. A VETERAN! RED SAMMY'S YOUR MAN!

Red Sammy was lying on the bare ground outside The Tower with his head under a truck while a gray monkey about a foot high, chained to a small chinaberry tree, chattered nearby. The monkey sprang back into the tree and got on the highest limb as soon as he saw the children jump out of the car and run toward him.

Inside, The Tower was a long dark room with a counter at one end and tables at the other and dancing space in the middle. They all sat down at a broad table next to the nickelodeon and Red Sam's wife, a tall burnt-brown woman with hair and eyes lighter than her skin, came and took their order. The children's mother put a dime in the machine and played "The Tennessee Waltz," and the grandmother said that tune always made her want to dance. She asked Bailey if he would like to dance but he only glared at her. He didn't have a naturally sunny disposition like she did and trips made him nervous. The grandmother's brown eyes were very bright. She swayed her head from side to side and pretended she was dancing in her chair. June Star said play something she could tap to so the children's mother put in another dime and played a fast number and June Star stepped out onto the dance floor and did her tap routine.

"Ain't she cute?" Red Sam's wife said, leaning over the counter. "Would you like to come be my little girl?"

"No I certainly wouldn't," June Star said. "I wouldn't live in a broken-down place like this for a million bucks!" and she ran back to the table.

"Ain't she cute?" the woman repeated, stretching her mouth politely.

"Aren't you ashamed?" hissed the grandmother.

Red Sam came in and told his wife to quit lounging on the counter and hurry up with these people's order. His khaki trousers reached just to his hip bones and his stomach hung over them like a sack of meal swaying under his shirt. He came over and sat down at a table nearby and let out a combination sigh and yodel. "You can't win," he said. "You can't win," and he wiped his sweating red face off with a gray handkerchief. "These days you don't know who to trust," he said. "Ain't that the truth?"

"People are certainly not nice like they used to be," said the grandmother.

"Two fellers come in here last week," Red Sammy said, "driving a Chrysler. It was a old beat-up car but it was a good one and these boys looked all right to me. Said they worked at the mill and you know I let them fellers charge the gas they bought? Now why did I do that?"

"Because you're a good man!" the grandmother said at once.

"Yes'm, I suppose so," Red Sam said as if he were struck with this answer.

His wife brought the orders, carrying the five plates all at once without a tray, two in each hand and one balanced on her arm. "It isn't a soul in this green world of God's that you can trust," she said. "And I don't count nobody out of that, not nobody," she repeated, looking at Red Sammy.

"Did you read about that criminal, The Misfit, that's escaped?" asked the grandmother.

"I wouldn't be a bit surprised if he didn't attact this place right here," said the woman. "If he hears about it being here, I wouldn't be none surprised to see him. If he hears it's two cent in the cash register, I wouldn't be a tall surprised if he . . ."

"That'll do," Red Sam said. "Go bring these people their Co'Colas," and the woman went off to get the rest of the order.

"A good man is hard to find," Red Sammy said. "Everything is getting terrible. I remember the day you could go off and leave your screen door unlatched. Not no more."

He and the grandmother discussed better times. The old lady said that in her opinion Europe was entirely to blame for the way things were now. She said the way Europe acted you would think we were made of money and Red Sam said it was no use talking about it, she was exactly right. The children ran outside into the white sunlight and looked at the monkey in the lacy chinaberry tree. He was busy catching fleas on himself and biting each one carefully between his teeth as if it were a delicacy.

They drove off again into the hot afternoon. The grandmother took cat naps and woke up every few minutes with her own snoring. Outside of Toombsboro she woke up and recalled an old plantation that she had visited in this neighborhood once when she was a young lady. She said the house had six white columns across the front and that there was an avenue of oaks leading up to it and two little wooden trellis arbors on either side in front where you sat down with your suitor after a stroll in the garden. She recalled exactly which road to turn off to get to it. She knew that Bailey would not be willing to lose any time looking at an old house, but the more she talked about it, the more she wanted to see it once again and find out if the little twin arbors were still standing. "There was a secret panel in this house," she said craftily, not telling the truth but wishing that she were, "and the story went that all the family silver was hidden in it when Sherman came through but it was never found . . ."

"Hey!" John Wesley said. "Let's go see it! We'll find it! We'll poke all the woodwork and find it! Who lives there? Where do you turn off at? Hey Pop, can't we turn off there?"

"We never have seen a house with a secret panel!" June Star shrieked. "Let's go to the house with the secret panel! Hey, Pop, can't we go see the house with the secret panel!"

"It's not far from here, I know," the grandmother said. "It wouldn't take over twenty minutes."

Bailey was looking straight ahead. His jaw was as rigid as a horseshoe. "No," he said.

The children began to yell and scream that they wanted to see the house with the secret panel. John Wesley kicked the back of the front seat and June Star hung over her mother's shoulder and whined desperately into her ear that they never had any fun even on their vacation, that they could never do what THEY wanted to do. The baby began to scream and John Wesley kicked the back of the seat so hard that his father could feel the blows in his kidney.

"All right!" he shouted and drew the car to a stop at the side of the road. "Will you all shut up? Will you all just shut up for one second? If you don't shut up, we won't go anywhere."

"It would be very educational for them," the grandmother murmured.

"All right," Bailey said, "but get this. This is the only time we're going to stop for anything like this. This is the one and only time."

"The dirt road that you have to turn down is about a mile back," the grandmother directed. "I marked it when we passed."

"A dirt road," Bailey groaned.

After they had turned around and were headed toward the dirt road, the grandmother recalled other points about the house, the beautiful glass over the front doorway and the candle-lamp in the hall. John Wesley said that the secret panel was probably in the fireplace.

"You can't go inside this house," Bailey said. "You don't know who lives there."

"While you all talk to the people in front, I'll run around behind and get in a window," John Wesley suggested.

"We'll all stay in the car," his mother said.

They turned onto the dirt road and the car raced roughly along in a swirl of pink dust. The grandmother recalled the times when there were no paved roads and thirty miles was a day's journey. The dirt road was hilly and there were sudden washes in it and sharp curves on dangerous embankments. All at once they would be on a hill, looking down over the blue tops of trees for miles around, then the next minute, they would be in a red depression with the dust-coated trees looking down on them.

"This place had better turn up in a minute," Bailey said, "or I'm going to turn around."

The road looked as if no one had traveled on it in months.

"It's not much farther," the grandmother said and just as she said it, a horrible thought came to her. The thought was so embarrassing that she turned red in the face and her eyes dilated and her feet jumped up, upsetting her valise in the corner. The instant the valise moved, the newspaper top she had over the basket under it rose with a snarl and Pitty Sing, the cat, sprang onto Bailey's shoulder.

The children were thrown to the floor and their mother, clutching the baby, was thrown out the door onto the ground; the old lady was thrown into the front seat. The car turned over once and landed right-side-up in a gulch on the side of the road. Bailey remained in the driver's seat with the cat—gray-striped with a broad white face and an orange nose—clinging to his neck like a caterpillar.

As soon as the children saw they could move their arms and legs, they scrambled out of the car, shouting, "We've had an ACCIDENT!" The grandmother was curled up under the dashboard, hoping she was injured so that Bailey's wrath would not come down on her all at once. The horrible thought she had had before the accident was that the house she had remembered so vividly was not in Georgia but in Tennessee.

Bailey removed the cat from his neck with both hands and flung it out the window against the side of a pine tree. Then he got out of the car and started looking for the children's mother. She was sitting against the side of the red gutted ditch, holding the screaming baby, but she only had a cut down her face and a broken shoulder. "We've had an ACCIDENT!" the children screamed in a frenzy of delight.

"But nobody's killed," June Star said with disappointment as the grandmother limped out of the car, her hat still pinned to her head but the broken front brim standing up at jaunty angle and the violet spray hanging off the side. They all sat down in the ditch, except the children, to recover from the shock. They were all shaking.

"Maybe a car will come along," said the children's mother hoarsely.

"I believe I have injured an organ," said the grandmother, pressing her side, but no one answered her. Bailey's teeth were clattering. He had on a yellow sport shirt with bright blue parrots designed in it and his face was as yellow as the shirt. The grandmother decided that she would not mention that the house was in Tennessee.

The road was about ten feet above and they could see only the tops of the trees on the other side of it. Behind the ditch they were sitting in there were more woods, tall and dark and deep. In a few minutes they saw a car some distance away on top of a hill, coming slowly as if the occupants were watching them. The grandmother stood up and waved both arms dramatically to attract their attention. The car continued to come on slowly, disappeared around a bend and appeared again, moving even slower, on top of the hill they had gone over. It was a big black battered hearse-like automobile. There were three men in it.

It came to a stop just over them and for some minutes, the driver looked down with a steady expressionless gaze to where they were sitting, and didn't speak. Then he turned his head and muttered something to the other two and they got out. One was a fat boy in black trousers and a red sweat shirt with a silver stallion embossed on the front of it. He moved around on the right side of them and stood staring, his mouth partly open in a kind of loose grin. The other had on khaki pants and a blue striped coat and a gray hat pulled down very low, hiding most of his face. He came around slowly on the left side. Neither spoke.

The driver got out of the car and stood by the side of it, looking down at them. He was an older man than the other two. His hair was just beginning to gray and he wore silver-rimmed spectacles that gave him a scholarly look. He had a long creased face and didn't have on any shirt or undershirt. He had on blue jeans that were too tight for him and was holding a black hat and a gun. The two boys also had guns.

"We've had an ACCIDENT!" the children screamed.

The grandmother had the peculiar feeling that the bespectacled man was someone she knew. His face was as familiar to her as if she had known him all her life but she could not recall who he was. He moved away from the car and began to come down the embankment, placing his feet carefully so that he wouldn't slip. He had on tan and white shoes and no socks, and his ankles were red and thin. "Good afternoon," he said. "I see you all had you a little spill."

"We turned over twice!" said the grandmother.

"Oncet," he corrected. "We see it happen. Try their car and see will it run, Hiram," he said quietly to the boy with the gray hat.

"What you got that gun for?" John Wesley asked. "Whatcha gonna do with that gun?"

"Lady," the man said to the children's mother, "would you mind calling them children to sit down by you? Children make me nervous. I want all you all to sit down right together there where you're at."

"What are you telling US what to do for?" June Star asked.

Behind them the line of woods gaped like a dark open mouth. "Come here," said their mother.

"Look here now," Bailey began suddenly, "we're in a predicament! We're in . . ."

The grandmother shrieked. She scrambled to her feet and stood staring.

"You're The Misfit!" she said. "I recognized you at once!"

"Yes'm," the man said, smiling slightly as if he were pleased in spite of himself to be known, "but it would have been better for all of you, lady, if you hadn't of reckernized me."

Bailey turned his head sharply and said something to his mother that shocked even the children. The old lady began to cry and The Misfit reddened.

"Lady," he said, "don't you get upset. Sometimes a man says things he don't mean. I don't reckon he meant to talk to you thataway."

"You wouldn't shoot a lady, would you?" the grandmother said and removed a clean handkerchief from her cuff and began to slap at her eyes with it.

The Misfit pointed the toe of his shoe into the ground and made a little hole and then covered it up again. "I would hate to have to," he said.

"Listen," the grandmother almost screamed, "I know you're a good man. You don't look a bit like you have common blood. I know you must come from nice people!"

"Yes mam," he said, "finest people in the world." When he smiled he showed a row of strong white teeth. "God never made a finer woman than my mother and my daddy's heart was pure gold," he said. The boy with the red sweat shirt had come around behind them and was standing with his gun at his hip. The Misfit squatted down on the ground. "Watch them children, Bobby Lee," he said. "You know they make me nervous." He looked at the six of them huddled together in front of him and he seemed to be embarrassed as if he couldn't think of anything to say. "Ain't a cloud in the sky," he remarked, looking up at it. "Don't see no sun but don't see no cloud neither."

"Yes, it's a beautiful day," said the grandmother. "Listen," she said, "you shouldn't call yourself The Misfit because I know you're a good man at heart. I can just look at you and tell."

"Hush!" Bailey yelled. "Hush! Everybody shut up and let me handle this!" He was squatting in the position of a runner about to sprint forward but he didn't move.

"I pre-chate that, lady," The Misfit said and drew a little circle in the ground with the butt of his gun.

"It'll take a half a hour to fix this here car," Hiram called, looking over the raised hood of it.

"Well, first you and Bobby Lee get him and that little boy to step over yonder with you," The Misfit said, pointing to Bailey and John Wesley. "The boys want to ast you something," he said to Bailey. "Would you mind stepping back in them woods there with them?"

"Listen," Bailey began, "we're in a terrible predicament! Nobody realizes what this is," and his voice cracked. His eyes were as blue and intense as the parrots in his shirt and he remained perfectly still.

The grandmother reached up to adjust her hat brim as if she were going to the woods with him but it came off in her hand. She stood staring at it and after a second she let it fall on the ground. Hiram pulled Bailey up by the arm as if he were assisting an old man. John Wesley caught hold of his father's hand and Bobby Lee followed. They went off toward the woods and just as they reached the dark edge, Bailey turned and supporting himself against a gray naked pine trunk, he shouted, "I'll be back in a minute, Mamma, wait on me!"

"Come back this instant" his mother shrilled but they all disappeared into the woods.

"Bailey Boy!" the grandmother called in a tragic voice but she found she was looking at The Misfit squatting on the ground in front of her. "I just know you're a good man," she said desperately. "You're not a bit common!"

"Nome, I ain't a good man," The Misfit said after a second as if he had considered her statement carefully, "but ain't the worst in the world neither. My daddy said I was different breed of dog from my brothers and sisters. 'You know,' Daddy said, 'it's some that can live their whole life out without asking about it and it's others has to know why it is, and this boy is one of the latters. He's going to be into everything!' " He put on his black hat and looked up suddenly and then away deep into the woods as if he were embarrassed again. "I'm sorry I don't have on a shirt before you ladies," he said, hunching his shoulders slightly. "We buried our clothes that we had on when we escaped and we're just making do until we can get better. We borrowed these from some folks we met," he explained.

"That's perfectly all right," the grandmother said. "Maybe Bailey has an extra shirt in his suitcase."

"I'll look and see terrectly," The Misfit said.

"Where are they taking him?" the children's mother screamed.

"Daddy was a card himself," The Misfit said. "You couldn't put anything over on him. He never got in trouble with the Authorities though. Just had the knack of handling them."

"You could be honest too if you'd only try," said the grandmother. "Think how wonderful it would be to settle down and live a comfortable life and not have to think about somebody chasing you all the time."

The Misfit kept scratching in the ground with the butt of his gun as if he were thinking about it. "Yes'm, somebody is always after you," he murmured.

The grandmother noticed how thin his shoulder blades were just behind his hat because she was standing up looking down on him. "Do you ever pray?" she asked.

He shook his head. All she saw was thc black hat wiggle between his shoulder blades. "Nome," he said.

There was a pistol shot from the woods, followed closely by another. Then silence. The old lady's head jerked around. She could hear the wind move through the tree tops like a long satisfied insuck of breath. "Bailey Boy!" she called.

"I was a gospel singer for a while," The Misfit said. "I been most everything. Been in the arm service, both land and sea, at home and abroad, been twict married, been an undertaker, been with the railroads, plowed Mother Earth, been in a tornado, seen a man burnt alive oncet," and he looked up at the children's mother and the little girl who were sitting close together, their faces white and their eyes glassy; "I even seen a woman flogged," he said.

"Pray, pray," the grandmother began, "pray, pray . . ."

"I never was a bad boy that I remember of," The Misfit said in an almost dreamy voice, "but somewheres along the line I done something wrong and got sent to the penitentiary. I was buried alive," and he looked up and held her attention to him by a steady stare.

"That's when you should have started to pray," she said. "What did you do to get sent to the penitentiary that first time?"

"Turn to the right, it was a wall," The Misfit said, looking up again at the cloudless sky. "Turn to the left, it was a wall. Look up it was a ceiling, look down it was a floor. I forget what I done, lady. I set there and set there, trying to remember what it was I done and I ain't recalled it to this day. Oncet in a while, I would think it was coming to me, but it never come."

"Maybe they put you in by mistake," the old lady said vaguely.

"Nome," he said. "It wasn't no mistake. They had the papers on me."

"You must have stolen something," she said.

The Misfit sneered slightly. "Nobody had nothing I wanted," he said. "It was a head-doctor at the penitentiary said what I had done was kill my daddy but I known that for a lie. My daddy died in nineteen ought nineteen of the epidemic flu and I never had a thing to do with it. He was buried in the Mount Hopewell Baptist churchyard and you can go there and see for yourself."

"If you would pray," the old lady said, "Jesus would help you."

"That's right," The Misfit said.

"Well then, why don't you pray?" she asked trembling with delight suddenly.

"I don't want no help," he said. "I'm doing all right by myself."

Bobby Lee and Hiram came ambling back from the woods. Bobby Lee was dragging a yellow shirt with bright blue parrots in it.

"Throw me that shirt, Bobby Lee," The Misfit said. The shirt came flying at him and landed on his shoulder and he put it on. The grandmother couldn't name what the shirt reminded her of. "No, lady," The Misfit said while he was buttoning it up, "I found out the crime don't matter. You can do one thing or you can do another, kill a man or take a tire off his car, because sooner or later you're going to forget what it was you done and just be punished for it."

The children's mother had begun to make heaving noises as if she couldn't get her breath. "Lady," he asked, "would you and that little girl like to step off yonder with Bobby Lee and Hiram and join your husband?"

"Yes, thank you," the mother said faintly. Her left arm dangled helplessly and she was holding the baby, who had gone to sleep, in the other. "Hep that lady up, Hiram," The Misfit said as she struggled to climb out of the ditch, "and Bobby Lee, you hold onto that little girl's hand."

"I don't want to hold hands with him," June Star said. "He reminds me of a pig."

The fat boy blushed and laughed and caught her by the arm and pulled her off into the woods after Hiram and her mother.

Alone with The Misfit, the grandmother found that she had lost her voice. There was not a cloud in the sky nor any sun. There was nothing around her but woods. She wanted to tell him that he must pray. She opened and closed her mouth several times before anything came out. Finally she found herself saying, "Jesus. Jesus," meaning, Jesus will help you, but the way she was saying it, it sounded as if she might be cursing.

"Yes'm," The Misfit said as if he agreed. "Jesus thown everything off balance. It was the same case with Him as with me except He hadn't committed any crime and they could prove I had committed one because they had the papers on me. Of course," he said, "they never shown me my papers. That's why I sign myself now. I said long ago, you get you a signature and sign everything you do and keep a copy of it. Then you'll know what you done and you can hold up the crime to the punishment and see do they match and in the end you'll have something to prove you ain't been treated right. I call myself The Misfit," he said, "because I can't make what all I done wrong fit what all I gone through in punishment."

There was a piercing scream from the woods, followed closely by a pistol report. "Does it seem right to you, lady, that one is punished a heap and another ain't punished at all?"

"Jesus!" the old lady cried. "You've got good blood! I know you wouldn't shoot a lady! I know you come from nice people! Pray! Jesus, you ought not to shoot a lady. I'll give you all the money I've got!"

"Lady," The Misfit said, looking beyond her far into the woods, "there never was a body that give the undertaker a tip."

There were two more pistol reports and the grandmother raised her head like a parched old turkey hen crying for water and called, "Bailey Boy, Bailey Boy!" as if her heart would break.

"Jesus was the only One that ever raised the dead," The Misfit continued, "and He shouldn't have done it. He thown everything off balance. If He did what He said, then it's nothing for you to do but thow away everything and follow Him, and if He didn't then it's nothing for you to do but enjoy the few minutes you got left the best way you can—by killing somebody or burning down his house or doing some other meanness to him. No pleasure but meanness," he said and his voice had become almost a snarl.

"Maybe He didn't raise the dead," the old lady mumbled, not knowing what she was saying and feeling so dizzy that she sank down in the ditch with her legs twisted under her.

"I wasn't there so I can't say He didn't," The Misfit said. "I wisht I had of been there," he said, hitting the ground with his fist. "It ain't right I wasn't there because if I had of been there I would of known. Listen lady," he said in a high voice, "if I had of been there I would of known and I wouldn't be like I am now." His voice seemed about to crack and the grandmother's head cleared for an instant. She saw the man's face twisted close to her own as if he were going to cry and she murmured, "Why, you're one of my babies. You're one of my own children!" She reached out and touched him on the shoulder. The Misfit sprang back as if a snake had bitten him and shot her three times through the chest. Then he put his gun down on the ground and took off his glasses and began to clean them.

Hiram and Bobby Lee returned from the woods and stood over the ditch, looking down at the grandmother who half sat and half lay in a puddle of blood with her legs crossed under her like a child's and her face smiling up at the cloudless sky.

Without his glasses, The Misfit's eyes were red-rimmed and pale and defenseless-looking. "Take her off and thow her where you thown the others," he said, picking up the cat that was rubbing itself against his leg.

"She was a talker, wasn't she?" Bobby Lee said, sliding down the ditch with a yodel.

"She would of been a good woman," The Misfit said, "if it had been somebody there to shoot her every minute of her life."

"Some fun!" Bobby Lee said.

"Shut up, Bobby Lee," the Misfit said. "It's no real pleasure in life."

FLANNERY O'CONNOR

The Artificial Nigger

Mr. Head awakened to discover that the room was full of moonlight. He sat up and stared at the floor boards—the color of silver—and then at the ticking on his pillow, which might have been brocade, and after a second, he saw half of the moon five feet away in his shaving mirror, paused as if it were waiting for his permission to enter. It rolled forward and cast a dignifying light on everything. The straight chair against the wall looked stiff and attentive as if it were awaiting an order and Mr. Head's trousers, hanging to the back of it, had an almost noble air, like the garment some great man had just flung to his servant; but the face on the moon was a grave one. It gazed across the room and out the window where it floated over the horse stall and appeared to contemplate itself with the look of a young man who sees his old age before him.

Mr. Head could have said to it that age was a choice blessing and that only with years does a man enter into that calm understanding of life that makes him a suitable guide for the young. This, at least, had been his own experience.

He sat up and grasped the iron posts at the foot of his bed and raised himself until he could see the face on the alarm clock which sat on an overturned bucket beside the chair. The hour was two in the morning. The alarm on the clock did not work but he was not dependent on any mechanical means to awaken him. Sixty years had not dulled his responses; his physical reactions, like his moral ones, were guided by his will and strong character, and these could be seen plainly in his features. He had a long tube-like face with a long rounded open jaw and a long depressed nose. His eyes were alert but quiet, and in the miraculous moonlight they had a look of composure and of ancient wisdom as if they belonged to one of the great guides of men. He might have been Vergil summoned in the middle of the night to go to Dante, or better, Raphael, awakened by a blast of God's light to fly to the side of Tobias. The only dark spot in the room was Nelson's pallet, underneath the shadow of the window.

Nelson was hunched over on his side, his knees under his chin and his heels under his bottom. His new suit and hat were in the boxes that they had been sent in and these were on the floor at the foot of the pallet where he could get his hands on them as soon as he woke up. The slop jar, out of the shadow and made snow-white in the moonlight, appeared to stand guard over him like a small personal angel. Mr. Head lay back down, feeling entirely confident that he could carry out the moral mission of the coming day. He meant to be up before Nelson and to have the breakfast cooking by the time he awakened. The boy was always irked when Mr. Head was the first up. They would have to leave the house at four to get to the railroad junction by five-thirty. The train was to stop for them at five forty-five and they had to be there on time for this train was stopping merely to accommodate them.

This would be the boy's first trip to the city though he claimed it would be his second because he had been born there. Mr. Head had tried to point out to him that when he was born he didn't have the intelligence to determine his whereabouts but this had made no impression on the child at all and he continued to insist that this was to be his second trip. It would be Mr. Head's third trip. Nelson had said, "I will've already been there twict and I ain't but ten."

Mr. Head had contradicted him.

"If you ain't been there in fifteen years, how you know you'll be able to find your way about?" Nelson had asked. "How you know it hasn't changed some?"

"Have you ever," Mr. Head had asked, "seen me lost?"

Nelson certainly had not but he was a child who was never satisfied until he had given an impudent answer and he replied, "It's nowhere around here to get lost at."

"The day is going to come," Mr. Head prophesied, "when you'll find you ain't as smart as you think you are." He had been thinking about this trip for several months but it was for the most part in moral terms that he conceived it. It was to be a lesson that the boy would never forget. He was to find out from it that he had no cause for pride merely because he had been born in a city. He was to find out that the city is not a great place. Mr. Head meant him to see everything there is to see in a city so that he would be content to stay at home for the rest of his life. He fell asleep thinking how the boy would at last find out that he was not as smart as he thought he was.

He was awakened at three-thirty by the smell of fatback frying and he leaped off his cot. The pallet was empty and the clothes boxes had been thrown open. He put on his trousers and ran into the other room.

The boy had a corn pone on cooking and had fried the meat. He was sitting in the half-dark at the table, drinking cold coffee out of a can. He had on his new suit and his new gray hat pulled low over his eyes. It was too big for him but they had ordered it a size large because they expected his head to grow. He didn't say anything but his entire figure suggested satisfaction at having arisen before Mr. Head.

Mr. Head went to the stove and brought the meat to the table in the skillet. "It's no hurry," he said. "You'll get there soon enough and it's no guarantee you'll like it when you do neither," and he sat down across from the boy whose hat teetered back slowly to reveal a fiercely expressionless face, very much the same shape as the old man's. They were grandfather and grandson but they looked enough alike to be brothers and brothers not too far apart in age, for Mr. Head had a youthful expression by daylight, while the boy's look was ancient, as if he knew everything already and would be pleased to forget it.

Mr. Head had once had a wife and daughter and when the wife died, the daughter ran away and returned after an interval with Nelson. Then one morning, without getting out of bed, she died and left Mr. Head with sole care of the year-old child. He had made the mistake of telling Nelson that he had been born in Atlanta. If he hadn't told him that, Nelson couldn't have insisted that this was going to be his second trip.

"You may not like it a bit," Mr. Head continued. "It'll be full of niggers."

The boy made a face as if he could handle a nigger.

"All right," Mr. Head said. "You ain't ever seen a nigger."

"You wasn't up very early," Nelson said.

"You ain't ever seen a nigger," Mr. Head repeated. "There hasn't been a nigger in this country since we run that one out twelve years ago and that was before you were born." He looked at the boy as if he were daring him to say he had ever seen a Negro.

"How you know I never saw a nigger when I lived there before?" Nelson asked. "I probably saw a lot of niggers."

"If you seen one you didn't know what he was," Mr. Head said, completely exasperated. "A six-month-old child don't know a nigger from anybody else."

"I reckon I'll know a nigger if I see one," the boy said and got up and straightened his slick sharply creased gray hat and went outside to the privy.

They reached the junction some time before the train was due to arrive and stood about two feet from the first set of tracks. Mr. Head carried a paper sack with some biscuits and a can of sardines in it for their lunch. A coarse-looking orange-colored sun coming up behind the east range of mountains was making the sky a dull red behind them, but in front of them it was still gray and they faced a gray transparent moon, hardly stronger than a thumbprint and completely without light. A small tin switch box and a black fuel tank were all there was to mark the place as a junction; the tracks were double and did not converge again until they were hidden behind the bends at either end of the clearing. Trains passing appeared to emerge from a tunnel of trees and, hit for a second by the cold sky, vanish terrified into the woods again. Mr. Head had had to make special arrangements with the ticket agent to have this train stop and he was secretly afraid it would not, in which case, he knew Nelson would say, "I never thought no train was going to stop for you." Under the useless morning moon the tracks looked white and fragile. Both the old man and the child stared ahead as if they were awaiting an apparition.

Then suddenly, before Mr. Head could make up his mind to turn back, there was a deep warning bleat and the train appeared, gliding very slowly, almost silently around the bend of trees about two hundred yards down the track, with one yellow front light shining. Mr. Head was still not certain it would stop and he felt it would make an even bigger idiot of him if it went by slowly. Both he and Nelson, however, were prepared to ignore the train if it passed them.

The engine charged by, filling their noses with the smell of hot metal and then the second coach came to a stop exactly where they were standing. A conductor with the face of an ancient bloated bulldog was on the step as if he expected them, though he did not look as if it mattered one way or the other to him if they got on or not. "To the right," he said.

Their entry took only a fraction of a second and the train was already speeding on as they entered the quiet car. Most of the travelers were still sleeping, some with their heads hanging off the chair arms, some stretched across two seats, and some sprawled out with their feet in the aisle. Mr. Head saw two unoccupied seats and pushed Nelson toward them. "Get in there by the winder," he said in his normal voice which was very loud at this hour of the morning. "Nobody cares if you sit there because it's nobody in it. Sit right there."

"I heard you," the boy muttered. "It's no use in you yelling," and he sat down and turned his head to the glass. There he saw a pale ghost-like face scowling at him beneath the brim of a pale ghost-like hat. His grandfather, looking quickly too, saw a different ghost, pale but grinning, under a black hat.

Mr. Head sat down and settled himself and took out his ticket and started reading aloud everything that was printed on it. People began to stir. Several woke up and stared at him. "Take off your hat," he said to Nelson and took off his own and put it on his knee. He had a small amount of white hair that had turned tobacco-colored over the years and this lay flat across the back of his head. The front of his head was bald and creased. Nelson took off his hat and put it on his knee and they waited for the conductor to come ask for their tickets.

The man across the aisle from them was spread out over two seats, his feet propped on the window and his head jutting into the aisle. He had on a light blue suit and a yellow shirt unbuttoned at the neck. His eyes had just opened and Mr. Head was ready to introduce himself when the conductor came up from behind and growled, "Tickets."

When the conductor had gone, Mr. Head gave Nelson the return half of his ticket and said, "Now put that in your pocket and don't lose it or you'll have to stay in the city."

"Maybe I will," Nelson said as if this were a reasonable suggestion.

Mr. Head ignored him. "First time this boy has ever been on a train," he explained to the man across the aisle, who was sitting up now on the edge of his seat with both feet on the floor.

Nelson jerked his hat on again and turned angrily to the window.

"He's never seen anything before," Mr. Head continued. "Ignorant as the day he was born, but I mean for him to get his fill once and for all."

The boy leaned forward, across his grandfather and toward the stranger. "I was born in the city," he said. "I was born there. This is my second trip." He said it in a high positive voice but the man across the aisle didn't look as if he understood. There were heavy purple circles under his eyes.

Mr. Head reached across the aisle and tapped him on the arm. "The thing to do with a boy," he said sagely, "is to show him all it is to show. Don't hold nothing back."

"Yeah," the man said. He gazed down at his swollen feet and lifted the left one about ten inches from the floor. After a minute he put it down and lifted the other. All through the car people began to get up and move about and yawn and stretch. Separate voices could be heard here and there and then a general hum. Suddenly Mr. Head's serene expression changed. His mouth almost closed and a light, fierce and cautious both, came into his eyes. He was looking down the length of the car. Without turning, he caught Nelson by the arm and pulled him forward. "Look," he said.

A huge coffee-colored man was coming slowly forward. He had on a light suit and a yellow satin tie with a ruby pin in it. One of his hands rested on his stomach which rode majestically under his buttoned coat, and in the other he held the head of a black walking stick that he picked up and set down with a deliberate outward motion each time he took a step. He was proceeding very slowly, his large brown eyes gazing over the heads of the passengers. He had a small white mustache and white crinkly hair. Behind him there were two young women, both coffee-colored, one in a yellow dress and one in a green. Their progress was kept at the rate of his and they chatted in low throaty voices as they followed him.

Mr. Head's grip was tightening insistently on Nelson's arm. As the procession passed them, the light from a sapphire ring on the brown hand that picked up the cane reflected in Mr. Head's eye, but he did not look up nor did the tremendous man look at him. The group proceeded up the rest of the aisle and out of the car. Mr. Head's grip on Nelson's arm loosened. "What was that?" he asked.

"A man," the boy said and gave him an indignant look as if he were tired of having his intelligence insulted.

"What kind of a man?" Mr. Head persisted, his voice expressionless.

"A fat man," Nelson said. He was beginning to feel that he had better be cautious.

"You don't know what kind?" Mr. Head said in a final tone.

"An old man," the boy said and had a sudden foreboding that he was not going to enjoy the day.

"That was a nigger," Mr. Head said and sat back.

Nelson jumped up on the seat and stood looking backward to the end of the car but the Negro had gone.

"I'd of thought you'd know a nigger since you seen so many when you was in the city on your first visit," Mr. Head continued. "That's his first nigger," he said to the man across the aisle.

The boy slid down into the seat. "You said they were black," he said in an angry voice. "You never said they were tan. How do you expect me to know anything when you don't tell me right?"

"You're just ignorant is all," Mr. Head said and he got up and moved over in the vacant seat by the man across the aisle.

Nelson turned backward again and looked where the Negro had disappeared. He felt that the Negro had deliberately walked down the aisle in order to make a fool of him and he hated him with a fierce raw fresh hate; and also, he understood now why his grandfather disliked them. He looked toward the window and the face there seemed to suggest that he might be inadequate to the day's exactions. He wondered if he would even recognize the city when they came to it.

After he had told several stories, Mr. Head realized that the man he was talking to was asleep and he got up and suggested to Nelson that they walk over the train and see the parts of it. He particularly wanted the boy to see the toilet so they went first to the men's room and examined the plumbing. Mr. Head demonstrated the ice-water cooler as if he had invented it and showed Nelson the bowl with the single spigot where the travelers brushed their teeth. They went through several cars and came to the diner.

This was the most elegant car in the train. It was painted a rich egg-yellow and had a wine-colored carpet on the floor. There were wide windows over the tables and great spaces of the rolling view were caught in miniature in the sides of the coffee pots and in the glasses. Three very black Negroes in white suits and aprons were running up and down the aisle, swinging trays and bowing and bending over the travelers eating breakfast. One of them rushed up to Mr. Head and Nelson and said, holding up two fingers, "Space for two!" but Mr. Head replied in a loud voice, "We eaten before we left!"

The waiter wore large brown spectacles that increased the size of his eye whites. "Stan' aside then please," he said with an airy wave of the arm as if he were brushing aside flies.

Neither Nelson nor Mr. Head moved a fraction of an inch. "Look," Mr. Head said.

The near corner of the diner, containing two tables, was set off from the rest by a saffron-colored curtain. One table was set but empty but at the other, facing them, his back to the drape, sat the tremendous Negro. He was speaking in a soft voice to the two women while he buttered a muffin. He had a heavy sad face and his neck bulged over his white collar on either side. "They rope them off," Mr. Head explained. Then he said, "Let's go see the kitchen," and they walked the length of the diner but the black waiter was coming fast behind them.

"Passengers are not allowed in the kitchen!" he said in a haughty voice. "Passengers are NOT allowed in the kitchen!"

Mr. Head stopped where he was and turned. "And there's good reason for that," he shouted into the Negro's chest, "because the cockroaches would run the passengers out!"

All the travelers laughed and Mr. Head and Nelson walked out, grinning. Mr. Head was known at home for his quick wit and Nelson felt a sudden keen pride in him. He realized the old man would be his only support in the strange place they were approaching. He would be entirely alone in the world if he were ever lost from his grandfather. A terrible excitement shook him and he wanted to take hold of Mr. Head's coat and hold on like a child.

As they went back to their seats they could see through the passing windows that the countryside was becoming speckled with small houses and shacks and that a highway ran alongside the train. Cars sped by on it, very small and fast. Nelson felt that there was less breath in the air than there had been thirty minutes ago. The man across the aisle had left and there was no one near for Mr. Head to hold a conversation with so he looked out the window, through his own reflection, and read aloud the names of the buildings they were passing. "The Dixie Chemical Corp!" he announced. "Southern Maid Flour! Dixie Doors! Southern Belle Cotton Products! Patty's Peanut Butter! Southern Mammy Cane Syrup!"

"Hush up!" Nelson hissed.

All over the car people were beginning to get up and take their luggage off the overhead racks. Women were putting on their coats and hats. The conductor stuck his head in the car and snarled, "Firstoppppppmry," and Nelson lunged out of his sitting position, trembling. Mr. Head pushed him down by the shoulder.

"Keep your seat," he said in dignified tones. "The first stop is on the edge of town. The second stop is at the main railroad station." He had come by this knowledge on his first trip when he had got off at the first stop and had had to pay a man fifteen cents to take him into the heart of town. Nelson sat back down, very pale. For the first time in his life, he understood that his grandfather was indispensable to him.

The train stopped and let off a few passengers and glided on as if it had never ceased moving. Outside, behind rows of brown rickety houses, a line of blue buildings stood up, and beyond them a pale rose-gray sky faded away to nothing. The train moved into the railroad yard. Looking down, Nelson saw lines and lines of silver tracks multiplying and criss-crossing. Then before he could start counting them, the face in the window started out at him, gray but distinct, and he looked the other way. The train was in the station. Both he and Mr. Head jumped up and ran to the door. Neither noticed that they had left the paper sack with the lunch in it on the seat.

They walked stiffly through the small station and came out of a heavy door into the squall of traffic. Crowds were hurrying to work. Nelson didn't know where to look. Mr. Head leaned against the side of the building and glared in front of him.

Finally Nelson said, "Well, how do you see what all it is to see?"

Mr. Head didn't answer. Then as if the sight of people passing had given him the clue, he said, "You walk," and started off down the street. Nelson followed, steadying his hat. So many sight and sounds were flooding in on him that for the first block he hardly knew what he was seeing. At the second corner, Mr. Head turned and looked behind him at the station they had left, a putty-colored terminal with a concrete dome on top. He thought that if he could keep the dome always in sight, he would be able to get back in the afternoon to catch the train again.

As they walked along, Nelson began to distinguish details and take note of the store windows, jammed with every kind of equipment—hardware, drygoods, chicken feed, liquor. They passed one that Mr. Head called his particular attention to where you walked in and sat on a chair with your feet upon two rests and let a Negro polish your shoes. They walked slowly and stopped and stood at the entrances so he could see what went on in each place but they did not go into any of them. Mr. Head was determined not to go into any city store because on his first trip here, he had got lost in a large one and had found his way out only after many people had insulted him.

They came in the middle of the next block to a store that had a weighing machine in front of it and they both in turn stepped up on it and put in a penny and received a ticket. Mr. Head's ticket said, "You weigh 120 pounds. You are upright and brave and all your friends admire you." He put the ticket in his pocket, surprised that the machine should have got his character correct but his weight wrong, for he had weighed on a grain scale not long before and knew he weighed 110. Nelson's ticket said, "You weigh 98 pounds. You have a great destiny ahead of you but beware of dark women." Nelson did not know any women and he weighed only 68 pounds but Mr. Head pointed out that the machine had probably printed the number upside down, meaning the 9 for a 6.

They walked on and at the end of five blocks the dome of the terminal sank out of sight and Mr. Head turned to the left. Nelson could have stood in front of every store window for an hour if there had not been another more interesting one next to it. Suddenly he said, "I was born here!" Mr. Head turned and looked at him with horror. There was a sweaty brightness about his face. "This is where I come from!" he said.

Mr. Head was appalled. He saw the moment had come for drastic action. "Lemme show you one thing you ain't seen yet," he said and took him to the corner where there was a sewer entrance. "Squat down," he said, "and stick you head in there," and he held the back of the boy's coat while he got down and put his head in the sewer. He drew it back quickly, hearing a gurgling in the depths under the sidewalk. Then Mr. Head explained the sewer system, how the entire city was underlined with it, how it contained all the drainage and was full of rats and how a man could slide into it and be sucked along down endless pitchblack tunnels. At any minute any man in the city might be sucked into the sewer and never heard from again. He described it so well that Nelson was for some seconds shaken. He connected the sewer passages with the entrance to hell and understood for the first time how the world was put together in its lower parts. He drew away from the curb.

Then he said, "Yes, but you can stay away from the holes," and his face took on that stubborn look that was so exasperating to his grandfather. "This is where I come from!" he said.

Mr. Head was dismayed but he only muttered, "You'll get your fill," and they walked on. At the end of two more blocks he turned to the left, feeling that he was circling the dome; and he was correct for in a half-hour they passed in front of the railroad station again. At first Nelson did not notice that he was seeing the same stores twice but when they passed the one where you put your feet on the rests while the Negro polished your shoes, he perceived that they were walking in a circle.

"We done been here!" he shouted. "I don't believe you know where you're at!"

"The direction just slipped my mind for a minute," Mr. Head said and they turned down a different street. He still did not intend to let the dome get too far away and after two blocks in their new direction, he turned to the left. This street contained two and three-story wooden dwellings. Anyone passing on the sidewalk could see into the rooms and Mr. Head, glancing through one window, saw a woman lying on an iron bed, looking out, with a sheet pulled over her. Her knowing expression shook him. A fierce-looking boy on a bicycle came driving down out of nowhere and he had to jump to the side to keep from being hit. "It's nothing to them if they knock you down," he said. "You better keep closer to me."

They walked on for some time on streets like this before he remembered to turn again. The houses they were passing now were all unpainted and the wood in them looked rotten; the street between was narrower. Nelson saw a colored man. Then another. Then another. "Niggers live in these houses," he observed.

"Well come on and we'll go somewheres else," Mr. Head said. "We didn't come to look at niggers," and they turned down another street but they continued to see Negroes everywhere. Nelson's skin began to prickle and they stepped along at a faster pace in order to leave the neighborhood as soon as possible. There were colored men in their undershirts standing in the doors and colored women rocking on the sagging porches. Colored children played in the gutters and stopped what they were doing to look at them. Before long they began to pass rows of stores with colored customers in them but they didn't pause at the entrances of these. Black eyes in black faces were watching them from every direction. "Yes," Mr. Head said, "this is where you were born—right here with all these niggers."

Nelson scowled. "I think you done got us lost," he said.

Mr. Head swung around sharply and looked for the dome. It was nowhere in sight. "I ain't got us lost either," he said. "You're just tired of walking."

"I ain't tired, I'm hungry," Nelson said. "Give me a biscuit."

They discovered then that they had lost the lunch.

"You were the one holding the sack," Nelson said. "I would have kepaholt of it."

"If you want to direct this trip, I'll go on by myself and leave you right here," Mr. Head said and was pleased to see the boy turn white. However, he realized they were lost and drifting farther every minute from the station. He was hungry himself and beginning to be thirsty and since they had been in the colored neighborhood, they had both begun to sweat. Nelson had on his shoes and he was unaccustomed to them. The concrete sidewalks were very hard. They both wanted to find a place to sit down but this was impossible and they kept on walking, the boy muttering under his breath, "First you lost the sack and then you lost the way," and Mr. Head growling from time to time, "Anybody wants to be from this nigger heaven can be from it!"

By now the sun was well forward in the sky. The odor of dinners cooking drifted out to them. The Negroes were all at their doors to see them pass. "Whyn't you ast one of these niggers the way?" Nelson said. "You got us lost."

"This is where you were born," Mr. Head said. "You can ast one yourself if you want to."

Nelson was afraid of the colored men and he didn't want to be laughed at by the colored children. Up ahead he saw a large colored woman leaning in a doorway that opened onto the sidewalk. Her hair stood straight out from her head for about four inches all around and she was resting on bare brown feet that turned pink at the sides. She had on a pink dress that showed her exact shape. As they came abreast of her, she lazily lifted one hand to her head and her fingers disappeared into her hair.

Nelson stopped. He felt his breath drawn up by the woman's dark eyes. "How do you get back to town?" he said in a voice that did not sound like his own.

After a minute she said, "You in town now," in a rich low tone that made Nelson feel as if a cool spray had been turned on him.

"How do you get back to the train?" he said in the same reed-like voice.

"You can catch you a car," she said.

He understood she was making fun of him but he was too paralyzed even to scowl. He stood drinking in every detail of her. His eyes traveled up from her great knees to her forehead and then made a triangular path from the glistening sweat on her neck down and across her tremendous bosom and over her bare arm back to where her fingers lay hidden in her hair. He suddenly wanted her to reach down and pick him up and draw him against her and then he wanted to feel her breath on his face. He wanted to look down and down into her eyes while she held him tighter and tighter. He had never had such a feeling before. He felt as if he were reeling down through a pitchblack tunnel.

"You can go a block down yonder and catch you a car take you to the railroad station, Sugarpie," she said.

Nelson would have collapsed at her feet if Mr. Head had not pulled him roughly away. "You act like you don't have any sense!" the old man growled.

They hurried down the street and Nelson did not look back at the woman. He pushed his hat sharply forward over his face which was already burning with shame. The sneering ghost he had seen in the train window and all the foreboding feelings he had on the way returned to him and he remembered that his ticket from the scale had said to beware of dark women and that his grandfather's had said he was upright and brave. He took hold of the old man's hand, a sign of dependence that he seldom showed.

They headed down the street toward the car tracks where a long yellow rattling trolley was coming. Mr. Head had never boarded a streetcar and he let that one pass. Nelson was silent. From time to time his mouth trembled slightly but his grandfather, occupied with his own problems, paid him no attention. They stood on the corner and neither looked at the Negroes who were passing, going about their business just as if they had been white, except that most of them stopped and eyed Mr. Head and Nelson. It occurred to Mr. Head that since the streetcar ran on tracks, they could simply follow the tracks. He gave Nelson a slight push and explained that they would follow the tracks on into the railroad station, walking, and they set off.

Presently to their great relief they began to see white people again and Nelson sat down on the sidewalk against the wall of a building. "I got to rest myself some," he said. "You lost the sack and the direction. You can just wait on me to rest myself."

"There's the tracks in front of us," Mr. Head said. "All we got to do is keep them in sight and you could have remembered the sack as good as me. This is where you were born. This is your old home town. This is your second trip. You ought to know how to do," and he squatted down and continued in this vein but the boy, easing his burning feet out of his shoes, did not answer.

"And standing there grinning like a chim-pan-zee while a nigger woman gives you direction. Great Gawd!" Mr. Head said.

"I never said I was nothing but born here," the boy said in a shaky voice. "I never said I would or wouldn't like it. I never said I wanted to come. I only said I was born here and I never had nothing to do with that. I want to go home. I never wanted to come in the first place. It was all your big idea. How you know you ain't following the tracks in the wrong direction?"

This last had occurred to Mr. Head too. "All these people are white," he said.

"We ain't passed here before," Nelson said. This was a neighborhood of brick buildings that might have been lived in or might not. A few empty automobiles were parked along the curb and there was an occasional passerby. The heat of the pavement came up through Nelson's thin suit. His eyelids began to droop, and after a few minutes his head tilted forward. His shoulders twitched once or twice and then he fell over on his side and lay sprawled in an exhausted fit of sleep.

Mr. Head watched him silently. He was very tired himself but they could not both sleep at the same time and he could not have slept anyway because he did not know where he was. In a few minutes Nelson would wake up, refreshed by his sleep and very cocky, and would begin complaining that he had lost the sack and the way. You'd have a mighty sorry time if I wasn't here, Mr. Head thought; and then another idea occurred to him. He looked at the sprawled figure for several minutes; presently he stood up. He justified what he was going to do on the grounds that it is sometimes necessary to teach a child a lesson he won't forget, particularly when the child is always reasserting his position with some new impudence. He walked without a sound to the corner about twenty feet away and sat down on a covered garbage can in the alley where he could look out and watch Nelson wake up alone.

The boy was dozing fitfully, half conscious of vague noises and black forms moving up from some dark part of him into the light. His face worked in his sleep and he had pulled his knees up under his chin. The sun shed a dull dry light on the narrow street; everything looked like exactly what it was. After a while Mr. Head, hunched like an old monkey on the garbage can lid, decided that if Nelson didn't wake up soon, he would make a loud noise by bamming his foot against the can. He looked at his watch and discovered that it was two o'clock. Their train left at six and the possibility of missing it was too awful for him to think of. He kicked his foot backwards on the can and a hollow boom reverberated in the alley.

Nelson shot up onto his feet with a shout. He looked where his grandfather should have been and stared. He seemed to whirl several times and then, picking up his feet and throwing his head back, he dashed down the street like a wild maddened pony. Mr. Head jumped off the can and galloped after but the child was almost out of sight. He saw a streak of gray disappearing diagonally a block ahead. He ran as fast as he could, looking both ways down every intersection, but without sight of him again. Then as he passed the third intersection, completely winded, he saw about half a block down the street a scene that stopped him altogether. He crouched behind a trash box to watch and get his bearings.

Nelson was sitting with both legs spread out and by his side lay an elderly woman, screaming. Groceries were scattered about the sidewalk. A crowd of women had already gathered to see justice done and Mr. Head distinctly heard the old woman on the pavement shout, "You've broken my ankle and your daddy'll pay for it! Every nickel! Police! Police!" Several of the women were plucking at Nelson's shoulder but the boy seemed too dazed to get up.

Something forced Mr. Head from behind the trash box and forward, but only at a creeping pace. He had never in his life been accosted by a policeman. The women were milling around Nelson as if they might suddenly all dive on him at once and tear him to pieces, and the old woman continued to scream that her ankle was broken and to call for an officer. Mr. Head came on so slowly that he could have been taking a backward step after each forward one, but when he was about ten feet away, Nelson saw him and sprang. The child caught him around the hips and clung panting against him.

The women all turned on Mr. Head. The injured onc sat up and shouted, "You sir! You'll pay every penny of my doctor's bill that your boy has caused. He's a juve-nile delinquent! Where is an officer? Somebody take this man's name and address!"

Mr. Head was trying to detach Nelson's fingers from the flesh in the back of his legs. The old man's head had lowered itself into his collar like a turtle's; his eyes were glazed with fear and caution.

"Your boy has broken my ankle!" the old woman shouted. "Police!"

Mr. Head sensed the approach of the policeman from behind. He stared straight ahead at the women who were massed in their fury like a solid wall to block his escape. "This is not my boy," he said. "I never seen him before."

He felt Nelson's fingers fall out of his flesh.

The women dropped back, staring at him with horror, as if they were so repulsed by a man who would deny his own image and likeness that they could not bear to lay hands on him. Mr. Head walked on, through a space they silently cleared, and left Nelson behind. Ahead of him he saw nothing but a hollow tunnel that had once been the street.

The boy remained standing where he was, his neck craned forward and his hands hanging by his sides. His hat was jammed on his head so that there were no longer any creases in it. The injured woman got up and shook her fist at him and the others gave him pitying looks, but he didn't notice any of them. There was no policeman in sight.

In a minute he began to move mechanically, making no effort to catch up with his grandfather but merely following at about twenty paces. They walked on for five blocks in this way. Mr. Head's shoulders were sagging and his neck hung forward at such an angle that it was not visible from behind. He was afraid to turn his head. Finally he cut a short hopeful glance over his shoulder. Twenty feet behind him, he saw two small eyes piercing into his back like pitchfork prongs.

The boy was not of a forgiving nature but this was the first time he had ever had anything to forgive. Mr. Head had never disgraced himself before. After two more blocks, he turned and called over his shoulder in a high desperately gay voice, "Let us go get us a Co' Cola somewheres!"

Nelson, with a dignity he had never shown before, turned and stood with his back to his grandfather.

Mr. Head began to feel the depth of his denial. His face as they walked on became all hollows and bare ridges. He saw nothing they were passing but he perceived that they had lost the car tracks. There was no dome to be seen anywhere and the afternoon was advancing. He knew that if dark overtook them in the city, they would be beaten and robbed. The speed of God's justice was only what he expected for himself, but he could not stand to think that his sins would be visited upon Nelson and that even now, he was leading the boy to his doom.

They continued to walk on block after block through an endless section of small brick houses until Mr. Head almost fell over a water spigot sticking up about six inches off the edge of a grass plot. He had not had a drink of water since early morning but felt he did not deserve it now. Then he thought that Nelson would be thirsty and they would both drink and be brought together. He squatted down and put his mouth to the nozzle and turned a cold stream of water into his throat. Then he called out in the high desperate voice, "Come on and getcher some water!"

This time the child stared through him for nearly sixty seconds. Mr. Head got up and walked on as if he had drunk poison. Nelson, though he had not had water since some he had drunk out of a paper cup on the train, passed by the spigot, disdaining to drink where his grandfather had. When Mr. Head realized this, he lost all hope. His face in the waning afternoon light looked ravaged and abandoned. He could feel the boy's steady hate, traveling at an even pace behind him and he knew that (if by some miracle they escaped being murdered in the city) it would continue just that way for the rest of his life. He knew that now he was wandering into a black strange place where nothing was like it had ever been before, a long old age without respect and an end that would be welcome because it would be the end.

As for Nelson, his mind had frozen around his grandfather's treachery as if he were trying to preserve it intact to present at the final judgment. He walked without looking to one side or the other, but every now and then his mouth would twitch and this was when he felt, from some remote place inside himself, a black mysterious form reach up as if it would melt his frozen vision in one hot grasp.

The sun dropped down behind a row of houses and hardly noticing, they passed into an elegant suburban section where mansions were set back from the road by lawns with birdbaths on them. Here everything was entirely deserted. For blocks they didn't pass even a dog. The big white houses were like partially submerged icebergs in the distance. There were no sidewalks, only drives, and these wound around and around in endless ridiculous circles. Nelson made no move to come nearer to Mr. Head. The old man felt that if he saw a sewer entrance he would drop down into it and let himself be carried away; and he could imagine the boy standing by, watching with only a slight interest, while he disappeared.

A loud bark jarred him to attention and he looked up to see a fat man approaching with two bulldogs. He waved both arms like someone shipwrecked on a desert island. "I'm lost!" he called. "I'm lost and can't find my way and me and this boy have got to catch this train and I can't find the station. Oh Gawd I'm lost! Oh help me Gawd I'm lost!"

The man, who was bald-headed and had on golf knickers, asked him what train he was trying to catch and Mr. Head began to get out his tickets, trembling so violently he could hardly hold them. Nelson had come up to within fifteen feet and stood watching.

"Well," the fat man said, giving him back the tickets, "you won't have time to get back to town to make this but you can catch it at the suburb stop. That's three blocks from here," and he began explaining how to get there.

Mr. Head stared as if he were slowly returning from the dead and when the man had finished and gone off with the dogs jumping at his heels, he turned to Nelson and said breathlessly, "We're going to get home!"

The child was standing about ten feet away, his face bloodless under the gray hat. His eyes were triumphantly cold. There was no light in them, no feeling, no interest. He was merely there, a small figure, waiting. Home was nothing to him.

Mr. Head turned slowly. He felt he knew now what time would be like without seasons and what heat would be like without light and what man would be like without salvation. He didn't care if he never made the train and if it had not been for what suddenly caught his attention, like a cry out of the gathering dusk, he might have forgotten there was a station to go to.

He had not walked five hundred yards down the road when he saw, within reach of him, the plaster figure of a Negro sitting bent over on a low yellow brick fence that curved around a wide lawn. The Negro was about Nelson's size and he was pitched forward at an unsteady angle because the putty that held him to the wall had cracked. One of his eyes was entirely white and he held a piece of brown watermelon.

Mr. Head stood looking at him silently until Nelson stopped at a little distance. Then as the two of them stood there, Mr. Head breathed, "An artificial nigger!"

It was not possible to tell if the artificial Negro were meant to be young or old; he looked too miserable to be either. He was meant to look happy because his mouth was stretched up at the corners but the chipped eye and the angle he was cocked at gave him a wild look of misery instead.

"An artificial nigger!" Nelson repeated in Mr. Head's exact tone.

The two of them stood there with their necks forward at almost the same angle and their shoulders curved in almost exactly the same way and their hands trembling identically in their pockets. Mr. Head looked like an ancient child and Nelson like a miniature old man. They stood gazing at the artificial Negro as if they were faced with some great mystery, some monument to another's victory that brought them together in their common defeat. They could both feel it dissolving their differences like an action of mercy. Mr. Head had never known before what mercy felt like because he had been too good to deserve any, but he felt he knew now. He looked at Nelson and understood that he must say something to the child to show that he was still wise and in the look the boy returned he saw a hungry need for that assurance. Nelson's eyes seemed to implore him to explain once and for all the mystery of existence.

Mr. Head opened his lips to make a lofty statement and heard himself say, "They ain't got enough real ones here. They got to have an artificial one."

After a second, the boy nodded with a strange shivering about his mouth, and said, "Let's go home before we get ourselves lost again."

Their train glided into the suburb stop just as they reached the station and they boarded it together, and ten minutes before it was due to arrive at the junction, they went to the door and stood ready to jump off if it did not stop; but it did, just as the moon, restored to its full splendor, sprang from a cloud and flooded the clearing with light. As they stepped off, the sage grass was shivering gently in shades of silver and the clinkers under their feet glittered with a fresh black light. The treetops, fencing the junction like the protecting walls of a garden, were darker than the sky which was hung with gigantic white clouds illuminated like lanterns.

Mr. Head stood very still and felt the action of mercy touch him again but this time he knew that there were no words in the world that could name it. He understood that it grew out of agony, which is not denied to any man and which is given in strange ways to children. He understood it was all a man could carry into death to give his Maker and he suddenly burned with shame that he had so little of it to take with him. He stood appalled, judging himself with the thoroughness of God, while the action of mercy covered his pride like a flame and consumed it. He had never thought himself a great sinner before but he saw now that his true depravity had been hidden from him lest it cause him despair. He realized that he was forgiven for sins from the beginning of time, when he had conceived of his own heart the sin of Adam, until the present, when he had denied poor Nelson. He saw that no sin was too monstrous for him to claim as his own, and since God loved in proportion as He forgave, he felt ready at that instant to enter Paradise.

Nelson, composing his expression under the shadow of his hat brim, watched him with a mixture of fatigue and suspicion, but as the train glided past them and disappeared like a frightened serpent into the woods, even his face lightened and he muttered, "I'm glad I've went once, but I'll never go back again!"

EUDORA WELTY

Death of a Traveling Salesman

R. J. Bowman, who for fourteen years had traveled for a shoe company through Mississippi, drove his Ford along a rutted dirt path. It was a long day! The time did not seem to clear the noon hurdle and settle into soft afternoon. The sun, keeping its strength here even in winter, stayed at the top of the sky, and every time Bowman stuck his head out of the dusty car to stare up the road, it seemed to reach a long arm down and push against the top of his head, right through his hat—like the practical joke of an old drummer, long on the road. It made him feel all the more angry and helpless. He was feverish, and he was not quite sure of the way.

This was his first day back on the road after a long siege of influenza. He had had very high fever, and dreams, and had become weakened and pale, enough to tell the difference in the mirror, and he could not think clearly. . . . All afternoon, in the midst of his anger, and for no reason, he had thought of his dead grandmother. She had been a comfortable soul. Once more Bowman wished he could fall into the big feather bed that had been in her room. . . . Then he forgot her again.

This desolate hill country! And he seemed to be going the wrong way—it was as if he were going back, far back. There was not a house in sight. . . . There was no use wishing he were back in bed, though. By paying the hotel doctor his bill he had proved his recovery. He had not even been sorry when the pretty trained nurse said good-bye. He did not like illness, he distrusted it, as he distrusted the road without signposts. It angered him. He had given the nurse a really expensive bracelet, just because she was packing up her bag and leaving.

But now—what if in fourteen years on the road he had never been ill before and never had an accident? His record was broken, and he had even begun almost to question it. . . . He had gradually put up at better hotels, in the bigger towns, but weren't they all, eternally, stuffy in summer and drafty in winter? Women? He could only remember little rooms within little rooms, like a nest of Chinese paper boxes, and if he thought of one woman he saw the worn loneliness that the furniture of that room seemed built of. And he himself—he was a man who always wore rather wide-brimmed black hats, and in the wavy hotel mirrors had looked something like a bullfighter, as he paused for that inevitable instant on the landing, walking downstairs to supper. . . . He leaned out of the car again, and once more the sun pushed at his head.

Bowman had wanted to reach Beulah by dark, to go to bed and sleep off his fatigue. As he remembered, Beulah was fifty miles away from the last town, on a graveled road. This was only a cow trail. How had he ever come to such a place? One hand wiped the sweat from his face, and he drove on.

He had made the Beulah trip before. But he had never seen this hill or this petering-out path before—or that cloud, he thought shyly, looking up and then down quickly—any more than he had seen this day before. Why did he not admit he was simply lost and had been for miles? . . . He was not in the habit of asking the way of strangers, and these people never knew where the very roads they lived on went to; but then he had not even been close enough to anyone to call out. People standing in the fields now and then, or on top of the haystacks, had been too far away, looking like leaning sticks or weeds, turning a little at the solitary rattle of his car across their countryside, watching the pale sobered winter dust where it chunked out behind like big squashes down the road. The stares of these distant people had followed him solidly like a wall, impenetrable, behind which they turned back after he had passed.

The cloud floated there to one side like a bolster on his grandmother's bed. It went over a cabin on the edge of a hill, where two bare chinaberry trees clutched at the sky. He drove through a heap of dead oak leaves, his wheels stirring their weightless sides to make a silvery melancholy whistle as the car passed through their bed. No car had been along this way ahead of him. Then he saw that he was on the edge of a ravine that fell away, a red erosion, and that this was indeed the road's end.

He pulled the brake. But it did not hold, though he put all his strength into it. The car, tipped toward the edge, rolled a little. Without doubt, it was going over the bank.

He got out quietly, as though some mischief had been done him and he had his dignity to remember. He lifted his bag and sample case out, set them down, and stood back and watched the car roll over the edge. He heard something—not the crash he was listening for, but a slow, un-uproarious crackle. Rather distastefully he went to look over, and he saw that his car had fallen into a tangle of immense grapevines as thick as his arm, which caught it and held it, rocked it like a grotesque child in a dark cradle, and then, as he watched, concerned somehow that he was not still inside it, released it gently to the ground.

He sighed.

Where am I? he wondered with a shock. Why didn't I do something? All his anger seemed to have drifted away from him. There was the house, back on the hill. He took a bag in each hand and with almost childlike willingness went toward it. But his breathing came with difficulty, and he had to stop to rest.

It was a shotgun house, two rooms and an open passage between, perched on the hill. The whole cabin slanted a little under the heavy heaped-up vine that covered the roof, light and green, as though forgotten from summer. A woman stood in the passage.

He stopped still. Then all of a sudden his heart began to behave strangely. Like a rocket set off, it began to leap and expand into uneven patterns of beats which showered into his brain, and he could not think. But in scattering and falling it made no noise. It shot up with great power, almost elation, and fell gently, like acrobats into nets. It began to pound profoundly, then waited irresponsibly, hitting in some sort of inward mockery first at his ribs, then against his eyes, then under his shoulder blades, and against the roof of his mouth when he tried to say, "Good afternoon, madam." But he could not hear his heart—it was as quiet as ashes falling. This was rather comforting; still, it was shocking to Bowman to feel his heart beating at all.

Stock-still in his confusion, he dropped his bags, which seemed to drift in slow bulks gracefully through the air and to cushion themselves on the gray prostrate grass near the doorstep.

As for the woman standing there, he saw at once that she was old. Since she could not possibly hear his heart, he ignored the pounding and now looked at her carefully, and yet in his distraction dreamily, with his mouth open.

She had been cleaning the lamp, and held it, half blackened, half clear, in front of her. He saw her with the dark passage behind her. She was a big woman with a weather-beaten but unwrinkled face; her lips were held tightly together, and her eyes looked with a curious dulled brightness into his. He looked at her shoes, which were like bundles. If it were summer she would be barefoot. . . . Bowman, who automatically judged a woman's age on sight, set her age at fifty. She wore a formless garment of some gray coarse material, rough-dried from a washing, from which her arms appeared pink and unexpectedly round. When she never said a word, and sustained her quiet pose of holding the lamp, he was convinced of the strength in her body.

"Good afternoon, madam," he said.

She stared on, whether at him or at the air around him he could not tell, but after a moment she lowered her eyes to show that she would listen to whatever he had to say.

"I wonder if you would be interested—" He tried once more. "An accident—my car . . ."

Her voice emerged low and remote, like a sound across a lake. "Sonny he ain't here."

"Sonny?"

"Sonny ain't here now."

Her son—a fellow able to bring my car up, he decided in blurred relief. He pointed down the hill. "My car's in the bottom of the ditch. I'll need help."

"Sonny ain't here, but he'll be here."

She was becoming clearer to him and her voice stronger, and Bowman saw that she was stupid.

He was hardly surprised at the deepening postponement and tedium of his journey. He took a breath, and heard his voice speaking over the silent blows of his heart. "I was sick. I am not strong yet. . . . May I come in?"

He stooped and laid his big black hat over the handle on his bag. It was a humble motion, almost a bow, that instantly struck him as absurd and betraying of all his weakness. He looked up at the woman, the wind blowing his hair. He might have continued for a long time in this unfamiliar attitude; he had never been a patient man, but when he was sick he had learned to sink submissively into the pillows, to wait for his medicine. He waited on the woman.

Then she, looking at him with blue eyes, turned and held open the door, and after a moment Bowman, as if convinced in his action, stood erect and followed her in.

Inside, the darkness of the house touched him like a professional hand, the doctor's. The woman set the half-cleaned lamp on a table in the center of the room and pointed, also like a professional person, a guide, to a chair with a yellow cowhide seat. She herself crouched on the hearth, drawing her knees up under the shapeless dress.

At first he felt hopefully secure. His heart was quieter. The room was enclosed in the gloom of yellow pine boards. He could see the other room, with the foot of an iron bed showing, across the passage. The bed had been made up with a red-and-yellow pieced guilt that looked like a map or a picture, a little like his grandmother's girlhood painting of Rome burning.

He had ached for coolness, but in this room it was cold. He stared at the hearth with dead coals lying on it and iron pots in the corners. The hearth and smoked chimney were of the stone he had seen ribbing the hills, mostly slate. Why is there no fire? he wondered.

And it was so still. The silence of the fields seemed to enter and move familiarly through the house. The wind used the open hall. He felt that he was in a mysterious, quiet, cool danger. It was necessary to do what? . . . To talk.

"I have a nice line of women's low-priced shoes . . ." he said.

But the woman answered, "Sonny'll be here. He's strong. Sonny'll move your car."

"Where is he now?"

"Farms for Mr. Redmond."

Mr. Redmond. Mr. Redmond. That was someone he would never have to encounter, and he was glad. Somehow the name did not appeal to him. . . . In a flare of touchiness and anxiety, Bowman wished to avoid even mention of unknown men and their unknown farms.

"Do you two live here alone?" He was surprised to hear his old voice, chatty, confidential, inflected for selling shoes, asking a question like that—a thing he did not even want to know.

"Yes. We are alone."

He was surprised at the way she answered. She had taken a long time to say that. She had nodded her head in a deep way too. Had she wished to affect him with some sort of premonition? he wondered unhappily. Or was it only that she would not help him, after all, by talking with him? For he was not strong enough to receive the impact of unfamiliar things without a little talk to break their fall. He had lived a month in which nothing had happened except in his head and his body—an almost inaudible life of heartbeats and dreams that came back, a life of fever and privacy, a delicate life which had left him weak to the point of—what? Of begging. The pulse in his palm leapt like a trout in a brook.

He wondered over and over why the woman did not go ahead with cleaning the lamp. What prompted her to stay there across the room, silently bestowing her presence upon him? He saw that with her it was not a time for doing little tasks. Her face was grave; she was feeling how right she was. Perhaps it was only politeness. In docility he held his eyes stiffly wide; they fixed themselves on the woman's clasped hands as though she held the cord they were strung on.

Then, "Sonny's coming," she said.

He himself had not heard anything, but there came a man passing the window and then plunging in at the door, with two hounds beside him. Sonny was a big enough man, with his belt slung low about his hips. He looked at least thirty. He had a hot, red face that was yet full of silence. He wore muddy blue pants and an old military coat stained and patched.

World War? Bowman wondered. Great God, it was a Confederate coat. On the back of his light hair he had a wide filthy black hat which seemed to insult Bowman's own. He pushed down the dogs from his chest. He was strong, with dignity and heaviness in his way of moving. . . . There was the resemblance to his mother.

They stood side by side. . . . He must account again for his presence here.

"Sonny, this man, he had his car to run off over the prec'pice an' wants to know if you will git it out for him," the woman said after a few minutes.

Bowman could not even state his case.

Sonny's eyes lay upon him.

He knew he should offer explanations and show money—at least appear either penitent or authoritative. But all he could do was to shrug slightly.

Sonny brushed by him going to the window, followed by the eager dogs, and looked out. There was effort even in the way he was looking, as if he could throw his sight out like a rope. Without turning Bowman felt that his own eyes could have seen nothing: it was too far.

"Got me a mule out there an' got me a block an' tackle," said Sonny meaningfully. "I *could* catch me my mule an' git me my ropes, an' before long I'd git your car out of the ravine."

He looked completely around the room, as if in meditation, his eyes roving in their own distance. Then he pressed his lips firmly and yet shyly together, and with the dogs ahead of him this time, he lowered his head and strode out. The hard earth sounded, cupping to his powerful way of walking—almost a stagger.

Mischievously, at the suggestion of those sounds, Bowman's heart leapt again. It seemed to walk about inside him.

"Sonny's goin' to do it," the woman said. She said it again, singing it almost, like a song. She was sitting in her place by the hearth.

Without looking out, he heard some shouts and the dogs barking and the pounding of hoofs in short runs on the hill. In a few minutes Sonny passed under the window with a rope, and there was a brown mule with quivering, shining, purple-looking ears. The mule actually looked in the window. Under its eyelashes it turned target-like eyes into his. Bowman averted his head and saw the woman looking serenely back at the mule, with only satisfaction in her face.

She sang a little more, under her breath. It occurred to him, and it seemed quite marvelous, that she was not really talking to him, but rather following the thing that came about with words that were unconscious and part of her looking.

So he said nothing, and this time when he did not reply he felt a curious and strong emotion, not fear, rise up in him.

This time, when his heart leapt, something—his soul—seemed to leap too, like a little colt invited out of a pen. He stared at the woman while the frantic nimbleness of his feeling made his head sway. He could not move; there was nothing he could do, unless perhaps he might embrace this woman who sat there growing old and shapeless before him.

But he wanted to leap up, to say to her, I have been sick and I found out then, only then, how lonely I am. Is it too late? My heart puts up a struggle inside me, and you may have heard it, protesting against emptiness. . . . It should be full, he would rush on to tell her, thinking of his heart now as a deep lake, it should be holding love like other hearts. It should be flooded with love. There would be a warm spring day. . . . Come and stand in my heart, whoever you are, and a whole river would cover your feet and rise higher and take your knees in whirlpools, and draw you down to itself, your whole body, your heart too.

But he moved a trembling hand across his eyes, and looked at the placid crouching woman across the room. She was still as a statue. He felt ashamed and exhausted by the thought that he might, in one more moment, have tried by simple words and embraces to communicate some strange thing—something which seemed always to have just escaped him. . . .

Sunlight touched the furthest pot on the hearth. It was late afternoon. This time tomorrow he would be somewhere on a good graveled road, driving his car past things that happened to people, quicker than their happening. Seeing ahead to the next day, he was glad, and knew that this was no time to embrace an old woman. He could feel in his pounding temples the readying of his blood for motion and for hurrying away.

"Sonny's hitched up your car by now," said the woman. "He'll git it out the ravine right shortly."

"Fine!" he cried with his customary enthusiasm.

Yet it seemed a long time that they waited. It began to get dark. Bowman was cramped in his chair. Any man should know enough to get up and walk around while he waited. There was something like guilt in such stillness and silence.

But instead of getting up, he listened. . . . His breathing restrained, his eyes powerless in the growing dark, he listened uneasily for a warning sound, forgetting in wariness what it would be. Before long he heard something—soft, continuous, insinuating.

"What's that noise?" he asked, his voice jumping into the dark. Then wildly he was afraid it would be his heart beating so plainly in the quiet room, and she would tell him so.

"You might hear the stream," she said grudgingly.

Her voice was closer. She was standing by the table. He wondered why she did not light the lamp. She stood there in the dark and did not light it.

Bowman would never speak to her now, for the time was past. I'll sleep in the dark, he thought, in his bewilderment pitying himself.

Heavily she moved on to the window. Her arm, vaguely white, rose straight from her full side and she pointed out into the darkness.

"That white speck's Sonny," she said, talking to herself.

He turned unwillingly and peered over her shoulder; he hesitated to rise and stand beside her. His eyes searched the dusky air. The white speck floated smoothly toward her finger, like a leaf on a river, growing whiter in the dark. It was as if she had shown him something secret, part of her life, but had offered no explanation. He looked away. He was moved almost to tears, feeling for no reason that she had made a silent declaration equivalent to his own. His hand waited upon his chest.

Then a step shook the house, and Sonny was in the room. Bowman felt how the woman left him there and went to the other man's side.

"I done got your car out, mister," said Sonny's voice in the dark. "She's settin' a-awaitin' in the road, turned to go back where she come from."

"Fine!" said Bowman, projecting his own voice to loudness. "I'm surely much obliged—I could never have done it myself—I was sick. . . ."

"I could do it easy," said Sonny.

Bowman could feel them both waiting in the dark, and he could hear the dogs panting out in the yard, waiting to bark when he should go. He felt strangely helpless and resentful. Now that he could go, he longed to stay. From what was he being deprived? His chest was rudely shaken by the violence of his heart. These people cherished something here that he could not see, they withheld some ancient promise of food and warmth and light. Between them they had a conspiracy. He thought of the way she had moved away from him and gone to Sonny, she had flowed toward him. He was shaking with cold, he was tired, and it was not fair. Humbly and yet angrily he stuck his hand into his pocket.

"Of course I'm going to pay you for everything—"

"We don't take money for such," said Sonny's voice belligerently.

"I want to pay. But do something more . . . Let me stay—tonight. . . ." He took another step toward them. If only they could see him, they would know his sincerity, his real need! His voice went on, "I'm not very strong yet, I'm not able to walk far, even back to my car, maybe, I don't know—I don't know exactly where I am—"

He stopped. He felt as if he might burst into tears. What would they think of him!

Sonny came over and put his hands on him. Bowman felt them pass (they were professional too) across his chest, over his hips. He could feel Sonny's eyes upon him in the dark.

"You ain't no revenuer come sneakin' here, mister, ain't got no gun?"

To this end of nowhere! And yet *he* had come. He made a grave answer. "No."

"You can stay."

"Sonny," said the woman, "you'll have to borry some fire."

"I'll go git it from Redmond's," said Sonny.

"What?" Bowman strained to hear their words to each other.

"Our fire, it's out, and Sonny's got to borry some, because it's dark an' cold," she said.

"But matches—I have matches—"

"We don't have no need for 'em," she said proudly. "Sonny's goin' after his own fire."

"I'm going to Redmond's," said Sonny with an air of importance, and he went out.

After they had waited a while, Bowman looked out the window and saw a light moving over the hill. It spread itself out like a little fan. It zigzagged along the field, darting and swift, not like Sonny at all. . . . Soon enough, Sonny staggered in, holding a burning stick behind him in tongs, fire flowing in his wake, blazing light into the corners of the room.

"We'll make a fire now," the woman said, taking the brand.

When that was done she lit the lamp. It showed its dark and light. The whole room turned golden-yellow like some sort of flower, and the walls smelled of it and seemed to tremble with the quiet rushing of the fire and the waving of the burning lampwick in its funnel of light.

The woman moved among the iron pots. With the tongs she dropped hot coals on top of the iron lids. They made a set of soft vibrations, like the sound of a bell far away.

She looked up and over at Bowman, but he could not answer. He was trembling. . . .

"Have a drink, mister?" Sonny asked. He had brought in a chair from the other room and sat astride it with his folded arms across the back. Now we are all visible to one another, Bowman thought, and cried, "Yes sir, you bet, thanks!"

"Come after me and do just what I do," said Sonny.

It was another excursion into the dark. They went through the hall, out to the back of the house, past a shed and a hooded well. They came to a wilderness of thicket.

"Down on your knees," said Sonny.

"What?" Sweat broke out on his forehead.

He understood when Sonny began to crawl through a sort of tunnel that the bushes made over the ground. He followed, startled in spite of himself when a twig or a thorn touched him gently without making a sound, clinging to him and finally letting him go.

Sonny stopped crawling and, crouched on his knees, began to dig with both his hands into the dirt. Bowman shyly struck matches and made a light. In a few minutes Sonny pulled up a jug. He poured out some of the whisky into a bottle from his coat pocket, and buried the jug again. "You never know who's liable to knock at your door," he said, and laughed. "Start back," he said, almost formally. "Ain't no need for us to drink outdoors, like hogs."

At the table by the fire, sitting opposite each other in their chairs, Sonny and Bowman took drinks out of the bottle, passing it across. The dogs slept; one of them was having a dream.

"This is good," said Bowman. "This is what I needed." It was just as though he were drinking the fire off the hearth.

"He makes it," said the woman with quiet pride.

She was pushing the coals off the pots, and the smells of corn bread and coffee circled the room. She set everything on the table before the men, with a bone-handled knife stuck into one of the potatoes, splitting out its golden fiber. Then she stood for a minute looking at them, tall and full above them where they sat. She leaned a little toward them.

"You all can eat now," she said, and suddenly smiled.

Bowman had just happened to be looking at her. He set his cup back on the table in unbelieving protest. A pain pressed at his eyes. He saw that she was not an old woman. She was young, still young. He could think of no number of years for her. She was the same age as Sonny, and she belonged to him. She stood with the deep dark corner of the room behind her, the shifting yellow light scattering over her head and her gray formless dress, trembling over her tall body when it bent over them in its sudden communication. She was young. Her teeth were shining and her eyes glowed. She turned and walked slowly and heavily out of the room, and he heard her sit down on the cot and then lie down. The pattern on the quilt moved.

"She's going to have a baby," said Sonny, popping a bite into his mouth.

Bowman could not speak. He was shocked with knowing what was really in this house. A marriage, a fruitful marriage. That simple thing. Anyone could have had that.

Somehow he felt unable to be indignant or protest, although some sort of joke had certainly been played upon him. There was nothing remote or mysterious here—only something private. The only secret was the ancient communication between two people. But the memory of the woman's waiting silently by the cold hearth, of the man's stubborn journey a mile away to get fire, and how they finally brought out their food and drink and filled the room proudly with all they had to show, was suddenly too clear and too enormous within him for response. . . .

"You ain't as hungry as you look," said Sonny.

The woman came out of the bedroom as soon as the men had finished, and ate her supper while her husband stared peacefully into the fire.

Then they put the dogs out, with the food that was left.

"I think I'd better sleep here by the fire, on the floor," said Bowman.

He felt that he had been cheated, and that he could afford now to be generous. Ill though he was, he was not going to ask them for their bed. He was through with asking favors in this house, now that he understood what was there.

"Sure, mister."

But he had not known yet how slowly he understood. They had not meant to give him their bed. After a little interval they both rose and looking at him gravely went into the other room.

He lay stretched by the fire until it grew low and dying. He watched every tongue of blaze lick out and vanish. "There will be special reduced prices on all footwear during the month of January," he found himself repeating quietly, and then he lay with his lips tight shut.

How many noises the night had! He heard the stream running, the fire dying, and he was sure now that he heard his heart beating, too, the sound it made under his ribs. He heard breathing, round and deep, of the man and his wife in the room across the passage. And that was all. But emotion swelled patiently within him, and he wished that the child were his.

He must get back to where he had been before. He stood weakly before the red coals and put on his overcoat. It felt too heavy on his shoulders. As he started out he looked and saw that the woman had never got through with cleaning the lamp. On some impulse he put all the money from his billfold under its fluted glass base, almost ostentatiously.

Ashamed, shrugging a little, and then shivering, he took his bags and went out. The cold of the air seemed to lift him bodily. The moon was in the sky.

On the slope he began to run, he could not help it. Just as he reached the road, where his car seemed to sit in the moonlight like a boat, his heart began to give off tremendous explosions like a rifle, bang bang bang.

He sank in fright onto the road, his bags falling about him. He felt as if all this had happened before. He covered his heart with both hands to keep anyone from hearing the noise it made.

But nobody heard it.

8

CONTRAST AND BALANCE

The flood of short story anthologies on today's market is testimony to the number of possible approaches to the "study" of fiction. This text has chosen to approach the story from the point of view of technique, of the methods which writers employ in order to achieve their purposes. If a text like this is not going to run to unreasonable lengths, this approach demands sometimes arbitrary selection. We could, for example, have included sections on such other technical aspects of fiction as description, atmosphere, tone, pace, and texture. We might even have included a section on the very crucial matter of the literary convention, for as readers we should be aware of the fact that literary fashions change, that what will "work" in one time and place will not "work" in another, and that a story writer like Bret Harte would very probably not be able to find a publisher in the 1970s. But because of the very central part which it plays in fiction, we have chosen to conclude our consideration of technique with this discussion of contrast and balance.

Any reader must soon become aware of the fact that *contrast* is one of the ever-present ingredients in fiction. It is to be found in every element of fiction and on every possible level of effect or meaning. It is the necessary a priori characteristic of all conflict, external or internal; the very concept of antagonist and protagonist presupposes contrast. It is frequently one of the most important methods of defining and realizing character. The use of *foils* in stories is only one of the least subtle ways by which through contrast writers realize "people." In an earlier discussion of irony, we pointed out how crucial contrast can be to the intelligent realization of a valid theme. No reader can overlook for long the part that contrast plays in communicating emotional effect: the juxtapositioning of two contrasting emotions, the use of understatement or exaggeration in such a way that style contrasts with content, the movement in a story from one emotion to an opposite emotion all testify to the importance of contrast in making us feel experience in fiction.

All of these uses of contrast we have already observed. What we wish to focus on in the stories that follow is the very important part that contrast plays in the *structure* of fiction. Hence, the term *balance* in our title to this section.

Contrast, of course, is always the balancing of one story element against another—one kind of character against another kind of character, one emotional effect against a contrasting emotional effect, one idea against an opposite idea. In the carefully constructed story, this balancing will frequently emerge as an over-all story pattern. Let us point to only one or two common instances.

One problem which the writer faces is to achieve the effect of unity—to leave the reader with the feeling that the story is all one piece, complete and self-contained, "finished." In the story in which conflict or plot is the dominant element, this presents little problem; the development and plausible resolution of a conflict will provide this effect. But the story in which conflict is not the dominant element can present problems which balancing can, in part, solve. For example, a writer can "frame" such a story. If, for example, a writer uses the same symbol in the opening and ending, we will have a framed story; if, in addition, he presents that symbol in identical or even similar phrasing, he will have emphasized his frame.

There are more subtle ways of employing balance. A story must not only give us the effect of unity; it must also give us the effect of progression, of going somewhere. Again, in the story in which conflict is not the dominant emphasis, balancing can help to provide this effect. If a story moves in careful steps from one emotion to an opposite emotion, the effect of progress will be present; and if we analyze that movement, we are likely to discover that it is primarily achieved by careful balance and contrast. In stories in which either character revelation or theme predominate, you will frequently find this kind of pattern emerging.

In the three stories which follow, you will discover that pattern through contrast and balance is perhaps the basic method by which three writers achieve their purpose. In one, character revelation and motivation are accomplished by means of a very careful employment of balance and contrast. In the second, both character and theme are realized in the same way. In the third we have a clear example of a "framed" story; beyond this, the story is internally an excellent example of theme achieved through a pattern of contrast and balance. And your analysis of this structural technique can lead you to the realization that other stories which you have already read have in part managed their effects or meanings by means of these same structural principles.

JAMES JOYCE

Counterparts

The bell rang furiously and, when Miss Parker went to the tube, a furious voice called out in a piercing North of Ireland accent:

"Send Farrington here!"

Miss Parker returned to her machine, saying to a man who was writing at a desk:

"Mr. Alleyne wants you upstairs."

The man muttered "*Blast* him!" under his breath and pushed back his chair to stand up. When he stood up he was tall and of great bulk. He had a hanging face, dark wine-coloured, with fair eyebrows and moustache: his eyes bulged forward slightly and the whites of them were dirty. He lifted up the counter and, passing by the clients, went out of the office with a heavy step.

He went heavily upstairs until he came to the second landing, where a door bore a brass plate with the inscription *Mr. Alleyne.* Here he halted, puffing with labour and vexation, and knocked. The shrill voice cried:

"Come in!"

The man entered Mr. Alleyne's room. Simultaneously Mr. Alleyne, a little man wearing gold-rimmed glasses on a clean-shaven face, shot his head up over a pile of documents. The head itself was so pink and hairless it seemed like a large egg reposing on the papers. Mr. Alleyne did not lose a moment:

"Farrington? What is the meaning of this? Why have I always to complain of you? May I ask you why you haven't made a copy of that contract between Bodley and Kirwan? I told you it must be ready by four o'clock."

"But Mr. Shelley said, sir—"

"*Mr. Shelley said, sir. . . .* Kindly attend to what I say and not to what *Mr. Shelley says, sir.* You have always some excuse or another for shirking work. Let me tell you that if the contract is not copied before this evening I'll lay the matter before Mr. Crosbie. . . . Do you hear me now?"

"Yes, sir."

"Do you hear me now? . . . Ay and another little matter! I might as well be talking to the wall as talking to you. Understand once for all that you get a half an hour for your lunch and not an hour and a half. How many courses do you want, I'd like to know. . . . Do you mind me now?"

"Yes, sir."

Mr. Alleyne bent his head again upon his pile of papers. The man stared fixedly at the polished skull which directed the affairs of Crosbie & Alleyne, gauging its fragility. A spasm of rage gripped his throat for a few moments and then passed, leaving after it a sharp sensation of thirst. The man recognized the sensation and felt that he must have a good night's drinking. The middle of the month was passed and, if he could get the copy done in time, Mr. Alleyne might give him an order on the cashier. He stood still, gazing fixedly at the head upon the pile of papers. Suddenly Mr. Alleyne began to upset all the papers, searching for something. Then, as if he had been unaware of the man's presence till that moment, he shot up his head again, saying:

"Eh? Are you going to stand there all day? Upon my word, Farrington, you take things easy!"

"I was waiting to see . . ."

"Very good, you needn't wait to see. Go downstairs and do your work."

The man walked heavily towards the door and, as he went out of the room, he heard Mr. Alleyne cry after him that if the contract was not copied by evening Mr. Crosbie would hear of the matter.

He returned to his desk in the lower office and counted the sheets which remained to be copied. He took up his pen and dipped it in the ink but he continued to stare stupidly at the last words he had written: *In no case shall the said Bernard Bodley be* . . . The evening was falling and in a few minutes they would be lighting the gas: then he could write. He felt that he must slake the thirst in his throat. He stood up from his desk and, lifting the counter as before, passed out of the office. As he was passing out the chief clerk looked at him inquiringly.

"It's all right, Mr. Shelley," said the man, pointing with his finger to indicate the objective of his journey.

The chief clerk glanced at the hat-rack, but, seeing the row complete, offered no remark. As soon as he was on the landing the man pulled a shepherd's plaid cap out of his pocket, put it on his head and ran quickly down the rickety stairs. From the street door he walked on furtively on the inner side of the path towards the corner and all at once dived into a doorway. He was now safe in the dark snug of O'Neill's shop, and, filling up the little window that looked into the bar with his inflamed face, the colour of dark wine or dark meat, he called out:

"Here, Pat, give us a g.p., like a good fellow."

The curate brought him a glass of plain porter. The man drank it at a gulp and asked for a caraway seed. He put his penny on the counter and, leaving the curate to grope for it in the gloom, retreated out of the snug as furtively as he had entered it.

Darkness, accompanied by a thick fog, was gaining upon the dusk of February and the lamps in Eustace Street had been lit. The man went up by the houses until he reached the door of the office, wondering whether he could finish his copy in time. On the stairs a moist pungent odour of perfumes saluted his nose: evidently Miss Delacour had come while he was out in O'Neill's. He crammed his cap back again into his pocket and re-entered the office, assuming an air of absent-mindedness.

"Mr. Alleyne has been calling for you," and the chief clerk severely. "Where were you?"

The man glanced at the two clients who were standing at the counter as if to intimate that their presence prevented him from answering. As the clients were both male the chief clerk allowed himself a laugh.

"I know that game," he said. "Five times in one day is a little bit. . . . Well, you better look sharp and get a copy of our correspondence in the Delacour case for Mr. Alleyne."

This address in the presence of the public, his run upstairs and the porter he had gulped down so hastily confused the man and, as he sat down at his desk to get what was required, he realised how hopeless was the task of finishing his copy of the contract before half past five. The dark damp night was coming and he longed to spend it in the bars, drinking with his friends amid the glare of gas and the clatter of glasses. He got out the Delacour correspondence and passed out of the office. He hoped Mr. Alleyne would not discover that the last two letters were missing.

The moist pungent perfume lay all the way up to Mr. Alleyne's room. Miss Delacour was a middle-aged woman of Jewish appearance. Mr. Alleyne was said to be sweet on her or on her money. She came to the office often and stayed a long time when she came. She was sitting beside his desk now in an aroma of perfumes, smoothing the handle of her umbrella and nodding the great black feather in her hat. Mr. Alleyne had swivelled his chair round to face her and thrown his right foot jauntily upon his left knee. The man put the correspondence on the desk and bowed respectfully but neither Mr. Alleyne nor Miss Delacour took any notice of his bow. Mr. Alleyne tapped a finger on the correspondence and then flicked it towards him as if to say: *"That's all right: you can go."*

The man returned to the lower office and sat down again at his desk. He stared intently at the incomplete phrase: *In no case shall the said Bernard Bodley be . . .* and thought how strange it was that the last three words began with the same letter. The chief clerk began to hurry Miss Parker, saying she would never have the letters typed in time for post. The man listened to the clicking of the machine for a few minutes and then set to work to finish his copy. But his head was not clear and his mind wandered away to the glare and rattle of the public-house. It was a night for hot punches. He struggled on with his copy, but when the clock struck five he had still fourteen pages to write. Blast it! He couldn't finish it in time. He longed to execrate aloud, to bring his fist down on something violently. He was so enraged that he wrote *Bernard Bernard* instead of *Bernard Bodley* and had to begin again on a clean sheet.

He felt strong enough to clear out the whole office single-handed. His body ached to do something, to rush out and revel in violence. All the indignities of his life enraged him. . . . Could he ask the cashier privately for an advance? No, the cashier was no good, no damn good: he wouldn't give an advance. . . . He knew where he would meet the boys: Leonard and O'Halloran and Nosey Flynn. The barometer of his emotional nature was set for a spell of riot.

His imagination had so abstracted him that his name was called twice before he answered. Mr. Alleyne and Miss Delacour were standing outside the counter and all the clerks had turned round in anticipation of something. The man got up from his desk. Mr. Alleyne began a tirade of abuse, saying that two letters were missing. The man answered that he knew nothing about them, that he had made a faithful copy. The tirade continued: it was so bitter and violent that the man could hardly restrain his fist from descending upon the head of the manikin before him:

"I know nothing about any other two letters," he said stupidly.

"*You—know—nothing.* Of course you know nothing," said Mr. Alleyne. "Tell me," he added, glancing first for approval to the lady beside him, "do you take me for a fool? Do you think me an utter fool?"

The man glanced from the lady's face to the little egg-shaped head and back again; and, almost before he was aware of it, his tongue had found a felicitous moment:

"I don't think, sir," he said, "that that's a fair question to put to me."

There was a pause in the very breathing of the clerks. Everyone was astounded (the author of the witticism no less than his neighbours) and Miss Delacour, who was a stout amiable person, began to smile broadly. Mr. Alleyne flushed to the hue of a wild rose and his mouth twitched with a dwarf's passion. He shook his fist in the man's face till it seemed to vibrate like the knob of some electric machine:

"You impertinent ruffian! You impertinent ruffian! I'll make short work of you! Wait till you see! You'll apologise to me for your impertinence or you'll quit the office instanter! You'll quit this, I'm telling you, or you'll apologise to me!"

He stood in a doorway opposite the office watching to see if the cashier would come out alone. All the clerks passed out and finally the cashier came out with the chief clerk. It was no use trying to say a word to him when he was with the chief clerk. The man felt that his position was bad enough. He had been obliged to offer an abject apology to Mr. Alleyne for his impertinence but he knew what a hornet's nest the office would be for him. He could remember the way in which Mr. Alleyne had hounded little Peake out of the office in order to make room for his own nephew. He felt savage and thirsty and revengeful, annoyed with himself and with everyone else. Mr. Alleyne would never give him an hour's rest; his life would be a hell to him. He had made a proper fool of himself this time. Could he not keep his tongue in his cheek? But they had never pulled together from the first, he and Mr. Alleyne, ever since the day Mr. Alleyne had overheard him mimicking his North of Ireland accent to amuse Higgins and Miss Parker; that had been the beginning of it. He might have tried Higgins for the money, but sure Higgins never had anything for himself. A man with two establishments to keep up, of course he couldn't. . . .

He felt his great body again aching for the comfort of the public-house. The fog had begun to chill him and he wondered could he touch Pat in O'Neill's. He could not touch him for more than a bob—and a bob was no use. Yet he must get money somewhere or other: he had spent his last penny for the g.p. and soon it would be too late for getting money anywhere. Suddenly, as he was fingering his watch-chain, he thought of Terry Kelly's pawn-office in Fleet Street. That was the dart! Why didn't he think of it sooner?

He went through the narrow alley of Temple Bar quickly, muttering to himself that they could all go to hell because he was going to have a good night of it. The clerk in Terry Kelly's said *A crown!* but the consignor held out for six shillings; and in the end the six shillings was allowed him literally. He came out of the pawn-office joyfully, making a little cylinder of the coins between his thumb and fingers. In Westmoreland Street the footpaths were crowded with young men and women returning from business and ragged urchins ran here and there yelling out the names of the evening editions. The man passed through the crowd, looking on the spectacle generally with proud satisfaction and staring masterfully at the office-girls. His head was full of the noises of tram-gongs and swishing trolleys and his nose already sniffed the curling fumes of punch. As he walked on he preconsidered the terms in which he would narrate the incident to the boys:

"So, I just looked at him—coolly, you know, and looked at her. Then I looked back at him again—taking my time, you know. 'I don't think that that's a fair question to put to me,' says I."

Nosey Flynn was sitting up in his usual corner of Davy Byrne's and, when he heard the story, he stood Farrington a half-one, saying it was as smart a thing as ever he heard. Farrington stood a drink in his turn. After a while O'Halloran and Paddy Leonard came in and the story was repeated to them. O'Halloran stood tailors of malt hot all round and told the story of the retort he had made to the chief clerk when he was in Callan's of Fownes's Street; but, as the retort was after the manner of the liberal shepherds in the eclogues, he had to admit that it was not as clever as Farrington's retort. At this Farrington told the boys to polish off that and have another.

Just as they were naming their poisons who should come in but Higgins! Of course he had to join in with the others. The men asked him to give his version of it, and he did so with great vivacity for the sight of five small hot whiskies was very exhilarating. Everyone roared laughing when he showed the way in which Mr. Alleyne shook his fist in Farrington's face. Then he imitated Farrington, saying, *"And here was my nabs, as cool as you please,"* while Farrington looked at the company out of his heavy dirty eyes, smiling and at times drawing forth stray drops of liquor from his moustache with the aid of his lower lip.

When that round was over there was a pause. O'Halloran had money but neither of the other two seemed to have any; so the whole party left the shop somewhat regretfully. At the corner of Duke Street Higgins and Nosey Flynn bevelled off to the left while the other three turned back towards the city. Rain was drizzling down on the cold streets and, when they reached the Ballast Office, Farrington suggested the Scotch House. The bar was full of men and loud with the noise of tongues and glasses. The three men pushed past the whining match-sellers at the door and formed a little party at the corner of the counter. They began to exchange stories. Leonard introduced them to a young fellow named Weathers who was performing at the Tivoli as an acrobat and knockabout *artiste.* Farrington stood a drink all round. Weathers said he would take a small Irish and Apollinaris. Farrington, who had definite notions of what was what, asked the boys would they have an Apollinaris too; but the boys told Tim to make theirs hot. The talk became theatrical. O'Halloran stood a round and then Farrington stood another round, Weathers protesting that the hospitality was too Irish. He promised to get them in behind the scenes and introduce them to some nice girls. O'Halloran said that he and

Leonard would go, but that Farrington wouldn't go because he was a married man; and Farrington's heavy dirty eyes leered at the company in token that he understood he was being chaffed. Weathers made them all have just one little tincture at his expense and promised to meet them later on at Mulligan's in Poolbeg Street.

When the Scotch House closed they went round to Mulligan's. They went into the parlour at the back and O'Halloran ordered small hot specials all around. They were all beginning to feel mellow. Farrington was just standing another round when Weathers came back. Much to Farrington's relief he drank a glass of bitter this time. Funds were getting low but they had enough to keep them going. Presently two young women with big hats and a young man in a check suit came in and sat at a table close by. Weathers saluted them and told the company that they were out of the Tivoli. Farrington's eyes wandered at every moment in the direction of one of the young women. There was something striking in her appearance. An immense scarf of peacock-blue muslin was wound round her hat and knotted in a great bow under her chin; and she wore bright yellow gloves, reaching to the elbows. Farrington gazed admiringly at the plump arm which she moved very often and with much grace; and when, after a little time, she answered his gaze he admired still more her large dark brown eyes. The oblique staring expression in them fascinated him. She glanced at him once or twice and, when the party was leaving the room, she brushed against his chair and said *"O, pardon!"* in a London accent. He watched her leave the room in the hope that she would look back at him, but he was disappointed. He cursed his want of money and cursed all the rounds he had stood, particularly all the whiskies and Apollinaris which he had stood to Weathers. If there was one thing that he hated it was a sponge. He was so angry that he lost count of the conversation of his friends.

When Paddy Leonard called him he found that they were talking about feats of strength. Weathers was showing his biceps muscle to the company and boasting so much that the other two had called on Farrington to uphold the national honour. Farrington pulled up his sleeve accordingly and showed his biceps muscle to the company. The two arms were examined and compared and finally it was agreed to have a trial of strength. The table was cleared and the two men rested their elbows on it, clasping hands. When Paddy Leonard said *"Go!"* each was to try to bring down the other's hand on to the table. Farrington looked very serious and determined.

The trial began. After about thirty seconds Weathers brought his opponent's hand slowly down on to the table. Farrington's dark wine-coloured face flushed darker still with anger and humiliation at having been defeated by such a stripling.

"You're not to put the weight of your body behind it. Play fair," he said.

"Who's not playing fair?" said the other.

"Come on again. The two best out of three."

The trial began again. The veins stood out on Farrington's forehead, and the pallor of Weathers' complexion changed to peony. Their hands and arms trembled under the stress. After a long struggle Weathers again brought his opponent's hand slowly on to the table. There was a murmur of applause from the spectators. The curate, who was standing beside the table, nodded his red head towards the victor and said with stupid familiarity:

"Ah! that's the knack!"

"What the hell do you know about it?" said Farrington fiercely, turning on the man. "What do you put in your gab for?"

"Sh, sh!" said O'Halloran, observing the violent expression of Farrington's face. "Pony up, boys. We'll have just one little smahan more and then we'll be off."

A very sullen-faced man stood at the corner of O'Connell Bridge waiting for the little Sandymount tram to take him home. He was full of smouldering anger and revengefulness. He felt humiliated and discontented; he did not even feel drunk; and he had only two-pence in his pocket. He cursed everything. He had done for himself in the office, pawned his watch, spent all his money; and he had not even got drunk. He began to feel thirsty again and he longed to be back again in the hot reeking public-house. He had lost his reputation as a strong man, having been defeated twice by a mere boy. His heart swelled with fury and, when he thought of the woman in the big hat who had brushed against him and said *Pardon!* his fury nearly choked him.

His tram let him down at Shelbourne Road and he steered his great body along the shadow of the wall of the barracks. He loathed returning to his home. When he went in by the side-door he found the kitchen empty and the kitchen fire nearly out. He bawled upstairs:

"Ada! Ada!"

His wife was a little sharp-faced woman who bullied her husband when he was sober and was bullied by him when he was drunk. They had five children. A little boy came running down the stairs.

"Who is that?" said the man, peering through the darkness.

"Me, pa."

"Who are you? Charlie?"

"No, pa. Tom."

"Where's your mother?"

"She's out at the chapel."

"That's right. . . . Did she think of leaving any dinner for me?"

"Yes, pa. I—"

"Light the lamp. What do you mean by having the place in darkness? Are the other children in bed?"

The man sat down heavily on one of the chairs while the little boy lit the lamp. He began to mimic his son's flat accent, saying half to himself: *"At the chapel. At the chapel, if you please!"* When the lamp was lit he banged his fist on the table and shouted:

"What's for my dinner?"

"I'm going . . . to cook it, pa," said the little boy.

The man jumped up furiously and pointed to the fire.

"On that fire! You let the fire out! By God, I'll teach you to do that again!"

He took a step to the door and seized the walking-stick which was standing behind it.

"I'll teach you to let the fire out!" he said, rolling up his sleeve in order to give his arm free play.

The little boy cried *"O, pa!"* and ran whimpering round the table, but the man followed him and caught him by the coat. The little boy looked about him wildly but, seeing no way to escape, fell upon his knees.

"Now, you'll let the fire out the next time!" said the man, striking at him vigorously with the stick. "Take that, you little whelp!"

The boy uttered a squeal of pain as the stick cut his thigh. He clasped his hands together in the air and his voice shook with fright.

"O, pa!" he cried. "Don't beat me, pa! And I'll . . . I'll say a *Hail Mary* for you. . . . I'll say a *Hail Mary* for you, pa, if you don't beat me. . . . I'll say a *Hail Mary*. . . ."

EUDORA WELTY

Livvie

Solomon carried Livvie twenty-one miles away from her home when he married her. He carried her away up on the Old Natchez Trace into the deep country to live in his house. She was sixteen—an only girl, then. Once people said he thought nobody would ever come along there. He told her himself that it had been a long time, and a day she did not know about, since that road was a traveled road with *people* coming and going. He was good to her, but he kept her in the house. She had not thought that she could not get back. Where she came from, people said an old man did not want anybody in the world to ever find his wife, for fear they would steal her back from him. Solomon asked her before he took her, "Would she be happy?"—very dignified, for he was a colored man that owned his land and had it written down in the courthouse; and she said, "Yes, sir," since he was an old man and she was young and just listened and answered. He asked her, if she was choosing winter, would she pine for spring, and she said, "No indeed." Whatever she said, always, was because he was an old man . . . while nine years went by. All the time, he got old, and he got so old he gave out. At least he slept the whole day in bed, and she was young still.

It was a nice house, inside and outside both. In the first place, it had three rooms. The front room was papered in holly paper, with green palmettos from the swamp spaced at careful intervals over the walls. There was fresh newspaper cut with fancy borders on the mantleshelf, on which were propped photographs of old or very young men printed in faint yellow—Solomon's people. Solomon had a houseful of furniture. There was a double settee, a tall scrolled rocker and an organ in the front room, all around a three-legged table with a pink marble top, on which was set a lamp with three gold feet, besides a jelly glass with pretty hen feathers in it. Behind the front room, the other room had the bright iron bed with the polished knobs like a throne, in which Solomon slept all day. There were snow-white curtains of wiry lace at the window, and a lace bedspread belonged on the bed. But what old Solomon slept sound under was a big feather-stitched piece-quilt in the pattern "Trip Around the World," which had twenty-one different colors, four hundred and forty pieces, and a thousand yards of thread, and that was what Solomon's mother made in her life and old age. There was a table holding the Bible, and a trunk with a key. On the wall were two calendars, and a diploma from somewhere in Solomon's family, and under that Livvie's one possession was nailed, a picture of the little white baby of the family she worked for, back in Natchez before she was married. Going through that room and on to the kitchen, there was a big wood stove and a big round table always with a wet top and with the knives and forks in one jelly glass and the spoons in another, and a cut-glass vinegar bottle between, and going out from those, many shallow dishes of pickled peaches, fig preserves, water-melon pickles and blackberry jam always sitting there. The churn sat in the sun, the doors of the safe were always both shut, and there were four baited mouse-traps in the kitchen, one in every corner.

The outside of Solomon's house looked nice. It was not painted, but across the porch was an even balance. On each side there was one easy chair with high springs, looking out, and a fern basket hanging over it from the ceiling, and a dishpan of zinnia seedlings growing at its foot on the floor. By the door was a plow-wheel, just a pretty iron circle, nailed up on one wall and a square mirror on the other, a turquoise-blue comb stuck up in the frame, with the wash stand beneath it. On the door was a wooden knob with a pearl in the end, and Solomon's black hat hung on that, if he was in the house.

Out front was a clean dirt yard with every vestige of grass patiently uprooted and the ground scarred in deep whorls from the strike of Livvie's broom. Rose bushes with tiny blood-red roses blooming every month grew in threes on either side of the steps. On one side was a peach tree, on the other a pomegranate. Then coming around up the path from the deep cut of the Natchez Trace below was a line of bare crape-myrtle trees with every branch of them ending in a colored bottle, green or blue. There was no word that fell from Solomon's lips to say what they were for, but Livvie knew that there could be a spell put in trees, and she was familiar from the time she was born with the way bottle trees kept evil spirits from coming into the house—by luring them inside the colored bottles, where they cannot get out again. Solomon had made the bottle trees with his own hands over the nine years, in labor amounting to about a tree a year, and without a sign that he had any uneasiness in his heart, for he took as much pride in his precautions against spirits coming in the house as he took in the house, and sometimes in the sun the bottle trees looked prettier than the house did.

It was a nice house. It was in a place where the days would go by and surprise anyone that they were over. The lamplight and the firelight would shine out the door after dark, over the still and breathing country, lighting the roses and the bottle trees, and all was quiet there.

But there was nobody, nobody at all, not even a white person. And if there had been anybody, Solomon would not have let Livvie look at them, just as he would not let her look at a field hand, or a field hand look at her. There was no house near, except for the cabins of the tenants that were forbidden to her, and there was no house as far as she had been, stealing away down the still, deep Trace. She felt as if she waded a river when she went, for the dead leaves on the ground reached as high as her knees, and when she was all scratched and bleeding she said it was not like a road that went anywhere. One day, climbing up the high bank, she had found a graveyard without a church; with ribbon-grass growing about the foot of an angel (she had climbed up because she thought she saw angel wings), and in the sun, trees shining like burning flames through the great caterpillar nets which enclosed them. Scarey thistles stood looking like the prophets in the Bible in Solomon's house. Indian paint brushes grew over her head, and the mourning dove made the only sound in the world. Oh for a stirring of the leaves, and a breaking of the nets! But not by a ghost, prayed Livvie, jumping down the bank. After Solomon took to his bed, she never went out, except one more time.

Livvie knew she made a nice girl to wait on anybody. She fixed things to eat on a tray like a surprise. She could keep from singing when she ironed, and to sit by a bed and fan away the flies, she could be so still she could not hear herself breathe. She could clean up the house and never drop a thing, and wash the dishes without a sound, and she would step outside to churn, for churning sounded too sad to her, like sobbing, and if it made her home-sick and not Solomon, she did not think of that.

But Solomon scarcely opened his eyes to see her, and scarcely tasted his food. He was not sick or paralyzed or in any pain that he mentioned, but he was surely wearing out in the body, and no matter what nice hot thing Livvie would bring him to taste, he would only look at it now, as if he were past seeing how he could add anything more to himself. Before she could beg him, he would go fast asleep. She could not surprise him any more, if he would not taste, and she was afraid that he was never in the world going to taste another thing she brought him—and so how could he last?

But one morning it was breakfast time and she cooked his eggs and grits, carried them in on a tray, and called his name. He was sound asleep. He lay in a dignified way with his watch beside him, on his back in the middle of the bed. One hand drew the quilt up high, though it was the first day of spring. Through the white lace curtains a little puffy wind was blowing as if it came from round cheeks. All night the frogs had sung out in the swamp, like a commotion in the room, and he had not stirred, though she lay wide awake and saying "Shh, frogs!" for fear he would mind them.

He looked as if he would like to sleep a little longer, and so she put back the tray and waited a little. When she tiptoed and stayed so quiet, she surrounded herself with a little reverie, and sometimes it seemed to her when she was so stealthy that the quiet she kept was for a sleeping baby, and that she had a baby and was its mother. When she stood at Solomon's bed and looked down at him, she would be thinking, "He sleeps so well," and she would hate to wake him up. And in some other way, too, she was afraid to wake him up because even in his sleep he seemed to be such a strict man.

Of course, nailed to the wall over the bed—only she would forget who it was—there was a picture of him when he was young. Then he had a fan of hair over his forehead like a king's crown. Now his hair lay down on his head, the spring had gone out of it. Solomon had a lightish face, with eyebrows scattered but rugged, the way privet grows, strong eyes, with second sight, a strict mouth, and a little gold smile. This was the way he looked in his clothes, but in bed in the daytime he looked like a different and smaller man, even when he was wide awake, and holding the Bible. He looked like somebody kin to himself. And then sometimes when he lay in sleep and she stood fanning the flies away, and the light came in, his face was like new, so smooth and clear that it was like a glass of jelly held to the window, and she could almost look through his forehead and see what he thought.

She fanned him and at length he opened his eyes and spoke her name, but he would not taste the nice eggs she had kept warm under a pan.

Back in the kitchen she ate heartily, his breakfast and hers, and looked out the open door at what went on. The whole day, and the whole night before, she had felt the stir of spring close to her. It was as present in the house as a young man would be. The moon was in the last quarter and outside they were turning the sod and planting peas and beans. Up and down the red fields, over which smoke from the brush-burning hung showing like a little skirt of sky, a white horse and a white mule pulled the plow. At intervals hoarse shouts came through the air and roused her as if she dozed neglectfully in the shade, and they were telling her, "Jump up!" She could see how over each ribbon of field were moving men and girls, on foot and mounted on mules, with hats set on their heads and bright with tall hoes and forks as if they carried streamers on them and were going to some place on a journey—and how as if at a signal now and then they would all start at once shouting, hollering, cajoling, calling and answering back, running, being leaped on and breaking away, flinging to earth with a shout and lying motionless in the trance of twelve o'clock. The old women came out of the cabins and brought them food they had ready for them, and they all worked together, spread evenly out. The little children came too, like a bouncing stream overflowing the fields, and set upon the men, the women, the dogs, the rushing birds and the wave-like rows of earth, their little voices almost too high to be heard. In the middle distance like some white-and-gold towers were the haystacks, with black cows coming around to eat their edges. High above everything, the wheel of fields, house, and cabins, and the deep road surrounding like a moat to keep them in, was the turning sky, blue with long, far-flung white mare's-tail clouds, serene and still as high flames. And sound asleep while all this went around him that was his, Solomon was like a little still spot in the middle.

Even in the house the earth was sweet to breathe. Solomon had never let Livvie go any farther than the chicken house and the well. But what if she would walk now into the heart of the fields and take a hoe and work until she fell stretched out and drenched with her efforts, like other girls, and laid her cheek against the laid-open earth, and shamed the old man with her humbleness and delight? To shame him! A cruel wish could come in uninvited and so fast while she looked out the back door. She washed the dishes and scrubbed the table. She could hear the cries of the little lambs. Her mother, that she had not seen since her wedding day, had said one time, "I rather a man be anything, than a woman be mean."

So all morning she kept tasting the chicken broth on the stove, and when it was right she poured a nice cupful. She carried it in to Solomon, and there he lay having a dream. Now what did he dream about? For she saw him sigh gently as if not to disturb some whole thing he held round in his mind, like a fresh egg. So even an old man dreamed about something pretty. Did he dream of her, while his eyes were shut and sunken, and his small hand with the wedding ring curled close in sleep around the quilt? He might be dreaming of what time it was, for even through his sleep he kept track of it like a clock, and knew how much of it went by, and waked up knowing where the hands were even before he consulted the silver watch that he never let go. He would sleep with the watch in his palm, and even holding it to his cheek like a child that loves a plaything. Or he might dream of journeys and travels on a steamboat to Natchez. Yet she thought he dreamed of her; but even while she scrutinized him, the rods of the foot of the bed seemed to rise up like a rail fence between them, and she could see that people never could be sure of anything as long as one of them was asleep and the other awake. To look at him dreaming of her when he might be going to die frightened her a little, as if he might carry her with him that way, and she wanted to run out of the room. She took hold of the bed and held on, and Solomon opened his eyes and called her name, but he did not want anything. He would not taste the good broth.

Just a little after that, as she was taking up the ashes in the front room for the last time in the year, she heard a sound. It was somebody coming. She pulled the curtains together and looked through the slit.

Coming up the path under the bottle trees was a white lady. At first she looked young, but then she looked old. Marvelous to see, a little car stood steaming like a kettle out in the field-track—it had come without a road.

Livvie stood listening to the long, repeated knockings at the door, and after a while she opened it just a little. The lady came in through the crack, though she was more than middle-sized and wore a big hat.

"My name is Miss Baby Marie," she said.

Livvie gazed respectfully at the lady and at the little suitcase she was holding close to her by the handle until the proper moment. The lady's eyes were running over the room, from palmetto to palmetto, but she was saying, "I live at home . . . out from Natchez . . . and get out and show these pretty cosmetic things to the white people and the colored people both . . . all around . . . years and years . . . Both shades of powder and rouge. . . . It's the kind of work a girl can do and not go clear 'way from home . . ." And the harder she looked, the more she talked. Suddenly she turned up her nose and said, "It is not Christian or sanitary to put feathers in a vase," and then she took a gold key out of the front of her dress and began unlocking the locks on her suitcase. Her face drew the light, the way it was covered with intense white and red, with a little patty-cake of white between the wrinkles by her upper lip. Little red tassels of hair bobbed under the rusty wires of her picture-hat, as with an air of triumph and secrecy she now drew open her little suitcase and brought out bottle after bottle and jar after jar, which she put down on the table, the mantle-piece, the settee, and the organ.

"Did you ever see so many cosmetics in your life?" cried Miss Baby Marie.

"No'm," Livvie tried to say, but the cat had her tongue.

"Have you ever applied cosmetics?" asked Miss Baby Marie next.

"No'm," Livvie tried to say.

"Then look!" she said, and pulling out the last thing of all, "Try this!" she said. And in her hand was unclenched a golden lipstick which popped open like magic. A fragrance came out of it like incense, and Livvie cried out suddenly. "Chinaberry flowers!"

Her hand took the lipstick, and in an instant she was carried away in the air through the spring, and looking down with a half-drowsy smile from a purple cloud she saw from above a chinaberry tree, dark and smooth and neatly leaved, neat as a guinea hen in the dooryard, and there was her home that she had left. On one side of the tree was her mama holding up her heavy apron, and she could see it was loaded with ripe figs, and on the other side was her papa holding a fish-pole over the pond, and she could see it transparently, the little clear fishes swimming up to the brim.

"Oh, no, not chinaberry flowers—secret ingredients," said Miss Baby Marie. "My cosmetics have secret ingredients—not chinaberry flowers."

"It's purple," Livvie breathed, and Miss Baby Marie said, "Use it freely. Rub it on."

Livvie tiptoed out to the wash stand on the front porch and before the mirror put the paint on her mouth. In the wavery surface her face danced before her like a flame. Miss Baby Marie followed her out, took a look at what she had done, and said, "That's it."

Livvie tried to say "Thank you" without moving her parted lips where the paint lay so new.

By now Miss Baby Marie stood behind Livvie and looked in the mirror over her shoulder, twisting up the tassels of her hair. "The lipstick I can let you have for only two dollars," she said, close to her neck.

"Lady, but I don't have no money, never did have," said Livvie.

"Oh, but you don't pay the first time. I make another trip, that's the way I do. I come back again—later."

"Oh," said Livvie, pretending she understood everything so as to please the lady.

"But if you don't take it now, this may be the last time I'll call at your house," said Miss Baby Marie sharply. "It's far away from anywhere, I'll tell you that. You don't live close to anywhere."

"Yes'm. My husband, he keep the *money*," said Livvie, trembling. "He is strict as he can be. He don't know *you* walk in here—Miss Baby Marie!"

"Where is he?"

"Right now, he in yonder sound asleep, an old man. I wouldn't ever ask him for anything."

Miss Baby Marie took back the lipstick and packed it up. She gathered up the jars for both black and white and got them all inside the suitcase, with the same little fuss of triumph with which she had brought them out. She started away.

"Goodbye," she said, making herself look grand from the back, but at the last minute she turned around in the door. Her old hat wobbled as she whispered, "Let me see your husband."

Livvie obediently went on tiptoe and opened the door to the other room. Miss Baby Marie came behind her and rose on her toes and looked in.

"My, what a little tiny old, old man!" she whispered, clasping her hands and shaking her head over them. "What a beautiful quilt! What a tiny old, old man!"

"He can sleep like that all day," whispered Livvie proudly.

They looked at him awhile so fast asleep, and then all at once they looked at each other. Somehow that was as if they had a secret, for he had never stirred. Livvie then politely, but all at once, closed the door.

"Well! I'd certainly like to leave you with a lipstick!" said Miss Baby Marie vivaciously. She smiled in the door.

"Lady, but I told you I don't have no money, and never did have."

"And never will?" In the air and all around, like a bright halo around the white lady's nodding head, it was a true spring day.

"Would you take eggs, lady?" asked Livvie softly.

"No, I have plenty of eggs—plenty," said Miss Baby Marie.

"I still don't have no money," said Livvie, and Miss Baby Marie took her suitcase and went on somewhere else.

Livvie stood watching her go, and all the time she felt her heart beating in her left side. She touched the place with her hand. It seemed as if her heart beat and her whole face flamed from the pulsing color of her lips. She went to sit by Solomon and when he opened his eyes he could not see a change in her. "He's fixin' to die," she said inside. That was the secret. That was when she went out of the house for a little breath of air.

She went down the path and down the Natchez Trace a way, and she did not know how far she had gone, but it was not far, when she saw a sight. It was a man, looking like a vision—she standing on one side of the Old Natchez Trace and he standing on the other side.

As soon as this man caught sight of her, he began to look himself over. Starting at the bottom with his pointed shoes, he began to look up, lifting his peg-top pants the higher to see fully his bright socks. His coat long and wide and leaf-green he opened like doors to see his high-up tawny pants and his pants he smoothed downward from the points of his collar, and he wore a luminous baby-pink satin shirt. At the end, he reached gently above his wide platter-shaped round hat, the color of a plum, and one finger touched at the feather, emerald green, blowing in the spring winds.

No matter how she looked, she could never look so fine as he did, and she was not sorry for that, she was pleased.

He took three jumps, one down and two up, and was by her side.

"My name is Cash," he said.

He had a guinea pig in his pocket. They began to walk along. She stared on and on at him, as if he were doing some daring spectacular thing, instead of just walking beside her. It was not simply the city way he was dressed that made her look at him and see hope in its insolence looking back. It was not only the way he moved along kicking the flowers as if he could break through everything in the way and destroy anything in the world, that made her eyes grow bright. It might be, if he had not appeared the way he did appear that day she would never have looked so closely at him, but the time people come makes a difference.

They walked through the still leaves of the Natchez Trace, the light and the shade falling through trees about them, the white irises shining like candles on the banks and the new ferns shining like green stars up in the oak branches. They came out at Solomon's house, bottle trees and all. Livvie stopped and hung her head.

Cash began whistling a little tune. She did not know what it was, but she had heard it before from a distance, and she had a revelation. Cash was a field hand. He was a transformed field hand. Cash belonged to Solomon. But he had stepped out of his overalls into this. There in front of Solomon's house he laughed. He had a round head, a round face, all of him was young, and he flung his head up, rolled it against the mare's-tail sky in his round hat, and he could laugh just to see Solomon's house sitting there. Livvie looked at it, and there was Solomon's black hat hanging on the peg on the front door, the blackest thing in the world.

"I been to Natchez," Cash said, wagging his head around against the sky. "*I* taken a trip, *I* ready for Easter!"

How was it possible to look so fine before the harvest? Cash must have stolen the money, stolen it from Solomon. He stood in the path and lifted his spread hand high and brought it down again and again in his laughter. He kicked up his heels. A little chill went through her. It was as if Cash was bringing that strong hand down to beat a drum or to rain blows upon a man, such an abandon and menace were in his laugh. Frowning, she went closer to him and his swinging arm drew her in at once and the fright was crushed from her body, as a little match-flame might be smothered out by what it lighted. She gathered the folds of his coat behind him and fastened her red lips to his mouth, and she was dazzled by herself then, the way he had been dazzled at himself to begin with.

In that instant she felt something that could not be told—that Solomon's death was at hand, that he was the same to her as if he were dead now. She cried out, and uttering little cries turned and ran for the house.

At once Cash was coming, following after, he was running behind her. He came close, and half-way up the path he laughed and passed her. He even picked up a stone and sailed it into the bottle trees. She put her hands over her head, and sounds clattered through the bottle trees like cries of outrage. Cash stamped and plunged zigzag up the front steps and in at the door.

When she got there, he had stuck his hands in his pockets and was turning slowly about in the front room. The little guinea pig peeped out. Around Cash, the pinned-up palmettos looked as if a lazy green monkey had walked up and down and around the walls leaving green prints of his hands and feet.

She got through the room and his hands were still in his pockets, and she fell upon the closed door to the other room and pushed it open. She ran to Solomon's bed, calling "Solomon! Solomon!" The little shapc of the old man never moved at all, wrapped under the quilt as if it were winter still.

"Solomon!" She pulled the quilt away, but there was another one under that, and she fell on her knees beside him. He made no sound except a sigh, and then she could hear in the silence the light springy steps of Cash walking and walking in the front room, and the ticking of Solomon's silver watch, which came from the bed. Old Solomon was far away in his sleep, his face looked small, relentless, and devout, as if he were walking somewhere where she could imagine the snow falling.

Then there was a noise like a hoof pawing the floor, and the door gave a creak, and Cash appeared beside her. When she looked up, Cash's face was so black it was bright, and so bright and bare of pity that it looked sweet to her. She stood up and held up her head. Cash was so powerful that his presence gave her strength even when she did not need any.

Under their eyes Solomon slept. People's faces tell of things and places not known to the one who looks at them while they sleep, and while Solomon slept under the eyes of Livvie and Cash his face told them like a mythical story that all his life he had built, little scrap by little scrap, respect. A beetle could not have been more laborious or more ingenious in the task of its destiny. When Solomon was young, as he was in his picture overhead, it was the infinite thing with him, and he could see no end to the respect he would contrive and keep in a house. He had built a lonely house, the way he would make a cage, but it grew to be the same with him as a great monumental pyramid and sometimes in his absorption of getting it erected he was like the builder-slaves of Egypt who forgot or never knew the origin and meaning of the thing to which they gave all the strength of their bodies and used up all their days. Livvie and Cash could see that as a man might rest from a life-labor he lay in his bed, and they could hear how, wrapped in his quilt, he sighed to himself comfortably in sleep, while in his dreams he might have been an ant, a beetle, a bird, an Egyptian, assembling and carrying on his back and building with his hands, or he might have been an old man of India or a swaddled baby, about to smile and brush all away.

Then without warning old Solomon's eyes flew wide open under the hedgelike brows. He was wide awake.

And instantly Cash raised his quick arm. A radiant sweat stood on his temples. But he did not bring his arm down—it stayed in the air, as if something might have taken hold.

It was not Livvie—she did not move. As if something said "Wait," she stood waiting. Even while her eyes burned under motionless lids, her lips parted in a stiff grimace, and with her arms stiff at her sides she stood above the prone old man and the panting young one, erect and apart.

Movement when it came came in Solomon's face. It was an old and strict face, a frail face, but behind it, like a covered light, came an animation that could play hide and seek, that would dart and escape, had always escaped. The mystery flickered in him, and invited from his eyes. It was that very mystery that Cash with his quick arm would have to strike, and that Livvie could not weep for. But Cash only stood holding his arm in the air, when the gentlest flick of his great strength, almost a puff of his breath, would have been enough, if he had known how to give it, to send the old man over the obstruction that kept him away from death.

If it could not be that the tiny illumination in the fragile and ancient face caused a crisis, a mystery in the room that would not permit a blow to fall, at least it was certain that Cash, throbbing in his Easter clothes, felt a pang of shame that the vigor of a man would come to such an end that he could not be struck without warning. He took down his hand and stepped back behind Livvie, like a round-eyed schoolboy on whose unsuspecting head the dunce cap has been set.

"Young ones can't wait," said Solomon.

Livvie shuddered violently, and then in a gush of tears she stooped for a glass of water and handed it to him, but he did not see her.

"So here come the young man Livvie wait for. Was no prevention. No prevention. Now I lay eyes on young man and it come to be somebody I know all the time, and been knowing since he were born in a cotton patch, and watched grow up year to year, Cash McCord, growed to size, growed up to come in my house in the end—ragged and barefoot."

Solomon gave a cough of distaste. Then he shut his eyes vigorously, and his lips began to move like a chanter's.

"When Livvie married, her husband were already somebody. He had paid great cost for his land. He spread sycamore leaves over the ground from wagon to door, day he brought her home, so her foot would not have to touch ground. He carried her through his door. Then he growed old and could not lift her, and she were still young."

Livvie's sobs followed his words like a soft melody repeating each thing as he stated it. His lips moved for a little without sound, or she cried too fervently, and unheard he might have been telling his whole life, and then he said, "God forgive Solomon for sins great and small. God forgive Solomon for carrying away too young girl for wife and keeping her away from her people and from all the young people would clamor for her back."

Then he lifted up his right hand toward Livvie where she stood by the bed and offered her his silver watch. He dangled it before her eyes, and she hushed crying; her tears stopped. For a moment the watch could be heard ticking as it always did, precisely in his proud hand. She lifted it away. Then he took hold of the quilt; then he was dead.

Livvie left Solomon dead and went out of the room. Stealthily, nearly without noise, Cash went beside her. He was like a shadow, but his shiny shoes moved over the floor in spangles, and the green downy feather shone like a light in his hat. As they reached the front room, he seized her deftly as a long black cat and dragged her hanging by the waist round and round him, while he turned in a circle, his face bent down to hers. The first moment, she kept one arm and its hand stiff and still, the one that held Solomon's watch. Then the fingers softly let go, all of her was limp, and the watch fell somewhere on the floor. It ticked away in the still room, and all at once there began outside the full song of a bird.

They moved around and around the room and into the brightness of the open door, then he stopped and shook her once. She rested in silence in his trembling arms, unprotesting as a bird on a nest. Outside the redbirds were flying and criss-crossing, the sun was in all the bottles on the prisoned trees, and the young peach was shining in the middle of them with the bursting light of spring.

NADINE GORDIMER

The Train from Rhodesia

The train came out of the red horizon and bore down toward them over the single straight track.

The stationmaster came out of his little brick station with its pointed chalet roof, feeling the creases in his serge uniform in his legs as well. A stir of preparedness rippled through the squatting native vendors waiting in the dust; the face of a carved wooden animal, eternally surprised, stuck out of a sack. The stationmaster's barefoot children wandered over. From the gray mud huts with the untidy heads that stood within a decorated mud wall, chickens, and dogs with their skin stretched like parchment over their bones, followed the piccanins down to the track. The flushed and perspiring west cast a reflection, faint, without heat, upon the station, upon the tin shed marked "Goods," upon the walled kraal, upon the gray tin house of the stationmaster and upon the sand, that lapped all around, from sky to sky, cast little rhythmical cups of shadow, so that the sand became the sea, and closed over the children's black feet softly and without imprint.

The stationmaster's wife sat behind the mesh of her verandah. Above her head the hunk of a sheep's carcass moved slightly, dangling in a current of air.

They waited.

The train called out, along the sky; but there was no answer; and the cry hung on: I'm coming . . . I'm coming . . .

The engine flared out now, big, whisking a dwindling body behind it; the track flared out to let it in.

Creaking, jerking, jostling, gasping, the train filled the station.

Here, let me see that one—the young woman curved her body further out of the corridor window. Missus? smiled the old boy, looking at the creatures he held in his hand. From a piece of string on his gray finger hung a tiny woven basket; he lifted it, questioning. No, no, she urged, leaning down toward him, across the height of the train, toward the man in the piece of old rug; that one, that one, her hand commanded. It was a lion, carved out of soft dry wood that looked like spongecake; heraldic, black and white, with impressionistic detail burnt in. The old man held it up to her still smiling, not from the heart, but at the customer. Between its Vandyke teeth, in the mouth opened in an endless roar too terrible to be heard, it had a black tongue. Look, said the young husband, if you don't mind! And round the neck of the thing, a piece of fur (rat? rabbit? meerkat?); a real mane, majestic, telling you somehow that the artist had delight in the lion.

All up and down the length of the train in the dust the artists sprang, walking bent, like performing animals, the better to exhibit the fantasy held toward the faces on the train. Buck, startled and stiff, staring with round black and white eyes. More lions, standing erect, grappling with strange, thin, elongated warriors who clutched spears and showed no fear in their slits of eyes. How much, they asked from the train, how much?

Give me penny, said the little ones with nothing to sell. The dogs went and sat, quite still, under the dining car, where the train breathed out the smell of meat cooking with onion.

A man passed beneath the arch of reaching arms meeting gray-black and white in the exchange of money for the staring wooden eyes, the stiff wooden legs sticking up in the air; went along under the voices and the bargaining, interrogating the wheels. Past the dogs; glancing up at the dining car where he could stare at the faces, behind glass, drinking beer, two by two, on either side of a uniform railway vase with its pale dead flower. Right to the end, to the guard's van, where the stationmaster's children had just collected their mother's two loaves of bread; to the engine itself, where the stationmaster and the driver stood talking against the steaming complaint of the resting beast.

The man called out to them, something loud and joking. They turned to laugh, in a twirl of steam. The two children careered over the sand, clutching the bread, and burst through the iron gate and up the path through the garden in which nothing grew.

Passengers drew themselves in at the corridor windows and turned into compartments to fetch money, to call someone to look. Those sitting inside looked up: suddenly different, caged faces, boxed in, cut off, after the contact of outside. There was an orange a piccanin would like. . . . What about that chocolate? It wasn't very nice. . . .

A young girl had collected a handful of the hard kind, that no one liked, out of the chocolate box, and was throwing them to the dogs, over at the dining car. But the hens darted in, and swallowed the chocolates, incredibly quick and accurate, before they had even dropped in the dust, and the dogs, a little bewildered, looked up with their brown eyes, not expecting anything.

—No, leave it, said the girl, don't take it. . . .

Too expensive, too much, she shook her head and raised her voice to the old boy, giving up the lion. He held it up where she had handed it to him. No, she said, shaking her head. Three-and-six? insisted her husband, loudly. Yes baas! laughed the boy. *Three-and-six?*—the young man was incredulous. Oh leave it—she said. The young man stopped. Don't you want it? he said, keeping his face closed to the boy. No, never mind, she said, leave it. The old native kept his head on one side, looking at them sideways, holding the lion. Three-and-six, he murmured, as old people repeat things to themselves.

The young woman drew her head in. She went into the coupé and sat down. Out of the window, on the other side, there was nothing; sand and bush; a thorn tree. Back through the open doorway, past the figure of her husband in the corridor, there was the station, the voices, wooden animals waving, running feet. Her eye followed the funny little valance of scrolled wood that outlined the chalet roof of the station; she thought of the lion and smiled. That bit of fur round the neck. But the wooden buck, the hippos, the elephants, the baskets that already bulked out of their brown paper under the seat and on the luggage rack! How will they look at home? Where will you put them? What will they mean away from the places you found them? Away from the unreality of the last few weeks? The man outside. But he is not part of the unreality; he is for good now. Odd . . . somewhere there was an idea that he, that living with him, was part of the holiday, the strange places.

Outside, a bell rang. The stationmaster was leaning against the end of the train, green flag rolled in readiness. A few men who had got down to stretch their legs sprang on to the train, clinging to the observation platforms, or perhaps merely standing on the iron step, holding the rail; but on the train, safe from the one dusty platform, the one tin house, the empty sand.

There was a grunt. The train jerked. Through the glass the beer drinkers looked out, as if they could not see beyond it. Behind the fly-screen, the stationmaster's wife sat facing back at them beneath the darkening hunk of meat.

There was a shout. The flag drooped out. Joints not yet coordinated, the segmented body of the train heaved and bumped back against itself. It began to move; slowly the scrolled chalet moved past it, the yells of the natives, running alongside, jetted up into the air, fell back at different levels. Staring wooden faces waved drunkenly, there, then gone, questioning for the last time at the windows. Here, one-and-six baas!—As one automatically opens a hand to catch a thrown ball, a man fumbled wildly down his pocket, brought up the shilling and sixpence and threw them out; the old native, gasping, his skinny toes splaying the sand, flung the lion.

The piccanins were waving, the dogs stood, tails uncertain, watching the train go: past the mud huts, where a woman turned to look, up from the smoke of the fire, her hand pausing on her hip.

The stationmaster went slowly in under the chalet.

The old native stood, breath blowing out the skin between his ribs, feet tense, balanced in the sand, smiling and shaking his head. In his opened palm, held in the attitude of receiving, was the retrieved shilling and sixpence.

The blind end of the train was being pulled helplessly out of the station.

The young man swung in from the corridor, breathless. He was shaking his head with laughter and triumph. Here! he said. And waggled the lion at her. One-and-six!

What? she said.

He laughed. I was arguing with him for fun, bargaining—when the train had pulled out already, he came tearing after. . . . One-and-six baas! So there's your lion.

She was holding it away from her, the head with the open jaws, the pointed teeth, the black tongue, the wonderful ruff of fur facing her. She was looking at it with an expression of not seeing, of seeing something different. Her face was drawn up, wryly, like the face of a discomforted child. Her mouth lifted nervously at the corner. Very slowly, cautious, she lifted her finger and touched the mane, where it was joined to the wood.

But how could you, she said. He was shocked by the dismay of her face.

Good Lord, he said, what's the matter?

If you wanted the thing, she said, her voice rising and breaking with the shrill impotence of anger, why didn't you buy it in the first place? If you wanted it, why didn't you pay for it? Why didn't you take it decently, when he offered it? Why did you have to wait for him to run after the train with it, and give him one-and-six? One-and-six!

She was pushing it at him, trying to force him to take it. He stood astonished, his hands hanging at his sides.

But you wanted it! You liked it so much!

—It's a beautiful piece of work, she said fiercely, as if to protect it from him.

You liked it so much! You said yourself it was too expensive—

Oh *you*—she said, hopeless and furious. *You*. . . . She threw the lion on to the seat.

He stood looking at her.

She sat down again in the corner and, her face slumped in her hand, stared out of the window. Everything was turning round inside her. One-and-six. One-and-six. One-and-six for the wood and the carving and the sinews of the legs and the switch of the tail. The mouth open like that and the teeth. The black tongue, rolling, like a wave. The mane round the neck. To give one-and-six for that. The heat of shame mounted through her legs and body and sounded in her ears like the sound of sand pouring. Pouring, pouring. She sat there, sick. A weariness, a tastelessness, the discovery of a void made her hands slacken their grip, atrophy emptily, as if the hour was not worth their grasp. She was feeling like this again. She had thought it was something to do with singleness, with being alone and belonging too much to oneself.

She sat there not wanting to move or speak, or to look at anything, even; so that the mood should be associated with nothing, no object, word or sight that might recur and so recall the feeling again. . . . Smuts blew in grittily, settled on her hands. Her back remained at exactly the same angle, turned against the young man sitting with his hands drooping between his sprawled legs, and the lion, fallen on its side in the corner.

The train had cast the station like a skin. It called out to the sky, I'm coming, I'm coming; and again, there was no answer.

9

STORIES FOR FURTHER STUDY

Perhaps the following questions have occurred to the reader of the preceding eight discussions of fictional theory: Where do these principles come from? Who legislates these "rules" for writing stories? This final section may provide at least a partial answer.

The answer, of course, is that no one makes these "rules"; rather, they are deduced from an analysis of short stories themselves. The critical process is primarily a comparative process. A critic reads a number of stories; he finds that some "work" and that others do not; he asks himself why this story is successful where that one is a failure; and he ultimately emerges with a generalization that successful short stories *usually* follow this or that principle, employ this or that method of accomplishing their aims. The term *usually* is, here, a crucial one, for the very wide reader of fiction will inevitably discover that no "rule" and no "principle" is ever universal; like theme in fiction, to be valid a critical principle must be carefully modified. To be sure, the presence of stock characters in a story or the use of coincidence in resolving a conflict or the employment of clichés and platitudes will ordinarily result in an inferior (that is, an ineffective) story. Yet one can find extremely effective stories which disregard these and most other critical principles. The case here is analogous to the high school English teacher who insists that the sentence "I ain't got no money" is "incorrect." In a department meeting it probably is; as a line of dialogue in a short story it may be exactly right.

The stories which follow, then, are chosen and grouped as they are with two ends in mind: first, they are designed to give you your first formal and concentrated experience in comparison and contrast; second, it is hoped that through your comparison you will discover the fact that ultimately the only "rule" for fiction might well be that there are no rules. For in any final analysis, the only relevant question we can ask of fiction is, "Does it work or doesn't it work?" And here is one instance in which the end justifies the means.

If you are relatively new to literary criticism, the process of comparison may present some problems. One can only compare things that are in some way alike. In a sense all short stories share similarities, and with enough experience, one can probably compare any short story to any other short story, regardless of how radically different their purposes, methods, forms, emphases, or results might be. But for the reader who is relatively new to literary comparison, such is not the case. Hence, in this section we have chosen stories because they share certain striking similarities. We could have made our choice on any number of bases, of course. We might, for example, have chosen stories with identical purposes which employ radically different methods of achieving those purposes. Or we might have chosen stories which employ similar methods in order to arrive at different ends. What we have done is to choose stories which seem to have been based on an identical germinal idea. In your comparison of these stories, you will probably discover what inevitably happens when a number of writers use an identical "plot." You will also, it is hoped, discover that some stories in each group work better than others, and perhaps you will be able to deduce why. If so, you will have experienced your first adventure in genuine literary criticism.

GROUP ONE

NATHANIEL HAWTHORNE

Wakefield

In some old magazine or newspaper I recollect a story, told as truth, of a man—let us call him Wakefield—who absented himself for a long time from his wife. The fact, thus abstractedly stated, is not very uncommon, nor—without a proper distinction of circumstances—to be condemned either as naughty or nonsensical. Howbeit, this, though far from the most aggravated, is perhaps the strangest instance on record of marital delinquency; and, moreover, as remarkable a freak as may be found in the whole list of human oddities. The wedded couple lived in London. The man, under pretence of going a journey, took lodgings in the next street to his own house, and there, unheard of by his wife or friends, and without the shadow of a reason for such self-banishment, dwelt upwards of twenty years. During that period, he beheld his home every day, and frequently the forlorn Mrs. Wakefield. And after so great a gap in his matrimonial felicity—when his death was reckoned certain, his estate settled, his name dismissed from memory, and his wife, long, long ago, resigned to her autumnal widowhood—he entered the door one evening, quietly, as from a day's absence, and became a loving spouse till death.

This outline is all that I remember. But the incident, though of the purest originality, unexampled, and probably never to be repeated, is one, I think, which appeals to the generous sympathies of mankind. We know, each for himself, that none of us would perpetrate such a folly, yet feel as if some other might. To my own contemplations, at least, it has often recurred, always exciting wonder, but with a sense that the story must be true, and a conception of its hero's character. Whenever any subject so forcibly affects the mind, time is well spent in thinking of it. If the reader choose, let him do his own meditation; or if he prefer to ramble with me through the twenty years of Wakefield's vagary, I bid him welcome; trusting that there will be a pervading spirit and a moral, even should we fail to find them, done up neatly, and condensed into the final sentence. Thought has always its efficacy, and every striking incident its moral.

What sort of a man was Wakefield? We are free to shape out our own idea, and call it by his name. He was now in the meridian of life; his matrimonial affections, never violent, were sobered into a calm, habitual sentiment; of all husbands, he was likely to be the most constant, because a certain sluggishness would keep his heart at rest, wherever it might be placed. He was intellectual, but not actively so; his mind occupied itself in long and lazy musings, that ended to no purpose, or had not vigor to attain it; his thoughts were seldom so energetic as to seize hold of words. Imagination, in the proper meaning of the term, made no part of Wakefield's gifts. With a cold but not depraved nor wandering heart, and a mind never feverish with riotous thoughts, nor perplexed with originality, who could have anticipated that our friend would entitle himself to a foremost place among the doers of eccentric deeds? Had his acquaintances been asked, who was the man in London the surest to perform nothing today which should be remembered on the morrow, they would have thought of Wakefield. Only the wife of his bosom might have hesitated. She, without having analyzed his character, was partly aware of a quiet selfishness, that had rusted into his inactive mind; of a peculiar sort of vanity, the most uneasy attribute about him; of a disposition to craft which had seldom produced more positive effects than the keeping of petty secrets, hardly worth revealing; and, lastly, of what she called a little strangeness, sometimes, in the good man. This latter quality is indefinable, and perhaps non-existent.

Let us now imagine Wakefield bidding adieu to his wife. It is the dusk of an October evening. His equipment is a drab great-coat, a hat covered with an oilcloth, top-boots, an umbrella in one hand and a small portmanteau in the other. He has informed Mrs. Wakefield that he is to take the night coach into the country. She would fain inquire the length of his journey, its object, and the probable time of his return; but, indulgent to his harmless love of mystery, interrogates him only by a look. He tells her not to expect him positively by the return coach, nor to be alarmed should he tarry three or four days; but, at all events, to look for him at supper on Friday evening. Wakefield himself, be it considered, has no suspicion of what is before him. He holds out his hand, she gives her own, and meets his parting kiss in the matter-of-course way of a ten years' matrimony; and forth goes the middle-aged Mr. Wakefield, almost resolved to perplex his good lady by a whole week's absence. After the door has closed behind him, she perceives it thrust partly open, and a vision of her husband's face, through the aperture, smiling on her, and gone in a moment. For the time, this little incident is dismissed without a thought. But, long afterwards, when she has been more years a widow than a wife, that smile recurs, and flickers across all her reminiscences of Wakefield's visage. In her many musings, she surrounds the original smile with a multitude of fantasies, which make it strange and awful: as, for instance, if she imagines him in a coffin, that parting look is frozen on his pale features; or, if she dreams of him in heaven, still his blessed spirit wears a quiet and crafty smile. Yet, for its sake, when all others have given him up for dead, she sometimes doubts whether she is a widow.

But our business is with the husband. We must hurry after him along the street, ere he lose his individuality, and melt into the great mass of London life. It would be vain searching for him there. Let us follow close at his heels, therefore, until, after several superfluous turns and doublings, we find him comfortably established by the fireside of a small apartment, previously bespoken. He is in the next street to his own, and at his journey's end. He can scarcely trust his good fortune, in having got thither unperceived—recollecting that, at one time, he was delayed by the throng, in the very focus of a lighted lantern; and, again, there were footsteps that seemed to tread behind his own, distinct from the multitudinous tramp around him; and, anon, he heard a voice shouting afar, and fancied that it called his name. Doubtless, a dozen busybodies had been watching him, and told his wife the whole affair. Poor Wakefield! Little knowest thou thine own insignificance in this great world! No mortal eye but mine has traced thee. Go quietly to thy bed, foolish man; and, on the morrow, if thou wilt be wise, get thee home to good Mrs. Wakefield, and tell her the truth. Remove not thyself, even for a little week, from thy place in her chaste bosom. Were she, for a single moment, to deem thee dead, or lost, or lastingly divided from her, thou wouldst be woefully conscious of a change in thy true wife forever after. It is perilous to make a chasm in human affections; not that they gape so long and wide—but so quickly close again!

Almost repenting of his frolic, or whatever it may be termed, Wakefield lies down betimes, and starting from his first nap, spreads forth his arms into the wide and solitary waste of the unaccustomed bed. "No,"—thinks he, gathering the bedclothes about him,—"I will not sleep alone another night."

In the morning he rises earlier than usual, and sets himself to consider what he really means to do. Such are his loose and rambling modes of thought that he has taken this very singular step with the consciousness of a purpose, indeed, but without being able to define it sufficiently for his own contemplation. The vagueness of the project, and the convulsive effort with which he plunges into the execution of it, are equally characteristic of a feeble-minded man. Wakefield sifts his ideas, however, as minutely as he may, and finds himself curious to know the progress of matters at home—how his exemplary wife will endure her widowhood of a week; and, briefly, how the little sphere of creatures and circumstances, in which he was a central object, will be affected by his removal. A morbid vanity, therefore, lies nearest the bottom of the affair. But, how is he to attain his ends? Not, certainly, by keeping close in this comfortable lodging, where, though he slept and awoke in the next street to his home, he is as effectually abroad as if the stage-coach had been whirling him away all night. Yet, should he reappear, the whole project is knocked in the head. His poor brains being hopelessly puzzled with this dilemma, he at length ventures out, partly resolving to cross the head of the street, and send one hasty glance towards his forsaken domicile. Habit—for he is a man of habits—takes him by the hand, and guides him, wholly unaware, to his own door, where, just at the critical moment, he is aroused by the scraping of his foot upon the step. Wakefield! whither are you going?

At that instant his fate was turning on the pivot. Little dreaming of the doom to which his first backward step devotes him, he hurries away, breathless with agitation hitherto unfelt, and hardly dares turn his head at the distant corner. Can it be that nobody caught sight of him? Will not the whole household—the decent Mrs. Wakefield, the smart maid servant, and the dirty little footboy—raise a hue and cry, through London streets, in pursuit of their fugitive lord and master? Wonderful escape! He gathers courage to pause and look homeward, but is perplexed with a sense of change about the familiar edifice, such as affects us all, when, after a separation of months or years, we again see some hill or lake, or work of art, with which we were friends of old. In ordinary cases, this indescribable impression is caused by the comparison and contrast between our imperfect reminiscences and the reality. In Wakefield, the magic of a single night has wrought a similar transformation, because, in that brief period, a great moral change has been effected. But this is a secret from himself. Before leaving the spot, he catches a far and momentary glimpse of his wife, passing athwart the front window, with her face turned towards the head of the street. The crafty nincompoop takes to his heels, scared with the idea that, among a thousand such atoms of mortality, her eye must have detected him. Right glad is his heart, though his brain be somewhat dizzy, when he finds himself by the coal fire of his lodgings.

So much for the commencement of this long whimwham. After the initial conception, and the stirring up of the man's sluggish temperament to put it in practice, the whole matter evolves itself in a natural train. We may suppose him, as the result of deep deliberation, buying a new wig, of reddish hair, and selecting sundry garments, in a fashion unlike his customary suit of brown, from a Jew's old-clothes bag. It is accomplished. Wakefield is another man. The new system being now established, a retrograde movement to the old would be almost as difficult as the step that placed him in his unparalleled position. Furthermore, he is rendered obstinate by a sulkiness occasionally incident to his temper, and brought on at present by the inadequate sensation which he conceives to have been produced in the bosom of Mrs. Wakefield. He will not go back until she be frightened half to death. Well; twice or thrice has she passed before his sight, each time with a heavier step, a paler cheek, and more anxious brow; and in the third week of his nonappearance he detects a portent of evil entering the house, in the guise of an apothecary. Next day the knocker is muffled. Towards nightfall comes the chariot of a physician, and deposits its big-wigged and solemn burden at Wakefield's door, whence, after a quarter of an hour's visit, he emerges, perchance the herald of a funeral. Dear woman! Will she die? By this time, Wakefield is excited to something like energy of feeling, but still lingers away from his wife's bedside, pleading with his conscience that she must not be disturbed at such a juncture. If aught else restrains him, he does not know it. In the course of a few weeks she gradually recovers; the crisis is over; her heart is sad, perhaps, but quiet; and, let him return soon or late, it will never be feverish for him again. Such ideas glimmer through the mist of Wakefield's mind, and render him indistinctly conscious that an almost impassable gulf divides his hired apartment from his former home. "It is but in the next street!" he sometimes says. Fool! it is in another world. Hitherto, he has put off his return from one particular day to another; henceforward, he leaves the precise time undetermined. Not tomorrow—probably next week—pretty soon. Poor man! The dead have nearly as much chance of revisiting their earthly homes as the self-banished Wakefield.

Would that I had a folio to write, instead of an article of a dozen pages! Then might I exemplify how an influence beyond our control lays its strong hand on every deed which we do, and weaves its consequences into an iron tissue of necessity. Wakefield is spellbound. We must leave him, for ten years or so, to haunt around his house, without once crossing the threshold, and to be faithful to his wife, with all the affection of which his heart is capable, while he is slowly fading out of hers. Long since, it must be remarked, he had lost the perception of singularity in his conduct.

Now for a scene! Amid the throng of a London street we distinguish a man, now waxing elderly, with few characteristics to attract careless observers, yet bearing, in his whole aspect, the handwriting of no common fate, for such as have the skill to read it. He is meagre; his low and narrow forehead is deeply wrinkled; his eyes, small and lustreless, sometimes wander apprehensively about him, but oftener seem to look inward. He bends his head, and moves with an indescribable obliquity of gait, as if unwilling to display his full front to the world. Watch him long enough to see what we have described, and you will allow that circumstances—which often produce remarkable men from nature's ordinary handiwork—have produced one such here. Next, leaving him to sidle along the footwalk, cast your eyes in the opposite direction, where a portly female, considerably in the wane of life, with a prayer-book in her hand, is proceeding to yonder church. She has the placid mien of settled widowhood. Her regrets have either died away, or have become so essential to her heart, that they would be poorly exchanged for joy. Just as the lean man and well-conditioned woman are passing, a slight obstruction occurs, and brings these two figures directly in contact. Their hands touch; the pressure of the crowd forces her bosom against his shoulder; they stand face to face, staring into each other's eyes. After a ten years' separation, thus Wakefield meets his wife!

The throng eddies away, and carries them asunder. The sober widow, resuming her former pace, proceeds to church, but pauses in the portal, and throws a perplexed glance along the street. She passes in, however, opening her prayer-book as she goes. And the man! with so wild a face that busy and selfish London stands to gaze after him, he hurries to his lodgings, bolts the door, and throws himself upon the bed. The latent feelings of years break out; his feeble mind acquires a brief energy from their strength; all the miserable strangeness of his life is revealed to him at a glance; and he cries out, passionately, "Wakefield! Wakefield! You are mad!"

Perhaps he was so. The singularity of his situation must have so moulded him to himself, that, considered in regard to his fellow-creatures and the business of life, he could not be said to possess his right mind. He had contrived, or rather he had happened, to dissever himself from the world—to vanish—to give up his place and privileges with living men, without being admitted among the dead. The life of a hermit is nowise parallel to his. He was in the bustle of the city, as of old; but the crowd swept by and saw him not; he was, we may figuratively say, always beside his wife and at his hearth, yet must never feel the warmth of the one nor the affection of the other. It was Wakefield's unprecedented fate to retain his original share of human sympathies, and to be still involved in human interests, while he had lost his reciprocal influence on them. It would be a most curious speculation to trace out the effect of such circumstances on his heart and intellect, separately, and in unison. Yet, changed as he was, he would seldom be conscious of it, but deem himself the same man as ever; glimpses of the truth, indeed, would come, but only for the moment; and still he would keep saying, "I shall soon go back!"—nor reflect that he had been saying so for twenty years.

I conceive, also, that these twenty years would appear, in the retrospect, scarcely longer than the week to which Wakefield had at first limited his absence. He would look on the affair as no more than an interlude in the main business of his life. When, after a little while more, he should deem it time to reënter his parlor, his wife would clap her hands for joy on beholding the middle-aged Mr. Wakefield. Alas, what a mistake! Would

Time but await the close of our favorite follies, we should be young men, all of us, and till Doomsday.

One evening, in the twentieth year since he vanished, Wakefield is taking his customary walk towards the dwelling which he still calls his own. It is a gusty night of autumn, with frequent showers that patter down upon the pavement, and are gone before a man can put up his umbrella. Pausing near the house, Wakefield discerns, through the parlor windows of the second floor, the red glow and the glimmer and fitful flash of a comfortable fire. On the ceiling appears a grotesque shadow of good Mrs. Wakefield. The cap, the nose and chin, and the broad waist form an admirable caricature, which dances, moreover, with the up-flickering and down-sinking blaze, almost too merrily for the shade of an elderly widow. At this instant a shower chances to fall, and is driven, by the unmannerly gust, full into Wakefield's face and bosom. He is quite penetrated with its autumnal chill. Shall he stand wet and shivering here, when his own hearth has a good fire to warm him, and his own wife will run to fetch the gray coat and small-clothes, which, doubtless, she has kept carefully in the closet of their bed-chamber? No! Wakefield is no such fool. He ascends the steps—heavily!—for twenty years have stiffened his legs since he came down—but he knows it not. Stay, Wakefield! Would you go to the sole home that is left you? Then step into your grave! The door opens. As he passes in, we have a parting glimpse of his visage, and recognize the crafty smile, which was the precursor of the little joke that he has ever since been playing off at his wife's expense. How unmercifully has he quizzed the poor woman! Well, a good night's rest to Wakefield!

This happy event—supposing it to be such—could only have occurred at an unpremeditated moment. We will not follow our friend across the threshold. He has left us much food for thought, a portion of which shall lend its wisdom to a moral, and be shaped into a figure. Amid the seeming confusion of our mysterious world, individuals are so nicely adjusted to a system, and systems to one another and to a whole, that, by stepping aside for a moment, a man exposes himself to a fearful risk of losing his place forever. Like Wakefield, he may become, as it were, the Outcast of the Universe.

SAMUEL YELLEN

The Passionate Shepherd

Have you ever stopped in the middle of a sentence to see if the person you were talking to was paying any attention? I don't recommend it, unless you brace yourself beforehand for a jolt. That is precisely what I did at a cocktail party last October, seven months ago. I was engaged in conversation with a good-looking young brunette, Rose Matthews, whose husband had just joined our faculty. I even remember (as if I could forget) what I was saying at the time, though I hesitate to repeat it here. It was the sort of thing my friends the psychologists would call verbalizing, a piece of cocktail party prattle which I had lifted from Marlowe: "Come live with me, and be my love, and we will all the pleasures prove. And I assure you this passionate shepherd will—" Some sudden caprice which I still cannot account for made me break off at that point. To my chagrin, the Passionate Shepherd discovered that his love was simply not listening and Marlowe's poesy was wasted on the smoke-laden air. Her ears, her eyes, her whole being were bent elsewhere. What stood there before me was only the empty shell. And even though the shell itself was, as we say, not at all bad, being endowed, for example, with full and firm breasts, I must confess that Professor Cyrus Richard Gray suffered a sharp pain near the heart. Yes, it was a veritable stab of pain, and I am sure that I grew pale. At that moment, while a needle caught in a groove of my brain kept playing *pleasures prove pleasures prove pleasures prove pleasures prove,* I had my first intimation that I did not exist.

It was the usual faculty cocktail party held in the usual faculty home during the Saturday twilight after a football game. The furniture was all straight lines and angles in chromium plate and blond wood. On the walls hung the ubiquitous Sunflowers of Van Gogh, two studies of ballet girls by Degas, and a number of Cubist abstractions tardily executed in water colors by our hostess. Seen through the pall of cigarette smoke, the fifty men and women standing jammed in the small living room and adjoining dining room were shades clamoring in the mists for a sip of the life-giving blood. Except that *these* shades were drinking Martinis and Manhattans. Perhaps my parallel is too lurid, and the illustrator should be not Doré, but Hogarth or Daumier. However, the scene was pathetic, almost tragic, rather than comic. The climate was one of desperation. But not the *quiet* desperation Thoreau speaks of. Far from it. Shrieks, screams, and squeals rebounded from wall and ceiling. Everyone seemed intent on a most frantic search for *something,* something without substance, without form, without name. Wives in their forties and fifties ogled, winked, grimaced, flirted with a frenzied gaiety, as if to give the lie to wrinkle, crow's foot, wattle, and hairy mole. Husbands with dewlap and sagging paunch embraced waists, only to recoil at flaccid breast or inflexibly ribbed girdle. Our host was busy saving on his liquor bill by going heavy on the vermouth. Our hostess, her face stamped with a bright fixed smile, was worrying about cigarette butts and spilled drinks, and wishing the party were over and done with. It was a motley assemblage, the kind you get when the hostess is wiping out her accumulation of social obligations in order to begin the new season with a clean sheet. Otherwise, how account for the presence of E. Feverell Dobson, Professor of Salesmanship (pause for raucous laughter) in our School of Commerce?

I realize that I must sound the petty academic snob indigenous to our large state universities. But that was not it at all. No, my attitude does not derive from the traditional respectability of my position as Professor of History (actually I took my doctorate at Harvard in American Civilization). Dobson *qua* Dobson is without significance in my story. True, he was hollow brass, undoubtedly an ignoramus, a hail fellow well met given to off-color limericks and guffaws. Likewise true, his title to local fame lay in a great collection of gaudy shirts and Countess Mara ties. Nevertheless, all of that was only his manner of saying to the world, *Regardez! I exist!* Others of my colleagues took other ways of making the same assertion. Some grew beards, some drove around in flashy yellow or crimson convertibles, some issued statements to the press, some dressed in tartan jackets, some cultivated eccentricities, some were constantly and ostentatiously off to Washington on mysterious topdrawer business, some never wore the same suit twice in a month, some never wore anything but the same suit month after month. And even *my* own unobtrusive behavior and dress, invariably, like my name, a neutral gray which rendered me almost invisible against the academic foliage, may have been, after all, nothing more than the reverse side of the medal. Without getting hopelessly lost in the maze of the ego, who can be sure that Dobson was not right? At least, his brassy loudness was a sign of his *presence.* It indicated *his* existence. And certainly at this party he was the gorgeous prismatic cock around whom the silly hens fluttered.

Let me hasten to add that any bitterness expressed above was really a symptom of inner discontent and pain. In part, I suppose, it was pique at the fact that Rose Matthews was not even conscious of disregarding me. Perhaps mine was the occupational sensitivity of the professor. But I think not. It was something else. When Rose Matthews stood before me, all attention fixed, as if by a tropism, on E. Feverell Dobson, I suddenly was simply not there. She had wiped me out of existence. It happened to be a time when I was particularly vulnerable. I had just turned fifty-six. I was raw, without integument to shield me. No longer could I delude myself that the sixties, hemorrhages of the brain, palsy, and *finis* were not breathing hard down my neck. Of course, the handwriting had always been up there on the wall, but now, myopic as I might be, I had come close enough to read it. Moreover, the season of the year vibrated sympathetically, and each leaf falling desiccated and crumpled to the earth echoed my dismal thoughts. Standing there with the Matthews woman, I was stricken with panic. I looked across the room and observed my wife shrilling to some blurred figure who had an arm around her. During the rest of the party, I moved along, an automaton somehow making the expected response to the anticipated stimulus.

As we were driving home that evening, my wife said, "That Rose Matthews is an extremely attractive woman, don't you think?"

Before answering, I waited a minute as though to consider. "Yes, I suppose some would think she is."

I foresaw not only what Helen would say next, but the valiantly matter-of-fact tone she would employ. "Well, I noticed that the men seemed to be taken with her."

Why we skirmished thus I don't understand. I am sure that she could predict my reply and the inflection of my voice as accurately as I could predict hers. Nevertheless, I pursed my lips and said, "She's a bit flamboyant for *my* taste, but *de gustibus*—" I shrugged my shoulders.

Helen should have known that the problem was not Rose Matthews, nor any of the other women whose sting she tried to neutralize by such epithets as "attractive" or "charming" or "beautiful." And yet, perhaps she did know well enough, and she was herself helpless before the compulsion to beat ineffectually against the ruins of time.

In the quiet streets, the lights of the car caught the leaves drifting down. There was no end to them, falling, falling, falling; and what they whispered as they fluttered in the air and their clatter as they dropped to the ground seemed, for the moment, to drown out the purr of the motor. In alarm I glanced quickly at Helen. She was staring ahead, her sharp chin lifted high to undo the half-a-century folds in her throat, her thin straight hair drawn close to the skull into a tight little knot at the back of her neck. My heart suddenly ached with pity. That face, which once launched a thousand ships each time I looked at it, now would no longer launch a single small vessel. And I remembered the fragrance of her young body when she first undressed for me, shy and yet in her pride wanting me to behold the flower which had bloomed in secret. Even that beauty had fallen victim to physiology and chemical equations. Maybe each commonplace reassurance I gave her helped temper the icy wind of truth. We had reached, I felt, a moment of high silent communion. But perversely that was the very moment Helen chose to turn eagerly to me. "Cy, I heard something interesting this afternoon. Guess who's going to get a divorce." I was not the sentient being, Cyrus Richard Gray. I was merely a patient and capacious ear to pour her post-party gossip into. Again I had the sensation that I did not exist.

That night at home I was unable to fall asleep. I lay in our bed as still as possible in order not to awaken Helen. The bed was spacious and obese, the kind without footboard called, I believe, a "Hollywood bed," which Helen had seen in *House Beautiful.* Had I not known her deficiency in the sense of humor, I might have thought she had got this voluptuous couch meant for an unmatrimonial orgy of fleshy passions as a piece of mockery for the decorous conjugality we had declined into. Getting up finally, I slipped out and closed the door carefully behind me. I tiptoed past the bedrooms of Joan and Ned, down the stairs, and into my study. There I sat for a time in a cocoon of silence trying to analyze the disturbing sensation which had come on me. But the longer I pondered the more elusive became my identity. At last I went into the bathroom and got a sleeping pill to give myself the relief of temporary oblivion. As I was shutting the medicine cabinet, there in the mirror was my image. I studied it closely. Each separate item in the physiognomy was itself familiar enough—the rumpled and ragged slate-colored hair streaked with gray, the regularity of chin and nose, the pale gray eyes, the liverish skin. (Indeed, so ordinary were the items that I wished for a moment I might have some Dickensian grotesquerie of feature to serve as a handle for my identity, so that I might think of myself as the Man with the Red Bulbous Nose or the Man with the Black Beetling Brow.) And yet the total image was that of a stranger. There was about it a suggestion of distortion, as if the parts had been jarred slightly after being assembled, or as if the mirror had some minute flaws. I could not be sure whether the image represented reality or phantom. But I felt that I was on the verge of discovering the real person. Within that gray outwardness I seemed to remember a younger face and a boyish head. Underneath that cracked and peeling surface I thought I could almost see brighter and fresher colors. With a little more effort—no, it was no use. I kept slipping away from myself. And I could not persuade myself to believe that the stranger in the mirror existed. "Well," I said to him, "*gnothi seauton,* Passionate Shepherd, know thyself! That great Thespian, Cyrus Richard Gray, will now enact a little morality quaintly entitled *Passion Redivivus, or the Shepherd in Search of Himself.*"

During the following days, while burning leaves spiced the air, a strange unrest took hold of me. My hands often trembled violently as they lifted a cup of coffee, a semaphore ticked unceasingly in my left eyelid, and fever patches blazed through the liverish skin over my cheekbones. I could not rid myself of the conviction that I had somehow, somewhere lost my inner self, that I was nothing but an empty container moving mechanically on fixed tracks. In my desperation, I crept back into the deepest recesses of the shell which had given me shelter in the past during fits of fluttering uncertainty. Like a neurotic straightening books, pictures, dishes, furniture in an effort to padlock his indefinable anxiety, I sought refuge in the formula of routine. Twenty-four years of treading the same invariable paths had rendered my motions automatic. In the morning I met my freshman class in the Introduction to Western Civilization, my advanced class in The Experimental Society in America, or my graduate seminar in The Brook Farm Group, obediently opening and shutting my mouth to the tintinnabulation of bells. The rest of the morning was taken up with correspondence, reading blue books and term papers, conferring with students, and filling out the official forms that streamed from the robots over in Administration. At noon I lunched in the Faculty Club. After lunch I glanced at the *New York Times* or played a hand of bridge. Then came the period of the day, from one-thirty to four o'clock, which twenty years before I had dedicated to research. The small basement room in the Library where I spent those two and a half hours had become my second home. There every afternoon without fail I added the grain of sand to the slowly but steadily growing mound out of which had already come five monographs and nineteen shorter articles. The hour from four to five was given over to faculty meetings and committees. Dinner at home was followed by an evening concert, a lecture, a movie, a visit, or reading the *Saturday Evening Post* serial.

For how many thousands of days this not unpleasant routine had fitted me comfortably! Yet now I sank unaccountably into absent states, from which I would come to with the blood thundering to my head as after a faint. Fortunately (praise be to William James for Habit!) I always found myself performing the proper task at the customary time and place. Nevertheless, these spells worried me, and presently I realized that the Matthews woman was haunting my thoughts. Not, mind you, in the role of femme fatale, but rather as if she had stolen something I needed desperately to get back. It was this necessity, I suppose, which compelled me now and again to walk slowly past her house in one of the side streets off the campus. To my irrational temper, it seemed that the sight of her might restore whatever it was I had lost, might furnish me with the precious clue. At any moment during the day (even in the period sacrosanct to research), like a somnambulist, I would be driven to take my foolish peripatetic exercise. Of course, I never caught so much as a glimpse of Rose Matthews.

In my increasing agitation, there was no one I could turn to for help. Helen did look anxiously at me for a while. But I easily threw her off the scent by allowing myself to be caught in the kitchen furtively mixing myself a bicarbonate of soda, and my malady was, I am sure, soon diagnosed and dismissed as a bout of indigestion. How long this state of affairs might have gone on I can only guess. For it came to an abrupt end one afternoon as I was seated in my basement cell at the Library (such is the treachery of the familiar) reading the letters of Charles Lamb. Unless my memory fails me, it was a letter to Coleridge. *Unless my memory fails me*—now there's an expression! Vestigium of exquisite academic dishonesty! Not only does my memory not fail me, but the very date of the letter—May 20, 1803—is engraved in red upon my private calendar. The fatal words sprang forward from the page to meet my eye: "He seems to have run the whole scenery of life, and now rests as the formal precisian of non-existence."

Even now, so ingrained are the accustomed academic gestures, I find myself obliged to explain why I was reading Lamb, what I was doing, as we like to say, outside my field. (As though it still matters that one of my colleagues might think I was spreading myself thin.) I must first make clear that my specialty is (or was) early Utopian experiments in America. Indeed, two of my monographs, those on New Harmony and Brook Farm, are, with due modesty, not entirely unknown to the world of scholarship. At the time, I was following up some leads on the pantisocracy which Coleridge, Southey, and Lovell had planned to establish on the banks of the Susquehanna. Since many of Lamb's letters were written to Coleridge and Southey, I inevitably encountered the passage that was to open my eyes. For a minute, I recall, I took *precisian* to be a misspelling, until I realized that it was the noun not for the quality, but for the person. On the instant, I recognized that I had been brought unto Lamb to see what he would call me, and I had been named. I, *I,* Cyrus Richard Gray, was the formal precisian of non-existence. I was the vacant outline, with the Roman numerals, capital letters, Arabic numerals, and lower case letters all correctly indented and set forth. The *content* had faded out of the realm of being. I felt stagnant, lusterless, inert. My heart began to quiver. But that, I told myself, was only because the creature of habit was fearful at the threat to his smug routine. *Creature* of habit? No, I was simply the habit itself. I was that old coat which William James describes as falling into its habitual folds and wrinkles. And no one was inside.

As I sat with the volume of Lamb's letters open on the table before me, I looked around at the old familiar face of my cloister. *There* was the whole scenery of my life. The walls were painted a dull rough gray, and the surface bulged and billowed to the ridges and whorls of the plaster underneath. My long table, strewn with books, pamphlets, note cards, and pads of paper, stood in the center of the worn pine floor. The two large rickety bookcases were loaded with dusty books, piles of off-prints sent me by colleagues, the thirty or so of those mottled black-and-gray cardboard boxes, each neatly labeled, in which the industrious scholar files his note cards. Ah, those boxes! Those boxes! In them reposed what thousands upon thousands of cards, each one covered with my small precise backward-slanting hand. Cards of two sizes, two colors—three-by-five for bibliographical data, four-by-six for notes on my reading, white for the factual or objective, yellow for my own comments and suggestions. Over the years it had been my sustaining faith that each card contributed its mite to the sum total of human knowledge. What a silly farce—written, staged, played, and directed by Vanity! No, each card was the measure of a certain number of pulse beats lost and never to be recaptured. In those mottled black-and-gray caskets were interred the bones of my youth and enthusiasm. There came to my mind the story of the Harvard professor who, on his death, left hundreds of boxes and baskets of notes, choking his shelves and even suspended by pulleys from the ceiling. For his university they were an embarrassment, and not of riches. They were the indecent remains of a corpse which finally had to be disposed of hugger-mugger. I could imagine how, after my departure from this vale of tears, *my* boxes would perplex the university. What to do with them? Whom to entrust them to? Certainly my colleagues would want nothing to do with them: each one was diligently storing up his own boxes of note cards.

I went over to the window, whose sill was level with the ground, and looked through the ancient fly specks and grime. The cold November sun painted the skeleton trees upon the earth, with pen-and-ink punctilio for the filigree of twig. A host of shriveled brown leaves scuttled like chipmunks before the wind. Some students came along the campus walk outside the Library, the bare legs of the coeds smooth, strong, and shapely. I could almost hear the crunch of the dead leaves being trodden down by those merciless feet. No one is more aware than the college professor of the hungry generations. No one can have a keener sense of how quickly and impatiently youth discards age. When it came my turn to go, who would there be to know the difference? Assuredly not my students. Those young egotists at the most egotistical hour of life hardly conceded existence to their teachers. Some of the more fatuous among my colleagues talked fervidly about *reaching* their students. I could not help remembering the student who had sat through an entire semester of my course under the impression that I was Professor *Thompson!* No, I could not flatter myself that I so much as cracked the glaze of those young egotists. And yet, distant as I was from my students, I was in many ways closer to them than to my own children. Joan and Ned no longer needed me. To them, I was an old stick of furniture that got in the way around the house. The language they spoke might as well have been one of those African tongues, all clicks and grunts. Joan, a senior at the university, was engaged to an accounting major, and already knew that callow brash stranger much better than she had ever known me. As for Ned, he was a sophomore wrapped up in his fraternity's hell week, pajama parties, and other such foolishness. Whenever I tried to enter their world, they merely waited with ill-concealed patience for me to make a more or less graceful exit.

Standing there at the window feeling a twinge of pity for old Shepherd Gray, I realized that I was whistling a tune under my breath while my fingers drummed a rhythm on the sill. The tune was very familiar, and yet I could not place it. Yes, a thing might be too familiar to be in focus. Surely, if anyone knew me, it was Helen. And yet I could go through a crisis like this without her being aware of it. While the tune teased me with its elusive familiarity, I let my thoughts play about Helen. She had been, in her way, a good wife and would, no doubt, notice my absence from the scene. But how soon she would get over it, and go on with her household concerns, her clubs, her teas, bridges, and luncheons. I watched the leaves scamper along outside. That tune nagged at me in a most distracting way. I recalled the cases of colleagues who had suddenly and inexplicably thrown overboard family, friends, position in the community, hard-earned academic security and reputation. Of Dewhirst, who had deserted a wife and three children to run off to Mexico with a coed. Of the professor of Latin whose name I had forgotten, who had joined an African safari and never returned. Of Templeton, who had gone berserk and shot two of his colleagues. Of Baker, who had simply disappeared into the ether and left no trace. Somehow they were never the E. Feverell Dobsons, but always the quiet ones, the unobtrusive ones. About each one, the rest of us would shake our heads and ask over a cocktail glass, "What*ever* got into him?" Well, now I knew. Just then, I identified the nagging tune, and at the same moment I realized that the semaphore had stopped ticking in my left eyelid. It was a gay tune, the patter song from *The Mikado*. "He never would be missed," I sang aloud. "I'm sure he'd not be missed."

It is not at all difficult to disappear. Indeed, I believe that I could now write a successful handbook for weary academics on *How to Vanish and Leave Not a Rack Behind.* Of course, having time and place which I did not have to account for was of great help. No one ever questioned what I was doing each afternoon between one-thirty and four, and so seldom did anyone else, even the janitor, enter my basement room at the Library that I could have safely kept a chorus girl there. My preparations took only a few days and carried me into the first week of December. I had never realized that Professor Gray had it in him to be such a man of action. I withdrew five hundred dollars from the bank, knowing that Helen would not miss the money until the beginning of the next month. Then down on the levee (a row of secondhand stores, saloons, greasyspoon restaurants, and disreputable hotels facing the railroad tracks) I bought an old brown suit, a battered brown hat, two woolen work shirts, a heavy sweater, a worn pair of brown shoes, and a cheap black cardboard suitcase, spreading my purchases over three stores. The chief risk I ran was getting these things into the Library. However, luck accommodated me. A little-used side door leads directly to the basement, and no one happened to see me enter that afternoon. My briefcase served to bring over some underwear, socks, and handkerchiefs, a few pieces each day.

On the appointed morning, as I said goodby to Joan and Ned and kissed Helen, I savored to the full the irony of being as perfunctory as usual. In fact, everything was as usual as usual, even the beating of my heart. I met my classes, answered some letters at the office, had lunch at the Faculty Club, played a hand of bridge, and strolled over to my secluded cloister. There I set about transforming myself. Most of my predecessors in the fine art of fading away into thin air had, I decided, tried too hard to disguise themselves and, since nothing is so unoriginal as efforts at originality, had used the very ham-actor stencils foreseen by the police. My commonplace face and figure, my undistinguished dress and manner, the absence of any oddity of feature were in my favor. I did not resort to artificial scars, dark glasses, moustache, or limp. All I did was to remove my glasses and comb my hair in a pompadour instead of parting it as I ordinarily did. Then I changed to the woolen work shirt and brown suit and hat, and put the clothes I had been wearing into the suitcase. A study of my reflection in the grimy window showed me that the metamorphosis was adequate. I was still unobtrusive enough to be completely overlooked. Nevertheless, I must confess that my heart was thumping when I left the Library by the side door, carrying the suitcase. However, on the walk outside the door one of my colleagues passed by me without so much as a second glance. That restored my confidence.

Of course, I had already picked out my destination, and without hesitating I caught the bus which crosses the railroad tracks over into the West

Side. During the 1880's and 1890's, that had been the fashionable section of town, and my interest in nineteenth-century domestic architecture had taken me there on occasional walks to view the dozen or so homes in the General Grant style still standing, though now converted into funeral parlors or rooming houses. One of the latter, need I say, was my *immediate* destination. Again luck was obliging to me, for I found a room at the first house I tried. I gave my name as George Brown and paid a week's rent in advance. The room, up in the square central tower which marks the General Grant house, was shabbily furnished, but clean enough, large, and well-lighted. For two weeks I holed up there, going out to the levee for my meals. Actually I did not stay close to my room, nor otherwise behave furtively. I took long walks through the streets of the West Side, over to the gas works, the cemetery, the furniture factory, or the slaughter house. I felt as if I were a tourist in a foreign town. And in a sense I was. For even a city of only sixty-three thousand is really a cluster of quite separate towns, each with its own economy, culture, social strata, flora and fauna.

My chief occupation was studying the local paper to keep track of my *alter idem*. It did not surprise me that my disappearance was not announced until the third day. I could surmise the quiet and discreet efforts of Helen and the university officials to locate me before deciding that they could no longer put off calling the police in. After the news broke, I read and reread the accounts avidly. I enjoyed observing the skill of our publicity director, who always succeeded in balancing the disgrace to the university of having one of its professors turn into an irresponsible missing person by some reference to the "important" research done by the "noted authority" on early Utopian experiments. I had become a problem in public relations. I also enjoyed following the activities of the police, who broadcast descriptions of me and bustled around the university interviewing my colleagues. And the embarrassment of the officers who "found" me in Chicago, New Orleans, and St. Louis furnished me with a perverse amusement.

However, the irony soon doubled back on me. It was something of a shock, yes, a blow to my self-esteem, to see how quickly all the fuss died down. In four days I passed from the front page to a spot among the advertisements for trusses and rheumatism remedies. In another three days I slipped from the news altogether, except for an occasional brief notice that police had begun to suspect foul play and were about to ask the FBI for assistance. Sometimes, with an understandable reluctance to vanish completely from the scene, I tried to chat about the *affaire Gray* with my landlady or with the waitress at the restaurant, but it was amazing how little interest the aborigines of the West Side had in the university and the mysterious disappearance of one of its distinguished professors. I could guess that the crescendo of chatter at the cocktail parties had passed its peak. Sitting for hours at a time in my room, I found that I thought seldom about Helen, and even less about the children. Joan and Ned were well on the way to taking care of themselves. As for Helen, she would have security enough. The house was paid for, our savings were considerable, and in due time she would draw benefits from our insurance policies and the ample pension fund which I had accumulated. I knew, moreover, that the university always found some clerical or secretarial job for its widows and abandoned wives. No, if anything, my desertion might prove a good thing for her. Occasionally I considered my own destiny, what I would do with myself and how I would go about making a living. But most often, I thought despairingly of my lost identity. Where and when would I recover myself? How many other formal precisians of non-existence had engaged in the same frantic search in that very room? While a phantom troop of forlorn figures paced the threadbare flowered carpet, sat brooding in the horsehair chairs, or lay despondently upon the tarnished brass bed, Descartes' first postulate, slightly altered, twanged in my head: *Credo ergo sum. If* I could believe, I would be.

During recent years I had often wondered how an underground was able to flourish in the very teeth of enemy occupation. Now I could see that it might be managed. Even with the police, so to speak, hot on my trail, establishing myself as an approved member of society took but a few minutes. I applied for a job in one of the limestone quarries south of town, saying that I had come from a farm in the hills of Tennessee near Murfreesboro. Without much ado, I was given a social security card and number, as well as a membership card in the stone workers' union. By signing my name half-a-dozen times, I became George Edward Brown. What surprised me was the ease with which I adapted myself. From the first I got along well with the men, who were soon calling me Tennessee. Somewhere Emerson says that the truck driver and the college professor give themselves away by their speech. The Sage of Concord was mistaken. The secret is not to try to speak unlike yourself. The men I worked with accepted me at face value, and whatever formality there was in my speech or manner they attributed to my supposed Southern origin. The work itself was hard in the beginning. But I liked it, and relished the sense of physical exhaustion each night. I slept soundly, and without benefit of pills. Although the pay was low (I *was* inexperienced labor and at what is called an advanced age), it was sufficient for my simple needs. All in all, the life was good. And I well remember the thrill I felt one morning when, clinging shakily to the iron cables, I took my first ride on a huge block of limestone swung high in the air by the derrick. All around me the sheer limestone walls dazzled my eyes with a brilliant display of color. I had not known that there could be so many tints of brown and yellow and orange and purple in such a variety of stippling and shading. Far below was the engine, crowned with a coiling plume of smoke. And (as though to provide the fitting touch for the Passionate Shepherd), on a nearby hillside, in the cold pastoral landscape surrounding the quarry, huddled a flock of sheep.

January and February brought snow, frost, and ice. My hands and face put forth a leathery weatherbeaten skin, and I became quite tough physically. My days were little else than work and sleep. Sometimes after the whistle blew at four o'clock, I accompanied some of the men to a cafe in the vicinity of the quarries for a glass of beer and a game of checkers or dominoes. Since I was tired at the end of the day and went to bed early, the evening passed quickly and I had little time for speculation. Aside from the *Post* and the local paper, I read almost nothing. Now and then I managed to get hold of the campus newspaper, and through it I kept an eye on my family and my deserted track at the university. Frequently I had heard people say that they would like to visit the earth after their death to see whether they were missed and how they were spoken of. That was the position I was in, a ghost haunting the scenes of his former life. And I can testify that I needed all the comfort I could suck from ironic detachment. For a while, it was entertaining to see who would be put into my slot. From various items in the campus paper, I learned that young Bob Hendricks had taken over my advanced course and graduate seminar, and also my seat on three or four special committees. Except that he had already launched himself in early railroad history, I suppose that he might even have been willing to inherit my thirty caskets of note cards. I had a picture of him, gradually taking on my manner, my dress, my neutral gray coloration. Indeed, I began to feel that it would be no more than proper for him to move in with Helen and take my place in that Hollywood bed.

There was undeniably an element of hurt in seeing how soon my shoes were filled. Nevertheless, watching young Hendricks pour, like raw molten metal, into the channels and molds so long occupied by Professor Gray was to have, in the long run, a wholesome effect upon me. I no longer had a carapace to crawl back into. Young Hendricks had cut off my retreat. George Edward Brown was now absolutely on his own. This realization first struck me just a couple of weeks ago, as the calendar wheeled away from Winter. March came in with a roar of wind and a flurry of soggy snow that soaked into the frozen earth. I could almost hear the iron bonds cracking and falling apart. These presentiments of Spring persuaded me to buy a bright red plaid mackinaw and the kind of scarlet cap worn by deer hunters. And it was only last Saturday that, impelled by some unnamed yearning, instead of having a beer and a game of checkers, I donned my new outfit and loitered on the courthouse square, not the fashionable east side with its expensive shops like Mademoiselle, but the west side where were the five-and-tens, the hardware stores, and the loan sharks. This plebeian side swarmed with farmers and laborers on Saturday afternoon, and I felt safely camouflaged as I lounged against a store front. The yearning which had seized me was, I admitted to myself, for someone to take cognizance of *me,* to fill my void with a sense of being. Had Helen come by then, I might even have revealed myself to her. But that futility was avoided. The thread by which fate hung held firm. It was rare for Helen to come to that side of the square. However, two of my former colleagues *did* pass by and fail to recognize me. And then suddenly my heart began to pound furiously. There, coming along my side of the street, was Rose Matthews. Her figure, I now noticed, was even more abundant, riper, than I had remembered. As she passed, without thinking I gave a low whistle. She halted.

"Pleasures prove," I said. "Pleasures prove."

She turned back uncertainly and looked at me. Then I saw that she was not Rose Matthews at all, but another woman I had never seen before. Without glasses, my eyes had played me a trick. The woman was not even a brunette, but a decided blonde.

"What was that you said?" she demanded.

There was a roughness to her voice which I found exciting. For a full minute we looked at each other, hardly conscious of the crowds passing by. Unlike Rose Matthews at the cocktail party, this woman really knew I was there. Not *credo ergo sum,* I suddenly understood, but *credis ergo sum. You* believe, therefore I am. In that moment the distressing conviction of non-existence dropped away from me like a sloughed skin. I felt alive, as you do on shipboard with a new companion to whom nothing about you is old shoe. I studied the woman's face before replying. It was round and lush, with the blood about to flood into the fair skin. Her nose was a saucy pug, and her full chin was pertly dimpled. A little hat perched on her honey-colored hair, and her blue eyes were examining me with a mixture of interest and puzzlement. No doubt, the bright red mackinaw and the cap were doing their work. I gave her body a bold up-and-down glance. I said, "Treasure trove, treasure trove."

She hesitated for an instant, and then smiled. "Now, Daddy," she said with mock reproach. "Behave yourself, Daddy." She gave my arm a pat and walked on, flipping her tail provocatively. I was sure that I would see her again.

GROUP TWO

W. SOMERSET MAUGHAM

The Outstation

The new assistant arrived in the afternoon. When the Resident, Mr. Warburton, was told that the prahu was in sight he put on his solar topee and went down to the landing-stage. The guard, eight little Dyak soldiers, stood to attention as he passed. He noted with satisfaction that their bearing was martial, their uniforms neat and clean, and their guns shining. They were a credit to him. From the landing-stage he watched the bend of the river round which in a moment the boat would sweep. He looked very smart in his spotless ducks and white shoes. He held under his arm a gold-headed Malacca cane which had been given him by the Sultan of Perak. He awaited the newcomer with mingled feelings. There was more work in the district than one man could properly do, and during his periodical tours of the country under his charge it had been inconvenient to leave the station in the hands of a native clerk, but he had been so long the only white man there that he could not face the arrival of another without misgiving. He was accustomed to loneliness. During the war he had not seen an English face for three years; and once when he was instructed to put up an afforestation officer he was seized with panic, so that when the stranger was due to arrive, having arranged everything for his reception, he wrote a note telling him he was obliged to go up-river, and fled; he remained away till he was informed by a messenger that his guest had left.

Now the prahu appeared in the broad reach. It was manned by prisoners, Dyaks under various sentences, and a couple of warders were waiting on the landing-stage to take them back to jail. They were sturdy fellows, used to the river, and they rowed with a powerful stroke. As the boat reached the side a man got out from under the attap awning and stepped on shore. The guard presented arms.

"Here we are at last. By God, I'm as cramped as the devil. I've brought you your mail."

He spoke with exuberant joviality. Mr. Warburton politely held out his hand.

"Mr. Cooper, I presume?"

"That's right. Were you expecting any one else?"

The question had a facetious intent, but the Resident did not smile.

"My name is Warburton. I'll show you your quarters. They'll bring your kit along."

He preceded Cooper along the narrow pathway and they entered a compound in which stood a small bungalow.

"I've had it made as habitable as I could, but of course no one has lived in it for a good many years."

It was built on piles. It consisted of a long living-room which opened on to a broad verandah, and behind, on each side of a passage, were two bedrooms.

"This'll do me all right," said Cooper.

"I daresay you want to have a bath and a change. I shall be very much pleased if you'll dine with me tonight. Will eight o'clock suit you?"

"Any old time will do for me."

The Resident gave a polite, but slightly disconcerted, smile and withdrew. He returned to the Fort where his own residence was. The impression which Allen Cooper had given him was not very favorable, but he was a fair man, and he knew that it was unjust to form an opinion on so brief a glimpse. Cooper seemed to be about thirty. He was a tall, thin fellow, with a sallow face in which there was not a spot of color. It was a face all in one tone. He had a large, hooked nose and blue eyes. When, entering the bungalow, he had taken off his topee and flung it to a waiting boy, Mr. Warburton noticed that his large skull, covered with short, brown hair, contrasted somewhat oddly with a weak, small chin. He was dressed in khaki shorts and a khaki shirt, but they were shabby and soiled; and his battered topee had not been cleaned for days. Mr. Warburton reflected that the young man had spent a week on a coasting steamer and had passed the last forty-eight hours lying in the bottom of a prahu.

"We'll see what he looks like when he comes in to dinner."

He went into his room where his things were as neatly laid out as if he had an English valet, undressed, and, walking down the stairs to the bathhouse, sluiced himself with cool water. The only concession he made to the climate was to wear a white dinner-jacket; but otherwise, in a boiled shirt and a high collar, silk socks and patent-leather shoes, he dressed as formally as though he were dining at his club in Pall Mall. A careful host, he went into the dining-room to see that the table was properly laid. It was gay with orchids and the silver shone brightly. The napkins were folded into elaborate shapes. Shaded candles in silver candlesticks shed a soft light. Mr. Warburton smiled his approval and returned to the sitting-room to await his guest. Presently he appeared. Cooper was wearing the khaki shorts, the khaki shirt, and the ragged jacket in which he had landed. Mr. Warburton's smile of greeting froze on his face.

"Hulloa, you're all dressed up," said Cooper. "I didn't know you were going to do that. I very nearly put on a sarong."

"It doesn't matter at all. I daresay your boys were busy."

"You needn't have bothered to dress on my account, you know."

"I didn't. I always dress for dinner."

"Even when you're alone?"

"Especially when I'm alone," replied Mr. Warburton, with a frigid stare.

He saw a twinkle of amusement in Cooper's eyes, and he flushed an angry red. Mr. Warburton was a hot-tempered man; you might have guessed that from his red face with its pugnacious features and from his red hair, now growing white; his blue eyes, cold as a rule and observing, could flush with sudden wrath; but he was a man of the world and he hoped a just one. He must do his best to get on with this fellow.

"When I lived in London I moved in circles in which it would have been just as eccentric not to dress for dinner every night as not to have a bath every morning. When I came to Borneo I saw no reason to discontinue so good a habit. For three years, during the war, I never saw a white man. I never omitted to dress on a single occasion on which I was well enough to come in to dinner. You have not been very long in this country; believe me, there is no better way to maintain the proper pride which you should have in yourself. When a white man surrenders in the slightest degree to the influences that surround him he very soon loses his self-respect, and when he loses his self-respect you may be quite sure that the natives will soon cease to respect him."

"Well, if you expect me to put on a boiled shirt and a stiff collar in this heat I'm afraid you'll be disappointed."

"When you are dining in your own bungalow you will, of course, dress as you think fit, but when you do me the pleasure of dining with me, perhaps you will come to the conclusion that it is only polite to wear the costume usual in civilized society."

Two Malay boys, in sarongs and songkoks, with smart white coats and brass buttons, came in, one bearing gin pahits, and the other a tray on which were olives and anchovies. Then they went in to dinner. Mr. Warburton flattered himself that he had the best cook, a Chinese, in Borneo, and he took great trouble to have as good food as in the difficult circumstances was possible. He exercised much ingenuity in making the best of his materials.

"Would you care to look at the menu?" he said, handing it to Cooper.

It was written in French and the dishes had resounding names. They were waited on by the two boys. In opposite corners of the room two more waved immense fans, and so gave movement to the sultry air. The fare was sumptuous and the champagne excellent.

"Do you do yourself like this every day?" said Cooper.

Mr. Warburton gave the menu a careless glance.

"I have not noticed that the dinner is any different from usual," he said. "I eat very little myself, but I make a point of having a proper dinner served to me every night. It keeps the cook in practice and it's good discipline for the boys."

The conversation proceeded with effort. Mr. Warburton was elaborately courteous, and it may be that he found a slightly malicious amusement in the embarrassment which he thereby occasioned in his companion. Cooper had not been more than a few months in Sembulu, and Mr. Warburton's inquiries about friends of his in Kuala Solor were soon exhausted.

"By the way," he said presently, "did you meet a lad called Hennerlay? He's come out recently, I believe."

"Oh, yes, he's in the police. A rotten bounder."

"I should hardly have expected him to be that. His uncle is my friend Lord Barraclough. I had a letter from Lady Barraclough only the other day asking me to look out for him."

"I heard he was related to somebody or other. I suppose that's how he got the job. He's been to Eton and Oxford and he doesn't forget to let you know it."

"You surprise me," said Mr. Warburton. "All his family have been at Eton and Oxford for a couple of hundred years. I should have expected him to take it as a matter of course."

"I thought him a damned prig."

"To what school did you go?"

"I was born in Barbados. I was educated there."

"Oh, I see."

Mr. Warburton managed to put so much offensiveness into his brief reply that Cooper flushed. For a moment he was silent.

"I've had two or three letters from Kuala Solor," continued Mr. Warburton, "and my impression was that young Hennerley was a great success. They say he's a first-rate sportsman."

"Oh, yes, he's very popular. He's just the sort of fellow they would like in K.S. I haven't got much use for the first-rate sportsman myself. What does it amount to in the long run that a man can play golf and tennis better than other people? And who cares if he can make a break of seventy-five at billiards? They attach a damned sight too much importance to that sort of thing in England."

"Do you think so? I was under the impression that the first-rate sportsman had come out of the war certainly no worse than any one else."

"Oh, if you're going to talk of the war then I do know what I'm talking about. I was in the same regiment as Hennerley and I can tell you that the men couldn't stick him at any price."

"How do you know?"

"Because I was one of the men."

"Oh, you hadn't got a commission."

"A fat chance I had of getting a commission. I was what was called a Colonial. I hadn't been to a public school and I had no influence. I was in the ranks the whole damned time."

Cooper frowned. He seemed to have difficulty in preventing himself from breaking into violent invective. Mr. Warburton watched him, his little blue eyes narrowed, watched him and formed his opinion. Changing the conversation, he began to speak to Cooper about the work that would be required of him, and as the clock struck ten he rose.

"Well, I won't keep you any more. I daresay you're tired by your journey."

They shook hands.

"Oh, I say, look here," said Cooper, "I wonder if you can find me a boy. The boy I had before never turned up when I was starting from K.S. He took my kit on board and all that and then disappeared. I didn't know he wasn't there till we were out of the river."

"I'll ask my head-boy. I have no doubt he can find you some one."

"All right. Just tell him to send the boy along and if I like the look of him I'll take him."

There was a moon, so that no lantern was needed. Cooper walked across from the Fort to his bungalow.

"I wonder why on earth they've sent me a fellow like that?" reflected Mr. Warburton. "If that's the kind of man they're going to get out now I don't think much of it."

He strolled down his garden. The Fort was built on the top of a little hill and the garden ran down to the river's edge; on the bank was an arbor, and hither it was his habit to come after dinner to smoke a cheroot. And often from the river that flowed below him a voice was heard, the voice of some Malay too timorous to venture into the light of day, and a complaint or an accusation was softly wafted to his ears, a piece of information was whispered to him or a useful hint, which otherwise would never have come into his official ken. He threw himself heavily into a long rattan chair. Cooper! An envious, ill-bred fellow, bumptious, self-assertive and vain. But Mr. Warburton's irritation could not withstand the silent beauty of the night. The air was scented with the sweet-smelling flowers of a tree that grew at the entrance to the arbor, and the fireflies, sparkling dimly, flew with their slow and silvery flight. The moon made a pathway on the broad river for the light feet of Siva's bride, and on the further bank a row of palm trees was delicately silhouetted against the sky. Peace stole into the soul of Mr. Warburton.

He was a queer creature and he had had a singular career. At the age of twenty-one he had inherited a considerable fortune, a hundred thousand pounds, and when he left Oxford he threw himself into the gay life which in those days (now Mr. Warburton was a man of four and fifty) offered itself to the young man of good family. He had his flat in Mount Street, his private hansom, and his hunting-box in Warwickshire. He went to all the places where the fashionable congregate. He was handsome, amusing and generous. He was a figure in the society of London in the early nineties, and society then had not lost its exclusiveness nor its brilliance. The Boer War which shook it was unthought of; the Great War which destroyed it was prophesied only by the pessimists. It was no unpleasant thing to be a rich young man in those days, and Mr. Warburton's chimney-piece during the season was packed with cards for one great function after another. Mr. Warburton displayed them with complacency. For Mr. Warburton was a snob. He was not a timid snob, a little ashamed of being impressed by his betters, nor a snob who sought the intimacy of persons who had acquired celebrity in politics or notoriety in the arts, nor the snob who was dazzled by riches; he was the naked, unadulterated common snob who dearly loved a lord. He was touchy and quick-tempered, but he would much rather have been snubbed by a person of quality than flattered by a commoner. His name figured insignificantly in *Burke's Peerage,* and it was marvelous to watch the ingenuity he used to mention his distant relationship to the noble family he belonged to; but never a word did he say of the honest Liverpool manufacturer from whom, through his mother, a Miss Gubbins, he had come by his fortune. It was the terror of his fashionable life that at Cowes, maybe, or at Ascot, when he was with a duchess or even with a prince of the blood, one of these relatives would claim acquaintance with him.

His failing was too obvious not soon to become notorious, but its extravagance saved it from being merely despicable. The great whom he adored laughed at him, but in their hearts felt his adoration not unnatural. Poor Warburton was a dreadful snob, of course, but after all he was a good fellow. He was always ready to back a bill for an impecunious nobleman, and if you were in a tight corner you could safely count on him for a hundred pounds. He gave good dinners. He played whist badly, but never minded how much he lost if the company was select. He happened to be a gambler, an unlucky one, but he was a good loser, and it was impossible not to admire the coolness with which he lost five hundred pounds at a sitting. His passion for cards, almost as strong as his passion for titles, was the cause of his undoing. The life he led was expensive and his gambling losses were formidable. He began to plunge more heavily, first on horses, and then on the Stock Exchange. He had a certain simplicity of character and the unscrupulous found him an ingenuous prey. I do not know if he ever realized that his smart friends laughed at him behind his back, but I think he had an obscure instinct that he could not afford to appear other than careless of his money. He got into the hands of money-lenders. At the age of thirty-four he was ruined.

He was too much inbued with the spirit of his class to hesitate in the choice of his next step. When a man in his set had run through his money he went out to the colonies. No one heard Mr. Warburton repine. He made no complaint because a noble friend had advised a disastrous speculation, he pressed nobody to whom he had lent money to repay it, he paid his debts (if he had only known it, the despised blood of the Liverpool manufacturer came out in him there), sought help from no one, and, never having done a stroke of work in his life, looked for a means of livelihood. He remained cheerful, unconcerned and full of humor. He had no wish to make any one with whom he happened to be uncomfortable by the recital of his misfortune. Mr. Warburton was a snob, but he was also a gentleman.

The only favor he asked of any of the great friends in whose daily company he had lived for years was a recommendation. The able man who was at that time Sultan of Sembulu took him into his service. The night before he sailed he dined for the last time at his club.

"I hear you're going away, Warburton," the old Duke of Hereford said to him.

"Yes, I'm going to Borneo."

"Good God, what are you going there for?"

"Oh, I'm broke."

"Are you? I'm sorry. Well, let us know when you come back. I hope you have a good time."

"Oh, yes. Lots of shooting, you know."

The Duke nodded and passed on. A few hours later Mr. Warburton watched the coast of England recede into the mist, and he left behind everything which to him made life worth living.

Twenty years had passed since then. He kept up a busy correspondence with various great ladies and his letters were amusing and chatty. He never lost his love for titled persons and paid careful attention to the announcements in *The Times* (which reached him six weeks after publication) of their comings and goings. He perused the column which records births, deaths, and marriages, and he was always ready with his letter of congratulation or condolence. The illustrated papers told him how people looked and on his periodical visits to England, able to take up the threads as though they had never been broken, he knew all about any new person who might have appeared on the social surface. His interest in the world of fashion was as vivid as when he himself had been a figure in it. It still seemed to him the only thing that mattered.

But insensibly another interest had entered into his life. The position he found himself in flattered his vanity; he was no longer the sycophant craving the smiles of the great, he was the master whose word was law. He was gratified by the guard of Dyak soldiers who presented arms as he passed. He liked to sit in judgment on his fellow men. It pleased him to compose quarrels between rival chiefs. When the head-hunters were troublesome in the old days he set out to chastise them with a thrill of pride in his own behavior. He was too vain not to be of dauntless courage, and a pretty story was told of his coolness in adventuring singlehanded into a stockaded village and demanding the surrender of a blood-thirsty pirate. He became a skilful administrator. He was strict, just and honest.

And little by little he conceived a deep love for the Malays. He interested himself in their habits and customs. He was never tired of listening to their talk. He admired their virtues, and with a smile and a shrug of the shoulders condoned their vices.

"In my day," he would say, "I have been on intimate terms with some of the greatest gentlemen in England, but I have never known finer gentlemen than some well-born Malays whom I am proud to call my friends."

He liked their courtesy and their distinguished manners, their gentleness and their sudden passions. He knew by instinct exactly how to treat them. He had a genuine tenderness for them. But he never forgot that he was an English gentleman and he had no patience with the white men who yielded to native customs. He made no surrenders. And he did not imitate so many of the white men in taking a native woman to wife, for an intrigue of this nature, however sanctified by custom, seemed to him not only shocking but undignified. A man who had been called George by Albert Edward, Prince of Wales, could hardly be expected to have any connection with a native. And when he returned to Borneo from his visits to England it was now with something like relief. His friends, like himself, were no longer young, and there was a new generation which looked upon him as a tiresome old man. It seemed to him that the England of today had lost a good deal of what he had loved in the England of his youth. But Borneo remained the same. It was home to him now. He meant to remain in the service as long as was possible, and the hope in his heart was that he would die before at last he was forced to retire. He had stated in his will that wherever he died he wished his body to be brought back to Sembulu and buried among the people he loved within sound of the softly flowing river.

But these emotions he kept hidden from the eyes of men; and no one, seeing this spruce, stout, well-set-up man, with his clean-shaven strong face and his whitening hair, would have dreamed that he cherished so profound a sentiment.

He knew how the work of the station should be done, and during the next few days he kept a suspicious eye on his assistant. He saw very soon that he was painstaking and competent. The only fault he had to find with him was that he was brusque with the natives.

"The Malays are shy and very sensitive," he said to him. "I think you will find that you will get much better results if you take care always to be polite, patient and kindly."

Cooper gave a short grating laugh.

"I was born in Barbados and I was in Africa in the war. I don't think there's much about niggers that I don't know."

"I know nothing," said Mr. Warburton acidly. "But we were not talking of them. We were talking of Malays."

"Aren't they niggers?"

"You are very ignorant," replied Mr. Warburton.

He said no more.

On the first Sunday after Cooper's arrival he asked him to dinner. He did everything ceremoniously, and though they had met on the previous day in the office and later, on the Fort verandah where they drank a gin and bitters together at six o'clock, he sent a polite note across to the bungalow by a boy. Cooper, however unwillingly, came in evening dress and Mr. Warburton, though gratified that his wish was respected, noticed with disdain that the young man's clothes were badly cut and his shirt ill-fitting. But Mr. Warburton was in a good temper that evening.

"By the way," he said to him, as he shook hands, "I've talked to my head-boy about finding you some one and he recommends his nephew. I've seen him and he seems a bright and willing lad. Would you like to see him?"

"I don't mind."

"He's waiting now."

Mr. Warburton called his boy and told him to send for his nephew. In a moment a tall, slender youth of twenty appeared. He had large dark eyes and a good profile. He was very neat in his sarong, a little white coat, and a fez, without a tassel, of plum-colored velvet. He answered to the name of Abas. Mr. Warburton looked on him with approval, and his manner insensibly softened as he spoke to him in fluent and idiomatic Malay. He was inclined to be sarcastic with white people, but with the Malays he had a happy mixture of condescension and kindliness. He stood in the place of the Sultan. He knew perfectly how to preserve his own dignity, and at the same time put a native at his ease.

"Will he do?" said Mr. Warburton, turning to Cooper.

"Yes, I daresay he's no more of a scoundrel than any of the rest of them."

Mr. Warburton informed the boy that he was engaged and dismissed him.

"You're very lucky to get a boy like that," he told Cooper. "He belongs to a very good family. They came over from Malacca nearly a hundred years ago."

"I don't much mind if the boy who cleans my shoes and brings me a drink when I want it has blue blood in his veins or not. All I ask is that he should do what I tell him and look sharp about it."

Mr. Warburton pursed his lips, but made no reply.

They went in to dinner. It was excellent, and the wine was good. Its influence presently had its effect on them and they talked not only without acrimony, but even with friendliness. Mr. Warburton liked to do himself well, and on Sunday night he made it a habit to do himself even a little better than usual. He began to think he was unfair to Cooper. Of course he was not a gentleman, but that was not his fault, and when you got to know him it might be that he would turn out a very good fellow. His faults, perhaps, were faults of manner. And he was certainly good at his work, quick, conscientious and thorough. When they reached the dessert Mr. Warburton was feeling kindly disposed towards all mankind.

"This is your first Sunday and I'm going to give you a very special glass of port. I've only got about two dozen of it left and I keep it for special occasions."

He gave his boy instructions and presently the bottle was brought. Mr. Warburton watched the boy open it.

"I got this port from my old friend Charles Hollington. He'd had it for forty years and I've had it for a good many. He was well known to have the best cellar in England."

"Is he a wine merchant?"

"Not exactly," smiled Mr. Warburton. "I was speaking of Lord Hollington of Castle Reagh. He's one of the richest peers in England. A very old friend of mine. I was at Eton with his brother."

This was an opportunity that Mr. Warburton could never resist and he told a little anecdote of which the only point seemed to be that he knew an earl. The port was certainly very good; he drank a glass and then a second. He lost all caution. He had not talked to a white man for months. He began to tell stories. He showed himself in the company of the great. Hearing him you would have thought that at one time ministries were formed and policies decided on his suggestion whispered into the ear of a duchess or thrown over the dinner-table to be gratefully acted on by the confidential adviser of the sovereign. The old days at Ascot, Goodwood and Cowes lived again for him. Another glass of port. There were the great house-parties in Yorkshire and in Scotland to which he went every year.

"I had a man called Foreman then, the best valet I ever had, and why do you think he gave me notice? You know in the Housekeeper's Room the ladies' maids and the gentlemen's gentlemen sit according to the precedence of their masters. He told me he was sick of going to party after party at which I was the only commoner. It meant that he always had to sit at the bottom of the table and all the best bits were taken before a dish reached him. I told the story to the old Duke of Hereford and he roared. 'By God, sir,' he said, 'if I were King of England I'd make you a viscount just to give your man a chance.' 'Take him yourself, Duke,' I said. 'He's the best valet I've ever had.' 'Well, Warburton,' he said, 'if he's good enough for you he's good enough for me. Send him along.' "

Then there was Monte Carlo, where Mr. Warburton and the Grand Duke Fyodor, playing in partnership, had broken the bank one evening; and there was Marienbad. At Marienbad Mr. Warburton had played baccarat with Edward VII.

"He was only Prince of Wales then, of course. I remember him saying to me, 'George, if you draw on a five you'll lose your shirt.' He was right; I don't think he ever said a truer word in his life. He was a wonderful man. I always said he was the greatest diplomatist in Europe. But I was a young fool in those days, I hadn't the sense to take his advice. If I had, if I'd never drawn on a five, I daresay I shouldn't be here today."

Cooper was watching him. His brown eyes, deep in their sockets, were hard and supercilious, and on his lips was a mocking smile. He had heard a good deal about Mr. Warburton in Kuala Solor. Not a bad sort, and he ran his district like clockwork, they said, but by heaven, what a snob! They laughed at him good-naturedly, for it was impossible to dislike a man who was so generous and so kindly, and Cooper had already heard the story of the Prince of Wales and the game of baccarat. But Cooper listened without indulgence. From the beginning he had resented the Resident's manner. He was very sensitive and he writhed under Mr. Warburton's polite sarcasms. Mr. Warburton had a knack of receiving a remark of which he disapproved with a devastating silence. Cooper had lived little in England and he had a peculiar dislike of the English. He resented especially the public-school boy since he always feared that he was going to patronize him. He was so much afraid of others putting on airs with him that, in order as it were to get in first, he put on such airs as to make every one think him insufferably conceited.

"Well, at all events the war has done one good thing for us," he said at last. "It's smashed up the power of the aristocracy. The Boer War started it, and 1914 put the lid on."

"The great families of England are doomed," said Mr. Warburton with the complacent melancholy of an *émigré* who remembered the court of Louis XV. "They cannot afford any longer to live in their splendid palaces and their princely hospitality will soon be nothing but a memory."

"And a damned good job too in my opinion."

"My poor Cooper, what can you know of the glory that was Greece and the grandeur that was Rome?"

Mr. Warburton made an ample gesture. His eyes for an instant grew dreamy with a vision of the past.

"Well, believe me, we're fed up with all that rot. What we want is a business government by business men. I was born in a Crown Colony and I've lived practically all my life in the colonies. I don't give a row of pins for a lord. What's wrong with England is snobbishness. And if there's anything that gets my goat it's a snob."

A snob! Mr. Warburton's face grew purple and his eyes blazed with anger. That was a word that had pursued him all his life. The great ladies whose society he had enjoyed in his youth were not inclined to look upon his appreciation of themselves as unworthy, but even great ladies are sometimes out of temper and more than once Mr. Warburton had had the dreadful word flung in his teeth. He knew, he could not help knowing, that there were odious people who called him a snob. How unfair it was! Why, there was no vice he found so detestable as snobbishness. After all, he liked to mix with people of his own class, he was only at home in their company, and how in heaven's name could any one say that was snobbish? Birds of a feather.

"I quite agree with you," he answered. "A snob is a man who admires or despises another because he is of a higher social rank than his own. It is the most vulgar failing of our English middle class."

He saw a flicker of amusement in Cooper's eyes. Cooper put up his hand to hide the broad smile that rose to his lips, and so made it more noticeable. Mr. Warburton' hands trembled a little.

Probably Cooper never knew how greatly he had offended his chief. A sensitive man himself, he was strangely insensitive to the feelings of others.

Their work forced them to see one another for a few minutes now and then during the day, and they met at six to have a drink on Mr. Warburton's verandah. This was an old-established custom of the country which Mr. Warburton would not for the world have broken. But they ate their meals separately, Cooper in his bungalow and Mr. Warburton at the Fort. After the office work was over they walked till dusk fell, but they walked apart. There were but few paths in this country, where the jungle pressed close upon the plantations of the village, and when Mr. Warburton caught sight of his assistant passing along with his loose stride, he would make a circuit in order to avoid him. Cooper, with his bad manners, his conceit in his own judgment and his intolerance, had already got on his nerves; but it was not till Cooper had been on the station for a couple of months that an incident happened which turned the Resident's dislike into bitter hatred.

Mr. Warburton was obliged to go up-country on a tour of inspection, and he left the station in Cooper's charge with more confidence, since he had definitely come to the conclusion that he was a capable fellow. The only thing he did not like was that he had no indulgence. He was honest, just and painstaking, but he had no sympathy for the natives. It bitterly amused Mr. Warburton to observe that this man, who looked upon himself as every man's equal, should look upon so many men as his own inferiors. He was hard, he had no patience with the native mind, and he was a bully. Mr. Warburton very quickly realized that the Malays disliked and feared him. He was not altogether displeased. He would not have liked it very much if his assistant had enjoyed a popularity which might rival his own. Mr. Warburton made his elaborate preparations, set out on his expedition, and in three weeks returned. Meanwhile the mail had arrived. The first thing that struck his eyes when he entered his sitting-room was a great pile of open newspapers. Cooper had met him, and they went into the room together. Mr. Warburton turned to one of the servants who had been left behind and sternly asked him what was the meaning of those open papers. Cooper hastened to explain.

"I wanted to read all about the Wolverhampton murder and so I borrowed your *Times*. I brought them back again. I knew you wouldn't mind."

Mr. Warburton turned on him, white with anger.

"But I do mind. I mind very much."

"I'm sorry," said Cooper, with composure. "The fact is, I simply couldn't wait till you came back."

"I wonder you didn't open my letters as well."

Cooper, unmoved, smiled at his chief's exasperation.

"Oh, that's not quite the same thing. After all, I couldn't imagine you'd mind my looking at your newspapers. There's nothing private in them."

"I very much object to any one reading my paper before me." He went up to the pile. There were nearly thirty numbers there. "I think it extremely impertinent of you. They're all mixed up."

"We can easily put them in order," said Cooper, joining him at the table.

"Don't touch them," cried Mr. Warburton.

"I say, it's childish to make a scene about a little thing like that."

"How dare you speak to me like that?"

"Oh, go to hell," said Cooper, and he flung out of the room.

Mr. Warburton, trembling with passion, was left contemplating his papers. His greatest pleasure in life had been destroyed by those callous, brutal hands. Most people living in out-of-the-way places when the mail comes tear open impatiently their papers and taking the last ones first glance at the latest news from home. Not so Mr. Warburton. His newsagent had instructions to write on the outside of the wrapper the date of each paper he despatched and when the great bundle arrived Mr. Warburton looked at these dates and with his blue pencil numbered them. His head-boy's orders were to place one on the table every morning in the verandah with the early cup of tea, and it was Mr. Warburton's especial delight to break the wrapper as he sipped his tea, and read the morning paper. It gave him the illusion of living at home. Every Monday morning he read the Monday *Times* of six weeks back and so went through the week. On Sunday he read *The Observer*. Like his habit of dressing for dinner it was a tie to civilization. And it was his pride that no matter how exciting the news was he had never yielded to the temptation of opening a paper before its allotted time. During the war the suspense sometimes had been intolerable, and when he read one day that a push was begun he had undergone agonies of suspense which he might have saved himself by the simple expedient of opening a later paper which lay waiting for him on a shelf. It had been the severest trial to which he had ever exposed himself, but he victoriously surmounted it. And that clumsy fool had broken open those neat tight packages because he wanted to know whether some horrid woman had murdered her odious husband.

Mr. Warburton sent for his boy and told him to bring wrappers. He folded up the papers as neatly as he could, placed a wrapper round each and numbered it. But it was a melancholy task.

"I shall never forgive him," he said. "Never."

Of course his boy had been with him on his expedition; he never traveled without him, for his boy knew exactly how he liked things, and Mr. Warburton was not the kind of jungle traveler who was prepared to dispense with his comforts; but in the interval since their arrival he had been gossiping in the servants' quarters. He had learnt that Copper had had trouble with his boys. All but the youth Abas had left him. Abas had desired to go too, but his uncle had placed him there on the instructions of the Resident, and he was afraid to leave without his uncle's permission.

"I told him he had done well, Tuan," said the boy. "But he is unhappy. He says it is not a good house and he wishes to know if he may go as the others have gone."

"No, he must stay. The tuan must have servants. Have those who went been replaced?"

"No, Tuan, no one will go."

Mr. Warburton frowned. Cooper was an insolent fool, but he had an official position and must be suitably provided with servants. It was not seemly that his house should be improperly conducted.

"Where are the boys who ran away?"

"They are in the kampong, Tuan."

"Go and see them tonight and tell them that I expect them to be back in Tuan Cooper's house at dawn to-morrow."

"They say they will not go, Tuan."

"On my order?"

The boy had been with Mr. Warburton for fifteen years, and he knew every intonation of his master's voice. He was not afraid of him, they had gone through too much together, once in the jungle the Resident had saved his life and once, upset in some rapids, but for him the Resident would have been drowned; but he knew when the Resident must be obeyed without question.

"I will go to the kampong," he said.

Mr. Warburton expected that his subordinate would take the first opportunity to apologize for his rudeness, but Cooper had the ill-bred man's inability to express regret; and when they met next morning in the office he ignored the incident. Since Mr. Warburton had been away for three weeks it was necessary for them to have a somewhat prolonged interview. At the end of it Mr. Warburton dismissed him.

"I don't think there's anything else, thank you." Cooper turned to go, but Mr. Warburton stopped him. "I understand you've been having some trouble with your boys."

Cooper gave a harsh laugh.

"They tried to blackmail me. They had the damned cheek to run away, all except that incompetent fellow Abas—he knew when he was well off—but I just sat tight. They've all come to heel again."

"What do you mean by that?"

"This morning they were all back on their jobs, the Chinese cook and all. There they were, as cool as cucumbers; you would have thought they owned the place. I suppose they'd come to the conclusion that I wasn't such a fool as I looked."

"By no means. They came back on my express order."

Cooper flushed slightly.

"I should be obliged if you wouldn't interfere with my private concerns."

"They're not your private concerns. When your servants run away it makes you ridiculous. You are perfectly free to make a fool of yourself, but I cannot allow you to be made a fool of. It is unseemly that your house should not be properly staffed. As soon as I heard that your boys had left you, I had them told to be back in their places at dawn. That'll do."

Mr. Warburton nodded to signify that the interview was at an end. Cooper took no notice.

"Shall I tell you what I did? I called them and gave the whole bally lot the sack. I gave them ten minutes to get out of the compound."

Mr. Warburton shrugged his shoulders.

"What makes you think you can get others?"

"I've told my own clerk to see about it."

Mr. Warburton reflected for a moment.

"I think you behaved very foolishly. You will do well to remember in future that good masters make good servants."

"Is there anything else you want to teach me?"

"I should like to teach you manners, but it would be an arduous task, and I have not the time to waste. I will see that you get boys."

"Please don't put yourself to any trouble on my account. I'm quite capable of getting them for myself."

Mr. Warburton smiled acidly. He had an inkling that Cooper disliked him as much as he disliked Cooper, and he knew that nothing is more galling than to be forced to accept the favors of a man you detest.

"Allow me to tell you that you have no more chance of getting Malay or Chinese servants here now than you have of getting an English butler or a French chef. No one will come to you except on an order from me. Would you like me to give it?"

"No."

"As you please. Good morning."

Mr. Warburton watched the development of the situation with acrid humor. Cooper's clerk was unable to persuade Malay, Dyak or Chinese to enter the house of such a master. Abas, the boy who remained faithful to him, knew how to cook only native food, and Cooper, a coarse feeder, found his gorge rise against the everlasting rice. There was no watercarrier, and in that great heat he needed several baths a day. He cursed Abas, but Abas opposed him with sullen resistance and would not do more than he chose. It was galling to know that the lad stayed with him only because the Resident insisted. This went on for a fortnight and then, one morning, he found in his house the very servants whom he had previously dismissed. He fell into a violent rage, but he had learnt a little sense, and this time, without a word, he let them stay. He swallowed his humiliation, but the impatient contempt he had felt for Mr. Warburton's idiosyncrasies changed into a sullen hatred; the Resident with this malicious stroke had made him the laughing-stock of all the natives.

The two men now held no communication with one another. They broke the time-honored custom of sharing, notwithstanding personal dislike, a drink at six o'clock with any white man who happened to be at the station. Each lived in his own house as though the other did not exist. Now that Cooper had fallen into the work, it was necessary for them to have little to do with one another in the office. Mr. Warburton used his orderly to send any message he had to give his assistant, and his instructions he sent by formal letter. They saw one another constantly, that was inevitable, but did not exchange half a dozen words in a week. The fact that they could not avoid catching sight of one another got on their nerves. They brooded over their antagonism and Mr. Warburton, taking his daily walk, could think of nothing but how much he detested his assistant.

And the dreadful thing was that in all probability they would remain thus, facing each other in deadly enmity, till Mr. Warburton went on leave. It might be three years. He had no reason to send in a complaint to headquarters: Cooper did his work very well, and at that time men were hard to get. True, vague complaints reached him and hints that the natives found Cooper harsh. There was certainly a feeling of dissatisfaction among them. But when Mr. Warburton looked into specific cases, all he could say was that Cooper had shown severity where mildness would not have been misplaced and had been unfeeling when himself would have been sympathetic. He had done nothing for which he could be taken to task. But Mr. Warburton watched him. Hatred will often make a man clear-sighted, and he had a suspicion that Cooper was using the natives without consideration, yet keeping within the law, because he felt that thus he could exasperate his chief. One day perhaps he would go too far. None knew better than Mr. Warburton how irritable the incessant heat could make a man and how difficult it was to keep one's self-control after a sleepless night. He smiled softly to himself. Sooner or later Cooper would deliver himself into his hand.

When at last the opportunity came Mr. Warburton laughed aloud. Cooper had charge of the prisoners; they made roads, built sheds, rowed when it was necessary to send the prahu up- or down-stream, kept the town clean and otherwise usefully employed themselves. If well-behaved they even on occasion served as house-boys. Cooper kept them hard at it. He liked to see them work. He took pleasure in devising tasks for them; and seeing quickly enough that they were being made to do useless things the prisoners worked badly. He punished them by lengthening their hours. This was contrary to the regulations, and as soon as it was brought to the attention of Mr. Warburton, without referring the matter back to his subordinate, he gave instructions that the old hours should be kept; Cooper, going out for his walk, was astounded to see the prisoners strolling back to the jail; he had given instructions that they were not to knock off till dusk. When he asked the warder in charge why they had left off work he was told that it was the Resident's bidding.

White with rage he strode to the Fort. Mr. Warburton, in his spotless white ducks and his neat topee, with a walking-stick in his hand, followed by his dogs, was on the point of starting out on his afternoon stroll. He had watched Cooper go and knew that he had taken the road by the river. Cooper jumped up the steps and went straight up to the Resident.

"I want to know what the hell you mean by countermanding my order that the prisoners were to work till six," he burst out, beside himself with fury.

Mr. Warburton opened his cold blue eyes very wide and assumed an expression of great surprise.

"Are you out of your mind? Are you so ignorant that you do not know that that is not the way to speak to your official superior?"

"Oh, go to hell. The prisoners are my pidgin and you've got no right to interfere. You mind your business and I'll mind mine. I want to know what the devil you mean by making a damned fool of me. Every one in the place will know that you've countermanded my order."

Mr. Warburton kept very cool.

"You had no power to give the order you did. I countermanded it because it was harsh and tyrannical. Believe me, I have not made half such a damned fool of you as you have made of yourself."

"You disliked me from the first moment I came here. You've done everything you could to make the place impossible for me because I wouldn't lick your boots for you. You got your knife into me because I wouldn't flatter you."

Cooper, sputtering with rage, was nearing dangerous ground, and Mr. Warburton's eyes grew on a sudden colder and more piercing.

"You are wrong. I thought you were a cad, but I was perfectly satisfied with the way you did your work."

"You snob. You damned snob. You thought me a cad because I hadn't been to Eton. Oh, they told me in K.S. what to expect. Why, don't you know that you're the laughing-stock of the whole country? I could hardly help bursting into a roar of laughter when you told your celebrated story about the Prince of Wales. My God, how they shouted at the club when they told it. By God, I'd rather be the cad I am than the snob you are."

He got Mr. Warburton on the raw.

"If you don't get out of my house this minute I shall knock you down," he cried.

The other came a little closer to him and put his face in his.

"Touch me, touch me," he said. "By God, I'd like to see you hit me. Do you want me to say it again? Snob. Snob."

Cooper was three inches taller than Mr. Warburton, a strong, muscular young man. Mr. Warburton was fat and fifty-four. His clenched fist shot out. Cooper caught him by the arm and pushed him back.

"Don't be a damned fool. Remember I'm not a gentleman. I know how to use my hands."

He gave a sort of hoot, and, grinning all over his pale, sharp face, jumped down the verandah steps. Mr. Warburton, his heart in his anger pounding against his ribs, sank exhausted into a chair. His body tingled as though he had prickly heat. For one horrible moment he thought he was going to cry. But suddenly he was conscious that his head-boy was on the verandah and instinctively regained control of himself. The boy came forward and filled him a glass of whisky and soda. Without a word Mr. Warburton took it and drank it to the dregs.

"What do you want to say to me?" asked Mr. Warburton, trying to force a smile on to his strained lips.

"Tuan, the assistant tuan is a bad man. Abas wishes again to leave him."

"Let him wait a little. I shall write to Kuala Solor and ask that Tuan Cooper should go elsewhere."

"Tuan Cooper is not good with the Malays."

"Leave me."

The boy silently withdrew. Mr. Warburton was left alone with his thoughts. He saw the club at Kuala Solor, the men sitting round the table in the window in their flannels, when the night had driven them in from golf and tennis, drinking whiskies and gin pahits and laughing when they told the celebrated story of the Prince of Wales and himself at Marienbad. He was hot with shame and misery. A snob! They all thought him a snob. And he had always thought them very good fellows, he had always been gentleman enough to let it make no difference to him that they were of very second-rate position. He hated them now. But his hatred for them was nothing compared with his hatred for Cooper. And if it had come to blows Cooper could have thrashed him. Tears of mortification ran down his red, fat face. He sat there for a couple of hours smoking cigarette after cigarette, and he wished he were dead.

At last the boy came back and asked him if he would dress for dinner. Of course! He always dressed for dinner. He rose wearily from his chair and put on his stiff shirt and the high collar. He sat down at the prettily decorated table and was waited on as usual by the two boys while two others waved their great fans. Over there in the bungalow, two hundred yards away, Cooper was eating a filthy meal clad only in a sarong and a baju. His feet were bare and while he ate he probably read a detective story. After dinner Mr. Warburton sat down to write a letter. The Sultan was away, but he wrote, privately and confidentially, to his representative. Cooper did his work very well, he said, but the fact was that he couldn't get on with him. They were getting dreadfully on each other's nerves and he would look upon it as a very great favor if Cooper could be transferred to another post.

He despatched the letter next morning by special messenger. The answer came a fortnight later with the month's mail. It was a private note and ran as follows:

"MY DEAR WARBURTON:

"I do not want to answer your letter officially and so I am writing you a few lines myself. Of course if you insist I will put the matter up to the Sultan, but I think you would be much wiser to drop it. I know Cooper is a rough diamond, but he is capable, and he had a pretty thin time in the war, and I think he should be given every chance. I think you are a little too much inclined to attach importance to a man's social position. You must remember that times have changed. Of course it's a very good thing for a man to be a gentleman, but it's better that he should be competent and hard-working. I think if you'll exercise a little tolerance you'll get on very well with Cooper.

"Yours very sincerely,

"RICHARD TEMPLE."

The letter dropped from Mr. Warburton's hand. It was easy to read between the lines. Dick Temple, whom he had known for twenty years, Dick Temple, who came from quite a good county family, thought him a snob and for that reason had no patience with his request. Mr. Warburton felt on a sudden discouraged with life. The world of which he was a part had passed away, and the future belonged to a meaner generation. Cooper represented it and Cooper he hated with all his heart. He stretched out his hand to fill his glass and at the gesture his head-boy stepped forward.

"I didn't know you were there."

The boy picked up the official letter. Ah, that was why he was waiting.

"Does Tuan Cooper go, Tuan?"

"No."

"There will be a misfortune."

For a moment the words conveyed nothing to his lassitude. But only for a moment. He sat up in his chair and looked at the boy. He was all attention.

"What do you mean by that?"

"Tuan Cooper is not behaving rightly with Abas."

Mr. Warburton shrugged his shoulders. How should a man like Cooper know how to treat servants? Mr. Warburton knew the type: he would be grossly familiar with them at one moment and rude and inconsiderate the next.

"Let Abas go back to his family."

"Tuan Cooper holds back his wages so that he may not run away.

He has paid him nothing for three months. I tell him to be patient. But he is angry, he will not listen to reason. If the tuan continues to use him ill there will be a misfortune."

"You were right to tell me."

The fool! Did he know so little of the Malays as to think he could safely injure them? It would serve him damned well right if he got a kris in his back. A kris. Mr. Warburton's heart seemed on a sudden to miss a beat. He had only to let things take their course and one fine day he would be rid of Cooper. He smiled faintly as the phrase, a masterly inactivity, crossed his mind. And now his heart beat a little quicker, for he saw the man he hated lying on his face in a pathway of the jungle with a knife in his back. A fit end for the cad and the bully. Mr. Warburton sighed. It was his duty to warn him and of course he must do it. He wrote a brief and formal note to Cooper asking him to come to the Fort at once.

In ten minutes Cooper stood before him. They had not spoken to one another since the day when Mr. Warburton had nearly struck him. He did not now ask him to sit down.

"Did you wish to see me?" Cooper asked.

He was untidy and none too clean. His face and hands were covered with little red blotches where mosquitoes had bitten him and he had scratched himself till the blood came. His long, thin face bore a sullen look.

"I understand that you are again having trouble with your servants. Abas, my head-boy's nephew, complains that you have held back his wages for three months. I consider it a most arbitrary proceeding. The lad wishes to leave you, and I certainly do not blame him. I must insist on your paying what is due to him."

"I don't choose that he should leave me. I am holding back his wages as a pledge of his good behavior."

"You do not know the Malay character. The Malays are very sensitive to injury and ridicule. They are passionate and revengeful. It is my duty to warn you that if you drive this boy beyond a certain point you run a great risk."

Cooper gave a contemptuous chuckle.

"What do you think he'll do?"

"I think he'll kill you."

"Why should you mind?"

"Oh, I wouldn't," replied Mr. Warburton, with a faint laugh. "I should bear it with the utmost fortitude. But I feel the official obligation to give you a proper warning."

"Do you think I'm afraid of a damned nigger?"

"It's a matter of entire indifference to me."

"Well, let me tell you this, I know how to take care of myself; that boy Abas is a dirty, thieving rascal, and if he tries any monkey tricks on me, by God, I'll wring his bloody neck."

"That was all I wished to say to you," said Mr. Warburton. "Good evening."

Mr. Warburton gave him a little nod of dismissal. Cooper flushed, did not for a moment know what to say or do, turned on his heel and stumbled out of the room. Mr. Warburton watched him go with an icy smile on his lips. He had done his duty. But what would he have thought had he known that when Copper got back to his bungalow, so silent and cheerless, he threw himself down on his bed and in his bitter loneliness on a sudden lost all control of himself? Painful sobs tore his chest and heavy tears rolled down his thin cheeks.

After this Mr. Warburton seldom saw Cooper, and never spoke to him. He read his *Times* every morning, did his work at the office, took his exercise, dressed for dinner, dined and sat by the river smoking his cheroot. If by chance he ran across Cooper he cut him dead. Each, though never for a moment unconscious of the propinquity, acted as though the other did not exist. Time did nothing to assuage their animosity. They watched one another's actions and each knew what the other did. Though Mr. Warburton had been a keen shot in his youth, with age he had acquired a distaste for killing the wild things of the jungle, but on Sundays and holidays Cooper went out with his gun: if he got something it was a triumph over Mr. Warburton; if not, Mr. Warburton shrugged his shoulders and chuckled. These counter-jumpers trying to be sportsmen! Christmas was a bad time for both of them: they ate their dinners alone, each in his own quarters, and they got deliberately drunk. They were the only white men within two hundred miles and they lived within shouting distance of each other. At the beginning of the year Cooper went down with fever, and when Mr. Warburton caught sight of him again he was surprised to see how thin he had grown. He looked ill and worn. The solitude, so much more unnatural because it was due to no necessity, was getting on his nerves. It was getting on Mr. Warburton's too, and often he could not sleep at night. He lay awake brooding. Cooper was drinking heavily and surely the breaking point was near; but in his dealings with the natives he took care to do nothing that might expose him to his chief's rebuke. They fought a grim and silent battle with one another. It was a test of endurance. The months passed, and neither gave sign of weakening. They were like men dwelling in regions of eternal night, and their souls were oppressed with the knowledge that never would the day dawn for them. It looked as though their lives would continue for ever in this dull and hideous monotony of hatred.

And when at last the inevitable happened it came upon Mr. Warburton with all the shock of the unexpected. Cooper accused the boy Abas of stealing some of his clothes, and when the boy denied the theft took him by the scruff of the neck and kicked him down the steps of the bungalow. The boy demanded his wages, and Cooper flung at his head every word of abuse he knew. If he saw him in the compound in an hour he would hand him over to the police. Next morning the boy waylaid him outside the Fort when he was walking over to his office, and again demanded his wages. Cooper struck him in the face with his clenched fist. The boy fell to the ground and got up with blood streaming from his nose.

Cooper walked on and set about his work. But he could not attend to it. The blow had calmed his irritation, and he knew that he had gone too far. He was worried. He felt ill, miserable and discouraged. In the adjoining office sat Mr. Warburton, and his impulse was to go and tell him what he had done; he made a movement in his chair, but he knew with what icy scorn he would listen to the story. He could see his patronizing smile. For a moment he had an uneasy fear of what Abas might do. Warburton had warned him all right. He sighed. What a fool he had been! But he shrugged his shoulders impatiently. He did not care; a fat lot he had to live for. It was all Warburton's fault; if he hadn't put his back up nothing like this would have happened. Warburton had made life a hell for him from the start. The snob. But they were all like that: it was because he was a Colonial. It was a damned shame that he had never got his commission in the war; he was as good as any one else. They were a lot of dirty snobs. He was damned if he was going to knuckle under now. Of course Warburton would hear of what had happened; the old devil knew everything. He wasn't afraid. He wasn't afraid of any Malay in Borneo, and Warburton could go to blazes.

He was right in thinking that Mr. Warburton would know what had happened. His head-boy told him when he went in to tiffin.

"Where is your nephew now?"

"I do not know, Tuan. He has gone."

Mr. Warburton remained silent. After luncheon as a rule he slept a little, but today he found himself very wide awake. His eyes involuntarily sought the bungalow where Cooper was now resting.

The idiot! Hesitation for a little was in Mr. Warburton's mind. Did the man know in what peril he was? He supposed he ought to send for him. But each time he had tried to reason with Cooper, Cooper had insulted him. Anger, furious anger welled up suddenly in Mr. Warburton's heart, so that the veins on his temples stood out and he clenched his fists. The cad had had his warning. Now let him take what was coming to him. It was no business of his and if anything happened it was not his fault. But perhaps they would wish in Kuala Solor that they had taken his advice and transferred Cooper to another station.

He was strangely restless that night. After dinner he walked up and down the verandah. When the boy went away to his own quarters, Mr. Warburton asked him whether anything had been seen of Abas.

"No, Tuan, I think maybe he has gone to the village of his mother's brother."

Mr. Warburton gave him a sharp glance, but the boy was looking down and their eyes did not meet. Mr. Warburton went down to the river and sat in his arbor. But peace was denied him. The river flowed ominously silent. It was like a great serpent gliding with sluggish movement towards the sea. And the trees of the jungle over the water were heavy with a breathless menace. No bird sang. No breeze ruffled the leaves of the cassias. All around him it seemed as though something waited.

He walked across the garden to the road. He had Cooper's bungalow in full view from there. There was a light in his sitting-room and across the road floated the sound of rag-time. Cooper was playing his gramophone. Mr. Warburton shuddered; he had never got over his instinctive dislike of that instrument. But for that he would have gone over and spoken to Cooper. He turned and went back to his own house. He read late into the night, and at last he slept. But he did not sleep very long, he had terrible dreams, and he seemed to be awakened by a cry. Of course that was a dream too, for no cry—from the bungalow for instance—could be heard in his room. He lay awake till dawn. Then he heard hurried steps and the sound of voices, his head-boy burst into the room without his fez, and Mr. Warburton's heart stood still.

"Tuan, Tuan."

Mr. Warburton jumped out of bed.

"I'll come at once."

He put on his slippers; and in his sarong and pyjama-jacket walked across his compound and into Cooper's. Cooper was lying in bed, with his mouth open, and a kris sticking in his heart. He had been killed in his sleep. Mr. Warburton started, but not because he had not expected to see just such a sight, he started because he felt in himself a sudden glow of exultation. A great burden had been lifted from his shoulders.

Cooper was quite cold. Mr. Warburton took the kris out of the wound, it had been thrust in with such force that he had to use an effort to get it out, and looked at it. He recognized it. It was a kris that a dealer had offered him some weeks before and which he knew Cooper had bought.

"Where is Abas?" he asked sternly.

"Abas is at the village of his mother's brother."

The sergeant of the native police was standing at the foot of the bed.

"Take two men and go to the village and arrest him."

Mr. Warburton did what was immediately necessary. With set face he gave orders. His words were short and peremptory. Then he went back to the Fort. He shaved and had his bath, dressed and went into the dining-room. By the side of his plate *The Times* in its wrapper lay waiting for him. He helped himself to some fruit. The head-boy poured out his tea while the second handed him a dish of eggs. Mr. Warburton ate with a good appetite. The head-boy waited.

"What is it?" asked Mr. Warburton.

"Tuan, Abas, my nephew, was in the house of his mother's brother all night. It can be proved. His uncle will swear that he did not leave the kampong."

Mr. Warburton turned upon him with a frown.

"Tuan Cooper was killed by Abas. You know it as well as I know it. Justice must be done."

"Tuan, you would not hang him?"

Mr. Warburton hesitated an instant, and though his voice remained set and stern a change came into his eyes. It was a flicker which the Malay was quick to notice and across his own eyes flashed an answering look of understanding.

"The provocation was very great. Abas will be sentenced to a term of imprisonment." There was a pause while Mr. Warburton helped himself to marmalade. "When he has served a part of his sentence in prison I will take him into this house as a boy. You can train him in his duties. I have no doubt that in the house of Tuan Cooper he got into bad habits."

"Shall Abas give himself up, Tuan?"

"It would be wise of him."

The boy withdrew. Mr. Warburton took his *Times* and neatly slit the wrapper. He loved to unfold the heavy, rustling pages. The morning, so fresh and cool, was delicious and for a moment his eyes wandered out over his garden with a friendly glance. A great weight had been lifted from his mind. He turned to the columns in which were announced the births, deaths, and marriages. That was what he always looked at first. A name he knew caught his attention. Lady Ormskirk had had a son at last. By George, how pleased the old dowager must be! He would write her a note of congratulation by the next mail.

Abas would make a very good house-boy.

That fool Cooper!

JOSEPH CONRAD

An Outpost of Progress

I

There were two white men in charge of the trading station. Kayerts, the chief, was short and fat; Carlier, the assistant, was tall, with a large head and a very broad trunk perched upon a long pair of thin legs. The third man on the staff was a Sierra Leone nigger, who maintained that his name was Henry Price. However, for some reason or other, the natives down the river had given him the name of Makola, and it stuck to him through all his wanderings about the country. He spoke English and French with a warbling accent, wrote a beautiful hand, understood bookkeeping, and cherished in his innermost heart the worship of evil spirits. His wife was a negress from Loanda, very large and very noisy. Three children rolled about in sunshine before the door of his low, shed-like dwelling. Makola, taciturn and impenetrable, despised the two white men. He had charge of a small clay store house with a dried-grass roof, and pretended to keep a correct account of beads, cotton cloth, red kerchiefs, brass wire, and other trade goods it contained. Besides the storehouse and Makola's hut, there was only one large building in the cleared ground of the station. It was build neatly of reeds, with a veranda on all the four sides. There were three rooms in it. The one in the middle was the living room, and had two rough tables and a few stools in it. The other two were the bedrooms for the white men. Each had a bedstead and a mosquito net for all furniture. The plank floor was littered with the belongings of the white men; open half-empty boxes, torn wearing apparel, old boots, all the things dirty, and all the things broken, that accumulate mysteriously round untidy men. There was also another dwelling place some distance away from the buildings. In it, under a tall cross much out of the perpendicular, slept the man who had seen the beginning of all this; who had

From *Tales of Unrest* by Joseph Conrad. Reprinted by permission of J. M. Dent & Sons Ltd. and the Trustees of the Joseph Conrad Estate.

planned and had watched the construction of this outpost of progress. He had been, at home, an unsuccessful painter who, weary of pursuing fame on an empty stomach, had gone out there through high protections. He had been the first chief of that station. Makola had watched the energetic artist die of fever in the just finished house with his usual kind of "I told you so" indifference. Then, for a time, he dwelt alone with his family, his account books, and the Evil Spirit that rules the lands under the equator. He got on very well with his god. Perhaps he had propitiated him by a promise of more white men to play with, by and by. At any rate the director of the Great Trading Company, coming up in a steamer that resembled an enormous sardine box with a flat-roofed shed erected on it, found the station in good order, and Makola as usual quietly diligent. The director had the cross put up over the first agent's grave, and appointed Kayerts to the post. Carlier was told off as second in charge. The director was a man ruthless and efficient, who at times, but very imperceptibly, indulged in grim humor. He made a speech to Kayerts and Carlier, pointing out to them the promising aspect of their station. The nearest trading post was about three hundred miles away. It was an exceptional opportunity for them to distinguish themselves and to earn percentages on the trade. This appointment was a favor done to beginners. Kayerts was moved almost to tears by his director's kindness. He would, he said, by doing his best, try to justify the flattering confidence, etc., etc. Kayerts had been in the Administration of the Telegraphs, and knew how to express himself correctly. Carlier, an ex-noncommissioned officer of cavalry in an army guaranteed from harm by several European powers, was less impressed. If there were commissions to get, so much the better; and, trailing a sulky glance over the river, the forests, the impenetrable bush that seemed to cut off the station from the rest of the world, he muttered between his teeth, "We shall see, very soon."

Next day, some bales of cotton goods and a few cases of provisions having been thrown on shore, the sardine-box steamer went off, not to return for another six months. On the deck the director touched his cap to the two agents, who stood on the bank waving their hats, and turning to an old servant of the Company on his passage to headquarters, said, "Look at those two imbeciles. They must be mad at home to send me such specimens. I told those fellows to plant a vegetable garden, build new storehouses and fences, and construct a landing stage. I bet nothing will be done! They won't know how to begin. I always thought the station on this river useless, and they just fit the station!"

"They will form themselves there," said the old stager with a quiet smile.

"At any rate, I am rid of them for six months," retorted the director.

The two men watched the steamer round the bend, then, ascending arm in arm the slope of the bank, returned to the station. They had been in this vast and dark country only a very short time, and as yet always in the midst of other white men, under the eye and guidance of their superiors. And now, dull as they were to the subtle influences of surroundings, they felt themselves very much alone, when suddenly left unassisted to face the wilderness; a wilderness rendered more strange, more incomprehensible by the mysterious glimpse of the vigorous life it contained. They were two perfectly insignificant and incapable individuals, whose existence is only rendered possible through the high organization of civilized crowds. Few men realize that their life, the very essence of their character, their capabilities and their audacities, are only the expression of their belief in the safety of their surroundings. The courage, the composure, the confidence; the emotions and principles; every great and every insignificant thought belongs not to the individual but to the crowd: to the crowd that believes blindly in the irresistible force of its institutions and of its morals, in the power of its police and of its opinion. But the contact with pure unmitigated savagery, with primitive nature and primitive man, brings sudden and profound trouble into the heart. To the sentiment of being alone of one's kind, to the clear perception of the loneliness of one's thoughts, of one's sensations—to the negation of the habitual, which is safe, there is added the affirmation of the unusual, which is dangerous; a suggestion of things vague, uncontrollable, and repulsive, whose discomposing intrusion excites the imagination and tries the civilized nerves of the foolish and the wise alike.

Kayerts and Carlier walked arm in arm, drawing close to one another as children do in the dark; and they had the same, not altogether unpleasant, sense of danger which one half suspects to be imaginary. They chatted persistently in familiar tones. "Our station is prettily situated," said one. The other assented with enthusiasm, enlarging volubly on the beauties of the situation. Then they passed near the grave. "Poor devil!" said Kayerts. "He died of fever, didn't he?" muttered Carlier, stopping short. "Why," retorted Kayerts, with indignation, "I've been told that the fellow exposed himself recklessly to the sun. The climate here, everybody says, is not at all worse than at home, as long as you keep out of the sun. Do you hear that, Carlier? I am chief here, and my orders are that you should not expose yourself to the sun!" He assumed his superiority jocularly, but his meaning was serious. The idea that he would, perhaps, have to bury Carlier and remain alone, gave him an inward shiver. He felt suddenly that this Carlier was more precious to him here, in the center of Africa, than a brother could be anywhere else. Carlier, entering into the spirit of the thing, made a military salute and answered in a brisk tone. "Your orders shall be attended to, chief!" Then he burst out laughing, slapped Kayerts on the back and shouted, "We shall let life run easily here! Just sit still and gather in the ivory those savages will bring. This country has its good points, after all!" They both laughed loudly while Carlier thought: "That poor Kayerts; he is so fat and unhealthy. It would be awful if I had to bury him here. He is a man I respect." . . . Before they reached the veranda of their house they called one another "my dear fellow."

The first day they were very active, pottering about with hammers and nails and red calico, to put up curtains, make their house habitable and pretty; resolved to settle down comfortably to their new life. For them an impossible task. To grapple effectually with even purely material problems requires more serenity of mind and more lofty courage than people generally imagine. No two beings could have been more unfitted for such a struggle. Society, not from any tenderness, but because of its strange needs, had taken care of those two men, forbidding them all independent thought, all initiative, all departure from routine; and forbidding it under pain of death. They could only live on condition of being machines. And now, released from the fostering care of men with pens behind the ears, or of men with gold lace on the sleeves, they were like those lifelong prisoners who, liberated after many years, do not know what use to make of their freedom. They did not know what use to make of their faculties, being both, through want of practice, incapable of independent thought.

At the end of two months Kayerts often would say, "If it was not for my Melie, you wouldn't catch me here." Melie was his daughter. He had thrown up his post in the Administration of the Telegraphs, though he had been for seventeen years perfectly happy there, to earn a dowry for his girl. His wife was dead, and the child was being brought up by his sisters. He regretted the streets, the pavements, the cafés, his friends of many years; all the things he used to see, day after day; all the thoughts suggested by familiar things—the thoughts effortless, monotonous, and soothing of a Government clerk; he regretted all the gossip, the small enmities, the mild venom, and the little jokes of Government offices. "If I had had a decent brother-in-law," Carlier would remark, "a fellow with a heart, I would not be here." He had left the army and had made himself so obnoxious to his family by his laziness and impudence, that an exasperated brother-in-law had made superhuman efforts to procure him an appointment in the Company as a second-class agent. Having not a penny in the world he was compelled to accept this means of livelihood as soon as it became quite clear to him that there was nothing more to squeeze out of his relations. He, like Kayerts, regretted his old life. He regretted the clink of saber and spurs on a fine afternoon, the barrack-room witticisms, the girls of garrison towns; but, besides, he had also a sense of grievance. He was evidently a much ill-used man. This made him moody, at times. But the two men got on well together in the fellowship of their stupidity and laziness. Together they did nothing, absolutely nothing, and enjoyed the sense of the idleness for which they were paid. And in time they came to feel something resembling affection for one another.

They lived like blind men in a large room, aware only of what came in contact with them (and of that only imperfectly), but unable to see the general aspect of things. The river, the forest, all the great land throbbing with life, were like a great emptiness. Even the brilliant sunshine disclosed nothing intelligible. Things appeared and disappeared before their eyes in an unconnected and aimless kind of way. The river seemed to come from nowhere and flow nowhither. It flowed through a void. Out of that void, at times, came canoes, and men with spears in their hands would suddenly crowd the yard of the station. They were naked, glossy black, ornamented with snowy shells and glistening brass wire, perfect of limb. They made an uncouth babbling noise when they spoke, moved in a stately manner, and sent quick, wild glances out of their startled, never-resting eyes. Those warriors would squat in long rows, four or more deep, before the veranda, while their chiefs bargained for hours with Makola over an elephant tusk. Kayerts sat on his chair and looked down on the proceedings, understanding nothing. He stared at them with his round blue eyes, called out to Carlier, "Here, look! look at that fellow there—and that other one, to the left. Did you ever see such a face? Oh, the funny brute!"

Carlier, smoking native tobacco in a short wooden pipe, would swagger up twirling his mustaches, and surveying the warriors with haughty indulgence, would say:

"Fine animals. Brought any bone? Yes? It's not any too soon. Look at the muscles of that fellow—third from the end. I wouldn't care to get a punch on the nose from him. Fine arms, but legs no good below the knee. Couldn't make cavalry men of them." And after glancing down complacently at his own shanks, he always concluded. "Pah! Don't they stink! You, Makola! Take that herd over to the fetish" (the storehouse was in every station called the fetish, perhaps because of the spirit of civilization it contained) "and give them up some of the rubbish you keep there. I'd rather see it full of bone than full of rags."

Kayerts approved.

"Yes, yes! Go and finish that palaver over there, Mr. Makola. I will come round when you are ready, to weight the tusk. We must be careful." Then turning to his companion: "This is the tribe that lives down the river; they are rather aromatic. I remember, they had been once before here. D'ya hear that row? What a fellow has got to put up with in this dog of a country! My head is split."

Such profitable visits were rare. For days the two pioneers of trade and progress would look on their empty courtyard in the vibrating brilliance of vertical sunshine. Below the high bank, the silent river flowed on glittering and steady. On the sands in the middle of the stream, hippos and alligators sunned themselves side by side. And stretching away in all directions, surrounding the insignificant cleared spot of the trading post, immense forests, hiding fateful complications of fantastic life, lay in the eloquent silence of mute greatness. The two men understood nothing, cared for nothing but for the passage of days that separated them from the steamer's return. Their predecessor had left some torn books. They took up these wrecks of novels, and, as they had never read anything of the kind before, they were surprised and amused. Then during long days there were interminable and silly discussions about plots and personages. In the center of Africa they made acquaintance of Richelieu and of d'Artagnan, of Hawk's Eye and of Father Goriot, and of many other people. All these imaginary personages became subjects for gossip as if they had been living friends. They discounted their virtues, suspected their motives, decried their successes; were scandalized at their duplicity or were doubtful about their courage. The accounts of crimes filled them with indignation, while tender or pathetic passages moved them deeply. Carlier cleared his throat and said in a soldierly voice, "What nonsense!" Kayerts, his round eyes suffused with tears, his fat cheeks quivering, rubbed his bald head, and declared, "This is a splendid book. I had no idea there were such clever fellows in the world." They also found some old copies of a home paper. That print discussed what it was pleased to call "Our Colonial Expansion" in high-flown language. It spoke much of the rights and duties of civilization, of the sacredness of the civilizing work, and extolled the merits of those who went about bringing light, and faith and commerce to the dark places of the earth. Carlier and Kayerts read, wondered, and began to think better of themselves. Carlier said one evening, waving his hand about, "In a hundred years, there will be perhaps a town here. Quays, and warehouses, and barracks, and—and—billiard rooms. Civilization, my boy, and virtue—and all. And then, chaps will read that two good fellows, Kayerts and Carlier, were the first civilized men to live in this very spot!" Kayerts nodded, "Yes, it is a consolation to think of that." They seemed to forget their dead predecessor; but, early one day, Carlier went out and replanted the cross firmly. "It used to make me squint whenever I walked that way," he explained to Kayerts over the morning coffee. "It made me squint, leaning over so much. So I just planted it upright. And solid, I promise you! I suspended myself with both hands to the crosspiece. Not a move. Oh, I did that properly."

At times Gobila came to see them. Goblia was the chief of the neighboring villages. He was a gray-headed savage, thin and black, with a white cloth round his loins and a mangy panther skin hanging over his back. He came up with long strides of his skeleton legs, swinging a staff as tall as himself, and, entering the common room of the station, would squat on his heels to the left of the door. There he sat, watching Kayerts, and now and then making a speech which the other did not understand. Kayerts, without interrupting his occupation, would from time to time say in a friendly manner: "How goes it, you old image?" and they would smile at one another. The two whites had a liking for that old and incomprehensible creature, and called him Father Gobila. Gobila's manner was paternal, and he seemed really to love all white men. They all appeared to him very young, indistinguishably alike (except for stature), and he knew that they were all brothers, and also immortal. The death of the artist, who was the first white man whom he knew intimately, did not disturb this belief, because he was firmly convinced that the white stranger had pretended to die and got himself buried for some mysterious purpose of his own, into which it was useless to inquire. Perhaps it was his way of going home to his own country? At any rate, these were his brothers, and he transferred his absurd affection to them. They returned it in a way. Carlier slapped him on the back, and recklessly struck off matches for his amusement. Kayerts was always ready to let him have a sniff at the ammonia bottle. In short, they behaved just like that other white creature that had hidden itself in a hole in the ground. Gobila considered them attentively. Perhaps they were the same being with the other—or one of them was. He couldn't decide—clear up that mystery; but he remained always very friendly. In consequence of that friendship the women of Gobila's village walked in single file through the reedy grass, bringing every morning to the station, fowls, and sweet potatoes, and palm wine, and sometimes a goat. The Company never provisions the stations fully, and the agents required those local supplies to live. They had them through the good will of Gobila, and lived well. Now and then one of them had a bout of fever, and the other nursed him with gentle devotion. They did not think much of it. It left them weaker, and their appearance changed for the worse. Carlier was hollow-eyed and irritable. Kayerts showed a drawn, flabby face above the rotundity of his stomach, which gave him a weird aspect. But being constantly together, they did not notice the change that took place gradually in their appearance, and also in their dispositions.

Five months passed in that way.

Then, one morning, as Kayerts and Carlier, lounging in their chairs under the veranda, talked about the approaching visit of the steamer, a knot of armed men came out of the forest and advanced towards the station. They were strangers to that part of the country. They were tall, slight, draped classically from neck to heel in blue fringed cloths, and carried percussion muskets over their bare right shoulders. Makola showed signs of excitement, and ran out of the storehouse (where he spent all his days) to meet these visitors. They came into the courtyard and looked about them with steady, scornful glances. Their leader, a powerful and determined-looking Negro with bloodshot eyes, stood in front of the veranda and made a long speech. He gesticulated much and ceased very suddenly.

There was something in his intonation, in the sounds of the long sentences he used, that startled the two whites. It was like a reminiscence of something not exactly familiar, and yet resembling the speech of civilized men. It sounded like one of those impossible languages which sometimes we hear in our dreams.

"What lingo is that?" said the amazed Carlier. "In the first moment I fancied the fellow was going to speak French. Anyway, it is a different kind of gibberish to what we ever heard."

"Yes," replied Kayerts. "Hey, Makola, what does he say? Where do they come from? Who are they?"

But Makola, who seemed to be standing on hot bricks, answered hurriedly, "I don't know. They come from very far. Perhaps Mrs. Price will understand. They are perhaps bad men."

The leader, after waiting for a while, said something sharply to Makola, who shook his head. Then the man, after looking round, noticed Makola's hut and walked over there. The next moment Mrs. Makola was heard speaking with great volubility. The other strangers—they were six in all—strolled about with an air of ease, put their heads through the door of the storeroom, congregated round the grave, pointed understandingly at the cross and generally made themselves at home.

"I don't like those chaps—and, I say, Kayerts, they must be from the coast, they've got firearms," observed the sagacious Carlier.

Kayerts also did not like those chaps. They both, for the first time, became aware that they lived in conditions where the unusual may be dangerous, and that there was no power on earth outside of themselves to stand between them and the unusual. They became uneasy, went in and loaded their revolvers. Kayerts said, "We must order Makola to tell them to go away before dark."

The strangers left in the afternoon, after eating a meal prepared for them by Mrs. Makola. The immense woman was excited, and talked much with the visitors. She rattled away shrilly, pointing here and there at the forests and at the river. Makola sat apart and watched. At times he got up and whispered to his wife. He accompanied the strangers across the ravine at the back of the station-ground, and returned slowly looking very thoughtful. When questioned by the white men he was very strange, seemed not to understand, seemed to have forgotten French—seemed to have forgotten how to speak altogether. Kayerts and Carlier agreed that the nigger had had too much palm wine.

There was some talk about keeping a watch in turn, but in the evening everything seemed so quiet and peaceful that they retired as usual. All night they were disturbed by a lot of drumming in the villages. A deep, rapid roll near by would be followed by another far off—then all ceased. Soon short appeals would rattle out here and there, then all mingle together, increase, become vigorous and sustained, would spread out over the forest, roll through the night, unbroken and ceaseless, near and far, as if the whole land had been one immense drum booming out steadily an appeal to heaven. And through the deep and tremendous noise sudden yells that resembled snatches of songs from a madhouse darted shrill and high in discordant jets of sound which seemed to rush far above the earth and drive all peace from under the stars.

Carlier and Kayerts slept badly. They both thought they had heard shots fired during the night—but they could not agree as to the direction. In the morning Makola was gone somewhere. He returned about noon with one of yesterday's strangers, and eluded all Kayerts' attempts to close with him: had become deaf apparently. Kayerts wondered. Carlier, who had been fishing off the bank, came back and remarked while he showed his catch, "The niggers seem to be in a deuce of a stir; I wonder what's up. I saw about fifteen canoes cross the river during the two hours I was there fishing." Kayerts, worried, said, "Isn't this Makola very queer today?" Carlier advised, "Keep all our men together in case of some trouble."

II

There were ten station men who had been left by the Director. Those fellows, having engaged themselves to the Company for six months (without having any idea of a month in particular and only a very faint notion of time in general), had been serving the cause of progress for upwards of two years. Belonging to a tribe from a very distant part of the land of darkness and sorrow, they did not run away, naturally supposing that as wandering strangers they would be killed by the inhabitants of the country; in which they were right. They lived in straw huts on the slope of a ravine overgrown with reedy grass, just behind the station buildings. They were not happy, regretting the festive incantations, the sorceries, the human sacrifices of their own land; where they also had parents, brothers, sisters, admired chiefs, respected magicians, loved friends, and other ties supposed generally to be human. Besides, the rice rations served out by the Company did not agree with them, being a food unknown to their land, and to which they could not get used. Consequently they were unhealthy and miserable. Had they been of any other tribe they would have made up their minds to die—for nothing is easier to certain savages than suicide—and so have escaped from the puzzling difficulties of existence. But belonging, as they did, to a warlike tribe with filed teeth, they had more grit, and went on stupidly living through disease and sorrow. They did very little work, and had lost their splendid physique. Carlier and Kayerts doctored them assiduously without being able to bring them back into condition again. They were mustered every morning and told off to different tasks—grass-cutting, fence-building, tree-felling, etc., etc., which no power on earth could induce them to execute efficiently. The two whites had practically very little control over them.

In the afternoon Makola came over to the big house and found Kayerts watching three heavy columns of smoke rising above the forests. "What is that?" asked Kayerts. "Some villages burn," answered Makola, who seemed to have regained his wits. Then he said abruptly: "We have got very little ivory; bad six months' trading. Do you like get a little more ivory?"

"Yes," said Kayerts, eagerly. He thought of percentages which were low.

"Those men who came yesterday are traders from Loanda who have got more ivory than they can carry home. Shall I buy? I know their camp."

"Certainly," said Kayerts. "What are those traders?"

"Bad fellows," said Makola, indifferently. "They fight with people, and catch women and children. They are bad men, and got guns. There is a great disturbance in the country. Do you want ivory?"

"Yes," said Kayerts. Makola said nothing for a while. Then: "Those workmen of ours are no good at all," he muttered, looking round. "Station in very bad order, sir. Director will growl. Better get a fine lot of ivory, then he say nothing."

"I can't help it; the men won't work," said Kayerts. "When will you get that ivory?"

"Very soon," said Makola. "Perhaps tonight. You leave it to me, and keep indoors, sir. I think you had better give some palm wine to our men to make a dance this evening. Enjoy themselves. Work better tomorrow. There's plenty palm wine—gone a little sour."

Kayerts said "yes," and Makola, with his own hands carried big calabashes to the door of his hut. They stood there till the evening, and Mrs. Makola looked into every one. The men got them at sunset. When Kayerts and Carlier retired, a big bonfire was flaring before the men's huts. They could hear their shouts and drumming. Some men from Gobila's village had joined the station hands, and the entertainment was a great success.

In the middle of the night, Carlier waking suddenly, heard a man shout loudly, then a shot was fired. Only one. Carlier ran out and met Kayerts on the veranda. They were both startled. As they went across the yard to call Makola, they saw shadows moving in the night. One of them cried, "Don't shoot! It's me, Price." Then Makola appeared close to them. "Go back, go back, please," he urged, "you spoil all." "There are strange men about," said Carlier. "Never mind; I know," said Makola. Then he whispered, "All right. Bring ivory. Say nothing! I know my business." The two white men reluctantly went back to the house, but did not sleep. They heard footsteps, whispers, some groans. It seemed as if a lot of men came in, dumped heavy things on the ground, squabbled a long time, then went away. They lay on their hard beds and thought: "This Makola is invaluable." In the morning Carlier came out, very sleepy, and pulled at the cord of the big bell. The station hands mustered every morning to the sound of the bell. That morning nobody came. Kayerts turned out also, yawning. Across the yard they saw Makola come out of his hut, a tin basin of soapy water in his hand. Makola, a civilized nigger, was very neat in his person. He threw the soapsuds skillfully over a wretched little yellow cur he had, then turning his face to the agent's house, he shouted from the distance, "All the men gone last night!"

They heard him plainly, but in their surprise they both yelled out together: "What!" Then they stared at one another. "We are in a proper fix now," growled Carlier. "It's incredible!" muttered Kayerts. "I will go to the huts and see," said Carlier, striding off. Makola coming up found Kayerts standing alone.

"I can hardly believe it," said Kayerts, tearfully. "We took care of them as if they had been our children."

"They went with the coast people," said Makola after a moment of hesitation.

"What do I care with whom they went—the ungrateful brutes!" exclaimed the other. Then with sudden suspicion, and looking hard at Makola, he added: "What do you know about it?"

Makola moved his shoulders, looking down on the ground. "What do I know? I think only. Will you come and look at the ivory I've got there? It is a fine lot. You never saw such."

He moved towards the store. Kayerts followed him mechanically, thinking about the incredible desertion of the men. On the ground before the door of the fetish lay six splendid tusks.

"What did you give for it?' asked Kayerts, after surveying the lot with satisfaction.

"No regular trade," said Makola. "They brought the ivory and gave it to me. I told them to take what they most wanted in the station. It is a beautiful lot. No station can show such tusks. Those traders wanted carriers badly, and our men were no good here. No trade, no entry in books; all correct."

Kayerts nearly burst with indignation. "Why!" he shouted, "I believe you have sold our men for these tusks!" Makola stood impassive and silent, "I—I—will—I," —stuttered Kayerts. "You fiend!" he yelled out.

"I did the best for you and the Company," said Makola, imperturbably. "Why you shout so much? Look at this tusk."

"I dismiss you! I will report you—I won't look at the tusk. I forbid you to touch them. I order you to throw them into the river. You—you!"

"You very red, Mr. Kayerts. If you are so irritable in the sun, you will get fever and die—like the first chief!" pronounced Makola impressively.

They stood still, contemplating one another with intense eyes, as if they had been looking with effort across immense distances. Kayerts shivered. Makola had meant no more than he said, but his words seemed to Kayerts full of ominous menace! He turned sharply and went away to the house. Makola retired into the bosom of his family; and the tusks, left lying before the store, looked very large and valuable in the sunshine.

Carlier came back on the veranda. "They're all gone, hey?" asked Kayerts from the far end of the common room in a muffled voice. "You did not find anybody?"

"Oh, yes," said Carlier, "I found one of Gobila's people lying dead before the huts—shot through the body. We heard that shot last night."

Kayerts came out quickly. He found his companion staring grimly over the yard at the tusks, away by the store. They both sat in silence for a while. Then Kayerts related his conversation with Makola. Carlier said nothing. At the midday meal they ate very little. They hardly exchanged a word that day. A great silence seemed to lie heavily over the station and press on their lips. Makola did not open the store; he spent the day playing with his children. He lay full-length on a mat outside his door, and the youngsters sat on his chest and clambered all over him. It was a touching picture. Mrs. Makola was busy cooking all day as usual. The white men made a somewhat better meal in the evening. Afterwards, Carlier smoking his pipe strolled over to the store; he stood for a long time over the tusks, touched one or two with his foot, even tried to lift the largest one by its small end. He came back to his chief, who had not stirred from the veranda, threw himself in the chair and said:

"I can see it! They were pounced upon while they slept heavily after drinking all that palm wine you've allowed Makola to give them. A put-up job! See? The worst is, some of Gobila's people were there, and got carried off too, no doubt. The least drunk woke up, and got shot for his sobriety. This is a funny country. What will you do now?"

"We can't touch it, of course," said Kayerts.

"Of course not," assented Carlier.

"Slavery is an awful thing," stammered out Kayerts in an unsteady voice.

"Frightful—the sufferings," grunted Carlier with conviction.

They believed their words. Everybody shows a respectful deference to certain sounds that he and his fellows can make. But about feelings people really know nothing. We talk with indignation or enthusiasm; we talk about oppression, cruelty, crime, devotion, self-sacrifice, virtue, and we know nothing real beyond the words. Nobody knows what suffering or sacrifice mean—except, perhaps the victims of the mysterious purpose of these illusions.

Next morning they saw Makola very busy setting up in the yard the big scales used for weighing ivory. By and by Carlier said: "What's that filthy scoundrel up to?" and lounged out into the yard. Kayerts followed. They stood watching. Makola took no notice. When the balance was swung true, he tried to lift a tusk into the scale. It was too heavy. He looked up helplessly without a word, and for a minute they stood round that balance as mute and still as three statues. Suddenly Carlier said: "Catch hold of the other end, Makola—you beast!" and together they swung the tusk up. Kayerts trembled in every limb. He muttered, "I say! O! I say!" and putting his hand in this pocket found there a dirty bit of paper and the stump of a pencil. He turned his back on the others, as if about to do something tricky, and noted stealthily the weights which Carlier shouted out to him with unnecessary loudness. When all was over Makola whispered to himself: "The sun's very strong here for the tusks." Carlier said to Kayerts in a careless tone: "I say, chief, I might just as well give him a lift with this lot into the store."

As they were going back to the house Kayerts observed with a sigh: "It had to be done." And Carlier said: "It's deplorable, but, the men being Company's men the ivory is Company's ivory. We must look after it." "I will report to the Director, of course," said Kayerts. "Of course; let him decide," approved Carlier.

At midday they made a hearty meal. Kayerts sighed from time to time. Whenever they mentioned Makola's name they always added to it an opprobrious epithet. It eased their conscience. Makola gave himself a half-holiday, and bathed his children in the river. No one from Gobila's villages came near the station that day. No one came the next day, and the next, nor for a whole week. Gobila's people might have been dead and buried for any sign of life they gave. But they were only mourning for those they had lost by the witchcraft of white men, who had brought wicked people into their country. The wicked people were gone, but fear remained. Fear always remains. A man may destroy everything within himself, love and hate and belief, and even doubt; but as long as he clings to life he cannot destroy fear: the fear, subtle, indestructible, and terrible, that pervades his being; that tinges his thoughts; that lurks in his heart; that watches on his lips the struggle of his last breath. In his fear, the mild old Gobila offered extra human sacrifices to all the Evil Spirits that had taken possession of his white friends. His heart was heavy. Some warriors spoke about burning and killing, but the cautious old savage dissuaded them. Who could foresee the woe those mysterious creatures, if irritated, might bring? They should be left alone. Perhaps in time they would disappear into the earth as the first one had disappeared. His people must keep away from them, and hope for the best.

Kayerts and Carlier did not disappear, but remained above on this earth, that, somehow, they fancied had become bigger and very empty. It was not the absolute and dumb solitude of the post that impressed them so much as an inarticulate feeling that something from within them was gone, something that worked for their safety, and had kept the wilderness from interfering with their hearts. The images of home; the memory of people like them, of men that thought and felt as they used to think and feel, receded into distances made indistinct by the glare of unclouded sunshine. And out of the great silence of the surrounding wilderness, its very hopelessness and savagery seemed to approach them nearer, to draw them gently, to look upon them, to envelop them with a solicitude irresistible, familiar, and disgusting.

Days lengthened into weeks, then into months. Gobila's people drummed and yelled to every new moon, as of yore, but kept away from the station. Makola and Carlier tried once in a canoe to open communications, but were received with a shower of arrows, and had to fly back to the station for dear life. That attempt set the country up and down the river into an uproar that could be very distinctly heard for days. The steamer was late. At first they spoke of delay jauntily, then anxiously, then gloomily. The matter was becoming serious. Stores were running short. Carlier cast his lines off the bank, but the river was low, and the fish kept out in the stream. They dared not stroll far away from the station to shoot. Moreover, there was no game in the impenetrable forest. Once Carlier shot a hippo in the river. They had no boat to secure it, and it sank. When it floated up it drifted away, and Gobila's people secured the carcass. It was the occasion for a national holiday, but Carlier had a fit of rage over it and talked about the necessity of exterminating all the niggers before the country could be made habitable. Kayerts mooned about silently; spent hours looking at the portrait of his Melie. It represented a little girl with long bleached tresses and a rather sour face. His legs were much swollen, and he could hardly walk. Carlier, undermined by fever, could not swagger any more, but kept tottering about, still with a devil-may-care air, as became a man who remembered his crack regiment. He had become hoarse, sarcastic, and inclined to say unpleasant things. He called it "being frank with you." They had long ago reckoned their percentages on trade, including in them that last deal of "this infamous Makola." They had also concluded not to say anything about it. Kayerts hesitated at first—was afraid of the Director.

"He has seen worse things done on the quiet," maintained Carlier, with a hoarse laugh. "Trust him! He won't thank you if you blab. He is no better than you or me. Who will talk if we hold our tongues? There is nobody here."

That was the root of the trouble! There was nobody there; and being left there alone with their weakness, they became daily more like a pair of accomplices than like a couple of devoted friends. They had heard nothing from home for eight months. Every evening they said, "Tomorrow we shall see the steamer." But one of the Company's steamers had been wrecked, and the Director was busy with the other, relieving very distant and important stations on the main river. He thought that the useless station, and the useless men, could wait. Meantime Kayerts and Carlier lived on rice boiled without salt, and cursed the Company, all Africa, and the day they were born. One must have lived on such diet to discover what ghastly trouble the necessity of swallowing one's food may become. There was literally nothing else in the station but rice and coffee; they drank the coffee without sugar. The last fifteen lumps Kayerts had solemnly locked away in his box, together with a half-bottle of cognac, "in case of sickness," he explained. Carlier approved. "When one is sick," he said, "any little extra like that is cheering."

They waited. Rank grass began to sprout over the courtyard. The bell never rang now. Days passed, silent, exasperating, and slow. When the two men spoke, they snarled; and their silences were bitter, as if tinged by the bitterness of their thoughts.

One day after a lunch of boiled rice, Carlier put down his cup untasted, and said: "Hang it all! Let's have a decent cup of coffee for once. Bring out that sugar, Kayerts!"

"For the sick," muttered Kayerts, without looking up.

"For the sick," mocked Carlier. "Bosh! . . . Well! I am sick."

"You are no more sick than I am, and I go without," said Kayerts in a peaceful tone.

"Come! Out with that sugar, you stingy old slave dealer."

Kayerts looked up quickly. Carlier was smiling with marked insolence. And suddenly it seemed to Kayerts that he had never seen that man before. Who was he? He knew nothing about him. What was he capable of? There was a surprising flash of violent emotion within him, as if in the presence of something undreamt-of, dangerous, and final. But he managed to pronounce with composure:

"That joke is in very bad taste. Don't repeat it."

"Joke!" said Carlier, hitching himself forward on his seat. "I am hungry—I am sick—I don't joke! I hate hypocrites. You are a hypocrite. You are a slave dealer. I am a slave dealer. There's nothing but slave dealers in this cursed country. I mean to have sugar in my coffee today, anyhow!"

"I forbid you to speak to me in that way," said Kayerts with a fair show of resolution.

"You!—What?" shouted Carlier, jumping up.

Kayerts stood up also. "I am your chief," he began, trying to master the shakiness of his voice.

"What?" yelled the other. "Who's chief? There's no chief here. There's nothing here: there's nothing but you and I. Fetch the sugar—you pot-bellied ass."

"Hold your tongue. Go out of this room," screamed Kayerts. "I dismiss you—you scoundrel!"

Carlier swung a stool. All at once he looked dangerously in earnest. "You flabby, good-for-nothing civilian—take that!" he howled.

Kayerts dropped under the table, and the stool struck the grass inner wall of the room. Then, as Carlier was trying to upset the table, Kayerts in desperation made a blind rush, head low, like a cornered pig would do, and overturning his friend, bolted along the veranda, and into his room. He locked the door, snatched his revolver, and stood panting. In less than a minute Carlier was kicking at the door furiously, howling, "If you don't bring out that sugar, I will shoot you at sight, like a dog. Now then—one—two—three. You won't? I will show you who's the master."

Kayerts thought the door would fall in, and scrambled through the square hole that served for a window in his room. There was then the whole breadth of the house between them. But the other was apparently not strong enough to break in the door, and Kayerts heard him running round. Then he also began to run laboriously on his swollen legs. He ran as quickly as he could, grasping the revolver, and unable yet to understand what was happening to him. He saw in succession Makola's house, the store, the river, the ravine, and the low bushes; and he saw all those things again as he ran for the second time round the house. Then again they flashed past him. That morning he could not have walked a yard without a groan.

And now he ran. He ran fast enough to keep out of sight of the other man.

Then as, weak and desperate, he thought, "Before I finish the next round I shall die," he heard the other man stumble heavily, then stop. He stopped also. He had the back and Carlier the front of the house, as before. He heard him drop into a chair cursing, and suddenly his own legs gave way and he slid down into a sitting posture with his back to the wall. His mouth was as dry as a cinder, and his face was wet with perspiration—and tears. What was it all about? He thought it must be a horrible illusion; he thought he was dreaming; he thought he was going mad! After a while he collected his senses. What did they quarrel about? That sugar! How absurd! He would give it to him—didn't want it himself.

And he began scrambling to his feet with a sudden feeling of security. But before he had fairly stood upright, a common-sense reflection occurred to him and drove him back into despair. He thought: "If I give way now to that brute of a soldier, he will begin this horror again tomorrow—and the day after—every day—raise other pretensions, trample on me, torture me, make me his slave—and I will be lost! Lost! The steamer may not come for days—may never come." He shook so that he had to sit down on the floor again. He shivered forlornly. He felt he could not, would not move any more. He was completely distracted by the sudden perception that the position was without issue—that death and life had in a moment become equally difficult and terrible.

All at once he heard the other push his chair back; and he leaped to his feet with extreme facility. He listened and got confused. Must run again! Right or left? He heard footsteps. He darted to the left, grasping his revolver, and at the very same instant, as it seemed to him, they came into violent collision. Both shouted with surprise. A loud explosion took place between them; a roar of red fire, thick smoke; and Kayerts, deafened and blinded, rushed back thinking: "I am hit—it's all over." He expected the other to come round—to gloat over his agony. He caught hold of an upright of the roof—"All over!" Then he heard a crashing fall on the other side of the house, as if somebody had tumbled headlong over a chair—then silence. Nothing more happened. He did not die. Only his shoulder felt as if it had been badly wrenched, and he had lost his revolver. He was disarmed and helpless! He waited for his fate. The other man made no sound. It was a stratagem. He was stalking him now! Along what side? Perhaps he was taking aim this very minute!

After a few moments of an agony frightful and absurd, he decided to go and meet his doom. He was prepared for every surrender. He turned the corner, steadying himself with one hand on the wall; made a few paces, and nearly swooned. He had seen on the floor, protruding past the other corner, a pair of turned-up feet. A pair of white naked feet in red slippers. He felt deadly sick, and stood for a time in profound darkness. Then Makola appeared before him, saying quietly: "Come along, Mr. Kayerts. He is dead." He burst into tears of gratitude; a loud, sobbing fit of crying. After a time he found himself sitting in a chair and looking at Carlier, who lay stretched on his back. Makola was kneeling over the body.

"Is this your revolver?" asked Makola, getting up.

"Yes," said Kayerts; then he added very quickly, "He ran after me to shoot me—you saw!"

"Yes, I saw," said Makola. "There is only one revolver; where's his?"

"Don't know," whispered Kayerts in a voice that had become suddenly very faint.

"I will go and look for it," said the other, gently. He made the round along the veranda, while Kayerts sat still and looked at the corpse. Makola came back empty-handed, stood in deep thought, then stepped quietly into the dead man's room, and came out directly with a revolver, which he held up before Kayerts. Kayerts shut his eyes. Everything was going round. He found life more terrible and difficult than death. He had shot an unarmed man.

After meditating for a while, Makola said softly, pointing at the dead man who lay there with his right eye blown out:

"He died of fever." Kayerts looked at him with a stony stare. "Yes," repeated Makola, thoughtfully, stepping over the corpse, "I think he died of fever. Bury him tomorrow."

And he went away slowly to his expectant wife, leaving the two white men alone on the veranda.

Night came, and Kayerts sat unmoving on his chair. He sat quiet as if he had taken a dose of opium. The violence of the emotions he had passed through produced a feeling of exhausted serenity. He had plumbed in one short afternoon the depths of horror and despair, and now found repose in the conviction that life had no more secrets for him: neither had death! He sat by the corpse thinking: thinking very actively, thinking very new thoughts. He seemed to have broken loose from himself altogether. His old thoughts, convictions, likes and dislikes, things he respected and things he abhorred, appeared in their true light at last! Appeared contemptible and childish, false and ridiculous. He reveled in his new wisdom while he sat by the man he had killed. He argued with himself about all things under heaven with that kind of wrong-headed lucidity which may be observed in some lunatics. Incidentally he reflected that the fellow dead there had been a noxious beast anyway; that men died every day in thousands; perhaps in hundreds of thousands—who could tell?—and that in the number, that one death could not possibly make any difference; couldn't have any importance, at least to a thinking creature. He, Kayerts, was a thinking creature. He had been all his life, till that moment, a believer in a lot of nonsense like the rest of mankind—who are fools; but now he thought! He knew! He was at peace; he was familiar with the highest wisdom! Then he tried to imagine himself dead, and Carlier sitting in his chair watching him; and his attempt met with such unexpected success, that in a very few moments he became not at all sure who was dead and who was alive. This extraordinary achievement of his fancy startled him, however, and by a clever and timely effort of mind he saved himself just in time from becoming Carlier. His heart thumped, and he felt hot all over at the thought of that danger. Carlier! What a beastly thing! To compose his now disturbed nerves—and no wonder!—he tried to whistle a little. Then, suddenly, he fell asleep, or thought he had slept; but at any rate there was a fog, and somebody had whistled in the fog.

He stood up. The day had come, and a heavy mist had descended upon the land: the mist penetrating, enveloping, and silent; the morning mist of tropical lands; the mist that clings and kills; the mist white and deadly, immaculate and poisonous. He stood up, saw the body, and threw his arms above his head with a cry like that of a man who, waking from a trance, finds himself immured forever in a tomb. *"Help! . . . My God!"*

A shriek inhuman, vibrating and sudden, pierced like a sharp dart the white shroud of that land of sorrow. Three short, impatient screeches followed, and then, for a time, the fog-wreaths rolled on, undisturbed, through a formidable silence. Then many more shrieks, rapid and piercing, like the yells of some exasperated and ruthless creature, rent the air. Progress was calling to Kayerts from the river. Progress and civilization and all the virtues. Society was calling to its accomplished child to come, to be taken care of, to be instructed, to be judged, to be condemned; it called him to return to that rubbish heap from which he had wandered away, so that justice could be done.

Kayerts heard and understood. He stumbled out of the veranda, leaving the other man quite alone for the first time since they had been thrown there together. He groped his way through the fog, calling in his ignorance upon the invisible heaven to undo its work. Makola flitted by in the mist, shouting as he ran:

"Steamer! Steamer! They can't see. They whistle for the station. I go ring the bell. Go down to the landing, sir. I ring."

He disappeared. Kayerts stood still. He looked upwards; the fog rolled low over his head. He looked round like a man who has lost his way; and he saw a dark smudge, a cross-shaped stain, upon the shifting purity of the mist. As he began to stumble towards it, the station bell rang in a tumultuous peal its answer to the impatient clamor of the steamer.

The Managing Director of the Great Civilizing Company (since we know that civilization follows trade) landed first, and incontinently lost sight of the steamer. The fog down by the river was exceedingly dense; above, at the station, the bell rang unceasing and brazen.

The Director shouted loudly to the steamer:

"There is nobody down to meet us; there may be something wrong, though they are ringing. You had better come, too!"

And he began to toil up the steep bank. The captain and the engine-driver of the boat followed behind. As they scrambled up the fog thinned, and they could see their Director a good way ahead. Suddenly they saw him start forward, calling to them over his shoulder: "Run! Run to the house! I've found one of them. Run, look for the other!

He had found one of them! And even he, the man of varied and startling experience, was somewhat discomposed by the manner of this finding. He stood and fumbled in his pockets (for a knife) while he faced Kayerts, who was hanging by a leather strap from the cross. He had evidently climbed the grave, which was high and narrow, and after tying the end of the strap to the arm, had swung himself off. His toes were only a couple of inches above the ground; his arms hung stiffly down; he seemed to be standing rigidly at attention, but with one purple cheek playfully posed on the shoulder. And, irreverently, he was putting out a swollen tongue at his Managing Director.

GROUP THREE

KAY BOYLE

Astronomer's Wife

There is an evil moment on awakening when all things seem to pause. But for women, they only falter and may be set in action by a single move: a lifted hand and the pendulum will swing, or the voice raised and through every room the pulse takes up its beating. The astronomer's wife felt the interval gaping and at once filled it to the brim. She fetched up her gentle voice and sent it warily down the stairs for coffee, swung her feet out upon the oval mat, and hailed the morning with her bare arms' quivering flesh drawn taut in rhythmic exercise: left, left, left my wife and fourteen children, right, right, right in the middle of the dusty road.

The day would proceed from this, beat by beat, without reflection, like every other day. The astronomer was still asleep, or feigning it, and she, once out of bed, had come into her own possession. Although scarcely ever out of sight of the impenetrable silence of his brow, she would be absent from him all the day in being clean, busy, kind. He was a man of other things, a dreamer. At times he lay still for hours, at others he sat upon the roof behind his telescope, or wandered down the pathway to the road and out across the mountains. This day, like any other, would go on from the removal of the spot left there from dinner on the astronomer's vest to the severe thrashing of the mayonnaise for lunch. That man might be each time the new arching wave, and woman the undertow that sucked him back, were things she had been told by his silence were so.

In spite of the earliness of the hour, the girl had heard her mistress's voice and was coming up the stairs. At the threshold of the bedroom she paused, and said: "Madame, the plumber is here."

The astronomer's wife put on her white and scarlet smock very quickly and buttoned it at the neck. Then she stepped carefully around the motionless spread of water in the hall.

"Tell him to come right up," she said. She laid her hands on the bannisters and stood looking down the wooden stairway. "Ah, I am Mrs. Ames," she said softly as she saw him mounting. "I am Mrs. Ames," she said softly, softly down the flight of stairs. "I am Mrs. Ames," spoken soft as a willow weeping. "The professor is still sleeping. Just step this way."

The plumber himself looked up and saw Mrs. Ames with her voice hushed, speaking to him. She was a youngish woman, but this she had forgotten. The mystery and silence of her husband's mind lay like a chiding finger on her lips. Her eyes were gray, for the light had been extinguished in them. The strange dim halo of her yellow hair was still uncombed and sideways on her head.

For all of his heavy boots, the plumber quieted the sound of his feet, and together they went down the hall, picking their way around the still lake of water that spread as far as the landing and lay docile there. The plumber was a tough, hardy man; but he took off his hat when he spoke to her and looked her fully, almost insolently in the eye.

"Does it come from the wash-basin," he said, "or from the other . . . ?"

"Oh, from the other," said Mrs. Ames without hesitation.

In this place the villas were scattered out few and primitive, and although beauty lay without there was no reflection of her face within. Here all was awkward and unfit; a sense of wrestling with uncouth forces gave everything an austere countenance. Even the plumber, dealing as does a woman with matters under hand, was grave and stately. The mountains round about seemed to have cast them into the shadow of great dignity.

Mrs. Ames began speaking of their arrival that summer in the little villa, mourning each event as it followed on the other.

"Then, just before going to bed last night," she said, "I noticed something was unusual."

The plumber cast down a folded square of sack-cloth on the brimming floor and laid his leather apron on it. Then he stepped boldly onto the heart of the island it shaped and looked long into the overflowing bowl.

"The water should be stopped from the meter in the garden," he said at last.

"Oh, I did that," said Mrs. Ames, "the very first thing last night. I turned it off at once, in my nightgown, as soon as I saw what was happening. But all this had already run in."

The plumber looked for a moment at her red kid slippers. She was standing just at the edge of the clear, pure-seeming tide.

"It's no doubt the soil lines," he said severely. "It may be that something has stopped them, but my opinion is that the water seals aren't working. That's the trouble often enough in such cases. If you had a valve you wouldn't be caught like this."

Mrs. Ames did not know how to meet this rebuke. She stood, swaying a little, looking into the plumber's blue relentless eye.

"I'm sorry—I'm sorry that my husband," she said, "is still—resting and cannot go into this with you. I'm sure it must be very interesting. . . ."

"You'll probably have to have the traps sealed," said the plumber grimly, and at the sound of this Mrs. Ames' hand flew in dismay to the side of her face. The plumber made no move, but the set of his mouth as he looked at her seemed to soften. "Anyway, I'll have a look from the garden end," he said.

"Oh, do," said the astronomer's wife in relief. Here was a man who spoke of action and object as simply as women did! But however hushed her voice had been, it carried clearly to Professor Ames who lay, dreaming and solitary, upon his bed. He heard their footsteps come down the hall, pause, and skip across the pool of overflow.

"Katherine!" said the astronomer in a ringing tone. "There's a problem worthy of your mettle!"

Mrs. Ames did not turn her head, but led the plumber swiftly down the stairs. When the sun in the garden struck her face, he saw there was a wave of color in it, but this may have been anything but shame.

"You see how it is," said the plumber, as if leading her mind away. "The drains run from these houses right down the hill, big enough for a man to stand upright in them, and clean as a whistle too." There they stood in the garden with the vegetation flowering in disorder all about. The plumber looked at the astronomer's wife. "They come out at the torrent on the other side of the forest beyond there," he said.

But the words the astronomer had spoken still sounded in her in despair. The mind of man, she knew, made steep and sprightly flights, pursued illusion, took foothold in the nameless things that cannot pass between the thumb and finger. But whenever the astronomer gave voice to the thoughts that soared within him, she returned in gratitude to the long expanses of his silence. Desert-like they stretched behind and before the articulation of his scorn.

Life, life is an open sea, she sought to explain it in sorrow, and to survive women cling to the floating débris on the tide. But the plumber had suddenly fallen upon his knees in the grass and had crooked his fingers through the ring of the drains' trap-door. When she looked down she saw that he was looking up into her face, and she saw too that his hair was as light as gold.

"Perhaps Mr. Ames," he said rather bitterly, "would like to come down with me and have a look around?"

"Down?" said Mrs. Ames in wonder.

"Into the drains," said the plumber brutally. "They're a study for a man who likes to know what's what."

"Oh, Mr. Ames," said Mrs. Ames in confusion. "He's still—still in bed, you see."

The plumber lifted his strong, weathered face and looked curiously at her. Surely it seemed to him strange for a man to linger in bed, with the sun pouring yellow as wine all over the place. The astronomer's wife saw his lean cheeks, his high, rugged bones, and the deep seams in his brow. His flesh was as firm and clean as wood, stained richly tan with the climate's rigor. His fingers were blunt, but comprehensible to her, gripped in the ring and holding the iron door wide. The backs of his hands were bound round and round with ripe blue veins of blood.

"At any rate," said the astronomer's wife, and the thought of it moved her lips to smile a little, "Mr. Ames would never go down there alive. He likes going up," she said. And she, in her turn, pointed, but impudently, towards the heavens. "On the roof. Or on the mountains. He's been up on the tops of them many times."

"It's a matter of habit," said the plumber, and suddenly he went down the trap. Mrs. Ames saw a bright little piece of his hair still shining, like a star, long after the rest of him had gone. Out of the depths, his voice, hollow and dark with foreboding, returned to her. "I think something has stopped the elbow," was what he said.

This was speech that touched her flesh and bone and made her wonder. When her husband spoke of height, having no sense of it, she could not picture it nor hear. Depth or magic passed her by unless a name were given. But madness in a daily shape, as elbow stopped, she saw clearly and well. She sat down on the grasses, bewildered that it should be a man who had spoken to her so.

She saw the weeds springing up, and she did not move to tear them up from life. She sat powerless, her senses veiled, with no action taking shape beneath her hands. In this way some men sat for hours on end, she knew, tracking a single thought back to its origin. The mind of man could balance and divide, weed out, destroy. She sat on the full, burdened grasses, seeking to think, and dimly waiting for the plumber to return.

Whereas her husband had always gone up, as the dead go, she knew now that there were others who went down, like the corporeal being of the dead. That men were then divided into two bodies now seemed clear to Mrs. Ames. This knowledge stunned her with its simplicity and took the uneasy motion from her limbs. She could not stir, but sat facing the mountains' rocky flanks, and harking in silence to lucidity. Her husband was the mind, this other man the meat, of all mankind.

After a little, the plumber emerged from the earth: first the light top of his head, then the burnt brow, and then the blue eyes fringed with whitest lash. He braced his thick hands flat on the pavings of the garden-path and swung himself completely from the pit.

"It's the soil lines," he said pleasantly. "The gases," he said as he looked down upon her lifted face, "are backing up the drains."

"What in the world are we going to do?" said the astronomer's wife softly. There was a young and strange delight in putting questions to which true answers would be given. Everything the astronomer had ever said to her was a continuous query to which there could be no response.

"Ah, come, now," said the plumber, looking down and smiling. "There's a remedy for every ill, you know. Sometimes it may be that," he said as if speaking to a child, "or sometimes the other thing. But there's always a help for everything a-miss."

Things come out of herbs and make you young again, he might have been saying to her; or the first good rain will quench any drought; or time of itself will put a broken bone together.

"I'm going to follow the ground pipe out right to the torrent," the plumber was saying. "The trouble's between here and there and I'll find it on the way. There's nothing at all that can't be done over for the caring," he was saying, and his eyes were fastened on her face in insolence, or gentleness, or love.

The astronomer's wife stood up, fixed a pin in her hair, and turned around towards the kitchen. Even while she was calling the servant's name, the plumber began speaking again.

"I once had a cow that lost her cud," the plumber was saying. The girl came out on the kitchen-step and Mrs. Ames stood smiling at her in the sun.

"The trouble is very serious, very serious," she said across the garden. "When Mr. Ames gets up, please tell him I've gone down."

She pointed briefly to the open door in the pathway, and the plumber hoisted his kit on his arm and put out his hand to help her down.

"But I made her another in no time," he was saying, "out of flowers and things and what-not."

"Oh," said the astronomer's wife in wonder as she stepped into the heart of the earth. She took his arm, knowing that what he said was true.

D. H. LAWRENCE

The Blind Man

Isabel Pervin was listening for two sounds—for the sound of wheels on the drive outside and for the noise of her husband's footsteps in the hall. Her dearest and oldest friend, a man who seemed almost indispensable to her living, would drive up in the rainy dusk of the closing November day. The trap had gone to fetch him from the station. And her husband, who had been blinded in Flanders, and who had a disfiguring mark on his brow, would be coming in from the outhouses.

He had been home for a year now. He was totally blind. Yet they had been very happy. The Grange was Maurice's own place. The back was a farmstead, and the Wernhams, who occupied the rear premises, acted as farmers. Isabel lived with her husband in the handsome rooms in front. She and he had been almost entirely alone together since he was wounded. They talked and sang and read together in a wonderful and unspeakable intimacy. Then she reviewed books for a Scottish newspaper, carrying on her old interest, and he occupied himself a good deal with the farm. Sightless, he could still discuss everything with Wernham, and he could also do a good deal of work about the place—menial work, it is true, but it gave him satisfaction. He milked the cows, carried in the pails, turned the separator, attended to the pigs and horses. Life was still very full and strangely serene for the blind man, peaceful with the almost incomprehensible peace of immediate contact in darkness. With his wife he had a whole world, rich and real and invisible.

They were newly and remotely happy. He did not even regret the loss of his sight in these times of dark, palpable joy. A certain exultance swelled his soul.

But as time wore on, sometimes the rich glamour would leave them. Sometimes, after months of this intensity, a sense of burden overcame Isabel, a weariness, a terrible *ennui,* in that silent house approached between a colonnade of tall-shafted pines. Then she felt she would go mad, for she could not bear it. And sometimes he had devastating fits of depression, which seemed to lay waste his whole being. It was worse than depression—a black misery, when his own life was a torture to him, and when his presence was unbearable to his wife. The dread went down to the roots of her soul as these black days recurred. In a kind of panic she tried to wrap herself up still further in her husband. She forced the old spontaneous cheerfulness and joy to continue. But the effort it cost her was almost too much. She knew she could not keep it up. She felt she would scream with the strain, and would give anything, anything, to escape. She longed to possess her husband utterly; it gave her inordinate joy to have him entirely to herself. And yet, when again he was gone in a black and massive misery, she could not bear him, she could not bear herself; she wished she could be snatched away off the earth altogether, anything rather than live at this cost.

Dazed, she schemed for a way out. She invited friends, she tried to give him some further connection with the outer world. But it was no good. After all their joy and suffering, after their dark, great year of blindness and solitude and unspeakable nearness, other people seemed to them both shallow, rattling, rather impertinent. Shallow prattle seemed presumptuous. He became impatient and irritated, she was wearied. And so they lapsed into their solitude again. For they preferred it.

But now, in a few weeks' time, her second baby would be born. The first had died, an infant, when her husband first went out to France. She looked with joy and relief to the coming of the second. It would be her salvation. But also she felt some anxiety. She was thirty years old, her husband was a year younger. They both wanted the child very much. Yet she could not help feeling afraid. She had her husband on her hands, a terrible joy to her, and a terrifying burden. The child would occupy her love and attention. And then, what of Maurice? What would he do? If only she could feel that he, too, would be at peace and happy when the child came! She did so want to luxuriate in a rich, physical satisfaction of maternity. But the man, what would he do? How could she provide for him, how avert those shattering black moods of his, which destroyed them both?

She sighed with fear. But at this time Bertie Reid wrote to Isabel. He was her old friend, a second or third cousin, a Scotchman, as she was a Scotchwoman. They had been brought up near to one another, and all her life he had been her friend, like a brother, but better than her own brothers. She loved him—though not in the marrying sense. There was a sort of kinship between them, an affinity. They understood one another instinctively. But Isabel would never have thought of marrying Bertie. It would have seemed like marrying in her own family.

Bertie was a barrister and a man of letters, a Scotchman of the intellectual type, quick, ironical, sentimental, and on his knees before the woman he adored but did not want to marry. Maurice Pervin was different. He came of a good old country family—the Grange was not a very great distance from Oxford. He was passionate, sensitive, perhaps oversensitive, wincing—a big fellow with heavy limbs and a forehead that flushed painfully. For his mind was slow, as if drugged by the strong provincial blood that beat in his veins. He was very sensitive to his own mental slowness, his feelings being quick and acute. So that he was just the opposite to Bertie, whose mind was much quicker than his emotions, which were not so very fine.

From the first the two men did not like each other. Isabel felt that they *ought* to get on together. But they did not. She felt that if only each could have the clue to the other there would be such a rare understanding between them. It did not come off, however. Bertie adopted a slightly ironical attitude, very offensive to Maurice, who returned the Scotch irony with English resentment, a resentment which deepened sometimes into stupid hatred.

This was a little puzzling to Isabel. However, she accepted it in the course of things. Men were made freakish and unreasonable. Therefore, when Maurice was going out to France for the second time, she felt that, for her husband's sake, she must discontinue her friendship with Bertie. She wrote to the barrister to this effect. Bertram Reid simply replied that in this, as in all others matters, he must obey her wishes, if these were indeed her wishes.

For nearly two years nothing had passed between the two friends. Isabel rather gloried in the fact; she had no compunction. She had one great article of faith, which was, that husband and wife should be so important to one another, that the rest of the world simply did not count. She and Maurice were husband and wife. They loved one another. They would have children. Then let everybody and everything else fade into insignificance outside this connubial felicity. She professed herself quite happy and ready to receive Maurice's friends. She was happy and ready: the happy wife, the ready woman in possession. Without knowing why, the friends retired abashed, and came no more. Maurice, of course, took as much satisfaction in this connubial absorption as Isabel did.

He shared in Isabel's literary activities, she cultivated a real interest in agriculture and cattle-raising. For she, being at heart perhaps an emotional enthusiast, always cultivated the practical side of life and prided herself on her mastery of practical affairs. Thus the husband and wife had spent the five years of married life. The last had been one of blindness and unspeakable intimacy. And now Isabel felt a great indifference coming over her, a sort of lethargy. She wanted to be allowed to bear her child in peace, to nod by the fire and drift vaguely, physically, from day to day.

Maurice was like an ominous thunder-cloud. She had to keep waking up to remember him.

When a little note came from Bertie, asking if he were to put up a tombstone to their dead friendship, and speaking of the real pain he felt on account of her husband's loss of sight, she felt a pang, a fluttering agitation of re-awakening. And she read the letter to Maurice.

"Ask him to come down," he said.

"Ask Bertie to come here!" she re-echoed.

"Yes—if he wants to."

Isabel paused for a few moments.

"I know he wants to—he'd only be too glad," she replied. "But what about you, Maurice? How would you like it?"

"I should like it."

"Well—in that case—— But I thought you didn't care for him——"

"Oh, I don't know. I might think differently of him now," the blind man replied. It was rather abstruse to Isabel.

"Well, dear," she said, "if you're quite sure——"

"I'm sure enough. Let him come," said Maurice.

So Bertie was coming, coming this evening, in the November rain and darkness. Isabel was agitated, racked with her old restlessness and indecision. She had always suffered from this pain of doubt, just an agonizing sense of uncertainty. It had begun to pass off, in the lethargy of maternity. Now it returned, and she resented it. She struggled as usual to maintain her calm, composed, friendly bearing, a sort of mask she wore over all her body.

A woman had lighted a tall lamp beside the table and spread the cloth. The long dining-room was dim, with its elegant but rather severe pieces of old furniture. Only the round table glowed softly under the light. It had a rich, beautiful effect. The white cloth glistened and dropped its heavy, pointed lace corners almost to the carpet, the china was old and handsome, creamy-yellow, with a blotched pattern of harsh red and deep blue, the cups large and bell-shaped, the teapot gallant. Isabel looked at it with superficial appreciation.

Her nerves were hurting her. She looked automatically again at the high, uncurtained windows. In the last dusk she could just perceive outside a huge fir-tree swaying its boughs: it was as if she thought it rather than saw it. The rain came flying on the window panes. Ah, why had she no peace? These two men, why did they tear at her? Why did they not come—why was there this suspense?

She sat in a lassitude that was really suspense and irritation. Maurice, at least, might come in—there was nothing to keep him out. She rose to her feet. Catching sight of her reflection in a mirror, she glanced at herself with a slight smile of recognition, as if she were an old friend to herself.

Her face was oval and calm, her nose a little arched. Her neck made a beautiful line down to her shoulder. With hair knotted loosely behind, she had something of a warm, maternal look. Thinking this of herself, she arched her eyebrows and her rather heavy eyelids, with a little flicker of a smile, and for a moment her grey eyes looked amused and wicked, a little sardonic, out of her transfigured Madonna face.

Then, resuming her air of womanly patience—she was really fatally self-determined—she went with a little jerk towards the door. Her eyes were slightly reddened.

She passed down the wide hall and through a door at the end. Then she was in the farm premises. The scent of dairy, and of farm-kitchen, and of farm-yard and of leather almost overcame her: but particularly the scent of dairy. They had been scalding out the pans. The flagged passage in front of her was dark, puddled, and wet. Light came out from the open kitchen door. She went forward and stood in the doorway. The farm-people were at tea, seated at a little distance from her, round a long, narrow table, in the centre of which stood a white lamp. Ruddy faces, ruddy hands holding food, red mouths working, heads bent over the tea-cups: men, land-girls, boys: it was tea-time, feeding-time. Some faces caught sight of her. Mrs. Wernham, going round behind the chairs with a large black teapot, halting slightly in her walk, was not aware of her for a moment. Then she turned suddenly.

"Oh, is it Madam!' 'she exclaimed. "Come in, then, come in! We're at tea." And she dragged forward a chair.

"No, I won't come in," said Isabel. "I'm afraid I interrupt your meal."

"No—no—not likely, Madam, not likely."

"Hasn't Mr. Pervin come in, do you know?"

"I'm sure I couldn't say! Missed him, have you, Madam?"

"No, I only wanted him to come in," laughed Isabel, as if shyly.

"Wanted him, did ye? Get up, boy—get up, now——"

Mrs. Wernham knocked one of the boys on the shoulder. He began to scrape to his feet, chewing largely.

"I believe he's in top stable," said another face from the table.

"Ah! No, don't get up. I'm going myself," said Isabel.

"Don't you go out of a dirty night like this. Let the lad go. Get along wi' ye, boy," said Mrs. Wernham.

"No, no," said Isabel, with a decision that was always obeyed. "Go on with your tea, Tom. I'd like to go across to the stable, Mrs. Wernham."

"Did ever you hear tell!" exclaimed the woman.

"Isn't the trap late?" asked Isabel.

"Why, no," said Mrs. Wernham, peering into the distance at the tall, dim clock. "No, Madam—we can give it another quarter or twenty minutes yet, good—yes, every bit of a quarter."

"Ah! It seems late when darkness falls so early," said Isabel.

"It do, that it do. Bother the days, that they draw in so," answered Mrs. Wernham. "Proper miserable!"

"They are," said Isabel, withdrawing.

She pulled on her overshoes, wrapped a large tartan shawl around her, put on a man's felt hat, and ventured out along the causeways of the first yard. It was very dark. The wind was roaring in the great elms behind the outhouses. When she came to the second yard the darkness seemed deeper. She was unsure of her footing. She wished she had brought a lantern. Rain blew against her. Half she liked it, half she felt unwilling to battle.

She reached at last the just visible door of the stable. There was no sign of a light anywhere. Opening the upper half, she looked in: into a simple well of darkness. The smell of horses, and ammonia, and of warmth was startling to her, in that full night. She listened with all her ears but could hear nothing save the night, and the stirring of a horse.

"Maurice!" she called, softly and musically, though she was afraid. "Maurice—are you there?"

Nothing came from the darkness. She knew the rain and wind blew in upon the horses, the hot animal life. Feeling it wrong, she entered the stable and drew the lower half of the door shut, holding the upper part close. She did not stir, because she was aware of the presence of the dark hind-quarters of the horses, though she could not see them, and she was afraid. Something wild stirred in her heart.

She listened intensely. Then she heard a small noise in the distance—far away, it seemed—the chink of a pan, and a man's voice speaking a brief word. It would be Maurice, in the other part of the stable. She stood motionless, waiting for him to come through the partition door. The horses were so terrifyingly near to her, in the invisible.

The loud jarring of the inner door-latch made her start; the door was opened. She could hear and feel her husband entering and invisibly passing among the horses near to her, darkness as they were, actively intermingled. The rather low sound of his voice as he spoke to the horses came velvety to her nerves. How near he was, and how invisible! The darkness seemed to be in a strange swirl of violent life, just upon her. She turned giddy.

Her presence of mind made her call, quietly and musically: "Maurice! Maurice—dea-ar!"

"Yes," he answered. "Isabel?"

She saw nothing, and the sound of his voice seemed to touch her. "Hello!" she answered cheerfully, straining her eyes to see him. He was still busy, attending to the horses near her, but she saw only darkness. It made her almost desperate.

"Won't you come in, dear?" she said.

"Yes, I'm coming. Just half a minute. *Stand over—now!* Trap's not come, has it?"

"Not yet," said Isabel.

His voice was pleasant and ordinary, but it had a slight suggestion of the stable to her. She wished he would come away. Whilst he was so utterly invisible, she was afraid of him.

"How's the time?" he asked.

"Not yet six," she replied. She disliked to answer into the dark. Presently he came very near to her, and she retreated out of doors.

"The weather blows in here," he said, coming steadily forward, feeling for the doors. She shrank away. At last she could dimly see him.

"Bertie won't have much of a drive," he said, as he closed the doors.

"He won't indeed!" said Isabel calmly, watching the dark shape at the door.

"Give me your arm, dear," she said.

She pressed his arm close to her, as she went. But she longed to see him, to look at him. She was nervous. He walked erect, with face rather lifted, but with a curious tentative movement of his powerful, muscular legs. She could feel the clever, careful, strong contact of his feet with the earth, as she balanced against him. For a moment he was a tower of darkness to her, as if he rose out of the earth.

In the house-passage he wavered and went cautiously, with a curious look of silence about him as he felt for the bench. Then he sat down heavily. He was a man with rather sloping shoulders, but with heavy limbs, powerful legs that seemed to know the earth. His head was small, usually carried high and light. As he bent down to unfasten his gaiters and boots he did not look blind. His hair was brown and crisp, his hands were large, reddish, intelligent, the veins stood out in the wrists; and his thighs and knees seemed massive. When he stood up his face and neck were surcharged with blood, the veins stood out on his temples. She did not look at his blindness.

Isabel was always glad when they had passed through the dividing door into their own regions of repose and beauty. She was a little afraid of him, out there in the animal grossness of the back. His bearing also changed, as he smelt the familiar indefinable odour that pervaded his wife's surroundings, a delicate, refined scent, very faintly spicy. Perhaps it came from the potpourri bowls.

He stood at the foot of the stairs, arrested, listening. She watched him, and her heart sickened. He seemed to be listening to fate.

"He's not here yet," he said. "I'll go up and change."

"Maurice," she said, "you're not wishing he wouldn't come, are you?"

"I couldn't quite say," he answered. "I feel myself rather on the qui vive."

"I can see you are," she answered. And she reached up and kissed his cheek. She saw his mouth relax into a slow smile.

"What are you laughing at?" she said roguishly.

"You consoling me," he answered.

"Nay," she answered. "Why should I console you? You know we love each other—you know *how* married we are! What does anything else matter?"

"Nothing at all, my dear."

He felt for her face and touched it, smiling.

"*You're* all right, aren't you?" he asked anxiously.

"I'm wonderfully all right, love," she answered. "It's you I am a little troubled about, at times."

"Why me?" he said, touching her cheeks delicately with the tips of his fingers. The touch had an almost hypnotizing effect on her.

He went away upstairs. She saw him mount into the darkness, unseeing and unchanging. He did not know that the lamps on the upper corridor were unlighted. He went on into the darkness with unchanging step. She heard him in the bath-room.

Pervin moved about almost unconsciously in his familiar surroundings, dark though everything was. He seemed to know the presence of objects before he touched them. It was a pleasure to him to rock thus through a world of things, carried on the flood in a sort of blood-prescience. He did not think much or trouble much. So long as he kept this sheer immediacy of blood-contact with the substantial world he was happy, he wanted no intervention of visual consciousness. In this state there was a certain rich positivity, bordering sometimes on rapture. Life seemed to move in him like a tide lapping, lapping, and advancing, enveloping all things darkly. It was a pleasure to stretch forth the hand and meet the unseen object, clasp it, and possess it in pure contact. He did not try to remember, to visualize. He did not want to. The new way of consciousness substituted itself in him.

The rich suffusion of this state generally kept him happy, reaching its culmination in the consuming passion for his wife. But at times the flow would seem to be checked and thrown back. Then it would beat inside him like a tangled sea, and he was tortured in the shattered chaos of his own blood. He grew to dread this arrest, this throw-back, this chaos inside himself, when he seemed merely at the mercy of his own powerful and conflicting elements. How to get some measure of control or surety, this was the question. And when the question rose maddening in him, he would clench his fists as if he would *compel* the whole universe to submit to him. But it was in vain. He could not even compel himself.

Tonight, however, he was still serene, though little tremors of unreasonable exasperation ran through him. He had to handle the razor very carefully, as he shaved, for it was not at one with him, he was afraid of it. His hearing also was too much sharpened. He heard the woman lighting the lamps on the corridor, and attending to the fire in the visitors' room. And then, as he went to his room, he heard the trap arrive. Then came Isabel's voice, lifted and calling, like a bell ringing:

"Is it you, Bertie? Have you come?"

And a man's voice answered out of the wind:

"Hello, Isabel! There you are."

"Have you had a miserable drive? I'm so sorry we couldn't send a closed carriage. I can't see you at all, you know."

"I'm coming. No, I liked the drive—it was like Perthshire. Well, how are you? You're looking fit as ever, as far as I can see."

"Oh, yes," said Isabel. "I'm wonderfully well. How are you? Rather thin, I think——"

"Worked to death—everybody's old cry. But I'm all right, Ciss. How's Pervin?—isn't he here?"

"Oh, yes, he's upstairs changing. Yes, he's awfully well. Take off your wet things; I'll send them to be dried."

"And how are you both, in spirits? He doesn't fret?"

"No—no, not at all. No, on the contrary, really. We've been wonderfully happy, incredibly. It's more than I can understand—so wonderful: the nearness, and the peace——"

"Ah! Well, that's awfully good news——"

They moved away. Pervin heard no more. But a childish sense of desolation had come over him, as he heard their brisk voices. He seemed shut out—like a child that is left out. He was aimless and excluded, he did not know what to do with himself. The helpless desolation came over him. He fumbled nervously as he dressed himself, in a state almost of childishness. He disliked the Scotch accent in Bertie's speech, and the slight response it found on Isabel's tongue. He disliked the slight purr of complacency in the Scottish speech. He disliked intensely the glib way in which Isabel spoke of their happiness and nearness. It made him recoil. He was fretful and beside himself like a child, he had almost a childish nostalgia to be included in the life circle. And at the same time he was a man, dark and powerful and infuriated by his own weakness. By some fatal flaw, he could not be by himself, he had to depend on the support of another. And this very dependence enraged him. He hated Bertie Reid, and at the same time he knew the hatred was nonsense, he knew it was the outcome of his own weakness.

He went downstairs. Isabel was alone in the dining-room. She watched him enter, head erect, his feet tentative. He looked so strong-blooded and healthy and, at the same time, cancelled. Cancelled—that was the word that flew across her mind. Perhaps it was his scar suggested it.

"You heard Bertie come, Maurice?" she said.

"Yes—isn't he here?"

"He's in his room. He looks very thin and worn."

"I suppose he works himself to death."

A woman came in with a tray—and after a few minutes Bertie came down. He was a little dark man, with a very big forehead, thin, wispy hair, and sad, large eyes. His expression was inordinately sad—almost funny. He had odd, short legs.

Isabel watched him hesitate under the door, and glance nervously at her husband. Pervin heard him and turned.

"Here you are, now," said Isabel. "Come, let us eat."

Bertie went across to Maurice.

"How are you, Pervin?" he said, as he advanced.

The blind man stuck his hand out into space, and Bertie took it.

"Very fit. Glad you've come," said Maurice.

Isabel glanced at them, and glanced away, as if she could not bear to see them.

"Come," she said. "Come to table. Aren't you both awfully hungry? I am, tremendously."

"I'm afraid you waited for me," said Bertie, as they sat down.

Maurice had a curious monolithic way of sitting in a chair, erect and distant. Isabel's heart always beat when she caught sight of him thus.

"No," she replied to Bertie. "We're very little later than usual. We're having a sort of high tea, not dinner. Do you mind? It gives us such a nice long evening, uninterrupted."

"I like it," said Bertie.

Maurice was feeling, with curious little movements, almost like a cat kneading her bed, for his plate, his knife and fork, his napkin. He was getting the whole geography of his cover into his consciousness. He sat erect and inscrutable, remote-seeming. Bertie watched the static figure of the blind man, the delicate tactile discernment of the large, ruddy hands, and the curious mindless silence of the brow, above the scar. With difficulty he looked away, and without knowing what he did, picked up a little crystal bowl of violets from the table, and held them to his nose.

"They are sweet-scented," he said. "Where do they come from?"

"From the garden—under the windows," said Isabel.

"So late in the year—and so fragrant! Do you remember the violets under Aunt Bell's south wall?"

The two friends looked at each other and exchanged a smile, Isabel's eyes lighting up.

"Don't I?" she replied. "*Wasn't* she queer!"

"A curious old girl," laughed Bertie. "There's a streak of freakishness in the family, Isabel."

"Ah—but not in you and me, Bertie," said Isabel. "Give them to

Maurice, will you?" she added, as Bertie was putting down the flowers. "Have you smelled the violets, dear? Do!—they are so scented."

Maurice held out his hand, and Bertie placed the tiny bowl against his large, warm-looking fingers. Maurices's hand closed over the thin white fingers of the barrister. Bertie carefully extricated himself. Then the two watched the blind man smelling the violets. He bent his head and seemed to be thinking. Isabel waited.

"Aren't they sweet, Maurice?" she said at last, anxiously.

"Very," he said. And he held out the bowl. Bertie took it. Both he and Isabel were a little afraid, and deeply disturbed.

The meal continued. Isabel and Bertie chatted spasmodically. The blind man was silent. He touched his food repeatedly, with quick, delicate touches of his knife-point, then cut irregular bits. He could not bear to be helped. Both Isabel and Bertie suffered: Isabel wondered why. She did not suffer when she was alone with Maurice. Bertie made her conscious of a strangeness.

After the meal the three drew their chairs to the fire, and sat down to talk. The decanters were put on a table near at hand. Isabel knocked the logs on the fire, and clouds of brilliant sparks went up the chimney. Bertie noticed a slight weariness in her bearing.

"You will be glad when your child comes now, Isabel?" he said.

She looked up to him with a quick wan smile.

"Yes, I shall be glad," she answered. "It begins to seem long. Yes, I shall be very glad. So will you, Maurice, won't you?" she added.

"Yes, I shall," replied her husband.

"We are both looking forward so much to having it," she said.

"Yes, of course," said Bertie.

He was a bachelor, three or four years older than Isabel. He lived in beautiful rooms overlooking the river, guarded by a faithful Scottish man-servant. And he had his friends among the fair sex—not lovers, friends. So long as he could avoid any danger of courtship or marriage, he adored a few good women with constant and unfailing homage, and he was chivalrously fond of quite a number. But if they seemed to encroach on him, he withdrew and detested them.

Isabel knew him very well, knew his beautiful constancy, and kindness, also his incurable weakness, which made him unable ever to enter into close contact of any sort. He was ashamed of himself because he could not marry, could not approach women physically. He wanted to do so. But he could not. At the centre of him he was afraid, helplessly and even brutally afraid. He had given up hope, had ceased to expect any more that he could escape his own weakness. Hence he was a brilliant and successful barrister, also a *littérateur* of high repute, a rich man, and a great social success. At the centre he felt himself neuter, nothing.

Isabel knew him well. She despised him even while she admired him.

She looked at his sad face, his little short legs, and felt contempt of him. She looked at his dark grey eyes, with their uncanny, almost childlike, intuition, and she loved him. He understood amazingly—but she had no fear of his understanding. As a man she patronized him.

And she turned to the impassive, silent figure of her husband. He sat leaning back, with folded arms, and face a little uptilted. His knees were straight and massive. She sighed, picked up the poker, and again began to prod the fire, to rouse the clouds of soft brilliant sparks.

"Isabel tells me," Bertie began suddenly, "that you have not suffered unbearably from the loss of sight."

Maurice straightened himself to attend but kept his arms folded.

"No," he said, "not unbearably. Now and again one struggles against it, you know. But there are compensations."

"They say it is much worse to be stone deaf," said Isabel.

"I believe it is," said Bertie. "Are there compensations?" he added, to Maurice.

"Yes. You cease to bother about a great many things." Again Maurice stretched his figure, stretched the strong muscles of his back, and leaned backwards, with uplifted face.

"And that is a relief," said Bertie. "But what is there in place of the bothering? What replaces the activity?"

There was a pause. At length the blind man replied, as out of a negligent, unattentive thinking:

"Oh, I don't know. There's a good deal when you're not active."

"Is there?" said Bertie. "What, exactly? It always seems to me that when there is no thought and no action, there is nothing."

Again Maurice was slow in replying.

"There is something," he replied. "I couldn't tell you what it is."

And the talk lapsed once more, Isabel and Bertie chatting gossip and reminiscence, the blind man silent.

At length Maurice rose restlessly, a big obtrusive figure. He felt tight and hampered. He wanted to go away.

"Do you mind," he said, "if I go and speak to Wernham?"

"No—go along, dear," said Isabel.

And he went out. A silence came over the two friends. At length Bertie said:

"Nevertheless, it is a great deprivation, Cissie."

"It is, Bertie. I know it is."

"Something lacking all the time," said Bertie.

"Yes, I know. And yet—and yet—Maurice is right. There is something else, something *there*, which you never knew was there, and which you can't express."

"What is there?" asked Bertie.

"I don't know—it's awfully hard to define it—but something strong and immediate. There's something strange in Maurice's presence—indefinable—but I couldn't do without it. I agree that it seems to put one's mind to sleep. But when we're alone I miss nothing; it seems awfully rich, almost splendid, you know."

"I'm afraid I don't follow," said Bertie.

They talked desultorily. The wind blew loudly outside, rain chattered on the window-panes, making a sharp drum-sound because of the closed, mellow-golden shutters inside. The logs burned slowly, with hot, almost invisible small flames. Bertie seemed uneasy, there were dark circles round his eyes. Isabel, rich with her approaching maternity, leaned looking into the fire. Her hair curled in odd, loose strands, very pleasing to the man. But she had a curious feeling of old woe in her heart, old, timeless night-woe.

"I suppose we're all deficient somewhere," said Bertie.

"I suppose so," said Isabel wearily.

"Damned, sooner or later."

"I don't know," she said, rousing herself. "I feel quite all right, you know. The child coming seems to make me indifferent to everything, just placid. I can't feel that there's anything to trouble about, you know."

"A good thing, I should say," he replied slowly.

"Well, there it is. I suppose it's just Nature. If only I felt I needn't trouble about Maurice, I should be perfectly content——"

"But you feel you must trouble about him?"

"Well—I don't know——" She even resented this much effort.

The night passed slowly. Isabel looked at the clock. "I say," she said. "It's nearly ten o'clock. Where can Maurice be? I'm sure they're all in bed at the back. Excuse me a moment."

She went out, returning almost immediately.

"It's all shut up and in darkness," she said. "I wonder where he is. He must have gone out to the farm——"

Bertie looked at her.

"I suppose he'll come in," he said.

"I suppose so," she said. "But it's unusual for him to be out now."

"Would you like me to go out and see?"

"Well—if you wouldn't mind. I'd go, but——" She did not want to make the physical effort.

Bertie put on an old overcoat and took a lantern. He went out from the side door. He shrank from the wet and roaring night. Such weather had a nervous effect on him: too much moisture everywhere made him feel almost imbecile. Unwilling, he went through it all. A dog barked violently at him. He peered in all the buildings. At last, as he opened the upper door of a sort of intermediate barn, he heard a grinding noise, and looking in, holding up his lantern, saw Maurice in his shirt-sleeves, standing listening, holding the handle of a turnip-pulper. He had been pulping sweet roots, a pile of which lay dimly heaped in a corner behind him.

"That you, Wernham?" said Maurice, listening.

"No, it's me," said Bertie.

A large, half-wild grey cat was rubbing at Maurice's leg. The blind man stooped to rub its sides. Bertie watched the scene, then unconsciously entered and shut the door behind him. He was in a high sort of barn-place, from which, right and left, ran off the corridors in front of the stalled cattle. He watched the slow, stooping motion of the other man, as he caressed the great cat.

Maurice straightened himself.

"You came to look for me?" he said.

"Isabel was a little uneasy," said Bertie.

"I'll come in. I like messing about doing these jobs."

The cat had reared her sinister, feline length against his leg, clawing at his thigh affectionately. He lifted her claws out of his flesh.

"I hope I'm not in your way at all at the Grange here," said Bertie, rather shy and stiff.

"My way? No, not a bit. I'm glad Isabel has somebody to talk to. I'm afraid it's I who am in the way. I know I'm not very lively company. Isabel's all right, don't you think? She's not unhappy, is she?"

"I don't think so."

"What does she say?"

"She says she's very content—only a little troubled about you."

"Why me?"

"Perhaps afraid that you might brood," said Bertie, cautiously.

"She needn't be afraid of that." He continued to caress the flattened grey head of the cat with his fingers. "What I am a bit afraid of," he resumed, "is that she'll find me a dead weight, always alone with me down here."

"I don't think you need think that," said Bertie, though this was what he feared himself.

"I don't know," said Maurice. "Sometimes I feel it isn't fair that she's saddled with me." Then he dropped his voice curiously. "I say," he asked, secretly struggling, "is my face much disfigured? Do you mind telling me?"

"There is the scar," said Bertie, wondering. "Yes, it is a disfigurement. But more pitiable than shocking."

"A pretty bad scar, though," said Maurice.

"Oh, yes."

There was a pause.

"Sometimes I feel I am horrible," said Maurice, in a low voice, talking as if to himself. And Bertie actually felt a quiver of horror.

"That's nonsense," he said.

Maurice again straightened himself, leaving the cat.

"There's no telling," he said. Then again, in an odd tone, he added: "I don't really know you, do I?"

"Probably not," said Bertie.

"Do you mind if I touch you?"

The lawyer shrank away instinctively. And yet, out of very philanthropy, he said, in a small voice: "Not at all."

But he suffered as the blind man stretched out a strong, naked hand to him. Maurice accidentally knocked off Bertie's hat.

"I thought you were taller," he said, starting. Then he laid his hand on Bertie Reid's head, closing the dome of the skull in a soft, firm grasp, gathering it, as it were; then, shifting his grasp and softly closing again, with a fine, close pressure, till he had covered the skull and the face of the smaller man, tracing the brows, and touching the full, closed eyes, touching the small nose and the nostrils, the rough, short moustache, the mouth, the rather strong chin. The hand of the blind man grasped the shoulder, the arm, the hand of the other man. He seemed to take him, in the soft, travelling grasp.

"You seem young," he said quietly, at last.

The lawyer stood almost annihilated, unable to answer.

"Your head seems tender, as if you were young," Maurice repeated. "So do your hands. Touch my eyes, will you?—touch my scar."

Now Bertie quivered with revulsion. Yet he was under the power of the blind man, as if hypnotized. He lifted his hand, and laid the fingers to the scar, on the scarred eyes. Maurice suddenly covered them with his own hand, pressed the fingers of the other man upon his disfigured eye-sockets, trembling in every fibre, and rocking slightly, slowly, from side to side. He remained thus for a minute or more, whilst Bertie stood as if in a swoon, unconscious, imprisoned.

Then suddenly Maurice removed the hand of the other man from his brow, and stood holding it in his own.

"Oh, my God," he said, "we shall know each other now, shan't we? We shall know each other now."

Bertie could not answer. He gazed mute and terror-struck, overcome by his own weakness. He knew he could not answer. He had an unreasonable fear, lest the other man should suddenly destroy him. Whereas Maurice was actually filled with hot, poignant love, the passion of friendship. Perhaps it was this very passion of friendship which Bertie shrank from most.

"We're all right together now, aren't we?" said Maurice. "It's all right now, as long as we live, so far as we're concerned?"

"Yes," said Bertie, trying by any means to escape.

Maurice stood with head lifted, as if listening. The new delicate fulfilment of mortal friendship had come as revelation and surprise to him, something exquisite and unhoped-for. He seemed to be listening to hear if it were real.

Then he turned for his coat.

"Come," he said, "we'll go to Isabel."

Bertie took the lantern and opened the door. The cat disappeared. The two men went in silence along the causeways. Isabel, as they came, thought their footsteps sounded strange. She looked up pathetically and anxiously for their entrance. There seemed a curious elation about Maurice. Bertie was haggard, with sunken eyes.

"What is it?" she asked.

"We've become friends," said Maurice, standing with his feet apart, like a strange colossus.

"Friends!" re-echoed Isabel. And she looked again at Bertie. He met her eyes with a furtive, haggard look; his eyes were as if glazed with misery.

"I'm so glad," she said, in sheer perplexity.

"Yes," said Maurice.

He was indeed so glad. Isabel took his hand with both hers, and held it fast.

"You'll be happier now, dear," she said.

But she was watching Bertie. She knew that he had one desire—to escape from this intimacy, this friendship, which had been thrust upon him. He could not bear it that he had been touched by the blind man, his insane reserve broken in. He was like a mollusc whose shell is broken.

GROUP FOUR

PETER TAYLOR

Reservations: A Love Story

It was arranged, of all things, that the bride and groom should make their escape from the country club through the little boys' locker room! But this was very reasonable, really. At nine o'clock on a night in January, the exit from the little boys' locker room to the swimming-pool terrace was the exit least likely to be congested. It was the exit also most likely to be overlooked by mischievous members of the wedding party. Every precaution had to be taken! No one was to be trusted!

In the lounge of the women's locker room, the bride got out of her gown in exactly thirty seconds. (She had taken an hour, more or less, to get into it.) She pushed the wedding dress into the hands of one of the club's maids and from the hands of another accepted the tweed travelling suit—puce-brown tweed trimmed with black velvet. Because it was imperative that no suspicion of her departure be roused among the guests, the bride was not attended by her mother or by her maid of honor. Her mother and all the bridal attendants remained upstairs at the party, where there was dancing, and where waiters moved about balancing trays of stemmed glasses. At two minutes to nine the bride ran on tiptoe along a service passageway that connected most of the rooms on the ground floor. She was accompanied now by the elder of the two maids who had assisted in the change from white satin to tweed. This woman was one of the club's veteran maids, a large, rather middle-aged person who, though she dyed her hair a lemon yellow and rouged her cheeks excessively, was known for her stalwart character and her incorruptibility. In the passageway, the bride chattered nervously to this companion who had been assigned to her. She told how she had written her name in the club's bride's book as "Franny Crowell," having forgotten momentarily that she was now Mrs. Miles Miller. The maid was not a very responsive sort, and said nothing.

But this didn't bother Franny; she went on to say, sometimes laughing while she spoke, that somehow she could not shake off the feeling that it was a pity and a shame to be slipping away from a party given in your own honor.

In one hand the maid held the key to a door down the passageway that would let the bride into the little boys' locker room. In the other hand she carried a pair of fur-trimmed galoshes. As they approached the locked door, the maid interrupted Franny's chatter. "Your father said tell you your fur coat's in the car, with your corsage pinned to it. He said be careful you don't sit on it." Simultaneously the maid held out the galoshes, giving them a little shake that indicated Franny should take them.

"What are those?" Franny chirped. "They're not mine."

"No, they're not yours, Mrs. Miller," said the maid, still pressing them on her.

"Well, I don't believe I'll want them," Franny said politely.

"Yes, your mother said so. It's snowing outside now—a nasty, wet snow, Mrs. Miller."

"But they're not mine, and they're not Mother's either. . . . How long has it been snowing?" She hoped to change the subject.

"Two hours off and on, Mrs. Miller. Ever since you got here from the church. It's not sticking, but there'll be slush underfoot."

"Well, whose are they?"

"Your mother snitched them from one of the guests—out of the cloakroom. She told me, 'Something borrowed.' "

Franny burst into laughter and took the galoshes. But she resolved not to put on the ugly things until after Miles had seen her and got the effect of her outfit.

While the maid fitted the key into the lock, Franny stood with her eyes lifted to the low basement ceiling. She heard the sound of the dancing overhead, and she speculated about which of the dancers upstairs these boots might belong to and thought of the pleasure it was sure to give some childhood friend of hers, or possibly some aunt or some woman friend of her parents, to learn that she had provided the bride with the one item that had been overlooked—the something borrowed.

Presently the door before her stood open. But Franny's eyes and thoughts were still directed toward the ceiling. "There you are," said the maid, obviously provoked by the bride's inattention.

Franny lowered her eyes. She looked at the woman beside her with a startled expression. Then she glanced briefly into the shadows of the unlighted locker room. And in the next moment she was clutching frantically at the starched sleeve of the maid's uniform. "But he is not here!" she exclaimed. Her tone was accusing; she eyed the maid suspiciously. Then, as if on further reflection, she spoke in a bewailing whisper: "He isn't hee-er!" According to the plan, he was to have been admitted to the little boys' locker room through a door from the adjoining men's locker room. But had he ever intended to be there? *He was gone! Of course he was! How else would it be?* Already Franny was thinking of what kind of poison she would administer to herself, of how she would manage to obtain the poison, of how she would look when they found her.

"What do you mean 'not here'?" said the maid, jerking her sleeve free.

Franny smiled coolly. She knew how she must carry it off. "Maybe I'll stay on for the party, after all," she said.

"What do you mean 'not here'?" the maid repeated. "He's standing there before your eyes."

Franny looked again, and of course there her bridegroom stood. "I didn't see him, it's so dark," she stammered.

But, instead of going to the bridegroom, suddenly the bride threw her arms about the woman with the lemon-yellow hair who had delivered her to him. This trustworthy woman had been known to Franny during most of her young life, but she was by no means a favorite of Franny's. And almost certainly Franny had never been a favorite of the woman's, either. . . . But still it seemed the thing to do. Somehow it was like embracing the whole wedding party or even the whole club membership, or possibly just simply her own mother. And, no doubt, in that moment this woman forgave Franny many an old score—forgave a little girl's criticism of sandwiches served toasted when they had been ordered untoasted, complaints about a bathing suit's not having been hung out to dry, and many another complaint besides. At any rate, the woman responded and returned the warm embrace. Then for an instant the two of them smiled at each other through the general mist of tears.

"Goodbye, little Miss 'Franny Crowell,' " the woman said.

"Goodbye, Bernice," said Franny, "and thanks for everything." Yes, the woman's name was Bernice. What a bother it had always been, trying to remember it, but now it had come out without Franny's having to try to think of it even.

Bernice took several steps backward, as if quitting a royal presence. At a respectful distance she turned her back, and in her white gum-soled shoes she retreated silently down the long passageway.

While waiting for the bride to come through the doorway to him, the bridegroom had literally stood dangling his little narrow-brimmed hat, shifting it from one hand to the other. He did not know what to make of that blank look she had given him at first, didn't know what to make of her saying "He is not here," didn't know what to make of her throwing herself into the arms of the hired help instead of into his own. . . . The embrace perhaps he understood better than the look. But anyway, she had come to him at last, which was what he wanted most in the world at the moment. Presently he had seated her on one of the rough wooden benches in the locker room and, on his knees before her, he was struggling to push her feet into the borrowed galoshes. Franny had held on to the galoshes through both her embraces, and as soon as she had handed them to Miles and was seated on the bench, she began to chatter again—about the galoshes now, about how her mother had positively stolen "the ugly things" from somebody upstairs.

It wasn't easy getting the galoshes on. They were a near-perfect fit, but Franny seemed incapable of being any help. Her little ankles had gone limp, like an absent-minded child's. But finally Miles managed to force both galoshes on. He zipped them up neatly, and then lifted his face to Franny and smiled. Franny extended one of her tiny gloved hands to him, as if she were going to pull him to his feet. Miles seized it, but he remained on one knee before her, pressing the hand firmly between the two of his. While he knelt there, Franny made a vague gesture with her free hand, a gesture that indicated the whole of the dark locker room. "I've never been in here before, Miles," she said.

"Neither have I, you know," Miles said playfully.

"Oh," Franny breathed, thoughtfully. "No, you probably haven't, have you."

Now she felt she understood. . . . *That* was why she had not been able to see him there at first. She had never *imagined* him there. It was because Miles Miller was not one of the local boys she had grown up with, wasn't one of that familiar group from whose number she had always assumed she would someday accept a husband. He was better than any of *those,* of course; he was her own, beloved, blue-eyed, black-haired, fascinating Miles Miller, whom she had recognized the first moment she ever saw him as the best-looking man she had ever laid eyes on (or ever would), as the man she must have for *hers*—and the very same Miles, of course, that at least half a dozen other girls of her year had thought they must have for *theirs.* Moreover, he was the young man who doesn't turn up in *every*body's year: the young bachelor from out of town, brought in from a distant region by one of the big corporations to fill a place in its local office, a young man without any local history of teen-age romances to annoy and perhaps worry the bride. And in Miles' case the circumstances were enhanced still further. He was an only child, and his parents had died while he was still in college. For his bride there would be no parents or brothers and sisters to be visited and adjusted to, and, since he had lived always on the West Coast and gone to Stanford, no prep-school friends, not even—at such a distance—a college roommate to be won over. Once they were married, Franny's family would be *their* family, her friends *their* friends. Besides all this, her Miles was at once the most modest and most self-assured human being imaginable. With one gentle look—gentle and yet reasonable and terribly penetrating—he could make her aware of the utter absurdity of something she said or did, and make her simultaneously aware of how little such absurdities mattered to someone who loved you.

Franny bent forward and kissed her husband gently on his smiling lips. He came up beside her on the bench, no longer smiling, and took Franny in his arms. For Franny it was as it had always been before—every time he had ever held her in his tender, confident way. It was as though she possessed at last, or was about to possess at last, what she had always wanted above everything else and had never dreamed she wanted—or, that is, never dreamed she wanted in quite the same way she wanted everything else. That was what seemed so incredible to her about it: *This* desire and *this* happiness differed only in degree from the other longings and other satisfactions one experienced. There was nothing at all unreal about it. And somehow the most miraculous part was that the man she was going to marry was not the man she had ever imagined herself marrying. On the contrary, he was the frightening stranger of her girlish daydreams—the dark, handsome man she was always going to meet on a train coming home from boarding school at Christmas or during the summer at Lake Michigan. In her daydreams she sometimes even bore that man a child, but there had always had to be a barrier to their marrying. The man was already married (perhaps to an invalid!), or he was a Jew, he was a Catholic—a French Canadian—or he was the foreign agent of a country committed to the destruction of her own country, or (when she was still younger) there was insanity or even a strain of Negro blood in his family! Yet the stranger had turned up after all—after she had almost forgotten him—and there was no barrier.

Still holding Franny close to him, Miles got to his feet and for a moment lifted his bride completely off the floor. "Franny, oh, 'little Miss Franny,' let's go!" he said. Franny laughed aloud. And to Miles she sounded for all the world like a delighted little girl of four or five. "Let's be on our way," he said, still holding her there. "Let's get out of here."

"Carry me to the car, Miles," she whispered.

"I will," he said. "You bet I will. Not this way, though. I'll set you down and get a good hold and then we'll dash."

But just as Franny's feet touched the floor, there came a great rattling sound from over toward the door to the terrace. Franny gave a little shriek that came out almost "Aha!" And then, in a quiet voice, in a tone of utter resignation, she said, "They've found us." She meant, of course, that the mischief-makers had found them. "We'll never get away."

"No, they haven't, darling," Miles said impatiently.

Franny turned away from him. At the far end of the room she saw a man's figure silhouetted against the glass door to the terrace. She realized at once that the man must be one of the club's waiters. It was he, she surmised, who had let Miles in from the men's locker room. He had been present all the while, and actually he was now holding the terrace door a little way open. The rattling noise had, plainly, come from the long Venetian blind on that door. But the source of the rattling no longer interested Franny; she was too angry with Miles for not having told her they weren't alone.

Suddenly her impulse was to turn back and deliver Miles a slap across the face. His inference that the waiter's presence hadn't mattered was insulting both to herself and to this man who had so faithfully performed the duties assigned him. But before she could turn or speak, Miles had seized her by the hand and the waiter had thrown open the door. Hand in hand, the bride and groom ran the length of the little boys' locker room. In the excitement of the moment, Miles had forgotten that he was going to carry Franny to the car. It was well for him that he had. Franny consented to let him hold her hand only in order to keep from embarrassing the waiter. Halfway to the door she made out just which of the club's waiters he was, and she could easily have called him by name. But instead she dropped her eyes, and she kept them lowered even when Miles paused in the doorway to slip a bill into the hand at the end of the white sleeve. In her pique with Miles, she wondered if the bill was of as large a denomination as it ought to be.

Outside, they ran along the edge of the gaping swimming pool and on in the direction of the tennis courts. Beyond the courts, Miles' new car was hidden. The wet snow was falling heavily, and it was beginning to stick now. It seemed to Franny that the snow might fill the empty swimming pool before the night was over. They went through the gate into the area of the tennis courts. From there Franny glanced back once at the lighted windows of the low, sprawling clubhouse. Through the snow it seemed miles away. They ran on across the courts and through the white shrubbery. Neither of them spoke until they were in the car. By then their rendezvous in the locker room seemed like something that had happened too long ago to mention. As Miles was helping her into her coat, and she was carefully protecting the big white orchid that she knew her father had pinned on the coat with his own hands, Franny said, "What are we going to do, Miles? I'm terrified. I hate snow. We can't get even as far as Bardstown tonight."

"Of course we can't, honey," he said. He had switched on the car lights and was starting the motor. "We'll have to stay here in town tonight. I telephoned the hotel a while ago. We'll have to stay there."

They had planned to spend the first night at Bardstown, which in good weather was only a few hours away, down in Kentucky, and where there was an attractive old inn. They had planned to make it to Natchez by the second night, and to be at the Gulf Coast by the third. Franny's father had urged them to fly down, or to take a train. But they were able to think only of what fun it would be to have their own car once they got to Biloxi. It had been silly of them, they acknowledged now, driving into town through the snow, but they did have the satisfaction of knowing that all planes would be grounded on such a night, anyway. And to both of them the idea of spending their wedding night in a Pullman berth seemed grotesque.

It took Miles three-quarters of an hour to get them through the snow and the traffic to the downtown hotel where he had managed to make reservations. Along the way, he apologized to Franny for putting them up at this particular hotel—the hotel, that is, where he had himself been living during the past year and a half. "As luck would have it," he explained, "there are two big conventions in town this week. I was lucky to find a room anywhere at all. I hope you don't mind too much."

"Why in the world should I mind?" Franny laughed. "We're a bona-fide married couple now."

Yet the moment she had passed through the revolving door into the marble-pillared lobby of the hotel, Franny rested a gloved hand on the sleeve of Miles' overcoat and said, "I *do* feel a little funny about it, after all."

"I was afraid you might feel funny about it," Miles said. They stood there a moment waiting for the boy with their luggage to follow them through the revolving door, and Miles began to apologize all over again. "The other hotels were all full up," he said. "It's only because I happen to hit it off so well with Bill Carlisle that I was able to get a room here. It wasn't easy for him even; he's just the assistant manager. Your father, or almost any of the guys in the wedding, might have found us something better. But it seemed worse, somehow, to have any of them—even your father—know exactly where we're spending the night, since we can't get out of town. I guessed you would feel the same way about it."

But Franny was not listening to Miles. She had become aware that she was the only woman in the lobby, and the mention of the assistant manager's name had further distracted her. Bill Carlisle had been invited to the wedding—she recalled addressing his invitation—but he had not been invited to the reception and supper dance. As for her own acquaintance with him, it was very slight. She had known him for a long time, however, and she knew that he knew just about everyone that she did. She interrupted Miles' apologies to say, "Do we have to see Bill Collier?"

"Who?" asked Miles.

"You know—the assistant manager."

"Of course we don't, darling," he said. "We don't even have to register. That's all set."

The boy with their luggage had joined them now. Another boy had appeared with their key and was beckoning them to follow him to the elevator. As they crossed the lobby, Franny began laughing to herself. Miles noticed, and asked what was funny.

"I was wondering," she said, "do you think he'll have put us in your room?"

"Will who have?"

"You know, your friend Bill—the assistant manager."

"At least it won't be that," said Miles. "There was someone waiting to take it over when I got the last of my possessions out this morning."

"What a shame," Franny whispered. "It would have been kind of interesting, and no one but Bill Cook need ever have known."

"Bill Carlisle's his name," Miles said rather petulantly. Then he added, "He's a pretty nice fellow, in case you care to know."

"Certainly he is," Franny said with a wink. "I've known him for years."

Franny stepped into the elevator, followed by Miles. Then the boy with the luggage got in, then one with the key. Franny observed that both the boys were mature men, and the key boy was even bald-headed. They kept their heads bowed, very courteously, not even looking up when presently they had occasion to speak to each other.

"Where's Jack?" the luggage boy asked quietly.

"He's coming," said the key boy.

"Who's Jack?" Franny asked Miles.

Thinking the question directed to him, the luggage boy replied, "He's the elevator boy." As he spoke, he glanced up at Franny. Probably he thought it was demanded of him. Unlike the key boy, he had a heavy head of hair, as dark and thick as Miles' own, and the face he lifted was youthful, almost handsome even, with a broad jaw and black, rather cruel eyes that seemed brimming with energy. As soon as he looked up he realized his mistake and bent his head again. But he had reminded Franny of someone—someone she didn't like. Or *did* like. Which was it? She couldn't think who it was, and felt vaguely that she didn't want to. And what would Jack, the elevator operator, be like, she wondered, when he turned up? Somehow she was sure he would be a redhead. Presently he would come running; he would hop into the elevator, close the door, push the button, and there she would be, locked in the elevator with Miles and with the three men in their dark-green livery and with the heap of luggage, and the elevator would shoot them up to their floor and stop with a sickening little bounce. She wished Miles would *say* something!

"Jack seems to have gotten lost," Miles said. Franny burst out laughing.

Immediately, Jack appeared, as if from nowhere. He was a Negro boy, but with light skin and a reddish tint to his hair.

Franny was conscious of Jack's arrival, and conscious of the color of his hair, but at the same time her real attention had been caught by a figure out in the lobby. It was the figure of a woman, and she was moving swiftly across the lobby toward this elevator, making her way between the heavier figures of the conventioners in their tweed overcoats and gray fedoras. (Most of them, it seemed to Franny, were smoking cigars, the way conventioners were supposed to.) The woman was wearing a navy-blue topcoat and hat, and carried an oversize handbag. "Wait!" Franny said to the elevator boy.

"What do you mean, 'Wait'?" Miles asked.

"Don't you see who that is trying to catch us?" Franny said, rising on her toes.

"I see who it is, but you don't know her, and I can promise you I don't either."

One of the hotel boys snorted, but he cut it off so short Franny couldn't tell for sure which of them it was. She suspected the bald-headed one.

"It's Bernice! The maid from the club!" Franny tried to recall whether she had forgotten anything essential. No, the woman must have an urgent message for her. Her father or her mother had been taken ill, or there had been some disaster at the club—a fire perhaps. She remembered distinctly having left a cigarette burning in the women's lounge.

"It's no such thing," Miles was saying. "Let's go, Jack!"

The woman was close enough now for Franny to see it was not Bernice. The long stride and the yellow hair sticking out from under the hat had deceived her. But she should have known, shouldn't she, that Bernice could not have worn such heels.

The elevator door was closing right in the woman's face, and even if the woman wasn't Bernice, this was more than Franny could bear. "Stop it!" she commanded, utterly outraged by the ungallant behavior of these men. "There's room for another person, easily!"

The boys looked at Miles. "Let the lady in," Miles thundered.

Jack slid the door open. But the woman hesitated. With a swift glance she seemed to have taken in every aspect of the situation—that it was a bride and groom she was intruding upon, that the bride had insisted upon holding the car for her, that the groom had protested. She now signalled Jack to go on without her, but with Miles' thundering command still in his ears Jack made no move to do so. Miles kept silent. And so did Franny, who in a last-minute glance as swift as the woman's had taken in *her* total situation—that she was a middle-aged prostitute late for an engagement. There was but one solution to the awful silence and to the irresolution of the elevator boy. The woman stepped into the elevator and abruptly turned her back to the other passengers.

As the car shot upward, Jack asked with easy nonchalance, "Your floor, please?"

Again there was silence. Finally Miles said, "What's our floor?"

The key boy looked up, showing his full face for the first time—eyes set close together, a small, puffy nose, ears flat against the bald head. Franny thought it the stupidest, most brutal face she had ever set eyes on. "*Your* floor is eight, Mr. Miller," he said, barely opening his swollen lips when he spoke.

After a moment Jack repeated, "Your floor, please?"

The woman now turned her face toward the elevator boy so that Franny saw her profile. Her face was plain—neither homely nor otherwise, really—and seemed devoid of expression. Only the fact that she had turned her face toward him showed that she knew the boy expected an answer from her. It occurred to Franny that in her agitation this poor creature had forgotten what floor she was going to. At last, and as if with great effort, she did speak. "Seven for me," she said.

With a long, bony forefinger Jack stabbed the seventh-floor button. The elevator stopped almost at once, and the door slid open. The woman stepped out into the hallway, where there was a broad mirror facing her between two metal cigarette urns. Instead of turning to left or right she stopped there just outside the elevator, and for one instant her pale eyes met Franny's in the glass. Then the door closed quietly between them.

Franny had not been aware of a bouncing sensation when the elevator stopped at that floor. But when it stopped at the floor above, the sensation so upset her equilibrium that she felt positively faint. Her two feet in their fur-trimmed galoshes seemed chilled to numbness. She felt that if she tried to take one step down the hallway in the direction of the bridal chamber her knees might buckle underneath her. She wondered how she would ever manage it.

To Miles Miller, his bride had seemed not herself at all, from the time they met in the shadows of the locker room at the country club until at last they were alone in the hotel room. But her confusion and nervousness were very understandable, he reasoned, in view of the upsetting change in their plans. And once they were alone in the room, she was indeed very much herself again. She was once again the vivacious, unaffected, ingenuous little being he had decided to marry after talking to her for five minutes during an intermission at a big début party last year. From the beginning, Miles had felt that he appreciated her special brand of innocence and even artlessness as no one else ever before had. One thing he had determined when he left college and entered upon his career in business was that he would not be the sort—the type—to marry the boss's daughter and further his career that way. He detested that type. He extended this pledge to himself even to include the daughters of prominent and influential men who might indirectly help him in his career. He extended it even to cover all the débutantes he had ever met or would ever meet. He had had no definite ideas about where he *would* find his wife, except one idea that was so childish he laughed at it himself: He had thought of meeting a perfectly unspoiled girl while vacationing in an unspoiled countryside—perhaps in the highland South, perhaps even somewhere in Europe. He had thought particularly of Switzerland. But when thinking more realistically Miles told himself simply that he would not marry for the sake of his business or social advancement. His marriage and his family life must be something altogether apart from his career.

And then, in his twenty-sixth year, he had met Franny Crowell and had had a wonderful insight. Franny was, in a most important sense, as beautifully innocent and provincial as any little mountain girl might have been. She delighted in her surroundings, accepted her relation to them without question, and would be content to remain where she was and as she was for the rest of her life. She had been practically nowhere away from home. For two years she went to boarding school in Virginia but hated dormitory life and thought it silly of girls to go East to college when they could be so much more comfortable staying at home. She had herself attended the local city university for two years and had relished meeting different kinds of people from her own home town. True, she had spent most of her summers at a resort on Lake Michigan, but even there most of her companions had been the same people she went to school with at home during the winter. Miles Miller recognized in Franny Crowell the flaxen-haired mountain girl of his childish imaginings. Her outward appearance might deceive the world but never him. She arranged her golden-brown hair always in the very latest, most sophisticated fashions. Last summer she had even let the beauty parlor put a blond streak in her hair. She plucked her eyebrows, even pencilled them. The shade of her lipstick paled or darkened according to whatever was newest. But Miles perceived that all of this was as innocent and natural in his Franny as plaiting flaxen pigtails might have been.

Miles and Franny had agreed in advance that they should each have only one glass of champagne at the club on their wedding night. But among the bags that they had had brought into the hotel was Miles' genuine Gucci liquor case—a present from the men at his office. Packed with ice in the plastic compartment of the elaborate leather case were two bottles of champagne of a somewhat earlier and better year than that offered the guests by the bride's father. And into Franny's makeup bag she had managed to fit two of their very own champagne glasses. Together they had thought of everything.

In their hotel room, they spent the first half hour making toasts. They drank to Betty Manville's début ball, where they had met, drank to their first date, to their first kiss, to the night he first proposed, to the night she accepted, to the night of the announcement party. Each toast had to be followed by a kiss. Each kiss inspired and motivated another reminiscence. Finally they turned to toasting people whom they associated with events of their courtship. Since Franny was a talented and tireless mimic, Miles encouraged her to "do" each of these people. She "did" Betty Manville's mother, her own father, and then one of her bridesmaids, who had once upon a time imagined *she* was going to have Miles Miller for herself. This last was the funniest of all to Miles. He was seated on the side of the bed, leaning on one elbow, and when he had witnessed Franny's version of that poor, misguided girl he set his champagne glass on the floor and fell back on the bed in a spasm of laughter. He threshed about, still laughing aloud, and all the while wiping tears from his eyes and begging Franny to stop.

When Franny promised to stop, Miles got control of himself and sat up in the center of the bed. Wiping his eyes with his handkerchief, he looked up again and found Franny sitting on the side of the bed with her thumb pressed against her nose so hard that her little nose was flattened on her face. Her eyes were squinted up and her mouth, which was normally small and tight, was stretched and spread into a wide ribbon across her face. "You know who this is?" she asked, barely moving her lips.

"I'm glad to say I don't," Miles said, as if offended by her ugliness.

"Oh, you do," Franny insisted.

"I don't, and it's not very attractive."

"Of course its not attractive," said Franny, keeping the thumb pressed against her nose. "It's that bald-headed bellboy, the one with the key."

"What's wrong with him?" Miles said, swinging his feet around to the other side of the bed and thus momentarily turning his back to Franny.

"You don't have to turn your back," Franny said. "See, it's still only me."

Miles looked around and smiled apologetically. Franny's face was her own again, and she was looking down at her hands very seriously. "Weren't all three of those bellboys grotesque?" she said.

"I don't think so," Miles said. "They're perfectly normal-looking human beings. I see them every day."

"Normal-looking!" Franny exclaimed, lifting her eyes to his. "How can you say so? The bald-headed one was really monstrous. And the one with the mop of hair had a really mad look in his eyes. And that pale Negro boy with the kinky red hair! How blind you are to people, Miles. You don't really *see* them."

"Maybe not," said Miles, meaning to dismiss the subject, since Franny seemed so emotional about it. Turning now, he let himself fall across the bed toward her, and again he took one of her hands between the two of his. But before he could speak the endearment he intended, something else occurred to him that he felt must be said first. It was in defense of his vision, or—he couldn't define it—in defense of something even more specially his own that had been disparaged. "Anyway," he said, "you must admit that not one of those bellhops was half as weird-looking as that painted-up creature you had your hug fest with when we were leaving the club. After the elevator ride, I don't have to tell you what *she* looked like." Though they had been in the room for more than half an hour, this was the first reference either of them had made to the woman in the elevator.

Franny withdrew her hand and stood up.

Miles said, "We're not going to quarrel about something so silly on our wedding night, are we?"

Franny was silent for a moment. Her eyes moved about the room as if taking it in for the first time. Then she bent over and kissed Miles on the top of his head. "We aren't *ever* going to quarrel again, are we, Miles?"

"Never," he said. He reached out a hand, but she pulled away. "Come back," he said in a whisper.

"Not until I've slipped into something more—more right." She smiled vaguely.

Miles lay with his head propped on one hand and watched her go to her little overnight bag and take out the folds of lace and peach silk that were her negligee and gown. Suddenly he leaped from the bed with outstretched arms. But the bride dashed through the open doorway to the bathroom and closed the door.

Miles had long since changed into his blue silk pajamas with the white monogram on the pocket when he saw the first turning and twisting of the doorknob. When Franny failed to appear at once—that is, when the knob ceased its twisting and the bathroom door didn't open—his vexation showed itself momentarily in one little horizontal crease in his smooth forehead. But the moment was so brief that even his eyes didn't reflect it, and soon a sly little smile came to his lips. . . . He would give her a signal that all was ready and waiting, and at the same time give her motivation and courage. Stepping over to the dresser he uncorked the second bottle of champagne. He managed it very expertly, taking satisfaction in his expertness. The pop was loud enough for Franny to hear and comprehend, yet there was not one bubble of wasteful overflow. The tiny golden bubbles came just to the mouth of the champagne bottle and no further. Miles had not even taken the precaution of having the two glasses handy. He was expert and he was confident of his expertness.

He watched the first bubbles appear and then shot a glance across the room at the doorknob. It was turning again. He stepped over to where the two glasses were, on the bedside table, filled them, and then returned the bottle to its ice. Still no Franny. But the doorknob was now turning back and forth rather rapidly. Miles watched it as if hypnotized. Finally he uttered a tentative "Franny?" There was no response except in the acceleration of the knob's turning. "Franny?" he repeated, striding toward the door. "What's the matter?" Still no answer. The turning was frenzied now. "Franny, do you hear me? What are you doing?"

"Of course I hear you!" Franny exclaimed through the door. "I'm trying to get out of here, you fool!"

Miles seized the knob and gave it a forceful twist.

"That's not going to help," said Franny, resentful of the overpowering yank to the knob she had been holding on to.

"The thing must be locked," Miles said, astonished. "Why did you lock it?"

Franny was silent. Then she said, "*I* didn't lock it."

"Well, *I* didn't." Miles laughed. "Anyway, try unlocking it."

"Do you think I haven't already?"

"What kind of lock is it? Is there a key?"

"No. It's one of those damned little eggs you turn."

"But why on earth would you have locked it?"

"If I did it, Miles, I did it without thinking."

Miles was now trying to see the bolt through the crack of the door. "But why would you?" he said absently.

"Why would I what?"

"Lock it without thinking."

"All decent people lock bathroom doors," she said with conviction.

"We didn't at our house," Miles said. He could definitely see the bolt through the crack. "My father used to throw away the key to the bathroom door as soon as we moved into a place."

"Don't start on your father *now,* Miles."

"My father was all right."

"Who said he wasn't? *Do* something, Miles, for God's sake."

"There's nothing to do but call the desk and have them take down the door."

Franny who had for a moment been leaning against the rim of the washbowl, now straightened and grasped the doorknob again. "Miles, you *wouldn't!*"

"Don't go to pieces, Franny."

"You'd let them send up those three stooges—"

Miles burst into laughter.

"How coarse you are, Miles," Franny said, her voice deepening.

"Oh, honey, there's a regular maintenance crew, and—"

"Maybe so," she broke in, her voice climbing the scale till it was much higher than Miles had ever heard it before. "But don't you know, Miles, that Bill Carlisle would certainly know about it? Oh, God, everybody in this town would know about it before tomorrow morning!"

"In God's name, Franny, what do you propose I do?"

"What kind of man are you, Miles? Take the door down yourself. You've been living in this hotel so long you depend on them for everything. You seem to think the world's just one big hotel and that you call in the maintenance crew for any and every thing."

"O.K., Franny, I'll try," Miles said amiably. "But have you ever tried taking down a locked door?"

"Why did you have to bring me to this dump?" Franny wailed.

"And why did you have to lock the door?" he countered.

Now they were both silent as Miles went to the closet door where his Valpak hung, and dug out a small gold pocketknife. His first effort to remove the pin in the upper door hinge was fruitless. The pin wouldn't budge. Neither would the pin in the lower hinge. He decided he needed a hammer to drive the knife blade upward against the heads of the pins, and he was just turning to go and fetch his shoe for that purpose when Franny spoke again.

"Miles," she began, speaking very slowly and in a tone so grave that it stopped him, "do you remember that night at Cousin Jane Thompson's party?"

He listened, waiting for her to continue. Then he realized she expected some response from him. "Yes, Franny," he said.

"That night at Cousin Jane's," she now went on in the same sepulchral tone, "when you said Sue Maynard's date was drunk and that she asked you to take her home." Sue Maynard was the bridesmaid who had thought *she* would have Miles for herself. Miles had been a stag at the party that night.

"Yes, I remember."

"You were lying."

"In a way, Franny—"

"In the worst way," she said flatly. "You thought I would think it was just Sue's lie and that you didn't know better, or that you knew better but were too honorable to give her away."

"Maybe."

"That's how you *thought* I would think. But I knew even that night,

Miles Miller, that you engineered it all. Her date was Puss Knowlton, and you had no trouble giving *him* the shove. And don't you think I know it's more than just necking that Sue Maynard goes in for? . . . And, Miles, the night last summer, *after* we were engaged, when you couldn't come for dinner at our house with Daddy's Aunt Caroline because of the report you had to write up—you didn't have any report to write up, Miles. You went someplace out on the South Side with a little creature named Becky Louise Johnson."

By the time Franny had finished, Miles had silently crossed the room to the bedside table and downed one of the two waiting glassfuls of champagne. He had listened intently to what she said, and the more he heard the more intent he had become on getting that damned door down. In his liquor case he found a bottle opener that he decided would work better than his knife. He returned to the door with his shoe and the bottle opener, and in no time he had the top pin out of its hinge.

"Miles—" Franny began again, still in the same tone.

"Shut up, Franny!" Miles said, and at once began hammering at the lower pin. It offered a little more resistance than the other, but was soon dislodged. The door was still firmly in place, however. Twice Miles jabbed the bottle opener into the crack on the hinge side, as though he might prize the door open. Then he laughed aloud at himself.

Franny heard him laugh, of course. "Is it funny? Is it really funny to you, Miles?" she said.

"Try giving it a push from in there, on the hinge side of the door," said Miles. Franny pushed. The door creaked, but that was all.

"Miles," Franny began once again, in a whisper now, and he could tell that she was leaning against the door and speaking into the crack. "I've thought of something else I've never confronted you with."

Miles felt the blood rush to his face. Suddenly he banged on the door with his fist. "Will you shut up, you little bitch! You know, I'm not above socking you in earnest if ever I get you out of there!"

"You would sock me just one time, Miles Miller."

"It would be the second time. Don't you forget that," he said.

They were really at it now, for he was reminding her of an occasion two days after their announcement party when he had found her kissing a college kid whose name he did not even know. He had struck her with his open hand on the back of her neck—not while she was kissing the kid but afterward, as he pushed her along the terrace there at the Polo Club. He had had too much to drink that night, and that was what saved them. Franny could claim that he had deserted her in favor of the bar. She also claimed that she had not really been kissing the boy and added that, anyway, he was an old, old, old friend and therefore meant nothing to her.

They hardly spoke to each other during the week following, though of course they continued going about together. And until now they had neither of them ever referred to the incident, as if by mutual agreement.

"You're no gentleman, Miles," Franny pronounced, carefully keeping away from the door now. "As Daddy said of you to start with, you have all the outward signs of a gentleman but that's no evidence you're one inside."

"I've already settled your father's hash, Franny."

"You mean he's settled yours."

It was an unfortunate word—"settled." And both of them were aware of it immediately. It quieted both of them for some time. It referred to another incident that was assumed to be closed. Franny's father had apparently suspected Miles of being a fortune hunter, and before the engagement was announced he had asked Miles frankly what kind of "settlement" he expected. Miles had stormed out of the house, and was reconciled with Mr. Crowell only after having it hammered home to him by Franny that what her father had done was merely the conventional, old-fashioned thing for a man in Mr. Crowell's position to do. Miles had finally accepted Franny's explanation, but only a few weeks ago he had had another stormy session over a similar matter. This time it was with both the bride's parents. At that very late date he had learned about certain letters of inquiry that had been sent out concerning his "background." The letters had been written to various family friends and relatives of the Crowells who had lived for many years in Santa Barbara and Laguna Beach. When Miles learned of these letters through a remark of Franny's, it was many months after the letters had been written and replied to. The revelation sent Miles into a rage. He was in such a state that Franny feared he might do real violence to her father, or even to her mother, who had actually written the letters.

She had let the cat out of the bag inadvertently. She and he were just going out to a movie one night. Franny had come down to the living room already wearing her coat and even with her gloves on, but Miles had wanted to linger and talk awhile. Before she came down, he had wandered about the room studying some family photographs taken thirty years before. These "portraits," in their upright frames on the mantelshelf and on the various tables, had reminded him of pictures in his own family's living room when he was growing up. He commenced talking to Franny about how his mother always placed the same pictures on the same tables and bureaus no matter where they were living, and then he went on to speak, as he had on several previous occasions, of how restless his father had been after he left the service. (Miles' father had been a West Point graduate and had remained in the Army until he had his first heart attack, just a few months before Pearl Harbor.) And now, as Miles had already done several times before, he began listing for Franny the towns they had lived in during and after the war. Franny, who was impatient to get on to the movie, didn't listen very carefully. When Miles hesitated, trying to think of which town it was he had omitted from his list, Franny absent-mindedly supplied "Palo Alto." But it was not Palo Alto he was trying to think of; it was San Jose.

"Palo Alto?" said Miles. "How did you know we ever lived in Palo Alto?"

"You've told me all this before," she answered.

But he had not told her about the spring in Palo Alto! It was then that his parents had quarrelled so endlessly, though he—and probably they—had never known just why. At any rate, he was always careful to leave Palo Alto out of his catalogue of towns. And he was not content now until he had wrung a confession of the whole business of the letters of inquiry out of Franny. Once she had confessed, he insisted upon taking the matter up with her parents that very night; he insisted upon *seeing* the letters. For a time, Mrs. Crowell maintained that she had already thrown away the letters. But at last she broke down. She went upstairs and returned with the packet of letters, all of which Miles read, sitting there in the family circle. He had known there couldn't be anything really bad in them, because just as there was nothing very good that could be said of his parents, there was nothing very bad, either. The worst the letters said of them was that they were "rootless people and apparently of restricted means." Miles found he could not even resent one lady's description of his mother as a "harmless little woman—pleasant enough—with a vague Southern background." The letters repeated each other with phrases like "thoroughly nice" and "well bred" and "well behaved." The sole reference to Palo Alto was "I think they lived at Palo Alto for a time. John's sister Laura met them there. She thought Major Miller very handsome. He had a small black mustache, if I recall."

The memory of all this and of the "settlement" episode occupied Miles' mind as he crossed the hotel room and picked up the glass of champagne that he had poured for Franny. The champagne had gone flat already, but he relished its flatness. He sipped it slowly, as if tasting in each sip a different unpleasant incident or aspect of their courtship and engagement—tasting all they had not tasted and toasted with the first bottle. Suddenly he put down the glass, leaving still a sip or two in the bottom, and stepped quickly over to the bathroom door. "Franny," he said, "it has just occurred to me! It wasn't your father's idea to talk about a settlement with me. You put him up to it! It was you who thought I might be after your family's money! If it had been your father's idea, he wouldn't have been so meek and mild when I called his hand. And, by God, you put your mother up to writing those letters, or she never would have given in and shown them to me."

He waited for Franny's denial, but none came. "And, Franny," he went on after a moment, "there's one more thing I know that you didn't know I knew. Your father went down to my office and asked about the likelihood of my staying on here or being transferred."

"I knew he did that, Miles."

"Darn right you knew it. You put him up to that, too. You didn't even want to take a chance on my moving you away from here." But before he had finished his last sentence, Miles heard the water running full force into the bathtub. "Franny, I'm not finished!" he shouted. "What are you doing?"

"If you don't get this door down within ten minutes"—she was speaking through the crack again—"and get it down without having Bill Carlisle up here to witness it, I'm going to drown myself in the damned bathtub."

As a matter of fact, she had begun running the water to drown out Miles' accusations, but as she spoke she became convinced that suicide really had been her original intention.

"Yes," Miles boomed, "you drown yourself in the bathtub and I'll jump out our eighth-floor window! Romeo and Juliet, that's us!"

Franny shut off the water. She opened her mouth to reply, but no words came. She burst into tears. And the poor little bride could not herself have said whether her tears were brought on by the heavy irony and sarcasm of her groom or by the thought of her dear Miles and her dear self lying dead in their caskets with their love yet unfulfilled.

Almost at once Miles began pleading with her not to cry. But it seemed that his every word brought increased volume to the wailing beyond the bathroom door. It was as if she had decided she could more effectively drown out the sound of his voice with tears than with the rush of bath water. But actually it wasn't the sound of her bridegroom's voice alone that she wished not to hear. There was the sound of another voice—other voices. She had first become aware of the other voices during one of hers and Miles' silences. Which silence she couldn't have said, because for some time afterward she tried to believe that she had only imagined hearing the other voices, or at least imagined that they sounded as near to her as they did. Finally, though, the persistence of the voices drew her attention to the fact of the other door. The other door, she finally acknowledged, must certainly lead into an adjoining room. And the voices—a man's and a woman's—came to her from that room. And now the ever-increasing volume of her own wailing was meant to conceal from herself that the woman's voice was addressing her directly through the door.

"Honey, I think we can help you." The offer was unmistakable.

"No, you can't, no, you can't!" Franny wailed.

"The gentlemen in here thinks he is pretty good with locks."

"No, no, please don't come in here," Franny begged, too frightened, too perplexed for more tears now.

"Franny, what's going on?" Miles seemed on the verge of tears himself. "Darling, I'll get a doctor, you'll be all right!"

"Miles, there's another door."

"Yes?"

"And there's someone over there. Oh, Miles, make them go away."

"Keep your head, Franny. What do they want?"

"It's a woman. She says there's a man in there who can get me out of here."

"You do want to get out, don't you, Franny?" It was as though he were speaking to someone on a window ledge.

"Not that way, I don't," said Franny. Now she was whispering through the door crack. "Miles, their voices sound familiar!"

"Now, Franny, cut it out!" scolded Miles, and Franny understood his full meaning. For a moment she listened to the other voices. From the start the man's voice had been no more than a low mumbling. He didn't want his voice recognized! The woman spoke more distinctly. Franny could hear them now discussing the problem. Presently the man said something and laughed. And the woman said, "Hush, the kid will hear you." Somehow this gave Franny courage. She stepped over to the other door and said bravely, "*Will* you help me?"

Hearing her, Miles gave a sigh of relief. Then he said, "Ask them to let me come around into their room—and help."

"Will you let my—my husband come around into your room?"

She heard them deliberating. The man was opposed. Finally, the woman said, "No. He can come and meet you outside our hall door if we get this one open."

She repeated this to Miles.

"Tell them O.K.," he commanded.

"O.K.," said Franny softly.

Now the man and woman were at the door. The man was still mumbling. "Is there a latch on your side?" the woman asked.

"Yes," said Franny. "A little sort of knob."

"Tell her to turn it," the man muttered.

"Turn it," said the woman.

Franny turned it. It moved easily. "I have," she said. She watched the big doorknob revolving, but the door didn't open. There was more discussion on the other side of the door.

"It's locked with a key," said the woman to Franny. "But that's how he's going to make hisself useful." Franny's deliverer was hard at work. She couldn't tell whether it was a skeleton key or some makeshift instrument he was using. Presently, she heard the click of the lock and heard the man say, "That's got it."

"Miles!" Franny called out. But Miles didn't answer. He was already waiting at their neighbors' hall door. There was the sound of footsteps hurriedly retreating, and then the door opened. The room itself was in darkness, but in the light from the bathroom Franny could see the man's figure outlined on the bed. The sheet was pulled up over his face. Franny looked at the woman. She was fully dressed, though barefoot, and she stood smiling at the ridiculous sight in the bed and probably at the memory of the male figure's racing across the room and jumping into the bed and pulling the sheet over its head.

"You're an angel," Franny said, without having known she was going to say it.

The woman acknowledged the compliment only by allowing the smile to fade from her lips. "He'll get up from there and try to open the other door for you in a minute," she said.

Franny gave her a grateful smile, and then she turned and walked with perfect poise toward the hall door. Her peach negligee was floor-length and its little train of lace swept gracefully along the dark carpet. When her hand was on the doorknob, she turned and said simply, "Good night." She might have been at home, turning to say a casual good night to her mother.

In the hallway, Miles had waited, fully expecting to have to carry his bride back to their room in his arms. When she appeared he was stunned by her radiance and self-possession. He had never seen her so beautiful. And Franny was equally stunned by Miles' manly beauty as he stood before her in his blue silk pajamas. For a moment they stood there beaming at one another. Finally Miles slipped his arm gently about his bride's waist and hurried her off to their room.

They found their bathroom door standing half open, and the door beyond it tightly closed. The two heavy pins still lay on the floor, but Miles quickly slipped them into the hinges. The door was now in perfect working order. Miles stood a moment gazing into the bright bathroom where Franny's clothes were heaped in one corner like a child's. "Well," he said at last, "that fellow worked fast."

"Miles," said Franny, also looking into the bathroom but with her eyes focussed on the door opposite, "did you see who it was?"

"What do you mean?"

"The woman over there—she was the woman on the elevator."

"Franny, Franny! . . . She got off at the seventh floor! How could you forget?"

"And the man—" Franny began.

"Franny, Franny, Franny," Miles interrupted, already having left her side to fetch the champagne glasses and refill them. "The man in that room is one of the conventioners from out of town. You never heard his voice or saw him before in your life."

She had been going to say that the man in the bed was Bill Carlisle. But she saw it was useless. And she knew she would never say it now. Miles came toward her slowly with the two glasses filled to the brim. They sipped their champagne, looking at one another over the glasses. In their hearts both of them were glad they had said all the things that they said through the door. As they gazed deep into each other's eyes, they believed that they had got all of that off their chests once and for all. There was nothing in the world to come between them now. They believed, really and truly, that neither of them would ever deceive or mistrust the other again. Silently they were toasting their own bliss and happiness, confident that it would never again be shadowed by the irrelevances of the different circumstances of their upbringings or by the possibly impure and selfish motives that had helped to bring them together.

JAMES JOYCE

The Boarding House

Mrs. Mooney was a butcher's daughter. She was a woman who was quite able to keep things to herself: a determined woman. She had married her father's foreman and opened a butcher's shop near Spring Gardens. But as soon as his father-in-law was dead Mr. Mooney began to go to the devil. He drank, plundered the till, ran head-long into debt. It was no use making him take the pledge: he was sure to break out again a few days after. By fighting his wife in the presence of customers and by buying bad meat he ruined his business. One night he went for his wife with the cleaver and she had to sleep in a neighbour's house.

After that they lived apart. She went to the priest and got a separation from him with care of the children. She would give him neither money nor food nor house-room; and so he was obliged to enlist himself as a sheriff's man. He was a shabby stooped little drunkard with a white face and a white moustache and white eyebrows, pencilled above his little eyes, which were pink-veined and raw; and all day long he sat in the bailiff's room, waiting to be put on a job. Mrs. Mooney, who had taken what remained of her money out of the butcher business and set up a boarding house in Harwicke Street, was a big imposing woman. Her house had a floating population made up of tourists from Liverpool and the Isle of Man and, occasionally, *artistes* from the music halls. Its resident population was made up of clerks from the city. She governed the house cunningly and firmly, knew when to give credit, when to be stern and when to let things pass. All the resident young men spoke of her as *The Madam*.

Mrs. Mooney's young men paid fifteen shillings a week for board and lodgings (beer or stout at dinner excluded). They shared in common tastes and occupations and for this reason they were very chummy with one another. They discussed with one another the chances of favourites and outsiders. Jack Mooney, the Madam's son, who was clerk to a commission agent in Fleet Street, had the reputation of being a hard case. He was fond of using soldiers' obscenities: usually he came home in the small hours. When he met his friends he had always a good one to tell them and he was always sure to be on to a good thing—that is to say, a likely horse or a likely *artiste*. He was also handy with the mits and sang comic songs. On Sunday nights there would often be a reunion in Mrs. Mooney's front drawing-room. The music-hall *artistes* would oblige; and Sheridan played waltzes and polkas and vamped accompaniments. Polly Mooney, the Madam's daughter, would also sing. She sang:

"I'm a . . . naughty girl.
You needn't sham:
You know I am."

Polly was a slim girl of nineteen; she had light soft hair and a small full mouth. Her eyes, which were grey with a shade of green through them, had a habit of glancing upwards when she spoke with anyone, which made her look like a little perverse madonna. Mrs. Mooney had first sent her daughter to be a typist in a corn-factor's office but, as a disreputable sheriff's man used to come every other day to the office, asking to be allowed to say a word to his daughter, she had taken her daughter home again and set her to do housework. As Polly was very lively the intention was to give her the run of the young men. Besides, young men like to feel that there is a young woman not very far away. Polly, of course, flirted with the young men but Mrs. Mooney, who was a shrewd judge, knew that the young men were only passing the time away: none of them meant business. Things went on so for a long time and Mrs. Mooney began to think of sending Polly back to typewriting when she noticed that something was going on between Polly and one of the young men. She watched the pair and kept her own counsel.

Polly knew that she was being watched, but still her mother's persistent silence could not be misunderstood. There had been no open complicity between mother and daughter, no open understanding but, though people in the house began to talk of the affair, still Mrs. Mooney did not intervene. Polly began to grow a little strange in her manner and the young man was evidently perturbed. At last, when she judged it to be the right moment, Mrs. Mooney intervened. She dealt with moral problems as a cleaver deals with meat: and in this case she had made up her mind.

It was a bright Sunday morning of early summer, promising heat, but with a fresh breeze blowing. All the windows of the boarding house were open and the lace curtains ballooned gently towards the street beneath the raised sashes. The belfry of George's Church sent out constant peals and worshippers, singly or in groups, traversed the little circus before the church, revealing their purpose by their self-contained demeanour no less than by the little volumes in their gloved hands. Breakfast was over in the boarding house and the table of the breakfast-room was covered with plates on which lay yellow streaks of eggs with morsels of bacon-fat and bacon-rind. Mrs. Mooney sat in the straw arm-chair and watched the servant Mary remove the breakfast things. She made Mary collect the crusts and pieces of broken bread to help to make Tuesday's bread-pudding. When the table was cleared, the broken bread collected, the sugar and butter safe under lock and key, she began to reconstruct the interview which she had had the night before with Polly. Things were as she had suspected: she had been frank in her questions and Polly had been frank in her answers. Both had been somewhat awkward, of course. She had been made awkward by her not wishing to receive the news in too cavalier a fashion or to seem to have connived and Polly had been made awkward not merely because allusions of that kind always made her awkward but also because she did not wish it to be thought that in her wise innocence she had divined the intention behind her mother's tolerance.

Mrs. Mooney glanced instinctively at the little gilt clock on the mantel-piece as soon as she had become aware through her revery that the bells of George's Church had stopped ringing. It was seventeen minutes past eleven: she would have lots of time to have the matter out with Mr. Doran and then catch short twelve at Marlborough Street. She was sure she would win. To begin with she had all the weight of social opinion on her side: she was an outraged mother. She had allowed him to live beneath her roof, assuming that he was a man of honour, and he had simply abused her hospitality. He was thirty-four or thirty-five years of age, so that youth could not be pleaded as his excuse; nor could ignorance be his excuse since he was a man who had seen something of the world. He had simply taken advantage of Polly's youth and inexperience: that was evident. The question was: What reparation would he make?

There must be reparation made in such case. It is all very well for the man: he can go his ways as if nothing had happened, having had his moment of pleasure, but the girl has to bear the brunt. Some mothers would be content to patch up such an affair for a sum of money; she had known cases of it. But she would not do so. For her only one reparation could make up for the loss of her daughter's honour: marriage.

She counted all her cards again before sending Mary up to Mr. Doran's room to say that she wished to speak with him. She felt sure she would win. He was a serious young man, not rakish or loud-voiced like the others. If it had been Mr. Sheridan or Mr. Meade or Bantam Lyons her task would have been much harder. She did not think he would face publicity. All the lodgers in the house knew something of the affair; details had been invented by some. Besides, he had been employed for thirteen years in a great Catholic wine-merchant's office and publicity would mean for him, perhaps, the loss of his job. Whereas if he agreed all might be well. She knew he had a good screw for one thing and she suspected he had a bit of stuff put by.

Nearly the half-hour! She stood up and surveyed herself in the pier-glass. The decisive expression of her great florid face satisfied her and she thought of some mothers she knew who could not get their daughters off their hands.

Mr. Doran was very anxious indeed this Sunday morning. He had made two attempts to shave but his hand had been so unsteady that he had been obliged to desist. Three days' reddish beard fringed his jaws and every two or three minutes a mist gathered on his glasses so that he had to take them off and polish them with his pocket-handkerchief. The recollection of his confession of the night before was a cause of acute pain to him; the priest had drawn out every ridiculous detail of the affair and in the end had so magnified his sin that he was almost thankful at being afforded a loophole of reparation. The harm was done. What could he do now but marry her or run away? He could not brazen it out. The affair would be sure to be talked of and his employer would be certain to hear of it. Dublin is such a small city: everyone knows everyone else's business. He felt his heart leap warmly in his throat as he heard in his excited imagination old Mr. Leonard calling out in his rasping voice: "Send Mr. Doran here, please."

All his long years of service gone for nothing! All his industry and diligence thrown away! As a young man he had sown his wild oats, of course; he had boasted of his free-thinking and denied the existence of God to his companions in public-houses. But that was all passed and done with . . . nearly. He still bought a copy of *Reynolds's Newspaper* every week but he attended to his religious duties and for nine-tenths of the year lived a regular life. He had money enough to settle down on; it was not that. But the family would look down on her. First of all there was her disreputable father and then her mother's boarding house was beginning to get a certain fame. He had a notion that he was being had. He could imagine his friends talking of the affair and laughing. She *was* a little vulgar; sometimes she said "I seen" and "If I had've known." But what would grammar matter if he really loved her? He could not make up his mind whether to like her or despise her for what she had done. Of course he had done it too. His instinct urged him to remain free, not to marry. Once you are married you are done for, it said.

While he was sitting helplessly on the side of the bed in shirt and trousers she tapped lightly at his door and entered. She told him all, that she had made a clean breast of it to her mother and that her mother would speak with him that morning. She cried and threw her arms round his neck, saying:

"O Bob! Bob! What am I to do? What am I to do at all?"

She would put an end to herself, she said.

He comforted her feebly, telling her not to cry, that it would be all right, never fear. He felt against his shirt the agitation of her bosom.

It was not altogether his fault that it had happened. He remembered well, with the curious patient memory of the celibate, the first casual caresses her dress, her breath, her fingers had given him. Then late one night as he was undressing for bed she had tapped at his door, timidly. She wanted to relight her candle at his for hers had been blown out by a gust. It was her bath night. She wore a loose open combing jacket of printed flannel. Her white instep shone in the opening of her furry slippers and the blood glowed warmly behind her perfumed skin. From her hands and wrists too as she lit and steadied her candle a faint perfume arose.

On nights when he came in very late it was she who warmed up his dinner. He scarcely knew what he was eating feeling her beside him alone, at night, in the sleeping house. And her thoughtfulness! If the night was anyway cold or wet or windy there was sure to be a little tumbler of punch ready for him. Perhaps they could be happy together. . . .

They used to go upstairs together on tiptoe, each with a candle, and on the third landing exchange reluctant good-nights. They used to kiss. He remembered well her eyes, the touch of her hand and his delirium. . . .

But delirium passes. He echoed her phrase, applying it to himself: *"What am I to do?"* The instinct of the celibate warned him to hold back. But the sin was there; even his sense of honour told him that reparation must be made for such a sin.

While he was sitting with her on the side of the bed Mary came to the door and said that the missus wanted to see him in the parlour. He stood up to put on his coat and waistcoat, more helpless than ever. When he was dressed he went over to her to comfort her. It would be all right, never fear. He left her crying on the bed and moaning softly: *"O my God!"*

Going down the stairs his glasses became so dimmed with moisture that he had to take them off and polish them. He longed to ascend through the roof and fly away to another country where he would never hear again of his trouble, and yet a force pushed him downstairs step by step. The implacable faces of his employer and of the Madam stared upon his discomfiture. On the last flight of stairs he passed Jack Mooney who was coming up from the pantry nursing two bottles of *Bass.* They saluted coldly; and the lover's eyes rested for a second or two on a thick bulldog face and a pair of thick short arms. When he reached the foot of the staircase he glanced up and saw Jack regarding him from the door of the return-room.

Suddenly he remembered the night when one of the music-hall *artistes,* a little blond Londoner, had made a rather free allusion to Polly.

The reunion had been almost broken up on account of Jack's violence. Everyone tried to quiet him. The music-hall *artiste,* a little paler than usual, kept smiling and saying that there was no harm meant: but Jack kept shouting at him that if any fellow tried that sort of a game on with his sister he'd bloody well put his teeth down his throat, so he would.

Polly sat for a little time on the side of the bed, crying. Then she dried her eyes and went over to the looking-glass. She dipped the end of the towel in the water-jug and refreshed her eyes with the cool water. She looked at herself in profile and readjusted a hairpin above her ear. Then she went back to the bed again and sat at the foot. She regarded the pillows for a long time and the sight of them awakened in her mind secret, amiable memories. She rested the nape of her neck against the cool iron bed-rail and fell into a revery. There was no longer any perturbation visible on her face.

She waited on patiently, almost cheerfully, without alarm, her memories gradually giving place to hopes and visions of the future. Her hopes and visions were so intricate that she no longer saw the white pillows on which her gaze was fixed or remembered that she was waiting for anything.

At last she heard her mother calling. She started to her feet and ran to the banisters.

"Polly! Polly!"

"Yes, mamma?"

"Come down, dear. Mr. Doran wants to speak to you."

Then she remembered what she had been waiting for.

BERNARD MALAMUD

The Magic Barrel

Not long ago there lived in uptown New York, in a small, almost meager room, though crowded with books, Leo Finkle, a rabbinical student in the Yeshivah University. Finkle, after six years of study, was to be ordained in June and had been advised by an acquaintance that he might find it easier to win himself a congregation if he were married. Since he had no present prospects of marriage, after two tormented days of turning it over in his mind, he called Pinye Salzman, a marriage broker whose two-line advertisement he had read in the *Forward*.

The matchmaker appeared one night out of the dark fourth-floor hallway of the graystone rooming house where Finkle lived, grasping a black, strapped portfolio that had been worn thin with use. Salzman, who had been long in the business, was of slight but dignified build, wearing an old hat, and an overcoat too short and tight for him. He smelled frankly of fish, which he loved to eat, and although he was missing a few teeth, his presence was not displeasing, because of an amiable manner curiously contrasted with mournful eyes. His voice, his lips, his wisp of beard, his bony fingers were animated, but give him a moment of repose and his mild blue eyes revealed a depth of sadness, a characteristic that put Leo a little at ease although the situation, for him, was inherently tense.

He at once informed Salzman why he had asked him to come, explaining that his home was in Cleveland, and that but for his parents, who had married comparatively late in life, he was alone in the world. He had for six years devoted himself almost entirely to his studies, as a result of which, understandably, he had found himself without time for a social life and the company of young women. Therefore he thought it the better part of trial and error—of embarrassing fumbling—to call in an experienced person to advise him on these matters. He remarked in passing that the function of the marriage broker was ancient and honorable, highly approved in the Jewish community, because it made practical the necessary without hindering joy. Moreover, his own parents had been brought together by a matchmaker. They had made, if not a financially profitable marriage—since neither had possessed any worldly goods to speak of—at least a successful one in the sense of their everlasting devotion to each other. Salzman listened in embarrassed surprise, sensing a sort of apology. Later, however, he experienced a glow of pride in his work, an emotion that had left him years ago, and he heartily approved of Finkle.

The two went to their business. Leo had led Salzman to the only clear place in the room, a table near a window that overlooked the lamp-lit city. He seated himself at the matchmaker's side but facing him, attempting by an act of will to suppress the unpleasant tickle in his throat. Salzman eagerly unstrapped his portfolio and removed a loose rubber band from a thin packet of much-handled cards. As he flipped through them, a gesture and sound that physically hurt Leo, the student pretended not to see and gazed steadfastly out the window. Although it was still February, winter was on its last legs, signs of which he had for the first time in years begun to notice. He now observed the round white moon, moving high in the sky through a cloud menagerie, and watched with half-open mouth as it penetrated a huge hen, and dropped out of her like an egg laying itself. Salzman, though pretending through eyeglasses he had just slipped on, to be engaged in scanning the writing on the cards, stole occasional glances at the young man's distinguished face, noting with pleasure the long, severe scholar's nose, brown eyes heavy with learning, sensitive yet ascetic lips, and a certain, almost hollow quality of the dark cheeks. He gazed around at shelves upon shelves of books and let out a soft, contented sigh.

When Leo's eyes fell upon the cards, he counted six spread out in Salzman's hand.

"So few?" he asked in disappointment.

"You wouldn't believe me how much cards I got in my office," Salzman replied. "The drawers are already filled to the top, so I keep them now in a barrel, but is every girl good for a new rabbi?"

Leo blushed at this, regretting all he had revealed of himself in a curriculum vitae he had sent to Salzman. He had thought it best to acquaint him with his strict standards and specifications, but in having done so, felt he had told the marriage broker more than was absolutely necessary.

He hesitantly inquired, "Do you keep photographs of your clients on file?"

"First comes family, amount of dowry, also what kind promises," Salzman replied, unbuttoning his tight coat and settling himself in the chair. "After comes pictures, rabbi."

"Call me Mr. Finkle. I'm not yet a rabbi."

Salzman said he would, but instead called him doctor, which he changed to rabbi when Leo was not listening too attentively.

Salzman adjusted his horn-rimmed spectacles, gently cleared his throat and read in an eager voice the contents of the top card:

"Sophie P. Twenty four years. Widow one year. No children. Educated high school and two years college. Father promises eight thousand dollars. Has wonderful wholesale business. Also real estate. On the mother's side comes teachers, also one actor. Well known on Second Avenue."

Leo gazed up in surprise. "Did you say a widow?"

"A widow don't mean spoiled, rabbi. She lived with her husband maybe four months. He was a sick boy she made a mistake to marry him."

"Marrying a widow has never entered my mind."

"This is because you have no experience. A widow, especially if she is young and healthy like this girl, is a wonderful person to marry. She will be thankful to you the rest of her life. Believe me, if I was looking now for a bride, I would marry a widow."

Leo reflected, then shook his head.

Salzman hunched his shoulders in an almost imperceptible gesture of disappointment. He placed the card down on the wooden table and began to read another:

"Lily H. High school teacher. Regular. Not a substitute. Has savings and new Dodge car. Lived in Paris one year. Father is successful dentist thirty-five years. Interested in professional man. Well Americanized family. Wonderful opportunity."

"I knew her personally," said Salzman. "I wish you could see this girl. She is a doll. Also very intelligent. All day you could talk to her about books and theater and what not. She also knows current events."

"I don't believe you mentioned her age?"

"Her age?" Salzman said, raising his brows. "Her age is thirty-two years."

Leo said after a while, 'I'm afraid that seems a little too old."

Salzman let out a laugh. "So how old are you, rabbi?"

"Twenty-seven."

"So what is the difference, tell me, between twenty-seven and thirty-two? My own wife is seven years older than me. So what did I suffer?—Nothing. If Rothschild's daughter wants to marry you, would you say on account her age, no?"

"Yes," Leo said dryly.

Salzman shook off the no in the yes. "Five years don't mean a thing. I give you my word that when you will live with her for one week you will forget her age. What does it mean five years—that she lived more and knows more than somebody who is younger? On this girl, God bless her, years are not wasted. Each one that it comes makes better the bargain."

"What subject does she teach in high school?"

"Languages. If you heard the way she speaks French, you will think it is music. I am in the business twenty-five years, and I recommend her with my whole heart. Believe me, I know what I'm talking, rabbi."

"What's on the next card?" Leo said abruptly.

Salzman reluctantly turned up the third card:

"Ruth K. Nineteen years. Honor student. Father offers thirteen thousand cash to the right bridegroom. He is a medical doctor. Stomach specialist with marvelous practice. Brother-in-law owns own garment business. Particular people."

Salzman looked as if he had read his trump card.

"Did you say nineteen?" Leo asked with interest.

"On the dot."

"Is she attractive?" He blushed. "Pretty?"

Salzman kissed his finger tips. "A little doll. On this I give you my word. Let me call the father tonight and you will see what means pretty."

But Leo was troubled. "You're sure she's that young?"

"This I am positive. The father will show you the birth certificate."

"Are you positive there isn't something wrong with her?" Leo insisted.

"Who says there is wrong?"

"I don't understand why an American girl her age should go to a marriage broker."

A smile spread over Salzman's face.

"So for the same reason you went, she comes."

Leo flushed. "I am pressed for time."

Salzman, realizing he had been tactless, quickly explained. "The father came, not her. He wants she should have the best, so he looks around himself. When we will locate the right boy he will introduce him and encourage. This makes a better marriage than if a young girl without experience takes for herself. I don't have to tell you this."

"But don't you think this young girl believes in love?" Leo spoke uneasily.

Salzman was about to guffaw but caught himself and said soberly, "Love comes with the right person, not before."

Leo parted dry lips but did not speak. Noticing that Salzman had snatched a glance at the next card, he cleverly asked, "How is her health?"

"Perfect," Salzman said, breathing with difficulty. "Of course, she is a little lame on her right foot from an auto accident that it happened to her when she was twelve years, but nobody notices on account she is so brilliant and also beautiful."

Leo got up heavily and went to the window. He felt curiously bitter and upbraided himself for having called in the marriage broker. Finally, he shook his head.

"Why not?" Salzman persisted, the pitch of his voice rising.

"Because I detest stomach specialists."

"So what do you care what is his business? After you marry her do you need him? Who says he must come every Friday night in your house?"

Ashamed of the way the talk was going, Leo dismissed Salzman, who went home with heavy, melancholy eyes.

Though he had felt only relief at the marriage broker's departure, Leo was in low spirits the next day. He explained it as arising from Salzman's failure to produce a suitable bride for him. He did not care for his type of clientele. But when Leo found himself hesitating whether to seek out another matchmaker, one more polished than Pinye, he wondered if it could be—his protestations to the contrary, and although he honored his father and mother—that he did not, in essence, care for the matchmaking institution? This thought he quickly put out of mind yet found himself still upset. All day he ran around in the woods—missed an important appointment, forgot to give out his laundry, walked out of a Broadway cafeteria without paying and had to run back with the ticket in his hand; had even not recognized his landlady in the street when she passed with a friend and courteously called out, "A good evening to you, Doctor Finkle." By nightfall, however, he had regained sufficient calm to sink his nose into a book and there found peace from his thoughts.

Almost at once there came a knock on the door. Before Leo could say enter, Salzman, commercial cupid, was standing in the room. His face was gray and meager, his expression hungry, and he looked as if he would expire on his feet. Yet the marriage broker managed, by some trick of the muscles, to display a broad smile.

"So good evening. I am invited?"

Leo nodded, disturbed to see him again, yet unwilling to ask the man to leave.

Beaming still, Salzman laid his portfolio on the table. "Rabbi, I got for you tonight good news."

"I've asked you not to call me rabbi. I'm still a student."

"Your worries are finished. I have for you a first-class bride."

"Leave me in peace concerning this subject." Leo pretended lack of interest.

"The world will dance at your wedding."

"Please, Mr. Salzman, no more."

"But first must come back my strength," Salzman said weakly. He fumbled with the portfolio straps and took out of the leather case an oily paper bag, from which he extracted a hard, seeded roll and a small, smoked white fish. With a quick motion of his hand he stripped the fish out of its skin and began ravenously to chew. "All day in a rush," he muttered.

Leo watched him eat.

"A sliced tomato you have maybe?" Salzman hesitantly inquired.

"No."

The marriage broker shut his eyes and ate. When he had finished he carefully cleaned up the crumbs and rolled up the remains of the fish, in the paper bag. His spectacled eyes roamed the room until he discovered, amid some piles of books, a one-burner gas stove. Lifting his hat he humbly asked, "A glass of tea you got, rabbi?"

Conscience-stricken, Leo rose and brewed the tea. He served it with a chunk of lemon and two cubes of lump sugar, delighting Salzman.

After he had drunk his tea, Salzman's strength and good spirits were restored.

"So tell me, rabbi," he said amiably, "you considered some more the three clients I mentioned yesterday?"

"There was no need to consider."

"Why not?"

"None of them suits me."

"What then suits you?"

Leo let it pass because he could give only a confused answer.

Without waiting for a reply, Salzman asked, "You remember this girl I talked to you—the high school teacher?"

"Age thirty-two?"

But, surprisingly, Salzman's face lit in a smile. "Age twenty-nine."

Leo shot him a look. "Reduced from thirty-two?"

"A mistake," Salzman avowed. "I talked today with the dentist. He took me to his safety deposit box and showed me the birth certificate. She was twenty-nine years last August. They made her a party in the mountains where she went for her vacation. When her father spoke to me the first time I forgot to write the age and I told you thirty-two, but now I remember this was a different client, a widow."

"The same one you told me about? I thought she was twenty-four?"

"A different. Am I responsible that the world is filled with widows?"

"No, but I'm not interested in them, nor for that matter, in school teachers."

Salzman pulled his clasped hands to his breast. Looking at the ceiling he devoutly exclaimed, "Yiddishe kinder, what can I say to somebody that he is not interested in high school teachers? So what then you are interested?"

Leo flushed but controlled himself.

"In what else will you be interested," Salzman went on, "if you not interested in this fine girl that she speaks four languages and has personally in the bank ten thousand dollars? Also her father guarantees futher twelve thousand. Also, she has a new car, wonderful clothes, talks on all subjects, and she will give you a first-class home and children. How near do we come in our life to paradise?"

"If she's so wonderful, why wasn't she married ten years ago?"

"Why?" said Salzman with a heavy laugh. "—Why? Because she is *partikiler*. This is why. She wants the *best*."

Leo was silent, amused at how he had entangled himself. But Salzman had aroused his interest in Lily H., and he began seriously to consider calling on her. When the marriage broker observed how intently Leo's mind was at work on the facts he had supplied, he felt certain they would soon come to an agreement.

Late Saturday afternoon, conscious of Salzman, Leo Finkle walked with Lily Hirschorn along Riverside Drive. He walked briskly and erectly, wearing with distinction the black fedora he had that morning taken with trepidation out of the dusty hat box on his closet shelf, and the heavy black Saturday coat he had thoroughly whisked clean. Leo also owned a walking stick, a present from a distant relative, but quickly put temptation aside and did not use it. Lily, petite and not unpretty, had on something signifying the approach of spring. She was au courant, animatedly, with all sorts of subjects, and he weighed her words and found her surprisingly sound—score another for Salzman, whom he uneasily sensed to be somewhere around, hiding perhaps high in a tree along the street, flashing the lady signals with a pocket mirror; or perhaps a cloven-hoofed Pan, piping nuptial ditties as he danced his invisible way before them, strewing wild buds on the walk and purple grapes in their path, symbolizing fruit of a union, though there was of course still none.

Lily startled Leo by remarking, "I was thinking of Mr. Salzman, a curious figure, wouldn't you say?"

Not certain what to answer, he nodded.

She bravely went on, blushing, "I for one am grateful for his introducing us. Aren't you?"

He courteously replied, "I am."

"I mean," she said with a little laugh—and it was all in good taste, or at least gave the effect of being not in bad—"do you mind that we came together so?"

He was not displeased with her honesty, recognizing that she meant to set the relationship aright, and understanding that it took a certain amount of experience in life, and courage, to want to do it quite that way. One had to have some sort of past to make that kind of beginning.

He said that he did not mind. Salzman's function was traditional and honorable—valuable for what it might achieve, which, he pointed out, was frequently nothing.

Lily agreed with a sigh. They walked on for a while and she said after a long silence, again with a nervous laugh, "Would you mind if I asked you something a little bit personal? Frankly, I find the subject fascinating." Although Leo shrugged, she went on half embarrassedly, "How was it that you came to your calling? I mean was it a sudden passionate inspiration?"

Leo, after a time, slowly replied, "I was always interested in the Law."

"You saw revealed in it the presence of the Highest?"

He nodded and changed the subject. "I understand that you spent a little time in Paris, Miss Hirschorn?"

"Oh, did Mr. Salzman tell you, Rabbi Finkle?" Leo winced but she went on, "It was ages ago and almost forgotten. I remember I had to return for my sister's wedding."

And Lily would not be put off. "When," she asked in a trembly voice, "did you become enamored of God?"

He stared at her. Then it came to him that she was talking not about Leo Finkle, but of a total stranger, some mystical figure, perhaps even passionate prophet that Salzman had dreamed up for her—no relation to the living or dead. Leo trembled with rage and weakness. The trickster had obviously sold her a bill of goods, just as he had him, who'd expected to become acquainted with a young lady of twenty-nine, only to behold, the moment he laid eyes upon her strained and anxious face, a woman past thirty-five and aging rapidly. Only his self control had kept him this long in her presence.

"I am not," he said gravely, "a talented religious person," and in seeking words to go on, found himself possessed by shame and fear. "I think," he said in a strained manner, "that I came to God not because I loved Him, but because I did not."

This confession he spoke harshly because its unexpectedness shook him.

Lily wilted. Leo saw a profusion of loaves of bread go flying like ducks high over his head, not unlike the winged loaves by which he had counted himself to sleep last night. Mercifully, then, it snowed, which he would not put past Salzman's machinations.

He was infuriated with the marriage broker and swore he would throw him out of the room the minute he reappeared. But Salzman did not come that night, and when Leo's anger had subsided, an unaccountable despair grew in its place. At first he thought this was caused by his disappointment in Lily, but before long it became evident that he had involved himself with Salzman without a true knowledge of his own intent. He gradually realized—with an emptiness that seized him with six hands—that he had called in the broker to find him a bride because he was incapable of doing it himself. This terrifying insight he had derived as a result of his meeting and conversation with Lily Hirschorn. Her probing questions had somehow irritated him into revealing—to himself more than her—the true nature of his relationship to God, and from that it had come upon him, with shocking force, that apart from his parents, he had never loved anyone. Or perhaps it went the other way, that he did not love God so well as he might, because he had not loved man. It seemed to Leo that his whole life stood starkly revealed and he saw himself for the first time as he truly was—unloved and loveless. This bitter but somehow not fully unexpected revelation brought him to a point of panic, controlled only by extraordinary effort. He covered his face with his hands and cried.

The week that followed was the worst of his life. He did not eat and lost weight. His beard darkened and grew ragged. He stopped attending seminars and almost never opened a book. He seriously considered leaving the Yeshivah, although he was deeply troubled at the thought of the loss of all his years of study—saw them like pages torn from a book, strewn over the city—and at the devastating effect of this decision upon his parents. But he had lived without knowledge of himself, and never in the Five Books and all the Commentaries—mea culpa—had the truth been revealed to him. He did not know where to turn, and in all this desolating loneliness there was no *to whom*, although he often thought of Lily but not once could bring himself to go downstairs and make the call. He became touchy and irritable, expecially with his landlady, who asked him all manner of personal questions; on the other hand, sensing his own disagreeableness, he waylaid her on the stairs and apologized abjectly, until mortified, she ran from him. Out of this, however, he drew the consolation that he was a Jew and that a Jew suffered. But gradually, as the long and terrible week drew to a close, he regained his composure and some idea of purpose in life: to go on as planned. Although he was imperfect, the idea was not. As for his quest of a bride, the thought of continuing afflicted him with anxiety and heartburn, yet perhaps with this new knowledge of himself he would be more successful than in the past. Perhaps love would now come to him and a bride to that love. And for this sanctified seeking who needed a Salzman?

The marriage broker, a skeleton with haunted eyes, returned that very night. He looked, withal, the picture of frustrated expectancy—as if he had steadfastly waited the week at Miss Lily Hirschorn's side for a telephone call that never came.

Casually coughing, Salzman came immediately to the point: "So how did you like her?"

Leo's anger rose and he could not refrain from chiding the matchmaker: "Why did you lie to me, Salzman?"

Salzman's pale face went dead white, the world had snowed on him.

"Did you not state that she was twenty-nine?" Leo insisted.

"I give you my word—"

"She was thirty-five, if a day. *At least* thirty-five."

"Of this don't be too sure. Her father told me—"

"Never mind. The worst of it was that you lied to her."

"How did I lie to her, tell me?"

"You told her things about me that weren't true. You made me out to be more, consequently less than I am. She had in mind a totally different person, a sort of semi-mystical Wonder Rabbi."

"All I said, you was a religious man."

"I can imagine."

Salzman sighed. "This is my weakness that I have," he confessed. "My wife says to me I shouldn't be a salesman, but when I have two fine people that they would be wonderful to be married, I am so happy that I talk too much." He smiled wanly. "This is why Salzman is a poor man."

Leo's anger left him. "Well, Salzman, I'm afraid that's all."

The marriage broker fastened hungry eyes on him.

"You don't want any more a bride?"

"I do," said Leo, "but I have decided to seek her in a different way. I am no longer interested in an arranged marriage. To be frank, I now admit the necessity of premarital love. That is, I want to be in love with the one I marry."

"Love?" said Salzman, astounded. After a moment he remarked, "For us, our love is our life, not for the ladies. In the ghetto they—"

"I know, I know," said Leo. "I've thought of it often. Love, I have said to myself, should be a by-product of living and worship rather than its own end. Yet for myself I find it necessary to establish the level of my need and fulfill it."

Salzman shrugged but answered, "Listen, rabbi, if you want love, this I can find for you also. I have such beautiful clients that you will love them the minute your eyes will see them."

Leo smiled unhappily. "I'm afraid you don't understand."

But Salzman hastily unstrapped his portfolio and withdrew a manila packet from it.

"Pictures," he said, quickly laying the envelope on the table.

Leo called after him to take the pictures away, but as if on the wings of the wind, Salzman had disappeared.

March came. Leo had returned to his regular routine. Although he felt not quite himself yet—lacked energy— he was making plans for a more active social life. Of course it would cost something, but he was an expert in cutting corners; and when there were no corners left he would make circles rounder. All the while Salzman's pictures had lain on the table, gathering dust. Occasionally as Leo sat studying, or enjoying a cup of tea, his eyes fell on the manila envelope, but he never opened it.

The days went by and no social life to speak of developed with a member of the opposite sex—it was difficult, given the circumstances of his situation. One morning Leo toiled up the stairs to his room and stared out the window at the city. Although the day was bright his view of it was dark. For some time he watched the people in the street below hurrying along and then turned with a heavy heart to his little room. On the table was the packet. With a sudden relentless gesture he tore it open. For a half-hour he stood by the table in a state of excitement, examining the photographs of the ladies Salzman had included. Finally, with a deep sigh he put them down. There were six, of varying degrees of attractiveness, but look at them long enough and they all became Lily Hirschorn: all past their prime, all starved behind bright smiles, not a true personality in the lot. Life, despite their frantic yoohooings, had passed them by; they were pictures in a brief case that stank of fish. After a while, however, as Leo attempted to return the photographs into the envelope, he found in it another, a snapshot of the type taken by a machine for a quarter. He gazed at it a moment and let out a cry.

Her face deeply moved him. Why, he could at first not say. It gave him the impression of youth—spring flowers, yet age—a sense of having been used to the bone, wasted; this came from the eyes, which were hauntingly familiar, yet absolutely strange. He had a vivid impression that he had met her before, but try as he might he could not place her although he could almost recall her name, as if he had read it in her own handwriting. No, this couldn't be; he would have remembered her. It was not, he affirmed, that she had an extraordinary beauty—no, though her face was attractive enough; it was that *something* about her moved him. Feature for feature, even some of the ladies of the photographs could do better; but she leaped forth to his heart—had *lived*, or wanted to—more than just wanted, perhaps regretted how she had lived—had somehow deeply suffered: it could be seen in the depths of those reluctant eyes, from the way the light enclosed and shone from her, and within her, opening realms of possibility: this was her own. Her he desired. His head ached and eyes narrowed with the intensity of his gazing, then as if an obscure fog had blown up in the mind, he experienced fear of her and was aware that he had received an impression, somehow, of evil. He shuddered, saying softly, it is thus with us all. Leo brewed some tea in a small pot and sat sipping it without sugar, to calm himself. But before he had finished drinking, again with excitement he examined the face and found it good: good for Leo Finkle. Only such a one could understand him and help him seek whatever he was seeking. She might, perhaps, love him. How she had happened to be among the discards in Salzman's barrel he could never guess, but he knew he must urgently go find her.

Leo rushed downstairs, grabbed up the Bronx telephone book, and searched for Salzman's home address. He was not listed nor was his office. Neither was he in the Manhattan book. But Leo remembered having written down the address on a slip of paper after he had read Salzman's advertisement in the "personals" column of the *Forward.* He ran up to his room and tore through his papers, without luck. It was exasperating. Just when he needed the matchmaker he was nowhere to be found. Fortunately Leo remembered to look in his wallet. There on a card he found his name written and a Bronx address. No phone number was listed, the reason—Leo now recalled—he had originally communicated with Salzman by letter. He got on his coat, put a hat on over his skull cap and hurried to the subway station. All the way to the far end of the Bronx he sat on the edge of his seat. He was more than once tempted to take out the picture and see if the girl's face was as he remembered it, but he refrained, allowing the snapshot to remain in his inside coat pocket, content to have her so close. When the train pulled into the station he was waiting at the door and bolted out. He quickly located the street Salzman had advertised.

The building he sought was less than a block from the subway, but it was not an office building, nor even a loft, nor a store in which one could rent office space. It was a very old tenement house. Leo found Salzman's name in pencil on a soiled tag under the bell and climbed three dark flights to his apartment. When he knocked, the door was opened by a thin, asthmatic, gray-haired woman, in felt slippers.

"Yes?" she said, expecting nothing. She listened without listening. He could have sworn he had seen her, too, before but knew it was an illusion.

"Salzman—does he live here? Pinye Salzman," he said, "the matchmaker?"

She stared at him a long minute. "Of course."

He felt embarrassed. "Is he in?"

"No." Her mouth, though left open, offered nothing more.

"The matter is urgent. Can you tell me where his office is?"

"In the air." She pointed upward.

"You mean he has no office?" Leo asked.

"In his socks."

He peered into the apartment. It was sunless and dingy, one large room divided by a half-open curtain, beyond which he could see a sagging metal bed. The near side of the room was crowded with rickety chairs, old bureaus, a three-legged table, racks of cooking utensils, and all the apparatus of a kitchen. But there was no sign of Salzman or his magic barrel, probably also a figment of the imagination. An odor of frying fish made Leo weak to the knees.

"Where is he?" he insisted. "I've got to see your husband."

At length she answered, "So who knows where he is? Every time he thinks a new thought he runs to a different place. Go home, he will find you."

"Tell him Leo Finkle."

She gave no sign she had heard.

He walked downstairs, depressed.

But Salzman, breathless, stood waiting at his door.

Leo was astounded and overjoyed. "How did you get here before me?"

"I rushed."

"Come inside."

They entered. Leo fixed tea, and a sardine sandwich for Salzman. As they were drinking he reached behind him for the packet of pictures and handed them to the marriage broker.

Salzman put down his glass and said expectantly, "You found somebody you like?"

"Not among these."

The marriage broker turned away.

"Here is the one I want." Leo held forth the snapshot.

Salzman slipped on his glasses and took the picture into his trembling hand. He turned ghastly and let out a groan.

"What's the matter?" cried Leo.

"Excuse me. Was an accident this picture. She isn't for you."

Salzman frantically shoved the manila packet into his portfolio. He thrust the snapshot into his pocket and fled down the stairs.

Leo, after momentary paralysis, gave chase and cornered the marriage broker in the vestibule. The landlady made hysterical outcries but neither of them listened.

"Give me back the picture, Salzman."

"No." The pain in his eyes was terrible.

"Tell me who she is then."

"This I can't tell you. Excuse me."

He made to depart, but Leo, forgetting himself, seized the matchmaker by his tight coat and shook him frenziedly.

"Please," sighed Salzman. *"Please."*

Leo ashamedly let him go. "Tell me who she is," he begged. "It's very important for me to know."

"She is not for you. She is a wild one—wild, without shame. This is not a bride for a rabbi."

"What do you mean wild?"

"Like an animal. Like a dog. For her to be poor was a sin. This is why to me she is dead now."

"In God's name, what do you mean?"

"Her I can't introduce to you," Salzman cried.

"Why are you so excited?"

"Why, he asks," Salzman said, bursting into tears. "This is my baby, my Stella, she should burn in hell."

Leo hurried up to bed and hid under the covers. Under the covers he thought his life through. Although he soon fell asleep he could not sleep her out of his mind. He woke, beating his breast. Though he prayed to be rid of her, his prayers went unanswered. Through days of torment he endlessly struggled not to love her; fearing success, he escaped it. He then concluded to covert her to goodness, himself to God. The idea alternately nauseated and exalted him.

He perhaps did not know that he had come to a final decision until he encounted Salzman in a Broadway cafeteria. He was sitting alone at a rear table, sucking the bony remains of a fish. The marriage broker appeared haggard, and transparent to the point of vanishing.

Salzman looked up at first without recognizing him. Leo had grown a pointed beard and his eyes were weighted with wisdom.

"Salzman," he said, "love has at last come to my heart."

"Who can love from a picture?" mocked the marriage broker.

"It is not impossible."

"If you can love her, then you can love anybody. Let me show you some new clients that they just sent me their photographs. One is a little doll."

"Just her I want," Leo murmured.

"Don't be a fool, doctor. Don't bother with her."

"Put me in touch with her, Salzman," Leo said humbly. "Perhaps I can be of service."

Salzman had stopped eating and Leo understood with emotion that it was now arranged.

Leaving the cafeteria, he was, however, afflicted by a tormenting suspicion that Salzman had planned it all to happen this way.

Leo was informed by letter that she would meet him on a certain corner, and she was there one spring night, waiting under a street lamp. He appeared, carrying a small bouquet of violets and rosebuds. Stella stood by the lamp post, smoking. She wore white with red shoes, which fitted his expectations, although in a troubled moment he had imagined the dress red, and only the shoes white. She waited uneasily and shyly. From afar he saw that her eyes—clearly her father's—were filled with desperate innocence. He pictured, in her, his own redemption. Violins and lit candles revolved in the sky. Leo ran forward with flowers outthrust.

Around the corner, Salzman, leaning against a wall, chanted prayers for the dead.

D. H. LAWRENCE

Wintry Peacock

There was thin, crisp snow on the ground, the sky was blue, the wind very cold, the air clear. Farmers were just turning out the cows for an hour or so in the midday, and the smell of cowsheds was unendurable as I entered Tible. I noticed the ash-twigs up in the sky were pale and luminous, passing into the blue. And then I saw the peacocks. There they were in the road before me, three of them, and tailless, brown, speckled birds, with dark-blue necks and ragged crests. They stepped archly over the filigree snow, and their bodies moved with slow motion, like small, light, flat bottomed boats. I admired them, they were curious. Then a gust of wind caught them, heeled them over as if they were three frail boats, opening their feathers like ragged sails. They hopped and skipped with discomfort, to get out of the draught of the wind. And then, in the lee of the walls, they resumed their arch, wintry motion, light and unballasted now their tails were gone, indifferent. They were indifferent to my presence. I might have touched them. They turned off to the shelter of an open shed.

As I passed the end of the upper house, I saw a young woman just coming out of the back door. I had spoken to her in the summer. She recognized me at once, and waved to me. She was carrying a pail, wearing a white apron that was longer than her preposterously short skirt, and she had on the cotton bonnet. I took off my hat to her and was going on. But she put down her pail and darted with a swift, furtive movement after me.

"Do you mind waiting a minute?" she said. "I'll be out in a minute."

She gave me a slight, odd smile, and ran back. Her face was long and sallow and her nose rather red. But her gloomy black eyes softened caressively to me for a moment, with that momentary humility which makes a man lord of the earth.

I stood in the road, looking at the fluffy, dark-red young cattle that mooed and seemed to bark at me. They seemed happy, frisky cattle, a little impudent, and either determined to go back into the warm shed, or determined not to go back. I could not decide which.

Presently the woman came forward again, her head rather ducked. But she looked up at me and smiled, with that odd, immediate intimacy, something witchlike and impossible.

"Sorry to keep you waiting," she said. "Shall we stand in this cart-shed—it will be more out of the wind."

So we stood among the shafts of the open cart-shed that faced the road. Then she looked down at the ground, a little sideways, and I noticed a small black frown on her brows. She seemed to brood for a moment. Then she looked straight into my eyes, so that I blinked and wanted to turn my face aside. She was searching me for something and her look was too near. The frown was still on her keen, sallow brow.

"Can you speak French?" she asked me abruptly.

"More or less," I replied.

"I was supposed to learn it at school," she said. "But I don't know a word." She ducked her head and laughed, with a slightly ugly grimace and a rolling of her black eyes.

"No good keeping your mind full of scraps," I answered.

But she had turned aside her sallow, long face, and did not hear what I said. Suddenly again she looked at me. She was searching. And at the same time she smiled at me, and her eyes looked softly, darkly, with infinite trustful humility into mine. I was being cajoled.

"Would you mind reading a letter for me, in French," she said, her face immediately black and bitter-looking. She glanced at me, frowning.

"Not at all," I said.

"It's a letter to my husband," she said, still scrutinizing.

I looked at her, and didn't quite realize. She looked too far into me, my wits were gone. She glanced round. Then she looked at me shrewdly. She drew a letter from her pocket, and handed it to me. It was addressed from France to Lance-Corporal Goyte, at Tible. I took out the letter and began to read it, as mere words. "Mon cher Alfred"—it might have been a bit of a torn newspaper. So I followed the script: the trite phrases of a letter from a French-speaking girl to an English soldier. "I think of you always, always. Do you think sometimes of me?" And then I vaguely realized that I was reading a man's private correspondence. And yet, how could one consider these trivial, facile French phrases private! Nothing more trite and vulgar in the world, than such a love-letter—no newspaper more obvious.

Therefore I read with a callous heart the effusions of the Belgian damsel. But then I gathered my attention. For the letter went on, "Notre cher petit bébé—our dear little baby was born a week ago. Almost I died, knowing you were far away, and perhaps forgetting the fruit of our perfect love. But the child comforted me. He has the smiling eyes and virile air of his English father. I pray to the Mother of Jesus to send me the dear father of my child, that I may see him with my child in his arms, and that we may be united in holy family love. Ah, my Alfred, can I tell you how I miss you, how I weep for you. My thoughts are with you always, I think of nothing but you, I live for nothing but you and our dear baby. If you do not come back to me soon, I shall die, and our child will die. But no, you cannot come back to me. But I can come to you, come to England with our child. If you do not wish to present me to your good mother and father, you can meet me in some town, some city, for I shall be so frightened to be alone in England with my child, and no one to take care of us. Yet I must come to you, I must bring my child, my little Alfred to his father, the big, beautiful Alfred that I love so much. Oh, write and tell me where I shall come. I have some money, I am not a penniless creature. I have money for myself and my dear baby—"

I read to the end. It was signed: "Your very happy and still more unhappy Elise." I suppose I must have been smiling.

"I can see it makes you laugh," said Mrs. Goyte, sardonically. I looked up at her.

"It's a love-letter, I know that," she said. "There's too many 'Alfreds' in it."

"One too many," I said.

"Oh, yes—And what does she say—Eliza? We know her name's Eliza, that's another thing." She grimaced a little, looking up at me with a mocking laugh.

"Where did you get this letter?" I said.

"Postman gave it me last week."

"And is your husband at home?"

"I expect him home to-night. He's been wounded, you know, and we've been applying for him home. He was home about six weeks ago—he's been in Scotland since then. Oh, he was wounded in the leg. Yes, he's all right, a great strapping fellow. But he's lame, he limps a bit. He expects he'll get his discharge—but I don't think he will. We married? We've been married six years—and he joined up the first day of the war. Oh, he thought he'd like the life. He'd been through the South African War. No, he was sick of it, fed up. I'm living with his father and mother—I've no home of my own now. My people had a big farm—over a thousand acres—in Oxfordshire. Not like here—no. Oh, they're very good to me, his father and mother. Oh, yes, they couldn't be better. They think more of me than of their own daughters. But it's not like being in a place of your own, is it? You can't *really* do as you like. No, there's only me and his father and mother at home. Before the war? Oh, he was anything. He's had a good education—but he liked the farming better. Then he was a chauffeur. That's how he knew French. He was driving a gentleman in France for a long time—"

At this point the peacocks came round the corner on a puff of wind.

"Hello, Joey!" she called, and one of the birds came forward, on delicate legs. Its grey speckled back was very elegant, it rolled its full, dark blue neck as it moved to her. She crouched down. "Joey, dear," she said, in an odd, saturnine caressive voice, "you're bound to find me, aren't you?" She put her face forward, and the bird rolled his neck, almost touching her face with his beak, as if kissing her.

"He loves you," I said.

She twisted her face up at me with a laugh.

"Yes," she said, "he loves me, Joey does,"—then, to the bird—"and I love Joey, don't I. I *do* love Joey." And she smoothed his feathers for a moment. Then she rose, saying: "He's an affectionate bird."

I smiled at the roll of her "bir-rrd."

"Oh, yes, he is," she protested. "He came with me from my home seven years ago. Those others are his descendants—but they're not like Joey—*are they, dee-urr?"* Her voice rose at the end with a witch-like cry.

Then she forgot the birds in the cart-shed and turned to business again.

"Won't you read that letter?" she said. "Read it, so that I know what it says."

"It's rather behind his back," I said.

"Oh, never mind him," she cried. "He's been behind my back long enough—all these four years. If he never did no worse things behind my back than I do behind his, he wouldn't have cause to grumble. You read me what it says."

Now I felt a distinct reluctance to do as she bid, and yet I began—" 'My dear Alfred'."

"I guessed that much," she said. "Eliza's dear Alfred." She laughed. "How do you say it in French? *Eliza?"*

I told her, and she repeated the name with great contempt—*Elise.*

"Go on," she said. "You're not reading."

So I began—" 'I have been thinking of you sometimes—have you been thinking of me?—' "

"Of several others as well, beside her, I'll wager," said Mrs. Goyte.

"Probably not," said I, and continued. " 'A dear little baby was born here a week ago. Ah, can I tell you my feelings when I take my darling little brother into my arms—' "

"I'll bet it's *his*," cried Mrs. Goyte.

"No," I said. "It's her mother's."

"Don't you believe it," she cried. "It's a blind. You mark, it's her own right enough—and his."

"No," I said, "it's her mother's. 'He has sweet smiling eyes, but not like your beautiful English eyes—' "

She suddenly struck her hand on her skirt with a wild motion, and bent down, doubled with laughter. Then she rose and covered her face with her hand.

"I'm forced to laugh at the beautiful English eyes," she said.

"Aren't his eyes beautiful?" I asked.

"Oh, yes—*very!* Go on!—*Joey, dear, dee-urr, Joey!"*—this to the peacock.

—"Er—'We miss you very much. We all miss you. We wish you were here to see the darling baby. Ah, Alfred, how happy we were when you stayed with us. We all loved you so much. My mother will call the baby Alfred so that we shall never forget you—' "

"Of course it's his right enough," cried Mrs. Goyte.

"No," I said. "It's the mother's. Er—'My mother is very well. My father came home yesterday—on leave. He is delighted with his son, my little brother, and wishes to have him named after you, because you were so good to us all in that terrible time, which I shall never forget. I must weep now when I think of it. Well, you are far away in England, and perhaps I shall never see you again. How did you find your dear mother and father? I am so happy that your wound is better, and that you can nearly walk—' "

"How did he find his dear *wife?*" cried Mrs. Goyte. "He never told her he had one. Think of taking the poor girl in like that!"

" 'We are so pleased when you write to us. Yet now you are in England you will forget the family you served so well—' "

"A bit too well—eh, *Joey?*" cried the wife.

" 'If it had not been for you we should not be alive now, to grieve and to rejoice in this life, that is so hard for us. But we have recovered some of our losses, and no longer feel the burden of poverty. The little Alfred is a great comfort to me. I hold him to my breast and think of the big, good Alfred, and I weep to think that those times of suffering were perhaps the times of a great happiness that is gone for ever'."

"Oh, but isn't it a shame, to take a poor girl in like that!" cried Mrs. Goyte. "Never to let on that he was married, and raise her hopes—I call it beastly, I do."

"You don't know," I said. "You know how anxious women are to fall in love, wife or no wife. How could he help it, if she was determined to fall in love with him?"

"He could have helped it if he'd wanted."

"Well," I said, "we aren't all heroes."

"Oh, but that's different! The big, good Alfred!—did ever you hear such tommy-rot in your life! Go on—what does she say at the end?"

"Er—'We shall be pleased to hear of your life in England. We all send many kind regards to your good parents. I wish you all happiness for your future days. Your very affectionate and ever-grateful, Elise'."

There was silence for a moment, during which Mrs. Goyte remained with her head dropped, sinister and abstracted. Suddenly she lifted her face, and her eyes flashed.

"Oh, but I call it beastly, I call it mean, to take a girl in like that."

"Nay," I said. "Probably he hasn't taken her in at all. Do you think those French girls are such poor innocent things? I guess she's a great deal more downy than he."

"Oh, he's one of the biggest fools that ever walked," she cried.

"There you are!" said I.

"But it's his child right enough," she said.

"I don't think so," said I.

"I'm sure of it."

"Oh, well," I said, "if you prefer to think that way."

"What other reason has she for writing like that—"

I went out into the road and looked at the cattle.

"Who is this driving the cows?" I said. She too came out.

"It's the boy from the next farm," she said.

"Oh, well," said I, "those Belgian girls! You never know where their letters will end. And, after all, it's his affair—you needn't bother."

"Oh—!" she cried, with rough scorn—"it's not *me* that bothers. But it's the nasty meanness of it—me writing him such loving letters"—she put her hand before her face and laughed malevolently—"and sending him parcels all the time. You bet he fed that gurrl on my parcels—I know he did. It's just like him. I'll bet they laughed together over my letters. I'll bet anything they did—"

"Nay," said I. "He'd burn your letters for fear they'd give him away."

There was a black look on her yellow face. Suddenly a voice was heard calling. She poked her head out of the shed, and answered coolly:

"All right!" Then turning to me: "That's his mother looking after me."

She laughed into my face, witch-like, and we turned down the road.

When I awoke, the morning after this episode, I found the house darkened with deep, soft snow, which had blown against the large west windows, covering them with a screen. I went outside, and saw the valley all white and ghastly below me, the trees beneath black and thin-looking like wire, the rock-faces dark between the glistening shroud, and the sky above sombre, heavy, yellowish-dark, much too heavy for this world below of hollow bluey whiteness figured with black. I felt I was in a valley of the dead. And I sensed I was a prisoner, for the snow was everywhere deep, and drifted in places. So all the morning I remained indoors, looking up the drive at the shrubs so heavily plumed with snow, at the gate-posts raised high with a foot or more of extra whiteness. Or I looked down into the white-and-black valley that was utterly motionless and beyond life, a hollow sarcophagus.

Nothing stirred the whole day—no plume fell off the shrubs, the valley was as abstracted as a grove of death. I looked over at the tiny, half-buried farms away on the bare uplands beyond the valley hollow, and I thought of Tible in the snow, of the black witch-like little Mrs. Goyte. And the snow seemed to lay me bare to influences I wanted to escape.

In the faint glow of the half-clear light that came about four o'clock in the afternoon, I was roused to see a motion in the snow away below, near where the thorn-trees stood very black and dwarfed, like a little savage group, in the dismal white. I watched closely. Yes, there was a flapping and a struggle—a big bird, it must be, labouring in the snow. I wondered. Our biggest birds, in the valley, were the large hawks that often hung flickering opposite my windows, level with me, but high above some prey on the steep valley-side. This was much too big for a hawk—too big for any known bird. I searched in my mind for the largest English wild birds, geese, buzzards.

Still it laboured and strove, then was still, a dark spot, then struggled again. I went out of the house and down the steep slope, at risk of breaking my leg between the rocks. I knew the ground so well—and yet I got well shaken before I drew near the thorn-trees.

Yes, it was a bird. It was Joey. It was the grey-brown peacock with a blue neck. He was snow-wet and spent.

"Joey—Joey, de-urr!" I said, staggering unevenly towards him. He looked so pathetic, rowing and struggling in the snow, too spent to rise, his blue neck stretching out and lying sometimes on the snow, his eye closing and opening quickly, his crest all battered.

"Joey dee-urr!" I said caressingly to him. And at last he lay still, blinking, in the surged and furrowed snow, whilst I came near and touched him, stroked him, gathered him under my arm. He stretched his long, wetted neck away from me as I held him, none the less he was quiet in my arm, too tired, perhaps, to struggle. Still he held his poor, crested head away from me, and seemed sometimes to droop, to wilt, as if he might suddenly die.

He was not so heavy as I expected, yet it was a struggle to get up to the house with him again. We set him down, not too near the fire, and gently wiped him with cloths. He submitted, only now and then stretched his soft neck away from us, avoiding us helplessly. Then we set warm food by him. I put it to his beak, tried to make him eat. But he ignored it. He seemed to be ignorant of what we were doing, recoiled inside himself inexplicably. So we put him in a basket with cloths, and left him crouching oblivious. His food we put near him. The blinds were drawn, the house was warm, it was night. Sometimes he stirred, but mostly he huddled still, leaning his queer crested head on one side. He touched no food, and took no heed of sounds or movements. We talked of brandy or stimulants. But I realized we had best leave him alone.

In the night, however, we heard him thumping about. I got up anxiously with a candle. He had eaten some food, and scattered more, making a mess. And he was perched on the back of a heavy arm-chair. So I concluded he was recovered, or recovering.

The next day was clear, and the snow had frozen, so I decided to carry him back to Tible. He consented, after various flappings, to sit in a big fish-bag with his battered head peeping out with wild uneasiness. And so I set off with him, slithering down into the valley, making good progress down in the pale shadow beside the rushing waters, then climbing painfully up the arrested white valley-side, plumed with clusters of young pine trees, into the paler white radiance of the snowy, upper regions, where the wind cut fine. Joey seemed to watch all the time with wide, anxious, unseeing eye, brilliant and inscrutable. As I drew near to Tible township he stirred violently in the bag, though I do not know if he had recognized the place. Then, as I came to the sheds, he looked sharply from side to side, and stretched his neck out long. I was a little afraid of him. He gave a loud, vehement yell, opening his sinister beak, and I stood still, looking at him as he struggled in the bag, shaken myself by his struggles, yet not thinking to release him.

Mrs. Goyte came darting past the end of the house, her head sticking forward in sharp scrutiny. She saw me, and came forward.

"Have you got Joey!" she cried sharply, as if I were a thief.

I opened the bag, and he flopped out, flapping as if he hated the touch of the snow now. She gathered him up, and put her lips to his beak. She was flushed and handsome, her eyes bright, her hair slack, thick, but more witch-like than ever. She did not speak.

She had been followed by a grey-haired woman with a round, rather sallow face and a slightly hostile bearing.

"Did you bring him with you, then?" she asked sharply. I answered that I had rescued him the previous evening.

From the background slowly approached a slender man with a grey moustache and large patches on his trousers.

"You've got 'im back' gain, ah see," he said to his daughter-in-law. His wife explained how I had found Joey.

"Ah," went on the grey man. "It wor our Alfred scarred him off, back your life. He must'a flyed over t'valley. Tha ma' thank thy stars as 'e wor fun, Maggie. 'E'd a bin froze. They a bit nesh, you know," he concluded to me.

"They are," I answered. "This isn't their country."

"No, it isna," replied Mr. Goyte. He spoke very slowly and deliberately, quietly, as if the soft pedal were always down in his voice. He looked at his daughter-in-law as she crouched, flushed and dark, before the peacock, which would lay its long blue neck for a moment along her lap. In spite of his grey moustache and thin grey hair, the elderly man had a face young and almost delicate, like a young man's. His blue eyes twinkled with some inscrutable source of pleasure, his skin was fine and tender, his nose delicately arched. His grey hair being slightly ruffled, he had a debonair look, as of a youth who is in love.

"We mun tell 'im it's come," he said slowly, and turning he called: "Alfred—Alfred! Wheer's ter gotten to?"

Then he turned again to the group.

"Get up then, Maggie, lass, get up wi' thee. Tha ma'es too much o'th' bod."

A young man approached, wearing rough khaki and knee-breeches. He was Danish-looking, broad at the loins.

"I's come back then," said the father to the son; "leastwise, he's bin browt back, flyed ower the Griff Low."

The son looked at me. He had a devil-may-care bearing, his cap on one side, his hands stuck in the front pockets of his breeches. But he said nothing.

"Shall you come in a minute, Master," said the elderly woman, to me.

"Ay, come in an' ha'e a cup o' tea or summat. You'll do wi' summat, carrin' that bod. Come on, Maggie wench, let's go in."

So we went indoors, into the rather stuffy, overcrowded living room, that was too cosy, and too warm. The son followed last, standing in the doorway. The father talked to me. Maggie put out the tea-cups. The mother went into the dairy again.

"Tha'lt rouse thysen up a bit again, now, Maggie," the father-in-law said—and then to me: " 'ers not bin very bright sin' Alfred come whoam, an' the bod flyed awee. 'E come whoam a Wednesday night, Alfred did. But ay, you knowed, didna yer. Ay, 'e comed 'a Wednesday—an' I reckon there wor a bit of a to-do between 'em, worn't there, Maggie?"

He twinkled maliciously to his daughter-in-law, who was flushed, brilliant and handsome.

"Oh, be quiet, Father. You're wound up, by the sound of you," she said to him, as if crossly. But she could never be cross with him.

" 'Ers got 'er colour back this mornin'," continued the father-in-law slowly. "It's bin heavy weather wi' 'er this last two days. Ay—'er's bin north-east sin 'er seed you a Wednesday."

"Father, do stop talking. You'd wear the leg off an iron pot. I can't think where you've found your tongue, all of a sudden," said Maggie, with caressive sharpness.

"Ah've found it wheer I lost it. Aren't goin' ter come in an' sit thee down, Alfred?"

But Alfred turned and disappeared.

" 'E's got th' monkey on 'is back ower this letter job," said the father secretly to me. "Mother, 'er knows nowt about it. Lot o' tom-foolery, isn't it? Ay! What's good o'makkin' a peak o' trouble over what's far enough off, an' ned niver come no nigher. No—not a smite o' use. That's what I tell'er. 'Er should ta'e no notice on it. Ty, what can y' expect."

The mother came in again, and the talk became general. Maggie flashed her eyes at me from time to time, complacent and satisfied, moving among the men. I paid her little compliments, which she did not seem to hear. She attended to me with a kind of sinister, witch-like graciousness, her dark head ducked between her shoulders, at once humble and powerful. She was happy as a child attending to her father-in-law and to me. But there was something ominous between her eyebrows, as if a dark moth were settled there—and something ominous in her bent, hulking bearing.

She sat on a low stool by the fire, near her father-in-law. Her head was dropped, she seemed in a state of abstraction. From time to time she would suddenly recover, and look up at us, laughing and chatting. Then she would forget again. Yet in her hulked black forgetting she seemed very near to us.

The door having been opened, the peacock came slowly in, prancing calmly. He went near to her and crouched down, coiling his blue neck. She glanced at him, but almost as if she did not observe him. The bird sat silent, seeming to sleep, and the woman also sat hulked and silent, seemingly oblivious. Then once more there was a heavy step, and Alfred entered. He looked at his wife, and he looked at the peacock crouching by her. He stood large in the doorway, his hands stuck in front of him, in his breeches pockets. Nobody spoke. He turned on his heel and went out again.

I rose also to go. Maggie started as if coming to herself.

"Must you go?" she asked, rising and coming near to me, standing in front of me, twisting her head sideways and looking up at me. "Can't you stop a bit longer? We can all be cosy to-day, there's nothing to do out-doors." And she laughed, showing her teeth oddly. She had a long chin.

I said I must go. The peacock uncoiled and coiled again his long blue neck, as he lay on the hearth. Maggie still stood close in front of me, so that I was acutely aware of my waistcoat buttons.

"Oh, well," she said, "you'll come again, won't you? Do come again."

I promised.

"Come to tea one day—yes, do!"

I promised—one day.

The moment I went out of her presence I ceased utterly to exist for her—as utterly as I ceased to exist for Joey. With her curious abstractedness she forgot me again immediately. I knew it as I left her. Yet she seemed almost in physical contact with me while I was with her.

The sky was all pallid again, yellowish. When I went out there was no sun; the snow was blue and cold. I hurried away down the hill, musing on Maggie. The road made a loop down the sharp face of the slope. As I went crunching over the laborious snow I became aware of a figure striding down the steep scarp to intercept me. It was a man with his hands in front of him, half stuck in his breeches pockets, and his shoulders square—a real farmer of the hills; Alfred, of course. He waited for me by the stone fence.

"Excuse me," he said as I came up.

I came to a halt in front of him and looked into his sullen blue eyes. He had a certain odd haughtiness on his brows. But his blue eyes stared insolently at me.

"Do you know anything about a letter—in French—that my wife opened—a letter of mine—?"

"Yes," said I. "She asked me to read it to her."

He looked square at me. He did not know exactly how to feel.

"What was there in it?" he asked.

"Why?" I said. "Don't you know?"

"She makes out she's burnt it," he said.

"Without showing it you?" I asked.

He nodded slightly. He seemed to be meditating as to what line of action he should take. He wanted to know the contents of the letter: he must know: and therefore he must ask me, for evidently his wife had taunted him. At the same time, no doubt, he would like to wreak untold vengeance on my unfortunate person. So he eyed me, and I eyed him, and neither of us spoke. He did not want to repeat his request to me. And yet I only looked at him, and considered.

Suddenly he threw back his head and glanced down the valley. Then he changed his position—he was a horse-soldier. Then he looked at me more confidentially.

"She burnt the blasted thing before I saw it," he said.

"Well," I answered slowly, "she doesn't know herself what was in it."

He continued to watch me narrowly. I grinned to myself.

"I didn't like to read her out what there was in it," I continued.

He suddenly flushed so that the veins in his neck stood out, and he stirred again uncomfortably.

"The Belgian girl said her baby had been born a week ago, and that they were going to call it Alfred," I told him.

He met my eyes. I was grinning. He began to grin, too.

"Good luck to her," he said.

"Best of luck," said I.

"And what did you tell *her*?" he asked.

"That the baby belonged to the old mother—that it was brother to your girl, who was writing to you as a friend of the family."

He stood smiling, with the long, subtle malice of a farmer.

"And did she take it in?" he asked.

"As much as she took anything else."

He stood grinning fixedly. Then he broke into a short laugh.

"Good for *her!*" he exclaimed cryptically.

And then he laughed aloud once more, evidently feeling he had won a big move in his contest with his wife.

"What about the other woman?" I asked.

"Who?"

"Elise."

"Oh"—he shifted uneasily—"she was all right—"

"You'll be getting back to her," I said.

He looked at me. Then he made a grimace with his mouth.

"Not me," he said. "Back your life it's a plant."

"You don't think the *cher petit bébé* is a little Alfred?"

"It might be," he said.

"Only might?"

"Yes—an' there's lots of mites in a pound of cheese." He laughed boisterously but uneasily.

"What did she say, exactly?" he asked.

I began to repeat, as well as I could, the phrases of the letter: "*Mon cher Alfred—Figure-toi comme je suis désolée—*"

He listened with some confusion. When I had finished all I could remember, he said:

"They know how to pitch you out a letter, those Belgian lasses."

"Practice," said I.

"They get plenty," he said.

There was a pause.

"Oh, well," he said. "I've never got that letter, anyhow."

The wind blew fine and keen, in the sunshine, across the snow. I blew my nose and prepared to depart.

"And *she* doesn't know anything?" he continued, jerking his head up the hill in the direction of Tible.

"She knows nothing but what I've said—that is, if she really burnt the letter."

"I believe she burnt it," he said, "for spite. She's a little devil, she is. But I shall have it out with her." His jaw was stubborn and sullen. Then suddenly he turned to me with a new note.

"Why?" he said. "Why didn't you wring that b— peacock's neck—that b— Joey?"

"Why?" I said. "What for?"

"I hate the brute," he said. "I had a shot at him—"

I laughed. He stood and mused.

"Poor little Elise," he murmured.

"Was she small—petite?" I asked. He jerked up his head.

"No," he said. "Rather tall."

"Taller than your wife, I suppose."

Again he looked into my eyes. And then once more he went into a loud burst of laughter that made the still, snow-deserted valley clap again.

"God, it's a knock-out!" he said, thoroughly amused. Then he stood at ease, one foot out, his hands in his breeches pockets, in front of him, his head thrown back, a handsome figure of a man.

"But I'll do that blasted Joey in—" he mused.

I ran down the hill, shouting with laughter.

GROUP FIVE

F. SCOTT FITZGERALD

Winter Dreams

Some of the caddies were poor as sin and lived in one-room houses with a neurasthenic cow in the front yard, but Dexter Green's father owned the second best grocery-store in Black Bear—the best one was "The Hub," patronized by the wealthy people from Sherry Island—and Dexter caddied only for pocket-money.

In the fall when the days became crisp and gray, and the long Minnesota winter shut down like the white lid of a box, Dexter's skis moved over the snow that hid the fairways of the golf course. At these times the country gave him a feeling of profound melancholy—it offended him that the links should lie in enforced fallowness, haunted by ragged sparrows for the long season. It was dreary, too, that on the tees where the gay colors fluttered in summer there were now only the desolate sand-boxes knee-deep in crusted ice. When he crossed the hills the wind blew cold as misery, and if the sun was out he tramped with his eyes squinted up against the hard dimensionless glare.

In April the winter ceased abruptly. The snow ran down into Black Bear Lake scarcely tarrying for the early golfers to brave the season with red and black balls. Without elation, without an interval of moist glory, the cold was gone.

Dexter knew that there was something dismal about this Northern spring, just as he knew there was something gorgeous about the fall. Fall made him clinch his hands and tremble and repeat idiotic sentences to himself, and make brisk abrupt gestures of command to imaginary audiences and armies. October filled him with hope which November raised to a sort of ecstatic triumph, and in this mood the fleeting brilliant impressions of the summer at Sherry Island were ready grist to his mill. He became a golf champion and defeated Mr. T. A. Hedrick in a marvellous match played a hundred times over the fairways of his imagination, a match each detail of which he changed about untiringly—sometimes he won with almost laughable ease, sometimes he came up magnificently from behind. Again, stepping from a Pierce-Arrow automobile, like Mr. Mortimer Jones, he strolled frigidly into the lounge of the Sherry Island Golf Club—or perhaps, surrounded by an admiring crowd, he gave an exhibition of fancy diving from the spring-board of the club raft. . . . Among those who watched him in open-mouthed wonder was Mr. Mortimer Jones.

And one day it came to pass that Mr. Jones—himself and not his ghost—came up to Dexter with tears in his eyes and said that Dexter was the — — best caddy in the club, and wouldn't he decide not to quit if Mr. Jones made it worth his while, because every other — — caddy in the club lost one ball a hole for him—regularly—

"No, sir," said Dexter decisively. "I don't want to caddy any more." Then, after a pause: "I'm too old."

"You're not more than fourteen. Why the devil did you decide just this morning that you wanted to quit? You promised that next week you'd go over to the state tournament with me."

"I decided I was too old."

Dexter handed in his "A Class" badge, collected what money was due him from the caddy master, and walked home to Black Bear Village.

"The best — — caddy I ever saw," shouted Mr. Mortimer Jones over a drink that afternoon. "Never lost a ball! Willing! Intelligent! Quiet! Honest! Grateful!"

The little girl who had done this was eleven—beautifully ugly as little girls are apt to be who are destined after a few years to be inexpressibly lovely and bring no end of misery to a great number of men. The spark, however, was perceptible. There was a general ungodliness in the way her lips twisted down at the corners when she smiled, and in the—Heaven help us!—in the almost passionate quality of her eyes. Vitality is born early in such women. It was utterly in evidence now, shining through her thin frame in a sort of glow.

She had come eagerly out on to the course at nine o'clock with a white linen nurse and five small new golf-clubs in a white canvas bag which the nurse was carrying. When Dexter first saw her she was standing by the caddy house, rather ill at ease and trying to conceal the fact by engaging her nurse in an obviously unnatural conversation graced by startling and irrelevant grimaces from herself.

"Well, it's certainly a nice day, Hilda," Dexter heard her say. She drew down the corners of her mouth, smiled, and glanced furtively around, her eyes in transit falling for an instant on Dexter.

Then to the nurse:

"Well, I guess there aren't very many people out here this morning, are there?"

The smile again—radiant, blatantly artificial—convincing.

"I don't know what we're supposed to do now," said the nurse, looking nowhere in particular.

"Oh, that's all right. I'll fix it up."

Dexter stood perfectly still, his mouth slightly ajar. He knew that if he moved forward a step his stare would be in her line of vision—if he moved backward he would lose his full view of her face. For a moment he had not realized how young she was. Now he remembered having seen her several times the year before—in bloomers.

Suddenly, involuntarily, he laughed, a short abrupt laugh—then, startled by himself, he turned and began to walk quickly away.

"Boy—"

Dexter stopped.

"Boy—"

Beyond question he was addressed. Not only that, but he was treated to that absurd smile, that preposterous smile—the memory of which at least a dozen men were to carry into middle age.

"Boy, do you know where the golf teacher is?"

"He's giving a lesson."

"Well, do you know where the caddy-master is?"

"He isn't here yet this morning."

"Oh." For a moment this baffled her. She stood alternately on her right and left foot.

"We'd like to get a caddy," said the nurse. "Mrs. Mortimer Jones sent us out to play golf, and we don't know how without we get a caddy."

Here she was stopped by an ominous glance from Miss Jones, followed immediately by the smile.

"There aren't any caddies here except me," said Dexter to the nurse, "and I got to stay here in charge until the caddy-master gets here."

"Oh."

Miss Jones and her retinue now withdrew, and at a proper distance from Dexter became involved in a heated conversation, which was concluded by Miss Jones taking one of the clubs and hitting it on the ground with violence. For further emphasis she raised it again and was about to bring it down smartly upon the nurse's bosom, when the nurse seized the club and twisted it from her hands.

"You damn little mean old *thing!*" cried Miss Jones wildly.

Another argument ensued. Realizing that the elements of the comedy were implied in the scene, Dexter several times began to laugh, but each time restrained the laugh before it reached audibility. He could not resist the monstrous conviction that the little girl was justified in beating the nurse.

The situation was resolved by the fortuitous appearance of the caddy-master, who was appealed to immediately by the nurse.

"Miss Jones is to have a little caddy, and this one says he can't go."

"Mr. McKenna said I was to wait here till you came," said Dexter quickly.

"Well, he's here now." Miss Jones smiled cheerfully at the caddy-master. Then she dropped her bag and set off at a haughty mince toward the first tee.

"Well?" The caddy-master turned to Dexter. "What you standing there like a dummy for? Go pick up the young lady's clubs.'"

"I don't think I'll go out to-day," said Dexter.

"You don't—"

"I think I'll quit."

The enormity of his decision frightened him. He was a favorite caddy, and the thirty dollars a month he earned through the summer were not to be made elsewhere around the lake. But he had received a strong emotional shock, and his perturbation required a violent and immediate outlet.

It is not so simple as that, either. As so frequently would be the case in the future, Dexter was unconsciously dictated to by his winter dreams.

II

Now, of course, the quality and the seasonability of these winter dreams varied, but the stuff of them remained. They persuaded Dexter several years later to pass up a business course at the state university—his father, prospering now, would have paid his way—for the precarious advantage of attending an older and more famous university in the East, where he was bothered by his scanty funds. But do not get the impression, because his winter dreams happened to be concerned at first with musings on the rich, that there was anything merely snobbish in the boy. He wanted not association with glittering things and glittering people—he wanted the glittering things themselves. Often he reached out for the best without knowing why he wanted it—and sometimes he ran up against the mysterious denials and prohibitions in which life indulges. It is with one of those denials and not with his career as a whole that this story deals.

He made money. It was rather amazing. After college he went to the city from which Black Bear Lake draws its wealthy patrons. When he was only twenty-three and had been there not quite two years, there were already people who liked to say: "Now *there's* a boy—" All about him rich men's sons were peddling bonds precariously, or investing patrimonies precariously, or plodding through the two dozen volumes of the "George Washington Commercial Course," but Dexter borrowed a thousand dollars on his college degree and his confident mouth, and bought a partnership in a laundry.

It was a small laundry when he went into it, but Dexter made a specialty of learning how the English washed fine woolen golf-stockings without shrinking them, and within a year he was catering to the trade that wore knickerbockers. Men were insisting that their Shetland hose and sweaters go to his laundry, just as they had insisted on a caddy who could find golf-balls. A little later he was doing their wives' lingerie as well—and running five branches in different parts of the city. Before he was twenty-seven he owned the largest string of laundries in his section of the country. It was then that he sold out and went to New York. But the part of his story that concerns us goes back to the days when he was making his first big success.

When he was twenty-three Mr. Hart—one of the gray-haired men who like to say "Now there's a boy"—gave him a guest card to the Sherry Island Golf Club for a week-end. So he signed his name one day on the register, and that afternoon played golf in a foursome with Mr. Hart and Mr. Sandwood and Mr. T. A. Hedrick. He did not consider it necessary to remark that he had once carried Mr. Hart's bag over this same links, and that he knew every trap and gully with his eyes shut—but he found himself glancing at the four caddies who trailed them, trying to catch a gleam or gesture that would remind him of himself, that would lessen the gap which lay between his present and his past.

It was a curious day, slashed abruptly with fleeting, familiar impressions. One minute he had the sense of being a trespasser—in the next he was impressed by the tremendous superiority he felt toward Mr. T. A. Hedrick, who was a bore and not even a good golfer any more.

Then, because of a ball Mr. Hart lost near the fifteenth green, an enormous thing happened. While they were searching the stiff grasses of the rough there was a clear call of "Fore!" from behind a hill in their rear. And as they all turned abruptly from their search a bright new ball sliced abruptly over the hill and caught Mr. T. A. Hedrick in the abdomen.

"By Gad!" cried Mr. T. A. Hedrick, "they ought to put some of these crazy women off the course. It's getting to be outrageous."

A head and a voice came up together over the hill:

"Do you mind if we go through?"

"You hit me in the stomach!" declared Mr. Hedrick wildly.

"Did I?" The girl approached the group of men. "I'm sorry. I yelled 'Fore!' "

Her glance fell casually on each of the men—then scanned the fairway for her ball.

"Did I bounce into the rough?"

It was impossible to determine whether this question was ingenuous or malicious. In a moment, however, she left no doubt, for as her partner came up over the hill she called cheerfully:

"Here I am! I'd have gone on the green except that I hit something."

As she took her stance for a short mashie shot, Dexter looked at her closely. She wore a blue gingham dress, rimmed at throat and shoulders with a white edging that accentuated her tan. The quality of exaggeration, of thinness, which had made her passionate eyes and down-turning mouth absurd at eleven, was gone now. She was arrestingly beautiful. The color in her cheeks was centred like the color in a picture—it was not a "high" color, but a sort of fluctuating and feverish warmth, so shaded that it seemed at any moment it would recede and disappear. This color and the mobility of her mouth gave a continual impression of flux, of intense life, of passionate vitality—balanced only partially by the sad luxury of her eyes.

She swung her mashie impatiently and without interest, pitching the ball into a sand-pit on the other side of the green. With a quick, insincere smile and a careless "Thank you!" she went on after it.

"That Judy Jones!" remarked Mr. Hedrick on the next tee, as they waited—some moments—for her to play on ahead. "All she needs is to be turned up and spanked for six months and then to be married off to an old-fashioned cavalry captain."

"My God, she's good-looking!" said Mr. Sandwood, who was just over thirty.

"Good-looking!" cried Mr. Hedrick contemptuously, "'she always looks as if she wanted to be kissed! Turning those big cow-eyes on every calf in town!"

It was doubtful if Mr. Hedrick intended a reference to the maternal instinct.

"She'd play pretty good golf if she'd try," said Mr. Sandwood.

"She has no form," said Mr. Hedrick solemnly.

"She has a nice figure," said Mr. Sandwood.

"Better thank the Lord she doesn't drive a swifter ball," said Mr. Hart, winking at Dexter.

Later in the afternoon the sun went down with a riotous swirl of gold and varying blues and scarlets, and left the dry, rustling night of Western summer. Dexter watched from the veranda of the Golf Club, watched the even overlap of the waters in the little wind, silver molasses under the harvest-moon. Then the moon held a finger to her lips and the lake became a clear pool, pale and quiet. Dexter put on his bathing-suit and swam out to the farthest raft, where he stretched dripping on the wet canvas of the springboard.

There was a fish jumping and a star shining and the lights around the lake were gleaming. Over on a dark peninsula a piano was playing the songs of last summer and of summers before that—songs from "Chin-Chin" and "The Count of Luxemburg" and "The Chocolate Soldier"—and because the sound of a piano over a stretch of water had always seemed beautiful to Dexter he lay perfectly quiet and listened.

The tune the piano playing at that moment had been gay and new five years before when Dexter was a sophomore at college. They had played it at a prom once when he could not afford the luxury of proms, and he had stood outside the gymnasium and listened. The sound of the tune precipitated in him a sort of ecstasy and it was with that ecstasy he viewed what happened to him now. It was a mood of intense appreciation, a sense that, for once, he was magnificently attune to life and that everything about him was radiating a brightness and a glamour he might never know again.

A low, pale oblong detached itself suddenly from the darkness of the Island, spitting forth the reverberate sound of a racing motorboat. Two white streamers of cleft water rolled themselves out behind it and almost immediately the boat was beside him, drowning out the hot tinkle of the piano in the drone of its spray. Dexter raising himself on his arms was aware of a figure standing at the wheel, of two dark eyes regarding him over the lengthening space of water—then the boat had gone by and was sweeping in an immense and purposeless circle of spray round and round in the middle of the lake. With equal eccentricity one of the circles flattened out and headed back toward the raft.

"Who's that?" she called, shutting off her motor. She was so near now that Dexter could see her bathing-suit, which consisted apparently of pink rompers.

The nose of the boat bumped the raft, and as the latter tilted rakishly he was precipitated toward her. With different degrees of interest they recognized each other.

"Aren't you one of those men we played through this afternoon?" she demanded.

He was.

"Well, do you know how to drive a motor-boat? Because if you do I wish you'd drive this one so I can ride on the surf-board behind. My name is Judy Jones"—she favored him with an absurd smirk—rather, what tried to be a smirk, for, twist her mouth as she might, it was not grotesque, it was merely beautiful—"and I live in a house over there on the Island, and in that house there is a man waiting for me. When he drove up at the door I drove out of the dock because he says I'm his ideal."

There was a fish jumping and a star shining and the lights around the lake were gleaming. Dexter sat beside Judy Jones and she explained how her boat was driven. Then she was in the water, swimming to the floating surfboard with a sinuous crawl. Watching her was without effort to the eye, watching a branch waving or a sea-gull flying. Her arms, burned to butternut, moved sinuously among the dull platinum ripples, elbow appearing first, casting the forearm back with a cadence of falling water, then reaching out and down, stabbing a path ahead.

They moved out into the lake; turning, Dexter saw that she was kneeling on the low rear of the now uptilted surfboard.

"Go faster," she called, "fast as it'll go."

Obediently he jammed the lever forward and the white spray mounted at the bow. When he looked around again the girl was standing up on the rushing board, her arms spread wide, her eyes lifted toward the moon.

"It's awful cold," she shouted. "What's your name?"

He told her.

"Well, why don't you come to dinner to-morrow night?" His heart turned over like a fly-wheel of the boat, and, for the second time, her casual whim gave a new direction to his life.

III

Next evening while he waited for her to come downstairs, Dexter peopled the soft deep summer room and the sun-porch that opened from it with the men who had already loved Judy Jones. He knew the sort of men they were—the men who when he first went to college had entered from the great prep schools with graceful clothes and the deep tan of healthy summers. He had seen that, in one sense, he was better than these men. He was newer and stronger. Yet in acknowledging to himself that he wished his children to be like them he was admitting that he was but the rough, strong stuff from which they eternally sprang.

When the time had come for him to wear good clothers, he had known who were the best tailors in America, and the best tailors in America had made him the suit he wore this evening. He had acquired that particular reserve peculiar to his university, that set it off from other universities. He recognized the value to him of such a mannerism and he had adopted it; he knew that to be careless in dress and manner required more confidence than to be careful. But carelessness was for his children. His mother's name had been Krimelich. She was a Bohemian of the peasant class and she had talked broken English to the end of her days. Her son must keep to the set patterns.

At a little after seven Judy Jones came down-stairs. She wore a blue silk afternoon dress, and he was disappointed at first that she had not put on something more elaborate. This feeling was accentuated when, after a brief greeting, she went to the door of a butler's pantry and pushing it open called: "You can serve dinner, Martha." He had rather expected that a butler would announce dinner, that there would be a cocktail. Then he put these thoughts behind him as they sat down side by side on a lounge and looked at each other.

"Father and mother won't be here," she said thoughtfully.

He remembered the last time he had seen her father, and he was glad the parents were not to be here to-night—they might wonder who he was. He had been born in Keeble, a Minnesota village fifty miles farther north, and he always gave Keeble as his home instead of Black Bear Village. Country towns were well enough to come from if they weren't inconveniently in sight and used as footstools by fashionable lakes.

They talked of his university, which she had visited frequently during the past two years, and of the near-by city which supplied Sherry Island with its patrons, and whither Dexter would return next day to his prospering laundries.

During dinner she slipped into a moody depression which gave Dexter a feeling of uneasiness. Whatever petulance she uttered in her throaty voice worried him. Whatever she smiled at—at him, at a chicken liver, at nothing—it disturbed him that her smile could have no root in mirth, or even in amusement. When the scarlet corners of her lips curved down, it was less a smile than an invitation to a kiss.

Then, after dinner, she led him out on the dark sun-porch and deliberately changed the atmosphere.

"Do you mind if I weep a little?" she said.

"I'm afraid I'm boring you," he responded quickly.

"You're not. I like you. But I've just had a terrible afternoon. There was a man I cared about, and this afternoon he told me out of a clear sky that he was poor as a church-mouse. He'd never even hinted it before. Does this sound horribly mundane?"

"Perhaps he was afraid to tell you."

"Suppose he was," she answered. "He didn't start right. You see, if I'd thought of him as poor—well, I've been mad about loads of poor men, and fully intended to marry them all. But in this case, I hadn't thought of him that way, and my interest in him wasn't strong enough to survive the shock. As if a girl calmly informed her fiancé that she was a widow. He might not object to widows, but—"

"Let's start right," she interrupted herself suddenly. "Who are you, anyhow?"

For a moment Dexter hesitated. Then:

"I'm nobody," he announced. "My career is largely a matter of futures."

"Are you poor?"

"No," he said frankly. "I'm probably making more money than any man my age in the Northwest. I know that's an obnoxious remark, but you advised me to start right."

There was a pause. Then she smiled and the corners of her mouth dropped and an almost imperceptible sway brought her closer to him, looking up into his eyes. A lump rose in Dexter's throat, and he waited breathless for the experiment, facing the unpredictable compound that would form mysteriously from the elements of their lips. Then he saw—she communicated her excitement to him, lavishly, deeply, with kisses that were not a promise but a fulfillment. They aroused in him no hunger demanding renewal but surfeit that would demand more surfeit . . . kisses that were like charity, creating want by holding back nothing at all.

It did not take him many hours to decide that he had wanted Judy Jones ever since he was a proud, desirous little boy.

IV

It began like that—and continued, with varying shades of intensity, on such a note right up to the dénouement. Dexter surrendered a part of himself to the most direct and unprincipled personality with which he had ever come in contact. Whatever Judy wanted, she went after with the full pressure of her charm. There was no divergence of method, no jockeying for position or premeditation of effects—there was a very little mental side to any of her affairs. She simply made men conscious to the highest degree of her physical loveliness. Dexter had no desire to change her. Her deficiencies were knit up with a passionate energy that transcended and justified them.

When, as Judy's head lay against his shoulder that first night, she whispered, "I don't know what's the matter with me. Last night I thought I was in love with a man and to-night I think I'm in love with you—"—it seemed to him a beautiful and romantic thing to say. It was the exquisite excitability that for the moment he controlled and owned. But a week later he was compelled to view this same quality in a different light. She took him in her roadster to a picnic supper, and after supper she disappeared, likewise in her roadster, with another man. Dexter became enormously upset and was scarcely able to be decently civil to the other people present. When she assured him that she had not kissed the other man he knew she was lying—yet he was glad that she had taken the trouble to lie to him.

He was, as he found before the summer ended, one of a varying dozen who circulated about her. Each of them had at one time been favored above all others—about half of them still basked in the solace of occasional sentimental revivals. Whenever one showed signs of dropping out through long neglect, she granted him a brief honeyed hour, which encouraged him to tag along for a year or so longer. Judy made these forays upon the helpless and defeated without malice, indeed half unconscious that there was anything mischievous in what she did.

When a new man came to town every one dropped out—dates were automatically cancelled.

The helpless part of trying to do anything about it was that she did it all herself. She was not a girl who could be "won" in the kinetic sense—she was proof against cleverness, she was proof against charm; if any of these assailed her too strongly she would immediately resolve the affair to a physical basis, and under the magic of her physical splendor the strong as well as the brilliant played her game and not their own. She was entertained only by the gratification of her desires and by the direct exercise of her own charm. Perhaps from so much youthful love, so many youthful lovers, she had come, in self-defense, to nourish herself wholly from within.

Succeeding Dexter's first exhilaration came restlessness and dissatisfaction. The helpless ecstasy of losing himself in her was opiate rather than tonic. It was fortunate for his work during the winter that those moments of ecstasy came infrequently. Early in their acquaintance it had seemed for a while that there was a deep and spontaneous mutual attraction—that first August, for example—three days of long evenings on her dusky veranda, of strange wan kisses through the late afternoon, in shadowy alcoves or behind the protecting trellises of the garden arbors, of mornings when she was fresh as a dream and almost shy at meeting him in the clarity of the rising day. There was all the ecstasy of an engagement about it, sharpened by his realization that there was no engagement. It was during those three days that, for the first time, he had asked her to marry him. She said "maybe some day," she said "kiss me," she said "I'd like to marry you," she said "I love you"—she said—nothing.

The three days were interrupted by the arrival of a New York man who visited at her house for half September. To Dexter's agony, rumor engaged them. The man was the son of the president of a great trust company. But at the end of a month it was reported that Judy was yawning. At a dance one night she sat all evening in a motor-boat with a local beau, while the New Yorker searched the club for her frantically. She told the local beau that she was bored with her visitor, and two days later he left. She was seen with him at the station, and it was reported that he looked very mournful indeed.

On this note the summer ended. Dexter was twenty-four, and he found himself increasingly in a position to do as he wished. He joined two clubs in the city and lived at one of them. Though he was by no means an integral part of the stag-lines at these clubs, he managed to be on hand at dances where Judy Jones was likely to appear. He could have gone out socially as much as he liked—he was an eligible young man, now, and popular with down-town fathers. His confessed devotion to Judy Jones had rather solidified his position. But he had no social aspirations and rather despised the dancing men who were always on tap for the Thursday or Saturday parties and who filled in at dinners with the younger married set. Already he was playing with the idea of going East to New York.

He wanted to take Judy Jones with him. No disillusion as to the world in which she had grown up could cure his illusion as to her desirability.

Remember that—for only in the light of it can what he did for her be understood.

Eighteen months after he first met Judy Jones he became engaged to another girl. Her name was Irene Scheerer, and her father was one of the men who had always believed in Dexter. Irene was light-haired and sweet and honorable, and a little stout, and she had two suitors whom she pleasantly reliquished when Dexter formally asked her to marry him.

Summer, fall, winter, spring, another summer, another fall—so much he had given of his active life to the incorrigible lips of Judy Jones. She had treated him with interest, with encouragement, with malice, with indifference, with contempt. She had inflicted on him the innumerable little slights and indignities possible in such a case—as if in revenge for having ever cared for him at all. She had beckoned him and yawned at him and beckoned him again and he had responded often with bitterness and narrowed eyes. She had brought him ecstatic happiness and intolerable agony of spirit. She had caused him untold inconvenience and not a little trouble. She had insulted him, and she had ridden over him, and she had played his interest in her against his interest in his work—for fun. She had done everything to him except to criticise him—this she had not done—it seemed to him only because it might have sullied the utter indifference she manifested and sincerely felt toward him.

When autumn had come and gone again it occurred to him that he could not have Judy Jones. He had to beat this into his mind but he convinced himself at last. He lay awake at night for a while and argued it over. He told himself the trouble and the pain she had caused him, he enumerated her glaring deficiencies as a wife. Then he said to himself that he loved her, and after a while he fell asleep. For a week, lest he imagine her husky voice over the telephone or her eyes opposite him at lunch, he worked hard and late, and at night he went to his office and plotted out his years.

At the end of a week he went to a dance and cut in on her once. For almost the first time since they had met he did not ask her to sit out with him or tell her that she was lovely. It hurt him that she did not miss these things—that was all. He was not jealous when he saw that there was a new man to-night. He had been hardened against jealousy long before.

He stayed late at the dance. He sat for an hour with Irene Scheerer and talked about books and about music. He knew very little about either. But he was beginning to be master of his own time now, and he had a rather priggish notion that he—the young and already fabulously successful Dexter Green—should know more about such things.

That was in October, when he was twenty-five. In January Dexter and Irene became engaged. It was to be announced in June, and they were to be married three months later.

The Minnesota winter prolonged itself interminably, and it was almost May when the winds came soft and the snow ran down into Black Bear Lake at last. For the first time in over a year Dexter was enjoying a certain tranquillity of spirit. Judy Jones had been in Florida, and afterward in Hot Springs, and somewhere she had been engaged, and somewhere she had broken it off. At first, when Dexter had definitely given her up, it had made him sad that people still linked them together and asked for news of her, but when he began to be placed at dinner next to Irene Scheerer people didn't ask him about her any more—they told him about her. He ceased to be an authority on her.

May at last. Dexter walked the streets at night when the darkness was damp as rain, wondering that so soon, with so little done, so much of ecstasy had gone from him. May one year back had been marked by Judy's poignant, unforgivable, yet forgiven turbulence—it had been one of those rare times when he fancied she had grown to care for him. That old penny's worth of happiness he had spent for this bushel of content. He knew that Irene would be no more than a curtain spread behind him, a hand moving among gleaming teacups, a voice calling to children . . . fire and loveliness were gone, the magic of nights and the wonder of the varying hours and seasons . . . slender lips, down-turning, dropping to his lips and bearing him up into a heaven of eyes. . . . The thing was deep in him. He was too strong and alive for it to die lightly.

In the middle of May when the weather balanced for a few days on the thin bridge that led to deep summer he turned in one night at Irene's house. Their engagement was to be announced in a week now—no one would be surprised at it. And to-night they would sit together on the lounge at the University Club and look on for an hour at the dancers. It gave him a sense of solidity to go with her—she was so sturdily popular, so intensely "great."

He mounted the steps of the brownstone house and stepped inside.

"Irene," he called.

Mrs. Scheerer came out of the living-room to meet him.

"Dexter," she said, "Irene's gone up-stairs with a splitting headache. She wanted to go with you but I made her go to bed."

"Nothing serious, I—"

"Oh, no. She's going to play golf with you in the morning. You can spare her for just one night, can't you, Dexter?"

Her smile was kind. She and Dexter liked each other. In the living-room he talked for a moment before he said good-night.

Returning to the University Club, where he had rooms, he stood in the doorway for a moment and watched the dancers. He leaned against the door-post, nodded at a man or two—yawned.

"Hello, darling."

The familiar voice at his elbow startled him. Judy Jones had left a man and crossed the room to him—Judy Jones, a slender enamelled doll in cloth of gold: gold in a band at her head, gold in two slipper points at her dress's hem. The fragile glow of her face seemed to blossom as she smiled at him. A breeze of warmth and light blew through the room. His hands in the pockets of his dinner-jacket tightened spasmodically. He was filled with a sudden excitement.

"When did you get back?" he asked casually.

"Come here and I'll tell you about it."

She turned and he followed her. She had been away—he could have wept at the wonder of her return. She had passed through enchanted streets, doing things that were like provocative music. All mysterious happenings, all fresh and quickening hopes, had gone away with her, come back with her now.

She turned in the doorway.

"Have you a car here? If you haven't, I have."

"I have a coupé."

In then, with a rustle of golden cloth. He slammed the door. Into so many cars she had stepped—like this—like that—her back against the leather, so—her elbow resting on the door—waiting. She would have been soiled long since had there been anything to soil her—except herself—but this was her own self outpouring.

With an effort he forced himself to start the car and back into the street. This was nothing, he must remember. She had done this before, and he had put her behind him, as he would have crossed a bad account from his books.

He drove slowly down-town and, affecting abstraction, traversed the deserted streets of the business section, peopled here and there where a movie was giving out its crowd or where consumptive or pugilistic youth lounged in front of pool halls. The clink of glasses and the slap of hands on the bars issued from saloons, cloisters of glazed glass and dirty yellow light.

She was watching him closely and the silence was embarrassing, yet in this crisis he could find no casual word with which to profane the hour. At a convenient turning he began to zigzag back toward the University Club.

"Have you missed me?" she asked suddenly.

"Everybody missed you."

He wondered if she knew of Irene Scheerer. She had been back only a day—her absence had been almost contemporaneous with his engagement.

"What a remark!" Judy laughed sadly—without sadness. She looked at him searchingly. He became absorbed in the dashboard.

"You're handsomer than you used to be," she said thoughtfully. "Dexter, you have the most rememberable eyes."

He could have laughed at this, but he did not laugh. It was the sort of thing that was said to sophomores. Yet it stabbed at him.

"I'm awfully tired of everything, darling." She called everyone darling, endowing the endearment with careless, individual camaraderie. "I wish you'd marry me."

The directness of this confused him. He should have told her now that he was going to marry another girl, but he could not tell her. He could as easily have sworn that he had never loved her.

"I think we'd get along," she continued, on the same note, "unless probably you've forgotten me and fallen in love with another girl."

Her confidence was obviously enormous. She had said, in effect, that she found such a thing impossible to believe, that if it were true he had merely committed a childish indiscretion—and probably to show off. She would forgive him, because it was not a matter of any moment but rather something to be brushed aside lightly.

"Of course you could never love anybody but me," she continued, "I like the way you love me. Oh, Dexter, have you forgotten last year?"

"No, I haven't forgotten."

"Neither have I!"

Was she sincerely moved—or was she carried along by the wave of her own acting?

"I wish we could be like that again," she said, and he forced himself to answer:

"I don't think we can."

"I suppose not. . . . I hear you're giving Irene Scheerer a violent rush."

There was not the faintest emphasis on the name, yet Dexter was suddenly ashamed.

"Oh, take me home," cried Judy suddenly; "I don't want to go back to that idiotic dance—with those children."

Then, as he turned up the street that led to the residence district, Judy began to cry quietly to herself. He had never seen her cry before.

The dark street lightened, the dwellings of the rich loomed up around them, he stopped his coupé in front of the great white bulk of the Mortimer Joneses' house, somnolent, gorgeous, drenched with the splendor of the damp moonlight. Its solidity startled him. The strong walls, the steel of the girders, the breadth and beam and pomp of it were there only to bring out the contrast with the young beauty beside him. It was sturdy to accentuate her slightness—as if to show what a breeze could be generated by a butterfly's wing.

He sat perfectly quiet, his nerves in wild clamor, afraid that if he moved he would find her irresistibly in his arms. Two tears had rolled down her wet face and trembled on her upper lip.

"I'm more beautiful than anybody else," she said brokenly, "why can't I be happy?" Her moist eyes tore at his stability—her mouth turned slowly downward with an exquisite sadness: "I'd like to marry you if you'll have me, Dexter. I suppose you think I'm not worth having, but I'll be so beautiful for you, Dexter."

A million phrases of anger, pride, passion, hatred, tenderness fought on his lips. Then a perfect wave of emotion washed over him, carrying off with it a sediment of wisdom, of convention, of doubt, of honor. This was his girl who was speaking, his own, his beautiful, his pride.

"Won't you come in?" He heard her draw in her breath sharply.

Waiting.

"All right," his voice was trembling, "I'll come in."

V

It was strange that neither when it was over nor a long time afterward did he regret that night. Looking at it from the perspective of ten years, the fact that Judy's flare for him endured just one month seemed of little importance. Nor did it matter that by his yielding he subjected himself to a deeper agony in the end and gave serious hurt to Irene Scheerer and to Irene's parents, who had befriended him. There was nothing sufficiently pictorial about Irene's grief to stamp itself on his mind.

Dexter was at bottom hard-minded. The attitude of the city on his action was of no importance to him, not because he was going to leave the city, but because any outside attitude on the situation seemed superficial. He was completely indifferent to popular opinion. Nor, when he had seen that it was no use, that he did not possess in himself the power to move fundamentally or to hold Judy Jones, did he bear any malice toward her. He loved her, and he would love her until the day he was too old for loving—but he could not have her. So he tasted the deep pain that is reserved only for the strong, just as he had tasted for a little while the deep happiness.

Even the ultimate falsity of the grounds upon which Judy terminated the engagement that she did not want to "take him away" from Irene—Judy who had wanted nothing else—did not revolt him. He was beyond any revulsion or any amusement.

He went East in February with the intention of selling out his laundries and settling in New York—but the war came to America in March and changed his plans. He returned to the West, handed over the management of the business to his partner, and went into the first officers' training-camp in late April. He was one of those young thousands who greeted the war with a certain amount of relief, welcoming the liberation from webs of tangled emotion.

VI

This story is not his biography, remember, although things creep into it which have nothing to do with those dreams he had when he was young. We are almost done with them and with him now. There is only one more incident to be related here, and it happens seven years farther on.

It took place in New York, where he had done well—so well that there were no barriers too high for him. He was thirty-two years old, and, except for one flying trip immediately after the war, he had not been West in seven years. A man named Devlin from Detroit came into his office to see him in a business way, and then and there this incident occurred, and closed out, so to speak, this particular side of his life.

"So you're from the Middle West," said the man Devlin with careless curiosity. "That's funny—I thought men like you were probably born and raised on Wall Street. You know—wife of one of my best friends in Detroit came from your city. I was an usher at the wedding."

Dexter waited with no apprehension of what was coming.

"Judy Simms," said Devlin with no particular interest; "Judy Jones she was once."

"Yes, I knew her." A dull impatience spread over him. He had heard, of course, that she was married—perhaps deliberately he had heard no more.

"Awfully nice girl," brooded Devlin meaninglessly, "I'm sort of sorry for her."

"Why?" Something in Dexter was alert, receptive, at once.

"Oh, Lud Simms has gone to pieces in a way. I don't mean he ill-uses her, but he drinks and runs around—"

"Doesn't she run around?"

"No. Stays at home with her kids."

"Oh."

"She's a little too old for him," said Devlin.

"Too old!" cried Dexter. "Why, man, she's only twenty-seven."

He was possessed with a wild notion of rushing out into the streets and taking a train to Detroit. He rose to his feet spasmodically.

"I guess you're busy," Devlin apologized quickly. "I didn't realize—"

"No, I'm not busy," said Dexter, steadying his voice. "I'm not busy at all. Not busy at all. Did you say she was—twenty seven? No, I said she was twenty-seven."

"Yes, you did," agreed Devlin dryly.

"Go on, then. Go on."

"What do you mean?"

"About Judy Jones."

Devlin looked at him helplessly.

"Well, that's—I told you all there is to it. He treats her like the devil. Oh, they're not going to get divorced or anything. When he's particularly outrageous she forgives him. In fact, I'm inclined to think she loves him. She was a pretty girl when she first came to Detroit."

A pretty girl! The phrase struck Dexter as ludicrous.

"Isn't she—a pretty girl any more?"

"Oh, she's all right."

"Look here," said Dexter, sitting down suddenly. "I don't understand. You say she was a 'pretty girl' and now you say she's 'all right.' I don't understand what you mean—Judy Jones wasn't a pretty girl, at all. She was a great beauty. Why, I knew her, I knew her. She was—"

Devlin laughed pleasantly.

"I'm not trying to start a row," he said. "I think Judy's a nice girl and I like her. I can't understand how a man like Lud Simms could fall madly in love with her, but he did." Then he added: "Most of the women like her."

Dexter looked closely at Devlin, thinking wildly that there must be a reason for this, some insensitivity in the man or some private malice.

"Lots of women fade just like *that,*" Devlin snapped his fingers. "You must have seen it happen. Perhaps I've forgotten how pretty she was at her wedding. I've seen her so much since then, you see. She has nice eyes."

A sort of dullness settled down upon Dexter. For the first time in his life he felt like getting very drunk. He knew that he was laughing loudly at something Devlin had said, but he did not know what it was or why it was funny. When, in a few minutes, Devlin went he lay down on his lounge and looked out the window at the New York sky-line into which the sun was sinking in dull lovely shades of pink and gold.

He had thought that having nothing else to lose he was invulnerable at last—but he knew that he had just lost something more, as surely as if he had married Judy Jones and seen her fade away before his eyes.

The dream was gone. Something had been taken from him. In a sort of panic he pushed the palms of his hands into his eyes and tried to bring up a picture of the waters lapping on Sherry Island and the moonlit veranda, and gingham on the golf-links and the dry sun and the gold color of her neck's soft down. And her mouth damp to his kisses and her eyes plaintive with melancholy and her freshness like new fine linen in the morning. Why, these things were no longer in the world! They had existed and they existed no longer.

For the first time in years the tears were streaming down his face. But they were for himself now. He did not care about mouth and eyes and moving hands. He wanted to care, and he could not care. For he had gone away and he could never go back any more. The gates were closed, the sun was gone down, and there was no beauty but the gray beauty of steel that withstands all time. Even the grief he could have borne was left behind in the country of illusion, of youth, of the richness of life, where his winter dreams had flourished.

"Long ago," he said, "long ago, there was something in me, but now that thing is gone. Now that thing is gone, that thing is gone. I cannot cry. I cannot care. That thing will come back no more."

WALLACE STEGNER

Maiden in a Tower

The highway entering Salt Lake City from the west curves around the southern end of Great Salt Lake past Black Rock and its ratty beaches, swings north away from the spouting smoke of the smelter towns, veers toward the onion-shaped domes of the Saltair Pavilion, and straightens out eastward again on the speedway. Ahead, across the white flats, the city and its mountains are a mirage, or a mural: metropolitan towers, then houses and trees and channeled streets, and then the mountain wall.

Driving into that, Kimball Harris began to feel like the newsreel diver whom the reversed projector sucks feet first out of his splash. Perhaps fatigue from the hard day and a half across the desert explained both the miragelike look of the city and his own sense that he was being run backward toward the beginning of the reel. But the feeling grew as he bored townward along the straight road, the same road out which, as a high-school boy, he had driven much too fast in a stripped-down Ford bug with screaming companions in the rumble seat. They must have driven back, too, but he remembered only the going out. To see the city head-on, like this, was strange to him.

Middle-aged, rather tired, but alert with the odd notion that he was returning both through distance and through time, he passed the airport and the fair grounds and slowed for the first streets of the city.

Twenty-five years had made little difference. The city had spread some, and he was surprised, after the desert, by the green luxuriance of the trees, but the streets were still a half mile wide, and water still ran in the gutters. It was a really good town, clean, with a freshness about it that revived him. Circling the Brigham Young monument, he nodded gravely to the figure with the outstretched hand, and like a native returning he went through the light and turned around the button in the middle of the block and came back to park before the Utah Hotel, careful to park well out from the curb so as not to block the flowing gutter. They gave you a ticket for that. It tickled him that he had remembered.

The doorman collared his bag, a bellhop climbed in to take the car around to the garage. Still running pleasantly backward into the reel, he went into the unchanged lobby and registered, and was carried up the unchanged elevators to the kind of room he remembered, such a room as they used to take when they held fraternity parties in the hotel, back in Prohibition times. During those years he had been on a diet for ulcers, and couldn't drink, but he had retired religiously with the boys, gargled raw Green River redeye, and spit it out again in the washbowl, only for the pleasure of lawbreaking and of carrying a distinguished breath back to the ballroom and the girls.

He shook his head, touched for a moment with his giddy and forgotten youth.

Later, fresh from the shower, with a towel around him, he picked up the telephone book, so dinky and provincial-seeming after the ponderous San Francisco directory that he caught himself feeling protective about it. But when he found the Merrill Funeral Parlors in the yellow pages he sat thinking, struck by the address. 363 East South Temple. On the Avenues side, just below Fourth East. He tried to visualize that once familiar street but it was all gone except for a general picture of tall stone and brick houses with high porches and lawns overtaken by plantain weeds. One, the one Holly had lived in, had a three-story stone tower.

That tower! With all the Jazz Age Bohemians crawling in and out. Havelock Ellis, Freud, Mencken, *The Memoirs of Fanny Hill, Love's Coming of Age, The Well of Loneliness,* Harry Kemp, Frank Harris. My Lord.

He was flooded with delighted recollection, they were all before him: reed-necked aesthetes, provincial cognoscenti, sad sexy yokels, lovers burning with a hard gemlike flame, a homosexual or two trying to look blasted and corroded by inward sin. Painters of bile-green landscapes, cubist photographers, poets and iconoclasts, scorners of the bourgeoisie, makers of cherished prose, dream-tellers, correspondence school psychoanalysts, they had swarmed through Holly's apartment and eddied around her queenly shape with noises like breaking china. He remembered her in her gold gown, a Proserpine or a Circe. For an instant she was slim and tall in his mind and he saw her laughing in the midst of the excitement she created, and how her hair was smooth black and her eyes very dark blue and how she wore massive gold hoops in her ears.

He wrote the number down and tucked it in the pocket of the suit laid out on the bed. But when he had dressed and gone down and was walking up South Temple past Beehive House, Lion House, Eagle Gate, the old and new apartment buildings, he began to look at numbers with a feeling that approached suspense, and he searched not so much for the Merrill Funeral Parlors as for the house with the round stone tower. Finally he saw it, lifting across the roof of a mansion gone to seed, and in another thirty paces he could see the sign and the new brass numbers on the riser of the top porch step. It was the very house.

Quickly he looked around for landmarks to restore and brace his memory. Some of the old maples and hickories he remembered along the sidewalk were gone, the terrace rolled down with an unfamiliar smooth nap of grass. The porch no longer carried its sagging swing, and porch and steps had been renewed and painted. The door was as he remembered it, with lozenges of colored glass above it, and the door knob's massive handful was an almost startling familiarity. But inside all was changed. Partitions had been gutted out. The stairs now mounted, or levitated, a spiral of white spokes and mahogany rails, from an expanse of plum-colored carpet. Instead of the cupping old parquetry his feet found softness, hushedness. The smells were of paint and flowers.

He was eying the stairs when a young man came out of an office on the left and bent his head a little leftward and said softly and pleasantly, "Yes, sir. Can I help?"

Harris brought himself dryly back to what he had driven eight hundred miles to do. He said, "I'm Kimball Harris. My aunt, Mrs. George Webb, died day before yesterday at the Julia Hicks Home. They telephoned me she would be here."

"We've been expecting you," the young man said, and put out his hand. "My name is McBride." A brief handshake, a moment when the young man regarded Harris with his head tilted. "Did you fly in?" he asked.

"Drove."

"All the way from San Francisco?"

"I slept a few hours in Elko."

"It wasn't so bad, then."

"Oh no," Harris said. "Not bad at all."

In his mind was a faint amusement: this young man might have been left over from one of Holly's parties. He looked better equipped to write fragile verses than deal with corpses.

"She's in the parlor just back here," McBride said. "Would you like to see her? She looks very nice."

That would be young McBride's function, of course. He would be the one who made them look nice. "Maybe later," Harris said. "I expect there are some details we ought to settle."

"Of course," McBride said. "If you'll just step in here. We can look at caskets after a minute. You have a family cemetery plot, I believe?

It will only take a minute for this. The details you can leave to us." He held the door wide, standing gracefully and deferentially back, and ushered Harris through.

A very few minutes seemed to settle the details. They rose, facing each other across the desk coolly glimmering in muted afternoon light. "Now would you like to see her?" McBride said.

Why, he takes pride, Harris thought. He probably stands back estimating his effects like a window dresser. Mister McBride, the Mortuary Max Factor. "All right," he said, "though it's not as if I had any tears to shed. I haven't seen her for twenty-five years, and she's been senile for ten."

McBride guided him around the unfamiliar stairs to where the plum carpet flowed smoothly into what had evidently once been a dining room. "She does look nice," he said. "Very sweet and peaceful."

Which is more than she did alive, Harris thought, and went forward to the table with the basket of chrysanthemums at its foot. To remind himself that this was his mother's sister, his last near relative, made him feel nothing. Not even a deliberate attempt to squeeze sentimental recollections out of the past and remember suppers at Aunt Margaret's, Christmas visits at Aunt Margaret's, times when Aunt Margaret had unexpectedly given him a quarter, made the wax figure any dearer or realer. His indifference was so marked that he separated it and noticed it, wondering with a tinge of shame if he was callous. He supposed that if he had been attached to the dead woman he might think her peaceful, touching, even terrible. All he could think as he looked at her was that she looked well-embalmed—but then she had probably been close to mummified before she died.

Old Aunt Margaret, never very lovable, never dear to him in his childhood, and in his maturity only a duty and an expense, thrust her sharp nose, sharp cheekbones, withered lips, up through the rouge and lipstick and was, if she was not a total stranger, only old Aunt Margaret, mercifully dead at eighty-three. Harris did not even feel the conventional disgust with young McBride, who tampered with the dead. Considering what he had to work with, McBride had done reasonably well.

Back in the hall again, he stood looking up the spiral stairs, apparently as unsupported as the Beanstalk, and remembered a time when Holly and three roommates—which three didn't matter, they changed so fast—came down the old shabby steps arguing about the proportions of the perfect female figure, and he met them on the second landing and like a chorus line they raised their skirts and thrust out their right legs before him, clamoring to know which was the most shapely. An undergraduate Paris and four demanding goddesses. He had picked Holly: why would he not?

McBride was in the office doorway. "We've just redone the whole place," he said. "It was the home of a Park City silver king originally, but it was all run down."

Harris was still looking up the stairs. McBride's words were no more important than the decorative changes, but upstairs there was something that *was* important, that pulled at him like an upward draft.

"I used to know this house twenty-five years ago," he said. "Some people I knew had an apartment on the third floor."

"Really? The front one or the back?"

"Front. The one with the round tower window."

"Oh yes," said McBride. "We haven't done much to that yet—just painted it."

"I wonder," Harris said, and made a little shrugging deprecatory motion and felt irritably ashamed, like a middle-aged man recalling last night's revels and his own unseemly capers and his pawing of the host's wife. It was fatuous to want to go up there, yet he did.

"Go on up if you want," McBride said. "The only thing, there's a woman laid out there."

"Well, then . . ."

"That wouldn't matter, if you don't mind. She's . . . presentable."

For a moment Harris hung on the word, and on the thought that McBride's professional vanity was one of the odder kinds, and on a little fit of irritability that a corpse should intrude upon a sentimental but perfectly legitimate impulse. Then he put his hand on the mahogany rail. "Maybe I will."

The second-floor hall, at whose doors he had knocked or entered, was as much changed as the ground floor, but up the second flight of stairs he mounted into a growing familiarity. And he climbed against the pressure of a crowd of ghosts. The carpet ended at the stairhead; he put his feet down softly and held back his breath with the wild notion that he heard voices from the door of Holly's old apartment. Up these stairs, a hundred, two hundred, three hundred times, through how long? a year? two years? he had come with books or bottles or manuscripts in his hands and (it seemed to him now) an incomparable capacity for enthusiasm in his heart. From the high burlap-hung windows of the apartment inside they had let their liquid ridicule fall on the streets of the bourgeois city. He half expected, as he moved into the doorway, to see their faces look up inquiringly from chair and couch and floor.

But in the room there was only the dead woman, and she was not looking at him.

She lay on a wheeled table, with beside her one stiff chair and a taboret bearing a bowl of flowers, all of it composed as if for a macabre still life. Looking toward the windows across the woman's body he saw how the gray light of the afternoon blurred in her carefully-waved hair.

For a minute or two, perhaps, he stood in the doorway, stopped partly by the body, and partly by the feeling of an obscure threat: he must summon and gather and recreate his recollections of this room; he was walking in a strange neighborhood and needed his own gang around him.

In Holly's time the tower bay had held an old upright piano, its backside exposed to the room like the hanging seat of a child's sleepers. Afternoons, evenings, Sunday and holiday mornings, there had been loud four-hand renderings of "Twelfth Street Rag," "St. Louis Blues," "Mood Indigo." On at least one Christmas morning they had even sung carols around it, syncopating them wickedly. That was the morning when he brought Holly the facsimile copy of *The Marriage of Heaven and Hell*—a mutinous book full of mottoes for their personalities and their times.

But what he remembered now, hanging in the doorway, was how in some lull in the bedlam that always went on there they had found themselves smiling foolishly at each other by the piano and she had put up her hands to his face and kissed him sweet and soft, a kiss like a happy child's. He realized now that he had recalled that kiss before, waking or sleeping, and that the memory of it had acquired a kind of caption, a fragment of the world's wisdom contributed to his adolescent store by a returned Mormon missionary: *"Das ewig Weibliche fuehrt uns hinan,"* that remembered moment said.

How they had flocked and gathered there, debated, kissed, lied, shocked and astonished and delighted each other, there in the tower with Holly at their center, there by the vanished piano: poets and athletes, Renaissance heroes, fearless Stoics and impassioned Epicureans and abandoned Hedonists, girls with a bloom on their loveliness, goddesses with Perfect Proportions, artists and iconoclasts, as delighted with their own wickedness as if it had meant something.

He felt the stairs in his legs, the years in his mind, as he went in softly past the woman who lay so quietly on her back, and when he had passed her he turned and searched her face, almost as if he might surprise in it some expression meaningful to this wry and confusing return.

She was a plain woman, perhaps fifty. McBride had not yet made her look nice with rouge and lipstick. She lay in a simple black dress, but she had a Navajo squash-blossom necklace around her throat. It struck him as a remarkable piece of realism—perhaps something she had especially liked and had stubbornly worn even past the age when costume jewelry became her. It gave her a touching. naïvely rakish air.

Yet she shed a chill around her, and her silence spread to fill the room. Hardly a sound came through the stone walls. In the old days there had always been the piano banging, the phonograph going, two or six or sixteen voices making cosmic conversation. And he never remembered daylight in the apartment. Holly had affected a romantic gloom; the windows were always shrouded by the artistically-frayed burlap, and the light was from lamps, most of them low on the floor and some of them at least with red globes in them. And always the smell of sandalwood.

Like a Chinese whorehouse. He shook his head, pitying and entranced, and sat down on the window seat overlooking the reach of South Temple. Directly across was a Five Minute Car Wash with a big apron of concrete and a spick dazzle of white paint and red tiles. In the times he remembered, that lot had held a Peewee Golf Course where men in shirt sleeves, women in summer dresses, young couples loud with laughter, putted little white balls along precise green alleys and across precise circles of green artificial grass and over gentle and predictable bridges and causeways into numbered holes.

"Look at them," Holly said to him once as they sat in the tower looking down at the after-dinner golfers moving under the bright floodlights. *"Toujours gai,* my God. Some day I'm going to build a miniature golf course with fairways six inches wide and rough all over the place. I'll fill the water holes with full-sized crocodiles and sow the sandtraps with sidewinders. How would it be to hide a black widow spider in every hole so that holing out and picking up your ball would earn you some excitement? What if you sawed the supports of all the little bridges nearly in two?"

Live it dangerously. It was strange to recall how essential that had seemed. Go boom, take chances. He touched the casement windows, thinking that this was the pose, sitting right here and looking out, that Holly had assumed when Tom Stead painted her in her gold velvet gown.

Probably that portrait wasn't anything special. It couldn't have been. The chances were that Tom Stead was painting signs somewhere now, if he hadn't drunk himself to death. But then, in this room, in the presence of its subject whose life overflowed upon them all, that slim golden shape with the velvet highlights was Lilith, Helen, Guenevere, *das ewig Weibliche.* And it was hardly a day before other girls, less fortunately endowed or graced, had begun dropping comments on how *warm* that Stead-Holly romance was getting, and hinting that there was hidden away somewhere a companion portrait—a nude.

Well, well, what a bunch of Bohemian puritans. Harris did not believe in any nude, or in its importance if there had been one, though at the time it had bothered him, and he had been malely offended, surprised that she would *lower* herself, you know?

Now, sitting bemused in the window, he reflected that what had truly shone out of that golden portrait, as out of Holly herself, was not so much glamour as innocence. Under the sheath she was positively virginal; if you cracked the enamel of her sophistication you found a delighted little girl playing Life.

Again he remembered the soft, childlike kiss by the piano on a Christmas morning, and he stood up so sharply that he startled himself with the sight of the dead woman. It *was* innocence. She could put away the predatory paws of college boys, twist laughing from the casual kiss, pass among the hot young Freudians as untouched as a nun, shed like water the propositions that were thrown at her seven to the week. There she sat in her gold gown by her window opening on the foam: a maiden in a tower.

He crossed the room and tried the bedroom door, wanting to look in on her intimately. In this room, now completely bare, aseptically painted, he had sat dozens of times when she was ill or when on Sunday mornings she made it a charming point of her sophistication to entertain in bed. While she lay propped with pillows he had read to her, talked to her, kissed her, had his hands fended away. The empty room was still charged with the vividness with which she invested everything. There was one night very late, two or three o'clock, when he had sat on one side of the bed and a mournful and lovesick jazz trumpeter had sat on the other, neither willing to leave the other alone there, and all that night he had read aloud into the smell of sandalwood the life story of a mad woman from Butte, Montana. *I, Mary MacLean,* that one was called.

What an occasion she made of it, laid up by flu, hemmed in by rival young men, covered to the chin in an absurd, high-necked, old-fashioned nightgown, taking aspirin with sips of ginger beer, laughing at them alternately or together with that face as vivid on the pillow as a flower laid against the linen. It was innocence. In that crackpot Bohemian pre-crash wonderful time, it was innocence.

How he and the trumpeter broke the deadlock, what had ever happened to the Tom Stead flurry, what had happened to any of Holly's string of admirers—all gone. She sent them away, or they quarreled at her over their bruised egos, or they grew huffy at finding her always in a crowd. Plenty of self-appointed humming-bird catchers, but no captures.

And yet, maybe . . .

Summer and winter, day and night, were telescoped in his memory. How old would he have been? Twenty? Twenty-one? It must have been near the end of Holly's reign in this apartment, before everything went sour and the delayed wave of the crash reached them and he left school to go to work and Holly herself went away. There was neither beginning nor end nor definite location in time to what he most vividly remembered. What they were doing, whether there had been a party there or whether they had been out on a date, whether she had roommates then or was living alone, none of that came back. But they were alone in a way they had seldom been.

They must have been talking, something must have led up to it, for there she was with the clarity of something floodlighted in his mind, Holly pressing against him and crying with her face against his chest, clinging and crying and saying—he heard only the refrain, not the garble against his chest—"Kim, Kim, get me out of here! I want to get out of this. This is all no good, I've got to, Kim, please!"

Both the tears and the way she clung excited him. But the game had been played so long by other rules that he went on in the old way, laughing, burlesquing gestures of consolation, patting the crow-wing hair, saying, "There there, little girl." Inanities, idiocies. . . . She wore an evening dress cut very low in the back, and he played his fingers up and down her spine. He slid his hand against her skin, slid it further, expecting the competent twist and shrug and fending and the laugh that would mean the emotional fit was over. But his hand went on around, clear around, and with a shock like an internal explosion he found it cupping the frantic softness of her breast.

Even remembering, all his sensations were shocking to him. He remembered how smoothly the curve of her side swelled upward, how astonishingly *consecutive* her body seemed. Also, also, and almost with revulsion, how rigid and demanding the nipple of her breast. Innocence—he had never touched a girl there, never imagined, or rather had imagined wrong. Stupefied by the sudden admission to her flesh, made uneasy by the way she crowded and clung, he stood wrapping her awkwardly, and kissed her and tasted her tears, and thought with alarm and conviction of Tom Stead and the rumored nude, and was anguished with eagerness to escape.

He could remember not a scrap, not a detail, of how he got away. She offered herself passionately in his memory, and that was all. The Peewee Golfer putting his little white ball up the little green alley of his youth came suddenly upon the sidewinder in the sandtrap, the crocodile in the artificial lake.

Harris closed the door on the ridiculous and humiliating memory. It had begun to occur to him that he had been an extraordinary young man, and very little of what had been extraordinary about himself pleased him. Innocence? Well, maybe, though there were more contemptuous names for it. He had been a fraud, a gargler of whiskey he would obediently not drink. A great yapper with the crowd, but when the cat stopped running, what a frantic sliding to a stop, what digging not to catch what he was after.

Weakly he tried to prop up the slack thing he had been. He told himself that it was a pose with all of them, the life that revolved around

Holly was an absurd and perhaps touching and certainly unimportant part of growing up. Or was it? What might he be at this moment, would he have more or less to regret, if he had taken Holly at her passionate word, married her, lived it, as she was determined to live it in her innocence, dangerously?

The last time he saw Holly she was boarding a train for Seattle, on her way to Shanghai and a job they all publicly envied but would probably not have risked taking themselves. Her life, whatever happened to her, would not have been dull. And yet it might have been more thoroughly wasted than at that moment he thought his own had been.

He had played it the other way, not so much from choice as from yielding to pressures, and he had done the best he could with it. How would he look to Holly now, at this very minute? How had he looked then?

Like a bubble of gas from something submerged and decaying in deep water there rose to the surface of his mind one of Blake's proverbs of Hell that they had admired together that long-gone Christmas morning. It burst, and it said, "Prudence is a rich ugly old maid courted by Incapacity."

It shamed him to remember, though he half repudiated it. From the life of prudence he had got a wife he loved and respected, children he adored, a job he could do with interest and almost with content. He regretted none of them. But he stood here remembering that moment when Holly stopped playing make-believe, and it seemed to him that his failure to take her when she offered herself was one of the saddest failures of his life. The fact that he might make all the same crucial choices the same way if he had them to make again helped not at all; it did him no good to remind himself that no one could turn in any direction without turning his back on something. The past had trapped him, and it held him like pain.

Angrily he looked at his watch. Past five. Starting for the door, he passed the dead woman's table and saw her calm pale face, the skin delicately wrinkled like the skin of a winter-kept apple, but soft-looking, as if it would be not unpleasant to touch. What was her name, what had she died of, what had she looked like when she wore expressions? Who mourned her, who had loved her, what things in her life did they regret or had she regretted? Would they think it disagreeable that a total stranger had been alone with her here staring into her dead face? And in that face what was it that the caution of death enclosed and hid?

The barbaric silver necklace seemed somehow to define her. What it said of frivolity, girlishness, love of ornament and of gaiety and of life, made him like her; the way it lay on the sober black crepe breast preached the saddest lesson he had ever derived.

He thought of how she had been transported and tampered with by McBride, and how further touches of disguise would complete her transfiguration from something real and terrible and lost to something serene, removed, bearable. Alone with her here, before the arrival of the others, before she went forth to be forgotten, he could feel a strange, real anguish for this woman he had never known, and a strange gratitude that he had been permitted to see her.

Gratitude, or something near it. And yet as he started for the door he threw a sick, apologetic glance around the room as quiet and empty as a chapel, and at the woman who lay so quietly at its center. He meant to tiptoe out, but he heard, almost with panic, the four quick raps his heels made on the bare floor before they found the consoling softness of the stairs.

CARSON McCULLERS

The Sojourner

The twilight border between sleep and waking was a Roman one this morning: splashing fountains and arched, narrow streets, the golden lavish city of blossoms and age-soft stone. Sometimes in this semi-consciousness he sojourned again in Paris, or German war rubble, or a Swiss skiing and a snow hotel. Sometimes, also, in a fallow Georgia field at hunting dawn. Rome it was this morning in the yearless region of dreams.

John Ferris awoke in a room in a New York hotel. He had the feeling that something unpleasant was awaiting him—what it was, he did not know. The feeling, submerged by matinal necessities, lingered even after he had dressed and gone downstairs. It was a cloudless autumn day and the pale sunlight sliced between the pastel skyscrapers. Ferris went into the next-door drugstore and sat at the end booth next to the window glass that overlooked the sidewalk. He ordered an American breakfast with scrambled eggs and sausage.

Ferris had come from Paris to his father's funeral which had taken place the week before in his home town in Georgia. The shock of death had made him aware of youth already passed. His hair was receding and the veins in his now naked temples were pulsing and prominent and his body was spare except for an incipient belly bulge. Ferris had loved his father and the bond between them had once been extraordinarily close—but the years had somehow unraveled this filial devotion; the death, expected for a long time, had left him with an unforseen dismay. He had stayed as long as possible to be near his mother and brothers at home. His plane for Paris was to leave the next morning.

Ferris pulled out his address book to verify a number. He turned the pages with growing attentiveness. Names and addresses from New York, the capitals of Europe, a few faint ones from his home state in the South. Faded, printed names, sprawled drunken ones. Betty Wills:

a random love, married now. Charlie Williams: wounded in the Hürtgen Forest, unheard of since. Grand old Williams—did he live or die? Don Walker: a B.T.O. in television, getting rich. Henry Green: hit the skids after the war, in a sanitarium now, they say. Cozie Hall: he had heard that she was dead. Heedless, laughing Cozie—it was strange to think that she too, silly girl, could die. As Ferris closed the address book, he suffered a sense of hazard, transience, almost of fear.

It was then that his body jerked suddenly. He was staring out of the window when there, on the sidewalk, passing by, was his ex-wife. Elizabeth passed quite close to him, walking slowly. He could not understand the wild quiver of his heart, nor the following sense of recklessness and grace that lingered after she was gone.

Quickly Ferris paid his check and rushed out to the sidewalk. Elizabeth stood on the corner waiting to cross Fifth Avenue. He hurried toward her meaning to speak, but the lights changed and she crossed the street before he reached her. Ferris followed. On the other side he could easily have overtaken her, but he found himself lagging unaccountably. Her fair hair was plainly rolled, and as he watched her Ferris recalled that once his father had remarked that Elizabeth had a "beautiful carriage." She turned at the next corner and Ferris followed, although by now his intention to overtake her had disappeared. Ferris questioned the bodily disturbance that the sight of Elizabeth aroused in him, the dampness of his hands, the hard heartstrokes.

It was eight years since Ferris had last seen his ex-wife. He knew that long ago she had married again. And there were children. During recent years he had seldom thought of her. But at first, after the divorce, the loss had almost destroyed him. Then after the anodyne of time, he had loved again, and then again. Jeannine, she was now. Certainly his love for his ex-wife was long since past. So why the unhinged body, the shaken mind? He knew only that his clouded heart was oddly dissonant with the sunny, candid autumn day. Ferris wheeled suddenly and, walking with long strides, almost running, hurried back to the hotel.

Ferris poured himself a drink, although it was not yet eleven o'clock. He sprawled out in an armchair like a man exhausted, nursing his glass of bourbon and water. He had a full day ahead of him as he was leaving by plane the next morning for Paris. He checked over his obligations: take luggage to Air France, lunch with his boss, buy shoes and an overcoat. And something—wasn't there something else? Ferris finished his drink and opened the telephone directory.

His decision to call his ex-wife was impulsive. The number was under Bailey, the husband's name, and he called before he had much time for self-debate. He and Elizabeth had exchanged cards at Christmastime, and Ferris had sent a carving set when he received the announcement of her wedding. There was no reason *not* to call. But as he waited, listening to the ring at the other end, misgiving fretted him.

Elizabeth answered; her familiar voice was a fresh shock to him. Twice he had to repeat his name, but when he was identified, she sounded glad. He explained he was only in town for that day. They had a theater engagement, she said—but she wondered if he would come by for an early dinner. Ferris said he would be delighted.

As he went from one engagement to another, he was still bothered at odd moments by the feeling that something necessary was forgotten. Ferris bathed and changed in the late afternoon, often thinking about Jeannine: he would be with her the following night. "Jeannine," he would say, "I happened to run into my ex-wife when I was in New York. Had dinner with her. And her husband, of course. It was strange seeing her after all these years."

Elizabeth lived in the East Fifties, and as Ferris taxied uptown he glimpsed at intersections the lingering sunset, but by the time he reached his destination it was already autumn dark. The place was a building with a marquee and a doorman, and the apartment was on the seventh floor.

"Come in, Mr. Ferris."

Braced for Elizabeth or even the unimagined husband, Ferris was astonished by the freckled red-haired child; he had known of the children, but his mind had failed somehow to acknowledge them. Surprise made him step back awkwardly.

"This is our apartment," the child said politely. "Aren't you Mr. Ferris? I'm Billy. Come in."

In the living room beyond the hall, the husband provided another surprise; he too had not been acknowledged emotionally. Bailey was a lumbering red-haired man with a deliberate manner. He rose and extended a welcoming hand.

"I'm Bill Bailey. Glad to see you. Elizabeth will be in, in a minute. She's finishing dressing."

The last words struck a gliding series of vibrations, memories of the other years. Fair Elizabeth, rosy and naked before her bath. Half-dressed before the mirror of her dressing table, brushing her fine, chestnut hair. Sweet, casual intimacy, the soft-fleshed loveliness indisputably possessed. Ferris shrank from the unbidden memories and compelled himself to meet Bill Bailey's gaze.

"Billy, will you please bring that tray of drinks from the kitchen table?"

The child obeyed promptly, and when he was gone Ferris remarked conversationally, "Fine boy you have there."

"We think so."

Flat silence until the child returned with a tray of glasses and a cocktail shaker of Martinis. With the priming drinks they pumped up conversation: Russia, they spoke of, and the New York rainmaking, and the apartment situation in Manhattan and Paris.

"Mr. Ferris is flying all the way across the ocean tomorrow," Bailey said to the little boy who was perched on the arm of his chair, quiet and well behaved. "I bet you would like to be a stowaway in his suitcase."

Billy pushed back his limp bangs. "I want to fly in an airplane and be a newspaperman like Mr. Ferris." He added with sudden assurance, "That's what I would like to do when I am big."

Bailey said, "I thought you wanted to be a doctor."

"I do!" said Billy. "I would like to be both. I want to be a atom-bomb scientist too."

Elizabeth came in carrying in her arms a baby girl.

"Oh, John!" she said. She settled the baby in the father's lap. "It's grand to see you. I'm awfully glad you could come."

The little girl sat demurely on Bailey's knees. She wore a pale pink crepe de Chine frock, smocked around the yoke with rose, and a matching silk hair ribbon tying back her pale soft curls. Her skin was summer tanned and her brown eyes flecked with gold and laughing. When she reached up and fingered her father's horn-rimmed glasses, he took them off and let her look through them a moment. "How's my old Candy?"

Elizabeth was very beautiful, more beautiful perhaps than he had ever realized. Her straight clean hair was shining. Her face was softer, glowing and serene. It was a madonna loveliness, dependent on the family ambiance.

"You've hardly changed at all," Elizabeth said, "but it has been a long time."

"Eight years." His hand touched his thinning hair self-consciously while further amenities were exchanged.

Ferris felt himself suddenly a spectator—an interloper among these Baileys. Why had he come? He suffered. His own life seemed so solitary, a fragile column supporting nothing amidst the wreckage of the years. He felt he could not bear much longer to stay in the family room.

He glanced at his watch. "You're going to the theater?"

"It's a shame," Elizabeth said, "but we've had this engagement for more than a month. But surely, John, you'll be staying home one of these days before long. You're not going to be an expatriate, are you?"

"Expatriate," Ferris repeated. "I don't much like the word."

"What's a better word?" she asked.

He thought for a moment. "Sojourner might do."

Ferris glanced again at his watch, and again Elizabeth apologized. "If only we had known ahead of time—"

"I just had this day in town. I came home unexpectedly. You see, Papa died last week."

"Papa Ferris is dead?"

"Yes, at Johns Hopkins. He had been sick there nearly a year. The funeral was down home in Georgia."

"Oh, I'm so sorry, John. Papa Ferris was always one of my favorite people."

The little boy moved from behind the chair so that he could look into his mother's face. He asked, "Who is dead?"

Ferris was oblivious to apprehension; he was thinking of his father's death. He saw again the outstretched body on the quilted silk within the coffin. The corpse flesh was bizarrely rouged and the familiar hands lay massive and joined above a spread of funeral roses. The memory closed and Ferris awakened to Elizabeth's calm voice.

"Mr. Ferris's father, Billy. A really grand person. Somebody you didn't know."

"But why did you call him *Papa* Ferris?"

Bailey and Elizabeth exchanged a trapped look. It was Bailey who answered the questioning child. "A long time ago," he said, "your mother and Mr. Ferris were once married. Before you were born—a long time ago."

"Mr. Ferris?"

The little boy stared at Ferris, amazed and unbelieving. And Ferris's eyes, as he returned the gaze, were somehow unbelieving too. Was it indeed true that at one time he had called this stranger, Elizabeth, Little Butterduck during nights of love, that they had lived together, shared perhaps a thousand days and nights and—finally—endured in the misery of sudden solitude the fiber by fiber (jealousy, alcohol and money quarrels) destruction of the fabric of married love?

Bailey said to the children, "It's somebody's suppertime. Come on now."

"But Daddy! Mama and Mr. Ferris—I—"

Billy's everlasting eyes—perplexed and with a glimmer of hostility—reminded Ferris of the gaze of another child. It was the young son of Jeannine—a boy of seven with a shadowed little face and knobby knees whom Ferris avoided and usually forgot.

"Quick march!" Bailey gently turned Billy toward the door. "Say good night now, son."

"Good night, Mr. Ferris." He added resentfully, "I thought I was staying up for the cake."

"You can come in afterward for the cake," Elizabeth said. "Run along now with Daddy for your supper."

Ferris and Elizabeth were alone. The weight of the situation descended on those first moments of silence. Ferris asked permission to pour himself another drink and Elizabeth set the cocktail shaker on the table at his side. He looked at the grand piano and noticed the music on the rack.

"Do you still play as beautifully as you used to?"

"I still enjoy it."

"Please play, Elizabeth."

Elizabeth arose immediately. Her readiness to perform when asked had always been one of her amiabilities; she never hung back, apologized. Now as she approached the piano there was the added readiness of relief.

She began with a Bach prelude and fugue. The prelude was as gaily iridescent as a prism in a morning room. The first voice of the fugue, an announcement pure and solitary, was repeated intermingling with a second voice, and again repeated within an elaborated frame, the multiple music, horizontal and serene, flowed with unhurried majesty. The principal melody was woven with two other voices, embellished with countless ingenuities—now dominant, again submerged, it had the sublimity of a single thing that does not fear surrender to the whole. Toward the end, the density of the material gathered for the last enriched insistence on the dominant first motif and with a chorded final statement the fugue ended. Ferris rested his head on the chair back and closed his eyes. In the following silence a clear, high voice came from the room down the hall.

"Daddy, how *could* Mama and Mr. Ferris—" A door was closed.

The piano began again—what was this music? Unplaced, familiar, the limpid melody had lain a long while dormant in his heart. Now it spoke to him of another time, another place—it was the music Elizabeth used to play. The delicate air summoned a wilderness of memory. Ferris was lost in the riot of past longings, conflicts, ambivalent desires. Strange that the music, catalyst for this tumultuous anarchy, was so serene and clear. The singing melody was broken off by the appearance of the maid.

"Miz Bailey, dinner is out on the table now."

Even after Ferris was seated at the table between his host and hostess, the unfinished music still overcast his mood. He was a little drunk.

"L'improvisation de la vie humaine," he said. "There's nothing that makes you so aware of the improvisation of human existence as a song unfinished. Or an old address book."

"Address book?" repeated Bailey. Then he stopped, noncommittal and polite.

"You're still the same old boy, Johnny," Elizabeth said with a trace of the old tenderness.

It was a Southern dinner that evening, and the dishes were his old favorites. They had fried chicken and corn pudding and rich, glazed candied sweet potatoes. During the meal Elizabeth kept alive a conversation when the silences were overlong. And it came about that Ferris was led to speak of Jeannine.

"I first knew Jeannine last autumn—about this time of the year—in Italy. She's a singer and she had an engagement in Rome. I expect we will be married soon."

The words seemed so true, inevitable, that Ferris did not at first acknowledge to himself the lie. He and Jeannine had never in that year spoken of marriage. And indeed, she was still married—to a White Russian money-changer in Paris from whom she had been separated for five years. But it was too late to correct the lie. Already Elizabeth was saying: "This really makes me glad to know. Congratulations, Johnny."

He tried to make amends with truth. "The Roman autumn is so beautiful. Balmy and blossoming." He added, "Jeannine has a little boy of six. A curious trilingual little fellow. We go to the Tuileries sometimes."

A lie again. He had taken the boy once to the gardens. The sallow foreign child in shorts that bared his spindly legs had sailed his boat in the concrete pond and ridden the pony. The child had wanted to go in to the puppet show. But there was not time, for Ferris had an engagement at the Scribe Hotel. He had promised they would go to the guignol another afternoon. Only once had he taken Valentin to the Tuileries.

There was a stir. The maid brought in a white-frosted cake with pink candles. The children entered in their night clothes. Ferris still did not understand.

"Happy birthday, John," Elizabeth said. "Blow out the candles."

Ferris recognized his birthday date. The candles blew out lingeringly and there was the smell of burning wax. Ferris was thirty-eight years old. The veins in his temples darkened and pulsed visibly.

"It's time you started for the theater."

Ferris thanked Elizabeth for the birthday dinner and said the appropriate good-byes. The whole family saw him to the door.

A high, thin moon shone above the jagged, dark skyscrapers. The streets were windy, cold. Ferris hurried to Third Avenue and hailed a cab. He gazed at the nocturnal city with the deliberate attentiveness of departure and perhaps farewell. He was alone. He longed for flighttime and the coming journey.

The next day he looked down on the city from the air, burnished in sunlight, toylike, precise. Then America was left behind and there was only the Atlantic and the distant European shore. The ocean was milky pale and placid beneath the clouds. Ferris dozed most of the day. Toward dark he was thinking of Elizabeth and the visit of the previous evening. He thought of Elizabeth among her family with longing, gentle envy and inexplicable regret. He sought the melody, the unfinished air, that had so moved him. The cadence, some unrelated tones, were all that remained;

the melody itself evaded him. He had found instead the first voice of the fugue that Elizabeth had played—it came to him, inverted mockingly and in a minor key. Suspended above the ocean the anxieties of transience and solitude no longer troubled him and he thought of his father's death with equanimity. During the dinner hour the plane reached the shore of France.

At midnight Ferris was in a taxi crossing Paris. It was a clouded night and mist wreathed the lights of the Place de la Concorde. The midnight bistros gleamed on the wet pavements. As always after a trans-ocean flight the change of continents was too sudden. New York at morning, this midnight Paris. Ferris glimpsed the disorder of his life: the succession of cities, of transitory loves; and time, the sinister glissando of the years, time always.

"Vite! Vite!" he called in terror. *"Dépêchez-vous."*

Valentin opened the door to him. The little boy wore pajamas and an outgrown red robe. His grey eyes were shadowed and, as Ferris passed into the flat, they flickered momentarily.

"J'attends Maman."

Jeannine was singing in a night club. She would not be home before another hour. Valentin returned to a drawing, squatting with his crayons over the paper on the floor. Ferris looked down at the drawing—it was a banjo player with notes and wavy lines inside a comic-strip balloon.

"We will go again to the Tuileries."

The child looked up and Ferris drew him closer to his knees. The melody, the unfinished music that Elizabeth had played, came to him suddenly. Unsought, the load of memory jettisoned—this time bringing only recognition and sudden joy.

"Monsieur Jean," the child said, "did you see him?"

Confused, Ferris thought only of another child—the freckled, family-loved boy. "See who, Valentin?"

"Your dead papa in Georgia." The child added, "Was he okay?"

Ferris spoke with rapid urgency: "We will go often to the Tuileries. Ride the pony and we will go into the guignol. We will see the puppet show and never be in a hurry any more."

"Monsieur Jean," Valentin said. "The guignol is now closed."

Again, the terror, the acknowledgment of wasted years and death. Valentin, responsive and confident, still nestled in his arms. His cheek touched the soft cheek and felt the brush of the delicate eyelashes. With inner desperation he pressed the child close—as though an emotion as protean as his love could dominate the pulse of time.

GROUP SIX

HENRY JAMES

The Jolly Corner

"Every one asks me what I 'think' of everything," said Spencer Brydon; "and I make answer as I can—begging or dodging the question, putting them off with any nonsense. It wouldn't matter to any of them really," he went on, "for, even were it possible to meet in that stand-and-deliver way so silly a demand on so big a subject, my 'thoughts' would still be almost altogether about something that concerns only myself." He was talking to Miss Staverton, with whom for a couple of months now he had availed himself of every possible occasion to talk; this disposition and this resource, this comfort and support, as the situation in fact presented itself, having promptly enough taken the first place in the considerable array of rather unattenuated surprises attending his so strangely belated return to America. Everything was somehow a surprise; and that might be natural when one had so long and so consistently neglected everything, taken pains to give surprises so much margin for play. He had given them more than thirty years—thirty-three, to be exact; and they now seemed to him to have organised their performance quite on the scale of that licence. He had been twenty-three on leaving New York—he was fifty-six today: unless indeed he were to reckon as he had sometimes, since his repatriation, found himself feeling; in which case he would have lived longer than is often allotted to man. It would have taken a century, he repeatedly said to himself, and said also to Alice Staverton, it would have taken a longer absence and a more averted mind than those even of which he had been guilty, to pile up the differences, the newnesses, the queernesses, above all the bignesses, for the better or the worse, that at present assaulted his vision wherever he looked.

The great fact all the while however had been the incalculability: since he *had* supposed himself, from decade to decade, to be allowing, and in the most liberal and intelligent manner, for brilliancy of change. He actually saw that he had allowed for nothing; he missed what he would have been sure of finding, he found what he would never have imagined. Proportions and values were upside-down; the ugly things he had expected, the ugly things of his far-away youth, when he had too promptly waked up to a sense of the ugly—these uncanny phenomena placed him rather, as it happened, under the charm; whereas the "swagger" things, the modern, the monstrous, the famous things, those he had more particularly, like thousands of ingenuous enquirers every year, come over to see, were exactly his sources of dismay. They were as so many set traps for displeasure, above all for reaction, of which his restless tread was constantly pressing the spring. It was interesting, doubtless, the whole show, but it would have been too disconcerting hadn't a certain finer truth saved the situation. He had distinctly not, in this steadier light, come over *all* for the monstrosities; he had come, not only in the last analysis but quite on the face of the act, under an impulse with which they had nothing to do. He had come—putting the thing pompously—to look at his "property," which he had thus for a third of a century not been within four thousand miles of; or, expressing it less sordidly, he had yielded to the humour of seeing again his house on the jolly corner, as he usually, and quite fondly, described it—the one in which he had first seen the light, in which various members of his family had lived and had died, in which the holidays of his overschooled boyhood had been passed and the few social flowers of his chilled adolescence gathered, and which, alienated then for so long a period, had, through the successive deaths of his two brothers and the termination of old arrangements, come wholly into his hands. He was the owner of another, not quite so "good"—the jolly corner having been, from far back, superlatively extended and consecrated; and the value of the pair represented his main capital, with an income consisting, in these later years, of their respective rents which (thanks precisely to their original excellent type) had never been depressingly low. He could live in "Europe," as he had been in the habit of living, on the product of these flourishing New York leases, and all the better since, that of the second structure, the mere number in its long row, having within a twelvemonth fallen in, renovation at a high advance had proved beautifully possible.

These were items of property indeed, but he had found himself since his arrival distinguishing more than ever between them. The house within the street, two bristling blocks westward, was already in course of reconstruction as a tall mass of flats; he had acceded, some time before, to overtures for this conversion—in which, now that it was going forward, it had been not the least of his astonishments to find himself able, on the spot, and though without a previous ounce of such experience, to participate with a certain intelligence, almost with a certain authority. He had lived his life with his back so turned to such concerns and his face addressed to those of so different an order that he scarce knew what to make of this lively stir, in a compartment of his mind never yet penetrated, of a capacity for business and a sense for construction. These virtues, so common all round him now, had been dormant in his own organism—where it might be said of them perhaps that they had slept the sleep of the just. At present, in the splendid autumn weather—the autumn at least was a pure boon in the terrible place—he loafed about his "work" undeterred, secretely agitated; not in the least "minding" that the whole proposition, as they said, was vulgar and sordid, and ready to climb ladders, to walk the plank, to handle materials and look wise about them, to ask questions, in fine, and challenge explanations and really "go into" figures.

It amused, it verily quite charmed him; and, by the same stroke, it amused, and even more, Alice Staverton, though perhaps charming her perceptibly less. She wasn't however going to be better off for it, as *he* was—and so astonishingly much: nothing was now likely, he knew, ever to make her better off than she found herself, in the afternoon of life, as the delicately frugal possessor and tenant of the small house in Irving Place to which she had subtly managed to cling through her almost unbroken New York career. If he knew the way to it now better than to any other address among the dreadful multiplied numberings which seemed to him to reduce the whole place to some vast ledger-page, overgrown, fantastic, of ruled and criss-crossed lines and figures—if he had formed, for his consolation, that habit, it was really not a little because of the charm of his having encountered and recognised, in the vast wilderness of the wholesale, breaking through the mere gross generalisation of wealth and force and success, a small still scene where items and shades, all delicate things, kept the sharpness of the notes of a high voice perfectly trained, and where economy hung about like the scent of a garden. His old friend lived with one maid and herself dusted her relics and trimmed her lamps and polished her silver; she stood off, in the awful modern crush, when she could, but she sallied forth and did battle when the challenge was really to "spirit," the spirit she after all confessed to, proudly and a little shyly, as to that of the better time, that of *their* common, their quite far-away and antediluvian social period and order. She made use of the street-cars when need be, the terrible things that people scrambled for as the panic-stricken at sea scramble for the boats; she affronted, inscrutably, under stress, all the public concussions and ordeals; and yet, with that slim mystifying grace of her appearance, which defied you to say if she were a fair young woman who looked older through trouble, or a fine smooth older one who looked young through successful indifference; with her precious reference, above all, to memories and histories into which he could enter, she was as exquisite for him as some pale pressed flower (a rarity to begin with), and, failing other sweetnesses, she was a sufficient reward of his effort. They had communities of knowledge, "their" knowledge (this discriminating possessive was always on her lips) of presences of the other age, presences all overlaid, in his case, by the experience of a man and the freedom of a wanderer, overlaid by pleasure, by infidelity, by passages of life that were strange and dim to her, just by "Europe" in short, but still unobscured, still exposed and cherished, under that pious visitation of the spirit from which she had never been diverted.

She had come with him one day to see how his "apartment-house" was rising; he had helped her over gaps and explained to her plans, and while they were there had happened to have, before her, a brief but lively discussion with the man in charge, the representative of the building-firm that had undertaken his work. He had found himself quite "standing-up" to his personage over a failure on the latter's part to observe some detail of one of their noted conditions, and had so lucidly urged his case that, besides ever so prettily flushing, at the time, for sympathy in his triumph, she had afterwards said to him (though to a slightly greater effect of irony) that he had clearly for too many years neglected a real gift. If he had but stayed at home he would have anticipated the inventor of the sky-scraper. If he had but stayed at home he would have discovered his genius in time really to start some new variety of awful architectural hare and run it till it burrowed in a gold-mine. He was to remember these words, while the weeks elapsed, for the small silver ring they had sounded over the queerest and deepest of his own lately most disguised and most muffled vibrations.

It had begun to be present to him after the first fortnight, it had broken out with the oddest abruptness, this particular wanton wonderment: it met him there—and this was the image under which he himself judged the matter, or at least, not a little, thrilled and flushed with it—very much as he might have been met by some strange figure, some unexpected occupant, at a turn of one of the dim passages of an empty house. The quaint analogy quite hauntingly remained with him, when he didn't indeed rather improve it by a still intenser form: that of his opening a door behind which he would have made sure of finding nothing, a door into a room shuttered and void, and yet so coming, with a great suppressed start, on some quite erect confronting presence, something planted in the middle of the place and facing him through the dusk. After that visit to the house in construction he walked with his companion to see the other and always so much the better one, which in the eastward direction formed one of the corners, the "jolly" one precisely, of the street now so generally dishonoured and disfigured in its westward reaches, and of the comparatively conservative Avenue. The Avenue still had pretensions, as Miss Staverton said, to decency; the old people had mostly gone, the old names were unknown, and here and there an old association seemed to stray, all vaguely, like some very aged person, out too late, whom you might meet and feel the impulse to watch or follow, in kindness, for safe restoration to shelter.

They went in together, our friends; he admitted himself with his key, as he kept no one there, he explained, preferring, for his reasons, to leave the place empty, under a simple arrangement with a good woman living in the neighbourhood and who came for a daily hour to open windows and dust and sweep. Spencer Brydon had his reasons and was growingly aware of them; they seemed to him better each time he was there, though he didn't name them all to his companion, any more than he told her as yet how often, how quite absurdly often, he himself came. He only let her see for the present, while they walked through the great blank rooms, that absolute vacancy reigned and that, from top to bottom, there was nothing but Mrs. Muldoon's broomstick, in a corner, to tempt the burglar. Mrs. Muldoon was then on the premises, and she loquaciously attended the visitors, preceding them from room to room and pushing back shutters and throwing up sashes—all to show them, as she remarked, how little there was to see. There was little indeed to see in the great gaunt shell where the main dispositions and the general apportionment of space, the style of an age of ampler allowances, had nevertheless for its master their honest pleading message, affecting him as some good old servant's, some lifelong retainer's appeal for a character, or even for a retiring-pension; yet it was also a remark of Mrs. Muldoon's that, glad as she was to oblige him by her noonday round, there was a request she greatly hoped he would never make of her. If he should wish her for any reason to come in after dark she would just tell him, if he "plased," that he must ask it of somebody else.

The fact that there was nothing to see didn't militate for the worthy woman against what one *might* see, and she put it frankly to Miss Staverton that no lady could be expected to like, could she? "craping up to thim top storeys in the ayvil hours." The gas and the electric light were off the house, and she fairly evoked a gruesome vision of her march through the great grey rooms—so many of them as there were too!—with her glimmering taper. Miss Staverton met her honest glare with a smile and the profession that she herself certainly would recoil from such an adventure. Spencer Brydon meanwhile held his peace—for the moment; the question of the "evil" hours in his old home had already become too grave for him. He had begun some time since to "crape," and he knew just why a packet of candles addressed to that pursuit had been stowed by his own hand, three weeks before, at the back of a drawer of the fine old sideboard that occupied, as a "fixture," the deep recess in the dining-room. Just now he laughed at his companions—quickly however changing the subject; for the reason that, in the first place, his laugh struck him even at that moment as starting the odd echo, the conscious human resonance (he scarcely knew how to qualify it) that sounds made while he was there alone sent back to his ear or his fancy; and that, in the second, he imagined Alice Staverton for the instant on the point of asking him, with a divination, if he ever so prowled. There were divinations he was unprepared for, and he had at all events averted enquiry by the time Mrs. Muldoon had left them, passing on to other parts.

There was happily enough to say, on so consecrated a spot, that could be said freely and fairly; so that a whole train of declarations was precipitated by his friend's having herself broken out, after a yearning look around: "But I hope you don't mean they want you to pull *this* to pieces!" His answer came, promptly, with his re-awakened wrath: it was of course exactly what they wanted, and what they were "at" him for, daily, with the iteration of people who couldn't for their life understand a man's liability to decent feelings. He had found the place, just as it stood and beyond what he could express, an interest and a joy. There were values other than the beastly rent-values, and in short, in short—! But it was thus Miss Staverton took him up. "In short you're to make so good a thing of your sky-scraper that, living in luxury on *those* ill-gotten gains, you can afford for a while to be sentimental here!" Her smile had for him, with the words, the particular mild irony with which he found half her talk suffused; an irony without bitterness and that came, exactly, from her having so much imagination—not, like the cheap sarcasms with which one heard most people, about the world of "society," bid for the reputation of cleverness, from nobody's really having any. It was agreeable to him at this very moment to be sure that when he had answered, after a brief demur, "Well yes: so, precisely, you may put it!" her imagination would still do him justice. He explained that even if never a dollar were to come to him from the other house he would nevertheless cherish this one; and he dwelt, further, while they lingered and wandered, on the fact of the stupefaction he was already exciting, the positive mystification he felt himself create.

He spoke of the value of all he read into it, into the mere sight of the walls, mere shapes of the room, mere sound of the floors, mere feel, in his hand, of the old silver-plated knobs of the several mahogany doors, which suggested the pressure of the palms of the dead; the seventy years of the past in fine that these things represented, the annals of nearly three generations, counting his grandfather's, the one that had ended there, and the impalpable ashes of his long-extinct youth, afloat in the very air like microscopic motes. She listened to everything; she was a woman who answered intimately but who utterly didn't chatter. She scattered abroad therefore no cloud of words; she could assent, she could agree, above all she could encourage, without doing that. Only at the last she went a little further than he had done himself. "And then how do you know? You may still, after all, want to live here." It rather indeed pulled him up, for it wasn't what he had been thinking, at least in her sense of the words. "You mean I may decide to stay on for the sake of it?"

"Well, *with* such a home—!" But quite beautifully, she had too much tact to dot so monstrous an *i,* and it was precisely an illustration of the way she didn't rattle. How could any one—of any wit—insist on any one else's "wanting" to live in New York?

"Oh," he said, "I *might* have lived here (since I had my opportunity early in life); I might have put in here all these years. Then everything would have been different enough—and, I dare say, 'funny' enough. But that's another matter. And then the beauty of it—I mean of my perversity, of my refusal to agree to a 'deal'—is just in the total absence of a reason. Don't you see that if I had a reason about the matter at all it would *have* to be the other way, and would then be inevitably a reason of dollars? There are no reasons here *but* of dollars. Let us therefore have none whatever—not the ghost of one."

They were back in the hall then for departure, but from where they stood the vista was large, through an open door, into the great square main saloon, with its almost antique felicity of brave spaces between windows. Her eyes came back from that reach and met his own a moment. "Are you very sure the 'ghost' of one doesn't, much rather, serve—?"

He had a positive sense of turning pale. But it was as near as they were then to come. For he made answer, he believed, between a glare and a grin: "Oh ghosts—of course the place must swarm with them! I should be ashamed of it if it didn't. Poor Mrs. Muldoon's right, and it's why I haven't asked her to do more than look in."

Miss Starverton's gaze again lost itself, and things she didn't utter, it was clear, came and went in her mind. She might even for the minute, off there in the fine room, have imagined some element dimly gathering. Simplified like the death-mask of a handsome face, it perhaps produced for her just then an effect akin to the stir of an expression in the "set" commemorative plaster. Yet whatever her impression may have been she produced instead a vague platitude. "'Well, if it were only furnished and lived in—!'"

She appeared to imply that in case of its being still furnished he might have been a little less opposed to the idea of a return. But she passed straight into the vestibule, as if to leave her words behind her, and the next moment he had opened the house-door and was standing with her on the steps. He closed the door and, while he re-pocketed his key, looking up and down, they took in the comparatively harsh actuality of the Avenue, which reminded him of the assault of the outer light of the Desert on the traveller emerging from an Egyptian tomb. But he risked before they stepped into the street his gathering answer to her speech. "For me it *is* lived in. For me it *is* furnished." At which it was easy for her to sigh "Ah yes—!" all vaguely and discreetly; since his parents and his favourite sister, to say nothing of other kin, in numbers, had run their course and met their end there. That represented, within the walls, ineffaceable life.

It was a few days after this that, during an hour passed with her again, he had expressed his impatience of the too flattering curiosity—among the people he met—about his appreciation of New York. He had arrived at none at all that was socially producible, and as for that matter of his "thinking" (thinking the better or the worse of anything there) he was wholly taken up with one subject of thought. It was mere vain egoism, and it was moreover, if she liked, a morbid obsession. He found all things come back to the question of what he personally might have been, how he might have led his life and "turned out," if he had not so, at the outset, given it up. And confessing for the first time to the intensity within him of this absurd speculation—which but proved also, no doubt, the habit of too selfishly thinking—he affirmed the impotence there of any other source of interest, any other native appeal. "What would it have made of me, what would it have made of me? I keep for ever wondering, all idiotically; as if I could possibly know! I see what it has made of dozens of others, those I meet, and it positively aches within me, to the point of exasperation, that it would have made something of me as well. Only I can't make out *what,* and the worry of it, the small rage of curiosity never to be satisfied, brings back what I remember to have felt, once or twice, after judging best, for reasons, to burn some important letter unopened. I've been sorry, I've hated it—I've never known what was in the letter. You may of course say it's a trifle—!"

"I don't say it's a trifle," Miss Staverton gravely interrupted.

She was seated by her fire, and before her, on his feet and restless, he turned to and fro between this intensity of his idea and a fitful and unseeing inspection, through his single eye-glass, of the dear little old objects on her chimney-piece. Her interruption made him for an instant look at her harder. "I shouldn't care if you did!" he laughed, however; "and it's only a figure, at any rate, for the way I now feel. *Not* to have followed my perverse young course—and almost in the teeth of my father's curse, as I may say; not to have kept it up, so, 'over there,' from that day to this, without a doubt or a pang; not, above all, to have liked it, to have loved it, so much, loved it, no doubt, with such an abysmal conceit of my own preference: some variation from *that,* I say, must have produced some different effect for my life and for my 'form.' I should have stuck here—if it had been possible; and I was too young, at twenty-three, to judge, *pour deux sous*, whether it *were* possible. If I had waited I might have seen it was, and then I might have been, by staying here, something nearer to one of these types who have been hammered so hard and made so keen by their conditions. It isn't that I admire them so much—the question of any charm in them, or of any charm, beyond that of the rank money-passion, exerted by their conditions *for* them, has nothing to do with the matter: it's only a question of what fantastic, yet perfectly possible, development of my own nature I mayn't have missed. It comes over me that I had then a strange *alter ego* deep down somewhere within me, as the full-blown flower is in the small tight bud, and that I just took the course, I just transferred him to the climate, that blighted him for once and for ever."

"And you wonder about the flower," Miss Staverton said. "So do I, if you want to know; and so I've been wondering these several weeks. I believe in the flower," she continued, "I feel it would have been quite splendid, quite huge and monstrous."

"Monstrous above all!" her visitor echoed; "and I imagine, by the same stroke, quite hideous and offensive."

"You don't believe that," she returned; "if you did you wouldn't wonder. You'd know, and that would be enough for you. What you feel—and what I feel *for* you—is that you'd have had power."

"You'd have liked me that way?" he asked.

She barely hung fire. "How should I not have liked you?"

"I see. You'd have liked me, have preferred me, a billionaire!"

"How should I not have liked you?" she simply again asked.

He stood before her still—her question kept him motionless. He took it in, so much there was of it; and indeed his not otherwise meeting it testified to that. "I know at least what I am," he simply went on; "the other side of the medal's clear enough. I've not been edifying—I believe I'm thought in a hundred quarters to have been barely decent. I've followed strange paths and worshipped strange gods; it must have come to you again and again—in fact you've admitted to me as much—that I was leading, at any time these thirty years, a selfish frivolous scandalous life. And you see what it has made of me."

She just waited, smiling at him. "You see what it has made of *me*."

"Oh you're a person whom nothing can have altered. You were born to be what you are, anywhere, anyway: you've the perfection nothing else could have blighted. And you don't see how, without my exile, I shouldn't have been waiting till now—?" But he pulled up for the strange pang.

"The great thing to see," she presently said, "seems to me to be that it has spoiled nothing. It hasn't spoiled your being here at last. It hasn't spoiled this. It hasn't spoiled your speaking—" She also however faltered.

He wondered at everything her controlled emotion might mean. "Do you believe then—too dreadfully!—that I *am* as good as I might ever have been?"

"Oh no! Far from it!" With which she got up from her chair and was nearer to him. "But I don't care," she smiled.

"You mean I'm good enough?"

She considered a little. "Will you believe it if I say so? I mean will you let that settle your question for you?" And then as if making out in his face that he drew back from this, that he had some idea which, however absurd, he couldn't yet bargain away: "Oh you don't care either—but very differently: you don't care for anything but yourself."

Spencer Brydon recognised it—it was in fact what he had absolutely professed. Yet he importantly qualified. *"He* isn't myself. He's the just so totally other person. But I do want to see him," he added. "And I can. And I shall."

Their eyes met for a minute while he guessed from something in hers that she divined his strange sense. But neither of them otherwise expressed it, and her apparent understanding, with no protesting shock, no easy derision, touched him more deeply than anything yet, constituting for his stifled perversity, on the spot, an element that was like breatheable air. What she said however was unexpected. "Well, *I've* seen him."

"You—?"

"I've seen him in a dream."

"Oh a 'dream'—!" It let him down.

"But twice over," she continued. "I saw him as I see you now."

"You've dreamed the same dream—?"

"Twice over," she repeated. "The very same."

This did somehow a little speak to him, as it also gratified him. "You dream about me at that rate?"

"Ah about *him!"* she smiled.

His eyes again sounded her. "Then you know all about him." And as she said nothing more: "What's the wretch like?"

She hesitated, and it was as if he were pressing her so hard that, resisting for reasons of her own, she had to turn away. ""I'll tell you some other time!"

II

It was after this that there was most of a virtue for him, most of a cultivated charm, most of a preposterous secret thrill, in the particular form of surrender to his obsession and of address to what he more and more believed to be his privilege. It was what in these weeks he was living for—since he really felt life to begin but after Mrs. Muldoon had retired from the scene and, visiting the ample house from attic to cellar, making sure he was alone, he knew himself in safe possession and, as he tacitly expressed it, let himself go. He sometimes came twice in the twenty-four hours; the moments he liked best were those of gathering dusk, of the short autumn twilight; this was the time of which, again and again, he found himself hoping most. Then he could, as seemed to him, most intimately wander and wait, linger and listen, feel his fine attention, never in his life before so fine, on the pulse of the great vague place: he preferred the lampless hour and only wished he might have prolonged each day the deep crepuscular spell. Later—rarely much before midnight, but then for a considerable vigil—he watched with his glimmering light; moving slowly, holding it high, playing it far, rejoicing above all, as much as he might, in open vistas, reaches of communication between rooms and by passages; the long straight chance or show, as he would have called it, for the revelation he pretended to invite. It was a practice he found he could perfectly "work" without exciting remark; no one was in the least the wiser for it; even Alice Staverton, who was moreover a well of discretion, didn't quite fully imagine.

He let himself in and let himself out with the assurance of calm proprietorship; and accident so far favoured him that, if a fat Avenue "officer" had happened on occasion to see him entering at eleven-thirty, he had never yet, to the best of his belief, been noticed as emerging at two. He walked there on the crisp November nights, arrived regularly at the evening's end; it was as easy to do this after dining out as to take his way to a club or to his hotel. When he left his club, if he hadn't been dining out, it was ostensibly to go to his hotel; and when he left his hotel, if he had spent a part of the evening there, it was ostensibly to go to his club. Everything was easy in fine; everything conspired and promoted: there was truly even in the strain of his experience something that glossed over, something that salved and simplified, all the rest of consciousness. He circulated, talked, renewed, loosely and pleasantly, old relations—met indeed, so far as he could, new expectations and seemed to make out on the whole that in spite of the career, of such different contacts, which he had spoken of to Miss Staverton as ministering so little, for those who might have watched it, to edification, he was positively rather liked than not. He was a dim secondary social success—and all with people who had truly not an idea of him. It was all mere surface sound, this murmur of their welcome, this popping of their corks—just as his gestures of response were the extravagant shadows, emphatic in proportion as they meant little, of some game of *ombres chinoises*.[1] He

[1] *ombres chinoises.* Galanty show; shadow play.

projected himself all day, in thought, straight over the bristling line of hard unconscious heads and into the other, the real, the waiting life; the life that, as soon as he had heard behind him the click of his great house-door, began for him, on the jolly corner, as beguilingly as the slow opening bars of some rich music follows the tap of the conductor's wand.

He always caught the first effect of the steel point of his stick on the old marble of the hall pavement, large black-and-white squares that he remembered as the admiration of his childhood and that had then made in him, as he now saw, for the growth of an early conception of style. This effect was the dim reverberating tinkle as of some far-off bell hung who should say where?—in the depths of the house, of the past, of that mystical other world that might have flourished for him had he not, for weal or woe, abandoned it. On this impression he did ever the same thing; he put his stick noiselessly away in a corner—feeling the place once more in the likeness of some great glass bowl, all precious concave crystal, set delicately humming by the play of a moist finger round its edge. The concave crystal held, as it were, this mystical other world, and the indescribably fine murmur of its rim was the sigh there, the scarce audible pathetic wail to his strained ear, of all the old baffled forsworn possibilities. What he did therefore by this appeal of his hushed presence was to wake them into such measure of ghostly life as they might still enjoy. They were shy, all but unappeasably shy, but they weren't really sinister; at least they weren't as he had hitherto felt them—before they had taken the Form he so yearned to make them take, the Form he at moments saw himself in the light of fairly hunting on tiptoe, the points of his evening-shoes, from room to room and from storey to storey.

That was the essence of his vision—which was all rank folly, if one would, while he was out of the house and otherwise occupied, but which took on the last verisimilitude as soon as he was placed and posted. He knew what he meant and what he wanted; it was as clear as the figure on a cheque presented in demand for cash. His *alter ego* "walked"—that was the note of his image of him, while his image of his motive for his own odd pastime was the desire to waylay him and meet him. He roamed, slowly, warily, but all restlessly, he himself did—Mrs. Muldoon had been right, absolutely, with her figure of their "craping"; and the presence he watched for would roam restlessly too. But it would be as cautious and as shifty; the conviction of its probable, in fact its already quite sensible, quite audible evasion of pursuit grew for him from night to night, laying on him finally a rigour to which nothing in his life had been comparable. It had been the theory of many superficially-judging persons, he knew, that he was wasting that life in a surrender to sensations, but he had tasted of no pleasure so fine as his actual tension, had been introduced to no sport that demanded at once the patience and the nerve of this stalking of a creature more subtle, yet at bay perhaps more formidable, than any beast of the forest. The terms, the comparisons, the very practices of the chase positively came again into play; there were even moments when passages of his occasional experience as a sportsman, stirred memories, from his younger time, of moor and mountain and desert, revived for him—and to the increase of his keenness—by the tremendous force of analogy. He found himself at moments—once he had placed his single light on some mantel-shelf or in some recess—stepping back into shelter or shade, effacing himself behind a door or in an embrasure, as he had sought of old the vantage of rock and tree; he found himself holding his breath and living in the joy of the instant, the supreme suspense created by big game alone.

He wasn't afraid (though putting himself to the question as he believed gentlemen on Bengal tiger-shoots or in close quarters with the great bear of the Rockies had been known to confess to having put it); and this indeed—since here at least he might be frank!—because of the impression, so intimate and so strange, that he himself produced as yet a dread, produced certainly a strain, beyond the liveliest he was likely to feel. They fell for him into categories, they fairly became familiar, the signs, for his own perception, of the alarm his presence and his vigilance created; though leaving him always to remark, portentously, on his probably having formed a relation, his probably enjoying a consciousness, unique in the experience of man. People enough, first and last, had been in terror of apparitions, but who had ever before so turned the tables and become himself, in the apparitional world, an incalculable terror? He might have found this sublime had he quite dared to think of it; but he didn't too much insist, truly, on that side of his privilege. With habit and repetition he gained to an extraordinary degree the power to penetrate the dusk of distances and the darkness of corners, to resolve back into their innocence the treacheries of uncertain light, the evil-looking forms taken in the gloom by mere shadows, by accidents of the air, by shifting effects of perspective; putting down his dim luminary he could still wander on without it, pass into other rooms and, only knowing it was there behind him in case of need, see his way about, visually project for his purpose a comparative clearness. It made him feel, this acquired faculty, like some monstrous stealthy cat; he wondered if he would have glared at these moments with large shining yellow eyes, and what it mightn't verily be, for the poor hard-pressed *alter ego,* to be confronted with such a type.

He liked however the open shutters; he opened everywhere those Mrs. Muldoon had closed, closing them as carefully afterwards, so that she shouldn't notice: he liked—oh this he did like, and above all in the upper rooms!—the sense of the hard silver of the autumn stars through the window-panes, and scarcely less the flare of the street-lamps below, the white electric lustre which it would have taken curtains to keep out. This was human actual social; this was of the world he had lived in, and he was more at his ease certainly for the countenance, coldly general and impersonal, that all the while and in spite of his detachment it seemed to give him. He had support of course mostly in the rooms at the wide front and the prolonged side; it failed him considerably in the central shades and the parts at the back. But if he sometimes, on his rounds, was glad of his optical reach, so none the less often the rear of the house affected him as the very jungle of his prey. The place was there more subdivided; a large "extension" in particular, where small rooms for servants had been multiplied, abounded in nooks and corners, in closets and passages, in the ramifications especially of an ample back staircase over which he leaned, many a time, to look far down—not deterred from his gravity even while aware that he might, for a spectator, have figured some solemn simpleton playing at hide-and-seek. Outside in fact he might himself make that ironic *rapprochement;* but with the walls, and in spite of the clear windows, his consistency was proof against the cynical light of New York.

It had belonged to that idea of the exasperated consciousness of his victim to become a real test for him; since he had quite put it to himself from the first that, oh distinctly! he could "cultivate" his whole perception. He had felt it as above all open to cultivation—which indeed was but another name for his manner of spending his time. He was bringing it on, bringing it to perfection, by practice; in consequence of which it had grown so fine that he was now aware of impressions, attestations of his general postulate, that couldn't have broken upon him at once. This was the case more specifically with a phenomenon at last quite frequent for him in the upper rooms, the recognition—absolutely unmistakeable, and by a turn dating from a particular hour, his resumption of his campaign after a diplomatic drop, a calculated absence of three nights—of his being definitely followed, tracked at a distance carefully taken and to the express end that he should the less confidently, less arrogantly, appear to himself merely to pursue. It worried, it finally quite broke him up, for it proved, of all the conceivable impressions, the one least suited to his book. He was kept in sight while remaining himself—as regards the essence of his position—sightless, and his only recourse then was in abrupt turns, rapid recoveries of ground. He wheeled about, retracing his steps, as if he might so catch in his face at least the stirred air of some other quick revolution. It was indeed true that his fully dislocalised thought of these maneuvres recalled to him Pantaloon, at the Christmas farce, buffeted and tricked from behind by ubiquitous Harlequin; but it left intact the influence of the conditions themselves each time he was re-exposed to them, so that in fact this association, had he suffered it to become constant, would on a certain side have ministered to his intenser gravity. He had made, as I have said, to create on the premises the baseless sense of a reprieve, his three absences; and the result of the third was to confirm the after-effect of the second.

On his return, that night—the night succeeding his last intermission—he stood in the hall and looked up the staircase with a certainty more intimate than any he had yet known. "He's *there,* at the top, and waiting—not, as in general, falling back for disappearance. He's holding his ground, and it's the first time—which is a proof, isn't it? that something has happened for him." So Brydon argued with his hand on the banister and his foot on the lowest stair; in which position he felt as never before the air chilled by his logic. He himself turned cold in it, for he seemed of a sudden to know what now was involved. "Harder pressed?—yes, he takes it in, with its thus making clear to him that I've come, as they say, 'to stay.' He finally doesn't like and can't bear it, in the sense, I mean, that his wrath, his menaced interest, now balances with his dread. I've hunted him till he has 'turned': that, up there, is what has happened—he's the fanged or the antlered animal brought at last to bay." There came to him, as I say—but determined by an influence beyond my notation!—the acuteness of this certainty; under which however the next moment he had broken into a sweat that he would as little have consented to attribute to fear as he would have dared immediately to act upon it for enterprise. It marked none the less a prodigious thrill, a thrill that represented sudden dismay, no doubt, but also represented, and with the selfsame throb, the strangest, the most joyous, possibly the next minute almost the proudest, duplication of consciousness.

"'He has been dodging, retreating, hiding, but now, worked up to anger, he'll fight!"—this intense impression made a single mouthful, as it were, of terror and applause. But what was wondrous was that the applause, for the felt fact, was so eager, since, if it was his other self he was running to earth, this ineffable identity was thus in the last resort not unworthy of him. It bristled there—somewhere near at hand, however unseen still—as the hunted thing, even as the trodden worm of the adage *must* at last bristle; and Brydon at this instant tasted probably of a sensation more complex than had ever before found itself consistent with sanity. It was as if it would have shamed him that a character so associated with his own should triumphantly succeed in just skulking, should to the end not risk the open, so that the drop of this danger was, on the spot, a great lift of the whole situation. Yet with another rare shift of the same subtlety he was already trying to measure by how much more he himself might now be in peril of fear; so rejoicing that he could, in another form, actively inspire that fear, and simultaneously quaking for the form in which he might passively know it.

The apprehension of knowing it must after a little have grown in him, and the strangest moment of his adventure perhaps, the most memorable or really most interesting, afterwards, of his crisis, was the lapse of certain instants of concentrated conscious *combat,* the sense of a need to hold on to something, even after the manner of a man slipping and slipping on some awful incline; the vivid impulse, above all, to move, to act, to charge, somehow and upon something—to show himself, in a word, that he wasn't afraid. The state of "holding-on" was thus the state to which he was momentarily reduced; if there had been anything, in the great vacancy, to seize, he would presently have been aware of having clutched it as he might under a shock at home have clutched the nearest chair-back. He had been surprised at any rate—of this he *was* aware—into something unprecedented since his original appropriation of the place; he had closed his eyes, held them tight, for a long minute, as with that instinct of dismay and that terror of vision. When he opened them the room, the other contiguous rooms, extraordinarily, seemed lighter—so light, almost, that at first he took the change for day. He stood firm, however that might be, just where he had paused; his resistance had helped him—it was as if there were something he had tided over. He knew after a little what this was—it had been in the imminent danger of flight. He had stiffened his will against going; without this he would have made for the stairs, and it seemed to him that, still with his eyes closed, he would have descended them, would have known how, straight and swiftly, to the bottom.

Well, as he had held out, here he was—still at the top, among the more intricate upper rooms and with the gauntlet of the others, of all the rest of the house, still to run when it should be his time to go. He would go at his time—only at his time: didn't he go every night very much at the same hour? He took out his watch—there was light for that: it was scarcely a quarter past one, and he had never withdrawn so soon. He reached his lodgings for the most part at two—with his walk of a quarter of an hour. He would wait for the last quarter—he wouldn't stir till then; and he kept his watch there with his eyes on it, reflecting while he held it that this deliberate wait, a wait with an effort, which he recognised, would serve perfectly for the attestation he desired to make. It would prove his courage—unless indeed the latter might most be proved by his budging at last from his place. What he mainly felt now was that, since he hadn't originally scuttled, he had his dignities—which had never in his life seemed so many—all to preserve and to carry aloft. This was before him in truth as a physical image, an image almost worthy of an age of greater romance. That remark indeed glimmered for him only to glow the next instant with a finer light, since what age of romance, after all, could have matched either the state of his mind or, "objectively," as they said, the wonder of his situation? The only difference would have been that, brandishing his dignities over his head as in a parchment scroll, he might then—that is in the heroic time—have proceeded downstairs with a drawn sword in his other grasp.

At present, really, the light he had set down on the mantel of the next room would have to figure his sword; which utensil, in the course of a minute, he had taken the requisite number of steps to possess himself of. The door between the rooms was open, and from the second another door opened to a third. These rooms, as he remembered, gave all three upon a common corridor as well, but there was a fourth, beyond them, without issue save through the preceding. To have moved, to have heard his step again, was appreciably a help; though even in recognising this he lingered once more a little by the chimney-piece on which his light had rested. When he next moved, just hesitating where to turn, he found himself considering a circumstance that, after his first and comparatively vague apprehension of it, produced in him the start that often attends some pang of recollection, the violent shock of having ceased happily to forget. He had come into sight of the door in which the brief chain of communication ended and which he now surveyed from the nearer threshold, the one not directly facing it. Placed at some distance to the left of this point, it would have admitted him to the last room of the four, the room without other approach or egress, had it not, to his intimate conviction, been closed *since* his former visitation, the matter probably of a quarter of an hour before. He stared with all his eyes at the wonder of the fact, arrested again where he stood and again holding his breath while he sounded its sense. Surely it had been *subsequently* closed—that is it had been on his previous passage indubitably open!

He took it full in the face that something had happened between—that he couldn't not have noticed before (by which he meant on his original tour of all the rooms that evening) that such a barrier had exceptionally presented itself. He had indeed since that moment undergone an agitation so extraordinary that it might have muddled for him any earlier view; and he tried to convince himself that he might perhaps then have gone into the room and, inadvertently, automatically, on coming out, have drawn the door after him. The difficulty was that this exactly was what he never did; it was against his whole policy, as he might have said, the essence of which was to keep vistas clear. He had them from the first, as he was well aware, quite on the brain: the strange apparition, at the far end of one of them, of his baffled "prey" (which had become by so sharp an irony so little the term now to apply!) was the form of success his imagination had most cherished, projecting into it always a refinement of beauty. He had known fifty times the start of perception that had afterwards dropped; had fifty times gasped to himself "There!"

under some fond brief hallucination. The house, as the case stood, admirably lent itself; he might wonder at the taste, the native architecture of the particular time, which could rejoice so in the multiplication of doors—the opposite extreme to the modern, the actual almost complete proscription of them; but it had fairly contributed to provoke this obsession of the presence encountered telescopically, as he might say, focussed and studied in diminishing perspective and as by a rest for the elbow.

It was with these considerations that his present attention was charged—they perfectly availed to make what he saw portentous. He *couldn't,* by any lapse, have blocked that aperture; and if he hadn't, if it was unthinkable, why what else was clear but that there had been another agent? Another agent?—he had been catching, as he felt, a moment back, the very breath of him; but when had he been so close as in this simple, this logical, this completely personal act? It was so logical, that is, that one might have *taken* it for personal; yet for what did Brydon take it, he asked himself, while, softly panting, he felt his eyes almost leave their sockets. Ah this time at last they *were,* the two, the opposed projections of him, in presence; and this time, as much as one would, the question of danger loomed. With it rose, as not before, the question of courage—for what he knew the blank face of the door to say to him was "Show us how much you have!" It stared, it glared back at him with that challenge; it put to him the two alternatives: should he just push it open or not? Oh to have this consciousness was to *think*—and to think, Brydon knew, as he stood there, was, with the lapsing moments, not to have acted! Not to have acted—that was the misery and the pang—was even still not to act; was in fact *all* to feel the thing in another, in a new and terrible way. How long did he pause and how long did he debate? There was presently nothing to measure it; for his vibration had already changed—as just by the effect of its intensity. Shut up there, at bay, defiant, and with the prodigy of the thing palpably proveably *done,* thus giving notice like some stark signboard—under that accession of accent the situation itself had turned; and Brydon at last remarkably made up his mind on what it had turned to.

It had turned altogether to a different admonition; to a supreme hint, for him, of the value of Discretion! This slowly dawned, no doubt—for it could take its time; so perfectly, on his threshold, had he been stayed, so little as yet had he either advanced or retreated. It was the strangest of all things that now when, by his taking ten steps and applying his hand to a latch, or even his shoulder and his knee, if necessary, to a panel, all the hunger of his prime need might have been met, his high curiosity crowned, his unrest assuaged—it was amazing, but it was also exquisite and rare, that insistence should have, at a touch, quite dropped from him. Discretion—he jumped at that; and yet not, verily, at such a pitch, because it saved his nerves or his skin, but because, much more valuably, it saved the situation. When I say he "jumped" at it I feel the consonance of this term with the fact that—at the end indeed of I know not how long—he did move again, he crossed straight to the door. He wouldn't touch it—it seemed now that he might *if* he would: he would only just wait there a little, to show, to prove, that he wouldn't. He had thus another station, close to the thin partition by which revelation was denied him; but with his eyes bent and his hands held off in a mere intensity of stillness. He listened as if there had been something to hear, but this attitude, while it lasted, was his own communication. "If you won't then—good: I spare you and I give up. You affect me as by the appeal positively for pity: you convince me that for reasons rigid and sublime—what do I know?—we both of us should have suffered. I respect them then, and, though moved and privileged as, I believe, it has never been given to man, I retire, I renounce—never, on my honour, to try again. So rest for ever—and let *me!*"

That, for Brydon was the deep sense of this last demonstration—solemn, measured, directed, as he felt it to be. He brought it to a close, he turned away; and now verily he knew how deeply he had been stirred. He retraced his steps, taking up his candle, burnt, he observed, well-nigh to the socket, and marking again, lighten it as he would, the distinctness of his footfall; after which, in a moment, he knew himself at the other side of the house. He did here what he had not yet done at these hours—he opened half a casement, one of those in the front, and let in the air of the night, a thing he would have taken at any time previous for a sharp rupture of his spell. His spell was broken now, and it didn't matter—broken by his concession and his surrender, which made it idle henceforth that he should ever come back. The empty street—its other life so marked even by the great lamplit vacancy—was within call, within touch; he stayed there as to be in it again, high above it though he was still perched; he watched as for some comforting common fact, some vulgar human note, the passage of a scavenger or a thief, some night-bird however base. He would have blessed that sign of life; he would have welcomed positively the slow approach of his friend the policeman, whom he had hitherto only sought to avoid, and was not sure that if the patrol had come into sight he mightn't have felt the impulse to get into relation with it, to hail it, on some pretext, from his fourth floor.

The pretext that wouldn't have been too silly or too compromising, the explanation that would have saved his dignity and kept his name, in such a case, out of the papers, was not definite to him: he was so occupied with the thought of recording his Discretion—as an effect of the vow he had just uttered to his intimate adversary—that the importance of this loomed large and something had overtaken all ironically his sense of proportion. If there had been a ladder applied to the front of the house, even one of the vertiginous perpendiculars employed by painters and roofers and sometimes left standing overnight, he would have managed somehow, astride of the window-sill, to compass by outstretched leg and arm that mode of descent. If there had been some such uncanny thing as he had found in his room at hotels, a workable fire-escape in the form of notched cable or a canvas shoot, he would have availed himself of it as a proof—well, of his present delicacy. He nursed that sentiment, as the question stood, a little in vain, and even—at the end of he scarce knew, once more, how long—found it, as by the action on his mind of the failure of response of the outer world, sinking back to vague anguish. It seemed to him he had waited an age for some stir of the great grim hush; the life of the town was itself under a spell—so unnaturally, up and down the whole prospect of known and rather ugly objects, the blankness and the silence lasted. Had they ever, he asked himself, the hard-faced houses, which had begun to look livid in the dim dawn, had they ever spoken so little to any need of his spirit? Great builded voids, great crowded stillnesses put on, often, in the heart of cities, for the small hours, a sort of sinister mask, and it was of this large collective negation that Brydon presently became conscious—all the more that the break of day was, almost incredibly, now at hand, proving to him what a night he had made of it.

He looked again at his watch, saw what had become of his time-values (he had taken hours for minutes—not, as in other tense situations, minutes for hours) and the strange air of the streets was but the weak, the sullen flush of a dawn in which everything was still locked up. His choked appeal from his own open window had been the sole note of life, and he could but break off at last as for a worse despair. Yet while so deeply demoralised he was capable again of an impulse denoting—at least by his present measure—extraordinary resolution; of retracing his steps to the spot where he had turned cold with the extinction of his last pulse of doubt as to there being in the place another presence than his own. This required an effort strong enough to sicken him; but he had his reason, which over-mastered for the moment everything else. There was the whole of the rest of the house to traverse, and how should he screw himself to that if the door he had seen closed were at present open? He could hold to the idea that the closing had practically been for him an act of mercy, a chance offered him to descend, depart, get off the ground and never again profane it. This conception held together, it worked; but what it meant for him depended now clearly on the amount of forbearance his recent action, or rather his recent inaction, had engendered. The image of the "presence," whatever it was, waiting there for him to go—this image had not yet been so concrete for his nerves as when he stopped short of the point at which certainty would have come to him. For, with all his resolution, or more exactly with all his dread, he did stop short—he hung back from really seeing. The risk was too great and his fear too definite: it took at this moment an awful specific form.

He knew—yes, as he had never known anything—that, *should* he see the door open, it would all too abjectly be the end of him. It would mean that the agent of his shame—for his shame was the deep abjection—was once more at large and in general possession; and what glared him thus in the face was the act that this would determine for him. It would send him straight about to the window he had left open, and by that window, be long ladder and dangling rope as absent as they would, he saw himself uncontrollably insanely fatally take his way to the street. The hideous chance of this he at least could avert; but he could only avert it by recoiling in time from assurance. He had the whole house to deal with, this fact was still there; only he now knew that uncertainty alone could start him. He stole back from where he had checked himself—merely to do so was suddenly like safety—and, making blindly for the greater staircase, left gaping rooms and sounding passages behind. Here was the top of the stairs, with a fine large dim descent and three spacious landings to mark off. His instinct was all for mildness, but his feet were harsh on the floors, and, strangely, when he had in a couple of minutes become aware of this, it counted somehow for help. He couldn't have spoken, the tone of his voice would have scared him, and the common conceit or resource of "whistling in the dark" (whether literally or figuratively) have appeared basely vulgar; yet he liked none the less to hear himself go, and when he had reached his first landing—taking it all with no rush, but quite steadily—that stage of success drew from him a gasp of relief.

The house, withal, seemed immense, the scale of space again inordinate; the open rooms to no one of which his eyes deflected, gloomed in their shuttered state like mouths of caverns; only the high skylight that formed the crown of the deep well created for him a medium in which he could advance, but which might have been, for queerness of colour, some watery under-world. He tried to think of something noble, as that his property was really grand, a splendid possession; but this nobleness took the form too of the clear delight with which he was finally to sacrifice it. They might come in now, the builders, the destroyers—they might come as soon as they would. At the end of two flights he had dropped to another zone, and from the middle of the third, with only one more left, he recognised the influence of the lower windows, of half-drawn blinds, of the occasional gleam of street-lamps, of the glazed spaces of the vestibule. This was the bottom of the sea, which showed an illumination of its own and which he even saw paved—when at a given moment he drew up to sink a long look over the banisters—with the marble squares of his childhood. By that time indubitably he felt, as he might have said in a commoner cause, better; it had allowed him to stop and draw breath, and the ease increased with the sight of the old black-and-white slabs. But what he most felt was that now surely, with the element of impunity pulling him as by hard firm hands, the case was settled for what he might have seen above had he dared that last look. The closed door, blessedly remote now, was still closed—and he had only in short to reach that of the house.

He came down further, he crossed the passage forming the access to the last flight; and if here again he stopped an instant it was almost for the sharpness of the thrill of assured escape. It made him shut his eyes—which opened again to the straight slope of the remainder of the stairs. Here was impunity still, but impunity almost excessive; inasmuch as the side-lights and the high fan-tracery of the entrance were glimmering straight into the hall; an appearance produced, he the next instant saw, by the fact that the vestibule gaped wide, that the hinged halves of the inner door had been thrown far back. Out of that again the *question* sprang at him, making his eyes, as he felt, half-start from his head, as they had done, at the top of the house, before the sign of the other door. If he had left that one open, hadn't he left this one closed, and wasn't he now in *most* immediate presence of some inconceivable occult activity? It was as sharp, the question, as a knife in his side, but the answer hung fire still and seemed to lose itself in the vague darkness to which the thin admitted dawn, glimmering archwise over the whole outer door, made a semicircular margin, a cold silvery nimbus that seemed to play a little as he looked—to shift and expand and contract.

It was as if there had been something within it, protected by indistinctness and corresponding in extent with the opaque surface behind, the painted panels of the last barrier to his escape, of which the key was in his pocket. The indistinctness mocked him even while he stared, affected him as somehow shrouding or challenging certitude, so that after faltering an instant on his step he let himself go with the sense that here *was* at last something to meet, to touch, to take, to know—something all unnatural and dreadful, but to advance upon which was the condition for him either of liberation or of supreme defeat. The penumbra, dense and dark, was the virtual screen of a figure which stood in it as still as some image erect in a niche or as some black-vizored sentinel guarding a treasure. Brydon was to know afterwards, was to recall and make out, the particular thing he had believed during the rest of his descent. He saw, in its great grey glimmering margin, the central vagueness diminish, and he felt it to be taking the very form toward which, for so many days, the passion of his curiosity had yearned. It gloomed, it loomed, it was something, it was somebody, the prodigy of a personal presence.

Rigid and conscious, spectral yet human, a man of his own substance and stature waited there to measure himself with his power to dismay. This only could it be—this only till he recognised, with his advance, that what made the face dim was the pair of raised hands that covered it and in which, so far from being offered in defiance, it was buried as for dark deprecation. So Brydon, before him, took him in; with every fact of him now, in the higher light, hard and acute—his planted stillness, his vivid truth, his grizzled bent head and white masking hands, his queer actuality of evening-dress, of dangling double eye-glass, of gleaming silk lappet and white linen, of pearl button and gold watch-guard and polished shoe. No portrait by a great modern master could have presented him with more intensity, thrust him out of his frame with more art, as if there had been "treatment," of the consummate sort, in his every shade and salience. The revulsion, for our friend, had become, before he knew it, immense—this drop, in the act of apprehension, to the sense of his adversary's inscrutable maneuvre. That meaning at least, while he gaped, it offered him; for he could but gape at his other self in this other anguish, gape as a proof that *he,* standing there for the achieved, the enjoyed, the triumphant life, couldn't be faced in his triumph. Wasn't the proof in the splendid covering hands, strong and completely spread?—so spread and so intentional that, in spite of a special verity that surpassed every other, the fact that one of these hands had lost two fingers, which were reduced to stumps, as if accidentally shot away, the face was effectually guarded and saved.

"Saved," though, *would* it be?—Brydon breathed his wonder till the very impunity of his attitude and the very insistence of his eyes produced, as he felt, a sudden stir which showed the next instant as a deeper portent, while the head raised itself, the betrayal of a braver purpose. The hands, as he looked, began to move, to open; then, as if deciding in a flash, dropped from the face and left it uncovered and presented. Horror, with the sight, had leaped into Brydon's throat, gasping there in a sound he couldn't utter; for the bared identity was too hideous as *his,* and his glare was the passion of his protest. The face, *that* face, Spencer Brydon's?—he searched it still, but looking away from it in dismay and denial, falling straight from his height of sublimity. It was unknown, inconceivable, awful, disconnected from any possibility—! He had been "sold," he inwardly moaned, stalking such game as this: the presence before him was a presence, the horror within him a horror, but the waste of his nights had been only grotesque and the success of his adventure an irony. Such an identity fitted his at *no* point, made its alternative monstrous. A thousand times yes, as it came upon him nearer now—the face was the face of a stranger. It came upon him nearer now, quite as one of those expanding fantastic images projected by the magic lantern of childhood; for the stranger, whoever he might be, evil, odious, blatant, vulgar, had advanced as for aggression, and he knew himself give ground. Then harder pressed still, sick with the force of his shock, and falling back as under the hot breath and the roused passion of a life larger than his own, a rage of personality before which his own collapsed, he felt the whole vision turn to darkness and his very feet give way. His head went round; he was going; he had gone.

III

What had next brought him back, clearly—though after how long?—was Mrs. Muldoon's voice, coming to him from quite near, from so near that he seemed presently to see her as kneeling on the ground before him while he lay looking up at her; himself not wholly on the ground, but half-raised and upheld—conscious, yes, of tenderness of support and, more particularly, of a head pillowed in extraordinary softness and faintly refreshing fragrance. He considered, he wondered, his wit but half at his service; than another face intervened, bending more directly over him, and he finally knew that Alice Staverton had made her lap an ample and perfect cushion to him, and that she had to this end seated herself on the lowest degree of the staircase, the rest of his long person remaining stretched on his old black-and-white slabs. They were cold, these marble squares of his youth; but *he* somehow was not, in this rich return of consciousness—the most wonderful hour, little by little, that he had ever known, leaving him, as it did, so gratefully, so abysmally passive, and yet as with a treasure of intelligence waiting all round him for quiet appropriation; dissolved, he might call it, in the air of the place and producing the golden glow of a late autumn afternoon. He had come back, yes—come back from further away than any man but himself had ever travelled; but it was strange how with this sense what he had come back *to* seemed really the great thing, and as if his prodigious journey had been all for the sake of it. Slowly but surely his consciousness grew, his vision of his state thus completing itself: he had been miraculously *carried* back—lifted and carefully borne as from where he had been picked up, the uttermost end of an interminable grey passage. Even with this he was suffered to rest, and what had now brought him to knowledge was the break in the long mild motion.

It had brought him to knowledge, to knowledge—yes, this was the beauty of his state; which came to resemble more and more that of a man who has gone to sleep on some news of a great inheritance, and then, after dreaming it away, after profaning it with matters strange to it, has waked up again to serenity of certitude and has only to lie and watch it grow. This was the drift of his patience—that he had only to let it shine on him. He must moreover, with intermissions, still have been lifted and borne; since why and how else should he have known himself, later on, with the afternoon glow intenser, no longer at the foot of his stairs—situated as these now seemed at that dark other end of his tunnel—but on a deep window-bench of his high saloon, over which had been spread, couch-fashion, a mantel of soft stuff lined with grey fur that was familiar to his eyes and that one of his hands kept fondly feeling as for its pledge of truth. Mrs. Muldoon's face had gone, but the other, the second he had recognised, hung over him in a way that showed how he was still propped and pillowed. He took it all in, and the more he took it the more it seemed to suffice: he was as much at peace as if he had had food and drink. It was the two women who had found him, on Mrs. Muldoon's having plied, at her usual hour, her latch-key—and on her having above all arrived while Miss Staverton still lingered near the house. She had been turning away, all anxiety, from worrying the vain bell-handle—her calculation having been of the hour of the good woman's visit; but the latter, blessedly, had come up while she was still there, and they had entered together. He had then lain, beyond the vestibule, very much as he was lying now—quite, that is, as he appeared to have fallen, but all so wondrously without bruise or gash; only in a depth of stupor. What he most took in, however, at present, with the steadier clearance, was that Alice Staverton had for a long unspeakable moment not doubted he was dead.

"It must have been that I *was*." He made it out as she held him. "Yes—I can only have died. You brought me literally to life. Only," he wondered, his eyes rising to her, "only, in the name of all the benedictions, how?"

It took her but an instant to bend her face and kiss him, and something in the manner of it, and in the way her hands clasped and locked his head while he felt the cool charity and viture of her lips, something in all this beatitude somehow answered everything. "And now I keep you," she said.

"Oh keep me, keep me!" he pleaded while her face still hung over him: in response to which it dropped again and stayed close, clingingly close. It was the seal of their situation—of which he tasted the impress for a long blissful moment in silence. But he came back. "Yet how did you know—?"

"I was uneasy. You were to have come, you remember—and you had sent no word."

"Yes, I remember—I was to have gone to you at one today." It caught on to their "old" life and relation—which were so near and so far. "I was still out there in my strange darkness—where was it, what was it? I must have stayed there so long." He could but wonder at the depth and the duration of his swoon.

"Since last night?" she asked with a shade of fear for her possible indiscretion.

"Since this morning—it must have been: the cold dim dawn of today. Where have I been," he vaguely wailed, "where have I been?" He felt her hold him close, and it was as if this helped him now to make in all security his mild moan. "What a long dark day!"

All in her tenderness she had waited a moment. "In the cold dim dawn?" she quavered.

But he had already gone on piecing together the parts of the whole prodigy. "As I didn't turn up you came straight—?"

She barely cast about. "I went first to your hotel—where they told me of your absence. You had dined out last evening and hadn't been back since. But they appeared to know you had been at your club."

"So you had the idea of *this*—?"

"Of what?" she asked in a moment.

"Well—of what has happened."

"I believe at least you'd have been here. I've known, all along," she said, "that you've been coming."

" 'Known' it—?"

"Well, I've believed it. I said nothing to you after that talk we had a month ago—but I felt sure. I knew you *would,*" she declared.

"That I'd persist, you mean?"

"That you'd see him."

"Ah but I didn't!" cried Brydon with his long wail. "There's somebody—an awful beast; whom I brought, too horribly, to bay. But it's not me."

At this she bent over him again, and her eyes were in his eyes. "No—it's not you." And it was as if, while her face hovered, he might have made out in it, hadn't it been so near, some particular meaning blurred by a smile. "No, thank heaven," she repeated—"it's not you! Of course it wasn't to have been."

"Ah but it *was,*" he gently insisted. And he stared before him now as he had been staring for so many weeks. "I was to have known myself."

"You couldn't!" she returned consolingly. And then reverting, and as if to account further for what she had herself done, "But it wasn't only *that,* that you hadn't been at home," she went on. "I waited till the hour at which we had found Mrs. Muldoon that day of my going with you; and she arrived, as I've told you, while, failing to bring any one to the door, I lingered in my despair on the steps. After a little, if she hadn't come, by such a mercy, I should have found means to hunt her up. But it wasn't," said Alice Staverton, as if once more with her fine intention—"it wasn't only that."

His eyes, as he lay, turned back to her. "What more then?"

She met it, the wonder she had stirred. "In the cold dim dawn, you say? Well, in the cold dim dawn of this morning I too saw you."

"Saw *me*—?"

"Saw *him,*" said Alice Staverton. "It must have been at the same moment."

He lay an instant taking it in—as if he wished to be quite reasonable. "At the same moment?"

"Yes—in my dream again, the same one I've named to you. He came back to me. Then I knew it for a sign. He had come to you."

At this Brydon raised himself; he had to see her better. She helped him when she understood his movement, and he sat up, steadying himself beside her there on the window-bench and with his right hand grasping her left. "*He* didn't come to me."

"You came to yourself," she beautifully smiled.

"Ah I've come to myself now—thanks to you, dearest. But this brute, with his awful face—this brute's a black stranger. He's none of *me*, even as I *might* have been," Brydon sturdily declared.

But she kept the clearness that was like the breath of infallibility. "Isn't the whole point that you'd have been different?"

He almost scowled for it. "As different as *that*—?"

Her look again was more beautiful to him than the things of this world. "Haven't you exactly wanted to know *how* different? So this morning," she said, "you appeared to me."

"Like *him?*"

"A black stranger!"

"Then how did you know it was I?"

"Because, as I told you weeks ago, my mind, my imagination, had worked so over what you might, what you mightn't have been—to show you, you see, how I've thought of you. In the midst of that you came to me—that my wonder might be answered. So I knew," she went on; "and believed that, since the question held you too so fast, as you told me that day, you too would see for yourself. And when this morning I again saw I knew it would be because you had—and also then, from the first moment, because you somehow wanted me. *He* seemed to tell me of that. So why," she strangely smiled, "shouldn't I like him?"

It brought Spencer Brydon to his feet. "You 'like' that horror—?"

"I *could* have liked him. And to me," she said, "he was no horror. I had accepted him."

" 'Accepted'—?" Brydon oddly sounded.

"Before, for the interest of his difference—yes. And as *I* didn't disown him, as *I* knew him—which you at last, confronted with him in his difference, so cruelly didn't, my dear—well, he must have been, you see, less dreadful to me. And it may have pleased him that I pitied him."

She was beside him on her feet, but still holding his hand—still with her arm supporting him. But though it all brought for him thus a dim light, "You 'pitied' him?" he grudgingly, resentfully asked.

"He has been unhappy; he has been ravaged," she said.

"And haven't I been unhappy? Am not I—you've only to look at me!—ravaged?"

"Ah I don't say I like him *better,*" she granted after a thought. "But he's grim, he's worn—and things have happened to him. He doesn't make shift, for sight, with your charming monocle."

"No"—it struck Brydon: "I couldn't have sported mine 'downtown.' They'd have guyed me there."

"His great convex pince-nez—I saw it, I recognised the kind—is for his poor ruined sight. And his poor right hand—!"

"Ah!" Brydon winced—whether for his proved identity or for his lost fingers. Then, "He has a million a year," he lucidly added. "But he hasn't you."

"And he isn't—no, he isn't—*you!*" she murmured as he drew her to his breast.

JOSEPH CONRAD

The Secret Sharer

I

On my right hand there were lines of fishing stakes resembling a mysterious system of half-submerged bamboo fences, incomprehensible in its division of the domain of tropical fishes, and crazy of aspect as if abandoned forever by some nomad tribe of fishermen now gone to the other end of the ocean; for there was no sign of human habitation as far as the eye could reach. To the left a group of barren islets, suggesting ruins of stone walls, towers, and blockhouses, had its foundations set in a blue sea that itself looked solid, so still and stable did it lie below my feet; even the track of light from the westering sun shone smoothly, without that animated glitter which tells of an imperceptible ripple. And when I turned my head to take a parting glance at the tug which had just left us anchored outside the bar, I saw the straight line of the flat shore joined to the stable sea, edge to edge, with a perfect and unmarked closeness, in one leveled floor half brown, half blue under the enormous dome of the sky. Corresponding in their significance to the islets of the sea, two small clumps of trees, one on each side of the only fault in the impeccable joint, marked the mouth of the river Meinam we had just left on the first preparatory stage of our homeward journey; and, far back on the inland level, a large and loftier mass, the grove surrounding the great Paknam pagoda, was the only thing on which the eye could rest from the vain task of exploring the monotonous sweep of the horizon. Here and there gleams as of a few scattered pieces of silver marked the windings of the great river; and on the nearest of them, just within the bar, the tug steaming right into the land became lost to my sight, hull and funnel and masts, as though the impassive earth had swallowed her up without an effort, without a tremor. My eye followed the light cloud of smoke, now here,

From *'Twixt Land and Sea* by Joseph Conrad. Reprinted by permission of J. M. Dent & Sons Ltd. and the Trustees of the Joseph Conrad Estate.

now there, above the plain, according to the devious curves of the steam, but always fainter and farther away, till I lost it at last behind the miter-shaped hill of the great pagoda. And then I was left alone with my ship, anchored at the head of the Gulf of Siam.

She floated at the starting point of a long journey, very still in an immense stillness, the shadows of her spars flung far to the eastward by the setting sun. At that moment I was alone on her decks. There was not a sound in her—and around us nothing moved, nothing lived, not a canoe on the water, not a bird in the air, not a cloud in the sky. In this breathless pause at the threshold of a long passage we seemed to be measuring our fitness for a long and arduous enterprise, the appointed task of both our existences to be carried out, far from all human eyes, with only sky and sea for spectators and for judges.

There must have been some glare in the air to interfere with one's sight, because it was only just before the sun left us that my roaming eyes made out beyond the highest ridge of the principal islet of the group something which did away with the solemnity of perfect solitude. The tide of darkness flowed on swiftly; and with tropical suddenness a swarm of stars came out above the shadowy earth, while I lingered yet, my hand resting lightly on my ship's rail as if on the shoulder of a trusted friend. But, with all that multitude of celestial bodies staring down at one, the comfort of quiet communion with her was gone for good. And there were also disturbing sounds by this time—voices, footsteps forward; the steward flitted along the main deck, a busily ministering spirit; a hand bell tinkled urgently under the poop deck. . . .

I found my two officers waiting for me near the supper table, in the lighted cuddy. We sat down at once, and as I helped the chief mate, I said:

"Are you aware that there is a ship anchored inside the islands? I saw her mastheads above the ridge as the sun went down."

He raised sharply his simple face, overcharged by a terrible growth of whisker, and emitted his usual ejaculations: "Bless my soul, sir! You don't say so!"

My second mate was a round-cheeked, silent young man, grave beyond his years, I thought; but as our eyes happened to meet I detected a slight quiver on his lips. I looked down at once. It was not my part to encourage sneering on board my ship. It must be said, too, that I knew very little of my officers. In consequence of certain events of no particular significance, except to myself, I had been appointed to the command only a fortnight before. Neither did I know much of the hands forward. All these people had been together for eighteen months or so, and my position was that of the only stranger on board. I mention this because it has some bearing on what is to follow. But what I felt most was my being a stranger to the ship; and if all the truth must be told, I was somewhat of a stranger to myself. The youngest man on board (barring the second mate), and untried as yet by a position of the fullest responsibility, I was willing to take the adequacy of the others for granted. They had simply to be equal to their tasks; but I wondered how far I should turn out faithful to that ideal conception of one's own personality every man sets up for himself secretly.

Meantime the chief mate, with an almost visible effect of collaboration on the part of his round eyes and frightful whiskers, was trying to evolve a theory of the anchored ship. His dominant trait was to take all things into earnest consideration. He was of a painstaking turn of mind. As he used to say, he "liked to account to himself" for practically everything that came in this way, down to a miserable scorpion he had found in his cabin a week before. The why and the wherefore of that scorpion—how it got on board and came to select his room rather than the pantry (which was a dark place and more what a scorpion would be partial to), and how on earth it managed to drown itself in the inkwell of his writing desk—had exercised him infinitely. The ship within the islands was much more easily accounted for; and just as we were about to rise from the table he made his pronouncement. She was, he doubted not, a ship from home lately arrived. Probably she drew too much water to cross the bar except at the top of spring tides. Therefore she went into that natural harbor to wait for a few days in preference to remaining in an open roadstead.

"That's so," confirmed the second mate, suddenly, in his slightly hoarse voice. "She draws over twenty feet. She's the Liverpool ship *Sephora* with a cargo of coal. Hundred and twenty-three days from Cardiff."

We looked at him in surprise.

"The tugboat skipper told me when he came on board for your letters, sir," explained the young man. "He expects to take her up the river the day after tomorrow."

After thus overwhelming us with the extent of his information he slipped out of the cabin. The mate observed regretfully that he "could not account for that young fellow's whims." What prevented him telling us all about it at once, he wanted to know.

I detained him as he was making a move. For the last two days the crew had had plenty of hard work, and the night before they had very little sleep. I felt painfully that I—a stranger—was doing something unusual when I directed him to let all hands turn in without setting an anchor watch. I proposed to keep on deck myself till one o'clock or thereabouts. I would get the second mate to relieve me at that hour.

"He will turn out the cook and the steward at four," I concluded, "and then give you a call. Of course at the slightest sign of any sort of wind we'll have the hands up and make a start at once."

He concealed his astonishment. "Very well, sir." Outside the cuddy he put his head in the second mate's door to inform him of my unheard-of caprice to take a five hours' anchor watch on myself. I heard the other raise his voice incredulously: "What? The captain himself?" Then a few more murmurs, a door closed, then another. A few moments later I went on deck.

My strangeness, which had made me sleepless, had prompted that unconventional arrangement, as if I had expected in those solitary hours of the night to get on terms with the ship of which I knew nothing, manned by men of whom I knew very little more. Fast alongside a wharf, littered like any ship in port with a tangle of unrelated things, invaded by unrelated shore people, I hardly seen her yet properly. Now, as she lay cleared for sea, the stretch of her main deck seemed to me very fine under the stars. Very fine, very roomy for her size, and very inviting. I descended the poop and paced the waist, my mind picturing to myself the coming passage through the Malay Archipelago, down the Indian Ocean, and up the Atlantic. All its phases were familiar enough to me, every characteristic, all the alternatives which were likely to face me on the high seas—everything! . . . except the novel responsibility of command. But I took heart from the reasonable thought that the ship was like other ships, the men like other men, and that the sea was not likely to keep any special surprises expressly for my discomfiture.

Arrived at the comforting conclusion, I bethought myself of a cigar and went below to get it. All was still down there. Everybody at the after end of the ship was sleeping profoundly. I came out again on the quarter-deck, agreeably at ease in my sleeping suit on that warm breathless night, barefooted, a glowing cigar in my teeth, and, going forward, I was met by the profound silence of the fore end of the ship. Only as I passed the door of the forecastle I heard a deep, quiet, trustful sigh of some sleeper inside. And suddenly I rejoiced in the great security of the sea as compared with the unrest of the land, in my choice of that untempted life presenting no disquieting problems, invested with an elementary moral beauty by the absolute straightforwardness of its appeal and by the singleness of its purpose.

The riding light in the fore-rigging burned with a clear, untroubled, as if symbolic, flame, confident and bright in the mysterious shades of the night. Passing on my way aft along the other side of the ship, I observed that the rope side ladder, put over, no doubt, for the master of the tug when he came to fetch away our letters, had not been hauled in as it should have been. I became annoyed at this, for exactitude in small matters is the very soul of discipline. Then I reflected that I had myself peremptorily dismissed my officers from duty, and by my own act had prevented the anchor watch being formally set and things properly attended to. I asked myself whether it was wise ever to interfere with the established routine of duties even from the kindest of motives. My action might have made me appear eccentric. Goodness only knew how that absurdly whiskered mate would "account" for my conduct, and what the whole ship thought of that informality of their new captain. I was vexed with myself.

Not from compunction certainly, but, as it were mechanically, I proceeded to get the ladder in myself. Now a side ladder of that sort is a light affair and comes in easily, yet my vigorous tug, which should have brought it flying on board, merely recoiled upon my body in a totally unexpected jerk. What the devil! . . . I was so astounded by the immovableness of that ladder that I remained stock-still, trying to account for it to myself like that imbecile mate of mine. In the end, of course, I put my head over the rail.

The side of the ship made an opaque belt of shadow on the darkling glassy shimmer of the sea. But I saw at once something elongated and pale floating very close to the ladder. Before I could form a guess a faint flash of phosphorescent light, which seemed to issue suddenly from the naked body of a man, flickered in the sleeping water with the elusive, silent play of summer lightning in a night sky. With a gasp I saw revealed to my stare a pair of feet, the long legs, a broad livid back immersed right up to the neck in a greenish cadaverous glow. One hand, awash, clutched the bottom rung of the ladder. He was complete but for the head. A headless corpse! The cigar dropped out of my gaping mouth with a tiny plop and a short hiss quite audible in the absolute stillness of all things under heaven. At that I suppose he raised up his face, a dimly pale oval in the shadow of the ship's side. But even then I could only barely make out down there the shape of his blackhaired head. However, it was enough for the horrid, frostbound sensation which had gripped me about the chest to pass off. The moment of vain exclamations was past, too. I only climbed on the spare spar and leaned over the rail as far as I could, to bring my eyes nearer to that mystery floating alongside.

As he hung by the ladder, like a resting swimmer, the sea lightning played about his limbs at every stir; and he appeared in it ghastly, silvery, fishlike. He remained as mute as a fish, too. He made no motion to get out of the water, either. It was inconceivable that he should not attempt to come on board, and strangely troubling to suspect that perhaps he did not want to. And my first words were prompted by just that troubled incertitude.

"What's the matter?" I asked in my ordinary tone; speaking down to the face upturned exactly under mine.

"Cramp," it answered, no louder. Then slightly anxious, "I say, no need to call anyone."

"I was not going to," I said.

"Are you alone on deck?"

"Yes."

I had somehow the impression that he was on the point of letting go the ladder to swim away beyond my ken—mysterious as he came. But, for the moment, this being appearing as if he had risen from the bottom of the sea (it was certainly the nearest land to the ship) wanted only to know the time. I told him. And he, down there, tentatively:

"I suppose your captain's turned in?"

"I am sure he isn't," I said.

He seemed to struggle with himself, for I heard something like the low, bitter murmur of doubt. "What's the good?" His next words came out with a hesitating effort.

"Look here, my man. Could you call him out quietly?"

I thought the time had come to declare myself.

"*I* am the captain."

I heard a "By Jove!" whispered at the level of the water. The phosphorescence flashed in the swirl of the water all about his limbs, his other hand seized the ladder.

"My name's Leggatt."

The voice was calm and resolute. A good voice. The self-possession of that man had somehow induced a corresponding state in myself. It was very quietly that I remarked:

"You must be a good swimmer."

"Yes. I've been in the water practically since nine o'clock. The question for me now is whether I am to let go this ladder and go on swimming till I sink from exhaustion, or—to come on board here."

I felt this was no mere formula of desperate speech, but a real alternative in the view of a strong soul. I should have gathered from this that he was young; indeed, it is only the young who are ever confronted by such clear issues. But at the time it was pure intuition on my part. A mysterious communication was established already between us too—in the face of that silent, darkened tropical sea. I was young, too; young enough to make no comment. The man in the water began suddenly to climb up the ladder, and I hastened away from the rail to fetch some clothes.

Before entering the cabin I stood still, listening in the lobby at the foot of the stairs. A faint snore came through the closed door of the chief mate's room. The second mate's door was on the hook, but the darkness in there was absolutely soundless. He, too, was young and could sleep like a stone. Remained the steward, but he was not likely to wake up before he was called. I got a sleeping suit out of my room and, coming back on deck, saw the naked man from the sea sitting on the main hatch, glimmering white in the darkness, his elbows on his knees and his head in his hands. In a moment he had concealed his damp body in a sleeping suit of the same gray-stripe pattern as the one I was wearing and followed me like my double on the poop. Together we moved right aft, barefooted, silent.

"What is it?" I asked in a deadened voice, taking the lighted lamp out of the binnacle, and raising it to his face.

"An ugly business."

He had rather regular features; a good mouth; light eyes under somewhat heavy, dark eyebrows; a smooth, square forehead; no growth on his cheeks; a small, brown mustache, and a well-shaped, round chin. His expression was concentrated, meditative, under the inspecting light of the lamp I held up to his face; such as a man thinking hard in solitude might wear. My sleeping suit was just right for his size. A well-knit young fellow of twenty-five at most. He caught his lower lip with the edge of white, even teeth.

"Yes," I said, replacing the lamp in the binnacle. The warm, heavy tropical night closed upon his head again.

"There's a ship over there," he murmured.

"Yes, I know. The *Sephora*. Did you know of us?"

"Hadn't the slightest idea. I am the mate of her—" He paused and corrected himself. "I should say I *was*."

"Aha! Something wrong?"

"Yes. Very wrong indeed. I've killed a man."

"What do you mean? Just now?"

"No, on the passage. Weeks ago. Thirty-nine south. When I say a man—"

"Fit of temper," I suggested, confidently.

The shadowy, dark head, like mine, seemed to nod imperceptably above the ghostly gray of my sleeping suit. It was, in the night, as though I had faced by my own reflection in the depths of a somber and immense mirror.

"A pretty thing to have to own up to for a *Conway* boy," murmured my double, distinctly.

"You're a *Conway* boy?"

"I am," he said, as if startled. Then, slowly . . . "Perhaps you too—"

It was so; but being a couple of years older I had left before he joined. After a quick interchange of dates a silence fell; and I thought suddenly of my absurd mate with his terrific whiskers and the "Bless my soul—you don't say so" type of intellect. My double gave me an inkling of his thoughts by saying:

"My father's a parson in Norfolk. Do you see me before a judge and jury on that charge? For myself I can't see the necessity. There are fellows that an angel from heaven— And I am not that. He was one of those creatures that are just simmering all the time with a silly sort of wickedness. Miserable devils that have no business to live at all. He wouldn't do his duty and wouldn't let anybody else do theirs. But what's the good of talking! You know well enough the sort of ill-conditioned snarling cur—"

He appealed to me as if our experiences had been as identical as our clothes. And I knew well enough the pestiferous danger of such a character where there are no means of legal repression. And I knew well enough also that my double there was no homicidal ruffian. I did not think of asking him for details, and he told me the story roughly in brusque, disconnected sentences. I needed no more. I saw it all going on as though I were myself inside that other sleeping suit.

"It happened while we were setting a reefed foresail, at dusk. Reefed foresail! You understand the sort of weather. The only sail we had left to keep the ship running; so you may guess what it had been like for days. Anxious sort of job, that. He gave me some of his cursed insolence at the sheet. I tell you I was overdone with this terrific weather that seemed to have no end to it. Terrific, I tell you—and a deep ship. I believe the fellow himself was half crazed with funk. It was no time for gentlemanly reproof, so I turned round and felled him like an ox. He up and at me. He closed just as an awful sea made for the ship. All hands saw it coming and took to the rigging, but I had him by the throat, and went on shaking him like a rat, the men above us yelling, 'Look out! look out!' Then a crash as if the sky had fallen on my head. They say that for over ten minutes hardly anything was to be seen of the ship—just the three masts and a bit of the forecastle head and of the poop all awash driving along in a smother of foam. It was a miracle that they found us, jammed together behind the forebits. It's clear that I meant business, because I was holding him by the throat still when they picked us up. He was black in the face. It was too much for them. It seems they rushed us aft together, gripped as we were, screaming 'Murder!' like a lot of lunatics, and broke into the cuddy. And the ship running for her life, touch and go all the time, any minute her last in a sea fit to turn your hair gray only a-looking at it. I understand that the skipper, too, started raving like the rest of them. The man had been deprived of sleep for more than a week, and to have this sprung on him at the height of a furious gale nearly drove him out of his mind. I wonder they didn't fling me overboard after getting the carcass of their precious shipmate out of my fingers. They had rather a job to separate us, I've been told. A sufficiently fierce story to make an old judge and a respectable jury sit up a bit. The first thing I heard when I came to myself was the maddening howling of that endless gale, and on that the voice of the old man. He was hanging on to my bunk, staring into my face out of his sou'wester.

" 'Mr. Leggatt, you have killed a man. You can act no longer as chief mate of this ship.' "

His care to subdue his voice made it sound monotonous. He rested a hand on the end of the skylight to steady himself with, and all that time did not stir a limb, so far as I could see. "Nice little tale for a quiet tea party," he concluded in the same tone.

One of my hands, too, rested on the end of the skylight; neither did I stir a limb, so far as I knew. We stood less than a foot from each other. It occurred to me that if old "Bless my soul—you don't say so" were to put his head up the companion and catch sight of us, he would think he was seeing double, or imagine himself come upon a scene of weird witchcraft; the strange captain having a quiet confabulation by the wheel with his own gray ghost. I became very much concerned to prevent anything of the sort. I heard the other's soothing undertone.

"My father's a parson in Norfolk," it said. Evidently he had forgotten he had told me this important fact before. Truly a nice little tale.

"You had better slip down into my stateroom now," I said, moving off stealthily. My double followed my movements; our bare feet made no sound; I let him in, closed the door with care, and, after giving a call to the second mate, returned on deck for my relief.

"Not much sign of any wind yet," I remarked when he approached.

"No sir. Not much," he assented, sleepily, in his hoarse voice, with just enough deference, no more, and barely suppressing a yawn.

"Well, that's all you have to look out for. You have got your orders."

"Yes, sir."

I paced a turn or two on the poop and saw him take up his position face forward with his elbow in the ratlines of the mizzen-rigging before I went below. The mate's faint snoring was still going on peacefully. The cuddy lamp was burning over the table on which stood a vase with flowers, a polite attention from the ship's provision merchant—the last flowers we should see for the next three months at the very least. Two bunches of bananas hung from the beam symmetrically, one on each side of the rudder casing. Everything was as before in the ship—except that two of her captain's sleeping suits were simultaneously in use, one motionless in the cuddy, the other keeping very still in the captain's stateroom.

It must be explained here that my cabin had the form of the capital letter L, the door being within the angle and opening into the short part of the letter. A couch was to the left, the bed-place to the right; my writing desk and the chronometers' table faced the door. But anyone opening it, unless he stepped right inside, had no view of what I call the long (or vertical) part of the letter. It contained some lockers surmounted by a book case; and a few clothes, a thick jacket or two, caps, oilskin coat, and such like, hung on hooks. There was at the bottom of that part a door opening into my bathroom, which could be entered also directly from the saloon. But that way was never used.

The mysterious arrival had discovered the advantage of this particular shape. Entering my room, lighted strongly by a big bulkhead lamp swung on gimbals above my writing desk, I did not see him anywhere till he stepped out quietly from behind the coats hung in the recessed part.

"I heard somebody moving about, and went in there at once," he whispered.

I, too, spoke under my breath.

"Nobody is likely to come in here without knocking and getting permission."

He nodded. His face was thin and the sunburn faded, as though he had been ill. And no wonder. He had been, I heard presently, kept under arrest in his cabin for nearly seven weeks. But there was nothing sickly in his eyes or in his expression. He was not a bit like me, really; yet, as we stood leaning over my bed-place, whispering side by side, with our dark heads together and our backs to the door, anybody bold enough to open it stealthily would have been treated to the uncanny sight of a double captain busy talking in whispers with his other self.

"But all this doesn't tell me how you came to hang on to our side ladder" I inquired, in the hardly audible murmurs we used, after he had told me something more of the proceedings on board the *Sephora* once the bad weather was over.

"When we sighted Java Head I had had time to think all those matters out several times over. I had six weeks of doing nothing else, and with only an hour or so every evening for a tramp on the quarter deck."

He whispered, his arms folded on the side of my bed-place, staring through the open port. And I could imagine perfectly the manner of this thinking out—a stubborn if not a steadfast operation; something of which I should have been perfectly incapable.

"I reckoned it would be dark before we closed with the land," he continued, so low that I had to strain my hearing, near as we were to each other, shoulder touching shoulder almost. "So I asked to speak to the old man. He always seemed very sick when he came to see me—as if he could not look me in the face. You know, that foresail saved the ship. She was too deep to have run long under bare poles. And it was I that managed to set it for him. Anyway, he came. When I had him in my cabin—he stood by the door looking at me as if I had the halter around my neck already—I asked him right away to leave my cabin door unlocked at night while the ship was going through Sunda Straits. There would be the Java coast within two or three miles, off Angier Point. I wanted nothing more. I've had a prize for swimming my second year in the *Conway*."

"I can believe it," I breathed out.

"God only knows why they locked me in every night. To see some of their faces you'd have thought they were afraid I'd go about at night strangling people. Am I a murdering brute? Do I look it? By Jove! if I had been he wouldn't have trusted himself like that into my room. You'll say I might have chucked him aside and bolted out, there and then—it was dark already. Well, no. And for the same reason I wouldn't think of trying to smash the door. There would have been a rush to stop me at the noise, and I did not mean to get into a confounded scrimmage. Somebody else might have gotten killed—for I would not have broken out only to get chucked back, and I did not want any more of that work. He refused, looking more sick than ever. He was afraid of the men, and also of that old second mate of his who had been sailing with him for years—a gray-headed old humbug; and his steward, too, had been with him devil knows how long—seventeen years or more—a dogmatic sort of loafer who hated me like poison, just because I was the chief mate. No chief mate ever made more than one voyage in the *Sephora*, you know. Those two old chaps ran the ship. Devil only knows what the skipper wasn't afraid of (all his nerve went to pieces altogether in that hellish spell of bad weather we had)—of what the law would do to him—of his wife, perhaps. Oh, yes! she's on board. Though I don't think she would have meddled. She would have been only too glad to have me out of the ship in any way. The 'brand of Cain' business, don't you see. That's all right. I was ready enough to go off wandering on the face of the earth—and that was price enough to pay for an Abel of that sort. Anyhow, he wouldn't listen to me. 'This thing must take its course. I represent the law here.' He was shaking like a leaf. 'So you won't?' 'No!' 'Then I hope you will be able to sleep on that,' I said, and turned my back on him. 'I wonder that *you* can,' cries he, and locks the door.

"Well, after that, I couldn't. Not very well. That was three weeks ago. We have had a slow passage through the Java Sea; drifted about Carimata for ten days. When we anchored here they thought, I suppose, it was all right. The nearest land (and that's five miles) is the ship's destination; the consul would soon set about catching me; and there would have been no object in bolting to these islets there. I don't suppose there's a drop of water on them. I don't know how it was, but tonight that steward, after bringing me my supper, went out to let me eat it, and left he door unlocked. And I ate it—all there was, too. After I had finished I strolled out on the quarter-deck. I don't know that I meant to do anything. A breath of fresh air was all I wanted, I believe. Then a sudden temptation came over me. I kicked off my slippers and was in the water before I had made up my mind fairly. Somebody heard the splash and they raised an awful hullabaloo. 'He's gone! Lower the boats! He's committed suicide! No, he's swimming.' Certainly I was swimming. It's not so easy for a swimmer like me to commit suicide by drowning. I landed on the nearest islet before the boat left the ship's side. I heard them pulling about in the dark, hailing, and so on, but after a bit they gave up. Everything quieted down and the anchorage became as still as death. I sat down on a stone and began to think. I felt certain they would start searching for me at daylight. There was no place to hide on those stony things—and if there had been, what would have been the good? But now I was clear of that ship, I was not going back. So after a while I took off all my clothes, tied them up in a bundle with a stone inside, and dropped them in the deep water on the outer side of that islet. That was suicide enough for me. Let them think what they liked, but I didn't mean to drown myself. I meant to swim till I sank—but that's not the same thing. I struck out for another of these little islands, and it was from that one that I first saw your riding light. Something to swim for. I went on easily, and on the way I came upon a flat rock a foot or two above water. In the daytime, I dare say, you might make it out with a glass from your poop. I scrambled up on it and rested myself for a bit. Then I made another start. That last spell must have been over a mile."

His whisper was getting fainter and fainter, and all the time he stared straight out through the porthole, in which there was not even a star to be seen. I had not interrupted him. There was something that made comment impossible in his narrative, or perhaps in himself; a sort of feeling, a quality, which I can't find a name for. And when he ceased, all I found was a futile whisper: "So you swam for our light?"

"Yes—straight for it. It was something to swim for. I couldn't see any stars low down because the coast was in the way, and I couldn't see the land, either. The water was like glass. One might have been swimming in a confounded thousand-feet deep cistern with no place for scrambling out anywhere; but what I didn't like was the notion of swimming round and round like a crazed bullock before I gave out; and as I didn't mean to go back . . . No. Do you see me being hauled back, stark naked, off one of these little islands by the scuff of the neck and fighting like a wild beast? Somebody would have got killed for certain, and I did not want any of that. So I went on. Then your ladder—"

"Why didn't you hail the ship?" I asked, a little louder.

He touched my shoulder lightly. Lazy footsteps came right over our heads and stopped. The second mate had crossed from the other side of the poop and might have been hanging over the rail, for all we knew.

"He couldn't hear us talking—could he?" My double breathed into my very ear, anxiously.

His anxiety was an answer, a sufficient answer, to the question I had put to him. An answer containing all the difficulty of that situation. I closed the porthole quietly, to make sure. A louder word might have been overheard.

"Who's that?" he whispered then.

"My second mate. But I don't know much more of the fellow than you do."

And I told him a little about myself. I had been appointed to take charge while I least expected anything of the sort, not quite a fortnight ago. I didn't know either the ship or the people. Hadn't had the time in port to look about me or size anybody up. And as to the crew, all they knew was that I was appointed to take the ship home. For the rest, I was almost as much of a stranger on board as himself, I said. And at the moment I felt it most acutely. I felt that it would take very little to make me a suspect person in the eyes of the ship's company.

He had turned about meantime; and we, the two strangers in the ship, faced each other in identical attitudes.

"Your ladder—" he murmured, after a silence. "Who'd have thought of finding a ladder hanging over at night in a ship anchored out here! I felt just then a very unpleasant faintness. After the life I've been leading for nine weeks, anybody would have got out of condition. I wasn't capable of swimming round as far as your rudder chains. And, lo and behold! there was a ladder to get hold of. After I gripped it I said to myself, 'What's the good?' When I saw a man's head looking over I thought I would swim away presently and leave him shouting—in whatever language it was. I didn't mind being looked at. I—liked it. And then you speaking to me so quietly—as if you had expected me—made me hold on a little longer. It had been a confounded lonely time—I don't mean while swimming. I was glad to talk a little to somebody that didn't belong to the *Sephora*. As to asking for the captain, that was a mere impulse. It could have been no use, with all the ship knowing about me and the other people pretty certain to be round here in the morning. I don't know—I wanted to be seen, to talk with somebody, before I went on. I don't know what I would have said. . . . 'Fine night, isn't it?' or something of the sort."

"Do you think they will be round here presently?" I asked with some incredulity.

"Quite likely," he said, faintly.

He looked extremely haggard all of a sudden. His head rolled on his shoulders.

"H'm. We shall see then. Meantime get into that bed," I whispered. "Want help? There."

It was a rather high bed-place with a set of drawers underneath. This amazing swimmer really needed the lift I gave him by seizing his leg. He tumbled in, rolled over on his back, and flung one arm across his eyes. And then, with his face nearly hidden, he must have looked exactly as

I used to look in that bed. I gazed upon my other self for a while before drawing across carefully the two green serge curtains which ran on a brass rod. I thought for a moment of pinning them together for greater safety, but I sat down on the couch, and once there I felt unwilling to rise and hunt for a pin. I would do it in a moment. I was extremely tired, in a peculiarly intimate way, by the strain of stealthiness, by the effort of whispering and the general secrecy of this excitement. It was three o'clock by now and I had been on my feet since nine, but I was not sleepy; I could not have gone to sleep. I sat there, fagged out, looking at the curtains, trying to clear my mind of the confused sensation of being in two places at once, and greatly bothered by an exasperating knocking in my head. It was a relief to discover suddenly that it was not in my head at all, but on the outside of the door. Before I could collect myself the words "Come in" were out of my mouth, and the steward entered with a tray, bringing in my morning coffee. I had slept, after all, and I was so frightened that I shouted, "This way! I am here, steward," as though he had been miles away. He put down the tray on the table next the couch and only then said, very quietly, "I can see you are here, sir." I felt him give me a keen look, but I dared not meet his eyes just then. He must have wondered why I had drawn the curtains of my bed before going to sleep on the couch. He went out, hooking the door open as usual.

I heard the crew washing decks above me. I knew I would have been told at once if there had been any wind. Calm, I thought, and I was doubly vexed. Indeed, I felt dual more than ever. The steward reappeared suddenly in the doorway. I jumped up from the couch so quickly that he gave a start.

"What do you want here?"

"Close your port, sir—they are washing decks."

"It is closed," I said, reddening.

"Very well, sir." But he did not move from the doorway and returned my stare in an extraordinary, equivocal manner for a time. Then his eyes wavered, all his expression change, and in a voice unusually gentle, almost coaxingly:

"May I come in to take the empty cup away, sir?"

"Of course!" I turned my back on him while he popped in and out. Then I unhooked and closed the door and even pushed the bolt. This sort of thing could not go on very long. The cabin was as hot as an oven, too. I took a peep at my double, and discovered that he had not moved, his arm was still over his eyes; but his chest heaved; his hair was wet; his chin glistened with perspiration. I reached over him and opened the port.

"I must show myself on deck," I reflected.

Of course, theoretically, I could do what I liked, with no one to say nay to me within the whole circle of the horizon; but to lock my cabin door and take the key away I did not dare. Directly I put my head out of the companion I saw the group of my two officers, the second mate barefooted, the chief mate in long india-rubber boots, near the break of the poop, and the steward halfway down the poop ladder talking to them eagerly. He happened to catch sight of me and dived, the second ran down on the main deck shouting some order or other, and the chief mate came to meet me, touching his cap.

There was a sort of curiosity in his eye that I did not like. I don't know whether the steward had told them that I was "queer" only, or downright drunk, but I know the man meant to have a good look at me. I watched him coming with a smile which, as he got into point-blank range, took effect and froze his very whiskers. I did not give him time to open his lips.

"Square the yards by lifts and braces before the hands go to breakfast."

It was the first particular order I had given on board that ship; and I stayed on deck to see it executed, too. I had felt the need of asserting myself without loss of time. That sneering young cub got taken down a peg or two on that occasion, and I also seized the opportunity of having a good look at the face of every foremast man as they filed past me to go to the after braces. After breakfast time, eating nothing myself, I presided with such frigid dignity that the two mates were only too glad to escape from the cabin as soon as decency permitted; and all the time the dual working of my mind distracted me almost to the point of insanity. I was constantly watching myself, my secret self, as dependent on my actions as my own personality, sleeping in that bed, behind that door which faced me as I sat at the head of the table. It was very much like being mad, only it was worse because one was aware of it.

I had to shake him for a solid minute, but when at last he opened his eyes it was in the full possession of his senses, with an inquiring look.

"All's well so far," I whispered. "Now you must vanish into the bathroom."

He did so, as noiseless as a ghost, and I then rang for the steward, and facing him boldly, directed him to tidy up my stateroom while I was having my bath—"and be quick about it." As my tone admitted of no excuses, he said, "Yes, sir," and ran off to fetch his dustpan and brushes. I took a bath and did most of my dressing, splashing, and whistling softly for the steward's edification, while the secret sharer of my life stood drawn up bolt upright in that little space, his face looking very sunken in daylight, his eyelids lowered under the stern, dark line of his eyebrows drawn together by a slight frown.

When I left him there to go back to my room the steward was finishing dusting. I sent for the mate and engaged him in some insignificant conversation. It was, as it were, trifling with the terrific character of his whiskers; but my object was to give him an opportunity for a good look at my cabin. And then I could at last shut, with a clear conscience, the door of my stateroom and get my double back into the recessed part. There was nothing else for it. He had to sit still on a small folding stool, half smothered by the heavy coats hanging there. We listened to the steward going into the bathroom out of the saloon, filling the water bottles there, scrubbing the bath, setting things to rights, whisk, bang, clatter—out again into the saloon—turn the key—click. Such was my scheme for keeping my second self invisible. Nothing better could be contrived under the circumstances. And there we sat; I at my writing desk ready to appear busy with some papers, he behind me, out of sight of the door. It would not have been prudent to talk in daytime; and I could not have stood the excitement of that queer sense of whispering to myself. Now and then, glancing over my shoulder, I saw him far back there, sitting rigidly on the low stool, his bare feet close together, his arms folded, his head hanging on his breast—and perfectly still. Anybody would have taken him for me.

I was fascinated by it myself. Every moment I had to glance over my shoulder. I was looking at him when a voice outside the door said:

"Beg pardon, sir."

"Well!" . . . I kept my eyes on him, and so, when the voice outside the door announced, "There's a ship's boat coming our way, sir," I saw him give a start—the first movement he had made for hours. But he did not raise his bowed head.

"All right. Get the ladder over."

I hesitated. Should I whisper something to him? But what? His immobility seemed to have been never disturbed. What could I tell him he did not know already? . . . Finally I went on deck.

II

The skipper of the *Sephora* had a thin red whisker all round his face, and the sort of complexion that goes with hair of that color; also the particular, rather smeary shade of blue in the eyes. He was not exactly a showy figure; his shoulders were high, his stature but middling—one leg slightly more bandy than the other. He shook hands, looking vaguely around. A spiritless tenacity was his main characteristic, I judged. I behaved with a politeness which seemed to disconcert him. Perhaps he was shy. He mumbled to me as if he were ashamed of what he was saying; gave his name (it was something like Archbold—but at this distance of years I hardly am sure), his ship's name, and a few other particulars of that sort, in the manner of a criminal making a reluctant and doleful confession. He had had terrible weather on the passage out—terrible—terrible—wife aboard, too.

By this time we were seated in the cabin and the steward brought in a tray with a bottle and glasses. "Thanks! No." Never took liquor. Would have some water, though. He drank two tumblerfuls. Terrible thirsty work. Ever since daylight had been exploring the islands round his ship.

"What was that for—fun?" I asked, with an appearance of polite interest.

"No!" He sighed. "Painful duty."

As he persisted in his mumbling and I wanted my double to hear every word, I hit upon the notion of informing him that I regretted to say I was hard of hearing.

"Such a young man, too!" he nodded, keeping his smeary blue, unintelligent eyes fastened upon me. What was the cause of it—some disease? he inquired, without the least sympathy and as if he thought that, if so, I'd got no more than I deserved.

"Yes; disease," I admitted in a cheerful tone which seemed to shock him. But my point was gained, because he had to raise his voice to give me his tale. It is not worth while to record that version. It was just over two months since all this had happened, and he had thought so much about it that he seemed completely muddled as to its bearings, but still immensely impressed.

"What would you think of such a thing happening on board your own ship? I've had the *Sephora* for these fifteen years. I am a well-known shipmaster."

He was densely distressed—and perhaps I should have sympathized with him if I had been able to detach my mental vision from the unsuspected sharer of my cabin as though he were my second self. There he was on the other side of the bulkhead, four or five feet from us, no more, as we sat in the saloon. I looked politely at Captain Archbold (if that was his name), but it was the other I saw, in a gray sleeping suit, seated on a low stool, his bare feet close together, his arms folded, and every word said between us falling into the ears of his dark head bowed on his chest.

"I have been at sea now, man and boy, for seven-and-thirty years, and I've never heard of such a thing happening in an English ship. And that it should be my ship. Wife on board, too."

I was hardly listening to him.

"Don't you think," I said, "'that the heavy sea which, you told me, came aboard just then might have killed the man? I have seen the sheer weight of a sea kill a man very neatly, by simply breaking his neck.'"

"Good God!" he uttered, impressively, fixing his smeary blue eyes on me. "The sea! No man killed by the sea ever looked like that." He seemed positively scandalized at my suggestion. And as I gazed at him, certainly not prepared for anything original on his part, he advanced his head close to mine and thrust his tongue out at me so suddenly that I couldn't help starting back.

After scoring over my calmness in this graphic way he nodded wisely. If I had seen the sight, he assured me, I would never forget it as long as I lived. The weather was too bad to give the corpse a proper sea burial. So next day at dawn they took it up on the poop, covering its face with a bit of bunting; he read a short prayer, and then, just as it was, in its oilskins and long boots, they launched it amongst those mountainous seas that seemed ready every moment to swallow up the ship herself and the terrified lives on board of her.

"That reefed foresail saved you," I threw in.

"Under God—it did," he exclaimed fervently. "It was by a special mercy, I firmly believe, that it stood some of those hurricane squalls."

"It was the setting of that sail which—" I began.

"God's own hand in it," he interrupted me. "Nothing less could have done it. I don't mind telling you that I hardly dared give the order. It seemed impossible that we could touch anything without losing it, and then our last hope would have been gone."

The terror of that gale was on him yet. I let him go on for a bit, then said, casually—as if returning to a minor subject:

"You were very anxious to give up your mate to the shore people, I believe?"

He was. To the law. His obscure tenacity on that point had in it something incomprehensible and a little awful; something, as it were, mystical, quite apart from his anxiety that he should not be suspected of "countenancing any doings of that sort." Seven-and-thirty virtuous years at sea, of which over twenty of immaculate command, and the last fifteen in the *Sephora,* seemed to have laid him under some pitiless obligation.

"And you know," he went on, groping shamefacedly amongst his feelings, "I did not engage that young fellow. His people had some interest with my owners. I was in a way forced to take him on. He looked very smart, very gentlemanly, and all that. But do you know—I never liked him, somehow. I am a plain man. You see, he wasn't exactly the sort for the chief mate of a ship like the *Sephora.*"

I had become so connected in thoughts and impressions with the secret sharer of my cabin that I felt as if I, personally, were being given to understand that I, too, was not the sort that would have done for the chief mate of a ship like the *Sephora.* I had no doubt of it in my mind.

"Not at all the style of man. You understand," he insisted superfluously, looking hard at me.

I smiled urbanely. He seemed at a loss for a while.

"I suppose I must report a suicide."

"Beg pardon?"

"Sui-cide! That's what I'll have to write to my owners directly I get in."

"Unless you manage to recover him before tomorrow," I assented, dispassionately. . . . "I mean, alive."

He mumbled something which I really did not catch, and I turned my ear to him in a puzzled manner. He fairly bawled:

"The land—I say, the mainland is at least seven miles off my anchorage."

"About that."

My lack of excitement, of curiosity, of surprise, of any sort of pronounced interest, began to arouse his distrust. But except for the felicitous pretense of deafness I had not tried to pretend anything. I had felt utterly incapable of playing the part of ignorance properly, and therefore was afraid to try. It is also certain that he had brought some ready-made suspicions with him, and that he viewed my politeness as a strange and unnatural phenomenon. And yet how else could I have received him? Not heartily! That was impossible for psychological reasons, which I need not state here. My only object was to keep off his inquiries. Surlily? Yes, but surliness might have provoked a point-blank question. From its novelty to him and from its nature, punctilious courtesy was the manner best calculated to restrain the man. But there was the danger of his breaking through my defense bluntly. I could not, I think, have met him by a direct lie, also for psychological (not moral) reasons. If he had only known how afraid I was of his putting my feeling of identity with the other to the test! But, strangely enough—(I thought of it only afterward)—I believe that he was not a little disconcerted by the reverse side of that weird situation, by something in me that reminded him of the man he was seeking—suggested a mysterious similitude to the young fellow he had distrusted and disliked from the first.

However that might have been, the silence was not very prolonged. He took another oblique step.

"I reckon I had no more than a two-mile pull to your ship. Not a bit more."

"And quite enough, too, in this awful heat," I said.

Another pause full of mistrust followed. Necessity, they say, is mother of invention, but fear, too, is not barren of ingenious suggestions. And I was afraid he would ask me point-blank for news of my other self.

"Nice little saloon, isn't it?" I remarked, as if noticing for the first time the way his eyes roamed from one closed door to the other. "And very well fitted out, too. Here, for instance," I continued, reaching over the back of my seat negligently and flinging the door open, "is my bathroom."

He made an eager movement, but hardly gave it a glance. I got up, shut the door of the bathroom, and invited him to have a look round, as if I were very proud of my accommodation. He had to rise and be shown round, but he went through the business without any raptures whatever.

"And now we'll have a look at my stateroom," I declared, in a voice as loud as I dared to make it, crossing the cabin to the starboard side with purposely heavy steps.

He followed me in and gazed around. My intelligent double had vanished. I played my part.

"Very convenient—isn't it?"

"Very nice. Very com . . ." He didn't finish, and went out brusquely as if to escape from some unrighteous wiles of mine. But it was not to be. I had been too frightened not to feel vengeful; I felt I had him on the run, and I meant to keep him on the run. My polite insistence must have had something menacing in it, because he gave in suddenly. And I did not let him off a single item; mate's room, pantry, storerooms, the very sail locker which was also under the poop—he had to look into them all. When at last I showed him out on the quarter-deck he drew a long, spiritless sigh, and mumbled dismally that he must really be going back to his ship now. I desired my mate, who had joined us, to see to the captain's boat.

The man of whiskers gave a blast on the whistle which he used to wear hanging round his neck, and yelled, "*Sephora* away!" My double down there in my cabin must have heard, and certainly could not feel more relieved than I. Four fellows came running out from somewhere forward and went over the side, while my own men, appearing on deck too, lined the rail. I escorted my visitor to the gangway ceremoniously, and nearly overdid it. He was a tenacious beast. On the very ladder he lingered, and in that unique, guiltily conscientious manner of sticking to the point:

"I say . . . you . . . you don't think that—"

I covered his voice loudly:

"Certainly not. . . . I am delighted. Good-by."

I had an idea of what he meant to say, and just saved myself by the privilege of defective hearing. He was too shaken generally to insist, but my mate, close witness of that parting, looked mystified and his face took on a thoughtful cast. As I did not want to appear as if I wished to avoid all communication with my officers, he had the opportunity to address me.

"Seems a very nice man. His boat's crew told our chaps a very extraordinary story, if what I am told by the steward is true. I suppose you had it from the captain, sir?"

"Yes. I had a story from the captain."

"A very horrible affair—isn't it, sir?"

"It is."

"Beats all these tales we hear about murders in Yankee ships."

"I don't think it beats them. I don't think it resembles them in the least."

"Bless my soul—you don't say so! But of course I've no acquaintance whatever with American ships, not I, so I couldn't go against your knowledge. It's horrible enough for me. . . . But the queerest part is that those fellows seemed to have some idea the man was hidden aboard here. They had really. Did you ever hear of such a thing?"

"Preposterous—isn't it?"

We were walking to and fro athwart the quarter-deck. No one of the crew forward could be seen (the day was Sunday), and the mate pursued:

"There was some little dispute about it. Our chaps took offense. 'As if we would harbor a thing like that,' they said. 'Wouldn't you like to look for him in our coal hole?' Quite a tiff. But they made it up in the end. I suppose he did drown himself. Don't you, sir?"

"I don't suppose anything."

"You have no doubt in the matter, sir?"

"None whatever."

I left him suddenly. I felt I was producing a bad impression, but with my double down there it was most trying to be on deck. And it was almost as trying to be below. Altogether a nerve-trying situation. But on the whole I felt less torn in two when I was with him. There was no one in the whole ship whom I dared take into my confidence. Since the hands had got to know his story, it would have been impossible to pass him off for anyone else, and an accidental discovery was to be dreaded now more than ever. . . .

The steward being engaged in laying the table for dinner, we could talk only with our eyes when I first went down. Later in the afternoon we had a cautious try at whispering. The Sunday quietness of the ship was against us; the stillness of air and water around her was against us; the elements, the men were against us—everything was against us in our secret partnership; time itself—for this could not go on forever. The very trust in Providence was, I suppose, denied to his guilt. Shall

I confess that this thought cast me down very much? And as to the chapter of accidents which counts for so much in the book of success, I could only hope that it was closed. For what favorable accident could be expected?

"Did you hear everything?" were my first words as soon as we took up our position side by side, leaning over my bed-place.

He had. And the proof of it was his earnest whisper, "The man told you he hardly dared to give the order."

I understood the reference to be to that saving foresail.

"Yes. He was afraid of it being lost in the setting."

"I assure you he never gave the order. He may think he did, but he never gave it. He stood there with me on the break of the poop after the maintopsail blew away, and whimpered about our last hope—positively whimpered about it and nothing else—and the night coming on! To hear one's skipper go on like that in such weather was enough to drive any fellow out of his mind. It worked me up into a sort of desperation. I just took it into my own hands and went away from him, boiling, and—. But what's the use telling you? *You* know! . . . Do you think that if I had not been pretty fierce with them I should have got the men to do anything? Not it! The bosun perhaps? Perhaps! It wasn't a heavy sea—it was a sea gone mad! I suppose the end of the world will be something like that; and a man may have the heart to see it coming once and be done with it—but to have to face it day after day—I don't blame anybody. I was precious little better than the rest. Only—I was an officer of that old coal-wagon, anyhow—"

"I quite understand," I conveyed that sincere assurance into his ear. He was out of breath with whispering; I could hear him pant slightly. It was all very simple. The same strung-up force which had given twenty-four men a chance, at least, for their lives, had, in a sort of recoil, crushed an unworthy mutinous existence.

But I had no leisure to weigh the merits of the matter—footsteps in the saloon, a heavy knock. "There's enough wind to get under way with, sir." Here was the call of a new claim upon my thoughts and even upon my feelings.

"Turn the hands up," I cried through the door. "I'll be on deck directly."

I was going out to make the acquaintance of my ship. Before I left the cabin our eyes met—the eyes of the only two strangers on board. I pointed to the recessed part where the little campstool awaited him and laid my finger on my lips. He made a gesture—somewhat vague—a little mysterious, accompanied by a faint smile, as if of regret.

This is not the place to enlarge upon the sensations of a man who feels for the first time a ship move under his feet to his own independent word. In my case they were not unalloyed. I was not wholly alone with my command; for there was that stranger in my cabin. Or rather, I was not completely and wholly with her. Part of me was absent. That mental feeling of being in two places at once affected me physically as if the mood of secrecy had penetrated my very soul. Before an hour had elapsed since the ship had begun to move, having occasion to ask the mate (he stood by my side) to take a compass bearing of the Pagoda, I caught myself reaching up to his ear in whispers, I say I caught myself, but enough had escaped to startle the man. I can't describe it otherwise than by saying that he shied. A grave, preoccupied manner, as though he were in possession of some perplexing intelligence, did not leave him henceforth. A little later I moved away from the rail to look at the compass with such a stealthy gait that the helmsman noticed it—and could not help noticing the unusual roundness of his eyes. These are trifling instances, though it's to no commander's advantage to be suspected of ludicrous eccentricities. But I was also more seriously affected. There are to a seaman certain words, gestures, that should in given conditions come as naturally, as instinctively as the winking of a menaced eye. A certain order should spring on to his lips without thinking; a certain sign should get itself made, so to speak, without reflection. But all unconscious alertness had abandoned me. I had to make an effort of will to recall myself back (from the cabin) to the conditions of the moment. I felt that I was appearing an irresolute commander to those people who were watching me more or less critically.

And, besides, there were the scares. On the second day out, for instance, coming off the deck in the afternoon (I had straw slippers on my bare feet) I stopped at the open pantry door and spoke to the steward. He was doing something there with his back to me. At the sound of my voice he nearly jumped out of his skin, as the saying is, and incidentally broke a cup.

"What on earth's the matter with you?" I asked astonished.

He was extremely confused. "Beg pardon, sir. I made sure you were in your cabin."

"You see I wasn't."

"No, sir. I could have sworn I had heard you moving in there not a moment ago. It's most extraordinary . . . very sorry, sir."

I passed on with an inward shudder. I was so identified with my secret double that I did not even mention the fact in those scanty, fearful whispers we exchanged. I suppose he had made some slight noise of some kind or other. It would have been miraculous if he hadn't at one time or another. And yet, haggard as he appeared, he looked always perfectly self-controlled, more than calm—almost invulnerable. On my suggestion he remained almost entirely in the bathroom, which, upon the whole, was the safest place. There could be really no shadow of an excuse for anyone ever wanting to go in there, once the steward had done with it. It was a very tiny place. Sometimes he reclined on the floor, his legs bent, his head sustained on one elbow. At others I would find him on the campstool, sitting in his gray sleeping suit and with his cropped dark hair like a patient, unmoved convict. At night I would smuggle him into my bed-place, and we would whisper together, with the regular footfalls of the officer of the watch passing and repassing over our heads. It was an infinitely miserable time. It was lucky that some tins of fine preserves were stowed in a locker in my stateroom; hard bread I could always get hold of; and so he lived on stewed chicken, paté de foie gras, asparagus, cooked oysters, sardines—on all sorts of abominable sham delicacies out of tins. My early morning coffee he always drank; and it was all I dared do for him in that respect.

Every day there was the horrible maneuvering to go through so that my room and then the bathroom should be done in the usual way. I came to hate the sight of the steward, to abhor the voice of that harmless man. I felt that it was he who would bring on the disaster of discovery. It hung like a sword over our heads.

The fourth day out, I think (we were then working down the east side of the Gulf of Siam, tack for tack, in light winds and smooth water)—the fourth day, I say, of this miserable juggling with the unavoidable, as we sat at our evening meal, that man, whose slightest movement I dreaded, after putting down the dishes ran upon deck busily. This could not be dangerous. Presently he came down again; and then it appeared that he had remembered a coat of mine which I had thrown over a rail to dry after having been wetted in a shower which had passed over the ship in the afternoon. Sitting stolidly at the head of the table I became terrified at the sight of the garment on his arm. Of course he made for my door. There was no time to lose.

"Steward," I thundered. My nerves were so shaken that I could not govern my voice and conceal my agitation. This was the sort of thing that made my terrifically whiskered mate tap his forehead with his forefinger. I had detected him using that gesture while talking on deck with a confidential air to the carpenter. It was too far to hear a word, but I had no doubt that this pantomime could only refer to the strange new captain.

"Yes, sir," the pale-faced steward turned resignedly to me. It was this maddening course of being shouted at, checked without rhyme or reason, arbitrarily chased out of my cabin, suddenly called into it, sent flying out of his pantry on incomprehensible errands, that accounted for the growing wretchedness of his expression.

"Where are you going with that coat?"

"To your room, sir."

"Is there another shower coming?"

"I'm sure I don't know, sir. Shall I go up again and see, sir?"

"No! Never mind."

My object was attained, as of course my other self in there would have heard everything that passed. During this interlude my two officers never raised their eyes off their respective plates; but the lip of that confounded cub, the second mate, quivered visibly.

I expected the steward to hook my coat on and come out at once. He was very slow about it; but I dominated my nervousness sufficiently not to shout after him. Suddenly I became aware (it could be heard plainly enough) that the fellow for some reason or other was opening the door of the bathroom. It was the end. The place was literally not big enough to swing a cat in. My voice died in my throat and I went stony all over. I expected to hear a yell of surprise and terror, and made a movement, but had not the strength to get on my legs. Everything remained still. Had my second self taken the poor wretch by the throat? I don't know what I would have done next moment if I had not seen the steward come out of my room, close the door, and then stand quietly by the sideboard.

Saved, I thought. But, no! Lost! Gone! He was gone!

I laid my knife and fork down and leaned back in my chair. My head swam. After a while, when sufficiently recovered to speak in a steady voice, I instructed my mate to put the ship round at eight o'clock himself.

"I won't come on deck," I went on. "I think I'll turn in, and unless the wind shifts I don't want to be disturbed before midnight. I feel a bit seedy."

"You did look middling bad a little while ago," the chief mate remarked without showing any great concern.

They both went out, and I stared at the steward clearing the table. There was nothing to be read on that wretched man's face. But why did he avoid my eyes I asked myself. Then I thought I should like to hear the sound of his voice.

"Steward!"

"Sir!" Startled as usual.

"Where did you hang up that coat?"

"In the bathroom, sir." The usual anxious tone. "'It's not quite dry yet, sir."

For some time longer I sat in the cuddy. Had my double vanished as he had come? But of his coming there was an explanation, whereas his disappearance would be inexplicable. . . . I went slowly into my dark room, shut the door, lighted the lamp, and for a time dared not turn round. When at last I did I saw him standing bolt upright in the narrow recessed part. It would not be true to say I had a shock, but an irresistible doubt of his bodily existence flitted through my mind. Can it be, I asked myself, that he is not visible to other eyes than mine? It was like being haunted. Motionless, with a grave face, he raised his hands slightly at me in a gesture which meant clearly, "Heavens! what a narrow escape!" Narrow indeed. I think I had come creeping quietly as near insanity as any man who has not actually gone over the border. That gesture restrained me, so to speak.

The mate with the terrific whiskers was now putting the ship on the other tack. In the moment of profound silence which follows upon the hands going to their stations I heard on the poop his raised voice: "Hard alee!" and the distant shout of the order repeated on the main-deck. The sails, in that light breeze, made but a faint fluttering noise. It ceased. The ship was coming round slowly; I held my breath in the renewed stillness of expectation; one wouldn't have thought that there was a single living soul on her decks. A sudden brisk shout, "Mainsail haul!" broke the spell, and in the noisy cries and rush overhead of the men running away with the main brace we two, down in my cabin, came together in our usual position by the bed-place.

He did not wait for my question. "I heard him fumbling here and just managed to squat myself down in the bath," he whispered to me. "The fellow only opened the door and put his arm in to hang the coat up. All the same—"

"I never thought of that," I whispered back, even more appalled than before at the closeness of the shave, and marveling at that something unyielding in his character which was carrying him through so finely. There was no agitation in his whisper. Whoever was being driven distracted, it was not he. He was sane. And the proof of his sanity was continued when he took up the whispering again.

"It would never do for me to come to life again."

It was something that a ghost might have said. But what he was alluding to was his old captain's reluctant admission of the theory of suicide. It would obviously serve his turn—if I had understood at all the view which seemed to govern the unalterable purpose of his action.

"You must maroon me as soon as ever you can get amongst these islands off the Cambodje shore," he went on.

"Maroon you! We are not living in a boy's adventure tale," I protested. His scornful whispering took me up.

"We aren't indeed! There's nothing of a boy's tale in this. But there's nothing else for it. I want no more. You don't suppose I am afraid of what can be done to me? Prison or gallows or whatever they may please. But you don't see me coming back to explain such things to an old fellow in a wig and twelve respectable tradesmen, do you? What can they know whether I am guilty or not—or of *what* I am guilty, either? That's my affair. What does the Bible say? 'Driven off the face of the earth.' Very well. I am off the face of the earth now. As I came at night so I shall go."

"Impossible!" I murmured. "You can't."

"Can't? . . . Not naked like a soul on the Day of Judgment. I shall freeze on to this sleeping suit. The Last Day is not yet—and . . . you have understood thoroughly. Didn't you?"

I felt suddenly ashamed of myself. I may say truly that I understood—and my hesitation in letting that man swim away from my ship's side had been a mere sham sentiment, a sort of cowardice.

"It can't be done now till next night," I breathed out. "The ship is on the offshore tack and the wind may fail us."

"As long as I know that you understand," he whispered. "But of course you do. It's a great satisfaction to have got somebody to understand. You seem to have been there on purpose." And in the same whisper, as if we two whenever we talked had to say things to each other which were not fit for the world to hear, he added, "It's very wonderful."

We remained side by side talking in our secret way—but sometimes silent or just exchanging a whispered word or two at long intervals.

And as usual he stared through the port. A breath of wind came now and again into our faces. The ship might have been moored in dock, so gently and on an even keel she slipped through the water, that did not murmur even at our passage, shadowy and silent like a phantom sea.

At midnight I went on deck, and to my mate's great surprise put the ship round on the other tack. His terrible whiskers flitted round me in silent criticism. I certainly should not have done it if it had been only a question of getting out of that sleepy gulf as quickly as possible. I believe he told the second mate, who relieved him, that it was a great want of judgment. The other only yawned. That intolerable cub shuffled about so sleepily and lolled against the rails in such a slack, improper fashion that I came down on him sharply.

"Aren't you properly awake yet?"

"Yes, sir! I am awake."

"Well, then, be good enough to hold yourself as if you were. And keep a lookout. If there's any current we'll be closing with some islands before daylight."

The east side of the gulf is fringed with islands, some solitary, others in groups. On the blue background of the high coast they seem to float on silvery patches of calm water, arid and gray, or dark green and rounded like clumps of evergreen bushes, with the larger ones, a mile or two long, showing the outlines of ridges, ribs of gray rock under the dark mantle of matted leafage. Unknown to trade, to travel, almost to geography, the manner of life they harbor is an unsolved secret. There must be villages—settlements of fishermen at least—on the largest of them, and some communication with the world is probably kept up by native craft. But all that forenoon, as we headed for them, fanned along by the faintest of breezes, I saw no sign of man or canoe in the field of the telescope I kept on pointing at the scattered group.

At noon I gave no orders for a change of course, and the mate's whiskers became much concerned and seemed to be offering themselves unduly to my notice. At last I said:

"I am going to stand right in. Quite in—as far as I can take her."

The stare of extreme surprise imparted an air of ferocity also to his eyes, and he looked truly terrific for a moment.

"We're not doing well in the middle of the gulf," I continued, casually. "I am going to look for the land breezes tonight."

"Bless my soul! Do you mean, sir, in the dark amongst the lot of all them islands and reefs and shoals?"

"Well—if there are any regular land breezes at all on this coast one must get close inshore to find them, mustn't one?"

"Bless my soul!" he exclaimed again under his breath. All that afternoon he wore a dreamy, contemplative appearance which in him was a mark of perplexity. After dinner I went into my stateroom as if I meant to take some rest. There we two bent our dark heads over a half-unrolled chart lying on my bed.

"There," I said. "It's got to be Koh-ring. I've been looking at it ever since sunrise. It has got two hills and a low point. It must be inhabited. And on the coast opposite there is what looks like the mouth of a biggish river—with some town, no doubt, not far up. It's the best chance for you that I can see."

"Anything. Koh-ring let it be."

He looked thoughtfully at the chart as if surveying chances and distances from a lofty height—and following with his eyes his own figure wandering on the blank land of Cochin-China, and then passing off that piece of paper clean out of sight into uncharted regions. And it was as if the ship had two captains to plan her course for her. I had been so worried and restless running up and down that I had not had the patience to dress that day. I had remained in my sleeping suit, with straw slippers and a soft floppy hat. The closeness of the heat in the gulf had been most oppressive, and the crew were used to see me wandering in that airy attire.

"She will clear the south point as she heads now," I whispered into his ear. "Goodness only knows when, though, but certainly after dark. I'll edge her in to half a mile, as far as I may be able to judge in the dark—"

"Be careful," he murmured, warningly—and I realized suddenly that all my future, the only future for which I was fit, would perhaps go irretrievably to pieces in any mishap to my first command.

I could not stop a moment longer in the room. I motioned him to get out of sight and made my way on the poop. That unplayful cub had the watch. I walked up and down for a while thinking things out, then beckoned him over.

"Send a couple of hands to open the two quarter-deck ports," I said, mildly.

He actually had the impudence, or else so forgot himself in his wonder at such an incomprehensible order, as to repeat:

"Open the quarter-deck ports! What for, sir?"

"The only reason you need concern yourself about is because I tell you to do so. Have them open wide and fastened properly."

He reddened and went off, but I believe made some jeering remarks to the carpenter as to the sensible practice of ventilating a ship's quarter-deck. I know he popped into the mate's cabin to impart the fact to him because the whiskers came on deck, as it were by chance, and stole glances at me from below—for signs of lunacy or drunkenness, I suppose.

A little before supper, feeling more restless than ever, I rejoined, for a moment, my second self. And to find him sitting so quietly was surprising, like something against nature, inhuman.

I developed my plan in a hurried whisper.

"I shall stand in as close as I dare and then put her round. I shall presently find means to smuggle you out of here into the sail locker, which communicates with the lobby. But there is an opening, a sort of square for hauling the sails out which gives straight on the quarter-deck and which is never closed in fine weather, so as to give air to the sails. When the ship's way is deadened in stays and all the hands are aft at the main braces you shall have a clear road to slip out and get overboard through the open quarter-deck port. I've had them both fastened up. Use a rope's end to lower yourself into the water so as to avoid a splash—you know. It could be heard and cause some beastly complication."

He kept silent for a while, then whispered, "I understand."

"I won't be there to see you go," I began with an effort. "The rest . . . I only hope I have understood, too."

"You have. From first to last," and for the first time there seemed to be a faltering, something strained in his whisper. He caught hold of my arm, but the ringing of the supper bell made me start. He didn't, though; he only released his grip.

After supper I didn't come below again till well past eight o'clock. The faint, steady breeze was loaded with dew; and the wet, darkened sails held all there was of propelling power in it. The night, clear and starry, sparkled darkly, and the opaque, lightless patches shifting slowly against the low stars were the drifting islets. On the port bow there was a big one more distant and shadowily imposing by the great space of sky it eclipsed.

On opening the door I had a back view of my very own self looking at a chart. He had come out of the recess and was standing near the table.

"Quite dark enough," I whispered.

He stepped back and leaned against my bed with a level, quiet glance. I sat on the couch. We had nothing to say to each other. Over our heads the officer of the watch moved here and there. Then I heard him move quickly. I knew what that meant. He was making for the companion; and presently his voice was outside my door.

"We are drawing in pretty fast, sir. Land looks rather close."

"Very well," I answered. "I am coming on deck directly."

I waited till he was gone out of the cuddy, then rose. My double moved too. The time had come to exchange our last whispers, for neither of us was ever to hear each other's natural voice.

"Look here!" I opened a drawer and took out three sovereigns. "Take this, anyhow. I've got six and I'd give you the lot, only I must keep a little money to buy some fruit and vegetables for the crew from native boats as we go through Sunda straits."

He shook his head.

"Take it," I urged him, whispering desperately. "No one can tell what—"

He smiled and slapped meaningly the only pocket of the sleeping jacket. It was not safe, certainly. But I produced a large old silk handkerchief of mine, and tying the three pieces of gold in a corner, pressed it on him. He was touched, I suppose, because he took it at last and tied it quickly round his waist under the jacket, on his bare skin.

Our eyes met; several seconds elapsed, till, our glances still mingled, I extended my hand and turned the lamp out. Then I passed through the cuddy, leaving the door of my room wide open. . . . "Steward!"

He was still lingering in the pantry in the greatness of his zeal, giving a rub-up to a plated cruet stand the last thing before going to bed. Being careful not to wake up the mate, whose room was opposite, I spoke in an undertone.

He looked round anxiously. "Sir!"

"Can you get me a little hot water from the galley?"

"I am afraid, sir, the galley fire's been out for some time now."

"Go and see."

He fled up the stairs.

"Now," I whispered, loudly, into the saloon—too loudly, perhaps, but I was afraid I couldn't make a sound. He was by my side in an instant—the double captain slipped past the stairs—through the tiny dark passage—a sliding door. We were in the sail locker, scrambling on our knees over the sails. A sudden thought struck me. I saw myself wandering barefooted, bareheaded, the sun beating on my dark poll. I snatched off my floppy hat and tried hurriedly in the dark to ram it on my other self. He dodged and fended off silently. I wonder what he thought had come to me before he understood and suddenly desisted. Our hands met gropingly, lingered united in a steady, motionless clasp for a second. . . . No word was breathed by either of us when they separated.

I was standing quietly by the pantry door when the steward returned.

"Sorry, sir. Kettle barely warm. Shall I light the spirit lamp?"

"Never mind."

I came out on deck slowly. It was now a matter of conscience to shave the land as close as possible—for now he must go overboard whenever the ship was put in stays. Must! There could be no going back for him. After a moment I walked over to leeward and my heart flew into my mouth at the nearness of the land on the bow. Under any other circumstances I would not have held on a minute longer. The second mate had followed me anxiously.

I looked on till I felt I could command my voice.

"She will weather," I said then in a quiet tone.

"Are you going to try that, sir?" he stammered out incredulously.

I took no notice of him and raised my tone just enough to be heard by the helmsman.

"Keep her good full."

"Good full, sir."

The wind fanned my cheek, the sails slept, the world was silent. The strain of watching the dark loom of the land grow bigger and denser was too much for me. I had shut my eyes—because the ship must go closer. She must! The stillness was intolerable. Were we standing still?

When I opened my eyes the second view started my heart with a thump. The black southern hill of Koh-ring seemed to hang right over the ship like a towering fragment of the everlasting night. On that enormous mass of blackness there was not a gleam to be seen, not a sound to be heard. It was gliding irresistibly toward us and yet seemed already within reach of the hand. I saw the vague figures of the watch grouped in the waist, gazing in awed silence.

"Are you going on, sir?" inquired an unsteady voice at my elbow.

I ignored it. I had to go on.

"Keep her full. Don't check her way. That won't do now," I said warningly.

"I can't see the sails very well," the helmsman answered me, in strange, quavering tones.

Was she close enough? Already she was, I won't say in the shadow of the land, but in the very blackness of it, already swallowed up as it were, gone too close to be recalled, gone from me altogether.

"Give the mate a call," I said to the young man who stood at my elbow as still as death. "And turn all hands up."

My tone had a borrowed loudness reverberated from the height of the land. Several voices cried out together: "We are all on deck, sir."

Then stillness again, with the great shadow gliding closer, towering higher, without a light, without a sound. Such a hush had fallen on the ship that she might have been a bark of the dead floating in slowly under the very gate of Erebus.

"My God! Where are we?"

It was the mate moaning at my elbow. He was thunderstruck, and as it were deprived of the moral support of his whiskers. He clapped his hands and absolutely cried out, "Lost!"

"Be quiet," I said sternly.

He lowered his tone, but I saw the shadowy gesture of his despair. "What are we doing here?"

"Looking for the land wind."

He made as if to tear his hair, and addressed me recklessly.

"She will never get out. You have done it, sir. I knew it'd end in something like this. She will never weather, and you are too close now to stay. She'll drift ashore before she's round. O my God!"

I caught his arm as he was raising it to batter his poor devoted head, and shook it violently.

"She's ashore already," he wailed, trying to tear himself away.

"Is she? . . . Keep good full there!"

"Good full, sir," cried the helmsman in a frightened, thin, childlike voice.

I hadn't let go the mate's arm and went on shaking it. "Ready about, do you hear? You go forward"—shake—"and stop there"—shake—"and hold your noise"—shake—"and see these head sheets properly overhauled"—shake, shake—shake.

And all the time I dared not look toward the land lest my heart should fail me. I released my grip at last and he ran forward as if fleeing for dear life.

I wondered what my double there in the sail locker thought of this commotion. He was able to hear everything—and perhaps he was able to understand why, on my conscience, it had to be thus close—no less. My first order, "Hard alee!" re-echoed ominously under the towering shadow of Koh-ring as if I had shouted in a mountain gorge. And then I watched the land intently. In that smooth water and light wind it was impossible to feel the ship coming-to. No! I could not feel her. And my second self was making now ready to slip out and lower himself overboard. Perhaps he was gone already . . . ?

The great black mass brooding over our very mastheads began to pivot away from the ship's side silently. And now I forgot the secret stranger ready to depart, and remembered only that I was a total stranger to the ship. I did not know her. Would she do it? How was she to be handled?

I swung the mainyard and waited helplessly. She was perhaps stopped, and her very fate hung in the balance, with the black mass of Koh-ring like the gate of the everlasting night towering over her taffrail. What would she do now? Had she way on her yet? I stepped to the side swiftly, and on the shadowy water I could see nothing except a faint phosphorescent flash revealing the glassy smoothness of the sleeping surface. It was impossible to tell—and I had not learned yet the feel of my ship. Was she moving? What I needed was something easily seen, a piece of paper, which I could throw overboard and watch. I had nothing on me. To run down for it I didn't dare. There was no time. All at once my strained, yearning stare distinguished a white object floating within a yard of the ship's side. White on the black water. A phosphorescent flash passed under it. What was that thing? . . . I recognized my own floppy hat. It must have fallen off his head . . . and he didn't bother. Now I had what I wanted—the saving mark for my eyes. But I hardly thought of my other self, now gone from the ship, to be hidden forever from all friendly faces, to be a fugitive and a vagabond on the earth, with no brand of the curse on his sane forehead to stay a slaying hand . . . too proud to explain.

And I watched the hat—the expression of my sudden pity for his mere flesh. It had been meant to save his homeless head from the dangers of the sun. And now—behold—it was saving the ship, by serving me for a mark to help out the ignorance of my strangeness. Ha! It was drifting forward, warning me just in time that the ship had gathered sternway.

"Shift the helm," I said in a low voice to the seaman standing still like a statue.

The man's eyes glistened wildly in the binnacle light as he jumped round to the other side and spun round the wheel.

I walked to the break of the poop. On the overshadowed deck all hands stood by the forebraces waiting for my order. The stars ahead seemed to be gliding from right to left. And all was so still in the world that I heard the quiet remark "She's round," passed in a tone of intense relief between two seamen.

"Let go and haul."

The foreyards ran round with a great noise, amidst cheery cries. And now the frightful whiskers made themselves heard giving various orders. Already the ship was drawing ahead. And I was alone with her. Nothing! no one in the world should stand now between us, throwing a shadow on the way of silent knowledge and mute affection, the perfect communion of a seaman with his first command.

Walking to the taffrail, I was in time to make out, on the very edge of a darkness thrown by a towering black mass like the very gateway of Erebus—yes, I was in time to catch an evanescent glimpse of my white hat left behind to mark the spot where the secret sharer of my cabin and of my thoughts, as though he were my second self, had lowered himself into the water to take his punishment: a free man, a proud swimmer striking out for a new destiny.

INDEX OF AUTHORS AND TITLES